A gift from NESFA.
If you enjoy this book,
visit us at www.nesfa.org.

The Queen of Air and Darkness

Volume Two

The Collected Short Works of Poul Anderson

Edited by Rick Katze

NESFA Press

Post Office Box 809
Framingham, MA 01701
www.nesfa.org/press
2009

FIRST EDITION, September 2009

ISBN-10: 1-886778-87-6
ISBN-13: 978-1-886778-87-0

Publication History

Editor's Introduction is original to this volume.

"Poul Anderson" by Mike Resnick is original to this volume.

"The Queen of Air and Darkness" first appeared in *The Magazine of Fantasy & Science Fiction,* November 1958.

"Jennifer's Lament" appeared in *Staves* (Jwindz Publishing 1993).

"Industrial Revolution" by Winston P. Sanders first appeared in *Analog Science Fiction / Science Fact,* September 1963.

"Cradle Song" appeared in *Staves*, (Jwindz Publishing 1993).

"Operation Afreet" first appeared in *The Magazine of Fantasy & Science Fiction*, September 1956.

"Science Fiction and Science: On Imaginary Science" first appeared in *Destinies*, April-June, 1979.

"Upon the Occasion of Being Asked at a Court of Love to Declare That About His Lady Which Pleases Him the Most" appeared in *Staves*, (Jwindz Publishing 1993).

"The Longest Voyage" first appeared in *Analog Science Fact–Fiction*, December 1960.

"Brave to Be a King" first appeared in *The Magazine of Fantasy & Science Fiction*, August 1959.

"Midsummer Song" appeared in *Staves*, (Jwindz Publishing 1993).

"Christa McAuliffe" appeared in *Staves*, (Jwindz Publishing 1993)

"Brake" first appeared in *Astounding Science Fiction*, August 1957.

"Jennifer's Song" appeared in *Staves*, (Jwindz Publishing 1993).

"Science Fiction and Science: The Hardness of Hard Science Fiction" first appeared in *Destinies*, January-February 1979.

"The Burning Bridge" first appeared in *Astounding Science Fiction,* January 1960.

"Veleda Speaks" appeared in *Staves*, (Jwindz Publishing 1993).

"Science Fiction and History" first appeared in *Amazing Stories,* January 1989.

"A World Called Maanerek" first appeared in *Galaxy Science Fiction,* July 1957.

"The Pirate" first appeared in *Analog Science Fiction / Science Fact,* October, 1968.

"To Build a World" first appeared in *Galaxy Magazine,* June 1964.

"Say It with Flowers" by Winston P. Sanders first appeared in *Analog Science Fiction / Science Fact,* September 1965.

"My Object All Sublime" first appeared in *Galaxy Magazine,* June 1961.

"Innocent at Large" by Poul and Karen Anderson first appeared in *Galaxy Science Fiction,* July 1958.

"Route Song of the Winged Folk" appeared in *Staves*, (Jwindz Publishing 1993).

"The Corkscrew of Space" first appeared in *Galaxy Science Fiction,* February 1956.

"A Little Knowledge" first appeared in *Analog Science Fiction / Science Fact,* August 1971.

"Marque and Reprisal" first appeared in *The Magazine of Fantasy & Science Fiction,* February 1965.

"Uncleftish Beholding" first appeared in *Analog Science Fiction / Science Fact,* Mid-December 1989.

"The Critique of Impure Reason" first appeared in *Worlds of If Science Fiction,* November 1962.

"Science and Creation" first appeared in *Analog Science Fiction / Science Fact*, September 1983.

"Of the Sea" appeared in *Staves*, (Jwindz Publishing 1993).

"Epilogue" first appeared in *Analog Science Fact / Science Fiction,* March 1962

"Tanka" appeared in *Staves*, (Jwindz Publishing 1993).

Contents

The Queen of Air and Darkness

Editor's Introduction

This is volume two of a multi-volume collection of Poul Anderson stories. You keep buying them; we'll keep printing them.

It is not intended as a compilation of any specific series that Poul wrote.

It is not intended to be a chronological collection of his works.

It is intended to preserve a significant portion of his short stories which appeared originally in magazine format. Many of these pulps are rapidly aging and decaying due to the lower quality of paper used to print them, thus making easy access to them next to impossible. As the years pass, the availability of the magazines in which to read these stories will continue to diminish. These hardback editions are printed on acid-free paper for a longer life.

One of the reviews of volume one of this collection noted that his favorite story, "The Longest Voyage", was not included in the first volume. It is presented here in volume two. And other stories that did not appear in the first two volumes will appear in later volumes. Please be patient. I do read the reviews and comments by others which help in selecting the stories for any given volume.

While the fiction which will appear in volume three which will be published in 2010 has been selected, volume four is still a blank slate. Comments and suggestions are always welcome

If I had intended to prepare one volume of the *best* science fiction written by Poul Anderson, the story selection would have been quite different. I would have started with all the stories which won either the Hugo or the Nebula, or both. The selection of additional material would have made for some hard choices. I am very happy that The New England Science Fiction Association has given me the luxury of a multi-volume collection.

This volume contains two Hugo winners—"The Queen of Air and Darkness" and "The Longest Voyage". And it contains many other worthy stories.

A single volume collection would not have had room for far to many *good* stories. As it is, I have the opportunity to mine a whole career's worth of writing and put volumes together of stories that, as a reader, I would want to read.

I would also like to mention that Baen Books is presently publishing compilations of some of Poul's series. They are also good books which should be bought and cherished.

Rick Katze
June 2009

Poul Anderson

by Mike Resnick

So let me tell you about one of science fiction's true Renaissance Men, because Poul Anderson never tooted his own horn, and as a result, while everyone knows he was a popular and prolific writer, most people don't know the truly profound effect he had on the fields of fantasy and science fiction.

Poul had a degree in physics. ("Don't all science fiction writers?" I hear you ask. Actually, you'd be surprised how many of us don't have degrees in anything.)

He was a founding member of the SCA, The Society for Creative Anachronism. (He and Randall Garrett boldly chose to defend John Campbell's honor in a joust on the lawn of the Claremont Hotel at the 1968 Worldcon. I must have been somewhere else at the moment, but Robert Silverberg still recalls how quickly the pair of them—Randy a little drunk, Poul a little short-sighted—were pounded into the ground by two of SCA's finest and most experienced swordsmen. Somehow John's honor survived anyway—and so, since they were firing with blank swords or the equivalent, did Poul and Randy.)

He was an early President of SFWA (Science Fiction and Fantasy Writers of America).

He was the Worldcon Guest of Honor in 1959.

He became a Gandalf Grand Master in 1978.

He became a SFWA Grand Master in 1991.

He won 7 Hugo Awards, and is tied for second on the all-time list among writers.

He won 3 Nebula Awards.

He won 4 Prometheus Awards, including a Lifetime Achievement one. (The Prometheus is for libertarian writing, a strain that is common in Poul's work.)

He won a John Campbell Memorial Award in 2000.

He won the Japanese "Seiun" and Russian "Strannik" awards

He even won a filksinging award, the Pegasus, in 1998, in collaboration with Anne Passavoy.

In my opinion, he wrote the ultimate hard science novel with *Tau Zero*. I know, I know, a lot of people would select Hal Clement's very fine *Mission of Gravity* for that honor, but *Mission of Gravity* is about Mesklinites (fascinating little wormlike critters) and *Tau Zero* is about *people*. And when all is said and done, people are what count.

This collection contains two of Poul's most famous stories: the Hugo-and-Nebula-winning "The Queen of Air and Darkness" and the Hugo-winning "The Longest Voyage". (So why didn't "The Longest Voyage" win the Nebula too? Easy. It came out in 1960, which is a few years before SFWA was formed, and the Nebula is SFWA's award.)

I recently attended the 2009 Nebula weekend, and got to spend some time with Poul's widow, Karen Anderson. Karen is an author in her own right (her own write?), was Poul's credited collaborator from time to time, and was his uncredited collaborator far more often. I told her that I'd been asked to introduce this collection, and that I hated the thought of just saying what the stories are about, because if you're reading this then it's clear that you're about to read them too. So what I wanted was Karen's reminiscences on exactly how Poul got the ideas for some of them.

(Isn't that what every science fiction writer is always being asked: "Where do you get your crazy ideas?")

So, from the source (Karen) through the middleman (me) to the reader (you):

Ed Emshwiller (who signed his paintings and drawings "Emsh") was the dominant science fiction artist in the 1950s and early 1960s, and one day Poul turned to Karen and said, "Tell me a cover, not specifying anything further." Karen asked what he meant, and he told her to describe a cover so he could write a story around it. Which cover did he have in mind, she wanted to know. Oh, not one that existed, answered Poul; So Karen described a non-existent Emsh painting that featured a robot sitting in an office, slaving away at a desk and smelling a flower—and Poul sat down and wrote "The Critique of Impure Reason."

When Poul wrote "Uncleftish Beholding," Karen says he decided to use Germanic-rooted words only. This kind of learned writing was actually named after him, and became known (don't wince) as Ander-Saxon.

Poul and Karen decided to plot a "biter-bit" story together and see just how many twists they could put into one story. It became "Innocent at Large."

Karen suggested that Poul base a story on Marlowe's *Tamerlaine*, perhaps one in which a time traveler gets stuck in ancient Persia and finds himself becoming unwillingly involved in local affairs. Poul took the idea and ran with it; you'll find it up ahead as "Brave to Be a King."

Karen didn't recall the genesis of "The Pirate," but tells me that upon finishing it, Poul claimed that no one under the age of 40 could ever truly understand it.

Poul came up with what he thought was a unique way to transmit a secret code. Karen suggested he borrow the structure of the story from one of their favorites, which almost no one remembered, a story titled "Mr. Glencannon Ignores the War". He did, and it became the very popular "Say It With Flowers."

And of course there's the biggie, "The Queen of Air and Darkness." Poul loved the title, which is the title of the second of the four parts of T. H. White's *The Once and Future King*—and then decided to write exactly the kind of story that you would *not* expect from such a title. He got some critical flak for treating it as science fiction rather than fantasy (given its awards, clearly not enough flak to matter), and his lyrics became a very popular filksong at conventions for the next decade.

He was quite a remarkable writer, equally skilled at science fiction, fantasy, folk tale, and myth. Of all his contemporaries, probably only Fritz Leiber displayed such range, and with no disrespect to Fritz, he couldn't write rigorous hard science the way Poul could. Poul could turn out carefully-reasoned science fiction, myth-inspired fantasy, could create characters like Nicholas van Rijn who was good for an entire series of books, and he was a pretty sharp parodist; when I was assembling an anthology of science fiction parodies more than two decades ago I bought a Conan parody from him that remains the funniest sword-and-sorcery parody I've read. And when he wasn't writing, he was starring; he showed up as the hero of a Philip K. Dick novelette, "Waterspider," that I bought for another anthology.

Poul, as I said at the start, was a modest man. I remember a day he spent driving me around Northern California, showing me the scenic highlights, and never once mentioned anything he'd written or anything he was going to write, any awards he'd won or hoped to win. He asked me about my own writing, and did everything he could to put me at ease—because while he was a modest man, he realized at some level that most of us were awed by his talent. Harry Turtledove is prompt to declare his debt to Poul; so are Jerry Pournelle, Greg Bear, Joe Haldeman, and a score of others. That debt may well have been greatest in his Hoka collaborator and close friend, Gordon R. Dickson.

We lost Poul to cancer in 2001, but thanks to NESFA Press we won't soon lose what made him so special to our field. So enough of my writing this introduction and your reading it; there are some wonderful futures and universes up ahead, just waiting for you to discover (or rediscover) them.

The Queen of Air and Darkness

The last glow of the last sunset would linger almost until midwinter. But there would be no more day, and the northlands rejoiced. Blossoms opened, flamboyance on firethorn trees, steelflowers rising blue from the brok and rainplant that cloaked all hills, shy whiteness of kiss-me-never down in the dales. Flitteries darted among them in iridescent wings; a crownbuck shook his horns and bugled. Between horizons the sky deepened from purple to sable. Both moons were aloft, nearly full, shining frosty on leaves and molten on waters. The shadows they made were blurred by an aurora, a great blowing curtain of light across half heaven. Behind it the earliest stars had come out.

A boy and a girl sat on Wolund's Barrow just under the dolmen it upbore. Their hair, which streamed halfway down their backs, showed startlingly forth, bleached as it was by summer. Their bodies, still dark from that season, merged with earth and bush and rock, for they wore only garlands. He played on a bone flute and she sang. They had lately become lovers. Their age was about sixteen, but they did not know this, considering themselves Outlings and thus indifferent to time, remembering little or nothing of how they had once dwelt in the lands of men.

His notes piped cold around her voice:

Cast a spell,
weave it well,
of dust and dew
and night and you.

A brook by the grave mound, carrying moonlight down to a hill-hidden river, answered with its rapids. A flock of hellbats passed black beneath the aurora.

A shape came bounding over Cloudmoor. It had two arms and two legs, but the legs were long and claw-footed and feathers covered it to the end of a tail and broad wings. The face was half-human, dominated by its eyes. Had Ayoch been able to stand wholly erect, he would have reached to the boy's shoulder.

The girl rose. "He carries a burden," she said. Her vision was not meant for twilight like that of a northland creature born, but she had learned how to use every sign her senses gave her. Besides the fact that ordinarily a pook would fly, there was a heaviness to his haste.

"And he comes from the south." Excitement jumped in the boy, sudden as a green flame that went across the constellation Lyrth. He sped down the mound. "Ohoi, Ayoch!" he called. "Me here, Mistherd!"

"And Shadow-of-a-Dream," the girl laughed, following.

The pook halted. He breathed louder than the soughing in the growth around him. A smell of bruised yerba lifted where he stood.

"Well met in winterbirth," he whistled. "You can help me bring this to Carheddin."

He held out what he bore. His eyes were yellow lanterns above. It moved and whimpered.

"Why, a child," Mistherd said.

"Even as you were, my son, even as you were. Ho, ho, what a snatch!" Ayoch boasted. "They were a score in yon camp by Fallowwood, armed, and besides watcher engines they had big ugly dogs aprowl while they slept. I came from above, however, having spied on them till I knew that a handful of dazedust—"

"The poor thing." Shadow-of-a-Dream took the boy and held him to her small breasts. "So full of sleep yet, aren't you?" Blindly, he sought a nipple. She smiled through the veil of her hair. "No, I am still too young, and you already too old. But come, when you wake in Carheddin under the mountain, you shall feast."

"Yo-ah," said Ayoch very softly. "She is abroad and has heard and seen. She comes." He crouched down, wings folded. After a moment Mistherd knelt, and then Shadow-of-a-Dream, though she did not let go the child.

The Queen's tall form blocked off the moons. For a while she regarded the three and their booty. Hill and moor sounds withdrew from their awareness until it seemed they could hear the northlights hiss.

At last Ayoch whispered, "Have I done well, Starmother?"

"If you stole a babe from a camp full of engines," said the beautiful voice, "then they were folk out of the far south who may not endure it as meekly as yeomen."

"But what can they do, Snowmaker?" the pook asked. "How can they track us?"

Mistherd lifted his head and spoke in pride. "Also, now they too have felt the awe of us."

"And he is a cuddly dear," Shadow-of-a-Dream said. "And we need more like him, do we not, Lady Sky?"

"It had to happen in some twilight," agreed she who stood above. "Take him onward and care for him. By this sign," which she made, "is he claimed for the Dwellers."

Their joy was freed. Ayoch cartwheeled over the ground till he reached a shiverleaf. There he swarmed up the trunk and out on a limb, perched half hidden by unrestful pale foliage, and crowed. Boy and girl bore the child toward Carheddin at an easy distance-devouring lope which let him pipe and her sing:

Wahaii, wahaii!
Wayala, laii!
Wing on the wind
high over heaven,
shrilly shrieking,
rush with the rainspears,
tumble through tumult,
drift to the moonhoar trees and the dream-heavy shadows beneath them,
and rock in, be one with the clinking wavelets of lakes where the starbeams drown.

As she entered, Barbro Cullen felt, through all grief and fury, stabbed by dismay. The room was unkempt. Journals, tapes, reels, codices, file boxes, bescribbled papers were piled on every table. Dust filmed most shelves and corners. Against one wall stood a laboratory setup, microscope and analytical equipment. She recognized it as compact and efficient, but it was not what you would expect in an office, and it gave the air a faint chemical reek. The rug was threadbare, the furniture shabby.

This was her final chance?

Then Eric Sherrinford approached. "Good day, Mrs. Cullen," he said. His tone was crisp, his handclasp firm. His faded gripsuit didn't bother her. She wasn't inclined to fuss about her own appearance except on special occasions. (And would she ever again have one, unless she got back Jimmy?) What she observed was a cat's personal neatness.

A smile radiated in crow's feet from his eyes. "Forgive my bachelor housekeeping. On Beowulf we have—we had, at any rate—machines for that, so I never acquired the habit myself, and I don't want a hireling disarranging my tools. More convenient to work out of my apartment than keep a separate office. Won't you be seated?"

"No, thanks. I couldn't," she mumbled.

"I understand. But if you'll excuse me, I function best in a relaxed position."

He jackknifed into a lounger. One long shank crossed the other knee. He drew forth a pipe and stuffed it from a pouch. Barbro wondered why he took tobacco in so ancient a way. Wasn't Beowulf supposed to have the up-to-date equipment that they still couldn't afford to build on Roland? Well, of course old customs might survive anyhow. They generally did in colonies, she remembered reading. People had moved starward in the hope of preserving such outmoded things as their mother tongues or constitutional government or rational-technological civilization...

Sherrinford pulled her up from the confusion of her weariness. "You must give me the details of your case, Mrs. Cullen. You've simply told me your son was kidnapped and your local constabulary did nothing. Otherwise, I know just a few obvious facts, such as your being widowed rather than divorced; and you're the daughter of outwayers in Olga Ivanoff Land who, nevertheless, kept in close telecommunication with Christmas Landing; and you're trained in one of the biological professions; and you had several years' hiatus in field work until recently you started again."

She gaped at the high-cheeked, beak-nosed, black-haired and gray-eyed countenance. His lighter made a *scrit* and a flare which seemed to fill the room. Quietness dwelt on this height above the city, and winter dusk was seeping through the windows. "How in cosmos do you know that?" she heard herself exclaim.

He shrugged and fell into the lecturer's manner for which he was notorious. "My work depends on noticing details and fitting them together. In more than a hundred years on Roland, tending to cluster according to their origins and thought habits, people have developed regional accents. You have a trace of the Olgan burr, but you nasalize your vowels in the style of this area, though you live in Portolondon. That suggests steady childhood exposure to metropolitan speech. You were part of Matsuyama's expedition, you told me, and took your boy along. They wouldn't have allowed any ordinary technician to do that; hence, you had to be valuable enough to get away with it. The team was conducting ecological research; therefore, you must be in the life sciences. For the same reason, you must have had previous field experience. But your skin is fair, showing none of the leatheriness one gets from prolonged exposure to this sun. Accordingly, you must have been mostly indoors for a good while before you went on your ill-fated trip. As for widowhood—you never mentioned a husband to me, but you have had a man whom you thought so highly of that you still wear both the wedding and the engagement ring he gave you."

Her sight blurred and stung. The last of those words had brought Tim back, huge, ruddy, laughterful and gentle. She must turn from this other person and stare outward. "Yes," she achieved saying, "you're right."

The apartment occupied a hilltop above Christmas Landing. Beneath it the city dropped away in walls, roofs, archaistic chimneys and lamplit streets, goblin lights of human-piloted vehicles, to the harbor, the sweep of Venture Bay, ships bound to and from the Sunward Islands and remoter regions of the Boreal Ocean, which glimmered like mercury in the afterglow of Charlemagne. Oliver was swinging rapidly higher, a mottled orange disc a full degree wide; closer to the zenith which it could never reach, it would shine the color of ice. Alde, half the seeming size, was a thin slow crescent near Sirius, which she remembered was near Sol, but you couldn't see Sol without a telescope—

"Yes," she said around the pain in her throat, "my husband is about four years dead. I was carrying our first child when he was killed by a stampeding monocerus. We'd been married three years before. Met while we were both at the University—'casts from School Central can only supply a basic education, you know—We founded our own team to do ecological studies under contract—you know, can a certain area be settled while maintaining a balance of nature, what crops will grow, what hazards, that sort of question—Well, afterward I did lab work for a fisher co-op in Portolondon. But the monotony, the...shut-in-ness... was eating me away. Professor Matsuyama offered me a position on the team he was organizing to examine Commissioner Hauch Land. I thought, God help me,

I thought Jimmy—Tim wanted him named James, once the tests showed it'd be a boy, after his own father and because of 'Timmy and Jimmy' and—Oh, I thought Jimmy could safely come along. I couldn't bear to leave him behind for months, not at his age. We could make sure he'd never wander out of camp. What could hurt him inside it? *I* had never believed those stories about the Outlings stealing human children. I supposed parents were trying to hide from themselves the fact they'd been careless, they'd let a kid get lost in the woods or attacked by a pack of satans or—Well, I learned better, Mr. Sherrinford. The guard robots were evaded and the dogs were drugged and when I woke, Jimmy was gone."

He regarded her through the smoke from his pipe. Barbro Engdahl Cullen was a big woman of thirty or so (Rolandic years, he reminded himself, ninety-five percent of Terrestrial, not the same as Beowulfan years), broad-shouldered, long-legged, full-breasted, supple of stride; her face was wide, straight nose, straightforward hazel eyes, heavy but mobile mouth; her hair was reddish-brown, cropped below the ears, her voice husky, her garment a plain street robe. To still the writhing of her fingers, he asked skeptically, "Do you now believe in the Outlings?"

"No. I'm just not so sure as I was." She swung about with half a glare for him. "And we have found traces."

"Bits of fossils," he nodded. "A few artifacts of a neolithic sort. But apparently ancient, as if the makers died ages ago. Intensive search has failed to turn up any real evidence for their survival."

"How intensive can search be, in a summer-stormy, winter-gloomy wilderness around the North Pole?" she demanded. "When we are, how many, a million people on an entire planet, half of us crowded into this one city?"

"And the rest crowding this one habitable continent," he pointed out.

"Arctica covers five million square kilometers," she flung back. "The Arctic Zone proper covers a fourth of it. We haven't the industrial base to establish satellite monitor stations, build aircraft we can trust in those parts, drive roads through the damned darklands and establish permanent bases and get to know them and tame them. Good Christ, generations of lonely outwaymen told stories about Graymantle, and the beast was never seen by a proper scientist till last year!"

"Still, you continue to doubt the reality of the Outlings?"

"Well, what about a secret cult among humans, born of isolation and ignorance, lairing in the wilderness, stealing children when they can for—" She swallowed. Her head dropped. "But you're supposed to be the expert."

"From what you told me over the visiphone, the Portolondon constabulary questions the accuracy of the report your group made, thinks the lot of you were hysterical, claims you must have omitted a due precaution, and the child toddled away and was lost beyond your finding."

His dry words pried the horror out of her. Flushing, she snapped, "Like any settler's kid? No. I didn't simply yell. I consulted Data Retrieval. A few too many such cases are recorded for accident to be a very plausible explanation. And shall we totally ignore the frightened stories about reappearances? But when I went back to the constabulary with my facts, they brushed me off. I suspect that was not entirely because they're undermanned. I think they're afraid too. They're recruited from country boys, and Portolondon lies near the edge of the unknown."

Her energy faded. "Roland hasn't got any central police force," she finished drably. "You're my last hope."

The man puffed smoke into twilight, with which it blent, before he said in a kindlier voice than hitherto: "Please don't make it a high hope, Mrs. Cullen. I'm the solitary private investigator on this world, having no resources beyond myself, and a newcomer to boot."

"How long have you been here?"

"Twelve years. Barely time to get a little familiarity with the relatively civilized coastlands. You settlers of a century or more—what do you, even, know about Arctica's interior?"

Sherrinford sighed. "I'll take the case, charging no more than I must, mainly for the sake of the experience," he said. "But only if you'll be my guide and assistant, however painful it will be for you."

"Of course! I dreaded waiting idle. Why me, though?"

"Hiring someone else as well qualified would be prohibitively expensive, on a pioneer planet where every hand has a thousand urgent tasks to do. Besides, you have a motive. And I'll need that. I, who was born on another world altogether strange to this one, itself altogether strange to Mother Earth, I am too dauntingly aware of how handicapped we are."

Night gathered upon Christmas Landing. The air stayed mild, but glimmer-lit tendrils of fog, sneaking through the streets, had a cold look, and colder yet was the aurora where it shuddered between the moons. The woman drew closer to the man in this darkening room, surely not aware that she did, until he switched on a fluoropanel. The same knowledge of Roland's aloneness was in both of them.

One lightyear is not much as galactic distances go. You could walk it in about 270 million years, beginning at the middle of the Permian Era, when dinosaurs belonged to the remote future, and continuing to the present day when spaceships cross even greater reaches. But stars in our neighborhood average some nine lightyears apart, and barely one percent of them have planets which are man-habitable, and speeds are limited to less than that of radiation. Scant help is given by relativistic time contraction and suspended animation en route. These make the journeys seem short, but history meanwhile does not stop at home.

Thus voyages from sun to sun will always be few. Colonists will be those who have extremely special reasons for going. They will take along germ plasm for exogenetic cultivation of domestic plants and animals—and of human infants, in order that population can grow fast enough to escape death through genetic drift. After all, they cannot rely on further immigration. Two or three times a century, a ship may call from some other colony. (Not from Earth. Earth has long ago sunk into alien concerns.) Its place of origin will be an old settlement. The young ones are in no position to build and man interstellar vessels.

Their very survival, let alone their eventual modernization, is in doubt. The founding fathers have had to take what they could get in a universe not especially designed for man.

Consider, for example, Roland. It is among the rare happy finds, a world where humans can live, breathe, eat the food, drink the water, walk unclad if they choose, sow their crops, pasture their beasts, dig their mines, erect their homes, raise their children and grandchildren. It is worth crossing three-quarters of a light-century to preserve certain dear values and strike new roots into the soil of Roland.

But the star Charlemagne is of type F9, forty percent brighter than Sol, brighter still in the treacherous ultraviolet and wilder still in the wind of charged particles that seethes from it. The planet has an eccentric orbit. In the middle of the short but furious northern summer, which includes periastron, total insolation is more than double what Earth gets; in the depth of the long northern winter, it is barely less than Terrestrial average.

Native life is abundant everywhere. But lacking elaborate machinery, not yet economically possible to construct for more than a few specialists, man can only endure the high latitudes. A ten-degree axial tilt, together with the orbit, means that the northern part of the Arctican continent spends half its year in unbroken sunlessness. Around the South Pole lies an empty ocean.

Other differences from Earth might superficially seem more important. Roland has two moons, small but close, to evoke clashing tides. It rotates once in thirty-two hours, which is endlessly, subtly disturbing to organisms evolved through gigayears of a quicker rhythm. The weather patterns are altogether unterrestrial. The globe is a mere 9500 kilometers in diameter; its surface gravity is 0.42 x 980 cm/sec^2; the sea level air pressure is slightly above one Earth atmosphere. (For actually Earth is the freak, and man exists because a cosmic accident blew away most of the gas that a body its size ought to have kept, as Venus has done.)

However, *Homo* can truly be called *sapiens* when he practices his specialty of being unspecialized. His repeated attempts to freeze himself into an all-answering pattern or culture or ideology, or whatever he has named it, have repeatedly brought ruin. Give him the pragmatic business of making his living, and he will usually do rather well. He adapts, within broad limits.

These limits are set by such factors as his need for sunlight and his being, necessarily and forever, a part of the life that surrounds him and a creature of the spirit within.

Portolondon thrust docks, boats, machinery, warehouses into the Gulf of Polaris. Behind them huddled the dwellings of its five thousand permanent inhabitants: concrete walls, storm shutters, high-peaked tile roofs. The gaiety of their paint looked forlorn amidst lamps; this town lay past the Arctic Circle.

Nevertheless Sherrinford remarked, "Cheerful place, eh? The kind of thing I came to Roland looking for."

Barbro made no reply. The days in Christmas Landing, while he made his preparations, had drained her. Gazing out the dome of the taxi that was whirring them downtown from the hydrofoil that brought them, she supposed he meant the lushness of forest and meadows along the road, brilliant hues and phosphorescence of flowers in gardens, clamor of wings overhead. Unlike Terrestrial flora in cold climates, Arctican vegetation spends every daylit hour in frantic growth and energy storage. Not till summer's fever gives place to gentle winter does it bloom and fruit; and estivating animals rise from their dens and migratory birds come home.

The view was lovely, she had to admit: beyond the trees, a spaciousness climbing toward remote heights, silvery-gray under a moon, an aurora, the diffuse radiance from a sun just below the horizon.

Beautiful as a hunting satan, she thought, and as terrible. That wilderness had stolen Jimmy. She wondered it she would at least be given to find his little bones and take them to his father.

Abruptly she realized that she and Sherrinford were at their hotel and that he had been speaking of the town. Since it was next in size after the capital, he must have visited here often before. The streets were crowded and noisy; signs flickered, music blared from shops, taverns, restaurants, sports centers, dance halls; vehicles were jammed down to molasses speed; the several-stories-high office buildings stood aglow. Portolondon linked an enormous hinterland to the outside world. Down the Gloria River came timber rafts, ores, harvest of farms whose owners were slowly making Rolandic life serve them, meat and ivory and furs gathered by rangers in the mountains beyond Troll Scarp. In from the sea came coastwise freighters, the fishing fleet, produce of the Sunward Islands, plunder of whole continents further south where bold men adventured. It clanged in Portolondon, laughed, blustered, swaggered, connived, robbed, preached, guzzled, swilled, toiled, dreamed, lusted, built, destroyed, died, was born, was happy, angry, sorrowful, greedy, vulgar, loving, ambitious, human. Neither the sun's blaze elsewhere nor the half year's twilight here—wholly night around midwinter—was going to stay man's hand.

Or so everybody said.

Everybody except those who had settled in the darklands. Barbro used to take for granted that they were evolving curious customs, legends and superstitions, which would die when the Outway had been completely mapped and controlled. Of late, she had wondered. Perhaps Sherrinford's hints, about a change in his own attitude brought about by his preliminary research, were responsible.

Or perhaps she just needed something to think about besides how Jimmy, the day before he went, when she asked him whether he wanted rye or French bread for a sandwich, answered in great solemnity—he was becoming interested in the alphabet—"I'll have a slice of what we people call the F bread."

She scarcely noticed getting out of the taxi, registering, being conducted to a primitively furnished room. But after she unpacked, she remembered Sherrinford had suggested a confidential conference. She went down the hall and knocked on his door. Her knuckles sounded less loud than her heart.

He opened the door, finger on lips, and gestured her toward a corner. Her temper bristled until she saw the image of Chief Constable Dawson in the visiphone. Sherrinford must have chimed him up and must have a reason to keep her out of scanner range. She found a chair and watched, nails digging into knees.

The detective's lean length refolded itself. "Pardon the interruption," he said. "A man mistook the number. Drunk, by the indications."

Dawson chuckled. "We get plenty of those." Barbro recalled his fondness for gabbing. He tugged the beard which he affected, as if he were an outwayer instead of a townsman. "No harm in them as a rule. They only have a lot of voltage to discharge, after weeks or months in the backlands."

"I've gathered that that environment—foreign in a million major and minor ways to the one that created man—I've gathered that it does do odd things to the personality." Sherrinford tamped his pipe. "Of course, you know my practice has been confined to urban and suburban areas. Isolated garths seldom need private investigators. Now that situation appears to have changed. I called to ask you for advice."

"Glad to help," Dawson said. "I've not forgotten what you did for us in the de Tahoe murder case." Cautiously: "Better explain your problem first."

Sherrinford struck fire. The smoke that followed cut through the green odors—even here, a paved pair of kilometers from the nearest woods—that drifted past traffic rumble through a crepuscular window. "This is more a scientific mission than a search for an absconding debtor or an industrial spy," he drawled. "I'm looking into two possibilities: that an organization, criminal or religious or whatever, has long been active and steals infants; or that the Outlings of folklore are real."

"Huh?" On Dawson's face Barbro read as much dismay as surprise. "You can't be serious!"

"Can't I?" Sherrinford smiled. "Several generations' worth of reports shouldn't be dismissed out of hand. Especially not when they become more frequent and consistent in the course of time, not less. Nor can we ignore the documented loss of babies and small children, amounting by now to over a hundred, and never a trace found afterward. Nor the finds which demonstrate that an intelligent species once inhabited Arctica and may still haunt the interior."

Dawson leaned forward as if to climb out of the screen. "Who engaged you?" he demanded. "That Cullen woman? We were sorry for her, naturally, but she wasn't making sense, and when she got downright abusive—"

"Didn't her companions, reputable scientists, confirm her story?"

"No story to confirm. Look, they had the place ringed with detectors and alarms, and they kept mastiffs. Standard procedure in country where a hungry sauroid or whatever might happen by. Nothing could've entered unbeknownst."

"On the ground. How about a flyer landing in the middle of camp?"

"A man in a copter rig would've roused everybody."

"A winged being might be quieter."

"A living flyer that could lift a three-year-old boy? Doesn't exist."

"Isn't in the scientific literature, you mean, Constable. Remember Graymantle; remember how little we know about Roland, a planet, an entire world. Such birds do exist on Beowulf—and on Rustum, I've read. I made a calculation from the local ratio of air density to gravity, and, yes, it's marginally possible here too. The child could have been carried off for a short distance before wing muscles were exhausted and the creature must descend."

Dawson snorted. "First it landed and walked into the tent where mother and boy were asleep. Then it walked away, toting him, after it couldn't fly further. Does that sound like a bird of prey? And the victim didn't cry out, the dogs didn't bark!"

"As a matter of fact," Sherrinford said, "those inconsistencies are the most interesting and convincing features of the whole account. You're right, it's hard to see how a human kidnapper could get in undetected, and an eagle type of creature wouldn't operate in that fashion. But none of this applies to a winged intelligent being. The boy could have been drugged. Certainly the dogs showed signs of having been."

"The dogs showed signs of having overslept. Nothing had disturbed them. The kid wandering by wouldn't do so. We don't need to assume one damn thing except, first, that he got restless and, second, that the alarms were a bit sloppily rigged—seeing as how no danger was expected from inside camp—and let him pass out. And, third, I hate to speak this way, but we must assume the poor tyke starved or was killed."

Dawson paused before adding: "If we had more staff, we could have given the affair more time. And would have, of course. We did make an aerial sweep, which risked the lives of the pilots, using instruments which would've spotted the kid anywhere in a fifty-kilometer radius, unless he was dead. You know how sensitive thermal analyzers are. We drew a complete blank. We have more important jobs than to hunt for the scattered pieces of a corpse."

He finished brusquely. "If Mrs. Cullen's hired you, my advice is you find an excuse to quit. Better for her, too. She's got to come to terms with reality."

Barbro checked a shout by biting her tongue.

"Oh, this is merely the latest disappearance of the series," Sherrinford said. She didn't understand how he could maintain his easy tone when Jimmy was lost. "More thoroughly recorded than any before, thus more suggestive. Usually an outwayer family has given a tearful but undetailed account of their child who vanished and must have been stolen by the Old Folk. Sometimes, years later, they'd tell about glimpses of what they swore must have been the grown child, not really human any longer, flitting past in murk or peering through a window or working mischief upon them. As you say, neither the authorities nor the scientists have had personnel or resources to mount a proper investigation. But as I say, the matter appears to be worth investigating. Maybe a private party like myself can contribute."

"Listen, most of us constables grew up in the outway. We don't just ride patrol and answer emergency calls; we go back there for holidays and reunions. If any gang of...of human sacrificers was around, we'd know."

"I realize that. I also realize that the people you came from have a widespread and deep-seated belief in nonhuman beings with supernatural powers. Many actually go through rites and make offerings to propitiate them."

"I know what you're leading up to," Dawson fleered. "I've heard it before, from a hundred sensationalists. The aborigines are the Outlings. I thought better of you. Surely you've visited a museum or three, surely you've read literature from planets which do have natives—or damn and blast, haven't you ever applied that logic of yours?"

He wagged a finger. "Think," he said. "What have we in fact discovered? A few pieces of worked stone; a few megaliths that might be artificial; scratchings on rock that seem to show plants and animals, though not the way any human culture would ever have shown them; traces of fires and broken bones; other fragments of bone that seem as if they might've belonged to thinking creatures, as if they might've been inside fingers or around big brains. If so, however, the owners looked nothing like men. Or angels, for that matter. Nothing! The most anthropoid reconstruction I've seen shows a kind of two-legged crocagator.

"Wait, let me finish. The stories about the Outlings—oh, I've heard them too, plenty of them. I believed them when I was a kid—the stories tell how there're different kinds, some winged, some not, some half human, some completely human except maybe for being too handsome—It's fairyland from ancient Earth all over again. Isn't it? I got interested once and dug into the Heritage Library microfiles, and be damned if I didn't find almost the identical yarns, told by peasants centuries before spaceflight.

"None of it squares with the scanty relics we have, if they are relics, or with the fact that no area the size of Arctica could spawn a dozen different intelligent species, or...hellfire, man, with the way your common sense tells you aborigines would behave when humans arrived!"

Sherrinford nodded. "Yes, yes," he said. "I'm less sure than you that the common sense of nonhuman beings is precisely like our own. I've seen so much variation within mankind. But, granted, your arguments are strong. Roland's too few scientists have more pressing tasks than tracking down the origins of what is, as you put it, a revived medieval superstition."

He cradled his pipe bowl in both hands and peered into the tiny hearth of it. "Perhaps what interests me most," he said softly, "is why—across that gap of centuries, across a barrier of machine civilization and its utterly antagonistic world view—no continuity of tradition whatsoever—why have hardheaded, technologically organized, reasonably well-educated colonists here brought back from its grave a belief in the Old Folk?"

"I suppose eventually, if the University ever does develop the psychology department they keep talking about, I suppose eventually somebody will get a thesis out of your question." Dawson spoke in a jagged voice, and he gulped when Sherrinford replied:

"I propose to begin now. In Commissioner Hauch Land, since that's where the latest incident occurred. Where can I rent a vehicle?"

"Uh, might be hard to do—"

"Come, come. Tenderfoot or not, I know better. In an economy of scarcity, few people own heavy equipment. But since it's needed, it can always be rented. I want a camper bus with a ground-effect drive suitable for every kind of terrain.

And I want certain equipment installed which I've brought along, and the top canopy section replaced by a gun turret controllable from the driver's seat. But I'll supply the weapons. Besides rifles and pistols of my own, I've arranged to borrow some artillery from Christmas Landing's police arsenal."

"Hoy? Are you genuinely intending to make ready for...a war...against a myth?"

"Let's say I'm taking out insurance, which isn't terribly expensive, against a remote possibility. Now, besides the bus, what about a light aircraft carried piggyback for use in surveys?"

"No." Dawson sounded more positive than hitherto. "That's asking for disaster. We can have you flown to a base camp in a large plane when the weather report's exactly right. But the pilot will have to fly back at once, before the weather turns wrong again. Meteorology's underdeveloped on Roland; the air's especially treacherous this time of year, and we're not tooled up to produce aircraft that can outlive every surprise." He drew breath. "Have you no idea of how fast a whirly-whirly can hit, or what size hailstones might strike from a clear sky, or—Once you're there, man, you stick to the ground." He hesitated. "That's an important reason our information is so scanty about the outway and its settlers are so isolated."

Sherrinford laughed ruefully. "Well, I suppose if details are what I'm after, I must creep along anyway."

"You'll waste a lot of time," Dawson said. "Not to mention your client's money. Listen, I can't forbid you to chase shadows, but—"

The discussion went on for almost an hour. When the screen finally blanked, Sherrinford rose, stretched and walked toward Barbro. She noticed anew his peculiar gait. He had come from a planet with a fourth again of Earth's gravitational drag, to one where weight was less than half Terrestrial. She wondered if he had flying dreams.

"I apologize for shuffling you off like that," he said. "I didn't expect to reach him at once. He was quite truthful about how busy he is. But having made contact, I didn't want to remind him overmuch of you. He can dismiss my project as a futile fantasy which I'll soon give up. But he might have frozen completely, might even have put up obstacles before us, if he'd realized through you how determined we are."

"Why should he care?" she asked in her bitterness.

"Fear of consequences, the worse because it is unadmitted fear of consequences, the more terrifying because they are unguessable." Sherrinford's gaze went to the screen, and thence out the window to the aurora pulsing in glacial blue and white immensely far overhead. "I suppose you saw I was talking to a frightened man. Down underneath his conventionality and scoffing, he believes in the Outlings—oh, yes, he believes."

The feet of Mistherd flew over yerba and outpaced windblown driftweed. Beside him, black and misshapen, hulked Nagrim the nicor, whose earthquake weight left a swath of crushed plants. Behind, luminous blossoms of a firethorn shone through the twining, trailing outlines of Morgarel the wraith.

Here Cloudmoor rose in a surf of hills and thickets. The air lay quiet, now and then carrying the distance-muted howl of a beast. It was darker than usual at winterbirth, the moons being down and aurora a wan flicker above the mountains on the northern world edge. But this made the stars keen, and their numbers crowded heaven, and Ghost Road shone among them as if it, like the leafage beneath, were paved with dew.

"Yonder!" bawled Nagrim. All four of his arms pointed. The party had topped a ridge. Far off glimmered a spark. "Hoah, hoah! 'Ull we right off stamp dem flat, or pluck dem apart slow?"

We shall do nothing of the sort, bonebrain, Morgarel's answer slid through their heads. *Not unless they attack us, and they will not unless we make them aware of us, and her command is that we spy out their purposes.*

"Gr-r-rum-m-m. I know deir aim. Cut down trees, stick plows in land, sow deir cursed seed in de clods and in deir shes. Less we drive dem into de bitterwater, and soon, soon, dey'll wax too strong for us."

"Not too strong for the Queen!" Mistherd protested, shocked.

Yet they do have new powers, it seems, Morgarel reminded him. *Carefully must we probe them.*

"Den carefully can we step on dem?" asked Nagrim.

The question woke a grin out of Mistherd's own uneasiness. He slapped the scaly back. "Don't talk, you," he said. "It hurts my ears. Nor think; that hurts your head. Come, run!"

Ease yourself, Morgarel scolded. *You have too much life in you, human-born.*

Mistherd made a face at the wraith, but obeyed to the extent of slowing down and picking his way through what cover the country afforded. For he traveled on behalf of the Fairest, to learn what had brought a pair of mortals questing hither.

Did they seek that boy whom Ayoch stole? (He continued to weep for his mother, though less and less often as the marvels of Carheddin entered him.) Perhaps. A birdcraft had left them and their car at the now-abandoned campsite, from which they had followed an outward spiral. But when no trace of the cub had appeared inside a reasonable distance, they did not call to be flown home. And this wasn't because weather forbade the farspeaker waves to travel, as was frequently the case. No, instead the couple set off toward the mountains of Moonhorn. Their course would take them past a few outlying invader steadings and on into realms untrodden by their race.

So this was no ordinary survey. Then what was it?

Mistherd understood now why she who reigned had made her adopted mortal children learn, or retain, the clumsy language of their forebears. He had hated that drill, wholly foreign to Dweller ways. Of course, you obeyed her, and in time you saw how wise she had been...

Presently he left Nagrim behind a rock—the nicor would only be useful in a fight—and crawled from bush to bush until he lay within manlengths of the humans. A rainplant drooped over him, leaves soft on his bare skin, and clothed him in darkness. Morgarel floated to the crown of a shiverleaf, whose unrest would better conceal his flimsy shape. He'd not be much help either. And that was the most troublous, the almost appalling thing here. Wraiths were among those who could not just sense and send thoughts, but cast illusions. Morgarel had reported that this time his power seemed to rebound off an invisible cold wall around the car.

Otherwise the male and female had set up no guardian engines and kept no dogs. Belike they supposed none would be needed, since they slept in the long vehicle which bore them. But such contempt of the Queen's strength could not be tolerated, could it?

Metal sheened faintly by the light of their campfire. They sat on either side, wrapped in coats against a coolness that Mistherd, naked, found mild. The male drank smoke. The female stared past him into a dusk which her flame-dazzled eyes must see as thick gloom. The dancing glow brought her vividly forth. Yes, to judge from Ayoch's tale, she was the dam of the new cub.

Ayoch had wanted to come too, but the Wonderful One forbade. Pooks couldn't hold still long enough for such a mission.

The man sucked on his pipe. His cheeks thus pulled into shadow while the light flickered across nose and brow, he looked disquietingly like a shearbill about to stoop on prey.

"—No, I tell you again, Barbro, I have no theories," he was saying. "When facts are insufficient, theorizing is ridiculous at best, misleading at worst."

"Still, you must have some idea of what you're doing," she said. It was plain that they had threshed this out often before. No Dweller could be as persistent as her or as patient as him. "That gear you packed—that generator you keep running—"

"I have a working hypothesis or two, which suggested what equipment I ought to take."

"Why won't you tell me what the hypotheses are?"

"They themselves indicate that that might be inadvisable at the present time. I'm still feeling my way into the labyrinth. And I haven't had a chance yet to hook everything up. In fact, we're really only protected against so-called telepathic influence—"

"What?" She started. "Do you mean...those legends about how they can read minds too..." Her words trailed off and her gaze sought the darkness beyond his shoulders.

He leaned forward. His tone lost its clipped rapidity, grew earnest and soft. "Barbro, you're racking yourself to pieces. Which is no help to Jimmy if he's alive, the more so when you may well be badly needed later on. We've a long trek before us, and you'd better settle into it."

She nodded jerkily and caught her lip between her teeth for a moment before she answered, "I'm trying."

He smiled around his pipe. "I expect you'll succeed. You don't strike me as a quitter or a whiner or an enjoyer of misery."

She dropped a hand to the pistol at her belt. Her voice changed; it came out of her throat like knife from sheath. "When we find them, they'll know what I am. What humans are."

"Put anger aside also," the man urged. "We can't afford emotions. If the Outlings are real, as I told you I'm provisionally assuming, they're fighting for their homes." After a short stillness he added: "I like to think that if the first explorers had found live natives, men would not have colonized Roland. But too late now. We can't go back if we wanted to. It's a bitter-end struggle, against an enemy so crafty that he's even hidden from us the fact that he is waging war."

"Is he? I mean, skulking, kidnapping an occasional child—"

"That's part of my hypothesis. I suspect those aren't harassments, they're tactics employed in a chillingly subtle strategy."

The fire sputtered and sparked. The man smoked awhile, brooding, until he went on:

"I didn't want to raise your hopes or excite you unduly while you had to wait on me, first in Christmas Landing, then in Portolondon. Afterward we were busy satisfying ourselves that Jimmy had been taken further from camp than he could have wandered before collapsing. So I'm only now telling you how thoroughly I studied available material on the...Old Folk. Besides, at first I did it on the principle of eliminating every imaginable possibility, however absurd. I expected no result other than final disproof. But I went through everything, relics, analyses, histories, journalistic accounts, monographs; I talked to outwayers who happened to be in town and to what scientists we have who've taken any interest in the matter. I'm a quick study. I flatter myself I became as expert as anyone—though God knows there's little to be expert on. Furthermore, I, a comparative stranger to Roland, maybe looked on the problem with fresh eyes. And a pattern emerged for me.

"If the aborigines had become extinct, why hadn't they left more remnants? Arctica isn't enormous, and it's fertile for Rolandic life. It ought to have supported a population whose artifacts ought to have accumulated over millennia. I've read that on Earth, literally tens of thousands of paleolithic hand axes were found, more by chance than archaeology.

"Very well. Suppose the relics and fossils were deliberately removed, between the time the last survey party left and the first colonizing ships arrived. I did find some support for that idea in the diaries of the original explorers. They were too preoccupied with checking the habitability of the planet to make catalogues of primitive monuments. However, the remarks they wrote down indicate they saw much more than later arrivals did. Suppose what we have found is just what the removers overlooked or didn't get around to.

"That argues a sophisticated mentality, thinking in long-range terms, doesn't it? Which in turn argues that the Old Folk were not mere hunters or neolithic farmers."

"But nobody ever saw buildings or machines or any such thing," Barbro protested.

"No. Most likely the natives didn't go through our kind of metallurgic-industrial evolution. I can conceive of other paths to take. Their full-fledged civilization might have begun, rather than ended, in biological science and technology. It might have developed potentialities of the nervous system, which might be greater in their species than in man. We have those abilities to some degree ourselves, you realize. A dowser, for instance, actually senses variations in the local magnetic field caused by a water table. However, in us, these talents are maddeningly rare and tricky. So we took our business elsewhere. Who needs to be a telepath, say, when he has a visiphone? The Old Folk may have seen it the other way around. The artifacts of their civilization may have been, may still be unrecognizable to men."

"They could have identified themselves to the men, though," Barbro said. "Why didn't they?"

"I can imagine any number of reasons. As, they could have had a bad experience with interstellar visitors earlier in their history. Ours is scarcely the sole race that has spaceships. However, I told you I don't theorize in advance of the facts. Let's say no more than that the Old Folk, if they exist, are alien to us."

"For a rigorous thinker, you're spinning a mighty thin thread."

"I've admitted this is entirely provisional." He squinted at her through a roil of campfire smoke. "You came to me, Barbro, insisting in the teeth of officialdom that your boy had been stolen, but your own talk about cultist kidnappers was ridiculous. Why are you reluctant to admit the reality of nonhumans?"

"In spite of the fact that Jimmy's being alive probably depends on it," she sighed. "I know." A shudder. "Maybe I don't dare admit it."

"I've said nothing thus far that hasn't been speculated about in print," he told her. "A disreputable speculation, true. In a hundred years, nobody has found valid evidence for the Outlings being more than a superstition. Still, a few people have declared it's at least possible that intelligent natives are at large in the wilderness."

"I know," she repeated. "I'm not sure, though, what has made you, overnight, take those arguments seriously."

"Well, once you got me started thinking, it occurred to me that Roland's outwayers are not utterly isolated medieval crofters. They have books, telecommunications, power tools, motor vehicles; above all, they have a modern science-oriented education. Why should they turn superstitious? Something must be causing it." He stopped. "I'd better not continue. My ideas go further than this; but if they're correct, it's dangerous to speak them aloud."

Mistherd's belly muscles tensed. There was danger for fair, in that shearbill head. The Garland Bearer must be warned. For a minute he wondered about summoning Nagrim to kill these two. If the nicor jumped them fast, their firearms might avail them naught. But no. They might have left word at home, or— He came back to his ears. The talk had changed course. Barbro was murmuring, "—why you stayed on Roland."

The man smiled his gaunt smile. "Well, life on Beowulf held no challenge for me. Heorot is—or was; this was decades past, remember—Heorot was densely populated, smoothly organized, boringly uniform. That was partly due to the lowland frontier, a safety valve that bled off the dissatisfied. But I lack the carbon dioxide tolerance necessary to live healthily down there. An expedition was being readied to make a swing around a number of colony worlds, especially those which didn't have the equipment to keep in laser contact. You'll recall its announced purpose, to seek out new ideas in science, arts, sociology, philosophy, whatever might prove valuable. I'm afraid they found little on Roland relevant to Beowulf. But I, who had wangled a berth, I saw opportunities for myself and decided to make my home here."

"Were you a detective back there, too?"

"Yes, in the official police. We had a tradition of such work in our family. Some of that may have come from the Cherokee side of it, if the name means anything to you. However, we also claimed collateral descent from one of the first private inquiry agents on record, back on Earth before spaceflight. Regardless of how true that may be, I found him a useful model. You see, an archetype—"

The man broke off. Unease crossed his features. "Best we go to sleep," he said. "We've a long distance to cover in the morning."

She looked outward. "Here is no morning."

They retired. Mistherd rose and cautiously flexed limberness back into his muscles. Before returning to the Sister of Lyrth, he risked a glance through a pane in the car. Bunks were made up, side by side, and the humans lay in them. Yet the man had not touched her, though hers was a bonny body, and nothing that had passed between them suggested he meant to do so.

Eldritch, humans. Cold and claylike. And they would overrun the beautiful wild world? Mistherd spat in disgust. It must not happen. It would not happen. She who reigned had vowed that.

The lands of William Irons were immense. But this was because a barony was required to support him, his kin and cattle, on native crops whose cultivation was still poorly understood. He raised some Terrestrial plants as well, by summerlight and in conservatories. However, these were a luxury. The true conquest of northern Arctica lay in yerba hay, in bathyrhiza wood, in pericoup and glycophyllon, and eventually, when the market had expanded with population and industry, in chalcanthemum for city florists and pelts of cage-bred rover for city furriers.

That was in a tomorrow Irons did not expect that he would live to see. Sherrinford wondered if the man really expected anyone ever would.

The room was warm and bright. Cheerfulness crackled in the fireplace. Light from fluoropanels gleamed off hand-carven chests and chairs and tables, off colorful draperies and shelved dishes. The outwayer sat solid in his high seat, stoutly clad, beard flowing down his chest. His wife and daughters brought coffee, whose fragrance joined the remnant odors of a hearty supper, to him, his guests and his sons.

But outside, wind hooted, lightning flared, thunder bawled, rain crashed on roof and walls and roared down to swirl among the courtyard cobblestones. Sheds and barns crouched against hugeness beyond. Trees groaned, and did a wicked undertone of laughter run beneath the lowing of a frightened cow? A burst of hailstones hit the tiles like knocking knuckles.

You could feel how distant your neighbors were, Sherrinford thought. And nonetheless they were the people whom you saw oftenest, did daily business with by visiphone (when a solar storm didn't make gibberish of their voices and chaos of their faces) or in the flesh, partied with, gossiped and intrigued with, intermarried with; in the end, they were the people who would bury you. The lights of the coastal towns were monstrously further away.

William Irons was a strong man. Yet when now he spoke, fear was in his tone. "You'd truly go over Troll Scarp?"

"Do you mean Hanstein Palisades?" Sherrinford responded, more challenge than question.

"No outwayer calls it anything but Troll Scarp," Barbro said.

And how had a name like that been reborn, lightyears and centuries from Earth's Dark Ages?

"Hunters, trappers, prospectors—rangers, you call them—travel in those mountains," Sherrinford declared.

"In certain parts," Irons said. "That's allowed, by a pact once made 'tween a man and the Queen after he'd done well by a jack-o'-the-hill that a satan had hurt. Wherever the plumablanca grows, men may fare, if they leave man-goods on the altar boulders in payment for what they take out of the land. Elsewhere—" one fist clenched on a chair arm and went slack again "—'s not wise to go."

"It's been done, hasn't it?"

"Oh, yes. And some came back all right, or so they claimed, though I've heard they were never lucky afterward. And some didn't; they vanished. And some who returned babbled of wonders and horrors, and stayed witlings the rest of their lives. Not for a long time has anybody been rash enough to break the pact and overtread the bounds." Irons looked at Barbro almost entreatingly. His woman and children stared likewise, grown still. Wind hooted beyond the walls and rattled the storm shutters. "Don't you."

"I've reason to believe my son is there," she answered.

"Yes, yes, you've told and I'm sorry. Maybe something can be done. I don't know what, but I'd be glad to, oh, lay a double offering on Unvar's Barrow this midwinter, and a prayer drawn in the turf by a flint knife. Maybe they'll return him." Irons sighed. "They've not done such a thing in man's memory, though. And he could have a worse lot. I've glimpsed them myself, speeding madcap through twilight. They seem happier than we are. Might be no kindness, sending your boy home again."

"Like in the Arvid song," said his wife.

Irons nodded. "M-hm. Or others, come to think of it."

"What's this?" Sherrinford asked. More sharply than before, he felt himself a stranger. He was a child of cities and technics, above all a child of the skeptical intelligence. This family *believed*. It was disquieting to see more than a touch of their acceptance in Barbro's slow nod.

"We have the same ballad in Olga Ivanoff Land," she told him, her voice less calm than the words. "It's one of the traditional ones, nobody knows who composed them, that are sung to set the measure of a ring dance in a meadow."

"I noticed a multilyre in your baggage, Mrs. Cullen," said the wife of Irons. She was obviously eager to get off the explosive topic of a venture in defiance of the Old Folk. A songfest could help. "Would you like to entertain us?"

Barbro shook her head, white around the nostrils. The oldest boy said quickly, rather importantly, "Well, sure, I can, if our guests would like to hear."

"I'd enjoy that, thank you." Sherrinford leaned back in his seat and stoked his pipe. If this had not happened spontaneously, he would have guided the conversation toward a similar outcome.

In the past he had had no incentive to study the folklore of the outway, and not much chance to read the scanty references on it since Barbro brought him her trouble. Yet more and more he was becoming convinced that he must get an understanding—not an anthropological study, but a feel from the inside out—of the relationship between Roland's frontiersmen and those beings which haunted them.

A bustling followed, rearrangement, settling down to listen, coffee cups refilled and brandy offered on the side. The boy explained, "The last line is the chorus. Everybody join in, right?" Clearly he too hoped thus to bleed off some of the tension. Catharsis through music? Sherrinford wondered, and added to himself: No; exorcism.

A girl strummed a guitar. The boy sang, to a melody which beat across the storm noise:

It was the ranger Arvid
rode homeward through the hills
among the shadowy shiverleafs,
along the chiming rills.
The dance weaves under the firethorn.

The night wind whispered around him
with scent of brok and rue.
Both moons rose high above him
and hills aflash with dew.
The dance weaves under the firethorn.

And dreaming of that woman
who waited in the sun,
he stopped, amazed by starlight,
and so he was undone.
The dance weaves under the firethorn.

For there beneath a barrow
that bulked athwart a moon,
the Outling folk were dancing
in glass and golden shoon.
The dance weaves under the firethorn.

The Outling folk were dancing
like water, wind and fire
to frosty-ringing harpstrings,

and never did they tire.
The dance weaves under the firethorn.

To Arvid came she striding
from where she watched the dance,
the Queen of Air and Darkness,
with starlight in her glance.
The dance weaves under the firethorn.

With starlight, love and terror
in her immortal eye,
the Queen of Air and Darkness—

"No!" Barbro leaped from her chair. Her fists were clenched and tears flogged her cheekbones. "You can't—pretend that—about the things that stole Jimmy!"
She fled from the chamber, upstairs to her guest bedroom.

But she finished the song herself. That was about seventy hours later, camped in the steeps where rangers dared not fare. She and Sherrinford had not said much to the Irons family, after refusing repeated pleas to leave the forbidden country alone. Nor had they exchanged many remarks at first as they drove north. Slowly, however, he began to draw her out about her own life. After a while she almost forgot to mourn, in her remembering of home and old neighbors. Somehow this led to discoveries—that he, beneath his professional manner, was a gourmet and a lover of opera and appreciated her femaleness; that she could still laugh and find beauty in the wild land around her—and she realized, half guiltily, that life held more hopes than even the recovery of the son Tim gave her.
"I've convinced myself he's alive," the detective said. He scowled. "Frankly, it makes me regret having taken you along. I expected this would be only a fact-gathering trip, but it's turning out to be more. If we're dealing with real creatures who stole him, they can do real harm. I ought to turn back to the nearest garth and call for a plane to fetch you."
"Like bottommost hell you will, mister," she said. "You need somebody who knows outway conditions, and I'm a better shot than average."
"M-m-m…it would involve considerable delay too, wouldn't it? Besides the added distance, I can't put a signal through to any airport before this current burst of solar interference has calmed down." Next "night" he broke out his remaining equipment and set it up. She recognized some of it, such as the thermal detector. Other items were strange to her, copied to his order from the advanced apparatus of his birthworld. He would tell her little about them. "I've explained my suspicion that the ones we're after have telepathic capabilities," he said in apology.
Her eyes widened. "You mean it could be true, the Queen and her people can read minds?"
"That's part of the dread which surrounds their legend, isn't it? Actually there's nothing spooky about the phenomenon. It was studied and fairly well defined

centuries ago, on Earth. I daresay the facts are available in the scientific microfiles at Christmas Landing. You Rolanders have simply had no occasion to seek them out, any more than you've yet had occasion to look up how to build power beamcasters or spacecraft."

"Well, how does telepathy work, then?"

Sherrinford recognized that her query asked for comfort as much as it did for facts and he spoke with deliberate dryness: "The organism generates extremely long-wave radiation which can, in principle, be modulated by the nervous system. In practice, the feebleness of the signals and their low rate of information transmission make them elusive, hard to detect and measure. Our prehuman ancestors went in for more reliable senses, like vision and hearing. What telepathic transceiving we do is marginal at best. But explorers have found extraterrestrial species that got an evolutionary advantage from developing the system further, in their particular environments. I imagine such species could include one which gets comparatively little direct sunlight—in fact, appears to hide from broad day. It could even become so able in this regard that, at short range, it can pick up man's weak emissions and make man's primitive sensitivities resonate to its own strong sendings."

"That would account for a lot, wouldn't it?" Barbro said faintly.

"I've now screened our car by a jamming field," Sherrinford told her, "but it reaches only a few meters past the chassis. Beyond, a scout of theirs might get a warning from your thoughts, if you knew precisely what I'm trying to do. I have a well-trained subconscious which sees to it that I think about this in French when I'm outside. Communication has to be structured to be intelligible, you see, and that's a different enough structure from English. But English is the only human language on Roland, and surely the Old Folk have learned it."

She nodded. He had told her his general plan, which was too obvious to conceal. The problem was to make contact with the aliens, if they existed. Hitherto, they had only revealed themselves, at rare intervals, to one or a few backwoodsmen at a time. An ability to generate hallucinations would help them in that. They would stay clear of any large, perhaps unmanageable expedition which might pass through their territory. But two people, braving all prohibitions, shouldn't look too formidable to approach. And...this would be the first human team which not only worked on the assumption that the Outlings were real but possessed the resources of modern, off-planet police technology.

Nothing happened at that camp. Sherrinford said he hadn't expected it would. The Old Folk seemed cautious this near to any settlement. In their own lands they must be bolder.

And by the following "night," the vehicle had gone well into yonder country. When Sherrinford stopped the engine in a meadow and the car settled down, silence rolled in like a wave.

They stepped out. She cooked a meal on the glower while he gathered wood, that they might later cheer themselves with a campfire. Frequently he glanced at his wrist. It bore no watch—instead, a radio-controlled dial, to tell what the instruments in the bus might register.

Who needed a watch here? Slow constellations wheeled beyond glimmering aurora. The moon Alde stood above a snowpeak, turning it argent, though this place lay at a goodly height. The rest of the mountains were hidden by the forest that crowded around. Its trees were mostly shiverleaf and feathery white plumablanca, ghostly amidst their shadows. A few firethorns glowed, clustered dim lanterns, and the underbrush was heavy and smelled sweet. You could see surprisingly far through the blue dusk. Somewhere nearby, a brook sang and a bird fluted.

"Lovely here," Sherrinford said. They had risen from their supper and not yet sat down again or kindled their fire.

"But strange," Barbro answered as low. "I wonder if it's really meant for us. If we can really hope to possess it."

His pipestem gestured at the stars. "Man's gone to stranger places than this."

"Has he? I...oh, I suppose it's just something left over from my outway childhood, but do you know, when I'm under them I can't think of the stars as balls of gas, whose energies have been measured, whose planets have been walked on by prosaic feet. No, they're small and cold and magical; our lives are bound to them; after we die, they whisper to us in our graves." Barbro glanced downward. "I realize that's nonsense."

She could see in the twilight how his face grew tight. "Not at all," he said. "Emotionally, physics may be a worse nonsense. And in the end, you know, after a sufficient number of generations, thought follows feeling. Man is not at heart rational. He could stop believing the stories of science if those no longer felt right."

He paused. "That ballad which didn't get finished in the house," he said, not looking at her. "Why did it affect you so?"

"I couldn't stand hearing *them*, well, praised. Or that's how it seemed. Sorry for the fuss."

"I gather the ballad is typical of a large class."

"Well, I never thought to add them up. Cultural anthropology is something we don't have time for on Roland, or more likely it hasn't occurred to us, with everything else there is to do. But—now you mention it, yes, I'm surprised at how many songs and stories have the Arvid motif in them."

"Could you bear to recite it?"

She mustered the will to laugh. "Why, I can do better than that if you want. Let me get my multilyre and I'll perform."

She omitted the hypnotic chorus line, though, when the notes rang out, except at the end. He watched her where she stood against moon and aurora.

—the Queen of Air and Darkness
cried softly under sky:

"Light down, you ranger Arvid,
and join the Outling folk.
You need no more be human,
which is a heavy yoke."

He dared to give her answer:
"I may do naught but run.
A maiden waits me, dreaming
in lands beneath the sun.

"And likewise wait me comrades
and tasks I would not shirk,
for what is ranger Arvid
if he lays down his work?

"So wreak your spells, you Outling,
and cast your wrath on me.
Though maybe you can slay me,
you'll not make me unfree."

The Queen of Air and Darkness
stood wrapped about with fear
and northlight-flares and beauty
he dared not look too near.

Until she laughed like harpsong
and said to him in scorn:
"I do not need a magic
to make you always mourn.

"I send you home with nothing
except your memory
of moonlight, Outling music,
night breezes, dew and me.

"And that will run behind you,
a shadow on the sun,
and that will lie beside you
when every day is done.

"In work and play and friendship
your grief will strike you dumb
for thinking what you are—and—
what you might have become.

"Your dull and foolish woman
treat kindly as you can.
Go home now, Ranger Arvid,
set free to be a man!"

In flickering and laughter
the Outling folk were gone.
He stood alone by moonlight
and wept until the dawn.
The dance weaves under the firethorn.

She laid the lyre aside. A wind rustled leaves. After a long quietness Sherrinford said, "And tales of this kind are part of everyone's life in the outway?"

"Well, you could put it thus," Barbro replied. "Though they're not all full of supernatural doings. Some are about love or heroism. Traditional themes."

"I don't think your particular tradition has arisen of itself." His tone was bleak. "In fact, I think many of your songs and stories were not composed by human beings."

He snapped his lips shut and would say no more on the subject. They went early to bed.

Hours later, an alarm roused them.

The buzzing was soft, but it brought them instantly alert. They slept in gripsuits, to be prepared for emergencies. Sky-glow lit them through the canopy. Sherrinford swung out of his bunk, slipped shoes on feet and clipped gun holster to belt. "Stay inside," he commanded.

"What's here?" Her pulse thudded.

He squinted at the dials of his instruments and checked them against the luminous telltale on his wrist. "Three animals," he counted. "Not wild ones happening by. A large one, homeothermic, to judge from the infrared, holding still a short ways off. Another…hm, low temperature, diffuse and unstable emission, as if it were more like a…a swarm of cells coordinated somehow…pheromonally?…hovering, also at a distance. But the third's practically next to us, moving around in the brush; and that pattern looks human."

She saw him quiver with eagerness, no longer seeming a professor. "I'm going to try to make a capture," he said. "When we have a subject for interrogation— Stand ready to let me back in again fast. But don't risk yourself, whatever happens. And keep this cocked." He handed her a loaded big-game rifle.

His tall frame poised by the door, opened it a crack. Air blew in, cool, damp, full of fragrances and murmurings. The moon Oliver was now also aloft, the radiance of both unreally brilliant, and the aurora seethed in whiteness and ice-blue.

Sherrinford peered afresh at his telltale. It must indicate the directions of the watchers, among those dappled leaves. Abruptly he sprang out. He sprinted past the ashes of the campfire and vanished under trees. Barbro's hand strained on the butt of her weapon.

Racket exploded. Two in combat burst onto the meadow. Sherrinford had clapped a grip on a smaller human figure. She could make out by streaming silver and rainbow flicker that the other was nude, male, long-haired, lithe and young. He fought demoniacally, seeking to use teeth and feet and raking nails, and meanwhile he ululated like a satan.

The identification shot through her: A changeling, stolen in babyhood and raised by the Old Folk. This creature was what they would make Jimmy into.

"Ha!" Sherrinford forced his opponent around and drove stiffened fingers into the solar plexus. The boy gasped and sagged. Sherrinford manhandled him toward the car.

Out from the woods came a giant. It might itself have been a tree, black and rugose, bearing four great gnarly boughs; but earth quivered and boomed beneath its leg-roots, and its hoarse bellowing filled sky and skulls.

Barbro shrieked. Sherrinford whirled. He yanked out his pistol, fired and fired, flat whipcracks through the half light. His free arm kept a lock on the youth. The troll shape lurched under those blows. It recovered and came on, more slowly, more carefully, circling around to cut him off from the bus. He couldn't move fast enough to evade it unless he released his prisoner—who was his sole possible guide to Jimmy—

Barbro leaped forth. "Don't!" Sherrinford shouted. "For God's sake, stay inside!" The monster rumbled and made snatching motions at her. She pulled the trigger. Recoil slammed her in the shoulder. The colossus rocked and fell. Somehow it got its feet back and lumbered toward her. She retreated. Again she shot, and again. The creature snarled. Blood began to drip from it and gleam oilily amidst dewdrops. It turned and went off, breaking branches, into the darkness that laired beneath the woods.

"Get to shelter!" Sherrinford yelled. "You're out of the jammer field!"

A mistiness drifted by overhead. She barely glimpsed it before she saw the new shape at the meadow edge. "Jimmy!" tore from her.

"Mother." He held out his arms. Moonlight coursed in his tears. She dropped her weapon and ran to him.

Sherrinford plunged in pursuit. Jimmy flitted away into the brush. Barbro crashed after, through clawing twigs. Then she was seized and borne away.

Standing over his captive, Sherrinford strengthened the fluoro output until vision of the wilderness was blocked off from within the bus. The boy squirmed beneath that colorless glare.

"You are going to talk," the man said. Despite the haggardness in his features, he spoke quietly.

The boy glared through tangled locks. A bruise was purpling on his jaw. He'd almost recovered ability to flee while Sherrinford chased and lost the woman. Returning, the detective had barely caught him. Time was lacking to be gentle, when Outling reinforcements might arrive at any moment. Sherrinford had knocked him out and dragged him inside. He sat lashed into a swivel seat.

He spat. "Talk to you, man-clod?" But sweat stood on his skin, and his eyes flickered unceasingly around the metal which caged him.

"Give me a name to call you by."

"And have you work a spell on me?"

"Mine's Eric. If you don't give me another choice, I'll have to call you...m-m-m...Wuddikins."

"What?" However eldritch, the bound one remained a human adolescent. "Mistherd, then." The lilting accent of his English somehow emphasized its sullenness. "That's not the sound, only what it means. Anyway, it's my spoken name, naught else."

"Ah, you keep a secret name you consider to be real?"

"She does. I don't know myself what it is. She knows the real names of everybody."

Sherrinford raised his brows. "She?"

"Who reigns. May she forgive me, I can't make the reverent sign when my arms are tied. Some invaders call her the Queen of Air and Darkness."

"So." Sherrinford got pipe and tobacco. He let silence wax while he started the fire. At length he said:

"I'll confess the Old Folk took me by surprise. I didn't expect so formidable a member of your gang. Everything I could learn had seemed to show they work on my race—and yours, lad—by stealth, trickery and illusion."

Mistherd jerked a truculent nod. "She created the first nicors not long ago. Don't think she has naught but dazzlements at her beck."

"I don't. However, a steel jacketed bullet works pretty well too, doesn't it?"

Sherrinford talked on, softly, mostly to himself: "I do still believe the, ah, nicors—all your half-humanlike breeds—are intended in the main to be seen, not used. The power of projecting mirages must surely be quite limited in range and scope as well as in the number of individuals who possess it. Otherwise she wouldn't have needed to work as slowly and craftily as she has. Even outside our mind-shield, Barbro—my companion—could have resisted, could have remained aware that whatever she saw was unreal…if she'd been less shaken, less frantic, less driven by need."

Sherrinford wreathed his head in smoke. "Never mind what I experienced," he said. "It couldn't have been the same as for her. I think the command was simply given us, 'You will see what you most desire in the world, running away from you into the forest.' Of course, she didn't travel many meters before the nicor waylaid her. I'd no hope of trailing them; I'm no Arctican woodsman, and besides, it'd have been too easy to ambush me. I came back to you." Grimly: "You're my link to your overlady."

"You think I'll guide you to Starhaven or Carheddin? Try making me, clodman."

"I want to bargain."

"I s'pect you intend more'n that." Mistherd's answer held surprising shrewdness. "What'll you tell after you come home?"

"Yes, that does pose a problem, doesn't it? Barbro Cullen and I are not terrified outwayers. We're of the city. We brought recording instruments. We'd be the first of our kind to report an encounter with the Old Folk, and that report would be detailed and plausible. It would produce action."

"So you see I'm not afraid to die," Mistherd declared, though his lips trembled a bit. "If I let you come in and do your man-things to my people, I'd have naught left worth living for."

"Have no immediate fears," Sherrinford said. "You're merely bait." He sat down and regarded the boy through a visor of calm. (Within, it wept in him: *Barbro, Barbro*!) "Consider. Your Queen can't very well let me go back, bringing my prisoner and telling about hers. She has to stop that somehow. I could try fighting my way through—this car is better armed than you know—but that wouldn't free anybody. Instead, I'm staying put. New forces of hers will get here as fast as they can. I assume they won't blindly throw themselves against a machine gun, a howitzer, a fulgurator. They'll parley first, whether their intentions are honest or not. Thus I make the contact I'm after."

"What d' you plan?" The mumble held anguish.

"First, this, as a sort of invitation." Sherrinford reached out to flick a switch. "There. I've lowered my shield against mind-reading and shapecasting. I daresay the leaders, at least, will be able to sense that it's gone. That should give them confidence."

"And next?"

"Next we wait. Would you like something to eat or drink'?"

During the time which followed, Sherrinford tried to jolly Mistherd along, find out something of his life. What answers he got were curt. He dimmed the interior lights and settled down to peer outward. That was a long few hours.

They ended at a shout of gladness, half a sob, from the boy. Out of the woods came a band of the Old Folk.

Some of them stood forth more clearly than moons and stars and northlights should have caused. He in the van rode a white crownbuck whose horns were garlanded. His form was manlike but unearthly beautiful, silverblond hair falling from beneath the antlered helmet, around the proud cold face. The cloak fluttered off his back like living wings. His frost-colored mail rang as he fared.

Behind him, to right and left, rode two who bore swords whereon small flames gleamed and flickered. Above, a flying flock laughed and trilled and tumbled in the breezes. Near then drifted a half-transparent mistiness. Those others who passed among trees after their chieftain were harder to make out. But they moved in quicksilver grace and as it were to a sound of harps and trumpets.

"Lord Luighaid." Glory overflowed in Mistherd's tone. "Her master Knower—himself."

Sherrinford had never done a harder thing than to sit at the main control panel, finger near the button of the shield generator, and not touch it. He rolled down a section of canopy to let voices travel. A gust of wind struck him in the face, bearing odors of the roses in his mother's garden. At his back, in the main body of the vehicle, Mistherd strained against his bonds till he could see the oncoming troop.

"Call to them," Sherrinford said. "Ask if they will talk with me."

Unknown, flutingly sweet words flew back and forth. "Yes," the boy interpreted. "He will, the Lord Luighaid. But I can tell you, you'll never be let go. Don't fight them. Yield. Come away. You don't know what 'tis to be alive till you've dwelt in Carheddin under the mountain."

The Outlings drew nigh.

Jimmy glimmered and was gone. Barbro lay in strong arms, against a broad breast, and felt the horse move beneath her. It had to be a horse, though only a few were kept any longer on the steadings and they only for special uses or love. She could feel the rippling beneath its hide, hear a rush of parted leafage and the thud when a hoof struck stone; warmth and living scent welled up around her through the darkness.

He who carried her said mildly, "Don't be afraid, darling. It was a vision. But he's waiting for us and we're bound for him."

She was aware in a vague way that she ought to feel terror or despair or something. But her memories lay behind her—she wasn't sure just how she had come to be here—she was borne along in a knowledge of being loved. At peace, at peace; rest in the calm expectation of joy...

After a while the forest opened. They crossed a lea where boulders stood gray-white under the moons, their shadows shifting in the dim hues which the aurora threw across them. Flitteries danced, tiny comets, above the flowers between. Ahead gleamed a peak whose top was crowned in clouds.

Barbro's eyes happened to be turned forward. She saw the horse's head and thought, with quiet surprise: Why, this is Sambo, who was mine when I was a girl. She looked upward at the man. He wore a black tunic and a cowled cape, which made his face hard to see. She could not cry aloud, here. "Tim," she whispered.

"Yes, Barbro."

"I buried you—"

His smile was endlessly tender. "Did you think we're no more than what's laid back into the ground? Poor torn sweetheart. She who's called us is the All Healer. Now rest and dream."

"Dream," she said, and for a space she struggled to rouse herself. But the effort was weak. Why should she believe ashen tales about...atoms and energies, nothing else to fill a gape of emptiness...tales she could not bring to mind...when Tim and the horse her father gave her carried her on to Jimmy? Had the other thing not been the evil dream, and this her first drowsy awakening from it?

As if he heard her thoughts, he murmured, "They have a song in Outling lands. The Song of the Men:

The world sails
to an unseen wind.
Light swirls by the bows.
The wake is night.
But the Dwellers have no such sadness.

"I don't understand," she said.

He nodded. "There's much you'll have to understand, darling, and I can't see you again until you've learned those truths. But meanwhile you'll be with our son."

She tried to lift her head and kiss him. He held her down. "Not yet," he said. "You've not been received among the Queen's people. I shouldn't have come for you, except that she was too merciful to forbid. Lie back, lie back."

Time blew past. The horse galloped tireless, never stumbling, up the mountain. Once she glimpsed a troop riding down it and thought they were bound for a last weird battle in the west against...who?...one who lay cased in iron and sorrow. Later she would ask herself the name of him who had brought her into the land of the Old Truth.

Finally spires lifted splendid among the stars, which are small and magical and whose whisperings comfort us after we are dead. They rode into a courtyard where candles burned unwavering, fountains splashed and birds sang. The air bore fragrance of brok and pericoup, of rue and roses, for not everything that man brought was horrible. The Dwellers waited in beauty to welcome her. Beyond their stateliness, pooks cavorted through the gloaming; among the trees darted children; merriment caroled across music more solemn.

"We have come—" Tim's voice was suddenly, inexplicably a croak. Barbro was not sure how he dismounted, bearing her. She stood before him and saw him sway on his feet.

Fear caught her. "Are you well?" She seized both his hands. They felt cold and rough. Where had Sambo gone? Her eyes searched beneath the cowl. In this brighter illumination, she ought to have seen her man's face clearly. But it was blurred, it kept changing. "What's wrong, oh, what's happened?"

He smiled. Was that the smile she had cherished? She couldn't completely remember. "I, I must go," he stammered, so low she could scarcely hear. "Our time is not ready." He drew free of her grasp and leaned on a robed form which had appeared at his side. A haziness swirled over both their heads. "Don't watch me go...back into the earth," he pleaded. "That's death for you. Till our time returns—There, our son!"

She had to fling her gaze around. Kneeling, she spread wide her arms. Jimmy struck her like a warm, solid cannonball. She rumpled his hair; she kissed the hollow of his neck; she laughed and wept and babbled foolishness; and this was no ghost, no memory that had stolen off when she wasn't looking. Now and again, as she turned her attention to yet another hurt which might have come upon him—hunger, sickness, fear—and found none, she would glimpse their surroundings. The gardens were gone. It didn't matter.

"I missed you so, Mother. Stay?"

"I'll take you home, dearest."

"Stay. Here's fun. I'll show. But you stay."

A sighing went through the twilight. Barbro rose. Jimmy clung to her hand. They confronted the Queen.

Very tall she was in her robes woven of northlights, and her starry crown and her garlands of kiss-me-never. Her countenance recalled Aphrodite of Milos, whose picture Barbro had often seen in the realms of men, save that the Queen's was more fair and more majesty dwelt upon it and in the night-blue eyes. Around her the gardens woke to new reality, the court of the Dwellers and the heaven-climbing spires.

"Be welcome," she spoke, her speaking a song, "forever."

Against the awe of her, Barbro said, "Moonmother, let us go home."

"That may not be."

"To our world, little and beloved," Barbro dreamed she begged, "which we build for ourselves and cherish for our children."

"To prison days, angry nights, works that crumble in the fingers, loves that turn to rot or stone or driftweed, loss, grief, and the only sureness that of the final nothingness. No. You too, Wanderfoot who is to be, will jubilate when the banners of the Outworld come flying into the last of the cities and man is made wholly alive. Now go with those who will teach you."

The Queen of Air and Darkness lifted an arm in summons. It halted, and none came to answer.

For over the fountains and melodies lifted a gruesome growling. Fires leaped, thunders crashed. Her hosts scattered screaming before the steel thing which boomed up the mountainside. The pooks were gone in a whirl of frightened wings. The nicors flung their bodies against the unalive invader and were consumed, until their Mother cried to them to retreat.

Barbro cast Jimmy down and herself over him. Towers wavered and smoked away. The mountain stood bare under icy moons, save for rocks, crags, and farther off a glacier in whose depths the auroral light pulsed blue. A cave mouth darkened a cliff. Thither folk streamed, seeking refuge underground. Some were human of blood, some grotesques like the pooks and nicors and wraiths; but most were lean, scaly, long-tailed, long-beaked, not remotely men or Outlings.

For an instant, even as Jimmy wailed at her breast—perhaps as much because the enchantment had been wrecked as because he was afraid—Barbro pitied the Queen who stood alone in her nakedness. Then that one also had fled, and Barbro's world shiverered apart.

The guns fell silent; the vehicle whirred to a halt. From it sprang a boy who called wildly, "Shadow-of-a-Dream, where are you? It's me, Mistherd. Oh, come, come!"—before he remembered that the language they had been raised in was not man's. He shouted in that until a girl crept out of a thicket where she had hidden. They stared at each other through dust, smoke and moonglow. She ran to him.

A new voice barked from the car, "Barbro, hurry!"

Christmas Landing knew day: short at this time of year, but sunlight, blue skies, white clouds, glittering water, salt breezes in busy streets, and the sane disorder of Eric Sherrinford's living room.

He crossed and uncrossed his legs where he sat, puffed on his pipe as if to make a veil, and said, "Are you certain you're recovered? You mustn't risk overstrain."

"I'm fine," Barbro Cullen replied, though her tone was flat. "Still tired, yes, and showing it, no doubt. One doesn't go through such an experience and bounce back in a week. But I'm up and about. And to be frank, I must know what's happened, what's going on, before I can settle down to regain my full strength. Not a word of news anywhere."

"Have you spoken to others about the matter?"

"No. I've simply told visitors I was too exhausted to talk. Not much of a lie. I assumed there's a reason for censorship."

Sherrinford looked relieved. "Good girl. It's at my urging. You can imagine the sensation when this is made public. The authorities agreed they need time to study the facts, think and debate in a calm atmosphere, have a decent policy ready to offer voters who're bound to become rather hysterical at first." His mouth quirked slightly upward. "Furthermore, your nerves and Jimmy's get their chance to heal before the journalistic storm breaks over you. How is he?"

"Quite well. He continues pestering me for leave to go play with his friends in the Wonderful Place. But at his age, he'll recover—he'll forget."

"He may meet them later anyhow."

"What? We didn't—" Barbro shifted in her chair. "I've forgotten too. I hardly recall a thing from our last hours. Did you bring back any kidnapped humans?"

"No. The shock was savage as it was, without throwing them straight into an...an institution. Mistherd, who's basically a sensible young fellow, assured me they'd get along, at any rate as regards survival necessities, till arrangements can be made." Sherrinford hesitated. "I'm not sure what the arrangements will be. Nobody is, at our present stage. But obviously they include those people—or many of them, especially those who aren't fullgrown—rejoining the human race. Though they may never feel at home in civilization. Perhaps in a way that's best, since we will need some kind of mutually acceptable liaison with the Dwellers."

His impersonality soothed them both. Barbro became able to say, "Was I too big a fool? I do remember how I yowled and beat my head on the floor."

"Why, no." He considered the big woman and her pride for a few seconds before he rose, walked over and laid a hand on her shoulder. "You'd been lured and trapped by a skillful play on your deepest instincts, at a moment of sheer nightmare. Afterward, as that wounded monster carried you off, evidently another type of being came along, one that could saturate you with close-range neuropsychic forces. On top of this, my arrival, the sudden brutal abolishment of every hallucination, must have been shattering. No wonder if you cried out in pain. Before you did, you competently got Jimmy and yourself into the bus, and you never interfered with me."

"What did you do?"

"Why, I drove off as fast as possible. After several hours, the atmospherics let up sufficiently for me to call Portolondon and insist on an emergency airlift. Not that that was vital. What chance had the enemy to stop us? They didn't even try-But quick transportation was certainly helpful."

"I figured that's what must have gone on." Barbro caught his glance. "No, what I meant was, how did you find us in the backlands?"

Sherrinford moved a little off from her. "My prisoner was my guide. I don't think I actually killed any of the Dwellers who'd come to deal with me. I hope not. The car simply broke through them, after a couple of warning shots, and afterward outpaced them. Steel and fuel against flesh wasn't really fair. At the cave entrance, I did have to shoot down a few of those troll creatures. I'm not proud of it."

He stood silent. Presently: "But you were a captive," he said. "I couldn't be sure what they might do to you, who had first claim on me." After another pause: "I don't look for any more violence."

"How did you make…the boy…cooperate?"

Sherrinford paced from her, to the window, where he stood staring out at the Boreal Ocean. "I turned off the mind-shield," he said. "I let their band get close, in full splendor of illusion. Then I turned the shield back on, and we both saw them in their true shapes. As we went northward, I explained to Mistherd how he and his kind had been hoodwinked, used, made to live in a world that was never really there. I asked him if he wanted himself and whomever he cared about to go on till they died as domestic animals—yes, running in limited freedom on solid hills, but always called back to the dream-kennel." His pipe fumed furiously. "May I never see such bitterness again. He had been taught to believe he was free."

Quiet returned, above the hectic traffic. Charlemagne drew nearer to setting; already the east darkened.

Finally Barbro asked, "Do you know why?"

"Why children were taken and raised like that? Partly because it was in the pattern the Dwellers were creating; partly in order to study and experiment on members of our species—minds, that is, not bodies; partly because humans have special strengths which are helpful, like being able to endure full daylight."

"But what was the final purpose of it all?"

Sherrinford paced the floor. "Well," he said, "of course the ultimate motives of the aborigines are obscure. We can't do more than guess at how they think, let alone how they feel. But our ideas do seem to fit the data.

"Why did they hide from man? I suspect they, or rather their ancestors—for they aren't glittering elves, you know; they're mortal and fallible too—I suspect the natives were only being cautious at first, more cautious than human primitives, though certain of those on Earth were also slow to reveal themselves to strangers. Spying, mentally eavesdropping, Roland's Dwellers must have picked up enough language to get some idea of how different man was from them, and how powerful; and they gathered that more ships would be arriving, bringing settlers. It didn't occur to them that they might be conceded the right to keep their lands. Perhaps they're still more fiercely territorial than we. They determined to fight, in their own way. I daresay, once we begin to get insight into that mentality, our psychological science will go through its Copernican revolution."

Enthusiasm kindled in him. "That's not the sole thing we'll learn, either," he went on. "They must have science of their own, a nonhuman science born on a planet that isn't Earth. Because they did observe us as profoundly as we've ever observed ourselves; they did mount a plan against us, one that would have taken another century or more to complete. Well, what else do they know? How do they support their civilization without visible agriculture or aboveground buildings or mines or anything? How can they breed whole new intelligent species to order? A million questions, ten million answers!"

"*Can* we learn from them?" Barbro asked softly. "Or can we only overrun them as you say they fear?"

Sherrinford halted, leaned elbow on mantel, hugged his pipe and replied, "I hope we'll show more charity than that to a defeated enemy. It's what they are. They tried to conquer us, and failed, and now in a sense we are bound to conquer them since they'll have to make their peace with the civilization of the machine rather than see it rust away as they strove for. Still, they never did us any harm as atrocious as what we've inflicted on our fellow men in the past. And, I repeat, they could teach us marvelous things; and we could teach them, too, once they've learned to be less intolerant of a different way of life."

"I suppose we can give them a reservation," she said, and didn't know why he grimaced and answered so roughly:

"Let's leave them the honor they've earned! They fought to save the world they'd always known from that"—he made a chopping gesture at the city—"and just possibly we'd be better off ourselves with less of it."

He sagged a trifle and sighed, "However, I suppose if Elfland had won, man on Roland would at last—peacefully, even happily—have died away. We live with our archetypes, but can we live in them?"

Barbro shook her head. "Sorry, I don't understand."

"What?" He looked at her in a surprise that drove out melancholy. After a laugh: "Stupid of me. I've explained this to so many politicians and scientists and commissioners and Lord knows what, these past days, I forgot I'd never explained to you. It was a rather vague idea of mine, most of the time we were traveling, and I don't like to discuss ideas prematurely. Now that we've met the Outlings and watched how they work, I do feel sure."

He tamped down his tobacco. "In limited measure," he said, "I've used an archetype throughout my own working life. The rational detective. It hasn't been a conscious pose—much—it's simply been an image which fitted my personality and professional style. But it draws an appropriate response from most people, whether or not they've ever heard of the original. The phenomenon is not uncommon. We meet persons who, in varying degrees, suggest Christ or Buddha or the Earth Mother, or, say, on a less exalted plane, Hamlet or d'Artagnan. Historical, fictional and mythical, such figures crystallize basic aspects of the human psyche, and when we meet them in our real experience, our reaction goes deeper than consciousness."

He grew grave again. "Man also creates archetypes that are not individuals. The Anima, the Shadow—and, it seems, the Outworld. The world of magic, of glamour—which originally meant enchantment—of half-human beings, some like Ariel and some like Caliban, but each free of mortal frailties and sorrows—therefore, perhaps, a little carelessly cruel, more than a little tricksy; dwellers, in dusk and moonlight, not truly gods but obedient to rulers who are enigmatic and powerful enough to be—Yes, our Queen of Air and Darkness knew well what sights to let lonely people see, what illusions to spin around them from time to time, what songs and legends to set going among them. I wonder how much she and her underlings gleaned from human fairy tales, how much they made up themselves, and how much men created all over again, all unwittingly, as the sense of living on the edge of the world entered them."

Shadows stole across the room. It grew cooler and the traffic noises dwindled. Barbro asked mutedly, "But what could this do?"

"In many ways," Sherrinford answered, "the outwayer is back in the Dark Ages. He has few neighbors, hears scanty news from beyond his horizon, toils to survive in a land he only partly understands, that may any night raise unforeseeable disasters against him and is bounded by enormous wildernesses. The machine civilization which brought his ancestors here is frail at best. He could lose it as the Dark Ages nations had lost Greece and Rome, as the whole of Earth seems to have lost it. Let him be worked on, long, strongly, cunningly, by the archetypical Outworld, until he has come to believe in his bones that the magic of the Queen of Air and Darkness is greater than the energy of engines; and first his faith, finally his deeds will follow her. Oh, it wouldn't happen fast. Ideally, it would happen too slowly to be noticed, especially by self-satisfied city people. But when in the end a hinterland gone back to the ancient way turned from them, how could they keep alive?"

Barbro breathed, "She said to me, when their banners flew in the last of our cities, we would rejoice."

"I think we would have, by then," Sherrinford admitted. "Nevertheless, I believe in choosing one's destiny."

He shook himself, as if casting off a burden. He knocked the dottle from his pipe and stretched, muscle by muscle. "Well," he said, "it isn't going to happen."

She looked straight at him. "Thanks to you."

A flush went up his thin cheeks. "In time, I'm sure somebody else would have—Anyhow, what matters is what we do next, and that's too big a decision for one individual or one generation to make."

She rose. "Unless the decision is personal, Eric," she suggested, feeling heat in her own face.

It was curious to see him shy. "I was hoping we might meet again."

"We will."

Ayoch sat on Wolund's Barrow. Aurora shuddered so brilliant, in such vast sheafs of light, as almost to hide the waning moons. Firethorn blooms had fallen; a few still glowed around the tree roots, amidst dry brok which crackled underfoot and smelled like woodsmoke. The air remained warm but no gleam was left on the sunset horizon.

"Farewell, fare lucky," the pook called. Mistherd and Shadow-of-a-Dream never looked back. It was as if they didn't dare. They trudged on out of sight, toward the human camp whose lights made a harsh new star in the south.

Ayoch lingered. He felt he should also offer good-bye to her who had lately joined him that slept in the dolmen. Likely none would meet here again for loving or magic. But he could only think of one old verse that might do. He stood and trilled:

Out of her breast
a blossom ascended.
The summer burned it.
The song is ended.

Then he spread his wings for the long flight away.

Jennifer's Lament

I hear the linnet and the lark declare
That we have seen all murkiness depart.
The flowers flaunt their hues through brilliant air,
And it is only raining in my heart.
When yesterday I heard how great the woe,
A lightning bolt struck lurid hellfire white;
I heard the thunder toll, the stormwind blow,
And nothing else through centuries of night.

But day must break, and gales lie down to rest,
And sunshine hunt the clouds across the sea.
Alone in nature is the human breast,
Where grief, like love, may dwell eternally.
Unless there come an ending of thy pain,
I must forever stand and wait in rain.

Industrial Revolution

"Well, yes," Amspaugh admitted, "it was a unique war in many ways, including its origin. However, there are so many analogies to other colonial revolutions—" His words trailed off as usual.

"I know. Earth's mercantile policies and so forth," said Lindgren. He fancies himself a student of interplanetary history. This has led to quite a few arguments since Amspaugh, who teaches in that field, joined the Club. Mostly they're good. I went to the bar and got myself another drink, listening as the mine owner's big voice went on:

"But what began it? When did the asterites first start realizing they weren't pseudopods of a dozen Terrestrial nations, but a single nation in their own right? There's the root of the revolution. And it can be pinned down, too."

" 'Ware metaphor!" cried someone at my elbow. I turned and saw Missy Blades. She'd come quietly into the lounge and started mixing a gin and bitters.

The view window framed her white head in Orion as she moved toward the little cluster of seated men. She took a fat cigar from her pocket, struck it on her shoe sole, and added her special contribution to the blue cloud in the room after she sat down.

"Excuse me," she said. "I couldn't help that. Please go on."

Which I hope relieves you of any fear that she's an Unforgettable Character. Oh, yes, she's old as Satan now; her toil and guts and conniving make up half the biography of the Sword; she manned a gun turret at Ceres, and was mate of the *Tyrfing* on some of the earliest Saturn runs when men took their lives between their teeth because they needed both hands free; her sons and grandsons fill the Belt with their brawling ventures; she can drink any ordinary man to the deck; she's one of the three women ever admitted to the Club. But she's also one of the few genuine ladies I've known in my life.

"Uh, well." Lindgren grinned at her. "I was saying, Missy, the germ of the revolution was when the Stations armed themselves. You see, that meant more than police powers. It implied a degree of sovereignty. Over the years, the implication grew."

"Correct." Orloff nodded his bald head. "I remember how the Governing Commission squalled when the Station managers first demanded the right. They foresaw trouble. But if the Stations belonging to one country put in space weapons, what else could the others do?"

"They should have stuck together and all been firm about refusing to allow it," Amspaugh said. "From the standpoint of their own best interests, I mean."

"They tried to," Orloff replied. "I hate to think how many communications we sent home from our own office, and the others must have done the same. But Earth was a long way off. The Station bosses were close. Inverse square law of political pressure."

"I grant you, arming each new little settlement proved important," Amspaugh said. "But really, it expressed nothing more than the first inchoate stirrings of asteroid nationalism. And the origins of that are much more subtle and complex. For instance…er..."

"You've got to have a key event somewhere," Lindgren insisted. "I say that this was it."

A silence fell, as will happen in conversation. I came back from the bar and settled myself beside Missy. She looked for a while into her drink, and then out to the stars. The slow spin of our rock had now brought the Dippers into view. Her faded eyes sought the Pole Star—but it's Earth's, not our own any more—and I wondered what memories they were sharing. She shook herself the least bit and said:

"I don't know about the sociological ins and outs. All I know is, a lot of things happened, and there wasn't any pattern to them at the time. We just slogged through as best we were able, which wasn't really very good. But I can identify one of those wriggling roots for you, Sigurd. I was there when the question of arming the Stations first came up. Or, rather, when the incident occurred that led directly to the question being raised."

Our whole attention went to her. She didn't dwell on the past as often as we would have liked.

A slow, private smile crossed her lips. She looked beyond us again. "As a matter of fact," she murmured, "I got my husband out of it." Then quickly, as if to keep from remembering too much:

"Do you care to hear the story? It was when the Sword was just getting started. They'd established themselves on SSC 45—oh, never mind the catalogue number. Sword Enterprises, because Mike Blades' name suggested it—what kind of name could you get out of Jimmy Chung, even if he was the senior partner? It'd sound too much like a collision with a meteorite—so naturally the asteroid also came to be called the Sword. They began on the borrowed shoestring that was usual in those days. Of course, in the Belt a shoestring has to be mighty long, and finances got stretched to the limit. The older men here will know how much had to be done by hand, in mortal danger, because machines were too expensive. But in spite of everything, they succeeded. The Station was functional and they were ready to start business when—"

It was no coincidence that the Jupiter craft were arriving steadily when the battleship came. Construction had been scheduled with this in mind, that the Sword should be approaching conjunction with the king planet, making direct shuttle service feasible, just as the chemical plant went into service. We need not consider how much struggle and heartbreak had gone into meeting that schedule. As for the battleship, she appeared because the fact that a Station in just this orbit was about to commence operations was news important enough to cross the Solar System and push through many strata of bureaucracy. The heads of the recently elected North American government became suddenly, fully aware of what had been going on.

Michael Blades was outside, overseeing the installation of a receptor, when his earplug buzzed. He thrust his chin against the turning plate, switching from gang to interoffice band. "Mike?" said Avis Page's voice. "You're wanted up front."

"Now?" he objected. "Whatever for?"

"Courtesy visit from the NASS *Altair.* You've lost track of time, my boy."

"What the...the jumping blue blazes are you talking about? We've had our courtesy visit. Jimmy and I both went over to pay our respects, and we had Rear Admiral Hulse here to dinner. What more do they expect, for Harry's sake?"

"Don't you remember? Since there wasn't room to entertain his officers, you promised to take them on a personal guided tour later. I made the appointment the very next watch. Now's the hour."

"Oh, yes, it comes back to me. Yeah. Hulse brought a magnum of champagne with him, and after so long a time drinking recycled water, my capacity was shot to pieces. I got a warm glow of good fellowship on, and offered—Let Jimmy handle it. I'm busy."

"The party's too large, he says. You'll have to take half of them. Their gig will dock in thirty minutes."

"Well, depute somebody else."

"That'd be rude, Mike. Have you forgotten how sensitive they are about rank at home?" Avis hesitated. "If what I believe about the mood back there is true, we can use the good will of high-level Navy personnel. And any other influential people in sight."

Blades drew a deep breath. "You're too blinking sensible. Remind me to fire you after I've made my first ten million bucks."

"What'll you do for your next ten million, then?" snipped his secretary-file clerk-confidante-advisor-et cetera.

"Nothing. I'll just squander the first."

"Goody! Can I help?"

"Uh...I'll be right along." Blades switched off. His ears felt hot, as often of late when he tangled with Avis, and he unlimbered only a few choice oaths.

"Troubles?" asked Carlos Odonaju.

Blades stood a moment, looking around, before he answered. He was on the wide end of the Sword, which was shaped roughly like a truncated pyramid. Beyond him and his half dozen men stretched a vista of pitted rock, jutting crags, gulf-black shadows, under the glare of floodlamps. A few kilometers away, the farthest horizon ended, chopped off like a cliff. Beyond lay the stars, crowding that night which never ends. It grew very still while the gang waited for his word. He could listen to his own lungs and pulse, loud in the spacesuit; he could even notice its interior smell, blend of plastic and oxygen cycle chemicals, flesh and sweat. He was used to the sensation of hanging upside down on the surface, gripsoled hoots holding him against that fractional gee by which the asteroid's rotation overcame its feeble gravity. But it came to him that this was an eerie bat-fashion way for an Oregon farm boy to stand.

Oregon was long behind him, though, not only the food factory where he grew up but the coasts where he had fished and the woods where he had tramped. No loss. There'd always been too many tourists. You couldn't escape from people on Earth. Cold and vacuum and raw rock and everything, the Belt was better. It annoyed him to be interrupted here.

Could Carlos take over as foreman? N-no, Blades decided, not yet. A gas receptor was an intricate piece of equipment. Carlos was a good man of his hands. Every one of the hundred-odd in the Station necessarily was. But he hadn't done this kind of work often enough.

"I have to quit," Blades said. "Secure the stuff and report to Buck Meyers over at the dock, the lot of you. His crew's putting in another recoil pier, as I suppose you know. They'll find jobs for you. I'll see you here again on your next watch."

He waved—being half the nominal ownership of this place didn't justify snobbery, when everyone must work together or die—and stepped off toward the nearest entry lock with that flowing spaceman's pace which always keeps one foot on the ground. Even so, he didn't unshackle his inward-reeling lifeline till he was inside the chamber.

On the way he topped a gaunt ridge and had a clear view of the balloons that were attached to the completed receptors. Those that were still full bulked enormous, like ghostly moons. The Jovian gases that strained their tough elastomer did not much blur the stars seen through them; but they swelled high enough to catch the light of the hidden sun and shimmer with it. The nearly discharged balloons hung thin, straining outward. Two full ones passed in slow orbit against the constellations. They were waiting to be hauled in and coupled fast, to release their loads into the Station's hungry chemical plant. But there were not yet enough facilities to handle them at once—and the *Pallas Castle* would soon be arriving with another—Blades found that he needed a few extra curses.

Having cycled through the air lock, he removed his suit and stowed it, also the heavy gloves which kept him from frostbite as he touched its space-cold exterior. Tastefully clad in a Navy surplus Long John, he started down the corridors.

Now that the first stage of burrowing within the asteroid had been completed, most passages went through its body, rather than being plastic tubes snaking across the surface. Nothing had been done thus far about facing them. They were merely shafts, two meters square, lined with doorways, ventilator grilles, and fluoropanels. They had no thermocoils. Once the nickel-iron mass had been sufficiently warmed up, the waste heat of man and his industry kept it that way. The dark, chipped-out tunnels throbbed with machine noises. Here and there a girlie picture or a sentimental landscape from Earth was posted. Men moved busily along them, bearing tools, instruments, supplies. They were from numerous countries, those men, though mostly North Americans, but they had acquired a likeness, a rangy leathery look and a free-swinging stride, that went beyond their colorful coveralls.

"Hi, Mike...How's she spinning?...Hey, Mike, you heard the latest story about the Martian and the bishop?...Can you spare me a minute? We got troubles in the separator manifolds...What's the hurry, Mike, your batteries overcharged?" Blades waved the hails aside. There was need for haste. You could move fast indoors, under the low weight which became lower as you approached the axis of rotation, with no fear of tumbling off. But it was several kilometers from the gas receptor end to the people end of the asteroid.

He rattled down a ladder and entered his cramped office out of breath. Avis Page looked up from her desk and wrinkled her freckled snub nose at him. "You ought to take a shower, but there isn't time," she said. "Here, use my antistinker." She threw him a spray cartridge with a deft motion. "I got your suit and beardex out of your cabin."

"Have I no privacy?" he grumbled, but grinned in her direction. She wasn't much to look at—not ugly, just small, brunette, and unspectacular—but she was a supernova of an assistant. Make somebody a good wife some day. He wondered why she hadn't taken advantage of the situation here to snaffle a husband. A dozen women, all but two of them married, and a hundred men, was a ratio even more lopsided than the norm in the Belt. Of course, with so much work to do, and with everybody conscious of the need to maintain cordial relations, sex didn't get much chance to rear its lovely head. Still—

She smiled back with the gentleness that he found disturbing when he noticed it. "Shoo," she said. "Your guests will be here any minute. You're to meet them in Jimmy's office."

Blades ducked into the tiny washroom. He wasn't any 3V star himself, he decided as he smeared cream over his face: big, homely, red-haired. *But not something you'd be scared to meet in a dark alley, either,* he added smugly. In fact, there had been an alley in Aresopolis...Things were expected to be going so smoothly by the time they approached conjunction with Mars that he could run over to that sinful ginful city for a vacation. Long overdue...whooee! He wiped off his whiskers, shucked the zipskin, and climbed into the white pants and high-collared blue tunic that must serve as formal garb.

Emerging, he stopped again at Avis' desk. "Any message from the *Pallas?"* he asked.

"No," the girl said. "But she ought to be here in another two watches, right on sked. You worry too much, Mike."

"Somebody has to, and I haven't got Jimmy's Buddhist ride-with-the-punches attitude."

"You should cultivate it." She grew curious. The brown eyes lingered on him. "Worry's contagious. You make me fret about you."

"Nothing's going to give me an ulcer but the shortage of booze on this rock. Uh, if Bill Mbolo should call about those catalysts while I'm gone, tell him—" He ran off a string of instructions and headed for the door.

Chung's hangout was halfway around the asteroid, so that one chief or the other could be a little nearer the scene of any emergency. Not that they spent much time at their desks. Shorthanded and undermechanized, they were forever having to help out in the actual construction. Once in a while Blades found himself harking wistfully back to his days as an engineer with Solar Metals: good pay, interesting if hazardous work on flying mountains where men had never trod before, and no further responsibilities. But most asterites had the dream of becoming their own bosses.

When he arrived, the *Altair* officers were already there, a score of correct young men in white dress uniforms. Short, squat, and placid looking, Jimmy Chung stood making polite conversation. "Ah, there," he said, "Lieutenant Ziska and gentlemen, my partner, Michael Blades, Mike, may I present—"

Blades' attention stopped at Lieutenant Ziska. He heard vaguely that she was the head quartermaster officer. But mainly she was tall and blond and blue-eyed, with a bewitching dimple when she smiled, and filled her gown the way a Cellini Venus doubtless filled its casting mold.

"Very pleased to meet you, Mr. Blades," she said as if she meant it. Maybe she did! He gulped for air.

"And Commander Liebknecht," Chung said across several light-years. "Commander Liebknecht. *Commander Liebknecht.*"

"Oh. Sure. 'Scuse." Blades dropped Lieutenant Ziska's hand in reluctant haste. "Hardjado, C'mander Liebfraumilch."

Somehow the introductions were gotten through. "I'm sorry we have to be so inhospitable," Chung said, "but you'll see how crowded we are. About all we can do is show you around, if you're interested."

"Of course you're interested," said Blades to Lieutenant Ziska. "I'll show you some gimmicks I thought up myself."

Chung scowled at him. "We'd best divide the party and proceed along alternate routes," he said. "We'll meet again in the mess for coffee. Lieutenant Ziska, would you like to—"

"Come with me? Certainly," Blades said.

Chung's glance became downright murderous. "I thought—" he began.

"Sure." Blades nodded vigorously. "You being the senior partner, you'll take the highest ranking of these gentlemen, and I'll be in Scotland before you. C'mon, let's get started. May I?" He offered the quartermistress his arm. She smiled and took it. He supposed that eight or ten of her fellows trailed them.

The first disturbing note was sounded on the verandah.

They had glanced at the cavelike dormitories where most of the personnel lived; at the recreation dome topside which made the life tolerable; at kitchen, sick bay, and the other service facilities; at the hydroponic tanks and yeast vats which supplied much of the Station's food; at the tiny cabins scooped out for the top engineers and the married couples. Before leaving this end of the asteroid, Blades took his group to the verandah. It was a clear dome jutting from the surface, softly lighted, furnished as a primitive officers' lounge, open to a view of half the sky.

"Oh-h," murmured Ellen Ziska. Unconsciously she moved closer to Blades.

Young Lieutenant Commander Gilbertson gave her a somewhat jaundiced look. "You've seen deep space often enough before," he said.

"Through a port or a helmet." Her eyes glimmered enormous in the dusk. "Never like this."

The stars crowded close in their wintry myriads. The galactic belt glistened, diamond against infinite darkness. Vision toppled endlessly outward, toward the far mysterious shimmer of the Andromeda Nebula; silence was not a mere absence of noise, but a majestic presence, the seething of suns.

"What about the observation terrace at Leyburg?" Gilbertson challenged.

"That was different," Ellen Ziska said. "Everything was safe and civilized. This is like being on the edge of creation."

Blades could see why Goddard House had so long resisted the inclusion of female officers on ships of the line, despite political pressure at home and the Russian example abroad. He was glad they'd finally given in. Now if only he could build himself up as a dashing, romantic type...But how long would the *Altair* stay? Her stopover seemed quite extended already, for a casual visit in the course of a routine patrol cruise. He'd have to work fast.

"Yes, we are pretty isolated," he said. "The Jupiter ships just unload their balloons, pick up the empties, and head right back for another cargo."

"I don't understand how you can found an industry here, when your raw materials only arrive at conjunction," Ellen said.

"Things will be different once we're in full operation," Blades assured her. "Then we'll be doing enough business to pay for a steady input, transshipped from whatever depot is nearest Jupiter at any given time."

"You've actually built this simply to process...gas?" Gilbertson interposed. Blades didn't know whether he was being sarcastic or asking a genuine question. It was astonishing how ignorant Earthsiders, even space-traveling Earthsiders, often were about such matters.

"Jovian gas is rich stuff," he explained. "Chiefly hydrogen and helium, of course; but the scoopships separate out most of that during a pickup. The rest is ammonia, water, methane, a dozen important organics, including some of the damn...doggonedest metallic complexes you ever heard of. We need them as the basis of a chemosynthetic industry, which we need for survival, which we need if we're to get the minerals that were the reason for colonizing the Belt in the first place." He waved his hand at the sky. "When we really get going, we'll attract settlement. This asteroid has companions, waiting for people to come and mine them. Homeships and orbital stations will be built. In ten years there'll be quite a little city clustered around the Sword."

"It's happened before," nodded tight-faced Commander Warburton of Gunnery Control.

"It's going to happen a lot oftener," Blades said enthusiastically. "The Belt's going to grow!" He aimed his words at Ellen. "This is the real frontier. The planets will never amount to much. It's actually harder to maintain human-type conditions on so big a mass, with a useless atmosphere around you, than on a lump in space like this. And the gravity wells are so deep. Even given nuclear power, the energy cost of really exploiting a planet is prohibitive. Besides which, the choice minerals are buried under kilometers of rock. On a metallic asteroid, you can find almost everything you want directly under your feet. No limit to what you can do."

"But your own energy expenditure—" Gilbertson objected.

"That's no problem." As if on cue, the worldlet's spin brought the sun into sight. Tiny but intolerably brilliant, it flooded the dome with harsh radiance. Blades lowered the blinds on that side. He pointed in the opposite direction, toward several sparks of equal brightness that had manifested themselves.

"Hundred-meter parabolic mirrors," he said. "Easy to make; you spray a thin metallic coat on a plastic backing. They're in orbit around us, each with a small geegee unit to control drift and keep it aimed directly at the sun. The focused radiation charges heavy-duty accumulators, which we then collect and use for our power source in all our mobile work."

"Do you mean you haven't any nuclear generator?" asked Warburton.

He seemed curiously intent about it. Blades wondered why, but nodded. "That's correct. We don't want one. Too dangerous for us. Nor is it necessary. Even at this distance from the sun, and allowing for assorted inefficiencies, a mirror supplies better than five hundred kilowatts, twenty-four hours a day, year after year, absolutely free."

"Hm-m-m. Yes." Warburton's lean head turned slowly about, to rake Blades with a look of calculation. "I understand that's the normal power system in Stations of this type. But we didn't know if it was used in your case, too."

Why should you care? Blades thought.

He shoved aside his faint unease and urged Ellen toward the dome railing. "Maybe we can spot your ship, Lieutenant, uh, Miss Ziska. Here's a telescope. Let me see, her orbit ought to run about so..."

He hunted until the *Altair* swam into the viewfield. At this distance the spheroid looked like a tiny crescent moon, dully painted; but he could make out the sinister shapes of a rifle turret and a couple of missile launchers. "Have a look," he invited. Her hair tickled his nose, brushing past him. It had a delightful sunny odor.

"How small she seems," the girl said, with the same note of wonder as before. "And how huge when you're aboard."

Big, all right, Blades knew, and loaded to the hatches with nuclear hellfire. But not massive. A civilian spaceship carried meteor plating, but since that was about as useful as wet cardboard against modern weapons, warcraft sacrificed it for the sake of mobility. The self-sealing hull was thin magnesium, the outer shell periodically renewed as cosmic sand eroded it.

"I'm not surprised we orbited, instead of docking," Ellen remarked. "We'd have butted against your radar and bellied into your control tower."

"Well, actually, no," said Blades. "Even half finished, our dock's big enough to accommodate you, as you'll see today. Don't forget, we anticipate a lot of traffic in the future. I'm puzzled why you didn't accept our invitation to use it."

"Doctrine!" Warburton clipped.

The sun came past the blind and touched the officers' faces with incandescence. Did some look startled, one or two open their mouths as if to protest and then snap them shut again at a warning look? Blades' spine tingled. *I never heard of any such doctrine,* he thought, *least of all when a North American ship drops in on a North American Station.*

"Is...er...is there some international crisis brewing?" he inquired.

"Why, no." Ellen straightened from the telescope. "I'd say relations have seldom been as good as they are now. What makes you ask?"

"Well, the reason your captain didn't—"

"Never mind," Warburton said. "We'd better continue the tour, if you please."

Blades filed his misgivings for later reference. He might have fretted immediately, but Ellen Ziska's presence forbade that. A sort of Pauli exclusion principle. One can't have two spins simultaneously, can one? He gave her his arm again. "Let's go on to Central Control," he proposed. "That's right behind the people section."

"You know, I can't get over it," she told him softly. "This miracle you've wrought. I've never been more proud of being human."

"Is this your first long space trip?"

"Yes. I was stationed at Port Colorado before the new Administration reshuffled armed service assignments."

"They did? How come?"

"I don't know. Well, that is, during the election campaign the Social Justice Party did talk a lot about old-line officers who were too hidebound to carry out modern policies effectively. But it sounded rather silly to me."

Warburton compressed his lips. "I do not believe it is proper for service officers to discuss political issues publicly," he said like a machine gun.

Ellen flushed. "S-sorry, commander."

Blades felt a helpless anger on her account. He wasn't sure why. What was she to him? He'd probably never see her again. A hell of an attractive target, to be sure; and after so much celibacy he was highly vulnerable; but did she really matter?

He turned his back on Warburton and his eyes on her—a five thousand per cent improvement—and diverted her from her embarrassment by asking, "Are you from Colorado, then, Miss Ziska?"

"Oh, no. Toronto."

"How'd you happen to join the Navy, if I may make so bold?"

"Gosh, that's hard to say. But I guess mostly I felt so crowded at home. So, pigeonholed. The world seemed to be nothing but neat little pigeonholes."

"Uh-huh. Same here. I was also a square pigeon in a round hole." She laughed. "Luckily," he added, "Space is too big for compartments."

Her agreement lacked vigor. The Navy must have been a disappointment to her. But she couldn't very well say so in front of her shipmates.

Hm-m·m...if she could be gotten away from them—"How long will you be here?" he inquired. His pulse thuttered.

"We haven't been told," she said.

"Some work must be done on the missile launchers," Warburton said. "That's best carried out here, where extra facilities are available if we need them. Not that I expect we will." He paused. "I hope we won't interfere with your own operations."

"Far from it." Blades beamed at Ellen. "Or, more accurately, this kind of interference I don't mind in the least."

She blushed and her eyelids fluttered. Not that she was a fluffhead, he realized. But to avoid incidents, Navy regulations enforced an inhuman correctness between personnel of opposite sexes. After weeks in the black, meeting a man who could pay a compliment without risking court-martial must be like a shot of adrenalin. Better and better!

"Are you sure?" Warburton persisted. "For instance, won't we be in the way when the next ship comes from Jupiter?"

"She'll approach the opposite end of the asteroid," Blades said. "Won't stay long, either."

"How long?"

"One watch, so the crew can relax a bit among those of us who're off duty. It'd be a trifle longer if we didn't happen to have an empty bag at the moment. But never very long. Even running under thrust the whole distance, Jupe's a good ways off. They've no time to waste."

"When is the next ship due?"

"The *Pallas Castle* is expected in the second watch from now."

"Second watch. I see." Warburton stalked on with a brooding expression on his Puritan face.

Blades might have speculated about that, but someone asked him why the Station depended on spin for weight. Why not put in an internal field generator, like a ship? Blades explained patiently that an Emett large enough to produce uniform pull through a volume as big as the Sword was rather expensive. "Eventually, when we're a few megabucks ahead of the game—"

"Do you really expect to become rich?" Ellen asked. Her tone was awed. No Earthsider had that chance any more, except for the great corporations. "*Individually* rich?"

"We can't fail to. I tell you, this is a frontier like nothing since the Conquistadores. We could very easily have been wiped out in the first couple of years—financially or physically—by any of a thousand accidents. But now we're too far along for that. We've got it made, Jimmy and I."

"What will you do with your wealth?"

"Live like an old-time sultan," Blades grinned. Then, because it was true as well as because he wanted to shine in her eyes: "Mostly, though, we'll go on to new things. There's so much that needs to be done. Not simply more asteroid mines. We need farms; timber; parks; passenger and cargo liners; every sort of machine. I'd like to try getting at some of that water frozen in the Saturnian System. Altogether, I see no end to the jobs. It's no good our depending on Earth for anything. Too expensive, too chancy. The Belt has to be made completely self-sufficient."

"With a nice rakeoff for Sword Enterprises," Gilbertson scoffed.

"Why, sure. Aren't we entitled to some return?"

"Yes. But not so out of proportion as the Belt companies seem to expect. They're only using natural resources that rightly belong to the people, and the accumulated skills and wealth of an entire society."

"Huh! The People didn't do anything with the Sword. Jimmy and I and our boys did. No Society was around here grubbing nickel-iron and riding out gravel storms; *we* were."

"Let's leave politics alone," Warburton snapped. But it was mostly Ellen's look of distress which shut Blades up.

To everybody's relief, they reached Central Control about then. It was a complex of domes and rooms, crammed with more equipment than Blades could put a name to. Computers were in Chung's line, not his. He wasn't able to answer all of Warburton's disconcertingly sharp questions.

But in a general way he could. Whirling through vacuum with a load of frail humans and intricate artifacts, the Sword must be at once machine, ecology, and unified organism. Everything had to mesh. A failure in the thermodynamic balance, a miscalculation in supply inventory, a few mirrors perturbed out of proper orbit, might spell Ragnarok. The chemical plant's purifications and syntheses were already a network too large for the human mind to grasp as a whole, and it was still growing. Even where men could have taken charge, automation was cheaper, more reliable, less risky of lives. The computer system housed in Central Control was not only the brain, but the nerves and heart of the Sword.

"Entirely cryotronic, eh?" Warburton commented. "That seems to be the usual practice at the Stations. Why?"

"The least expensive type for us," Blades answered. "There's no problem in maintaining liquid helium here."

Warburton's gaze was peculiarly intense. "Cryotronic systems are vulnerable to magnetic and radiation disturbances."

"Uh-huh. That's one reason we don't have a nuclear power plant. This far from the sun, we don't get enough emission to worry about. The asteroid's mass screens out what little may arrive. I know the TIMM system is used on ships; but if nothing else, the initial cost is more than we want to pay."

"What's TIMM?" inquired the *Altair's* chaplain.

"Thermally Integrated Micro-Miniaturized," Ellen said crisply. "Essentially, ultraminiaturized ceramic-to-metal-seal vacuum tubes running off thermionic generators. They're immune to gamma ray and magnetic pulses, easily shielded against particule radiation, and economical of power." She grinned. "Don't tell me there's nothing about them in Leviticus, Padre!"

"Very fine for a ship's autopilot," Blades agreed. "But as I said, we needn't worry about rad or mag units here, we don't mind sprawling a bit, and as for thermal efficiency, we *want* to waste some heat. It goes to maintain internal temperature."

"In other words, efficiency depends on what you need to effish," Ellen bantered. She grew grave once more and studied him for a while before she mused, "The same person who swung a pick, a couple of years ago, now deals with something as marvelous as this..." He forgot about worrying.

But he remembered later, when the gig had left and Chung called him to his office. Avis came too, by request. As she entered, she asked why.

"You were visiting your folks Earthside last year," Chung said. "Nobody else in the Station has been back as recently as that."

"What can I tell you?"

"I'm not sure. Background, perhaps. The feel of the place. We don't really know, out in the Belt, what's going on there. The beamcast news is hardly a trickle. Besides, you have more common sense in your left little toe than that big mick yonder has in his entire copperplated head."

They seated themselves in the cobwebby low-gee chairs around Chung's desk. Blades took out his pipe and filled the bowl with his tobacco ration for today. Wouldn't it be great, he thought dreamily, if this old briar turned out to be an Aladdin's lamp, and the smoke condensed into a blonde she-Canadian—?

"Wake up, will you?" Chung barked.

"Huh?" Blades started. "Oh. Sure. What's the matter? You look like a fish on Friday."

"Maybe with reason. Did you notice anything unusual with that party you were escorting?"

"Yes, indeed."

"What?"

"About one hundred seventy-five centimeters tall, yellow hair, blue eyes, and some of the smoothest fourth-order curves I ever—"

"Mike, stop that!" Avis sounded appalled. "This is serious."

"I agree. She'll be leaving in a few more watches."

The girl bit her lip. "You're too old for that mooncalf rot and you know it."

"Agreed again. I feel more like a bull." Blades made pawing motions on the desktop.

"There's a lady present," Chung said.

Blades saw that Avis had gone quite pale. "I'm sorry," he blurted. "I never thought...I mean, you've always seemed like—"

"One of the boys," she finished for him in a brittle tone. "Sure. Forget it. What's the problem, Jimmy?"

Chung folded his hands and stared at them. "I can't quite define that," he answered, word by careful word. "Perhaps I've simply gone spacedizzy. But when we called on Admiral Hulse, and later when he called on us, didn't you get the impression of, well, wariness? Didn't he seem to be watching and probing, every minute we were together?"

"I wouldn't call him a cheerful sort," Blades nodded. "Stiff as molasses on Pluto. But I suppose...supposed he's just naturally that way."

Chung shook his head. "It wasn't a normal standoffishness. You've heard me reminisce about the time I was on Vesta with the North American technical representative, when the Convention was negotiated."

"Yes, I've heard that story a few times," said Avis dryly.

"Remember, that was right after the Europa Incident. We'd come close to a space war—undeclared, but it would have been nasty. We were still close. Every delegate went to that conference cocked and primed.

"Hulse had the same manner."

A silence fell. Blades said at length, "Well, come to think of it, he did ask some rather odd questions. He seemed to twist the conversation now and then, so he could find out things like our exact layout, emergency doctrine, and so forth. It didn't strike me as significant, though."

"Nor me," Chung admitted. "Taken in isolation, it meant nothing. But these visitors today—Sure, most of them obviously didn't suspect anything untoward. But that Liebknecht, now. Why was he so interested in Central Control? Nothing new or secret there. Yet he kept asking for details like the shielding factor of the walls."

"So did Commander Warburton," Blades remembered. "Also, he wanted to know exactly when the *Pallas* is due, how long she'll stay...hm-m-m, yes, whether we have any radio linkage with the outside, like to Ceres or even the nearest Commission base—"

"Did you tell him that we don't?" Avis asked sharply.

"Yes. Shouldn't I have?"

"It scarcely makes any difference," Chung said in a resigned voice. "As thoroughly as they went over the ground, they'd have seen what we do and do not have installed so far."

He leaned forward. "Why are they hanging around?" he asked. "I was handed some story about overhauling the missile system."

"Me, too," Blades said.

"But you don't consider a job complete till it's been tested. And you don't fire a test shot, even a dummy, this close to a Station. Besides, what could have gone wrong? I can't see a ship departing Earth orbit for a long cruise without everything being in order. And they didn't mention any meteorites, any kind of trouble, en route. Furthermore, why do the work here? The Navy yard's at Ceres. We can't spare them any decent amount of materials or tools or help."

Blades frowned. His own half-formulated doubts shouldered to the fore, which was doubly unpleasant after he'd been considering Ellen Ziska. "They tell me the international situation at home is O.K.," he offered.

Avis nodded. "What newsfaxes we get in the mail indicate as much," she said. "So why this hanky-panky?" After a moment, in a changed voice: "Jimmy, you begin to scare me a little."

"I scare myself," Chung said.

"Every morning when you debeard," Blades said; but his heart wasn't in it. He shook himself and protested: "Damnation, they're our own countrymen. We're engaged in a lawful business. Why should they do anything to us?"

"Maybe Avis can throw some light on that," Chung suggested.

The girl twisted her fingers together. "Not me," she said. "I'm no politician."

"But you were home not so long ago. You talked with people, read the news, watched the 3V. Can't you at least give an impression?"

"N-no—Well, of course the preliminary guns of the election campaign were already being fired. The Social Justice Party was talking a lot about...oh, it seemed so ridiculous that I didn't pay much attention."

"They talked about how the government had been pouring billions and billions of dollars into space, while overpopulation produced crying needs in America's back yard," Chung said. "We know that much, even in the Belt. We know the appropriations are due to be cut, now the Essjays are in. So what?"

"We don't need a subsidy any longer," Blades remarked. "It'd help a lot, but we can get along without if we have to, and personally, I prefer that. Less government money means less government control."

"Sure," Avis said. "There was more than that involved, however. The Essjays were complaining about the small return on the investment. Not enough minerals coming back to Earth."

"Well, for Jupiter's sake," Blades exclaimed, "what do they expect? We have to build up our capabilities first."

"They even said, some of them, that enough reward never would be gotten. That under existing financial policies, the Belt would go in for its own expansion, use nearly everything it produced for itself and export only a trickle to America. I had to explain to several of my parents' friends that I wasn't really a socially irresponsible capitalist."

"Is that all the information you have?" Chung asked when she fell silent.

"I...I suppose so. Everything was so vague. No dramatic events. More of an atmosphere than a concrete thing."

"Still, you confirm my own impression," Chung said. Blades jerked his undisciplined imagination back from the idea of a Thing, with bug eyes and tentacles, cast in reinforced concrete, and listened as his partner summed up:

"The popular feeling at home has turned against private enterprise. You can hardly call a corporate monster like Systemic Developments a private enterprise! The new President and Congress share that mood. We can expect to see it manifested in changed laws and regulations. But what has this got to do with a battleship parked a couple of hundred kilometers from us?"

"If the government doesn't want the asterites to develop much further—" Blades bit hard on his pipestem. "They must know we have a caviar mine here. We'll be the only city in this entire sector,"

"But we're still a baby," Avis said. "We won't be important for years to come. Who'd have it in for a baby?"

"Besides, we're Americans, too," Chung said. "If that were a foreign ship, the story might be different—Wait a minute! Could they be thinking of establishing a new base here?"

"The Convention wouldn't allow," said Blades.

"Treaties can always be renegotiated, or even denounced. But first you have to investigate quietly, find out if it's worth your while."

"Hoo hah, what lovely money that'd mean!"

"And lovely bureaucrats crawling out of every file cabinet," Chung said grimly. "No, thank you. We'll fight any such attempt to the last lawyer. We've got a good basis, too, in our charter. If the suit is tried on Ceres, as I believe it has to be, we'll get a sympathetic court as well."

"Unless they bring in an Earthside judge," Avis warned.

"Yeah, that's possible. Also, they could spring proceedings on us without notice. We've got to find out in advance, so we can prepare. Any chance of pumping some of those officers?"

" 'Fraid not," Avis said. "The few who'd be in the know are safely back on shipboard."

"We could invite 'em here individually," said Blades. "As a matter of fact, I already have a date with Lieutenant Ziska."

"What?" Avis' mouth fell open.

"Yep," Blades said complacently. "End of the next watch, so she can observe the *Pallas* arriving. I'm to fetch her on a scooter." He blew a fat smoke ring. "Look, Jimmy, can you keep everybody off the porch for a while then? Starlight, privacy, soft music on the piccolo—who knows what I might find out?"

"You won't get anything from *her,*" Avis spat. "No secrets or, or anything."

"Still, I look forward to making the attempt. C'mon, pal, pass the word. I'll do as much for you sometime."

"Times like that never seem to come for me," Chung groaned.

"Oh, let him play around with his suicide blonde," Avis said furiously. "We others have work to do. I...I'll tell you what, Jimmy. Let's not eat in the mess tonight. I'll draw our rations and fix us something special in your cabin."

A scooter was not exactly the ideal steed for a knight to convey his lady. It amounted to little more than three saddles and a locker, set atop an accumulator-powered gyrogravitic engine, sufficient to lift you off an asteroid and run at low acceleration. There were no navigating instruments. You locked the autopilot's radar-gravitic sensors onto your target object and it took you there, avoiding any bits of debris which might pass near; but you must watch the distance indicator and press the deceleration switch in time. If the 'pilot was turned off, free maneuver became possible, but that was a dangerous thing to try before you were almost on top of your destination. Stereoscopic vision fails beyond six or seven meters, and the human organism isn't equipped to gauge cosmic moments.

Nevertheless, Ellen was enchanted. "This is like a dream," her voice murmured in Blades' earplug. "The whole universe, on every side of us. I could almost reach out and pluck those stars."

"You must have trained in powered spacesuits at the Academy," he said for lack of a more poetic rejoiner.

"Yes, but that's not the same. We had to stay near Luna's night side, to be safe from solar particles, and it bit a great chunk out of the sky. And then everything was so—regulated, disciplined—we did what we were ordered to do, and that was that. Here I feel free. You can't imagine how free." Hastily: "Do you use this machine often?"

"Well, yes, we have about twenty scooters at the Station. They're the most convenient way of flitting with a load: out to the mirrors to change accumulators, for instance, or across to one of the companion rocks where we're digging some ores that the Sword doesn't have. That kind of work." Blades would frankly rather have had her behind him on a motorskimmer, hanging on as they careened through a springtime countryside. He was glad when they reached the main forward air lock and debarked.

He was still gladder when the suits were off. Lieutenant Ziska in dress uniform was stunning, but Ellen in civvies, a fluffy low-cut blouse and close-fitting slacks, was a hydrogen blast. He wanted to roll over and pant, but settled for saying, "Welcome back" and holding her hand rather longer than necessary.

With a shy smile, she gave him a package. "I drew this before leaving," she said. "I thought, well, your life is so austere—"

"A demi of Sandeman," he said reverently. "I won't tell you you shouldn't have, but I will tell you you're a sweet girl."

"No, really." She flushed. "After we've put you to so much trouble."

"Let's go crack this," he said. "The *Pallas* has called in, but she won't be visible for a while yet."

They made their way to the verandah, picking up a couple of glasses enroute. Bless his envious heart, Jimmy had warned the other boys off as requested. *I hope Avis cooks him a Cordon Bleu dinner,* Blades thought. *Nice kid, Avis, if she'd quit trying to... what?... mother me?* He forgot about her, with Ellen to seat by the rail.

The Milky Way turned her hair frosty and glowed in her eyes. Blades poured the port with much ceremony and raised his glass. "Here's to your frequent return," he said.

Her pleasure dwindled a bit. "I don't know if I should drink to that. We aren't likely to be back, ever."

"Drink anyway. Gling, glang, gloria!" The rims tinkled together. "After all," said Blades, "this isn't the whole universe. We'll both be getting around. See you on Luna?"

"Maybe."

He wondered if he was pushing matters too hard. She didn't look at ease. "Oh, well," he said, "if nothing else, this has been a grand break in the monotony for us. I don't wish the Navy ill, but if trouble had to develop, I'm thankful it developed here."

"Yes—"

"How's the repair work progressing? Slowly, I hope."

"I don't know."

"You should have some idea, being in QM."

"No supplies have been drawn."

Blades stiffened.

"What's the matter?" Ellen sounded alarmed.

"Huh?" *A fine conspirator I make, if she can see my emotions on me in neon capitals!* "Nothing. Nothing. It just seemed a little strange, you know. Not taking any replacement units."

"I understand the work is only a matter of making certain adjustments."

"Then they should've finished a lot quicker, shouldn't they?"

"Please," she said unhappily. "Let's not talk about it. I mean, there are such things as security regulations."

Blades gave up on that tack. But Chung's idea might be worth probing a little. "Sure," he said. "I'm sorry, I didn't mean to pry." He took another sip as he hunted for suitable words. A beautiful girl, a golden wine...and vice versa...why couldn't he simply relax and enjoy himself? Did he have to go fretting about what was probably a perfectly harmless conundrum?...Yes. However, recreation might still combine with business.

"Permit me to daydream," he said, leaning close to her. "The Navy's going to establish a new base here, and the *Altair* will be assigned to it."

"Daydream indeed!" she laughed, relieved to get back to a mere flirtation. "Ever hear about the Convention of Vesta?"

"Treaties can be renegotiated," Blades plagiarized.

"What do we need an extra base for? Especially since the government plans to spend such large sums on social welfare. They certainly don't want to start an arms race besides."

Blades nodded. *Jimmy's notion did seem pretty thin,* he thought with a slight chill, *and now I guess it's completely whiffed.* Mostly to keep the conversation going, he shrugged and said, "My partner—and me, too, aside from the privilege of your company—wouldn't have wanted it anyhow. Not that we're unpatriotic, but there are plenty of other potential bases, and we'd rather keep government agencies out of here."

"Can you, these days?"

"Pretty much. We're under a new type of charter, as a private partnership. The first such charter in the Belt, as far as I know, though there'll be more in the future. The Bank of Ceres financed us. We haven't taken a nickel of federal money."

"Is that possible?"

"Just barely. I'm no economist, but I can see how it works. Money represents goods and labor. Hitherto those have been in mighty short supply out here. Government subsidies made up the difference, enabling us to buy from Earth. But now the asterites have built up enough population and industry that they have some capital surplus of their own, to invest in projects like this."

"Even so, frankly, I'm surprised that two men by themselves could get such a loan. It must be huge. Wouldn't the bank rather have lent the money to some corporation?"

"To tell the truth, we have friends who pulled wires for us. Also, it was done partly on ideological grounds. A lot of asterites would like to see more strictly homegrown enterprises, not committed to anyone on Earth. That's the only way we can grow. Otherwise our profits—our net production, that is—will continue to be siphoned off for the mother country's benefit."

"Well," Ellen said with some indignation, "that was the whole reason for planting asteroid colonies. You can't expect us to set you up in business, at enormous cost to ourselves—things we might have done at home—and get nothing but 'Ta' in return."

"Never fear, we'll repay you with interest," Blades said. "But whatever we make from our own work, over and above that, ought to stay here with us."

She grew angrier. "Your kind of attitude is what provoked the voters to elect Social Justice candidates."

"Nice name, that," mused Blades. "Who can be against social justice? But you know, I think I'll go into politics myself. I'll organize the North American Motherhood Party."

"You wouldn't be so flippant if you'd go see how people have to live back there."

"As bad as here? *Whew!*"

"Nonsense. You know that isn't true. But bad enough. And you aren't going to stick in these conditions. Only a few hours ago, you were bragging about the millions you intend to make."

"Millions *and* millions, if my strength holds out," leered Blades, thinking of the alley in Aresopolis. But he decided that that was then and Ellen was now, and what had started as a promising little party was turning into a dismal argument about politics.

"Let's not fight," he said. "We've got different orientations, and we'd only make each other mad. Let's discuss our next bottle instead...at the Coq d'Or in Paris, shall we say? Or Morraine's in New York."

She calmed down, but her look remained troubled. "You're right, we are different," she said low. "Isolated, living and working under conditions we can hardly imagine on Earth—and you can't really imagine our problems—yes, you're becoming another people. I hope it will never go so far that—No. I don't want to think about it." She drained her glass and held it out for a refill, smiling. "Very well, sir, when do you next plan to be in Paris?"

An exceedingly enjoyable while later, the time came to go watch the *Pallas Castle* maneuver in. In fact, it had somehow gotten past that time, and they were late; but they didn't hurry their walk aft. Blades took Ellen's hand, and she raised no objection. Schoolboyish, no doubt—however, he had reached the reluctant conclusion that for all his dishonorable intentions, this affair wasn't likely to go beyond the schoolboy stage. Not that he wouldn't keep trying.

As they glided through the refining and synthesizing section, which filled the broad half of the asteroid, the noise of pumps and regulators rose until it throbbed in their bones. Ellen gestured at one of the pipes which crossed the corridor overhead. "Do you really handle that big a volume at a time?" she asked above the racket.

"No," he said. "Didn't I explain before? The pipe's thick because it's so heavily armored."

"I'm glad you don't use that dreadful word 'cladded.' But why the armor? High pressure?"

"Partly. Also, there's an inertrans lining. Jupiter gas is hellishly reactive at room temperature. The metallic complexes especially; but think what a witch's brew the stuff is in every respect. Once it's been refined, of course, we have less trouble. That particular pipe is carrying it raw."

They left the noise behind and passed on to the approach control dome at the receptor end. The two men on duty glanced up and immediately went back to their instruments. Radio voices were staccato in the air. Blades led Ellen to an observation port.

She drew a sharp breath. Outside, the broken ground fell away to space and the stars. The ovoid that was the ship hung against them, lit by the hidden sun, a giant even at her distance but dwarfed by the balloon she towed. As that bubble tried ponderously to rotate, rainbow gleams ran across it, hiding and then revealing the constellations. Here, on the asteroid's axis, there was no weight, and one moved with underwater smoothness, as if disembodied. "Oh, a fairy tale," Ellen sighed.

Four sparks flashed out of the boat blisters along the ship's hull. "Scoopships," Blades told her. "They haul the cargo in, being so much more maneuverable. Actually, though, the mother vessel is going to park her load in orbit, while those boys bring in another one...see, there it comes into sight. We still haven't got the capacity to keep up with our deliveries."

"How many are there? Scoopships, that is."

"Twenty, but you don't need more than four for this job. They've got terrific power. Have to, if they're to dive from orbit down into the Jovian atmosphere, ram themselves full of gas, and come back. There they go."

The *Pallas Castle* was wrestling the great sphere she had hauled from Jupiter into a stable path computed by Central Control. Meanwhile the scoopships, small only by comparison with her, locked onto the other balloon as it drifted close. Energy poured into their drive fields. Spiraling downward, transparent globe and four laboring spacecraft vanished behind the horizon. The *Pallas* completed her own task, disengaged her towbars, and dropped from view, headed for the dock.

The second balloon rose again, like a huge glass moon on the opposite side of the Sword. Still it grew in Ellen's eyes, kilometer by kilometer of approach. So much mass wasn't easily handled, but the braking curve looked disdainfully smooth. Presently she could make out the scoopships in detail, elongated teardrops with the intake gates yawning in the blunt forward end, cockpit canopies raised very slightly above.

Instructions rattled from the men in the dome. The balloon veered clumsily toward the one free receptor. A derricklike structure released one end of a cable, which streamed skyward. Things that Ellen couldn't quite follow in this tricky light were done by the four tugs, mechanisms of their own extended to make their tow fast to the cable.

They did not cast loose at once, but continued to drag a little, easing the impact of centrifugal force. Nonetheless a slight shudder went through the dome as slack was taken up. Then the job was over. The scoopships let go and flitted off to join their mother vessel. The balloon was winched inward. Spacesuited men moved close, preparing to couple valves together.

"And eventually," Blades said into the abrupt quietness, "that cargo will become food, fabric, vitryl, plasti-board, reagents, fuels, a hundred different things. That's what we're here for."

"I've never seen anything so wonderful," Ellen said raptly. He laid an arm around her waist.

The intercom chose that precise moment to blare: "Attention! Emergency! All hands to emergency stations! Blades, get to Chung's office on the double! All hands to emergency stations!"

Blades was running before the siren had begun to howl.

Rear Admiral Barclay Hulse had come in person. He stood as if on parade, towering over Chung. The asterite was red with fury. Avis Page crouched in a corner, her eyes terrified.

Blades barreled through the doorway and stopped hardly short of a collision. "What's the matter?" he puffed.

"Plenty!" Chung snarled. "These incredible thumble-fumbed oafs—" His voice broke. *When he gets mad, it means something!*

Hulse nailed Blades with a glance. "Good day, sir," he clipped. "I have had to report a regrettable accident which will require you to evacuate the Station. Temporarily, I hope."

"Huh?"

"As I told Mr. Chung and Miss Page, a nuclear missile has escaped us. If it explodes, the radiation will be lethal, even in the heart of the asteroid."

"What...what—" Blades could only gobble at him.

"Fortunately, the *Pallas Castle* is here. She can take your whole complement aboard and move to a safe distance while we search for the object."

"How the *devil?"*

Hulse allowed himself a look of exasperation. "Evidently I'll have to repeat myself to you. Very well. You know we have had to make some adjustments on our launchers. What you did not know was the reason. Under the circumstances, I think it's permissible to tell you that several of them have a new and secret, experimental control system. One of our missions on this cruise was to carry out field tests. Well, it turned out that the system is still full of, ah, bugs. Gunnery Command has had endless trouble with it, has had to keep tinkering the whole way from Earth.

"Half an hour ago, while Commander Warburton was completing a reassembly—lower ranks aren't allowed in the test turrets—something happened. I can't tell you any guess as to what, but if you want to imagine that a relay got stuck, that will do for practical purposes. A missile was released under power. Not a dummy—the real thing. And release automatically arms the war head."

The news was like a hammerblow. Blades spoke an obscenity. Sweat sprang forth under his arms and trickled down his ribs.

"No such thing was expected," Hulse went on. "It's an utter disaster, and the designers of the system aren't likely to get any more contracts. But as matters were, no radar fix was gotten on it, and it was soon too far away for gyrogravitic pulse detection. The thrust vector is unknown. It could be almost anywhere now.

"Well, naval missiles are programmed to reverse acceleration if they haven't made a target within a given time. This one should be back in less than six hours. If it first detects our ship, everything is all right. It has optical recognition circuits that identify any North American warcraft by type, disarm the war head, and steer it home. But, if it first comes within fifty kilometers of some other mass—like this asteroid or one of the companion rocks—it will detonate. We'll make every effort to intercept, but space is big. You'll have to take your people to a safe distance. They can come back even after a blast, of course. There's no concussion in vacuum, and the fireball won't reach here. It's principally an anti-personnel weapon. But you must not be within the lethal radius of radiation."

"The hell we can come back!" Avis cried.

"I beg your pardon?" Hulse said.

"You imbecile! Don't you know Central Control here is cryotronic?"

Hulse did not flicker an eyelid. "So it is," he said expressionlessly. "I had forgotten."

Blades mastered his own shock enough to grate: "Well, we sure haven't. If that thing goes off, the gamma burst will kick up so many minority carriers in the transistors that the *p*-type crystals will act *n*-type, and the *n*-type act *p*-type, for a whole couple of microseconds. Everyone of 'em will flip simultaneously! The computers' memory and program data systems will be scrambled beyond hope of reorganization."

"Magnetic pulse, too," Chung said. "The fireball plasma will be full of inhomogeneities moving at several per cent of light speed. Their electromagnetic output, hitting our magnetic core units, will turn them from super to ordinary conduction. Same effect, total computer amnesia. We haven't got enough shielding against it. Your TIMM systems can take that kind of a beating. Ours can't!"

"Very regrettable," Hulse said. "You'd have to reprogram everything—"

"Reprogram what?" Avis retorted. Tears started forth in her eyes. "We've told you what sort of stuff our chemical plant is handling. We can't shut it down on that short notice. It'll run wild. There'll be sodium explosions, hydrogen and organic combustion, n-n-nothing left here but wreckage!"

Hulse didn't unbend a centimeter. "I offer my most sincere apologies. If actual harm does occur, I'm sure the government will indemnify you. And, of course, my command will furnish what supplies may be needed for the *Pallas Castle* to transport you to the nearest Commission base. At the moment, though, you can do nothing but evacuate and hope we will be able to intercept the missile."

Blades knotted his fists. A sudden comprehension rushed up in him and he bellowed, "There isn't going to be an interception! This wasn't an accident!"

Hulse backed a step and drew himself even straighter. "Don't get overwrought," he advised.

"You louse-bitten, egg-sucking, bloated faggot-porter! How stupid do you think we are? As stupid as your Essjay bosses? By heaven, we're staying! Then see if you have the nerve to murder a hundred people!"

"Mike...Mike—" Avis caught his arm.

Hulse turned to Chung. "I'll overlook that unseemly outburst," he said. "But in light of my responsibilities and under the provisions of the Constitution, I am hereby putting this asteroid under martial law. You will have all personnel aboard the *Pallas Castle* and at a minimum distance of a thousand kilometers within four hours of this moment, or be subject to arrest and trial. Now I have to get back and commence operations. The *Altair* will maintain radio contact with you. Good day." He bowed curtly, spun on his heel, and clacked from the room.

Blades started to charge after him. Chung caught his free arm. Together he and Avis dragged him to a stop. He stood cursing the air ultraviolet until Ellen entered.

"I couldn't keep up with you," she panted. "What's happened, Mike?"

The strength drained from Blades. He slumped into a chair and covered his face.

Chung explained in a few harsh words. "Oh-h-h," Ellen gasped. She went to Blades and laid her hands on his shoulders. "My poor Mike!"

After a moment she looked at the others. "I should report back, of course," she said, "but I won't be able to before the ship accelerates. So I'll have to stay with you till afterward. Miss Page, we left about half a bottle of wine on the verandah. I think it would be a good idea if you went and got it."

Avis bridled. "And why not you?"

"This is no time for personalities," Chung said. "Go on, Avis. You can be thinking what records and other paper we should take, while you're on your way. I've got to organize the evacuation. As for Miss Ziska, well, Mike needs somebody to pull him out of his dive."

"Her?" Avis wailed, and fled.

Chung sat down and flipped his intercom to Phone Central. "Get me Captain Janichevski aboard the *Pallas,*" he ordered. "Hello, Adam? About that general alarm—"

Blades raised a haggard countenance toward Ellen's."You better clear out, along with the women and any men who don't want to stay," he said. "But I think most of them will take the chance. They're on a profit-sharing scheme, they stand to lose too much if the place is ruined."

"What do you mean?"

"It's a gamble, but I don't believe Hulse's sealed orders extend to murder. If enough of us stay put, he'll have to catch that thing. He jolly well knows its exact trajectory."

"You forget we're under martial law," Chung said, aside to him. "If we don't go freely, he'll land some PP's and march us off at gunpoint. There isn't any choice. We've had the course."

"I don't understand," Ellen said shakily.

Chung went back to his intercom. Blades fumbled out his pipe and rolled it empty between his hands. "That missile was shot off on purpose," he said.

"What? No, you must be sick, that's impossible!"

"I realize you didn't know about it. Only three or four officers have been told. The job had to be done very, very secretly, or there'd be a scandal, maybe an impeachment. But it's still sabotage."

She shrank from him. "You're not making sense."

"Their own story doesn't make sense. It's ridiculous. A new missile system wouldn't be sent on a field trial clear to the Belt before it'd had enough tests closer to home to get the worst bugs out. A war-head missile wouldn't be stashed anywhere near something so unreliable, let alone be put under its control. The testing ship wouldn't hang around a civilian Station while her gunnery chief tinkered. And Hulse, Warburton, Liebknecht, they were asking in *such* detail about how radiation-proof we are."

"I can't believe it. Nobody will."

"Not back home. Communication with Earth is so sparse and garbled. The public will only know there was an accident; who'll give a hoot about the details? We couldn't even prove anything in an asteroid court. The Navy would say, 'Classified information!' and that'd stop the proceedings cold. Sure, there'll be a board of inquiry—composed of naval officers. Probably honorable men, too. But what are they going to believe, the sworn word of their Goddard House colleague, or the rantings of an asterite bum?"

"Mike, I know this is terrible for you, but you've let it go to your head." Ellen laid a hand over his. "Suppose the worst happens. You'll be compensated for your loss."

"Yeah. To the extent of our personal investment. The Bank of Ceres still has nearly all the money that was put in. We didn't figure to have them paid off for another ten years. They, or their insurance carrier, will get the indemnity. And after our fiasco, they won't make us a new loan. They were just barely talked into it, the first time around. I daresay Systemic Developments will make them a nice juicy offer to take this job over."

Ellen colored. She stamped her foot. "You're talking like a paranoiac. Do you really believe the government of North America would send a battleship clear out here to do you dirt?"

"Not the whole government. A few men in the right positions is all that's necessary. I don't know if Hulse was bribed or talked into this. But probably he agreed as a duty. He's the prim type."

"A duty—to destroy a North American business?"

Chung finished at the intercom in time to answer: "Not permanent physical destruction, Miss Ziska. As Mike suggested, some corporation will doubtless inherit the Sword and repair the damage. But a private, purely asterite business... yes, I'm afraid Mike's right. We are the target."

"In mercy's name, why?"

"From the highest motives, of course," Chung sneered bitterly. "You know what the Social Justice Party thinks of private capitalism. What's more important, though, is that the Sword is the first Belt undertaking not tied to Mother Earth's apron strings. We have no commitments to anybody back there. We can sell our output wherever we like. It's notorious that the asterites are itching to build up their own self-sufficient industries. Quite apart from sentiment, we can make bigger profits in the Belt than back home, especially when you figure the cost of sending stuff in and out of Earth's gravitational well. So certainly we'd be doing most of our business out here.

"Our charter can't simply be revoked. First a good many laws would have to be revised, and that's politically impossible. There is still a lot of individualist sentiment in North America, as witness the fact that businesses do get launched and that the Essjays did have a hard campaign to get elected. What the new government wants is something like the Eighteenth Century English policy toward America. Keep the colonies as a source of raw materials and as a market for manufactured goods, but don't let them develop a domestic industry. You can't come right out and say that, but you can let the situation develop naturally.

"Only...here the Sword is, obviously bound to grow rich and expand in every direction. If we're allowed to develop, to reinvest our profits, we'll become the nucleus of independent asterite enterprise. If, on the other hand, we're wiped out by an unfortunate accident, there's no nucleus; and a small change in the banking laws is all that's needed to prevent others from getting started. Q.E.D."

"I daresay Hulse does think he's doing his patriotic duty," said Blades. "He wants to guarantee North America our natural resources—in the long run, maybe, our allegiance. If he has to commit sabotage, too bad, but it won't cost him any sleep."

"No!" Ellen almost screamed.

Chung sagged in his chair. "We're very neatly trapped," he said like an old man. "I don't see any way out. Think you can get to work now, Mike? You can assign group leaders for the evacuation—"

Blades jumped erect. "I can fight!" he growled.

"With what? Can openers?"

"You mean you're going to lie down and let them break us?"

Avis came back. She thrust the bottle into Blades' hands as he paced the room. "Here you are," she said in a distant voice.

He held it out toward Ellen. "Have some," he invited.

"Not with you...you subversive!"

Avis brightened noticeably, took the bottle and raised it. "Then here's to victory," she said, drank, and passed it to Blades.

He started to gulp; but the wine was too noble, and he found himself savoring its course down his throat. *Why,* he thought vaguely, *do people always speak with scorn about Dutch courage? The Dutch have real guts. They fought themselves free of Spain and free of the ocean itself; when the French or Germans came, they made the enemy sea their ally—*

The bottle fell from his grasp. In the weak acceleration, it hadn't hit the floor when Avis rescued it. "Gimme that, you big butterfingers," she exclaimed. Her free hand clasped his arm. "Whatever happens, Mike," she said to him, "we're not quitting."

Still Blades stared beyond her. His fists clenched and unclenched. The noise of his breathing filled the room. Chung looked around in bewilderment; Ellen watched with waxing horror; Avis' eyes kindled.

"Holy smoking seegars," Blades whispered at last. "I really think we can swing it."

Captain Janichevski recoiled. "You're out of your skull!"

"Probably," said Blades. "Fun, huh?"

"You can't do this."

"We can try."

"Do you know what you're talking about? Insurrection, that's what. Quite likely piracy. Even if your scheme worked, you'd spend the next ten years in Rehab—at least."

"Maybe, provided the matter ever came to trial. But it won't."

"That's what you think. You're asking me to compound the felony, and misappropriate the property of my owners to boot." Janichevski shook his head. "Sorry, Mike. I'm sorry as hell about this mess. But I won't be party to making it worse."

"In other words," Blades replied, "you'd rather be party to sabotage. I'm proposing an act of legitimate self-defense."

"If there actually is a conspiracy to destroy the Station."

"Adam, you're a spaceman. You know how the Navy operates. Can you swallow that story about a missile getting loose by accident?"

Janichevski bit his lip. The sounds from outside filled the captain's cabin, voices, footfalls, whirr of machines and clash of doors, as the *Pallas Castle* readied for departure. Blades waited.

"You may be right," said Janichevski at length, wretchedly. "Though why Hulse should jeopardize his career—"

"He's not. There's a scapegoat groomed back home, you can be sure. Like some company that'll be debarred from military contracts for a while...and get nice fat orders in other fields. I've kicked around the System enough to know how that works."

"If you're wrong, though...if this is an honest blunder...then you risk committing treason."

"Yeah. I'll take the chance."

"Not I. No. I've got a family to support," Janichevski said.

Blades regarded him bleakly. "If the Essjays get away with this stunt, what kind of life will your family be leading, ten years from now? It's not simply that we'll be high-class peons in the Belt. But tied hand and foot to a shortsighted government, how much progress will we be able to make? Other countries have colonies out here too, remember, and some of them are already giving their people a freer hand than we've got. Do you want the Asians, or the Russians, or even the Europeans, to take over the asteroids?"

"I can't make policy."

"In other words, mama knows best. Believe, obey, anything put out by some bureaucrat who never set foot beyond Luna. Is that your idea of citizenship?"

"You're putting a mighty fine gloss on baling yourself out!" Janichevski flared.

"Sure, I'm no idealist. But neither am I a slave." Blades hesitated. "We've been friends too long, Adam, for me to try bribing you. But if worst comes to worst, we'll cover for you...somehow...and if contrariwise we win, then we'll soon be hiring captains for our own ships and you'll get the best offer any spaceman ever got."

"No. Scram. I've work to do."

Blades braced himself. "I didn't want to say this. But I've already informed a number of my men. They're as mad as I am. They're waiting in the terminal. A monkey wrench or a laser torch makes a pretty fair weapon. We can take over by force. That'll leave you legally in the clear. But with so many witnesses around, you'll have to prefer charges against us later on."

Janichevski began to sweat.

"We'll be sent up," said Blades. "But it will still have been worth it."

"Is it really that important to you?"

"Yes. I admit I'm no crusader. But this is a matter of principle."

Janichevski stared at the big redhaired man for a long while. Suddenly he stiffened. "O.K. On that account, and no other, I'll go along with you."

Blades wobbled on his feet, near collapse with relief. "Good man!" he croaked.

"But I will not have any of my officers or crew involved."

Blades rallied and answered briskly, "You needn't. Just issue orders that my boys are to have access to the scoopships. They can install the equipment, jockey the boats over to the full balloons, and even couple them on."

Janichevski's fears had vanished once he made his decision, but now a certain doubt registered. "That's a pretty skilled job."

"These are pretty skilled men. It isn't much of a maneuver, not like making a Jovian sky dive."

"Well, O.K., I'll take your word for their ability. But suppose the *Altair* spots those boats moving around?"

"She's already several hundred kilometers off, and getting farther away, running a search curve which I'm betting my liberty—and my honor; I certainly don't want to hurt my own country's Navy—I'm betting that search curve is guaranteed not to find the missile in time. They'll spot the *Pallas* as you depart—oh, yes, our people will be aboard as per orders—but no finer detail will show in so casual an observation."

"Again, I'll take your word. What else can I do to help ?"

"Nothing you weren't doing before. Leave the piratics to us. I'd better get back." Blades extended his hand. "I haven't got the words to thank you, Adam."

Janichevski accepted the shake. "No reason for thanks. You dragooned me." A grin crossed his face. "I must confess, though, I'm not sorry you did."

Blades left. He found his gang in the terminal, two dozen engineers and rockjacks clumped tautly together.

"What's the word?" Carlos Odonaju shouted.

"Clear track," Blades said. "Go right aboard."

"Good. Fine. I always wanted to do something vicious and destructive," Odonaju laughed.

"The idea is to prevent destruction," Blades reminded him, and proceeded toward the office.

Avis met him in Corridor Four. Her freckled countenance was distorted by a scowl. "Hey, Mike, wait a minute," she said, low and hurriedly. "Have you seen La Ziska?"

"The leftenant? Why, no. I left her with you, remember, hoping you could calm her down."

"Uh-huh. She was incandescent mad. Called us a pack of bandits and—But then she started crying. Seemed to break down completely. I took her to your cabin and went back to help Jimmy. Only, when I checked there a minute ago, she was gone."

"What? Where?"

"How should I know? But that she-devil's capable of anything to wreck our chances."

"You're not being fair to her. She's got an oath to keep."

"All right," said Avis sweetly. "Far be it from me to prevent her fulfilling her obligations. Afterward she may even write you an occasional letter. I'm sure that'll brighten your Rehab cell no end."

"What can she do?" Blades argued, with an uneasy sense of whistling in the dark. "She can't get off the asteroid without a scooter, and I've already got Sam's gang working on all the scooters."

"Is there no other possibility? The radio shack?"

"With a man on duty there. That's out." Blades patted the girl's arm.

"O.K., I'll get back to work. But…I'll be so glad when this is over, Mike!"

Looking into the desperate brown eyes, Blades felt a sudden impulse to kiss their owner. But no, there was too much else to do. Later, perhaps. He cocked a thumb upward. "Carry on."

Too bad about Ellen, he thought as he continued toward his office. *What an awful waste, to make a permanent enemy of someone with her kind of looks. And personality—Come off that stick, you clabberhead! She's probably the marryin' type anyway.*

In her shoes, though, what would I do? Not much; they'd pinch my feet. But—damnation, Avis is right. She's not safe to have running around loose. The radio shack? Sparks is not one of the few who've been told the whole story and co-opted into the plan. She could—

Blades cursed, whirled, and ran.

His way was clear. Most of the men were still in their dorms, preparing to leave. He traveled in huge low-gravity leaps.

The radio shack rose out of the surface near the verandah. Blades tried the door. It didn't budge. A chill went through him. He backed across the corridor and charged. The door was only plastiboard—

He hit with a thud and a grunt, and rebounded with a numbed shoulder. But it looked so easy for the cops on 3V!

No time to figure out the delicate art of forcible entry. He hurled himself against the panel, again and again, heedless of the pain that struck in flesh and bone. When the door finally, splinteringly gave way, he stumbled clear across the room beyond, fetched up against an instrument console, recovered his balance, and gaped.

The operator lay on the floor, swearing in a steady monotone. He had been efficiently bound with his own blouse and trousers, which revealed his predilection for maroon shorts with zebra stripes. There was a lump on the back of his head, and a hammer lay close by. Ellen must have stolen the tool and come in here with the thing behind her back. The operator would have had no reason to suspect her.

She had not left the sender's chair, not even while the door was under attack. Only a carrier beam connected the Sword with the *Altair*. She continued doggedly to fumble with dials and switches, trying to modulate it and raise the ship.

"Praises be...you haven't had advanced training...in radio," Blades choked. "That's...a long-range set…pretty special system—" He weaved toward her. "Come along, now."

She spat an unladylike refusal.

Theoretically, Blades should have enjoyed the tussle that followed. But he was in poor shape at the outset. And he was a good deal worse off by the time he got her pinioned.

"O.K.," he wheezed. "Will you come quietly?"

She didn't deign to answer, unless you counted her butting him in the nose. He had to yell for help to frog march her aboard ship.

"*Pallas Castle* calling NASS *Altair*. Come in, *Altair*."

The great ovoid swung clear in space, among a million cold stars. The asteroid had dwindled out of sight. A radio beam flickered across emptiness. Within the hull, the crew and a hundred refugees sat jammed together. The air was thick with their breath and sweat and waiting.

Blades and Chung, seated by the transmitter, felt another kind of thickness, the pull of the internal field. Earth-normal weight dragged down every movement; the enclosed cabin began to feel suffocatingly small. *We'd get used to it again pretty quickly,* Blades thought. *Our bodies would, that is. But our own selves, tied down to Earth forever—no.*

The vision screen jumped to life. "NASS *Altair* acknowledging *Pallas Castle,*" said the uniformed figure within.

"O.K., Charlie, go outside and don't let anybody else enter," Chung told his own operator.

The spaceman gave him a quizzical glance, but obeyed. "I wish to report that evacuation of the Sword is now complete," Chung said formally.

"Very good, sir," the Navy face replied. "I'll inform my superiors."

"Wait, don't break off yet. We have to talk with your captain."

"Sir? I'll switch you over to—"

"None of your damned chains of command," Blades interrupted. "Get me Rear Admiral Hulse direct, toot sweet, or I'll eat out whatever fraction of you he leaves unchewed. This is an emergency. I've got to warn him of an immediate danger only he can deal with."

The other stared, first at Chung's obvious exhaustion, then at the black eye and assorted bruises, scratches, and bites that adorned Blades' visage. "I'll put the message through Channel Red at once, sir." The screen blanked.

"Well, here we go," Chung said. "I wonder how the food in Rehab is these days."

"Want me to do the talking?" Blades asked. Chung wasn't built for times as hectic as the last few hours, and was worn to a nubbin. He himself felt immensely keyed up. He'd always liked a good fight.

"Sure." Chung pulled a crumpled cigarette from his pocket and began to fill the cabin with smoke. "You have a larger stock of rudeness than I."

Presently the screen showed Hulse, rigid at his post on the bridge. "Good day, gentlemen," he said. "What's the trouble?"

"Plenty," Blades answered. "Clear everybody else out of there; let your ship orbit free a while. And seal your circuit."

Hulse reddened. "Who do you think you are?"

"Well, my birth certificate says Michael Joseph Blades. I've got some news for you concerning that top-secret gadget you told us about. You wouldn't want unauthorized personnel listening in."

Hulse leaned forward till he seemed about to fall through the screen. "What's this about a hazard?"

"Fact. The *Altair* is in distinct danger of getting blown to bits."

"Have you gone crazy? Get me the captain of the *Pallas.*"

"Very small bits."

Hulse compressed his lips. "All right, I'll listen to you for a short time. You had better make it worth my while."

He spoke orders. Blades scratched his back while he waited for the bridge to be emptied and wondered if there was any chance of a hot shower in the near future.

"Done," said Hulse. "Give me your report."

Blades glanced at the telltale. "You haven't sealed your circuit, admiral."

Hulse said angry words, but complied. "Now will you talk?"

"Sure. This secrecy is for your own protection. You risk court-martial otherwise."

Hulse suppressed a retort.

"O.K., here's the word." Blades met the transmitted glare with an almost palpable crash of eyeballs. "We decided, Mr. Chung and I, that any missile rig as haywire as yours represents a menace to navigation and public safety. If you can't control your own nuclear weapons, you shouldn't be at large. Our charter gives us local authority as peace officers. By virtue thereof and so on and so forth, we ordered certain precautionary steps taken. As a result, if that warhead goes off, I'm sorry to say that NASS *Altair* will be destroyed."

"Are you...have you—" Hulse congealed. In spite of everything, he was a competent officer, Blades decided. "Please explain yourself," he said without tone.

"Sure," Blades obliged. "The Station hasn't got any armament, but trust the human race to juryrig that. We commandeered the scoopships belonging to this vessel and loaded them with Jovian gas at maximum pressure. If your missile detonates, they'll dive on you."

Something like amusement tinged Hulse's shocked expression. "Do you seriously consider that a weapon?"

"I seriously do. Let me explain. The ships are orbiting free right now, scattered through quite a large volume of space. Nobody's aboard them. What is aboard each one, though, is an autopilot taken from a scooter, hooked into the drive controls. Each 'pilot has its sensors locked onto your ship. You can't maneuver fast enough to shake off radar beams and mass detectors. You're the target object, and there's nothing to tell those idiot computers to decelerate as they approach you.

"Of course, no approach is being made yet. A switch has been put in every scooter circuit, and left open. Only the meteorite evasion units are operative right now. That is, if anyone tried to lay alongside one of those scoopships, he'd be detected and the ship would skitter away. Remember, a scoopship hasn't much mass, and she does have engines designed for diving in and out of Jupe's gravitational well. She can out-accelerate either of our vessels, or any boat of yours, and out-dodge any of your missiles. You can't catch her."

Hulse snorted. "What's the significance of this farce?"

"I said the autopilots were switched off at the moment, as far as heading for the target is concerned. But each of those switches is coupled to two other units. One is simply the sensor box. If you withdraw beyond a certain distance, the switches will close. That is, the 'pilots will be turned on if you try to go beyond range of the beams now locked onto you. The other unit we've installed in every boat is an ordinary two-for-a-dollar radiation meter. If a nuclear weapon goes off, anywhere within a couple of thousand kilometers, the switches will also close. In either of these cases, the scoopships will dive on you.

"You might knock out a few with missiles, before they strike. Undoubtedly you can punch holes in them with laser guns. But that won't do any good, except when you're lucky enough to hit a vital part. Nobody's aboard to be killed. Not even much gas will be lost, in so short a time.

"So to summarize, chum, if that rogue missile explodes, your ship will be struck by ten to twenty scoopships, each crammed full of concentrated Jovian air. They'll pierce that thin hull of yours, but since they're already pumped full beyond the margin of safety, the impact will split them open and the gas will whoosh out. Do you know what Jovian air does to substances like magnesium?

"You can probably save your crew, take to the boats and reach a Commission base. But your nice battleship will be *ganz kaput.* Is your game worth that candle?"

"You're totally insane! Releasing such a thing—"

"Oh, not permanently. There's one more switch on each boat, connected to the meteorite evasion unit and controlled by a small battery. When those batteries run down, in about twenty hours, the 'pilots will be turned off completely. Then we can spot the scoopships by radar and pick 'em up. And you'll be free to leave."

"Do you think for one instant that your fantastic claim of acting legally will stand up in court?"

"No, probably not. But it won't have to. Obviously you can't make anybody swallow your yarn if a *second* missile gets loose. And as for the first one, since it's failed in its purpose, your bosses aren't going to want the matter publicized. It'd embarrass them no end, and serve no purpose except revenge on Jimmy and me—which there's no point in taking, since the Sword would still be privately owned. You check with Earth, admiral, before shooting off your mouth. They'll tell you that both parties to this quarrel had better forget about legal action. Both would lose.

"So I'm afraid your only choice is to find that missile before it goes off."

"And yours? What are your alternatives?" Hulse had gone gray in the face, but he still spoke stoutly.

Blades grinned at him. "None whatsoever. We've burned our bridges. We can't do anything about those scoopships now, so it's no use trying to scare us or arrest us or whatever else may occur to you. What we've done is establish an automatic deterrent."

"Against an, an attempt...at sabotage...that only exists in your imagination!"

Blades shrugged. "That argument isn't relevant any longer. I do believe the missile was released deliberately. We wouldn't have done what we did otherwise. But there's no longer any point in making charges and denials. You'd just better retrieve the thing."

Hulse squared his shoulders. "How do I know you're telling the truth?"

"Well, you can send a man to the Station. He'll find the scooters lying gutted. Send another man over here to the *Pallas.* He'll find the scoopships gone. I also took a few photographs of the autopilots being installed and the ships being cast adrift. Go right ahead. However, may I remind you that the fewer people who have an inkling of this little intrigue, the better for all concerned."

Hulse opened his mouth, shut it again, stared from side to side, and finally slumped the barest bit. "Very well," he said, biting off the words syllable by syllable. "I can't risk a ship of the line. Of course, since the rogue is still farther away than your deterrent allows the *Altair* to go, we shall have to wait in space a while."

"I don't mind."

"I shall report the full story to my superiors at home...but unofficially."

"Good. I'd like them to know that we asterites have teeth."

"Signing off, then."

Chung stirred. "Wait a bit," he said. "We have one of your people aboard, Lieutenant Ziska. Can you send a gig for her?"

"She didn't collaborate with us," Blades added. "You can see the evidence of her loyalty, all over my mug."

"Good girl!" Hulse exclaimed savagely. "Yes, I'll send a boat. Signing off."

The screen blanked. Chung and Blades let out a long, ragged breath. They sat a while trembling before Chung muttered, "That skunk as good as admitted everything."

"Sure," said Blades. "But we won't have any more trouble from him.

Chung stubbed out his cigarette. Poise was returning to both men. "There could be other attempts, though, in the next few years." He scowled. "I think we should arm the Station. A couple of laser guns, if nothing else. We can say it's for protection in case of war. But it'll make our own government handle us more carefully, too."

"Well, you can approach the Commission about it." Blades yawned and stretched, trying to loosen his muscles. "Better get a lot of other owners and supervisors to sign your petition, though." The next order of business came to his mind. He rose. "Why don't you go tell Adam the good news?"

"Where are you bound?"

"To let Ellen know the fight is over."

"Is it, as far as she's concerned?"

"That's what I'm about to find out. Hope I won't need an armored escort." Blades went from the cubicle, past the watchful radioman, and down the deserted passageway beyond.

The cabin given her lay at the end, locked from outside. The key hung magnetically on the bulkhead. Blades unlocked the door and tapped it with his knuckles.

"Who's there?" she called.

"Me," he said. "May I come in?"

"If you must," she said freezingly.

He opened the door and stepped through. The overhead light shimmered off her hair and limned her figure with shadows. His heart bumped. "You, uh, you can come out now," he faltered. "Everything's O.K."

She said nothing, only regarded him from glacier-blue eyes.

"No harm's been done, except to me and Sparks, and we're not mad," he groped. "Shall we forget the whole episode?"

"If you wish."

"Ellen," he pleaded, "I had to do what seemed right to me."

"So did I."

He couldn't find any more words.

"I assume that I'll be returned to my own ship," she said. He nodded. "Then, if you will excuse me, I had best make myself as presentable as I can. Good day, Mr. Blades."

"What's good about it?" he snarled, and slammed the door on his way out.

Avis stood outside the jampacked saloon. She saw him coming and ran to meet him. He made swab-O with his fingers and joy blazed from her. "Mike," she cried, "I'm so happy!"

The only gentlemanly thing to do was hug her. His spirits lifted a bit as he did. She made a nice armful. Not bad looking, either.

"Well," said Amspaugh. "So that's the inside story. How very interesting. I never heard it before."

"No, obviously it never got into any official record," Missy said. "The only announcement made was that there'd been a near accident, that the Station tried to make counter-missiles out of scoopships, but that the quick action of NASS *Altair* was what saved the situation. Her captain was commended. I don't believe he ever got a further promotion, though."

"Why didn't you publicize the facts afterwards?" Lindgren wondered. "When the revolution began, that is. It would've made good propaganda."

"Nonsense," Missy said. "Too much else had happened since then. Besides, neither Mike nor Jimmy nor I wanted to do any cheap emotion-fanning. We knew the asterites weren't any little pink-bottomed angels, nor the people back sunward a crew of devils. There were rights and wrongs on both sides. We did what we could in the war, and hated every minute of it, and when it was over we broke out two cases of champagne and invited as many Earthsiders as we could get to the party. They had a lot of love to carry home for us."

A stillness fell. She took a long swallow from her glass and sat looking out at the stars.

"Yes," Lindgren said finally, "I guess that was the worst, fighting against our own kin."

"Well, I was better off in that respect than some," Missy conceded. "I'd made my commitment so long before the trouble that my ties were nearly all out here. Twenty years is time enough to grow new roots."

"Really?" Orloff was surprised. "I haven't met you often before, Mrs. Blades, so evidently I've had a false impression. I thought you were a more recent immigrant than that."

"Shucks, no," she laughed. "I only needed six months after the *Altair* incident to think things out, resign my commission and catch the next Belt-bound ship. You don't think I'd have let a man like Mike get away, do you?"

Cradle Song

Now that the daylight has gone to bed,
See what a gladness is overhead.
Capture it under your closing eyes.
Weave it well into my lullabies.

Little Boy Blue, come blow your horn
For all of the children about to be born.
Starry the fields where they shall reap
The harvest you sow for them as you sleep.

Weary and small in your cradle berth,
You shall yet slip from this heavy Earth.
Out of her darknesses, fare you free
Home to the Sea of Tranquillity.

Little Bo-Peep, so deep in sleep,
Go seek your dreams and find them.
May it be soon your feet on the moon
Leave dancer tracks behind them.

Wild are those ways and beset by dread,
Full of farewells; but hold high your head.
Child of my heart, may you someday go
Forth among worlds I shall never know.

Sing a song of spacefolk, a. pocket full of stars.
Play it on the trumpets, harmonicas, guitars.
When the sky was opened, mankind began to sing:
"Now's the time to leave the nest. The wind is on the wing!"

Operation Afreet

-1-

It was sheer bad luck, or maybe their Intelligence was better than we knew, but the last raid, breaking past our air defenses, had spattered the Weather Corps tent from here to hell. Supply problems being what they were, we couldn't get replacements for weeks, and meanwhile the enemy had control of the weather. Our only surviving Corpsman, Major Jackson, had to save what was left of his elementals to protect us against thunderbolts; so otherwise we took whatever they chose to throw at us. At the moment, it was rain.

There's nothing so discouraging as a steady week of cold rain. The ground turns liquid and runs up into your boots, which get so heavy you can barely lift them. Your uniform is a drenched rag around your shivering skin, the rations are soggy, the rifles have to have extra care, and always the rain drums down on your helmet till you hear it in dreams. You'll never forget that endless gray washing and beating; ten years later a rainstorm will make you feel depressed.

The one consolation, I thought, was that they couldn't very well attack us from the air while it went on. Doubtless they'd yank the cloud cover away when they were ready to strafe us, but our broomsticks could scramble as fast as their carpets could arrive. Meanwhile, we slogged ahead, a whole division of us with auxiliaries—the 45th, the Lightning Busters, pride of the United States Army, turned into a wet misery of men and dragons hunting through the Oregon hills for the invader.

I made a slow way through the camp. Water ran off tents and gurgled in slit trenches. Our sentries were, of course, wearing Tarnkappen, but I could see their footprints form in the mud and hear the boots squelch and the tired monotonous cursing.

I passed by the Air Force strip; they were bivouacked with us, to give support as needed. A couple of men stood on guard outside the knockdown hangar, not bothering with invisibility. Their blue uniforms were as mucked and bedraggled as my OD's, but they had shaved and their insignia—the winged broomstick and the anti-Evil Eye beads—were polished. They saluted me, and I returned the gesture idly. Esprit de corps, wild blue yonder, nuts.

Beyond was the armor. The boys had erected portable shelters for their beasts, so I only saw steam rising out of the cracks and caught the rank reptile smell. Dragons hate rain, and their drivers were having a hell of a time controlling them.

Nearby lay Petrological Warfare, with a pen full of hooded basilisks writhing and hissing and striking out with their crowned heads at the men feeding them. Personally, I doubted the practicality of that whole corps. You have to get a basilisk quite close to a man, and looking straight at him, for petrifaction; and the aluminum-foil suit and helmet you must wear to deflect the influence of your pets is an invitation to snipers. Then, too, when human carbon is turned to silicon, you have a radioactive isotope, and maybe get such a dose of radiation yourself that the medics have to give you St. John's Wort plucked from a graveyard in the dark of the moon.

So, in case you didn't know, cremation hasn't simply died out as a custom; it's become illegal under the National Defense Act. We have to have plenty of old-fashioned cemeteries. Thus does the age of science pare down our liberties.

I went on past the engineers, who were directing a gang of zombies carving another drainage ditch, and on to General Vanbrugh's big tent. When the guard saw my Tetragrammaton insigne, for the Intelligence Corps, and the bars on my shoulders, he saluted and let me in. I came to a halt before the desk and brought my own hand up.

"Captain Matuchek reporting, sir," I said.

Vanbrugh looked at me from beneath shaggy gray brows. He was a large man with a face like weathered rock, 103 percent Regular Army, but we liked him as well as you can like a buck general. "At ease," he said. "Sit down. This'll take a while."

I found a folding chair and lowered myself into it. Two others were already seated whom I didn't know. One was a plump man with a round red face and a fluffy white beard, a major bearing the crystal-ball emblem of the Signal Corps. The other was a young woman. In spite of my weariness, I blinked and looked twice at her. She was worth it—a tall green-eyed redhead with straight high-cheeked features and a figure too good for the WAC clothes or any other. Captain's bars, Cavalry spider...or Sleipnir, if you want to be official about it.

"Major Harrigan," grumbled the general. "Captain Graylock. Captain Matuchek. Let's get down to business."

He spread a map out before us. I leaned over and looked at it. Positions were indicated, ours and the enemy's. They still held the Pacific seaboard from Alaska halfway down through Oregon, though that was considerable improvement from a year ago, when the Battle of the Mississippi had turned the tide.

"Now then," said Vanbrugh, "I'll tell you the over-all situation. This is a dangerous mission, you don't have to volunteer, but I want you to know how important it is."

What I knew, just then, was that I'd been told to volunteer or else. That was the Army, at least in a major war like this, and in principle I couldn't object. I'd been a reasonably contented Hollywood actor when the Saracen Caliphate attacked us. I wanted to go back to more of the same, but that meant finishing the war.

"You can see we're driving them back," said the general, "and the occupied countries are primed and cocked to revolt as soon as they get a fighting chance. The British have been organizing the underground and arming them while readying for a cross-Channel jump. The Russians are set to advance from the north. But we have to give the enemy a decisive blow, break this whole front and roll 'em up. That'll be the signal. If we succeed, the war will be over this year. Otherwise, it might drag on for another three."

I knew it. The whole Army knew it. Official word hadn't been passed yet, but somehow you feel when a big push is impending.

His stumpy finger traced along the map. "The 9th Armored Division is here, the 12th Broomborne here, the 14th Cavalry here, the Salamanders here where we know they've concentrated their fire-breathers. The Marines are ready to establish a beachhead and retake Seattle, now that the Navy's bred enough Krakens. One good goose, and we'll have 'em running."

Major Harrigan snuffled into his beard and stared gloomily at a crystal ball. It was clouded and vague; the enemy had been jamming our crystals till they were no use whatsoever, though naturally we'd retaliated. Captain Graylock tapped impatiently on the desk with a perfectly manicured nail. She was so clean and crisp and efficient, I decided I didn't like her looks after all. Not while I had three days' beard bristling from my chin.

"But apparently something's gone wrong, sir," I ventured.

"Correct, damn it," said Vanbrugh. "In Trollburg."

I nodded. The Saracens held that town: a key position, sitting as it did on U.S. Highway 20 and guarding the approach to Salem and Portland.

"I take it we're supposed to seize Trollburg, sir," I murmured.

Vanbrugh scowled. "That's the job for the 45th," he grunted. "If we muff it, the enemy can sally out against the 9th, cut them off, and throw the whole operation akilter. But now Major Harrigan and Captain Graylock come from the 14th to tell me the Trollburg garrison has an afreet."

I whistled, and a chill crawled along my spine. The Caliphate had exploited the Powers recklessly—that was one reason why the rest of the Moslem world regarded them as heretics and hated them as much as we did—but I never thought they'd go as far as breaking Solomon's seal. An afreet getting out of hand could destroy more than anybody cared to estimate.

"I hope they haven't but one," I whispered.

"No, they don't," said the Graylock woman. Her voice was low and could have been pleasant if it weren't so brisk. "They've been dredging the Red Sea in hopes of finding another Solly bottle, but this seems to be the last one left."

"Bad enough," I said. The effort to keep my tone steady helped calm me down. "How'd you find out?"

"We're with the 14th," said Graylock unnecessarily. Her Cavalry badge had surprised me, however. Normally, the only recruits the Army can dig up to ride unicorns are pickle-faced schoolteachers and the like.

"I'm simply a liaison officer," said Major Harrigan in haste. "I go by broomstick myself." I grinned at that. No American male, unless he's in holy orders, likes to admit he's qualified to control a unicorn. He saw me and flushed angrily.

Graylock went on, as if dictating. She kept her tone flat, though little else. "We had the luck to capture a bimbashi in a commando attack. I questioned him."

"They're pretty close-mouthed, those noble sons of. . .um...the desert," I said. I'd bent the Geneva Convention myself, occasionally, but didn't relish the idea of breaking it completely—even if the enemy had no such scruples.

"Oh, we practiced no brutality," said Graylock. "We housed him and fed him very well. But the moment a bite of food was in his throat, I'd turn it into pork. He broke pretty fast, and spilled everything he knew."

I had to laugh aloud, and Vanbrugh himself chuckled; but she sat perfectly deadpan. Organic-organic transformation, which merely shuffles molecules around without changing atoms, has no radiation hazards but naturally requires a good knowledge of chemistry. That's the real reason the average dogface hates the technical corps: pure envy of a man who can turn K rations into steak and French fries. The quartermasters have enough trouble conjuring up the rations themselves, without branching into fancy dishes.

"Okay, you learned they have an afreet in Trollburg," said the general. "What about their strength otherwise?"

"A small division, sir. You can take the place handily, if that demon can be immobilized," said Harrigan.

"Yes, I know." Vanbrugh swiveled his eyes around to me. "Well, Captain, are you game? If you can carry the stunt off, it'll mean a Silver Star at least—pardon me, a Bronze."

"Uh—" I paused, fumbling after words. I was more interested in promotion and ultimate discharge, but that might follow too. Nevertheless...quite apart from my own neck, there was a practical objection. "Sir, I don't know a damn thing about the job. I nearly flunked Demonology 1 in college."

"That'll be my part," said Graylock.

"You!" I picked my jaw off the floor again, but couldn't find anything else to say.

"I was head witch of the Arcane Agency in New York before the war," she said coldly. Now I knew where she got that personality: the typical big-city career girl. I can't stand them. "I know as much about handling demons as anyone on this coast. Your task will be to escort me safely to the place and back."

"Yeah," I said weakly. "Yeah, that's all."

Vanbrugh cleared his throat. He didn't like sending a woman on such a mission, but time was too short for him to have any choice. "Captain Matuchek is one of the best werewolves in the business," he complimented me.

Ave, Caesar, morituri te salutant, I thought. No, that isn't what I mean, but never mind. I can figure out a better phrasing at my leisure after I'm dead.

I wasn't afraid, exactly. Besides the spell laid on me to prevent that, I had reason to believe my personal chances were no worse than those of any infantryman headed into a firefight. Nor would Vanbrugh sacrifice personnel on a mission he himself considered hopeless. But I did feel less optimistic about the prospects than he.

"I think two adepts can get past their guards," the general proceeded. "From then on, you'll have to improvise. If you can put that monster out of action, we attack at noon tomorrow." Grimly: "If I haven't got word to that effect by dawn, we'll have to regroup, start retreating, and save what we can. Okay, here's a geodetic survey map of the town and approaches—"

He didn't waste time asking me if I had really volunteered.

-2-

I guided Captain Graylock back to the tent I shared with two brother officers. Darkness was creeping across the long chill slant of rain. We plodded through the muck in silence until we were under canvas. My tentmates were out on picket duty, so we had the place to ourselves. I lit the saint-elmo and sat down on the sodden plank floor.

"Have a chair," I said, pointing to our one camp stool. It was an animated job we'd bought in San Francisco: not especially bright, but it would carry our duffel and come when called. It shifted uneasily at the unfamiliar weight, then went back to sleep.

Graylock took out a pack of Wings and raised her brows. I nodded my thanks, and the cigarette flapped over to my mouth. Personally, I smoke Luckies in the field: self-striking tobacco is convenient when your matches may be wet. When I was a civilian and could afford it, my brand was Philip Morris, because the little red-coated smoke sprite can also mix you a drink.

We puffed for a bit in silence, listening to the rain. "Well," I said at last, "I suppose you have transportation."

"My personal broomstick," she said. "I don't like this GI Willys. Give me a Cadillac anytime. I've souped it up, too."

"And you have your grimoires and powders and whatnot?"

"Just some chalk. No material agency is much use against a powerful demon."

"Yeah? What about the sealing wax on the Solly bottle?"

"It isn't the wax that holds an afreet in, but the seal. The spells are symbolic; in fact, it's believed their effect is purely psychosomatic." She hollowed the flat planes of her cheeks, sucking in smoke, and I saw what a good bony structure she had. "We may have a chance to test that theory tonight."

"Well, then, you'll want a light pistol loaded with silver slugs; they have weres of their own, you know. I'll take a grease gun and a forty-five and a few grenades."

"How about a squirter?"

I frowned. The notion of using holy water as a weapon has always struck me as blasphemous, though the chaplain said it was permissible against Low World critters. "No good to us," I said. "The Moslems don't have that ritual, so of course they don't use any beings that can be controlled by it. Let's see, I'll want my Polaroid flash too. And that's about it."

Ike Abrams stuck his big nose in the tent flap. "Would you and the lady captain like some eats, sir?" he asked.

"Why, sure," I said. Inwardly, I thought: Hate to spend my last night on Midgard standing in a chow line. When he had gone, I explained to the girl: "Ike's only a private, but we were friends in Hollywood—he was a prop man when I played in *Call of the Wild* and *Silver Chief*—and he's kind of appointed himself my orderly. He'll bring us some food here."

"You know," she remarked, "that's one good thing about the technological age. Did you know there used to be widespread anti-Semitism in this country? Not just among a few Johannine cranks; no, among ordinary respectable citizens."

"Fact?"

"Fact. Especially a false belief that Jews were cowards and never found in the front lines. Now, when religion forbids most of them to originate spells, and the Orthodox don't use goetics at all, the proportion of them who serve as dogfaces and Rangers is simply too high to ignore."

I myself had gotten tired of comic-strip supermen and pulp-magazine heroes having such monotonously Yiddish names—don't Anglo-Saxons belong to our culture too?—but she'd made a good point. And it showed she was a trifle more than a money machine. A bare trifle.

"What'd you do in civilian life?" I asked, chiefly to drown out the incessant noise of the rain.

"I told you," she snapped, irritable again. "I was with the Arcane Agency. Advertising, public relations, and so on."

"Oh, well," I said. "Hollywood is at least as phony, so I shouldn't sneer."

I couldn't help it, however. Those Madison Avenue characters gave me a pain in the rear end. Using the good Art to puff some self-important nobody, or to sell a product whose main virtue is its total similarity to other brands of the same. The SPCA has cracked down on training nixies to make fountains spell out words, or cramming young salamanders into glass tubes to light up Broadway, but I can still think of better uses for slick paper than trumpeting Ma Chère perfume. Which is actually a love potion anyway, though you know what postal regulations are.

"You don't understand," she said. "It's part of our economy—part of our whole society. Do you think the average backyard warlock is capable of repairing, oh, say a lawn sprinkler? Hell, no! He'd probably let loose the water elementals and flood half a township if it weren't for the inhibitory spells. And we, Arcane, undertook the campaign to convince the Hydros they had to respect our symbols. I told you it's psychosomatic when you're dealing with these really potent beings. For that job, I had to go down in an aqualung!"

I stared at her with more respect. Ever since mankind found how to degauss the ruinous effects of cold iron, and the goetic age began, the world has needed some pretty bold people. Apparently she was one of them.

Abrams brought in two plates of rations. He looked wistful, and I would have invited him to join us except that our mission was secret and we had to thresh out the details.

Captain Graylock 'chanted the coffee into martinis—not quite dry enough—and the dog food into steaks—a turn too well done; but you can't expect the finer sensibilities in a woman, and it was the best chow I'd had in a month. She relaxed a bit over the brandy, and I learned that her repellent crispness was simply armor against the slick types she dealt with, and we found out that our first names were Steven and Virginia. But then dusk had become dark outside, and we must be going.

-3-

You may think it was sheer lunacy, sending two people, one of them a woman, into an enemy division on a task like this. It would seem to call for a Ranger brigade, at least. But present-day science has transformed war as well as industry, medicine, and ordinary life. Our mission was desperate in any event, and we wouldn't have gained enough by numbers to make reinforcements worthwhile.

You see, while practically anyone can learn a few simple cantrips, to operate a presensitized broomstick or vacuum cleaner or turret lathe or whatever, only a small minority of the human race can qualify as adepts. Besides years of study and practice, that takes inborn talent. It's kind of like therianthropy: if you're one of the rare persons with chromosomes for that, you can change into your characteristic animal almost by instinct; otherwise you need a transformation performed on you by powerful outside forces.

My scientific friends tell me that the Art involves regarding the universe as a set of Cantorian infinities. Within any given class, the part is equal to the whole and so on. One good witch could do all the runing we were likely to need; a larger party would simply be more liable to detection, and would risk valuable personnel. So Vanbrugh had very rightly sent us two alone.

The trouble with sound military principles is that sometimes you personally get caught in them.

Virginia and I turned our backs on each other while we changed clothes. She got into an outfit of slacks and combat jacket, I into the elastic knit garment which would fit me as well in wolf-shape. We put on our helmets, hung our equipment around us, and turned about. Even in the baggy green battle garb she looked good.

"Well," I said tonelessly, "shall we go?"

I wasn't afraid, of course. Every recruit is immunized against fear when they put the geas on him. But I didn't like the prospect.

"The sooner the better, I suppose," she answered. Stepping to the entrance, she whistled.

Her stick swooped down and landed just outside. It had been stripped of the fancy chrome, but was still a neat job. The foam-rubber seats had good shock absorbers and well-designed back rests, unlike Army transport. Her familiar was a gigantic tomcat, black as a furry midnight, with two malevolent yellow eyes. He arched his back and spat indignantly. The weather-proofing spell kept rain off him, but be didn't like this damp air.

Virginia chucked him under the chin. "Oh, so, Svartalf," she murmured. "Good cat, rare sprite, prince of darkness, if we outlive this night you shall sleep on cloudy cushions and lap cream from a golden bowl." He cocked his ears and raced his motor.

I climbed into the rear seat, snugged my feet in the stirrups, and leaned back. The woman mounted in front of me and crooned to the stick. It swished upward, the ground fell away and the camp was hidden in gloom. Both of us had been given witch-sight—infra-red vision, actually—so we didn't need lights.

When we got above the clouds, we saw a giant vault of stars overhead and a swirling dim whiteness below. I also glimpsed a couple of P-56's circling on patrol, fast jobs with six brooms each to lift their weight of armor and machine guns. We left them behind and streaked northward. I rested the BAR on my lap and sat listening to the air whine past. Underneath us, in the rough-edged murk of the hills, I spied occasional flashes, an artillery duel. So far no one had been able to cast a spell fast enough to turn or implode a shell. I'd heard rumors that General Electric was developing a gadget which could recite the formula in microseconds, but meanwhile the big guns went on talking.

Trollburg was a mere few miles from our position. I saw it as a vague sprawling mass, blacked out against our cannon and bombers. It would have been nice to have an atomic weapon just then, but as long as the Tibetans keep those antinuclear warfare prayer wheels turning, such thoughts must remain merely science-fictional. I felt my belly muscles tighten. The cat bottled out his tail and swore. Virginia sent the broom-stick slanting down.

We landed in a clump of trees and she turned to me. "Their outposts must be somewhere near," she whispered. "I didn't dare try landing on a rooftop; we could have been seen too easily. We'll have to go in from here."

I nodded. "Okay. Gimme a minute."

I turned the flash on myself. How hard to believe that transforming had depended on a bright full moon till only ten years ago! Then Wiener showed that the process was simply one of polarized light of the right wavelengths, triggering the pineal gland, and the Polaroid Corporation made another million dollars or so from its WereWish Lens. It's not easy to keep up with this fearful and wonderful age we live in, but I wouldn't trade.

The usual rippling, twisting sensations, the brief drunken dizziness and half-ecstatic pain, went through me. Atoms reshuffled into whole new molecules, nerves grew some endings and lost others bone was briefly fluid and muscles like stretched rubber. Then I stabilized, shook myself, stuck my tail out the flap of the skin-tight pants, and nuzzled Virginia's hand.

She stroked my neck, behind the helmet. "Good boy," she whispered. "Go get 'em."

I turned and faded into the brush.

A lot of writers have tried to describe how it feels to be were, and every one of them has failed, because human language doesn't have the words. My vision was no longer acute, the stars were blurred above me and the world took on a colorless flatness. But I heard with a clarity that made the night almost a roar, way into the supersonic; and a universe of smells roiled in my nostrils, wet grass and teeming dirt, the hot sweet little odor of a scampering field mouse, the clean tang of oil and guns, a faint harshness of smoke—Poor stupefied humanity, half-dead to such earthy glories!

The psychological part is the hardest to convey. I was a wolf, with a wolf's nerves and glands and instincts, a wolf's sharp but limited intelligence. I had a man's memories and a man's purposes, but they were unreal, dreamlike. I must make an effort of trained will to hold to them and not go hallooing off after the nearest jackrabbit. No wonder weres had a bad name in the old days, before they themselves understood the mental changes involved and got the right habits drilled into them from babyhood.

I weigh a hundred and eighty pounds, and the conservation of mass holds good like any other law of nature, so I was a pretty big wolf. But it was easy to flow through the bushes and meadows and gullies, another drifting shadow. I was almost inside the town when I caught a near smell of man.

I flattened, the gray fur bristling along my spine, and waited. The sentry came by. He was a tall bearded fellow with gold earrings that glimmered wanly under the stars. The turban wrapped around his helmet bulked monstrous against the Milky Way.

I let him go and followed his path until I saw the next one. They were placed around Trollburg, each pacing a hundred-yard arc and meeting his opposite number at either end of it. No simple task to—

Something murmured in my ears. I crouched. One of their aircraft ghosted overhead. I saw two men and a couple of machine guns squatting on top of the carpet. It circled low and lazily, above the ring of sentries. Trollburg was well guarded.

Somehow, Virginia and I had to get through that picket. I wished the transformation had left me with full human reasoning powers. My wolf-impulse was simply to jump on the nearest man, but that would bring the whole garrison down on my hairy ears.

Wait—maybe that was what was needed!

I loped back to the thicket. The Svartalf cat scratched at me and zoomed up a tree. Virginia Graylock started, her pistol sprang into her hand, then she relaxed and laughed a bit nervously. I could work the flash hung about my neck, even as I was, but it went more quickly with her fingers.

"Well?" she asked when I was human again. "What'd you find out?"

I described the situation, and saw her frown and bite her lip. It was really too shapely a lip for such purposes. "Not so good," she reflected. "I was afraid of something like this."

"Look," I said, "can you locate that afreet in a hurry?"

"Oh, yes. I've studied at Congo U. and did quite well at witch-smelling. What of it?"

"If I attack one of those guards and make a racket doing it, their main attention will be turned that way. You should have an even chance to fly across the line unobserved, and once you're in the town your Tarnkappe—"

She shook her red head. "I didn't bring one. Their detection systems are as good as ours. Invisibility is actually obsolete."

"Mmm—yeah I suppose you're right. Well, anyhow, you can take advantage of the darkness to get to the afreet house. From there on, you'll have to play by ear."

"I suspected we'd have to do something like this," she replied. With a softness that astonished me: "But Steve, that's a long chance for you to take."

"Not unless they hit me with silver, and most of their cartridges are plain lead. They use a tracer principle like us; every tenth round is argent. I've got a ninety percent probability of getting home free."

"You're a liar," she said. "But a brave liar."

I wasn't brave at all. It's inspiring to think of Valley Forge, or the Alamo, or San Juan Hill or Casablanca where our outnumbered Army stopped three Panther divisions of von Ogerhaus' Afrika Korps—but only when you're safe and comfortable yourself. Down underneath the antipanic geas, a cold knot was in my guts. Still, I couldn't see any other way to do the job, and failure to attempt it would mean court-martial.

"I'll run their legs off once they start chasing me," I told her. "When I've shaken 'em, I'll try to circle back and join you."

"Okay." Suddenly she rose on tiptoe and kissed me. The impact was explosive.

I stood for a moment, looking at her. "What are you doing Saturday night?" I asked, a mite shakily.

She laughed. "Don't get ideas, Steve. I'm in the Cavalry."

"Yeah, but the war won't last forever." I grinned at her, a reckless fighting grin that made her eyes linger. Acting experience is often useful.

We settled the details as well as we could. She herself had no soft touch: the afreet would be well guarded, and was plenty dangerous in itself. The chances of us both seeing daylight were nothing to feel complacent about.

I turned back to wolf-shape and licked her hand. She rumpled my fur. I slipped off into the darkness.

I had chosen a sentry well off the highway, across which there would surely be barriers. A man could be seen to either side of my victim, tramping slowly back and forth. I glided behind a stump near the middle of his beat and waited for him.

When he came, I sprang. I caught a dark brief vision of eyes and teeth in the bearded face, I heard him yelp and smelled the upward spurt of his fear, then we shocked together. He went down on his back, threshing, and I snapped for the throat. My jaws closed on his arm, and blood was hot and salty on my tongue.

He screamed again. I sensed the call going down the line. The two nearest Saracens ran to help. I tore out the gullet of the first man and bunched myself for a leap at the next.

He fired. The bullet went through me in a jag of pain and the impact sent me staggering. But he didn't know how to deal with a were. He should have dropped on one knee and fired steadily till he got to the silver bullet; if necessary, he should have fended me off, even pinned me with his bayonet, while he shot. This one kept running toward me, calling on the Allah of his heretical sect.

My tissues knitted as I plunged to meet him. I got past the bayonet and gun muzzle, hitting him hard enough to knock the weapon loose but not to bowl him over. He braced his legs, grabbed my neck, and hung on.

I swung my left hind leg back of his ankle and shoved. He fell with me on top, the position an infighting werewolf always tries for. My head swiveled; I gashed open his arm and broke his grip.

Before I could settle the business, three others had piled on me. Their trench scimitars went up and down, in between my ribs and out again. Lousy training they'd had. I snapped my way free of the heap—half a dozen by then—and broke loose.

Through sweat and blood I caught the faintest whiff of Chanel No. 5, and something in me laughed. Virginia had sped past the confusion—riding her stick a foot above ground, and was inside Trollburg. My next task was to lead a chase and not stop a silver slug while doing so.

I howled, to taunt the men spilling from outlying houses, and let them have a good look at me before making off across the fields. My pace was easy, not to lose them at once; I relied on zigzags to keep me unpunctured. They followed, stumbling and shouting.

As far as they knew, this had been a mere commando raid. Their pickets would have re-formed and the whole garrison been alerted. But surely none except a few chosen officers knew about the afreet, and none of those knew we'd acquired the information. So they had no way of telling what we really planned. Maybe we would pull this operation off—

Something swooped overhead, one of their damned carpets. It rushed down on me like a hawk, guns spitting. I made for the nearest patch of woods.

Into the trees! Given half a break, I could—

They didn't give it. I heard a bounding behind me, caught the acrid smell, and whimpered. A weretiger could go as fast as I.

For a moment I remembered an old guide I'd had in Alaska, and wished to blazes he were here. He was a were-Kodiak bear. Then I whirled and met the tiger before he could pounce.

He was a big one, five hundred pounds at least. His eyes smoldered above the great fangs, and he lifted a paw that could crack my spine like a dry twig. I rushed in, snapping, and danced back before he could strike.

Part of me heard the enemy, blundering around in the underbrush trying to find us. The tiger leaped. I evaded him and bolted for the nearest thicket. Maybe I could go where he couldn't. He ramped through the woods behind me, roaring.

I saw a narrow space between a pair of giant oaks, too small for him, and hurried that way. But it was too small for me also. In the half second that I was stuck, he caught up. The lights exploded and went out.

-4-

I was nowhere and nowhen. My very body had departed from me, or I from it. How could I think of infinite eternal dark and cold and emptiness when I had no senses? How could I despair when I was nothing but a point in spacetime?...No, not even that, for there was nothing else, nothing to find or love or hate or fear or be related to in any way whatsoever. The dead were less alone than I, for I was all which existed.

This was my despair.

But on the instant, or after a quadrillion years, or both or neither, I came to know otherwise. I was under the regard of the Solipsist. Helpless in unconsciousness, I could but share that egotism so ultimate that it would yield no room even to hope. I swirled in the tides and storms of thoughts too remote, too alien, too vast for me to take in save as I might brokenly hear the polar ocean while it drowned me.

—danger, this one—he and those two—somehow they can be a terrible danger—not now (scornfully) *when they merely help complete the ruin of a plan already bungled into wreck—no, later, when the next plan is ripening, the great one of which this war was naught but an early leaf—something about them warns thinly of danger—could I only scan more clearly into time!—they must be diverted, destroyed, somehow dealt with before their potential has grown—but I cannot originate anything yet—maybe they will be slain by the normal chances of war—if not, I must remember them and try later—now I have too much else to do, saving those seeds I planted in the world—the birds of the enemy fly thick across my fields, hungry crows and eagles to guard them—*(with ever wilder hate) *my snares shall take you yet, birds—and the One Who loosed you!*

So huge was the force of that final malevolence that I was cast free.

-5-

I opened my eyes. For a while I was aware entirely of the horror. Physical misery rescued me, driving those memories back to where half-forgotten nightmares dwell. The thought flitted by me that shock must have made me briefly delirious.

A natural therianthrope in his beast shape isn't quite as invulnerable as most people believe. Aside from things like silver—biochemical poisons to a metabolism in that semifluid state—damage which stops a vital organ will stop life; amputations are permanent unless a surgeon is near to sew the part back on before its cells die; and so on and so on, no pun intended. We are a hardy sort, however. I'd taken a blow that probably broke my neck. The spinal cord not being totally severed, the damage had healed at standard therio speed.

The trouble was, they'd arrived and used my flash to make me human before the incidental hurts had quite gone away. My head drummed and I retched.

"Get up." Someone stuck a boot in my ribs.

I lurched erect. They'd removed my gear, including the flash. A score of them trained their guns on me.

Tiger Boy stood close. In man-shape he was almost seven feet tall and monstrously fat. Squinting through the headache, I saw he wore the insignia of an emir—which was a military rank these days rather than a title, but pretty important nevertheless.

"Come," he said. He led the way, and I was hustled along behind.

I saw their carpets in the sky and heard the howling of their own weres looking for spoor of other Americans. I was still too groggy to care very much.

We entered the town, its pavement sounding hollow under the boots, and went toward the center. Trollburg wasn't big, maybe five thousand population once. Most of the streets were empty. I saw a few Saracen troops, antiaircraft guns poking into the sky, a dragon lumbering past with flames flickering around its jaws and cannon projecting from the armored howdah. No trace of the civilians, but I knew what had happened to them. The attractive young women were in the officers' harems, the rest dead or locked away pending shipment to the slave markets.

By the time we got to the hotel where the enemy headquartered, my aches had subsided and my brain was clear. That was a mixed blessing under the circumstances. I was taken upstairs to a suite and told to stand before a table. The emir sat down behind it, half a dozen guards lined the walls, and a young pasha of Intelligence seated himself nearby.

The emir's big face turned to that one, and he spoke a few words—I suppose to the effect of "I'll handle this, you take notes." He looked back at me. His eyes were the pale tiger-green.

"Now then," he said in good English, "we shall have some questions. Identify yourself, please."

I told him mechanically that I was called Sherrinford Mycroft, Captain, AUS, and gave him my serial number.

"That is not your real name, is it?" he asked.

"Of course not!" I replied. "I know the Geneva Convention, and you're not going to cast name-spells on me. Sherrinford Mycroft is my official johnsmith."

"The Caliphate has not subscribed to the Geneva Convention," said the emir quietly, "and stringent measures are sometimes necessary in a jehad. What was the purpose of this raid?"

"I am not required to answer that," I said. Silence would have served the same end, delay to gain time for Virginia, but not as well.

"You may be persuaded to do so," he said.

If this had been a movie, I'd have told him I was picking daisies, and kept on wisecracking while they brought out the thumbscrews. In practice it would have fallen a little flat.

"All right," I said. "I was scouting."

"A single one of you?"

"A few others. I hope they got away." That might keep his boys busy hunting for a while.

"You lie," he said dispassionately.

"I can't help it if you don't believe me," I shrugged.

His eyes narrowed. "I shall soon know if you speak truth," he said. "If not, may Eblis have mercy on you."

I couldn't help it, I jerked where I stood and sweat pearled out on my skin. The emir laughed. He had an unpleasant laugh, a sort of whining growl deep in his fat throat, like a tiger playing with its kill.

"Think over your decision," he advised, and turned to some papers on the table.

It grew most quiet in that room. The guards stood as if cast in bronze. The young shavetail dozed beneath his turban. Behind the emir's back, a window looked out on a blankness of night. The sole sounds were the loud ticking of a clock and the rustle of papers. They seemed to deepen the silence.

I was tired, my head ached, my mouth tasted foul and thirsty. The sheer physical weariness of having to stand was meant to help wear me down. It occurred to me that the emir must be getting scared of us, to take this much trouble with a lone prisoner. That was kudos for the American cause, but small consolation to me.

My eyes flickered, studying the tableau. There wasn't much to see, standard hotel furnishings. The emir had cluttered his desk with a number of objects: a crystal ball useless because of our own jamming, a fine cut-glass bowl looted from somebody's house, a set of nice crystal wineglasses, a cigar humidor of quartz glass, a decanter full of what looked like good Scotch. I guess he just liked crystal.

He helped himself to a cigar, waving his hand to make the humidor open and a Havana fly into his mouth and light itself. As the minutes crawled by, an ashtray soared up from time to time to receive from him. I guessed that everything he had was 'chanted so it would rise and move easily. A man that fat, paying the price of being a really big werebeast, needed such conveniences.

It was very quiet. The light glared down on us. It was somehow hideously wrong to see a good ordinary GE saint-elmo shining on those turbaned heads.

I began to get the forlorn glimmerings of an idea. How to put it into effect I didn't yet know, but just to pass the time I began composing some spells.

Maybe half an hour had passed, though it seem more like half a century, when the door opened and a fennec, the small fox of the African desert, trotted in. The emir looked up as it went into a closet, to find darkness to use its flash. The fellow who came out was, naturally, a dwarf barely one foot high. He prostrated himself and spoke rapidly in a high thready voice.

"So." The emir's chins turned slowly around to me. "The report is that no trace was found of other tracks than yours. You have lied."

"Didn't I tell you?" I asked. My throat felt stiff and strange. "We used owls and bats. I was the lone wolf."

"Be still," he said tonelessly. "I know as well as you that the only werebats are vampires, and that vampires are—what you say—4-F in all armies."

That was true. Every so often, some armchair general asks why we don't raise a force of Draculas. The answer is routine: they're too light and flimsy; they can't endure sunshine; if they don't get a steady blood ration they're apt to turn on their comrades; and you can't possibly use them around Italian troops. I swore at myself, but my mind had been too numb to think straight.

"I believe you are concealing something," went on the emir. He gestured at his glasses and decanter, which supplied him with a shot of Scotch, and sipped judiciously. The Caliphate sect was also heretical with respect to strong drink; they maintained that while the Prophet forbade wine, he said nothing about beer, gin, whisky, brandy, rum, or akvavit.

"We shall have to use stronger measures," the emir said at last. "I was hoping to avoid them." He nodded at his guards.

Two held my arms. The pasha worked me over. He was good at that. The werefennec watched avidly, the emir puffed his cigar and went on with his paperwork. After a long few minutes, he gave an order. They let me go, and even set forth a chair for me, which I needed badly.

I sat breathing hard. The emir regarded me with a certain gentleness. "I regret this," he said. "It is not enjoyable." Oddly, I believed him. "Let us hope you will be reasonable before we have to inflict permanent injuries. Meanwhile, would you like a cigar?"

The old third degree procedure. Knock a man around for a while, then show him kindness. You'd be surprised how often that makes him blubber and break.

"We desire information about your troops and their plans," said the emir. "If you will cooperate and accept the true faith, you can have an honored position with us. We like good men in the Caliphate." He smiled. "After the war, you could select your harem out of Hollywood if you desired."

"And if I don't squeal—" I murmured.

He spread his hands. "You will have no further wish for a harem. The choice is yours."

"Let me think," I begged. "This isn't easy."

"Please do," he answered urbanely, and returned to his papers.

I sat as relaxed as possible, drawing my throat and letting strength flow back. The Army geas could be broken by their technicians only if I gave my free consent, and I didn't want to. I considered the window behind the emir. It was a two-story drop to the street.

Most likely, I'd just get myself killed. But that was preferable to any other offer I'd had.

I went over the spells I'd haywired. A real technician has to know at least one arcane language—Latin, Greek, classical Arabic, Sanskrit, Old Norse, or the like—for the standard reasons of sympathetic science. Paranatural phenomena are not strongly influenced by ordinary speech. But except for the usual tag-ends of incantations, the minimum to operate the gadgets of daily life, I was no scholar.

However, I knew one slightly esoteric dialect quite well. I didn't know if it would work, but I could try.

My muscles tautened as I moved. It was a shudder some effort to be casual. I knocked the end of ash on my cigar. As I lifted the thing again, it collected some ash from the emir's.

I got the rhyme straight in my mind, put the cigarette to my lips, and subvocalized the spell.

Ashes-way of the urningbay,
upward-way ownay eturningray,
as-way the arksspay do yflay,
ikestray imhay in the aye-way!"

I closed my right eye and brought the glowing cigar end almost against the lid.

The emir's El Fumo leaped up and ground itself into *his* right eye.

He screamed and fell backward. I soared to my feet. I'd marked the werefennec, and one stride brought me over to him. I broke his vile little neck with a backhanded cuff and yanked off the flash that hung from it.

The guards howled and plunged for me. I went over the table and down on top of the emir, snatching his decanter en route. He clawed at me, wild with pain, I saw the ghastliness in his eye socket, and meanwhile I was hanging on to the vessel and shouting:

Ingthay of ystalcray
ebay a istralmay!
As-way I-way owthray,
yflay ouyay osay!

As I finished, I broke free and hurled the decanter at the guards. It was lousy poetics, and might not have worked if the fat man hadn't already sensitized his stuff. As it was, the ball, the ashtray, the bowl, the glasses, the humidor, and the windowpanes all took off after the decanter. The air was full of flying glass.

I didn't stay to watch the results, but went out that window like an exorcised devil. I landed in a ball on the sidewalk, bounced up, and began running.

-6-

Soldiers were around. Bullets sleeted after me. I set a record reaching the nearest alley. My witch-sight showed me a broken window, and I wriggled through that. Crouching beneath the sill, I heard the pursuit go by.

This was the back room of a looted grocery store plenty dark for my purposes. I hung the flash around my neck, turned it on myself, and made the change over. They'd return in a minute, and I didn't want to be vulnerable to lead.

Wolf, I snuffled around after another exit. A rear door stood half open. I slipped through into a tour yard full of ancient packing cases. They made a good hideout. I lay there, striving to control my lupine nature, which wanted to pant, while they swarmed through the area.

When they were gone again, I tried to considered my situation. The temptation was to hightail out of this poor, damned place. I could probably make it and technically fulfilled my share of the mission but the job wasn't really complete, and Virginia was alone with the afreet—if she still lived—and—

When I tried to recall her, the image came as a she-wolf and a furry aroma. I shook my head angrily. Weariness and desperation were submerging my reason and letting the animal instincts take over. I'd better do whatever had to be done fast.

I cast about. The town smells were confusing, but I caught the faintest sulfurous whiff and trotted cautiously in that direction. I kept to the shadows, and was seen twice but not challenged. They must have supposed I was one of theirs. The brimstone reek grew stronger.

They kept the afreet in the courthouse, a good solid building. I went through the small park in front of it, snuffed the wind carefully, and dashed over street and steps. Four enemy soldiers sprawled on top, throats cut open, and the broomstick was parked by the door. It had a twelve-inch switchblade in the handle, and Virginia had used it like a flying lance.

The man side of me, which had been entertaining stray romantic thoughts, backed up in a cold sweat; but the wolf grinned. I poked at the door. She'd 'chanted the lock open and left it that way. I stuck my nose in, and almost had it clawed off before Svartalf recognized me. He jerked his tail curtly, and I passed by and across the lobby. The stinging smell was coming from upstairs. I followed it through a thick darkness.

Light glowed in a second-floor office. I thrust the door ajar and peered in. Virginia was there. She had drawn the curtains and lit the elmos to see by. She was still busy with her precautions, startled a little on spying me but went on with the chant. I parked my shaggy behind near the door and watched.

She'd chalked the usual figure, same as the Pentagon in Washington, and a Star of David inside that. The Solly bottle was at the center. It didn't look impressive, an old flask of hard-baked clay with its hollow handle bent over and returning inside—merely a Klein bottle, with Solomon's seal in red wax at the mouth. She'd loosened her hair, and it floated in a ruddy cloud about the pale beautiful face.

The wolf of me wondered why we didn't just make off with this crock of It. The man reminded him that undoubtedly the emir had taken precautions and would have sympathetic means to uncork it from afar. We had to put the demon out of action...somehow...but nobody on our side knew a great deal about his race.

Virginia finished her spell, drew the bung, and sprang outside the pentacle as smoke boiled from the flask. She almost didn't make it, the afreet came out in such a hurry. I stuck my tail between my legs and snarled. She was scared, too, trying hard not to show that but I caught the adrenalin odor.

The afreet must bend almost double under the ceiling. He was a monstrous gray thing, nude, more or less anthropoid but with wings and horns and long ears, a mouthful of fangs and eyes like hot embers. His assets were strength, speed, and physical near-invulnerability. Turned loose, he could break any attack of Vanbrugh's, and inflict frightful casualties on the most well-dug-in defense. Controlling him afterward, before he laid the countryside waste, would be a problem. But why should the Saracens care? They'd have exacted a geas from him, that he remain their ally, as the price of his freedom.

He roared something in Arabic. Smoke swirled from his mouth. Virginia looked tiny under those half unfurled bat membranes. Her voice was less cool than she would have preferred: "Speak English, Marid. Or are you too ignorant?"

The demon huffed indignantly. "O spawn of a thousand baboons!" My eardrums flinched from the volume. "O thou white and gutless infidel thing, which I could break with my least finger, come in to me if thou darest!"

I was frightened, less by the chance of his breaking loose than by the racket he was making. It could be heard for a quarter mile.

"Be still, accursed of God!" Virginia answered. That shook him a smidgen. Like most of the hell-breed, he was allergic to holy names, though only seriously so under conditions that we couldn't reproduce here. She stood hands on hips, head tilted, to meet the gaze that smoldered down upon her. "Suleiman bin Daoud, on whom be peace, didn't jug you for nothing, I see. Back to your prison and never come forth again, lest the anger of Heaven smite you!"

The afreet fleered. "Know that Suleiman the Wise is dead these three thousand years," he retorted. "Long and long have I brooded in my narrow cell, I who once raged free through earth and sky and will now at last be released to work my vengeance on the puny sons of Adam." He shoved at the invisible barrier, but one of that type has a rated strength of several million p.s.i. It would hold firm—till some adept dissolved it. "O thou shameless unveiled harlot with hair of hell, know that I am Rashid the Mighty, the glorious in power, the smiter of rocs! Come in here and fight like a man!"

I moved close to the girl, my hackles raised. The hand that touched my head was cold. "Paranoid type," she whispered. "A lot of these harmful Low Worlders are psycho. Stupid, though. Trickery's our single chance. I don't have any spells to compel him directly. But—Aloud, to him, she said: "Shut up, Rashid, and listen to me. I also am of your race, and to be respected as such."

"Thou?" He hooted with fake laughter. "Thou of the Marid race? Why, thou fish-faced antling, if thou'dst come in here I'd show thee thou'rt not even fit to—" The rest was graphic but not for any gentlewere to repeat.

"No, hear me," said the girl. "Look and hearken well." She made signs and uttered a formula. I recognized the self-geas against telling a falsehood in the particular conversation. Our courts still haven't adopted it—Fifth Amendment—but I'd seen it used in trials abroad.

The demon recognized it, too. I imagine the Saracen adept who pumped a knowledge of English into him, to make him effective in this war, had added other bits of information about the modern world. He grew more quiet and attentive.

Virginia intoned impressively: "I can speak nothing to you except the truth. Do you agree that the name is the thing?"

"Y-y-yes," the afreet rumbled. "That is common knowledge."

I scented her relief. First hurdle passed! He had *not* been educated in scientific goetics. Though the name is, of course, in sympathy with the object, which is the principle of nymic spells and the like—nevertheless, only in this century has Korzybski demonstrated that the word and its referent are not identical.

"Very well," she said. "My name is Ginny."

He started in astonishment. "Art thou indeed?"

"Yes. Now will you listen to me? I came to offer you advice, as one jinni to another. I have powers of my own, you know, albeit I employ them in the service of Allah, the Omnipotent, the Omniscient, the Compassionate."

He glowered, but supposing her to be one of his species, he was ready to put on a crude show of courtesy. She couldn't be lying about her advice. It did not occur to him that she hadn't said the counsel would be good.

"Go on, then, if thou wilst," he growled. "Knowest thou that tomorrow I fare forth to destroy the infidel host?" He got caught up in his dreams of glory. "Aye, well will I rip them, and trample them, and break and gut and flay them. Well will they learn the power of Rashid the bright-winged, the fiery, the merciless, the wise, the..."

Virginia waited out his adjectives, then said gently: "But Rashid, why must you wreak harm? You earn nothing thereby except hate."

A whine crept into his bass. "Aye, thou speakest sooth. The whole world hates me. Everybody conspires against me. Had he not had the aid of traitors, Suleiman had never locked me away. All which I have sought to do has been thwarted by envious ill-wishers—Aye, but tomorrow comes the day of reckoning!"

Virginia lit a cigarette with a steady hand and blew smoke at him. "How can you trust the emir and his cohorts?" she asked. "He too is your enemy. He only wants to make a cat's-paw of you. Afterward, back in the bottle!"

"Why...why..." The afreet swelled till the space-warp barrier creaked. Lightning crackled from his nostrils. It hadn't occurred to him before; his race isn't bright; but of course a trained psychologist would understand how to follow out paranoid logic.

"Have you not known enmity throughout your long days?" continued Virginia quickly. "Think back, Rashid. Was not the very first thing you remember the cruel act of a spitefully envious world?"

"Aye—it was." The maned head nodded, and the voice dropped very low. "On the day I was hatched...aye, my mother's wingtip smote me so I reeled."

"Perhaps that was accidental," said Virginia.

"Nay. Ever she favored my older brother—the lout!"

Virginia sat down cross-legged. "Tell me about it," she oozed. Her tone dripped sympathy.

I felt a lessening, of the great forces that surged within the barrier. The afreet squatted on his hams, eyes half-shut, going back down a memory trail of millennia. Virginia guided him, a hint here and there. I didn't know what she was driving at, surely you couldn't psychoanalyze the monster in half a night, but—

"—Aye, and I was scarce turned three centuries when I fell into a pit my foes must have dug for me."

"Surely you could fly out of it," she murmured.

The afreet's eyes rolled. His face twisted into still more gruesome furrows. "It was a pit, I say!"

"Not by any chance a lake?" she inquired.

"Nay!" His wings thundered. "No such damnable thing...'twas dark; and wet, but—nay, not wet either, a cold which burned...

I saw dimly that the girl had a lead. She dropped long lashes to hide the sudden gleam in her gaze. Even as a wolf, I could realize what a shock it must have been to an aerial demon, nearly drowning, his fires hissing into steam, and how he must ever after deny to himself that it had happened. But what use could she make of—

Svartalf the cat streaked in and skidded to a halt. Every hair on him stood straight, and his eyes blistered me. He spat something and went out again with me in his van.

Down in the lobby I heard voices. Looking through the door, I saw a few soldiers milling about. They come by, perhaps to investigate the noise, seen the dead guards, and now they must have sent for reinforcements.

Whatever Ginny was trying to do, she needed time for it. I went out that door in one gray leap and tangled with the Saracens. We boiled into a clamorous pile. I was almost pinned flat by their numbers, but kept my jaws free and used them. Then Svartalf rode that broomstick above the fight, stabbing.

We carried a few of their weapons back into the lobby in our jaws, and sat down to wait. I figured I'd do better to remain wolf and be immune to most things than have the convenience of hands. Svartalf regarded a tommy gun thoughtfully, propped it along a wall, and crouched over it.

I was in no hurry. Every minute we were left alone, or held off the coming attack, was a minute gained for Ginny. I laid my head on my forepaws and dozed off. Much too soon I heard hobnails rattle on pavement.

The detachment must have been a good hundred. I saw their dark mass, and the gleam of starlight off their weapons. They hovered for a while around the squad we'd liquidated. Abruptly they whooped and charged up the steps.

Svartalf braced himself and worked the tommy gun. The recoil sent him skating back across the lobby, swearing, but he got a couple. I met the rest in the doorway.

Slash, snap, leap in, leap out, rip them and gash them and howl in their faces! After a brief whirl of teeth they retreated. They left half a dozen dead and wounded.

I peered through the glass in the door and saw my friend the emir. He had a bandage over his eye, but lumbered around exhorting his men with more energy than I'd expected. Groups of them broke from the main bunch and ran to either side. They'd be coming in the windows and the other doors.

I whined as I realized we'd left the broomstick outside. There could be no escape now, not even for Ginny. The protest became a snarl when I heard glass breaking and rifles blowing off locks.

That Svartalf was a smart cat. He found the tommy gun again and somehow, clumsy though paws are, managed to shoot out the lights. He and I retreated to the stairway.

They came at us in the dark, blind as most men are. I let them fumble around, and the first one who groped to the stairs was killed quietly. The second had time to yell. The whole gang of them crowded after him.

They couldn't shoot in the gloom and press without potting their own people. Excited to mindlessness, they attacked me with scimitars, which I didn't object to. Svartalf raked their legs and I tore them apart—whick, snap, clash, Allah Akbar and teeth in the night!

The stair was narrow enough for me to hold, and their own casualties hampered them, but the sheer weight of a hundred brave men forced me back a tread at a time. Otherwise one could have tackled me and a dozen more have piled on top. As things were, we gave the houris a few fresh customers for every foot we lost.

I have no clear memory of the fight. You seldom do. But it must have been about twenty minutes before they fell back at an angry growl. The emir himself stood at the foot of the stairs, lashing his tail and rippling his gorgeously striped hide.

I shook myself wearily and braced my feet for the last round. The one-eyed tiger climbed slowly towards us. Svartalf spat. Suddenly he zipped down the banister past the larger cat and disappeared in the gloom. Well, he had his own neck to think about—

We were almost nose to nose when the emir lifted paw full of swords and brought it down. I dodged somehow and flew for his throat. All I got was a mouthful of baggy skin, but I hung on and tried to work my way inward.

He roared and shook his head till I swung like a bell clapper. I shut my eyes and clamped on tight. He raked my ribs with those long claws. I skipped away but kept my teeth where they were. Lunging, he fell on me. His jaws clashed shut. Pain jagged through my tail. I let go to howl.

He pinned me down with one paw, raising the other to break my spine. Somehow, crazed with the hurt, I writhed free and struck upward. His remaining eye was glaring at me, and I bit it out of his head.

He screamed! A sweep of one paw sent me kiting up to slam against the banister. I lay with the wind knocked from me while the blind tiger rolled over in his agony. The beast drowned the man, and he went down the stairs and wrought havoc among his own soldiers.

A broomstick whizzed above the melee. Good old Svartalf! He'd only gone to fetch our transportation. I saw him ride toward the door of the afreet, and rose groggily to meet the next wave of Saracens.

They were still trying to control their boss. I gulped for breath and stood watching and smelling and listening. My tail seemed, ablaze. Half of it was gone.

A tommy gun began stuttering. I heard blood rattle in the emir's lungs. He was hard to kill. *That's the end of you, Steve Matuchek,* thought the man of me. *They'll do what they should have done in the first place, stand beneath you and sweep you with their fire, every tenth round argent.*

The emir fell and lay gasping out his life. I waited for his men to collect their wits and remember me.

Ginny appeared on the landing, astride the broom-stick. Her voice seemed to come from very far away. "Steve! Quick! Here!"

I shook my head dazedly, trying to understand. I was too tired, too canine. She stuck her fingers in her mouth and whistled. That fetched me.

She slung me across her lap and hung on tight as Svartalf piloted the stick. A gun fired blindly from below. We went out a second-story window and into the sky.

A carpet swooped near. Svartalf arched his back and poured on the Power. That Cadillac had legs! We left the enemy sitting there, and I passed out.

-7-

When I came to, I was prone on a cot in a hospital tent. Daylight was bright outside; the earth lay wet and steaming. A medic looked around as I groaned. "Hello, hero," he said. "Better stay in that position for a while. How're you feeling?"

I waited till full consciousness returned before I accepted a cup of bouillon. "How am I?" I whispered; they'd humanized me, of course.

"Not too bad, considering. You had some infection of your wounds—a staphylococcus that can switch species for a human or canine host—but we cleaned the bugs out with a new antibiotic technique. Otherwise, loss of blood, shock, and plain old exhaustion. You should be fine in a week or two."

I lay thinking, my mind draggy, most of my attention on how delicious the bouillon tasted. A field hospital can't lug around the equipment to stick pins in model bacteria. Often it doesn't even have the enlarged anatomical dummies on which the surgeon can do a sympathetic operation. "What technique do you mean?" I asked.

"One of our boys has the Evil Eye. He looks at the germs through a microscope."

I didn't inquire further, knowing that *Reader's Digest* would be waxing lyrical about it in a few months. Something else nagged at me. "The attack...have they begun?"

"The—Oh. That! That was two days ago, Rin-Tin Tin. You've been kept under asphodel. We mopped 'em up along the entire line. Last I heard, they were across the Washington border and still running."

I sighed and went back to sleep. Even the noise as the medic dictated a report to his typewriter couldn't hold me awake.

Ginny came in the next day, with Svartalf riding he shoulder. Sunlight striking through the tent flap turned her hair to hot copper. "Hello, Captain Matuchek, she said. "I came to see how you were, soon as I could get leave."

I raised myself on my elbows, and whistled at the cigarette she offered. When it was between my lips, said slowly: "Come off it, Ginny. We didn't exactly go on a date that night, but I think we're properly introduced."

"Yes." She sat down on the cot and stroked my hair. That felt good. Svartalf purred at me, and I wished I could respond.

"How about the afreet?" I asked after a while.

"Still in his bottle." She grinned. "I doubt if anybody'll ever be able to get him out again, assuming anybody would want to."

"But what did you *do*?"

"A simple application of Papa Freud's principles. If it's ever written up, I'll have every Jungian in country on my neck, but it worked. I got him spinning out his memories and illusions, and found he had a hydrophobic complex—which is fear of water, Rover, not rabies—"

"You can call me Rover," I growled, "but if you call me Fido, Fido gives a paddling."

She didn't ask why I assumed I'd be sufficiently close in future for such laying on of hands. That encouraged me. Indeed, she blushed, but went on: "Having gotten the key to his personality, I found it simple to play on his phobia. I pointed out how common a substance water is and how difficult total dehydration is. He got more and more scared. When I showed him that all animal tissue, including his own, is about eighty percent water, that was that. He crept back into his bottle and went catatonic."

After a moment, she added thoughtfully: "I'd like to have him for my mantelpiece, but I suppose he'll wind up in the Smithsonian. So I'll simply write a little treatise on the military uses of psychiatry."

"Aren't bombs and dragons and elfshot gruesome enough?" I demanded with a shudder.

Poor simple elementals! They think they're fiendish, but ought to take lessons from the human race.

As for me, I could imagine certain drawbacks to getting hitched with a witch, but "C'mere, youse."

She did.

I don't have many souvenirs of the war. It was an ugly time and best forgotten. But one keepsake will always be with me, in spite of the plastic surgeons' best efforts. As a wolf, I've got a stumpy tail, and as a man I don't like to sit down in wet weather.

That's a hell of a thing to receive a Purple Heart for.

Science Fiction and Science: On Imaginary Science

In the last part of this series we considered hard science fiction and its relationship to science in a preliminary way. I would have preferred to call it "hard core science fiction," since it belongs so unequivocally to our field and is so central to it. However, that would have made too many present-day readers snicker. What are we going to do for a vocabulary, now that "adult," "exotic," and "explicit" all mean "pornographic"?

To recapitulate, hard science fiction is the kind which, ideally, confines the story assumptions to established facts. The author postulates no laws of nature, as yet undiscovered, which would allow things to happen. He reasons logically, sometimes mathematically, what the likely consequences are of the conditions he is setting up. (Or she does, of course; some fine work of this type comes nowadays from women.)

For instance, if he uses a Martian setting, he uses the latest findings about Mars and doesn't contradict any of them. If he puts an imaginary planet in orbit around a particular sort of star, he calculates, or at least estimates, what the results are, everything from the length of the year to the mean surface temperature. He avoids absurdities such as an atmosphere containing both free oxygen and free hydrogen.

To be sure, he might sketch out a plausible biochemistry which causes organisms on a world with free oxygen to give off hydrogen. Nevertheless, he'll be aware that to the extent the latter gas does not escape into space, it will be oxidized to water in a comparatively short time. The equilibrium concentration of it in the air cannot be very great. How much could be present and what kind of organic processes could produce it are left as an exercise for the reader. This author is tired.

Hard science fiction is not necessarily unimaginative. On the contrary, think of the dazzling creations of Hal Clement, to name only its most obvious practitioner. Though the writer sticks *by* the facts, he is not confined *to* them. Hence, while incorporating the Viking data about Mars, he might propose a possible life form which by its nature has escaped detection. Seeming limitations on him often become challenges. Thus, I've already mentioned how a suggestion by John Campbell showed me a way to have winged beings massive enough for big brains, on an Earthlike world, which had hitherto looked unbelievable. As for future technology, the writer is simply required to describe things which could be built in principle, *e.g.*, a fusion-powered plasma-jet spacecraft which can move at a full gravity or more of acceleration for months on end. He doesn't have to engineer the devices. If he could do that, he wouldn't be preparing stories but patent applications.

Nor need hard science fiction be unemotional. The scientific background of Ursula K. Le Guin's fine study of a human dilemma, "Nine Lives," is excellent. Mildred Downey Broxon had the consequences of a black hole wandering into a planetary system worked out with exactness before she started to write her tragic "Singularity." If I may cite myself again, though *Tau Zero* was called, by the late James Blish, the ultimate hard science novel, numerous readers, some of whom admitted being baffled by the technicalities, have told me they liked the people.

I mention that one because a point came up in the planning of it which may interest you. For the benefit of those who haven't read it, or did but have forgotten, it concerns a spaceship trapped into traveling closer and closer to the speed of light. (The basic idea for the vessel, a ramscoop, was proposed in the professional literature by a physicist, R. W. Bussard.) According to the laws of relativity, this meant that time onboard went more and more slowly with respect to the rest of the universe, until at last millions of years might go outside while someone drew a breath. Now how could any sense of that vastness be conveyed?

I turned to the works of Olaf Stapledon, two of which are unmatched in their awesome scale, to find out how he had made me feel it. That proved to be by a more or less logarithmic progression, which gets us accustomed to one order of magnitude before moving on to the next. Accordingly, I laid out my chapters likewise. The first occupies a few hours on the galactic clock, the second a few days, the third a few months, and so on. Each span is approximately ten times as long as the previous one. It seems to have worked pretty well, producing emotional impact. But the real credit belongs to Stapledon. And the real moral is that either there are no "two cultures," science *versus* the humanities, or if there are, this is unfortunate and unnecessary.

The book has been used to help teach relativity, which pleases me far more than if it were in an English course. Yet a few readers have argued the plausibility of certain things in it. For example, would not the increasing intensity of gravitational radiation come to shed energy as fast as the ship could gain it, thereby setting a speed limit? I don't know myself, but, again, I'm happy that knowledgeable individuals found my ideas worth that much consideration.

Being caught out in error is, of course, an occupational hazard of the hard science fiction writer. The out-and-out inevitability he faces is that the scientific picture he employed will change. Once the first Pioneer flyby had sent back its readings on Jupiter, virtually every story ever written about that planet or its moons, no matter how carefully constructed, went down in flames. Needless to say, we can still enjoy the good ones, as we can still enjoy G. K. Chesterton's *The*

Flying Inn and *The Napoleon of Notting Hill*, which are laid in future periods that are now behind us and never came to pass as the author imagined. However, we can no longer pretend that the old hard science fiction yarns depict something that might actually be.

Indeed, the assumption that what we know today, or think we know, is all that will ever concern us, even within the confines of a single story, is perhaps more unrealistic than the wildest flight of fancy. I love hard science fiction but it does, by definition, omit the crown of science—discovery of what is fundamentally new to us.

Besides, where do you draw the line between hewing to the facts and postulating additional facts which are not in today's scientific canon? Clement himself often allows faster-than-light travel, mainly because he needs it to get his characters to his alien worlds in reasonable time but partly, he has admitted, because of a feeling that it may be possible in spite of what most physicists say. Of late, work on the frontiers of relativity theory itself gives reason to suppose this could be the case (no proof...as yet).

Arthur Clarke's *Imperial Earth* is a splendid piece of hard science fiction, with all the technical details hanging together and ringing true. Just the same, he chose to power a spacecraft with a small black hole. Such may or may not exist; so far, we don't know. They ought to *if* conditions during the first few minutes of the universe's outward expansion were right. Cosmologists are still trying to establish precisely what went on then.

A few years ago I was asked to write a piece on "The Science" in science fiction for an anthology.[1] Seeking to clarify the subject, I set up four classes of story which look reasonable to me, though like all such they are very approximate and correspond to no sharp distinctions in reality.

The first class contains "hard science," as we have been considering at length. In the manner that I've attempted to show, it blends gradually into the next class, which employs "imaginary science." We can now go a little further into that.

I avoided the word "pseudoscience" because it has bad connotations that are frequently undeserved. Norman Spinrad coined the phrase "Rubber Sciences" in an essay on this literary device[2], but I'll stick to my own, if only to avoid plagiarism.

The most obvious imaginary science involves standard concepts such as faster-than-light travel, time travel, and parallel universes. They can be used routinely, loosely, or brilliantly. This has nothing to do with literary quality. Let's make time travel our exemplar.

Routine use takes the concept for granted in order to get on with the story. L. Sprague de Camp cast the hero of *Lest Darkness Fall* back into Ostrogothic Italy by a lightning bolt, the same as I threw a modern American soldier back into tenth-century Iceland in "The Man Who Came Early." In either case, as in many others, the tale was really about matters like intercultural conflict. Perhaps the most famous, because beautiful and haunting, is Robert Nathan's *Portrait of Jen-*

1 *Nebula Award Stories Seven*, Lloyd Biggle, Jr., ed. (Harper & Row 1973)

2 In *The Craft of Science Fiction*, Reginald Bretnor, ed. (Harper & Row 1976)

nie which brings in time travel by sheer fiat. Such handling of imaginary science is as legitimate as the witches in *Macbeth.* Shakespeare probably didn't believe in witches himself and certainly didn't stop to develop the logical implications of their existence. He just needed them to start the story and keep it going.

"Loose" employment of a concept means "some treatment of it for its own sake, but no rigor." Too often, it is sloppy. The author goofs. As a case in point, we have the ancient plot of the time traveler who becomes his own father or her own mother by the parent of opposite sex. No way could this happen, unless we rewrite the entire well-founded science of genetics. Ancestry would have to be rather more distant than that.

Sometimes, though, honorable fudging occurs. It may be for laughs, as in Fredric Brown's hilarious "Paradox Lost," wherein all time travelers are lunatics because only a lunatic can comprehend the theory of it, and have exterminated the dinosaurs by hunting them with slingshots. For the big dinosaurs, they used bigger slingshots.

William Tenn was equally funny in his "Brooklyn Project." There scientists worry that sending an object into the past might change the present; at the end, the world is totally altered, but of course nobody knows that and everybody takes for granted that no harm was done. Without the humor, I used the same general notion in *Guardians of Time.* If chronokinesis ever does come to be, I supposed that people would institute a patrol to regulate the traffic, and went into detail about its operations. The incentive to regulate was especially strong because history could in fact be diverted by someone who went back and affected a key point.

The looseness here consists not in violating such principles as causality—we can do that and still call ourselves honest craftsmen, if we know what we are about—but in omitting any real study of the consequences. Suppose you head off World War Two by visiting the year 1889 and strangling Hitler in his cradle. (Personally, if that was my aim, I'd try to keep Woodrow Wilson from getting elected President, but never mind.) Do you thereby create a whole new universe? If so, how, and what does this imply? (A. E. van Vogt asked that question in "Recruiting Station," and got a typically mind-boggling answer.) If you only create a new Earth—maybe, at first, only a new household in Braunau-am-Inn—how does this affect the rest of the cosmos? It doesn't take much thought to show how many more things need to be considered, and how many stories that consideration might bring forth.

My situation was that none of them was the story I wanted to tell. So I went ahead regardless, and seem to have been forgiven. The same is true of numerous colleagues, perhaps most notably Fritz Leiber, whose "Change War" series is rightly called classic.

Brilliant use is exemplified by Mark Twain's *Connecticut Yankee,* which first pointed out that intercultural conflicts would arise; H. G. Wells' *The Time Machine,* which first proposed that, if time travel is possible, people should be able to do it deliberately; and two novelettes by Robert Heinlein, "By His Bootstraps" and "All You Zombies." The first of these put time travel into a completely deterministic universe and showed, with merciless and hilarious precision, how cause and effect could get mixed up. The second went it one better, and even made it reasonable that a time traveler might be his/her own parent!

In short, "routine," "loose," and "brilliant" are neither swear words nor accolades; they merely refer to how the author treats his imaginary science for his particular narrative purposes. Already, then, we touch on what I have labeled "quasiscience," but let's not get into that for a while.

Imaginary sciences, fully developed, have provided the skeletons of many strong stories. Van Vogt and Charles L. Harness come immediately to mind as masters of the form, as Raymond F. Jones was earlier. In general, much of a tale like this consists of the characters' piece-by-piece discovery of a strange set of phenomena. (Occasionally the characters know all about it from the start, and it is the reader who gets the gradual revelation.) This does not mean that there can't be human beings involved. Consider Isaac Asimov's *The End of Eternity,* A. J. Budrys' *Rogue Moon,* or Samuel R. Delany's *The Einstein Intersection,* to name three works almost at random.

They are not quite at random, because, while their authors can write "hard" whenever they choose, they are perhaps best known for explorations of imaginary science as well as for literary qualities. For example, Asimov's robot stories may fall under this rubric. Though we don't know anything which would, in principle, forbid us designing such humanlike machines, we don't know for sure that it can be done, the way that we knew back in the 1930's that a spaceship able to land on the Moon could be built. Granted, this is a borderline case, which could arguably be put in the "hard science fiction" category. Asimov's psychohistory is more germane, but I'll come back to it later.

As Spinrad says in his essay, good "rubber science" requires that the author know real science and not violate it unless he is fully conscious of what he's doing and what it means. Thus, when Slipstick Libby in Heinlein's *Methuselah's Children* presented the spaceship he was on with a drive which, in effect, cancelled its inertia, his friend Lazarus Long worried about what that did to the conservation of energy. Libby replied—in a few sentences which repay close study, because they summarize a great deal of the philosophy of science—that conservation of energy is a generalization from a finite number of observations, and that there is no logical reason why the function which describes it cannot have points of discontinuity. I am rephrasing his colloquial language on purpose, in order to emphasize that this is not mere gobbledygook like "Harold Hero switched on the dreelsprail fantangler, which hypewangled him and Sue Submissive into the seventy-eighth chorp dimension." Heinlein makes a statement which, if true, would not deny what we know but would extend it. At the same time, he indicates what *is* true that certain extensions of knowledge imply that we must revise our entire image of reality—the kind of revision which relativity and quantum mechanics forced upon the Newtonian and Maxwellian schemes.

Doubtless the most overworked and otherwise maltreated imaginary science has been that group of notions lumped together as "psionics." Readers who came to science fiction much later than me have missed the excitement when some stunning new concepts or treatments first appeared; but they have also been spared some dismal periods. One of these occurred in the late 1950's and early 1960's, when it seemed that every second item in the magazines was a piece of hackwork about a telepath or a telekineticist who went to Las Vegas and won a fortune, or about a dogmatic Establishment scientist who denied that dowsing worked but was refuted...etc., etc., etc. We are as well rid of these things as we are well rid of the spate of stories which, slightly before, dealt with computers that suddenly acquired consciousness.

Nevertheless, at least one moving, memorable tale came out of the latter fashion, Oliver La Farge's "John the Revelator." As for psionics, the narrative possibilities have always been large, and have sometimes been realized. Several of Theodore Sturgeon's finest works, *e.g., More Than Human,* dealt with what it could mean to people to know each other so directly. This is only to mention one writer out of a number.

The imaginary science itself was explored in various interesting directions. Clement's "Impediment" suggested that it might do a telepathic alien little good to learn how to read the mind of a human being, because we are not a telepathic species and therefore each of us develops a unique interior language. Heinlein, with his usual convincing touches, showed telepaths being used in military communications (*If This Goes On,* also known as *Revolt in 2100 A.D.)* and elsewhere made a broader spectrum of psionic powers the entry to examining a Bishop Berkeley kind of universe (*Waldo*). Alfred Bester's detailed pictures of telepathy in *The Demolished Man* and teleportation in *The Stars My Destination* are science fiction landmarks, brilliant both in employment of the ideas and in style.

Let me omit further distinguished examples and mention two small things of my own, because they are my own and hence I know what went into them. In "Journeys End," I supposed that telepathy might occur as a great rarity—which in itself was nothing new—but, given our kind of society, the telepaths might find they had to shun each other because mind-reading was too deep a violation of privacy. (The story must have touched a nerve, because it's frequently been reprinted, though editors *will* put an apostrophe in the title. Anthony Boucher, who first published it, told me that he had to fight to keep that apostrophe out.) In "The Martyr" I developed the concept of psionic ability as something that evolves in a species and leads at last, in a rationalistic fashion, to survival of the personality after bodily death; but it turns out that we humans aren't that far evolved. (I'd intended the story as a chiller, but one young lady wrote to tell me that it was so beautiful that she spent the evening in tears. This writing game is full of surprises.)

In short, psionics is perfectly proper imaginary science. It simply got misused for a while in fiction, and the time may now be ripe for new insights about it. Frank Herbert's *Dune* trilogy and Gordon R. Dickson's "Childe" cycle certainly give us powerful modern cases.

Furthermore, just as real science can no longer quite scoff at faster-than-light travel, time travel, or parallel universes, so can it no longer quite scoff at psionics. While Martin Gardner, notably, has done a demolition job on the claims of people like J. B. Rhine, still, enough facts remain to show what ought to be obvious, that we don't know everything in this area either.

I am, myself, of skeptical temperament, and I cut my philosophical teeth on the most hard-boiled logical positivism. Nevertheless, I have witnessed water dowsing, in a limited way; it wasn't feasible to drill a well on the spot, but the rod twisted at the same place for about half the persons present, none of whom were credophiles[3] and one of whom later admitted that he meant to clown it up and got quite shaken when the rod seemed to take on a will of its own. The same object was inert in my hands. However, afterward John Campbell persuaded me to try dowsing a buried conduit and it worked, as he said it works for fifty percent of the population. I have subsequently experimented elsewhere and, in a somewhat imprecise fashion, can still do the trick. To her disappointment, my wife can't.

In short, I have reason to think there is something real here. It need not be occult, and in fact I would fiercely deny that it is. Marginal sensitivities to change in quantities like terrestrial magnetism may well explain it. Indeed, years ago Y. Rocard, a French physicist, made out an excellent case for this being what goes on in water dowsing.[4] I would go so far as to call the scientific establishment remiss in not encouraging intensive study of phenomena of this kind, because of the light they may throw on the workings of the nervous system.

About telepathy, telekinesis, and the rest, I have no personal information, nor any second-hand accounts that satisfy. A few legitimate scientists are looking into them, and in any event, they remain suitable material for science fiction—if handled right.

Part of the appeal of psionics, like the appeal of biology and anthropology, no doubt lies in the fact that they feel closely human. Spinrad says that with the "rubber sciences" we are not off in a chilly Newtonian universe as we are in hard science fiction, but into individual people. I disagree with the literary theory implied by his remark. Was there ever a more relentlessly Newtonian story than Stephen Crane's "The Open Boat," and have there been many that were more human? The same could be said, within science fiction and perhaps to a lesser degree, of Tom Godwin's "The Cold Equations." Nevertheless, I can't deny that hard science and imaginary science which touch us right where we live have a special power. In fact, earlier in this series I suggested that biological speculation may tend to get underplayed as such precisely because it leads so easily to emotional themes.

Now several recognized sciences are directly concerned with our own species. Some of them, even the most intolerant positivist must admit, are reasonably hard. For examples, we have modern prehistory, with its careful excavations, its statistical analyses, and its use of physics, chemistry, and biology. We have modern historiography. (When word-frequency studies show that St. Paul cannot

3 Thank you, L. Sprague de Camp, for that lovely word.

4 *Le Signal du Sourcier* (Dunod 1964). Michael Gauquelin's *The Cosmic Clocks;* Henry Regnery 1969; Avon paperback 1969) makes out a rational case for studying possible planetary influences on humans.

have written every one of the epistles traditionally attributed to him, that's getting pretty scientific!) Anthropology is less rigorous, because much of its material is necessarily anecdotal and no observations made on cultures can be exactly repeated, but still does have a scientific character. We can proceed to more controversial areas such as economics and psychology. Whatever one's opinions about these, the fact is undeniable that a few schemes in economics do have some predictive value, and various results in experimental psychology do make statistical sense—not to mention research now going on into things like brain chemistry.

All disciplines of this kind are vital nourishment for science fiction. Its writers need to know a fair amount of history, anthropology, economics, and the like. Jerry Pournelle has gone into this at length in his essay "The Construction of Believable Societies,"[5] and has applied the principles himself in many excellent stories.

For present purposes, though, I just want to point out that, because they are less quantitative than physics, these human sciences blend still more readily into the imaginary. Everybody agrees that we are far indeed from full comprehension of how our own affairs, public and private, work. Some thinkers hold that eventually we can come to a better, more exact understanding. Whether this be true or not, which only time will show, it is a potent theme for science fiction.

Asimov's *Foundation* series is surely the most famous case. There he assumed, for narrative purposes, that the kind of historical pattern described by Spengler, Toynbee, and other scholars is real, not merely something they read into the facts. He also assumed that the analysis can be carried much further than it has yet been, can be made mathematical—given large enough populations, as thermodynamics requires large enough numbers of molecules. Then it might become possible to set up initial conditions such that society *must* move in foreseeable directions…unless a freak like the Mule appears…

The stories are a landmark like Bester's, though, oddly, they too have not been quite what you would call seminal. That is, they haven't inspired many successor tales, exploring different aspects of the basic concept, in the way that *Frankenstein* and *R. U. R.* did. I don't know why. Certainly the psychohistoric motif seems a rich one.

I've had a go or two at it myself. In *Question and Answer* and related yarns, I suggested that the prospect of a science like this might generate a fatal *hubris.* In the "future history" which includes Nicholas van Rijn and Dominic Flandry I've employed a chronological scheme, with rationales, of rise-breakdown-decline-fall which draws on, several researchers into the subject. Others have done similarly, of course, not usually assuming historical cycles, but taking historiography, economics, and the rest of the human sciences as source material. Mack Reynolds probably has the primary reputation for doing this, but I'd say that Dickson, Herbert, Pournelle, and Jack Vance are equally capable, in their different manners (a non-exhaustive list).

Thus we find that science fiction, with its elements of pure imagination, is—on one side of the family, at lest—a child of science, which itself has elements of

5 In *The Craft of Science Fiction.*

the same pure imagination. Since the last part of that sentence may look outrageous to some readers, and may on the other hand encourage some readers of a different turn of mind to believe that anything goes, it requires explanation. I think we've reached the time for a closer look at real science, not so much the current findings as the underlying philosophy, and will attempt that in the next part of this series.

Upon the Occasion of Being Asked at a Court of Love to Declare That About His Lady Which Pleases Him the Most

Whereas they bid this minstrel count the ways
Wherein he finds his lady to excel.
All fingers will not serve to list each praise,
Nay, shoeless, he must use his toes as well.
And having thought upon her darling face,
With smiling lip, soft cheek, deep lightful eye,
The curve of breast and hip in strength and grace,
And other parts we'll come to by-and-by,
He then gives heed to what is different
And yet allied—the wealth within her heart
Of love, of loyalty, of merriment:
Whereon, if called to name her choicest part,
He can but say to her, "My dearest elf,
That which I treasure most is thine own self."

The Longest Voyage

When first we heard of the Sky Ship, we were on an island whose name, as nearly as Montalirian tongues can wrap themselves about so barbarous a noise, was Yarzik. That was almost a year after the *Golden Leaper* sailed from Lavre Town, and we judged we had come halfway round the world. So befouled was our poor caravel with weeds and shells that all sail could scarce drag her across the sea. What drinking water remained in the butts was turned green and evil, the biscuit was full of worms, and the first signs of scurvy had appeared on certain crewmen.

"Hazard or no," decreed Captain Rovic, "we must land somewhere." A gleam I remembered appeared in his eyes. He stroked his red beard and murmured, "Besides, it's long since we asked for the Aureate Cities. Perhaps this time they'll have intelligence of such a place."

Steering by that ogre planet which climbed daily higher as we bore westward, we crossed such an emptiness that mutinous talk broke out afresh. In my heart I could not blame the crew. Imagine, my lords. Day upon day upon day where we saw naught but blue waters, white foam, high clouds in a tropic sky; heard only the wind, *whoosh* of waves, creak of timbers, sometimes at night the huge sucking and rushing as a sea monster breached. These were terrible enough to common sailors, unlettered men who still thought the world must be flat. But then to have Tambur hang forever above the bowsprit, and climb, so that all could see we must eventually pass directly beneath that brooding thing…*and what upbore it?* the crew mumbled in the forecastle. Would an angered God not let fall down on us?

So a deputation waited on Captain Rovic. Very timid and respectful they were, those rough burly men, as they asked him to turn about. But their comrades massed below, muscled sun-blackened bodies taut in the ragged kilts, with daggers and belaying pins ready to hand. We officers on the quarterdeck had swords and pistols, true. But we numbered a mere six, including that frightened boy who was myself, and aged Froad the astrologue, whose robe and white beard were reverend to see but of small use in a fight.

Rovic stood mute for a long while after the spokesman had voiced this demand. The stillness grew, until the empty shriek of wind in our shrouds, the empty glitter of ocean out to the world's rim, became all there was. Most splendid our master looked, for he had donned scarlet hose and belltipped shoon when he knew the deputation was coming: as well as helmet and corselet polished to mirror brightness. The plumes blew around that blinding steel head and the diamonds on his fingers flashed against the rubies in his sword hilt. Yet when at last he spoke, it was not as a knight of the Queen's court, but in the broad Anday of his fisher boyhood.

"So 'tis back ye'd wend, lads? Wi' a fair wind an' a warm sun, liefer ye'd come about an' beat half round the globe? How ye're changed from yere fathers! Ken ye nay the legend, that once all things did as man commanded, an' 'twas an Andayman's lazy fault that now men must work? For see ye, 'twas nay too much that he told his ax to cut down a tree for him, an' told the faggots to walk home, but when he told 'em to carry him, then God was wroth an' took the power away. Though to be sure, as recompense God gave all Andaymen sea-luck, dice-luck, an' love-luck. What more d'ye ask for, lads?"

Bewildered at this response, the spokesman wrung his hands, flushed, looked at the deck, and stammered that we'd all perish miserably...starve, or thirst, or drown, or be crushed under that horrible moon, or sail off the world's edge...the *Golden Leaper* had come farther than ship had sailed since the Fall of Man, and if we returned at once, our fame would live forever—

"But can ye eat fame, Etien?" asked Rovic, still mild and smiling. "We've had fights an' storms, aye, an' merry carouses too; but devil an Aureate City we've seen, though well ye ken they lie out here someplace, stuffed wi' treasure for the first bold man who'll come plunder 'em. What ails yere gutworks, lad? Is't nay an easy cruise? What would the foreigners say? How will yon arrogant cavaliers o' Sathayn, yon grubby chapmen o' Woodland, laugh—nay alone at us, but at all Montalir—did we turn back!"

Thus he jollied them. Only once did he touch his sword, half drawing it, as if absent-mindedly, when he recalled how we had weathered the hurricane off Xingu. But they remembered the mutiny that followed then, and how that same sword had pierced three armed sailors who attacked him together. His dialect told them he would let bygones lie forgotten: if they would. His bawdy promises of sport among lascivious heathen tribes yet to be discovered, his recital of treasure legends, his appeal to their pride as seamen and Montalirians, soothed fear. And then in the end, when he saw them malleable, he dropped the provincial speech. He stood forth on the quarterdeck with burning casque and tossing plumes, and the flag of Montalir blew its sea-faded colors above him, and he said as the knights of the Queen say:

"Now you know I do not propose to turn back until the great globe has been rounded and we bring to Her Majesty that gift which is most peculiarly ours to give. The which is not gold or slaves, nor even that lore of far places that she and her most excellent Company of Merchant Adventurers desire. No, what we shall lift in our hands to give her, on that day when again we lie by the long docks of Lavre, shall be our achievement: that we did this thing which no men have dared in all the world erenow, and did it to her glory."

A while longer he stood, through a silence full of the sea's noise. Then he said quietly, "Dismissed," turned on his heel and went back into his cabin.

So we continued for some days more, the men subdued but not uncheerful, the officers taking care to hide their doubts. I found myself busied, not so much with the clerical duties for which I was paid or the study of captaincy for which I was apprenticed—both these amounting to little by now—as with assisting Froad the astrologue. In these balmy airs he could carry on his work even on shipboard. To him it scarce mattered whether we sank or swam; he had lived more than a common span of years already. But the knowledge of the heavens to be gained here, that was something else. At night, standing on the foredeck with quadrant, astrolabe, and telescope, drenched in the radiance from above, he resembled some frosty-bearded saint in the windows of Provien Minster.

"See there, Zhean." His thin hand pointed above seas that glowed and rippled with light, past the purple sky and the few stars still daring to show themselves, toward Tambur. Huge it was in full phase at midnight, sprawling over seven degrees of sky, a shield or barry of soft vert and azure, splotched with angry sable that could be seen to move across its face. The firefly moon we had named Siett twinkled near the hazy edge of the giant. Balant, espied rarely and low on the horizon in our part of the world, here stood high: a crescent, but with the dark part of the disk tinged by luminous Tambur.

"Observe," declared Froad, "there's no doubt left, one can *see* how it rotates on an axis, and how storms boil up in its air. Tambur is no longer the dimmest of frightened legends, nor a dreadful apparition seen to rise as we entered unknown waters; Tambur is real. A world like our own. Immensely bigger, certes, but still a spheroid in space: around which our own world moves, always turning the same hemisphere to her monarch. The conjectures of the ancients are triumphantly confirmed. Not merely that our world is round, *pouf,* that's obvious to anyone... but that we move about a greater center, which in turn has an annual path about the sun. But, then, how big is the sun?"

"Siett and Balant are inner satellites of Tambur," I rehearsed, struggling for comprehension. "Vieng, Darou, and the other moons commonly seen at home, have paths outside our own world's. Aye. But what holds it all up?"

"That I don't know. Mayhap the crystal sphere containing the stars exerts an inward pressure. The same pressure, maybe, that hurled mankind down onto the earth, at the time of the Fall From Heaven."

That night was warm, but I shivered, as if those had been winter stars. "Then," I breathed, "there may also be men on...Siett, Balant, Vieng...even on Tambur?"

"Who knows? We'll need many lifetimes to find out. And what lifetimes they'll be! Thank the good God, Zhean, that you were born in this dawn of the coming age."

Froad returned to making measurements. A dull business, the other officers thought; but by now I had learned enough of the mathematic arts to understand that from these endless tabulations might come the true size of the earth, of Tambur, sun and moons and stars, the path they took through space and the direction of Paradise. So the common sailors who muttered and made signs against evil as they passed our instruments, were closer to fact than Rovic's gentlemen: for indeed Froad practiced a most potent gramarye.

At length we saw weeds floating on the sea, birds, towering cloud masses, all the signs of land. Three days later we raised an island. It was an intense green under those calm skies. Surf, still more violent than in our hemisphere, flung against high cliffs, burst in a smother of foam and roared back down again. We coasted carefully, the palomers aloft to seek an approach, the gunners standing by our cannon with lighted matches. For not only were there unknown currents and shoals—familiar hazards—but we had had brushes with canoe-sailing cannibals in the past. Especially did we fear the eclipses. My lords can visualize how in that hemisphere the sun each day must go behind Tambur. In that longitude the occurrence was about midafternoon and lasted nearly ten minutes. An awesome sight: the primary planet—for so Froad now called it, a planet akin to Diell or Coint, with our own world humbled to a mere satellite thereof!—become a black disk encircled with red, up in a sky suddenly full of stars. A cold wind blew across the sea, and even the breakers seemed hushed. Yet so impudent is the soul of man that we continued about our duties, stopping only for the briefest prayer as the sun disappeared, thinking more about the chance of shipwreck in the gloom than of God's Majesty.

So bright is Tambur that we continued to work our way around the island at night. From sunup to sunup, twelve mortal hours, we kept the *Golden Leaper* slowly moving. Toward the second noon, Captain Rovie's persistence was rewarded. An opening in the cliffs revealed a long fjord. Swampy shores overgrown with saltwater trees told us that while the tides rose high in that bay, it was not one of those roosts so dreaded by mariners. The wind being against us, we furled sail and lowered the boats, towing in our caravel by the power of oars. This was a vulnerable moment, especially since we had perceived a village within the fjord. "Should we not stand out, master, and let them come first to us?" I ventured.

Rovic spat over the rail. "I've found it best never to show doubt," said he. "If a canoe fleet should assail us, we'll give 'em a whiff of grapeshot and trust to break their nerve. But I think, thus showing ourselves fearless of them from the very first, we're less likely to meet treacherous ambuscade later."

He proved right.

In the course of time, we learned we had come upon the eastern end of a large archipelago. The inhabitants were mighty seafarers, considering that they had only outrigger dugouts to travel in. These, however, were often a hundred feet long. With forty paddles, or with three bast-sailed masts, such a vessel could almost match our best speed, and was more maneuverable. However, the small cargo space limited their range of travel.

Though they lived in houses of wood and thatch, possessing only stone tools, the natives were cultivated folk. They farmed as well as fished; their priests had an alphabet. Tall and vigorous, somewhat darker and less hairy than we, they were impressive to behold: whether nude as was common, or in full panoply of cloth and feathers and shell ornaments. They had formed a loose empire throughout the archipelago, raided islands lying farther north and carried on a brisk trade within their own borders. Their whole nation they called the Hisagazi, and the island on which we had chanced was Yarzik.

This we learned slowly, as we mastered somewhat their tongue. For we were several weeks at that town. The duke of the island, Guzan, made us welcome, supplying us with food, shelter, and helpers as we required. For our part, we pleased them with glassware, bolts of Woondish cloth, and suchlike trade goods. Nonetheless we encountered many difficulties. The shore above highwater mark being too swampy for beaching a vessel as heavy as ours, we must build a drydock before we could careen. Numerous of us took a flux from some disease, though all recovered in time, and this slowed us further.

"Yet I think our troubles will prove a blessing," Rovic told me one night. As had become his habit, once he learned I was a discreet amanuensis, he confided certain thoughts in me. The captain is ever a lonely man; and Rovic, fisher lad, freebooter, self-taught navigator, victor over the Grand Fleet of Sathayn and ennobled by the Queen herself, must have found the keeping of that necessary aloofness harder than would a gentleman born.

I waited silent, there in the grass hut they had given him. A soapstone lamp threw wavering light and enormous shadows over us; something rustled the thatch. Outside, the damp ground sloped past houses on stilts and murmurous fronded trees, to the fjord where it shimmered under Tambur. Faintly I heard drums throb, a chant and stamping of feet around some sacrificial fire. Indeed the cool hills of Montalir seemed far.

Rovic leaned back his muscular form, y-clad a mere seaman's kilt in this heat. He had had them fetch him a civilized chair from the ship. "For see you, young fellow," he continued, "at other times we'd have established just enough communication to ask about gold. Well we might also try to get a few sailing directions. But all in all, we'd hear little except the old story—'aye, foreign lord, indeed there's a kingdom where the very streets are paved with gold…a hundred miles west'—anything to get rid of us, eh? But in this prolonged stay, I've asked out the duke and the idolater priests more subtly. I've been so coy about whence we came and what we already know, that they've let slip a gobbet of knowledge they'd not otherwise have disgorged on the rack itself."

"The Aureate Cities?" I cried.

"Hush! I'd not have the crew get excited and out of hand. Not yet."

His leathery, hooknosed face turned strange with thought. "I've always believed those cities an old wives' tale," he said. My shock must have been mirrored to his gaze, for he grinned and went on, "A useful one. Like a lodestone on a stick, it's dragging us around the world." His mirth faded. Again he got that look, which was not unlike the look of Froad considering the heavens. "Aye, of course I want gold, too. But if we find none on this voyage, I'll not care. I'll just capture a few ships of Eralia or Sathayn when we're back in home waters, and pay for the voyage thus. I spoke God's truth that day on the quarterdeck, Zhean, that this journey was its own goal; until I can give it to Queen Odela, who once gave me the kiss of ennoblement."

He shook himself out of his reverie and said in a brisk tone: "Having led him to believe I already knew the most of it, I teased from Duke Guzan the admission that on the main island of this Hisagazi empire is something I scarce dare think about. A ship of the gods, he says, and an actual live god who came from the stars therein. Any of the natives will tell you this much. The secret reserved to the noble folk is that this is no legend or mummery, but sober fact. Or so Guzan claims. I know not what to think. But...he took me to a holy cave and showed me an object from that ship. It was some kind of clockwork mechanism, I believe. What, I know not. But of a shining silvery metal such as I've never seen before. The priest challenged me to break it. That metal was not heavy; must have been thin. But it blunted my sword, splintered a rock I pounded with, and my diamond ring would not scratch it."

I made signs against evil. A chill went along me, spine and skin and scalp, until I prickled all over. For the drums were muttering in a jungle dark, and the waters lay like quicksilver beneath gibbous Tambur, and each afternoon that planet ate the sun. Oh, for the bells of Provien, across windswept Anday downs!

When the *Golden Leaper* was seaworthy again, Rovic had no trouble gaining permission to visit the Hisagazian emperor on the main island. He would, indeed, have found difficulty in not doing so. By now the canoes had borne word of us from one end of the realm to another, and the great lords were all agog to see these blue-eyed strangers. Sleek and content once more, we disentangled ourselves from the arms of tawny wenches and embarked. Up anchor, up sail, with chanties whose echoes sent sea birds whirling above the steeps, and we stood out to sea. This time we were escorted. Guzan himself was our pilot, a big middle-aged man whose handsomeness was not much injured by the livid green tattoos his folk affected on face and body. Several of his sons spread their pallets on our decks, while a swarm of warriors paddled alongside.

Rovic summoned Etien the boatswain to him in his cabin. "You're a man of some wit," he said. "I give you charge of keeping our crew alert, weapons ready, however peaceful this may look."

"Why, master!" The scarred brown face sagged with near dismay. "Think you the natives plot a treachery?"

"Who can tell?" said Rovic. "Now, say naught to the crew. They've no skill in dissembling. Did greed or fear rise among 'em, the natives would sense as much, and grow uneasy—which would worsen the attitude of our own men, until none but God's Daughter could tell what'd happen. Only see to it, as casually as you're able, that our arms are ever close by and that our folk stay together."

Etien collected himself, bowed, and left the cabin. I made bold to ask what Rovic had in mind.

"Nothing, yet," said he. "However, I did hold in these fists a piece of clockwork such as the Grand Ban of Giair never imagined; and yarns were spun me of a Ship which flew down from heaven, bearing a god or a prophet. Guzan thinks I know more than I do, and hopes we'll be a new, disturbing element in the balance of things, by which he may further his own ambitions. He did not take all those fighting men along by accident. As for me...I intend to learn more about this."

He sat a while at his table, staring at a sunbeam which sickled up and down the wainscot as the ship rocked. Finally: "Scripture tells us man dwelt beyond the stars before the Fall. The astrologues of the past generation or two have told us the planets are corporeal bodies like this earth. A traveler from Paradise—"

I left with my head in a roar.

We made an easy passage among scores of islands. After several days we raised the main one, Ulas-Erkila. It is about a hundred miles long, forty miles across at the widest, rising steep and green toward central mountains dominated by a volcanic cone. The Hisagazi worship two sorts of gods, watery and fiery, and believe this Mount Ulas houses the latter. When I saw that snowpeak afloat in the sky above emerald ridges, staining the blue with smoke, I could feel what the pagans did. The holiest act a man can perform among them is to cast himself into the burning crater of Ulas, and many an aged warrior is carried up the mountain that he may do so. Women are not allowed on the slopes.

Nikum, the royal seat, is situated at the head of a fjord like the village where we had been staying. But Nikum is rich and extensive, being about the size of Roann. Many houses are made from timber rather than thatch; there is also a massive basalt temple atop a cliff, overlooking the city, with orchards, jungle, and mountains at its back. So great are the tree trunks available to them for pilings, the Hisagazi have built here a regular set of docks like those at Lavre—instead of moorings and floats that can rise or fall with the tides, such as most harbors throughout the world are content with. We were offered a berth of honor at the central wharf, but Rovic made the excuse that our ship was awkward to handle and got us tied at the far end.

"In the middle, we'd have the watchtower straight above us," he muttered to me. "And they may not have discovered the bow here, but their javelin throwers are good. Also, we'd have an easy approach to our ship, plus a clutter of moored canoes between us and the bay mouth. Here, though, a few of us could hold the pier whilst the others ready for quick departure."

"But have we anything to fear, master?" I asked.

He gnawed his mustache. "I know not. Much depends on what they really believe about this god-ship of theirs...as well as what the truth is. But come all death and hell against us, we'll not return without that truth for Queen Odela."

Drums rolled and feathered spearmen leaped as our officers disembarked. A royal catwalk had been erected above highwater level. (Common townsfolk in this realm swim from house to house when the tide laps their thresholds, or take a coracle if they have burdens to carry.) Across the graceful span of vines and canes lay the palace, which was a long building made from logs, the roof pillars carved into fantastic god-shapes.

Iskilip, Priest-Emperor of the Hisagazi, was an old and corpulent man. A soaring headdress of plumes, a feather robe, a wooden scepter topped with a human skull, his own facial tattoos, his motionlessness, all made him seem unhuman. He sat on a dais, under sweet-smelling torches. His sons sat crosslegged at his feet, his courtiers on either side. Down the long walls were ranged his guardsmen. They had not our custom of standing to attention; but they were big supple young men, with shields and corselets of scaly seamonster leather, with flint axes and obsidian spears that could kill as easily as iron. Their heads were shaven, which made them look the fiercer.

Iskilip greeted us well, called for refreshment, bade us be seated on a bench not much lower than his dais. He asked many perceptive questions. Wide-ranging, the Hisagazi knew of islands far beyond their own chain. They could even point the direction and tell us roughly the distance of a many-castled country they named Yurakadak; though none of them had traveled that far himself. Judging by their third-hand description, what could this be but Giair, which the Wondish adventurer Hanas Tolasson had reached overland? It blazed in me that we were indeed rounding the world. Only after that glory had faded a little did I again heed the talk.

"As I told Guzan," Rovic was saying, "another thing which drew us hither was the tale that you were blessed with a Ship from heaven. And he showed me this was true."

A hissing went down the hall. The princes grew stiff, the courtiers blanked their countenances, even the guardsmen stirred and muttered. Remotely through the walls I heard the rumbling, nearing tide. When Iskilip spoke, through the mask of himself, his voice had gone whetted: "Have you forgotten that these things are not for the uninitiate to see, Guzan?"

"No, Holy One," said the duke. Sweat sprang forth among the devils on his face, but it was not the sweat of fear. "However, this captain knew. His people also...as nearly as I could learn...he still has trouble speaking so I can understand...his people are initiate too. The claim seems reasonable, Holy One. Look at the marvels they brought. The hard, shining stone-which-is-not-stone, as in this long knife I was given, is that not like the stuff of which the Ship is built? The tubes which make distance things look close at hand, such as he has given you, Holy One, is this not akin to the far-seer the Messenger possesses?"

Iskilip leaned forward, toward Rovic. His scepter hand trembled so much that the pegged jaws of the skull clattered together. "Did the Star People themselves teach you to make all this?" he cried. "I never imagined...The Messenger never spoke of any others—"

Rovic held up both palms. "Not so fast, Holy One, I pray you," said he. "We are poorly versed in your tongue. I couldn't recognize a word just now."

This was his deceit. All his officers had been ordered to feign a knowledge of Hisagazi less than they really possessed. (We had improved our command of it by secret practicing with each other.) Thus he had an unimpeachable device for equivocation.

"Best we talk of this in private, Holy One," suggested Guzan, with a glance at the courtiers. They returned him a jealous glare.

Iskilip slouched in his gorgeous regalia. His words fell blunt enough, but in the weak tone of an old, uncertain man. "I know not. If these strangers are already initiate, certes we can show them what we have. But otherwise—if profane ears heard the Messenger's own tale—"

Guzan raised a dominator's hand. Bold and ambitious, long thwarted in his petty province, he had taken fire this day. "Holy One," he said, "why has the full story been withheld all these years? In part to keep the commoners obedient, aye. But also, did you and your councillors not fear that all the world might swarm hither, greedy for knowledge, if it knew, and we should then be overwhelmed? Well, if we let the blue-eyed men go home with curiosity unsatisfied, I think they are sure to return in strength. So we have naught to lose by revealing the truth to them. If they have never had a Messenger of their own, if they can be of no real use to us, time enough to kill them. But if they have indeed been visited like us, what might we and they not do together!"

This was spoken fast and softly, so that we Montalirians should not understand. And indeed our gentlemen failed to do so. I, having young ears, got the gist; and Rovic preserved such a fatuous smile of incomprehension that I knew he was seizing every word.

So in the end they decided to take our leader—and my insignificant self, for no Hisagazian magnate goes anywhere quite unattended—up to the temple. Iskilip led the way in person, with Guzan and two brawny princes behind. A dozen spearmen brought up the rear. I thought Rovic's blade would be scant use if trouble came, but set my lips firmly together and made myself walk behind him. He looked as eager as a child on Thanksday Morning, teeth agleam in the pointed beard, a plumed bonnet slanted rakish over his brow. None would have thought him aware of any peril.

We left about sundown; in Tambur's hemisphere, folk make less distinction between day and night than our people must. Having observed Siett and Balant in high tide position, I was not surprised that Nikun lay nearly drowned. And yet, as we wound up the cliff trail toward the temple, methought I had never seen a view more alien.

Below us lay a sheet of water, on which the long grass roofs of the city appeared to float; the crowded docks, where our own ship's masts and spars raked above heathen figureheads; the fjord, winding between precipices toward its mouth, where the surf broke white and terrible on the skerries. The heights above us seemed altogether black, against a fire-colored sunset that filled nigh half the sky and bloodied the waters. Wan through those clouds I glimpsed the thick crescent of Tambur, banded in a heraldry no man could read. A basalt column chipped into the shape of a head loomed in outline athwart the planet. Right and left of the path grew sawtoothed grasses, summer-dry. The sky was pale at the zenith, dark purple in the east, where the first few stars had appeared. Tonight I found no comfort in the stars. We all walked silent. The bare native feet made no noise. My own shoes went *pad-pad* and the bells on Rovic's toes raised a tiny jingle.

The temple was a bold piece of work. Within a quadrangle of basalt walls guarded by tall stone heads lay several buildings of the same material. Only the fresh-cut fronds that roofed them were alive. With Iskilip to lead us, we brushed past acolytes and priests to a wooden cabin behind the sanctum. Two guardsmen stood watch at its door, but they knelt for Iskilip. The emperor rapped with his curious scepter.

My mouth was dry and my heart thunderous. I expected almost any being hideous or radiant to stand in the doorway as it was opened. Astonishing, then, to see just a man, and of no great stature. By lamplight within I discerned his room, clean, austere, but not uncomfortable; this could have been any Hisagazian dwelling. He himself wore a simple bast skirt. The legs beneath were bent and thin, old man's shanks. His body was also thin, but still erect, the white head proudly carried. In complexion he was darker than a Montalirian, lighter than a Hisagazian, with brown eyes and thin beard. His visage differed subtly, in nose and lips and slope of jaw, from any other race I had ever encountered. But he was human.

Naught else.

We entered the cabin, shutting out the spearmen. Iskilip doddered through a half-religious ceremony of introduction. I saw Guzan and the princes shift their stance, restless and unawed. Their class had long been party to this. Rovic's face was unreadable. He bowed with full courtliness to Val Nira, Messenger of Heaven, and explained our presence in a few words. But as he spoke, their eyes met and I saw him take the star man's measure.

"Aye, this is my home," said Val Nira. Habit spoke for him; he had given this account to so many young nobles that the edges were worn off it. As yet he had not observed our metallic instruments, or else had not grasped their significance to him "For...forty-three years, is that right. Iskilip? I have been treated as well as might be. If at times I was near screaming from loneliness, that is what an oracle must expect."

The emperor stirred, uneasy in his robe. "His demon left him," he explained. "Now he is simple human flesh. That's the real secret we keep. It was not ever thus. I remember when he first came. He prophesied immense things, and all the people wailed and went on their faces. But since his demon has gone back to the stars, and the once potent weapon he bore has equally been emptied of its force. The people would not believe this, however, so we still pretend otherwise, or there would be unrest among them."

"Affecting your own privileges," said Val Nira. His tone was tired and sardonic. "Iskilip was young then," he added to Rovic, "and the imperial succession was in doubt. I gave him my influence. He promised in return to do certain things for me."

"I tried, Messenger," said the monarch. "Ask all the sunken canoes and drowned men if I did nor try. But the will of the gods was otherwise."

"Evidently." Val Nira shrugged. "These islands have few ores, Captain Rovic, and no person capable of recognizing those I required. It's too far to the mainland for Hisagazian canoes. But I don't deny you tried, Iskilip...then." He cocked an eyebrow back at us. "This is the first time foreigners have been taken so deeply into the imperial confidence, my friends. Are you certain you can get back out again, alive?"

"Why, why, why, they're our guests," blustered Iskilip and Gzan, almost in each other's mouths.

"Besides," smiled Rovic, "I had most of the secret already. My own country has secrets of its own to set against this. Yes, I think we might well do business, Holy One."

The emperor trembled. His voice cracked across. "Have you indeed a Messenger too?"

"What?" For a numbed moment Val Nira stared at us. Red and white pursued each other across his countenance. Then he sat down on a bench and began to weep.

"Well, not precisely." Rovic laid a hand on the shaking shoulder, "I confess no heavenly vessel had docked at Montalir. But we've certain other secrets, belike equally valuable." Only I, who knew his moods somewhat, could sense the tautness in him. He locked eyes with Guzan and stared the duke down as a wild animal tamer does. And all the while, motherly gentle, he spoke with Val Nira. "I take it, friend, your Ship was wrecked on these shores, but could be repaired if you had certain materials?"

"Yes...yes...listen—" Stammering and gulping at the thought he might see his home again ere he died, Val Nira tried to explain.

The doctrinal implications of what he said are so astounding, even dangerous, that I feel sure my lords would not wish me to repeat much. However, I do not believe they are false. If the stars are indeed suns like our own, each attended by planets like our own, this demolishes the crystal-sphere theory. But Froad, when he was told later, did not think that mattered to the true religion. Scripture has never said in so many words that Paradise lies directly above the birthplace of God's Daughter; this was merely assumed, during those centuries when the earth was believed to be flat. Why should Paradise not be those planets of other suns, where men dwell in magnificence, men who possess all the ancient arts and flit from star to star as casually as we might go from Lavre to West Alayn?

Val Nira believed our ancestors had been cast away on this world, several thousand years ago. They must have been fleeing the consequences of some crime or heresy, to come so far from any human domain. Somehow their ship was wrecked, the survivors went back to savagery, only by degrees have their descendants regained a little knowledge. I cannot see where this explanation contradicts the dogma of the Fall. Rather, it amplifies it. The Fall was not the portion of all mankind, but only of a few—our own tainted blood—while the others continued to dwell prosperous and content in the heavens.

Even today, our world lies far off the trade lanes of the Paradise folk. Very few of them nowadays have any interest in seeking new worlds. Val Nira, though, was such a one. He traveled at hazard for months until he chanced upon our earth.

Then the curse seized him, too. Something went wrong. He descended upon Ulas-Erkila, and the Ship would fly no more.

"I know what the damage is," he said ardently. "I've not forgotten. How could I? No day has passed in all these years that I didn't recite to myself what must be done. A certain subtle engine in the Ship requires quicksilver." (He and Rovic must spend some time talking ere they deduced this must be what he meant by the word he used.) "When the engine failed, I landed so hard that its tanks burst. All the quicksilver, what I had in reserve as well as what I was employing, poured forth. So much, in that hot enclosed space, would have poisoned me. I fled outside, forgetting to close the doorway. The deck being canted, the quicksilver ran after me. By the time I had recovered from blind panic, a tropical rainstorm had carried off all the fluid metal. A series of unlikely accidents, yes, that's what's condemned me to a life's exile. It really would have made more sense to perish outright!"

He clutched Rovic's hand, staring up from his seat at the captain who stood. over him. "Can you actually get quicksilver?" he begged. "I need no more than the volume of a man's head. Only that, and a few repairs easily made with tools in the Ship. When this cult grew up around me, I must needs release certain things I possessed, that each provincial temple might have a relic. But I took care never to give away anything important. Whatever I need is all there. A gallon of quicksilver, and—Oh, God, my wife may even be alive, on Terra!"

Guzan, at least, had begun to understand the situation. He gestured to the princes, who hefted their axes and stepped a little closer. The door was shut on the guard escort, but a shout would bring their spears into this cabin. Rovic looked from Val Nira to Guzan, whose face was grown ugly with tension. My captain laid hand on hilt. In no other way did he seem to feel any nearness of trouble.

"I take it, milord," he said lightly, "you're willing that the Heaven Ship be made to fly again."

Guzan was jarred. He had never expected this. "Why, of course," he exclaimed. "Why not?"

"Your tame god would depart you. What then becomes of your power in Hisagazia?"

"I...I'd not thought of that," Iskilip stuttered.

Val Nira's eyes shuttled among us, as if watching a game of paddleball. His thin body shook. "No," he whimpered. "You can't. You can't keep me!"

Guzan nodded. "In a few more years," he said, not unkindly, "you would depart in death's canoe anyhow. If meanwhile we held you against your will, you might not speak the right oracles for us. Nay, be at ease; we'll get your flowing stone." With a slitted glance at Rovie: "Who shall fetch it?"

"My own folk," said the knight. "Our ship can readily reach Giair, where there are civilized nations who surely have the quicksilver. We could return within a year, I think."

"Accompanied by a fleet of adventurers, to help you seize the sacred vessel?" asked Guzan bluntly. "Or...once out of our islands...you might not proceed to

Yurakadak at all. You might continue the whole way home, and tell your Queen, and return with all the power she commands."

Rovic lounged against a roof post like a big pouncecat at its ease in ruffles and hose and scarlet cape. His right hand continued to rest on his sword pommel. "Only Val Nira could make that Ship go, I suppose," he drawled. "Does it matter who aids him in making repairs? Surely you don't think either of our nations could conquer Paradise!"

"The Ship is very easy to operate," chattered Val Nira. "Anyone can fly it in air. I showed many nobles what levers to use. It's navigating among the stars which is more difficult. No nation on this world could even reach my people unaided—let alone fight them—but why should you think of fighting? I've told you a thousand times, Iskilip, the dwellers in the Milky Way are dangerous to none, helpful to all. They have so much wealth they're hard put to find a use for most of it. Gladly would they spend large amounts to help all the peoples on this world become civilized again." With an anxious, half hysterical look at Rovic: "Fully civilized, I mean. We'll teach you our arts. We'll give you engines, automata, homunculi, that do all the toilsome work; and boats that fly through the air; and regular passenger service on those ships that ply between the stars—"

"These things you have promised for forty years," said Iskilip. "We've only your word."

"And, finally, a chance to confirm his word," I blurted.

Guzan said with calculated grimness: "Matters are not that simple, Holy One. I've watched these men from across the ocean for weeks, while they lived on Yarzik. Even on their best behavior, they're a fierce and greedy lot. I trust them no further than my eyes reach. This very night I see how they've befooled us. They know our language better than they ever admitted. And they misled us to believe they might have some inkling of a Messenger. If the Ship were indeed made to fly again, with them in possession, who knows what they might choose to do?"

Rovic's tone softened still further, "What do you propose, Guzan?"

"We can discuss that another time."

I saw knuckles tighten around stone axes. For a moment, only Val Nira's unsteady breathing was heard. Guzan stood heavy in the lamplight, rubbing his chin, the small black eyes turned downward in thoughtfulness. At last he shook himself. "Perhaps," he said crisply, "a crew mainly Hisagazian could sail your ship, Rovic, and fetch the flowing stone. A few of your men could go along to instruct ours. The rest could remain here as hostages."

My captain made no reply. Val Nira groaned, "You don't understand! You're squabbling over nothing! When my people come here, there'll be no more war, no more oppression, they'll cure you of all such diseases. They'll show friendship to all and favor to none. I beg you—"

"Enough," said Iskilip. His own words fell ragged. "We shall sleep on all this. If anyone can sleep after so much strangeness."

Rovic looked past the emperor's plumes, into the face of Guzan. "Before we decide anything—" His fingers tightened on the sword hilt till the nails turned white. Some thought had sprung up within him. But he kept his tone even. "First I want to see that Ship. Can we go there tomorrow?"

Iskilip was the Holy One, but he stood huddled in his feather robe. Guzan nodded agreement.

We bade our goodnights and went forth under Tambur. The planet was waxing toward full, flooding the courtyard with cold luminance, but the hut was shadowed by the temple. It remained a black outline, with a narrow lamplight rectangle of doorway in the middle. There was etched the frail body of Val Nira, who had come from the Stars. He watched us till we had gone out of sight.

On the way down the path, Guzan and Rovic bargained in curt words. The Ship lay two days' march inland, on the slopes of Mount Ulas. We would go in a joint party to inspect it, but a mere dozen Montalirians were to be allowed. Afterward we would debate our course of action.

Lanthorns glowed yellow at our caravel's poop. Refusing Iskilip's hospitality, Rovic and I returned thither for the night. A pikeman on guard at the gangway inquired what I had learned. "Ask me tomorrow," I said feebly. "My head's in too much of a whirl."

"Come into my cabin, lad, for a stoup ere we retire," the captain invited me.

God knows I needed wine. We entered the low little room, crowded with nautical instruments, with books, and with printed charts that looked quaint to me now I had seen a little of those spaces where the cartographer drew mermaids and windsprites. Rovic sat down behind his table, gestured me to a chair opposite, and poured from a carafe into two goblets of Quaynish crystal. Then I knew he had momentous thoughts in his head—far more than the problem of saving our lives.

We sipped a while, unspeaking. I heard the *lap-lap* of wavelets on our hull, the tramp of men on watch, the rustle of distant surf: otherwise nothing. At last Rovic leaned back, staring at the ruby wine on the table. I could not read his expression.

"Well, lad," said he, "what do you think?"

"I know not what to think, master."

"You and Froad are a little prepared for this idea that the stars are other suns. You're educated. As for me, I've seen so much eldritch in my day that this seems quite believable. The rest of our people, though—"

"An irony that barbarians like Guzan should long have been familiar with the concept—having had the old man from the sky to preach it privily to their class for more than forty years—Is he indeed a prophet, master?"

"He denies it. He plays prophet because he must, but it's evident all the dukes and earls of this realm know it's a trick. Iskilip is senile, more than half converted to his own artificial creed. He was mumbling about prophecies Val Nira made long ago, true prophecies. Bah! Tricks of memory and wishfulness. Val Nira is as human and fallible as I am. We Montalirians are the same flesh as these Hisagazi, even if we have learned the use of metal before they did. Val Nira's people know more in turn than us; but they're still mortals, by Heaven. I *must* remember that they are."

"Guzan remembers."

"Bravo, lad!" Rovic's mouth bent upward, one-sidedly. "He's a clever one, and bold. When he came, he saw his chance to stop stagnating as the petty lord of an outlying island. He'll not let that chance slip without a fight. Like many a double-dealer before him, he accuses us of plotting the very things he hopes to do."

"But what does he hope for?"

"My guess would be, he wants the Ship for himself. Val Nira said it was easy to fly. Navigation between the Stars would be too difficult for anyone save him; nor could any man in his right mind hope to play pirate along the Milky Way. However...if the Ship stayed right here, on this earth, rising no higher than a mile above ground...the warlord who used it might conquer more widely than Lame Darveth himself."

I was aghast. "Do you mean Guzan would not even try to seek out Paradise?"

Rovic scowled so blackly at his wine that I saw he wanted aloneness. I stole off to my bunk in the poop.

The captain was up before dawn, readying our folk. Plainly he had reached some decision, and it was not pleasant. But once he set a course, he seldom left it. He was long in conference with Etien, who came out of the cabin looking frightened. As if to reassure himself, the boatswain ordered the men about all the more harshly.

Our allowed dozen were to be Rovic, Froad, myself, Etien, and eight crewmen. All were supplied with helmets and corselets, muskets and edged weapons. Since Guzan had told us there was a beaten path to the Ship, we assembled a supply cart on the dock. Etien supervised its lading. I was astonished to see that nearly all it carried, till the axles groaned, was barrels of gunpowder. "But we're not taking cannon!" I protested.

"Skipper's orders," rapped Etien. He turned his back on me. After a glance at Rovic's face, no one ventured to ask him the reason. I remembered we would be going up a mountainside. A wagonful of powder, with lit fuse, set rolling down toward a hostile army, might win a battle. But did Rovic anticipate open conflict so soon?

Certes his orders to the men and officers remaining behind suggested as much. They were to stay aboard the *Golden Leaper* holding her ready for instant fight or flight.

As the sun rose, we said our morning prayers to God's Daughter and marched down the docks. The wood banged hollow under our boots. A few thin mists drifted on the bay; Tambur's crescent hung wan above. Nikum Town was hushed as we passed through.

Guzan met us at the temple. A son of Iskilip was supposedly in charge, But the duke ignored that youth as much as we did. They had a hundred guardsmen with them, scaly-coated, shaven-headed, tattooed with storms and dragons. The early sunlight gleamed off obsidian spearheads. Our approach was watched in silence. But when we drew up before those disorderly ranks, Guzan trod forth. He was also y-clad in leather, and carried the sword Rovic had given him on Yarzik. The dew shimmered on his feather cloak. "What have you in that wagon?" he demanded.

"Supplies," Rovic answered.

"For four days?"

"Send home all but ten of your men," said Rovic coolly, "and I'll send back this cart."

Their eyes clashed, until Guzan turned and gave his orders. We started off, a few Montalirians surrounded by pagan warriors. The jungle lay ahead of us, a deep and burning green, rising halfway up the slope of Ulas. Then the mountain became naked black, up to the snow that edged its smoking crater.

Val Nira walked between Rovic and Guzan. Strange, I thought, that the instrument of God's will for us was so shriveled. He ought to have walked tall and haughty, with a star on his brow.

During the day, at night when we made camp, and again the next day, Rovic and Froad questioned him eagerly about his home. Of course, all their talk was in fragments. Nor did I hear everything, since I must take my turn at pulling our wagon along that narrow, upward, damnable trail. The Hisagazi have no draft animals, therefore they make very little use of the wheel and have no proper roads. But what I did hear kept me long awake.

Ah, greater marvels than the poets have imagined for Elf Land! Entire cities built in a single tower half a mile high. The sky made to glow, so that there is no true darkness after sunset. Food not grown in the earth, but manufactured in alchemical laboratories. The lowest peasant owning a score of machines which serve him more subtly and humbly than might a thousand slaves—owning an aerial carriage which can fly him around his world in less than a day—owning a crystal window on which theatrical images appear, to beguile his abundant leisure. Argosies between suns, stuffed with the wealth of a thousand planets; yet every ship unarmed and unescorted, for there are no pirates and this realm has long ago come to such good terms with the other starfaring nations that war has also ceased. (These other countries, it seems, are more akin to the supernatural than Val Nira's, in that the races composing them are not human, though able to speak and reason.) In this happy land there is little crime. When it does occur, the criminal is soon captured by the arts of the provost corps; yet he is not hanged, nor even transported overseas. Instead, his mind is cured of the wish to violate any law. He returns home to live as an especially honored citizen, since all know he is now completely trustworthy. As for the government—but here I lost the thread of discourse. I believe it is in form a republic, but in practice a devoted fellowship of men, chosen by examination, who see the welfare of everyone else.

Surely, I thought, this was Paradise!

Our sailors listened with mouths agape. Rovic's mien was reserved, but he gnawed his mustaches incessantly. Guzan, to whom this was an old tale, grew rough of manner. Plain to see, he disliked our intimacy with Val Nira and the ease wherewith we grasped ideas that were spoken.

But then, we came of a nation which has long encouraged natural philosophy and improvement of all mechanic arts. I myself, in my short lifetime, had witnessed the replacement of the waterwheel in regions where there are few streams, by the modern form of windmill. The pendulum clock was invented the year before I was born. I had read many romances about the flying machines which no few men have tried to devise. Living at such a dizzy pace of progress, we Montalirians were well prepared to entertain still vaster concepts.

At night, sitting up with Froad and Etien around a campfire, I spoke somewhat of this to the savant. "Ah," he crooned, "today Truth stood unveiled before me. Did you hear what the starman said? The three laws of planetary motion about a sun, and the one great law of attraction which explains them? Dear saints, that law can be put in a single short sentence, and yet the development will keep mathematicians busy for three hundred years!"

He stared past the flames, and the other fires around which the heathen men slept, and the jungle gloom, and the angry volcanic glow in heaven. I started to query him. "Leave be, lad," grunted Etien. "Can ye nay tell when a man's in love?"

I shifted my position, a little closer to the boatswain's stolid, comforting bulk. "What do you think of all this?" I asked, softly, for the jungle whispered and croaked on every side.

"Me, I stopped thinking a while back," he said. "After yon day on the quarterdeck, when the skipper jested us into sailing wi' him though we went off the world's edge an' tumbled down in foam amongst the nether stars…well, I'm but a poor sailor man, an' my one chance o' regaining home is to follow the skipper."

"Even beyond the sky?"

"Less hazard to that, maybe, than sailing on around the world. The little man swore his vessel was safe, an' that there're no storms between the suns."

"Can you trust his word?"

"Oh, aye. Even a knocked-about old palomer like me has seen enough o' men to ken when a one's too timid an' eagersome to stand by a lie. I fear not the folk in Paradise, nor does the skipper. Except in some way—" Etien rubbed his bearded jaw, scowling. "In some way I can nay wholly grasp, they affright Rovic. He fears nay they'll come hither wi' torch an' sword; but there's somewhat else about 'em that frets him."

I felt the ground shudder, ever so faintly. Ulas had cleared his throat. "It does seem we'd be daring God's anger—"

"That's nay what gnaws on the skipper's mind, He was never an over-pious man." Etien scratched himself, yawned, and climbed to his feet. "Glad I am to be nay the skipper. Let him think over what's best to do. Time ye an' me was asleep."

But I slept little that night. Rovic, I think, rested well. Yet as the next day wore on, I could see haggardness on him. I wondered why. Did he think the Hisagazi would turn on us? If so, why had he come at all? As the slope steepened, the wagon grew so toilsome to push and drag that my fears died for lack of breath.

Yet when we came upon the Ship, toward evening, I forgot my weariness. And after one amazed volley of oaths, our mariners rested silent on their pikes. The Hisagazi, never talkative, crouched low in token of awe. Only Guzan remained erect among them. I glimpsed his expression as he stared at the marvel. It was a look of lust.

Wild was that place. We had gone above timberline, so the land was a green sea below us, edged with silvery ocean. Here we stood among tumbled black boulders, with cinders and spongy rufa underfoot. The mountain rose in steeps and scarps and ravines, up to the snows and the smoke, which rose another mile into a pale chilly sky. And here stood the Ship.

And the Ship was beauty.

I remember. In length—height, rather, since it stood on its tail—it was about equal to our own caravel, in form not unlike a lance head, in color a shining white untarnished after forty years. That was all. But, words are paltry, my lord. What can they show of clean soaring curves, of iridescence on burnished metal, of a thing which was proud and lovely and in its very shape aquiver to be off? How can I conjure back the glamor which hazed that Ship whose keel had cloven starlight?

We stood there a long time. My vision blurred. I wiped my eyes, angry to be seen so affected, until I noticed one tear glisten in Rovic's red beard. But the captain's visage was quite blank. When he spoke, he said merely, in a flat voice, "Come, let's make camp."

The Hisagazian guardsmen dared approach no closer than these several hundred yards, to so potent an idol as the ship had become. Our own mariners were glad enough to maintain the same distance. But after dark, when all else was in order, Val Nira led Rovic, Froad, Guzan, and myself to the vessel.

As we approached, a double door in the side swung noiselessly open and a metal gangplank descended therefrom. Glowing in Tambur's light, and in the dull clotted red reflected off the smoke clouds, the Ship was already as strange as I could endure. When it thus opened itself to me, as if a ghost stood guard, I whimpered and fled. The cinders crunched beneath my boots; I caught a whiff of sulfurous air.

But at the edge of camp I rallied myself enough to look again. The dark ground blotted all light, so that the Ship appeared alone with its grandeur. Presently I went back.

The interior was lit by luminous panels, cool to the touch. Val Nira explained that the great engine which drove it—as if the troll of folklore were put on a treadmill—was intact, and would furnish power at the flick of a lever. As nearly as I could understand what he said, this was done by changing the metallic part of ordinary salt into light…so I do not understand after all. The quicksilver was required for a part of the controls, which channeled power from the engine into another mechanism that hurtled the Ship skyward. We inspected the broken container. Enormous indeed had been the impact of landing, to twist and bend that thick alloy so. And yet Val Nira had been shielded by invisible forces, and the rest of the Ship had not suffered important damage. He fetched some tools, which flamed and hummed and whirled, and demonstrated a few repair operations on the broken part. Obviously he would have no trouble completing the work—and then he need only pour in a gallon of quicksilver, to bring his vessel alive again.

Much else did he show us that night. I shall say naught of this, for I cannot even remember such strangeness very dearly, let alone find words. Suffice it that Rovic, Froad, and Zhean spent a few hours in Elf Hill.

So, too, did Guzan, Though he had been taken here once before, as part of his initiation, he had never been shown this much erenow. Watching him, however, I saw less marveling in him than greed.

No doubt Rovic observed the same. There was little which Rovic did not observe. When we departed the Ship, his silence was not stunned like Froad's or my own. At the time, I thought in a vague fashion that he fretted over the trouble Guzan was certain to make. Now, looking back, I believe his mood was sadness.

Sure it is that long after we others were in our bedrolls, he stood alone, looking at the planetlit Ship.

Early in a cold dawn, Etien shook me awake. "Up, lad, we've work to do. Load yere pistols an' belt on yere dirk."

"What? What's to happen?" I fumbled with a hoarfrosted blanket. Last night seemed a dream.

"The skipper's nay said, but plainly he awaits a fight. Report to the wagon an' help us move into yon flying tower." Erien's thick form heel-squatted a moment longer beside me. Then, slowly: "Methinks Guzan has some idea o' murdering us all, here on the mountain. One officer an' a few crewmen can be made to sail the *Golden Leaper* for him, to Giair an' back. The rest o' us would be less trouble to him wi' our weasands slit."

I crawled forth, teeth clattering in my head. After arming myself, I snatched some food from the common store. The Hisagazi on the march carry dried fish and a sort of bread made from a powdered weed. Only the saints knew when I'd next get a chance to eat. I was the last to join Rovic at the cart. The natives were drifting sullenly toward us, unsure what we intended.

"Let's go, lads," said Rovic. He gave his orders. Four men started manhandling the wagon across the rocky trail toward the Ship, where this gleamed among mists. We others stood by, weapons ready. Almost at once Guzan hastened toward us, with Val Nira toiling in his wake.

Anger darkened his countenance. "What are you doing?" he barked.

Rovic gave him a calm stare. "Why, milord, as we may be here for some time, inspecting the wonders aboard the Ship—"

"What?" interrupted Guzan. "What do you mean? Have you not seen enough for one visit? We must get home again, and prepare to sail after the flowing stone."

"Go if you wish," said Rovic. "I choose to linger. And since you don't trust me, I reciprocate the feeling. My folk will stay in the Ship, which can be defended if necessary."

Guzan stormed and raged, but Rovic ignored him. Our men continued hauling the cart over the uneven ground. Guzan signaled his spearmen, who approached in a disordered but alert mass. Etien spoke a command. We fell into line. Pikes slanted forward, muskets took aim.

Guzan stepped back. We had demonstrated firearms for him at his own home island. Doubtless he could overwhelm us with sheer numbers, were he determined enough, but the cost would be heavy. "No reason to fight, is there?" purred Rovic. "I am only taking a sensible precaution. The Ship is a most valuable prize. It could bring Paradise for all…or dominion over this earth for one. There are those who'd prefer the latter. I've not accused you of being among them. However, in prudence I'd liefer keep the Ship for my hostage and my fortress, as long as it pleases me to remain here."

I think then I was convinced of Guzan's real intentions, not as a surmise of ours but as plain fact. Had he truly wished to attain the stars, his one concern would have been to keep the Ship safe. He would not have reached out, snatched little Val Nira in his powerful hands, and dragged he starman backward like a shield against our fire. Not that his intent matters, save to my own conscience. Wrath distorted his patterned visage. He screamed at us "Then I'll keep a hostage too! And much good may your shelter do you!"

The Hisagazi milled about, muttering, hefting their spears and axes, but not prepared to follow us. We grunted our way across the black mountainside. The sun strengthened. Froad twisted his beard. "Dear me, master captain," he said, "think you they'll lay siege to us?"

"I'd not advise anyone to venture forth alone," said Rovic dryly.

"But without Val Nira to explain things, what use for us to stay at the Ship? Best we go back. I've mathematic texts to consult—my head's aspin with the law that binds the turning planets—I must ask the man from Paradise what he knows of—"

Rovic interrupted with a gruff order to three men, that they help lift a wheel wedged between two stones. He was in a savage temper. I confess his action seemed mad to me. If Guzan intended treachery, we had gained little by immobilizing ourselves in the Ship, where he could starve us. Better to let him attack in the open, where we would have a chance of fighting our way through. On the other hand, if Guzan did not plan to fall on us in the jungle any other time—then this was senseless provocation on our part. But I dared not question.

When we had brought our wagon up to the Ship, its gangplank again descended for us. The sailors started and cursed. Rovic forced himself out of his own bitterness, to speak soothing word. "Easy, lads. I've been aboard already, ye ken. Naught harmful within. Now we must tote our powder thither, an' stow it as I've planned."

Being slight of frame, I was not set to carrying the heavy casks, but put at the foot of the gangplank to watch the Hisagazi. We were too far away to distinguish words, but I saw how Guzan stood up on a boulder and harangued them. They shook their weapons at us and whooped. But they did not venture to attack. I wondered wretchedly what this was all about. If Rovic had foreseen us besieged, that would explain why he brought so much powder along…no, it would not, for there was more than a dozen men could shoot off in weeks of musketry, even had we had enough lead along…and we had almost no food! I looked past the poisonous volcano clouds, to Tambur where storms raged that could engulf all our earth, and wondered what demons lurked here to possess men.

I sprang to alertness at an indignant shout from within. Froad! Almost, I ran up the gangway, then remembered my duty. I heard Rovic roar him down and order the crewfolk to carry on, Froad and Rovic must have gone alone into the pilot's compartment and talked for an hour or more. When the old man emerged, he protested no longer. But as he walked down the gangway, he wept.

Rovic followed, grimmer of countenance than I had ever seen a man erenow. The sailors filed after, some looking appalled, some relieved, but chiefly watching the Hisagazian camp. They were simple mariners; the Ship was little to them save an alien and disquieting thing. Last came Etien, walking backward down the metal plank as he uncoiled a long string.

"Form square!" barked Rovic, The men snapped into position. "Best get within, Zhean and Froad," said the captain. "You can better carry extra ammunition than fight." He placed himself in the van.

I tugged Froad's sleeve. "Please, I beg you, master, what's happening?" But he sobbed too much to answer.

Etien crouched with flint and steel in his hands. He heard me—for otherwise we were all deathly silent—and said in a hard voice: "We placed casks o' powder throughout this hull, lad, wi' powder trains to join 'em, Here's the fuse to the whole."

I could not speak, could not even think, so monstrous was this. As if from immensely far away, I heard the click of stone on steel in Etien's fingers, heard him blow on the spark and add: "A good idea, methinks. I said t'other eventide, I'd follow the skipper wi'out fear o' God's curse—but better 'tis not to tempt Him over much."

"Forward march!" Rovic's sword blazed clear of the scabbard.

Our feet scrunched loud and horrible on the mountain as we quick-stepped away. I did not look back. I could not. I was still fumbling in a nightmare. Since Guzan would have moved to intercept us anyhow, we proceeded straight toward his band. He stepped forward as we halted at the camp's edge. Val Nira slunk shivering after him. I heard the words dimly:

"Well, Rovic, what now? Are you ready to go home?"

"Yes," said the captain. His voice was dull. "All the way home."

Guzan squinted in rising suspiciousness. "Why did you abandon your wagon? What did you leave behind?"

"Supplies. Come, let's march."

Val Nira stared at the cruel shapes of our pikes. He must wet his lips a few times ere he could quaver, "What are you talking about? There's no reason to leave food there. It would spoil in all the time until…until—" He faltered as he looked into Rovic's eyes. The blood drained from him.

"What have you done?" he whispered.

Suddenly Rovic's free hand went up, to cover his face. "What I must," he said thickly. "Daughter of God, forgive me."

The starman regarded us an instant more. Then he turned and ran. Past the astonished warriors he burst, out onto the cindery slope, toward his Ship.

"Come back!" bellowed Rovic. "You fool. You'll never—"

He swallowed hard. As he looked after that small, stumbling, lonely shape, hurrying across a fire mountain toward the Beautiful One, the sword sank in his grasp. "Perhaps it's best," he said, like a benediction.

Guzan raised his own sword. In scaly coat and blowing feathers, he was a figure as impressive as steel-clad Rovic. "Tell me what you've done," he snarled, "or I'll kill you this moment!"

He paid our muskets no heed. He, too, had had dreams.

He, too, saw them end, when the Ship exploded.

Even that adamantine hull could not withstand a wagonload of carefully placed gunpowder, set off at one time. There came a crash that knocked me to my knees, and the hull cracked open. White-hot chunks of metal screamed across the slopes. I saw one of them strike a boulder and split it in twain. Val Nira vanished, destroyed too quickly to have seen what happened; so in the ultimate, God was merciful to him. Through the flames and smokes and the doomsday noise which followed, I saw the Ship fall. It rolled down the slope, strewing its own mangled guts behind. Then the mountainside grumbled and slid in pursuit, and buried it, and dust hid the sky.

More than this, I have no heart to remember.

The Hisagazi shrieked and fled. They must have thought all hell come to earth. Guzan stood his ground. As the dust enveloped us, hiding the grave of the Ship and the white volcano crater, turning the sun red, he sprang at Rovic. A musketeer raised his weapon. Etien slapped it down. We stood and watched those two men fight, up and over the shaken cinder land, and knew in our private darkness that this was their right. Sparks flew where the blades clamored togetber. At last Rovic's skill prevailed. He took Guzan in the throat.

We gave Guzan decent burial and went down through the jungle.

That night the guardsmen rallied their courage enough to attack us. We were aided by our muskets, but must chiefly use sword and pike. We hewed our way through them because we had no other place to go than the sea.

They gave up, but carried word ahead of us. When we reached Nikum, all the forces Iskilip could raise were besieging the *Golden Leaper* and waiting to oppose Rovic's entry. We formed a square again, and no matter how many thousands they had, only a score or so could reach us at any time. Nonetheless, we left six good men in the crimsoned mud of those streets. When our people on the caravel realized Rovic was coming back, they bombarded the town. This ignited the thatch roofs and distracted the enemy enough that a sortie from the ship was able to effect a juncture with us. We chopped our way to the pier, got aboard, and manned the capstan.

Outraged and very brave, the Hisagazi paddled their canoes up to our hull, where our cannon could not be brought to bear. They stood on each other's shoulders to reach our rail. One band forced itself aboard, and the fight was fierce which cleared them from the decks. That was when I got the shattered collarbone which plagues me to this day.

But in the end, we came out of the fjord. A fresh east wind was blowing. With all sail aloft, we outran the foe. We counted our dead, bound our wounds, and slept.

Next dawning, awakened by the pain of my shoulder and the worse pain within, I mounted the quarterdeck. The sky was overcast. The wind had stiffened; the sea ran cold and green, whitecaps our to a cloud-gray horizon. Timbers groaned and rigging skirled. I stood an hour facing aft, into the chill wind that numbs pain.

When I heard boots behind me I did not turn around. I knew they were Rovic's. He stood beside me a long while, bareheaded. I noticed that he was starting to turn gray.

Finally, not yet regarding me, still squinting into the air that lashed tears from our eyes, he said: "I had a chance to talk Froad over, that day. He was grieved, but owned I was right. Has he spoken to you about it?"

"No," I said.

"None of us are ever likely to speak of it much," said Rovic.

After another time: "I was not afraid Guzan or anyone else would seize the Ship and try to turn conqueror. We men of Montalir should well be able to deal with any such rogues. Nor was I afraid of the Paradise dwellers. That poor little man could only have been telling truth. They would never have harmed us…willingly. They would have brought precious gifts, and taught us their own esoteric arts, and let us visit all their stars."

"Then why?" I got out.

"Someday Froad's successors will solve the riddles of the universe," he said. "Someday our descendants will build their own Ship, and go forth to whatever destiny they wish."

Spume blew up and around us, until our hair was wet. I tasted the salt on my lips.

"Meanwhile," said Rovic. "we'll sail the seas of this earth, and walk its mountains, and chart and subdue and come to understand it. Do you see, Zhean? That is what the Ship would have taken from us."

Then I was also made able to weep. He laid his hand on my uninjured shoulder and stood with me while the *Golden Leaper,* all sail set, proceeded westward.

Brave to Be a King

-1-

On an evening in mid-twentieth-century New York, Manse Everard had changed into a threadbare lounging outfit and was mixing himself a drink. The doorbell interrupted. He swore at it. A tiring several days lay behind him and he wanted no other company than the lost narratives of Dr. Watson.

Well, maybe this character could be gotten rid of. He slippered across his apartment and opened the door, his expression mutinous. "Hello," he said coldly.

And then, all at once, it was as if he were aboard some early spaceship which had just entered free fall; he stood weightless and helpless in a blaze of stars.

"Oh," he said. "I didn't know...Come in."

Cynthia Denison paused a moment, looking past him to the bar. He had hung two crossed spears and a horse-plumed helmet from the Achaean Bronze Age over it. They were dark and shining and incredibly beautiful. She tried to speak with steadiness, but failed. "Could I have a drink, Manse? Right away?"

"Of course." He clamped his mouth shut and helped her off with her coat. She closed the door and sat down on a Swedish modern couch as clean and functional as the Homeric weapons. Her hands fumbled with her purse, getting out cigarettes. For a time she did not look at him, nor he at her.

"Do you still drink Irish on the rocks?" he asked. His words seemed to come from far away, and his body was awkward among bottles and glasses, forgetting how the Time Patrol had trained it.

"Yes," she said. "So you do remember." Her lighter snapped, unexpectedly loud in the room.

"It's been just a few months," he said, for lack of other phrases.

"Entropic time. Regular, untampered-with, twenty-four-hours-to-the-day time." She blew a cloud of smoke and stared at it. "Not much more than that for me. I've been in now almost continuously since my, my wedding. Just eight and a half months of my personal, biological, lifeline time since Keith and I...But how long has it been for you, Manse? How many years have you rung up, in how many different epochs, since you were Keith's best man?"

She had always had a rather high and thin voice. It was the only flaw he had ever found in her, unless you counted her being so small—barely five feet. So she could never put much expression into her tones. But he could hear that she was staving off a scream.

He gave her a drink. "Down the hatch," he said. "All of it." She obeyed, strangling a little. He got her a refill and completed his own Scotch and soda. Then he drew up a chair and took pipe and tobacco from the depths of his moth-eaten smoking jacket. His hands still shook, but so faintly he didn't think she would notice. It had been wise of her not to blurt whatever news she carried; they both needed a chance to get back their control.

Now he even dared to look straight at her. She hadn't changed. Her figure was almost perfect in a delicate way, as the black dress emphasized. Sunlight-colored hair fell to her shoulders; the eyes were blue and enormous, under arched brows, in a tip-tilted face with the lips always just a little parted. She hadn't enough makeup for him to tell for sure if she had cried lately. But she looked very near to it.

Everard became busy filling his pipe. "Okay, Cyn," he said. "Want to tell me?"

She shivered. Finally she got out: "Keith. He's disappeared."

"Huh?" Everard sat up straight. "On a mission?"

"Yes. Where else? Ancient Iran. He went back there and never returned. That was a week ago." She set her glass down on the couch arm and twisted her fingers together. "The Patrol searched, of course. I just heard the results today. They can't find him. They can't even find out what happened to him."

"Judas," whispered Everard.

"Keith always...always thought of you as his best friend," she said frantically. "You wouldn't believe how often he spoke of you. Honestly, Manse, I know we've neglected you, but you never seemed to be in any..."

"Of course," he said. "How childish do you think I am? I was busy. And after all, you two were newly married."

After I introduced you, that night beneath Mauna Loa and the moon. The Time Patrol doesn't bother with snobbishness. A youngster like Cynthia Cunningham, a mere clerk fresh out of the Academy and Attached to her own century, is quite free to see a ranking veteran...like myself, for instance...as often as they both wish, off duty. There is no reason why he should not use his skill at disguise to take her waltzing in Strauss's Vienna or *to the theater in Shakespeare's London—as well as exploring funny little bars in Tom Lehrer's New York or playing tag in the sun and surf of Hawaii a thousand years before the canoe men arrived. And a fellow member of the Patrol is equally free to join them both. And later to marry her. Sure.*

Everard got his pipe going. When his face was screened with smoke, he said: "Begin at the beginning. I've been out of touch with you for—two or three years of my own lifeline time—so I'm not certain precisely what Keith was working on."

"That long?" she asked wonderingly. "You never even spent your furloughs in this decade? We did want you to come visit us."

"Quit apologizing!" he snapped. "I could have dropped in if I'd wished." The elfin face looked as if he had slapped it. He backed up, appalled. "I'm sorry. Naturally I wanted to. But as I said...we Unattached agents are so damned busy, hopping around in all space-time like fleas on a griddle...Oh, hell." He tried to smile. "You know me, Cyn, tactless, but it doesn't mean anything. I originated a chimaera legend all by myself, back in Classic Greece. I was known as the *dilaiopod,* a curious monster with two left feet, both in its mouth."

She returned a dutiful quirk of lips and picked up her cigarette from the ashtray. "I'm still just a clerk in Engineering Studies," she said. "But it puts me in close contact with all the other offices in this entire milieu, including headquarters. So I know exactly what's been done about Keith...and it isn't enough! They're just abandoning him! Manse, if you won't help Keith is dead!"

She stopped, shakily. To give them both a little more time, Everard reviewed the career of Keith Denison.

Born Cambridge, Mass., 1927, to a moderately wealthy family, Ph.D. in archaeology with a distinguished thesis at the age of twenty-three, after having also taken a collegiate boxing championship and crossed the Atlantic in a thirty-foot ketch. Drafted in 1950, served in Korea with a bravery which would have earned him some fame in a more popular war. Yet you had to know him quite a while before you learned any of this. He spoke, with a gift of dry humor, about impersonal things, until there was work to be done. Then, without needless fuss, he did it. *Sure,* thought Everard, *the best man got the girl. Keith could've made Unattached easily, if he'd cared to. But he had roots here that I didn't. More stable, I guess.*

Discharged and at loose ends in 1952, Denison was contacted by a Patrol agent and recruited. He had accepted the fact of time travel more readily than most. His mind was supple and, after all, he was an archaeologist. Once trained, he found a happy coincidence of his own interests and the needs of the Patrol; he became a Specialist, East Indo-European Protohistory, and in many ways a more important man than Everard.

For the Unattached officer might rove up and down the time lanes, rescuing the distressed and arresting the lawbreaker and keeping the fabric of human destiny secure. But how could he tell what he was doing without a record? Ages before the first hieroglyphics there had been wars and wanderings, discoveries and achievements, whose consequences reached through all the continuum. The Patrol had to know them. Charting their course was a job for the Specialist ratings.

Besides all of which, Keith was a friend of mine.

Everard took the pipe from his mouth. "Okay, Cynthia," he said. "Tell me what did happen."

-2-

The little voice was almost dry now, so rigidly had she harnessed herself. "He was tracing the migrations of the different Aryan clans. They're very obscure, you know. You have to start at a point when the history is known for certain, and work backward. So on this last job, Keith was going to Iran in the year 558 B.C. That was near the close of the Median period, he said. He'd make inquiries among the people, learn their own traditions, and then afterward check back at a still earlier point, and so on...But you must know all about this, Manse. You helped him once, before we met. He often spoke about that."

"Oh, I just went along in case of trouble," shrugged Everard. "He was studying the prehistoric trek of a certain band from the Don over the Hindu Kush. We told their chief we were passing hunters, claimed hospitality, and accompanied the wagon train for a few weeks. It was fun."

He remembered steppes and enormous skies, a windy gallop after antelope and a feast by campfires and a certain girl whose hair had held the bittersweet of woodsmoke. For a while he wished he could have lived and died as one of those tribesmen.

"Keith went back alone this time," continued Cynthia. "They're always so shorthanded in his branch, in the entire Patrol, I suppose. So many thousands of years to watch and so few man-lifetimes to do it with. He'd gone alone before. I was always afraid to let him, but he said…dressed as a wandering shepherd with nothing worth stealing...he'd be safer in the Iranian highlands than crossing Broadway. Only this time he wasn't!"

"I take it, then," said Everard quickly, "he left—a week ago, did you say?—intending to get his information, report it to the clearinghouse of his specialty, and come back to the same day here as he'd left you." *Because only a blind buckethead would let more of your lifespan pass without being there himself.* "But he didn't."

"Yes." She lit another cigarette from the butt of the first. "I got worried right away. I asked the boss about it. He obliged me by querying himself a week ahead—today—and got the answer that Keith had not returned. The information clearinghouse said he never came to them. So we checked with Records in milieu headquarters. Their answer was...was...Keith never did come back and no trace of him was ever found."

Everard nodded with great care. "Then, of course, the search was ordered which MHQ has a record of."

Mutable time made for a lot of paradoxes, he reflected for the thousandth occasion.

In the case of a missing man, you were not required to search for him just because a record somewhere said you had done so. But how else would you stand a chance of finding him? You *might* possibly go back and thereby change events so that you did find him after all—in which case the report you filed would "always" have recorded your success, and you alone would know the "former" truth.

It could get very messed up. No wonder the Patrol was fussy, even about small changes which would not affect the main pattern.

"Our office notified the boys in the Old Iranian milieu, who sent a party to investigate the spot," foretold Everard. "They only knew the approximate site at which Keith had intended to materialize, didn't they? I mean, since he couldn't know exactly where he'd be able to hide the scooter, he didn't file precise coordinates." Cynthia nodded. "But what I don't understand is, why didn't they find the machine afterward? Whatever happened to Keith, the scooter would still be somewhere around, in some cave or whatever. The Patrol has detectors. They should have been able to track down the scooter, at least, and then work backwards from it to locate Keith."

She drew on her cigarette with a violence that caved in her cheeks. "They tried," she said. "But I'm told it's a wild, rugged country, hard to search. Nothing turned up. They couldn't find a trace. They might have, if they'd looked very, very hard—made a mile-by-mile, hour-by-hour search. But they didn't dare. You see, that particular milieu is critical. Mr. Gordon showed me the analysis. I couldn't follow all those symbols, but he said it was a *very* dangerous century to tamper with."

Everard closed one large hand on the bowl of his pipe. Its warmth was somehow comforting. Critical eras gave him the willies.

"I see," he said. "They couldn't search as thoroughly as they wanted, because it might disturb too many of the local yokels, which might make them act differently when the big crisis came. Uh-huh. But how about making inquiries in disguise, among the people?"

"Several Patrol experts did. They tried that for weeks, Persian time. And the natives never even gave them a hint. Those tribes are so wild and suspicious... maybe they feared our agents were spies from the Median king, I understand they didn't like his rule...No. The Patrol couldn't find a trace. And anyhow, there's no reason to think the pattern was affected. They believe Keith was murdered and his scooter vanished somehow. And what difference—" Cynthia sprang to her feet. Suddenly she yelled—"What difference does one more skeleton in one more gully make?"

Everard rose too, she came into his arms, and he let her have it out. For himself, he had never thought it would be this bad. He had stopped remembering her, except maybe ten times a day, but now she came to him and the forgetting would have to be done all over again.

"Can't they go back locally?" she pleaded. "Can't somebody hop back a week from now, just to tell him not to go, is that so much to ask? What kind of monsters made that law against it?"

"Ordinary men did," said Everard. "If we once started doubling back to tinker with our personal pasts, we'd soon get so tangled up that none of us would exist."

"But in a million years or more—there must be exceptions!"

Everard didn't answer. He knew that there were. He knew also that Keith Denison's case wouldn't be one of them. The Patrol was not staffed by saints, but its people dared not corrupt their own law for their own ends. You took your losses like any other corps, and raised a glass to the memory of your dead, and you did not travel back to look upon them again while they had lived.

Presently Cynthia left him, returned to her drink and tossed it down. The yellow locks swirled past her face as she did. "I'm sorry," she said. She got out a handkerchief and wiped her eyes. "I didn't mean to bawl."

"It's okay."

She stared at the floor. "You could try to help Keith. The regular agents have given up, but you could try."

It was an appeal from which he had no recourse. "I could," he told her. "I might not succeed. The existing records show that, if I tried, I failed. And any alteration of space-time is frowned on, even a trivial one like this."

"It isn't trivial to Keith," she said.

"You know, Cyn," he murmured, "you're one of the few women that ever lived who'd have phrased it that way. Most would have said, It isn't trivial to me."

Her eyes captured his, and for a moment she stood very quiet: Then, whispering:

"I'm sorry. Manse. I didn't realize...I thought, what with all the time that's gone past for you; you would have—"

"What are you talking about?" he defended himself.

"Can't the Patrol psychs do anything for you?" she asked. Her head drooped again. "I mean, if they can condition us so we just simply can't tell anyone unauthorized that time travel exists...I should think it would also be possible to, to condition a person out of—"

"Skip it," said Everard roughly.

He gnawed his pipestem a while. "Okay," he said at last. "I've an idea or two of my own that may not have been tried. If Keith can be rescued in any way, you'll get him back before tomorrow noon."

"Could you time-hop me up to that moment, Manse?" She was beginning to tremble.

"I could," he said, "but I won't. One way or another, you'll need to be rested tomorrow. I'll take you home now and see that you swallow a sleepy pill. And then I'll come back here and think about the situation." He twisted his mouth into a sort of grin. "Cut out that shimmy, huh? I told you I had to think."

"Manse..." Her hands closed about his.

He knew a sudden hope for which he cursed himself.

-3-

In the fall of the year 542 B.C., a solitary man came down out of the mountains and into the valley of the Kur. He rode a handsome chestnut gelding: bigger even than most cavalry horses, which might elsewhere have been an invitation to bandits; but the Great King had given so much law to his dominions that it was said a virgin with a sack of gold could walk unmolested across all Persia. It was one reason Manse Everard had chosen to hop to this date, sixteen years after Keith Denison's destination.

Another motive was to arrive long after any excitement which the time traveler had conceivably produced in 558 had died away. Whatever the truth about Keith's fate, it might be more approachable from the rear; at least, straightforward methods had failed.

Finally, according to the Achaemenid Milieu office, autumn 542 happened to be the first season of relative tranquility since the disappearance. The years

558-553 had been tense ones when the Persian king of Anshan, Kuru-sh (he whom the future knew as Koresh and Cyrus), was more and more at odds with his Median overlord Astyages. Then came three years when Cyrus revolted, civil war racked the empire, and the Persians finally overcame their northerly neighbors. But Cyrus was scarcely victorious before he must face counter-uprisings, as well as Turanian incursions; he spent four years putting down that trouble and extending his rule eastward. This alarmed his fellow monarchs; Babylon, Egypt, Lydia, and Sparta formed a coalition to destroy him, with King Croesus of Lydia leading an invasion in 546. The Lydians were broken and annexed, but they revolted and had to be broken all over again; the troublesome Greek colonies of Ionia, Carla, and Lycia must be settled with; and while his generals did all this in the west, Cyrus himself must war in the east, forcing back the savage horsemen who would otherwise burn his cities.

Now there was a breathing spell. Cilicia would yield without a fight, seeing that Persia's other conquests were governed with a humanity and a tolerance of local custom such as the world had not known before. Cyrus would leave the eastern marches to his nobles, and devote himself to consolidating what he had won. Not until 539 would the war with Babylon be taken up again and Mesopotamia acquired. And then Cyrus would have another time of peace, until the wild men grew too strong beyond the Aral Sea and the King rode forth against them to his death.

Manse Everard entered Pasargadae as if into a springtime of hope.

Not that any actual era lends itself to such flowery metaphors. He jogged through miles where peasants bent with sickles, loading creaky unpainted oxcarts, and dust smoked off the stubble fields into his eyes. Ragged children sucked their thumbs outside windowless mud huts and stared at him. A chicken squawked back and forth on the highway until the galloping royal messenger who had alarmed it was past and the chicken dead. A squad of lancers trotting by were costumed picturesquely enough, baggy pants and scaly armor, spiked or plumed helmets, gaily striped cloaks; but they were also dusty, sweaty, and swapping foul jokes. Behind adobe walls the aristocrats possessed large houses with very beautiful gardens, but an economy like this would not support many such estates. Pasargadae was ninety percent an Oriental town of twisted slimy streets between faceless hovels, greasy headcloths and dingy robes, screaming merchants in the bazaars, beggars displaying their sores, traders leading strings of battered camels and overloaded donkeys, dogs raiding offal heaps, tavern music like cat in a washing machine, men who windmilled their arms and screamed curses—whatever started this yarn about the inscrutable East?

"Alms, lord. Alms, for the love of Light! Alms, and Mithras will smile upon you!..."

"Behold sir! By my father's beard I swear that never was there finer work from a more skilled hand than the bridle which I offer to you, most fortunate of men, for the ridiculous sum of..."

"This way, master, this way, only four houses down to the finest sarai in all Persia—no, in all the world. Our pallets are stuffed with swan's down, my father serves wine fit for a Devi, my mother cooks a pilau whose fame has spread to the ends of the earth, and my sisters are three moons of delight available for a mere..."

Everard ignored the childish runners who clamored at his sides. One of them tugged his ankle, he swore and kicked, and the boy grinned without shame. The man hoped to avoid staying at an inn; the Persians were cleaner than most folk in this age, but there would still be insect life.

He tried not to feel defenseless. Ordinarily a Patrolman could have an ace in the hole: say, a thirtieth-century stun pistol beneath his coat and a midget radio to call the hidden space-time antigravity scooter to him. But not when he might be frisked. Everard wore a Greek outfit: tunic and sandals and long wool cloak, sword at waist, helmet and shield hung at the horse's crupper, and that was it; only the steel was anachronistic. He could turn to no local branch office if he got into trouble, for this relatively poor and turbulent transition epoch attracted no Temporal commerce; the nearest Patrol unit was milieu HQ in Persepolis, a generation futureward.

The streets widened as he pushed on, bazaars thinned out and houses grew larger. At last he emerged in a square enclosed by four mansions. He could see pruned trees above their outer walls. Guards, lean lightly armed youths, squatted beneath on their heels because standing at attention had not yet been invented. They rose, nocking wary arrows, as Everard approached. He might simply have crossed the plaza, but he veered and hailed a fellow who looked like a captain.

"Greetings, sir, may the sun fall bright upon you." The Persian which he had learned in an hour under hypno flowed readily off his tongue. "I seek hospitality from some great man who may care to hear my poor tales of foreign travel."

"May your days be many," said the guard. Everard remembered that he must not offer baksheesh: these Persians of Cyrus's own clans were a proud hardy folk, hunters, herdsmen, and warriors. All spoke with the dignified politeness common to their type throughout history. "I serve Croesus the Lydian, servant of the Great King. He will not refuse his roof to—"

"Meander from Athens," supplied Everard. It was an alias which would explain his large bones, light complexion, and short hair. He had, though, been forced to stick a realistic Van Dyke effect on his chin. Herodotus was not the first Greek globetrotter, so an Athenian would not be inconveniently outré. At the same time, half a century before Marathon, Europeans were still uncommon enough here to excite interest.

A slave was called, who got hold of the majordomo, who sent another slave, who invited the stranger through the gate. The garden beyond was as cool and green as hoped; there was no fear that anything would be stolen from his baggage in this household; the food and drink should be good; and Croesus himself would certainly interview the guest at length. *We're playing in luck, lad.* Everard assured himself, and accepted a hot bath, fragrant oils, fresh clothing, dates and wine brought to his austerely furnished room, a couch and a pleasant view. He only missed a cigar.

Of attainable things, that is.

To be sure, if Keith had unamendably died...

"Hell and purple frogs," muttered Everard. "Cut that out, will you?"

-4-

After sunset it grew chilly. Lamps were lit with much ceremony, fire being sacred, and braziers were blown up. A slave prostrated himself to announce that dinner was served. Everard accompanied him down a long hall where vigorous murals showed the Sun and the Bull of Mithras, past a couple of spearmen, and into a small chamber brightly lit, sweet with incense and lavish with carpeting. Two couches were drawn up in the Hellenic manner at a table covered with un-Hellenic dishes of silver and gold; slave waiters hovered in the background and Chinese-sounding music twanged from an inner door.

Croesus of Lydia nodded graciously. He had been handsome once, with regular features, but seemed to have aged a lot in the few years since his wealth and power were proverbial. Grizzled of beard and with long hair, he was dressed in a Grecian chlamys but wore rouge in the Persian manner. "Rejoice, Meander of Athens," he said in Greek, and lifted his face.

Everard kissed his cheek as indicated. It was nice of Croesus thus to imply that Meander's rank was but little inferior to his own, even if Croesus had been eating garlic. "Rejoice, master. I thank you for your kindness."

"This solitary meal was not to demean you," said the ex-king. "I only thought..." He hesitated. "I have always considered myself near kin to the Greeks, and we could talk seriously—"

"My lord honors me beyond my worth." They went through various rituals and finally got to the food. Everard spun out a prepared yarn about his travels; now and then Croesus would ask a disconcertingly sharp question, but a Patrolman soon learned how to evade that kind.

"Indeed times are changing, you are fortunate in coming at the very dawn of a new age," said Croesus. "Never has the world known a more glorious King than," etc., etc., doubtless for the benefit of any retainers who doubled as royal spies. Though it happened to be true.

"The very gods have favored our King," went on Croesus. "Had I known how they sheltered him—for truth, I mean, not for the mere fable which I believed it was—I should never have dared oppose myself to him. For it cannot be doubted, he is a Chosen One."

Everard maintained his Greek character by watering the wine and wishing he had picked some less temperate nationality. "What is that tale, lord?" he asked. "I knew only that the Great King was the son of Cambyses, who held this province as a vassal of Median Astyages. Is there more?"

Croesus leaned forward. In the uncertain light, his eyes held a curious bright look, a Dionysian blend of terror and enthusiasm which Everard's age had long forgotten. "Hear, and bring the account to your countrymen," he said. "Astyages wed his daughter Mandane to Cambyses, for he knew that the Persians were restless under his own heavy yoke and he wished to tie their leaders to his house. But Cambyses became ill and weak. If he died and his infant son Cyrus succeeded in Anshan, there would be a troublesome regency of Persian nobles not bound to Astyages. Dreams also warned the Median king that Cyrus would be the death of his dominion.

"Thereafter Astyages ordered his kinsman, the King's Eye Aurvagaush [Croesus rendered the name Harpagus, as he Hellenized all local names], to do away with the prince. Harpagus took the child despite Queen Mandane's protests; Cambyses lay too sick to help her, nor could Persia in any case revolt without preparation. But Harpagus could not bring himself to the deed. He exchanged the prince for the stillborn child of a herdsman in the mountains, whom he swore to secrecy. The dead baby was wrapped in royal clothes and left on a hillside; presently officials of the Median court were summoned to witness that it had been exposed, and buried it. Our lord Cyrus grew up as a herdsman.

"Cambyses lived for twenty years more without begetting other sons, not strong enough in his own person to avenge the firstborn. But at last he was plainly dying, with no successor whom the Persians would feel obliged to obey. Again Astyages feared trouble. At this time Cyrus came forth, his identity being made known through various signs. Astyages, regretting what had gone before, welcomed him and confirmed him as Cambyses's heir.

"Cyrus remained a vassal for five years, but found the tyranny of the Medes ever more odious. Harpagus in Ecbatana had also a dreadful thing to avenge: as punishment for his disobedience in the matter of Cyrus, Astyages made Harpagus eat his own son. So Harpagus conspired with certain Median nobles. They chose Cyrus as their leader, Persia revolted, and after three years of war Cyrus made himself the master of the two peoples. Since then, of course, he has added many others. When ever did the gods show their will more plainly?"

Everard lay quiet on the couch for a little. He heard autumn leaves rustle dryly in the garden, under a cold wind.

"This is true, and no fanciful gossip?" he asked.

"I have confirmed it often enough since I joined the Persian court. The King himself has vouched for it to me, as well as Harpagus and others who were directly concerned."

The Lydian could not be lying if he cited his ruler's testimony: the upper-class Persians were fanatics about truthfulness. And yet Everard had heard nothing so incredible in all his Patrol career. For it was the story which Herodotus recorded—with a few modifications to be found in the *Shah Nameh*—and anybody could spot that as a typical hero myth. Essentially the same yarn had been told about Moses, Romulus, Sigurd, a hundred great men. There was no reason to believe it held any fact, no reason to doubt that Cyrus had been raised in a perfectly normal manner at his father's house, had succeeded by plain right of birth and revolted for the usual reasons.

Only, this tall tale was sworn to by eyewitnesses!

There was a mystery here. It brought Everard back to his purpose. After appropriate marveling remarks, he led the conversation until he could say: "I have heard rumors that sixteen years ago a stranger entered Pasargadae, clad as a poor shepherd but in truth a mage who did miracles. He may have died here. Does my gracious host know anything of it?"

He waited then, tensed. He was playing a hunch, that Keith Denison had not been murdered by some hillbilly, fallen off a cliff and broken his neck, or come to grief in any such way. Because in that case, the scooter should still have been around when the Patrol searched. They might have gridded the area too loosely to find Denison himself, but how could their detectors miss a time hopper?

So, Everard thought, something more complicated had happened. And if Keith survived at all, he would have come down here to civilization.

"Sixteen years ago?" Croesus tugged his beard. "I was not here then. And surely in any case the land would have been full of portents, for that was when Cyrus left the mountains and took his rightful crown of Anshan. No, Meander, I know nothing of it."

"I have been anxious to find this person," said Everard, "because an oracle," etc., etc.

"You can inquire among the servants and townspeople," suggested Croesus. "I will ask at court on your behalf. You will stay here awhile, will you not? Perhaps the King himself will wish to see you; he is always interested in foreigners."

The conversation broke up soon after. Croesus explained with a rather sour smile that the Persians believed in early to bed, early to rise, and he must be at the royal palace by dawn. A slave conducted Everard back to his room, where he found a good-looking girl waiting with an expectant smile. He hesitated a moment, remembering a time twenty-four hundred years hence. But—the hell with that. A man had to take whatever the gods offered him, and they were a miserly lot.

-5-

It was not long after sunrise when a troop reined up in the plaza and shouted for Meander the Athenian. Everard left his breakfast to go out and stare up a gray stallion into the hard, hairy hawk-face of a captain of those guards called the Immortals. The men made a backdrop of restless horses, cloaks and plumes blowing, metal jingling and leather squeaking, the young sun ablaze on polished mail.

"You are summoned by the Chiliarch," rapped the officer. The title he actually used was Persian: commander of the guard and grand vizier of the empire.

Everard stood for a moment, weighing the situation. His muscles tightened. This was not a very cordial invitation. But he could scarcely plead a previous engagement.

"I hear and obey," he said. "Let me but fetch a small gift from my baggage, in token of the honor paid me."

"The Chiliarch said you were to come at once. Here is a horse."

An archer sentry offered cupped hands, but Everard pulled himself into the saddle without help, a trick it was useful to know in eras before stirrups were introduced. The captain nodded a harsh approval, whirled his mount, and led at a gallop off the plaza and up a wide avenue lined with sphinxes and the homes of the great. This was not as heavily trafficked as the bazaar streets, but there were enough riders, chariots, litters, and pedestrians scrambling out of the way. The Immortals stopped for no man. They roared through palace gates flung open before them. Gravel spurted under hoofs; they tore around a lawn where fountains sparkled, and clanged to a stop outside the west wing.

The palace, gaudily painted brick, stood on a wide platform with several lesser buildings. The captain himself sprang down, gestured curtly, and strode up a marble staircase. Everard followed, hemmed in by warriors who had taken the light battle axes from their saddlebows for his benefit. The party went among household slaves, robed and turbaned and flat on their faces, through a red and yellow colonnade, down a mosaic hall whose beauty Everard was in no mood to appreciate, and so past a squad of guards into a room where slender columns upheld a peacock dome and the fragrance of late-blooming roses entered through arched windows.

There the Immortals made obeisance. *What's good enough for them is good enough for you, son,* thought Everard, and kissed the Persian carpet. The man on the couch nodded. "Rise and attend," he said. "Fetch a cushion for the Greek." The soldiers took their stance by him. A Nubian bustled forth with a pillow, which he laid on the floor beneath his master's seat. Everard sat down on it, cross-legged; His mouth felt dry.

The Chiliarch, whom he remembered Croesus identifying as Harpagus, leaned forward. Against the tiger skin on the couch and the gorgeous red robe on his own gaunt frame, the Mede showed as an aging man, his shoulder-length hair the color of iron and his dark craggy-nosed face sunken into a mesh of wrinkles. But shrewd eyes considered the newcomer.

"Well," he said, his Persian having the rough accent of a North Iranian, "so you are the man from Athens. The noble Croesus spoke of your advent this morning and mentioned some inquiries you were making. Since the safety of the state may be involved, I would know just what it is you seek." He stroked his beard with a jewel-flashing hand and smiled frostily. "It may even be, if your search is harmless, that I can help it."

He had been careful not to employ the usual formulas of greeting, to offer refreshment, or otherwise give Meander the quasi-sacred status of guest. This was an interrogation. "Lord, what is it you wish to know?" asked Everard. He could well imagine, and it was a troublous anticipation.

"You sought a mage in shepherd guise, who entered Pasargadae sixteen summers ago. and did miracles." The voice was ugly with tension. "Why is this and what more have you heard of such matters? Do not pause to invent a lie—speak!"

"Great lord," said Everard, "the oracle at Delphi told me I should mend my fortunes if I learned the fate of a herdsman who entered the Persian capital in, er, the third year of the first tyranny of Pisistratus. More than that I have never known. My lord is aware how dark are the oracular sayings."

"Hm, hm." Fear touched the lean countenance and Harpagus drew the sign of the cross, which was a Mithraic sun-symbol. Then, roughly: "What have you discovered so far?"

"Nothing, great lord. No one could tell—"

"You lie!" snarled Harpagus. "All Greeks are liars. Have a care, for you touch on unholy matters. Who else have you spoken to?"

Everard saw a nervous tic lift the Chiliarch's mouth. His own stomach was a cold lump in him. He had stumbled on something which Harpagus had thought safely buried, something so big that the risk of a clash with Croesus, who was duty bound to protect a guest, became nothing. And the most reliable gag ever invented was a snickersnee...after rack and pincers had extracted precisely what the stranger knew...*But what the blue hell do I know?*

"None, my lord," he husked. "None but the oracle, and the Sun God whose voice the oracle is, and who sent me here, has heard of this before last night."

Harpagus sucked in a sharp breath, taken aback by the invocation. But then, almost visibly squaring his shoulders: "We have only your word, the word of a Greek, that you were told by an oracle—that you did not spy out state secrets. Or even if the God did indeed send you here, it may as well have been to destroy you for your sins. We shall ask further about this." He nodded at the captain. "Take him below. In the King's name."

The King!

It blazed upon Everard. He jumped to his feet.

"Yes, the King!" he shouted. "The God told me...there would be a sign...and then I should bear his word to the Persian King!"

"Seize him!" yelled Harpagus.

The guardsmen whirled to obey. Everard sprang back, yelling for King Cyrus as loudly as he could. Let them arrest him. Word would be carried to the throne and...Two men hemmed him against the wall, their axes raised. Others pressed behind them. Over their helmets, he saw Harpagus leap up on the couch.

"Take him out and behead him," ordered the Mede.

"My lord," protested the captain, "he called upon the King."

"To cast a spell! I know him now, the son of Zohak and agent of Ahriman! Kill him!"

"No, wait," cried Everard, "wait, can you not see, it is this traitor who would keep me from telling the King...Let go, you sod!"

A hand closed on his right arm. He had been prepared to sit a few hours in jail, till the big boss heard of the affair and bailed him out, but matters were a bit more urgent after all. He threw a left hook which ended in a squelching of nose. The guardsman staggered back. Everard plucked the ax from his hand, spun about, and parried the blow of the warrior on his left.

The Immortals attacked. Everard's ax clanged against metal, darted in and smashed a knuckle. He outreached most of these people; But he hadn't a cellophane snowball's chance in hell of standing them off. A blow whistled toward his head. He ducked behind a column; chips flew. An opening—he stiff-armed one man, hopped over the clashing mail-clad form as it fell, and got onto open floor under the dome. Harpagus scuttled up, drawing a saber from beneath his robe; the old bastard was brave enough. Everard twirled to meet him, so that the Chiliarch was between him and the guards. Ax and sword rattled together. Everard tried to close in...a clinch would keep the Persians from throwing their weapons at him, but they were circling to get at his rear. Judas, this might be the end of one more Patrolman...

"Halt! Fall on your faces! The King comes!"

Three times it was blared. The guardsmen froze in their tracks, stared at the gigantic scarlet-robed person who stood bellowing in the doorway, and hit the rug. Harpagus dropped his sword. Everard almost brained him; then, remembering, and hearing the hurried tramp of warriors in the hall, he let go his own weapon. For a moment, he and the Chiliarch panted into each other's faces.

"So...he got word...and came...at once," gasped Everard.

The Mede crouched like a cat and hissed back: "Have a care, then! I will be watching you. If you poison his mind there will be poison for you, or a dagger..."

"The King! The King!" bellowed the herald.

Everard joined Harpagus on the floor.

A band of Immortals trotted into the room and made an alley to the couch. A chamberlain dashed to throw a special tapestry over it. Then Cyrus himself entered, robe billowing around long muscular strides. A few courtiers followed, leathery men privileged to bear arms in the royal presence, and a slave MC wringing his hands in their wake at not having been given time to spread a carpet or summon musicians.

The King's voice rang through the silence: "What is this? Where is the stranger who called on me?"

Everard risked a peek. Cyrus was tall, broad of shoulder and slim of body, older-looking than Croesus's account suggested—he was forty-seven years old, Everard knew with a shudder—but kept supple by sixteen years of war and the chase. He had a narrow dark countenance with hazel eyes, a sword scar on the left cheekbone, a straight nose and full lips. His black hair faintly grizzled, was brushed back and his beard trimmed more closely than was Persian custom. He was dressed as plainly as his status allowed.

"Where is the stranger whom the slave ran to tell me of?"

"I am he, Great King," said Everard.

"Arise. Declare your name."

Everard stood up and murmured: "Hi, Keith."

-6-

Vines rioted about a marble pergola. They almost hid the archers who ringed it. Keith Denison slumped on a bench, stared at leaf shadows dappled onto the floor, and said wryly, "At least we can keep our talk private. The English language hasn't been invented yet."

After a moment he continued, with a rusty accent: "Sometimes I've thought that was the hardest thing to take about this situation, never having a minute to myself. The best I can do is throw everybody out of the room I'm in; but they stick around just beyond the door, under the windows, guarding, listening. I hope their dear loyal souls fry."

"Privacy hasn't been invented yet either," Everard reminded him. "And VIPs like you never did have much, in all history."

Denison raised a tired visage. "I keep wanting to ask how Cynthia is," he said, "but of course for her it has been—will be—not so long. A week, perhaps. Did you by any chance bring some cigarettes?"

"Left 'em in the scooter," said Everard. "I figured I'd have trouble enough without explaining that away. I never expected to find you running this whole shebang."

"I didn't myself." Denison shrugged. "It was the damnedest fantastic thing. The time paradoxes—"

"So what did happen?"

Denison rubbed his eyes and sighed. "I got myself caught in the local gears. You know, sometimes everything that went before seems unreal to me, like a dream. Were there ever such things as Christendom, contrapuntal music, or the Bill of Rights? Not to mention all the people I knew. You yourself don't belong here, Manse, I keep expecting to wake up...Well, let me think back.

"Do you know what the situation was? The Medes and the Persians are pretty near kin, racially and culturally, but the Medes were top dog then, and they'd picked up a lot of habits from the Assyrians which didn't sit so well in the Persian viewpoint. We're ranchers and freehold farmers, mostly, and of course it isn't right that we should be vassals—" Denison blinked. "Hey, there I go again! What do I mean 'we'? Anyhow, Persia was restless. King Astyages of Media had ordered the murder of little Prince Cyrus twenty years before, but now he regretted it, because Cyrus's father was dying and the dispute over succession could touch off a civil war.

"Well, I appeared in the mountains. I had to scout a little bit in both space and time-hopping through a few days and several miles to find a good hiding place for my scooter. That's why the Patrol couldn't locate it afterward...part of the reason. You see, I did finally park it in a cave and set out on foot, but right away I came to grief. A Median army was bound through that region to discourage the Persians from making trouble. One of their scouts saw me emerge, checked my back trail—first thing I knew, I'd been seized and their officer was grilling me about what that gadget was I had in the cave. His men took me for a magician of some kind and were in considerable awe, but more afraid of showing fear than they were of me. Naturally, the word ran like a brushfire through the ranks and across the countryside. Soon all the area knew that a stranger had appeared under remarkable circumstances.

"Their general was Harpagus himself, as smart and tough-minded a devil as the world has ever seen. He thought I could be used. He ordered me to make my brazen horse perform, but I wasn't allowed to mount it. However, I did get a chance to kick it into time-drive. That's why the search party didn't find the thing. It was only a few hours in this century, then it probably went clear back to the Beginning."

"Good work," said Everard.

"Oh, I knew the orders forbidding that degree of anachronism." Denison's lips twisted. "But I also expected the Patrol to rescue me. If I'd known they wouldn't,

I'm not so sure I'd have stayed a good self-sacrificing Patrolman. I might have hung on to my scooter, and played Harpagus's game till a chance came to escape on my own."

Everard looked at him a moment, somberly. Keith had changed, he thought: not just in age, but the years among aliens. had marked him more deeply than he knew. "If you risked altering the future," he said, "you risked Cynthia's existence."

"Yes. Yes, true. I remember thinking of that...at the time...How long ago it seems!"

Denison leaned forward, elbows on knees, staring into the pergola screen. His words continued, flat. "Harpagus spit rivets, of course. I thought for a while he was going to kill me. I was carried off, trussed up like butcher's meat. But as I told you, there were already rumors about me, which were losing nothing in repetition. Harpagus saw a still better chance. He gave me a choice, string along with him or have my throat cut. What else could I do? It wasn't even a matter of hazarding an alteration; I soon saw I was playing a role which history had *already* written.

"You see, Harpagus bribed a herdsman to support his tale, and produced me as Cyrus, son of Cambyses."

Everard nodded, unsurprised. "What's in it for him?" he asked.

"At the time, he only wanted to bolster the Median rule. A king in Anshan under his thumb would have to be loyal to Astyages, and thereby help keep all the Persians in line. I was rushed along, too bewildered to do more than follow his lead, still hoping minute by minute for a Patrol hopper to appear and get me out of the mess. The truth fetish of all these Iranian aristocrats helped us a lot—few of them suspected I perjured myself in swearing I was Cyrus, though I imagine Astyages quietly ignored the discrepancies. And he put Harpagus in his place by punishing him in an especially gruesome way for not having done away with Cyrus as ordered—even if Cyrus turned out to be useful now—and of course the double irony was that Harpagus really had followed orders, two decades before!

"As for me, in the course of five years I got more and more sickened by Astyages myself. Now, looking back, I see he wasn't really such a hound from hell, just a typical Oriental monarch of the ancient world, but that's kind of hard to appreciate when you're forced to watch a man being racked.

"So Harpagus, wanting revenge, engineered a revolt, and I accepted the leadership of it which he offered me." Denison grinned crookedly. "After all, I was Cyrus the Great, with a destiny to play out. We had a rough time at first, the Medes clobbered us again and again, but you know, Manse, I found myself enjoying it. Not like that wretched twentieth-century business of sitting in a foxhole wondering if the enemy barrage will ever let up. Oh, war is miserable enough here, especially if you're a buck private when disease breaks out, as it always does. But when you fight, by God, you fight, with your own hands! And I even found a talent for that sort of thing. We've pulled some gorgeous stunts." Everard watched life flow back into him: "like the time the Lydian cavalry had us outnumbered. We sent our baggage camels in the van, with the infantry behind and horse last. Croesus's nags got a whiff of the camels and stampeded. For all I know, they're running yet. We mopped him up!"

He jarred to silence, stared awhile into Everard's eyes, and bit his lip. "Sorry. I keep forgetting. Now and then, I remember I was not a killer at home—after a battle, when I see the dead scattered around, and worst of all the wounded. But I couldn't help it, Manse! I've had to fight! First there was the revolt. If I hadn't played along with Harpagus, how long do you think I'd have lasted, personally? And then there's been the realm itself. I didn't ask the Lydians to invade us, or the eastern barbarians. Have you ever seen a town sacked by Turanians, Manse? It's them or us, and when *we* conquer somebody we don't march them off in chains, they keep their own lands and customs and...For Mithras's sake, Manse, could I do anything else?"

Everard sat listening to the garden rustle under a breeze. At last: "No. I understand. I hope it hasn't been too lonesome."

"I got used to it," said Denison carefully. "Harpagus is an acquired taste, but interesting. Croesus turned out to be a very decent fellow. Kobad the Mage has some original thoughts, and he's the only man alive who dares beat me at chess. And there's the feasting, and hunting, and women..." He gave the other a defiant look. "Yeah. What else would you have me do?"

"Nothing," said Everard. "Sixteen years is a long time."

"Cassandane, my chief wife, is worth a lot of the trouble I've had. Though Cynthia—God in heaven, Manse!" Denison stood up and laid hands on Everard's shoulders. The fingers closed with bruising strength; they had held ax, bow, and bridle for a decade and a half. The King of the Persians shouted aloud:

"How are you going to get me out of here?"

-7-

Everard rose too, walked to the floor's edge and stared through lacy stonework, thumbs hooked in his belt and head lowered.

"I don't see how," he answered.

Denison smote a fist into one palm. "I've been afraid of that. Year by year I've grown more afraid that if the Patrol ever finds me it'll...You've got to help."

"I tell you, I can't!" Everard's voice cracked. He did not turn around. "Think it over. You must have done so already. You're not some lousy little barbarian chief whose career won't make a jot of difference a hundred years from now. You're Cyrus, the founder of the Persian Empire; a key figure in a key milieu. If Cyrus goes, so does the whole future! There won't have been any twentieth century with Cynthia in it."

"Are you certain?" pleaded the man at his back.

"I boned up on the facts before hopping here," said Everard through clenched jaws. "Stop kidding yourself. We're prejudiced against the Persians because at one time they were the enemies of Greece, and we happen to get some of the more conspicuous features of our own culture from Hellenic sources. But the Persians are at least as important!

"You've watched it happen. Sure, they're pretty brutal by your standards: the whole era is, including the Greeks. And they're not democratic, but you can't blame them for not making a European invention outside their whole mental horizon. What counts is this:

"Persia was the first conquering power which made an effort to respect and conciliate the people it took over; which obeyed its own laws; which pacified enough territory to open steady contact with the Far East; which created a viable world religion, Zoroastrianism, not limited to anyone race or locality. Maybe you don't know how much Christian belief and ritual is of Mithraic origin, but believe me, it's plenty. Not to mention Judaism, which you, Cyrus the Great, are personally going to rescue. Remember? You'll take over Babylon and allow those Jews who've kept their identity to return home; without you, they'd be swallowed up and lost in the general ruck as the ten other tribes already have been.

"Even when it gets decadent, the Persian Empire will be a matrix for civilization. What were most of Alexander's conquests but just taking over Persian territory? And that spread Hellenism through the known world! And there'll be Persian successor states: Pontus, Parthia, the Persia of Firdauzi and Omar and Hafiz, the Iran we know and the Iran of a future beyond the twentieth century..."

Everard turned on his heel. "If you quit," he said, "I can imagine them still building ziggurats and reading entrails—and running through the woods up in Europe, with America underdiscovered—three thousand years from now!"

Denison sagged. "Yeah," he answered. "I thought so."

He paced awhile, hands behind his back. The dark face looked older each minute. "Thirteen more years," he murmured, almost to himself. "In thirteen years I'll fall in battle against the nomads. I don't know exactly how. One way or another, circumstances will force me to it. Why not? They've forced me into everything else I've done, willy-nilly...In spite of everything I can do to train him, I know my own son Cambyses will turn out to be a sadistic incompetent and it will take Darius to save the empire—God!" He covered his face with a flowing sleeve. "Excuse me. I do despise self-pity, but I can't help this."

Everard sat down, avoiding the sight. He heard how the breath rattled in Denison's lungs.

Finally the King poured wine into two chalices, joined Everard on the bench and said in a dry tone: "Sorry. I'm okay now. And I haven't given up yet."

"I can refer your problem to headquarters," said Everard with a touch of sarcasm.

Denison echoed it: "Thanks, little chum. I remember their attitude well enough. We're expendable. They'll interdict the entire lifetime of Cyrus to visitors, just so I won't be tempted, and send me a nice message. They will point out that I'm the absolute monarch of a civilized people, with palaces, slaves, vintages, chefs, entertainers, concubines, and hunting grounds at my disposal in unlimited quantities, so what am I complaining about? No, Manse, this is something you and I will have to work out between us."

Everard clenched his fists till he felt the nails bite into the palms. "You're putting me in a hell of a spot, Keith," he said.

"I'm only asking you to think on the problem—and Ahriman damn you, you will!" Again the fingers closed on his flesh, and the conqueror of the East snapped forth a command. The old Keith would never have taken that tone, thought Everard, anger flickering up; and he thought:

If you don't come home, and Cynthia is told that you never will...She could come back and join you; one more foreign girl in the Kings harem won't affect history. But if I reported to headquarters before seeing her, reported the problem as insoluble, which it doubtless is in fact...why, then the reign of Cyrus would be interdicted and she could not join you.

"I've been over this ground before, with myself," said Denison more calmly. "I know the implications as well as you do. But look, I can show you the cave where my machine rested for those few hours. You could go back to the moment I appeared there and warn me."

"No," said Everard. "That's out. Two reasons. First the regulation against that sort of thing, which is a sensible one. They might make an exception under different circumstances, but there's a second reason too: you are Cyrus. They're not going to wipe out an entire future for one mans sake."

Would I do it for one woman's? I'm not sure. I hope not... Cynthia wouldn't have to know the facts. It would be kinder if she didn't. I could use my Unattached authority to keep the truth secret from lower echelons and tell her nothing except that Keith had irrevocably died under circumstances which forced us to shut off this period to time traffic. She'd grieve awhile, of course, but she's too healthy to mourn forever...Sure, it's a lousy trick. But wouldn't it be kinder in the long run than letting her come back here, to servile status, and share her man with at least the dozen princesses that politics forces him to be married to? Wouldn't it be better for her to make a clean break and a fresh start, among her own people?

"Uh-huh," said Denison. "I mentioned that idea only to dispose of it. But there must be some other way. Look, Manse, sixteen years ago a situation existed from which everything else has followed, not through human caprice but through the sheer logic of events. Suppose I had not showed up? Mightn't Harpagus have found a different pseudo-Cyrus? The exact identity of the King doesn't matter. Another Cyrus would have acted differently from me in a million day-to-day details. Naturally. But if he wasn't a hopeless moron or maniac, if he was a reasonably able and decent person—give me credit for being that much—then his career would have been the same as mine in all the important ways, the ways that got into the history books. You know that as well as I do. Except at the crucial points, time always reverts to its own shape. The small differences damp out in days or years, negative feedback. It's only at key instants that a positive feedback can be set up and the effects multiply with passing time instead of disappearing. You know that!"

"Sure," said Everard. "But judging from your own account, your appearance in the cave *was* crucial. It was that which put the idea in Harpagus's head. Without it, well, I can imagine a decadent Median Empire falling apart, maybe falling prey to Lydia, or to the Turanians, because the Persians wouldn't have had the kind of royal divine-right-by-birth leadership they needed...No. I wouldn't come near that moment in the cave without authorization from anyone less than a Danellian."

Denison looked at him over a raised chalice, lowered it and kept on looking. His face congealed into a stranger's. He said at last, very softly:

"You don't want me to come back, do you?"

Everard leaped off the bench. He dropped his own cup; it rang on the floor and wine ran from it like blood.

"Shut up!" he yelled.

Denison nodded. "I am the King," he said. "If I raise my finger, those guards will hack you in pieces."

"That's a hell of a way to get my help," growled Everard.

Denison's body jerked. He sat motionless for a while, before he got out: "I'm sorry. You don't realize what a shock...Oh, yes, yes, it hasn't been a bad life. It's had more color in it than most, and this business of being quasi-divine grows on you. I suppose that's why I'll take the field beyond the Jaxartes, thirteen years from now: because I can't do anything else, with all those young lion eyes on me. Hell, I may even think it was worth it."

His expression writhed smilewards. "Some of my girls have been absolute knockouts. And there's always Cassandane. I made her my chief wife because in a dark way she reminds me of Cynthia. I think. It's hard to tell, after all this time. The twentieth century isn't real to me. And there's more actual satisfaction in a good horse than a sports car...and I know my work here is valuable, which isn't a knowledge granted to many...Yeh. I'm sorry I barked at you. I know you'd help if you dared. Since you don't, and I don't blame you, you needn't regret it for my sake."

"Cut that out!" groaned Everard.

It felt as if there were gears in his brain, spinning against emptiness. Overhead he saw a painted roof, where a youth killed a bull, and the Bull was the Sun and the Man. Beyond columns and vines trod guards in dragonskin mailcoats, their bows strung, their faces like carved wood. The harem wing of the palace could be glimpsed, where a hundred or a thousand young women counted themselves fortunate to await the King's occasional pleasure. Beyond the city walls lay harvest fields where peasants readied sacrifice to an Earth Mother who was old in this land when the Aryans came, and that was in a dark predawn past. High over the walls floated the mountains, haunted by wolf, lion, boar, and demon. It was too alien a place. Everard had thought himself hardened to otherness, but now he wanted suddenly to run and hide, up to his own century and his own people and a forgetting.

He said in a careful voice, "Let me consult a few associates. We can check the whole period in detail. There might be some kind of switch point where...I'm not competent to handle this alone, Keith. Let me go back upstairs and get some advice. If we work out anything we'll return to...this very night."

"Where's your scooter?" asked Denison.

Everard waved a hand. "Up in the hills."

Denison stroked his beard. 'You aren't telling me more than that, eh? Well, it's wise. I'm not sure I'd trust myself, if I knew where a time machine could be gotten."

"I don't mean that!" shouted Everard.

"Oh, never mind. Let's not fight about it." Denison sighed. "Sure, go on home and see what you can do. Want an escort?"

"Better not. It isn't necessary, is it?"

"No. We've made this area safer than Central Park."

"That isn't saying much." Everard held out his hand. "Just get me back my horse. I'd hate to lose him: special Patrol animal, trained to time hop." His gaze closed with the other man's. "I'll return. In person. Whatever the decision is."

"Sure, Manse," said Denison.

They walked out together, to go through the various formalities of notifying guardsmen and gatekeepers. Denison indicated a palace bedchamber where he said he would be every night for a week, as a rendezvous. And then at last Everard kissed the King's feet, and when the royal presence had departed he got aboard his horse and jogged slowly out through the palace gates.

He felt empty inside. There was really nothing to be done; and he had promised to come back himself and pass that sentence upon the King.

-8-

Late that day he was in the hills, where cedars gloomed above cold, brawling brooks and the side road onto which he had turned became a rutted upward track. Though arid enough, the Iran of this age still had a few such forests. The horse plodded beneath him, worn down. He should find some herdsman's house and request lodging, simply to spare the creature. But no, there would be a full moon; he could walk if he must and reach the scooter before sunrise. He didn't think he could sleep.

A place of long sere grass and ripe berries did invite him to rest, though. He had food in the saddlebags, a wineskin, and a stomach unfilled since dawn. He clucked encouragingly to the horse and turned.

Something caught his eye. Far down the road, level sunlight glowed off a dust cloud. It grew bigger even as he watched. Several riders, he guessed, coming in one devil of a hurry. King's messengers? But why, into this section? Uneasiness tickled his nerves. He put on his helmet cap, buckled the helmet itself above, hung shield on arm and loosened the short sword in its sheath. Doubtless the party would just hurry on past him, but...

Now he could see that there were eight men. They had good horseflesh beneath them, and the rearmost led a string of remounts. Nevertheless the animals were pretty jaded; sweat had made streaks down their dusty flanks and manes were plastered to necks. It must have been a long gallop. The riders were decently clad in the usual full white pants, shirt, boots, cloak, and tall brimless hat: not courtiers or professional soldiers, but not bandits either. They were armed with swords, bows, and lariats.

Suddenly Everard recognized the greybeard at their head. It exploded in him: Harpagus!

And through whirling haze he could also see—even for ancient Iranians, the followers were a tough-looking crew.

"Oh-oh," said Everard, half aloud. "School's out."

His mind clicked over. There wasn't time to be afraid, only to think. Harpagus had no other obvious motive for hightailing into the hills than to catch the Greek Meander. Surely, in a court riddled with spies and blabbermouths, Harpagus would have learned within an hour that the King spoke to the stranger as an equal in some unknown tongue and let him go back northward. It would take the Chiliarch a while longer to manufacture some excuse for leaving the palace, round up his personal bully boys, and give chase. Why? Because "Cyrus" had once appeared in these uplands, riding some device which Harpagus had coveted. No fool, the Mede must never have been satisfied with the evasive yarn Keith had handed him. It would seem reasonable that one day another mage from the King's home country must appear; and this time Harpagus would not let the engine go from him so easily.

Everard paused no longer. They were only a hundred yards away. He could see the Chiliarch's eyes glitter beneath shaggy brows. He spurred his horse, off the road and across the meadow.

"Stop!" yelled a remembered voice behind him. "Stop, Greek!"

Everard got an exhausted trot out of his mount. The cedars threw long shadows across him.

"Stop or we shoot!...halt!...shoot, then! Not to kill! Get the steed!"

At the forest edge, Everard slipped from his saddle. He heard an angry whirr and a score of thumps. The horse screamed. Everard cast a glance behind the poor beast was on its knees. By God, somebody would pay for this! But he was one man and they were eight. He hurried under the trees. A shaft smote a trunk by his left shoulder, burying itself.

He ran, crouched, zigzag in a chilly sweet-smelling twilight. Now and then a low branch whipped across his face. He could have used more underbrush, there were some Algonquian stunts for a hunted man to try, but at least the soft floor was noiseless under his sandals. The Persians were lost to sight. Almost instinctively, they had tried to ride after him. Cracking and crashing and loud obscenities ripped the air to show how well that had worked.

They'd come on foot in a minute. He cocked his head. A faint rush of water... He moved in its direction, up a steep boulder-strewn slope. His hunters were not helpless urbanites, he thought. At least some of them were sure to be mountaineers, with eyes to read the dimmest signs of his passage. He had to break the trail; then he could hole up until Harpagus must return to court duties. The breath grew harsh in his throat. Behind him voices snapped forth, a note of decision, but he couldn't make out what was said. Too far. And the blood pounded so loudly in his ears.

If Harpagus had fired on the King's guest, then Harpagus surely did not intend that that guest should ever report it to the King. Capture, torture till he revealed where the machine lay and how to operate it, and a final mercy of cold steel were the program. *Judas,* thought Everard through the clamor in his veins, *I've mucked this operation up till it's a manual of how not to be a Patrolman. And the first item is, don't think so hard about a certain girl who isn't yours that you neglect elementary precautions.*

He came out on the edge of a high, wet bank. A brook roiled valleyward below him. They'd see he had come this far, but it would be a toss-up which way he splashed in the streambed...which should it be, anyhow?...the mud was cold and slippery on his skin as he scrambled down. Better go upstream. That would bring him closer to his scooter, and Harpagus might assume it more likely he'd try to double back to the King.

Stones bruised his feet and the water numbed them. The trees made a wall above either bank, so that he was roofed by a narrow strip of sky whose blue deepened momentarily. High up there floated an eagle. The air grew colder. But he had one piece of luck: the brook twisted like a snake in delirium and he had quickly slipped and stumbled his way from sight of his entry point. *I'll* go *on a mile or so,* he thought, *and maybe there'll be an overhanging branch I can grab so I won't leave an outgoing trail.* Slow minutes passed.

So I get to the scooter, he thought, *and go upstairs and ask my chiefs for help. I know damn well they aren't going to give me any. Why not sacrifice one man to insure their own existence and everything they care about? Therefore Keith is stuck here, with thirteen years to go till the barbarians cut him down. But Cynthia will still be young in thirteen years, and after so long a nightmare of exile and knowing her man's time to die, she'd be cut off, an alien in an interdicted era, alone in the frightened court of mad Cambyses II...No, I've got to keep the truth from her, keep her at home, thinking Keith is dead. He'd want it that way himself. And after a year or two she'd be happy again; I could teach her to be happy.*

He had stopped noticing how the rocks smashed at his thinly shod feet, how his body pitched and staggered or how noisy the water was. But then he came around a bend and saw the Persians.

There were two of them, wading downstream. Evidently his capture meant enough to overcome their religious prejudice against defiling a river. Two more walked above, threading between the trees on either bank. One of the latter was Harpagus. Their long swords hissed from the scabbards.

"Stop!" called the Chiliarch. "Halt, Greek! Yield!"

Everard stood death-still. The water purled about his ankles. The pair who splashed to meet him were unreal down here in a well of shadow, their faces blotted out so that he saw only white clothes and a shimmer along curved blades. It hit him in the belly: the pursuers had seen his trail down into the brook. So they split up, half in each direction, running faster on solid ground than he could move in the bed. Having gone beyond his possible range, they started working their way back, more slowly when they were bound to the stream's course but quite certain of their quarry.

"Take him alive," reminded Harpagus. "Hamstring him if you must, but take him alive."

Everard snarled and turned toward that bank. "Okay, buster, you asked for it," he said in English. The two men in the water yelled and began to run. One tripped and went on his face. The man opposite tobogganed down the slope on his backside.

The mud was slippery. Everard chopped the lower edge of his shield into it and toiled up. Harpagus moved coolly to await him. As he came near, the old noble's blade whirred, striking from above. Everard rolled his head and caught the blow on his helmet, which bonged. The edge slid down a cheekpiece and cut his right shoulder, but not badly. He felt only a sting and then was too busy to feel anything.

He didn't expect to win out. But he would make them kill him, and pay for the privilege.

He came onto grass and raised his shield just in time to protect his eyes. Harpagus probed for the knees. Everard beat that aside with his own short sword. The Median saber whistled. But at close quarters a lightly armed Asian hadn't a chance against the hoplite, as history was to prove a couple of generations hence. *By God,* thought Everard, *if only I had cuirass and greaves, I might be able to take all four of 'em!* He used his big shield with skill, put it in front of every blow and thrust, and always worked near to get beneath the longer blade and into Harpagus's defenseless guts.

The Chiliarch grinned tautly through tangled gray whiskers and skipped away. A play for time, of course. It succeeded. The other three men climbed the bank, shouted and rushed. It was a disorderly attack. Superb fighters as individuals, the Persians had never developed the mass discipline of Europe, on which they would break themselves at Marathon and Gaugamela. But four against unarmored one was impossible odds.

Everard got his back to a tree bole. The first man came in recklessly, sword clashing on the Greek shield. Everard's blade darted from behind the bronze oblong. There was a soft, somehow heavy resistance. He knew that feeling from other days, pulled his weapon out and stepped quickly aside. The Persian sat down, spilling out his life. He groaned once, saw he was a dead man, and raised his face toward the sky.

His mates were already at Everard, one to a side. Overhanging boughs made lassos useless; they would have to do battle. The Patrolman held off the left-hand blade with his shield. That exposed his right ribs, but since his opponents were ordered not to kill he could afford it. The right-hand man slashed at Everard's ankles. Everard sprang in the air and the sword hissed under his feet. The left-hand attacked, stabbed low. Everard sensed a dull shock and saw steel in his calf. He jerked free. A sunset ray came between bunched needles and touched the blood, making it an impossibly brilliant red. Everard felt that leg buckle under him.

"So, so," cried Harpagus, hovering ten feet away. "Chop him!"

Everard growled above his shield rim: "A task your jackal leader has no courage to attempt for himself, after I drove him back with his tail between his legs!"

It was calculated. The attack on him stopped a bare instant. He reeled forward. "If you Persians must be the dogs of a Mede," he croaked, "can you not choose a Mede who is a man, rather than this creature which betrayed its king and now runs from a single Greek?"

Even this far west and this long ago, an Oriental could not lose face in such a manner. Not that Harpagus had ever been a coward; Everard knew how unfair his taunts were. But the Chiliarch spat a curse and dashed at him. Everard had a moment's glimpse of eyes wild in a sunken hook-nosed face. He lumbered lopsidedly forward. The two Persians hesitated for a second more. That was long enough for Everard and Harpagus to meet The Median blade rose and fell, bounced off Greek helmet and shield, snaked sideways for another leg cut. A loose white tunic flapped before Everard's gaze. He hunched shoulders and drove his sword in.

He withdrew it with the cruel professional twist which assures a mortal wound, pivoted on his right heel, and caught a blow on his shield. For a minute he and one Persian traded fury. At the edge of an eye, he saw the other circling about to get behind him. Well, he thought in a remote way, he had killed the one man dangerous to Cynthia...

"Hold! Halt!"

The call was a weak flutter in the air, less loud than the mountain stream, but the warriors stepped back and lowered their weapons. Even the dying Persian took his eyes from heaven.

Harpagus struggled to sit up, in a puddle of his own blood. His skin was turned gray. "No...hold," he whispered. "Wait. There is a purpose here. Mithras would not have struck me down unless..."

He beckoned, a somehow lordly gesture. Everard dropped his sword, limped over and knelt by Harpagus. The Mede sank back into his arms.

"You are from the King's homeland," he rasped in the bloody beard. "Do not deny that But know...Aurvagaush the son of Khshayavarsha...is no traitor." The thin form stiffened itself, imperious, as if ordering death to wait upon its pleasure. "I knew there were powers—of heaven, of hell, I know not which to this day—powers behind the King's advent. I used them, I used him, not for myself, but because I had sworn loyalty to my own king, Astyages, and he needed a... a Cyrus...lest the realm be torn asunder. Afterward, by his cruelty, Astyages forfeited my oath. But I was still a Mede. I saw in Cyrus the only hope—the best hope—of Media. For he has been a good king to us also—we are honored in his domains second only to the Persians...Do you understand, you from the King's home?" Dim eyes rolled about, trying to see into Everard's but without enough control. "I wanted to capture you—to force your engine and its use from you, and then to kill you...yes...but not for my own gain. It was for the realm's. I feared you would take the King home, as I know he has longed to go. And what would become of us? Be merciful, as you too must hope for mercy."

"I shall," said Everard. "The King will remain."

"It is well," sighed Harpagus. "I believe you speak the truth...I dare not believe otherwise...Then I have atoned?" he asked in a thin anxious voice. "For the murder I did at my old king's behest—that I laid a helpless infant upon the mountainside and watched him die—have I atoned, King's countryman? For it was that prince's death...which brought the land close to ruin...but I found another Cyrus! I saved us! Have I atoned?"

"You have," said Everard, and wondered how much absolution it lay in his power to give.

Harpagus closed his eyes. "'Then leave me," he said like the fading echo of a command.

Everard laid him upon the earth and hobbled away. The two Persians knelt by their master, performing certain rites. The third man returned to his own contemplations. Everard sat down under a tree, tore a strip from his cloak and bandaged his hurts. The leg cut would need attention. Somehow he must get to the scooter. That wouldn't be fun, but he could manage it and then a Patrol doctor could repair him in a few hours with a medical science future to his home era. He'd go to some branch office in an obscure milieu, because there'd be too many questions in the twentieth century.

And he couldn't afford that. If his superiors knew what he planned, they would probably forbid it.

The answer had come to him not as a blinding revelation, but as a tired consciousness of knowledge which he might well have had subconsciously for a long time. He leaned back, getting his breath. The other four Persians arrived and were told what had happened. All of them ignored Everard, except for glances where terror struggled with pride, and made furtive signs against evil. The lifted their dead chief and their dying companion and bore them into the forest. Darkness thickened. Somewhere an owl hooted.

-9-

The Great King sat up in bed. He had heard a noise beyond the curtains.

Cassandane, the Queen, stirred invisibly. One slim hand touched his face. "What is it, sun of my heaven?" she asked.

"I do not know." He fumbled for the sword which lay always beneath his pillow. "Nothing."

Her palm slipped down over his breast. "No, it is much," she whispered, suddenly shaken. "Your heart goes like a war drum."

"Stay there." He trod out past the drapes.

Moonlight streamed from a deep-purple sky, through an arched window to the floor. It glanced almost blindingly off a bronze mirror. The air was cold upon bare skin.

A thing of dark metal, whose rider gripped two handlebars and touched tiny controls on a panel, drifted like another shadow. It landed on the carpet without a sound and the rider got off. He was a burly man in Grecian tunic and helmet. "Keith," he breathed.

"Manse!" Denison stepped into the moonlight. "You came!"

"Tell me more," snorted Everard sarcastically. "Think anybody will hear us? I don't believe I was noticed. Materialized directly over the roof and floated slowly down on antigrav."

"There are guards just outside the door," said Denison, "but they won't come in unless I strike that gong, or yell."

"Good. Put on some clothes."

Denison dropped his sword. He stood rigid for an instant, then it blazed from him: "You've got a way out?"

"Maybe. Maybe." Everard looked away from the other man, drummed fingers on his machine's control panel. "Look, Keith," he said at last, "I've an idea which might or might not work. I'll need your help to carry it out. If it does work, you can go home. The front office will accept a *fait accompli* and wink at any broken regulations. But if it fails, you'll have to come back to this very night and live out your life as Cyrus. Can you do that?"

Denison shivered with more than chill. Very low: "I think so."

"I'm stronger than you are," said Everard roughly, "and I'll have the only weapons. If necessary, I'll shanghai you back here. Please don't make me."

Denison drew a long breath. "I won't."

"Then let's hope the Norns cooperate. Come on, get dressed. I'll explain as we go. Kiss this year good-bye, and trust it isn't 'So long'—because if my notion pans out, neither you nor anyone else will ever see it again."

Denison, who had half turned to the garments thrown in a corner for a slave to replace before dawn, stopped. "What?" he said.

"We're going to try rewriting history," said Everard. "Or maybe to restore the history which was there in the first place. I don't know. Come on, hop to it!"

"But—"

"Quick, man, quick! D'you realize I came back to the same day as I left you, that at this moment I'm crawling through the mountains with one leg stabbed open, just to save you that extra time? Get moving!"

Decision closed upon Denison. His face was in darkness, but he spoke very low and clear: "I've got one personal good-bye to say."

"What?"

"Cassandane. She's been my wife here for, God, for fourteen years! She's borne me three children, and nursed me through two fevers and a hundred fits of despair, and once when the Medes were at our gates she led the women of Pasargadae out to rally us and we won...Give me five minutes, Manse."

"All right, all right. Though it'll take more than that to send a eunuch to her room and—"

"She's here."

Denison vanished behind the bed curtains.

Everard stood for a moment as if struck. *You expected me to come tonight,* he thought, *and you hoped I'd be able to take you back to Cynthia. So you sent for Cassandane.*

And then, when his fingertips had begun to hurt from the tightness of his grip on the sword hilt: *Oh, shut up, Everard, you smug self-righteous whelp.*

Presently Denison came back. He did not speak as he put on his clothes and mounted the rear seat on the scooter. Everard space-hopped, an instantaneous jump; the room vanished and moonlight flooded the hills far below. A cold gust searched around the men in the sky.

"Now for Ecbatana." Everard turned on his dashlight and adjusted controls according to notes scribbled on the pilot pad.

"Ec—Oh, you mean Hagmatan? The old Median capital?" Denison sounded astonished. "But it's only a summer residence now."

"I mean Ecbatana thirty-six years ago," said Everard.

"Huh?"

"Look, all the scientific historians in the future are convinced that the story of Cyrus's childhood as told by Herodotus and the Persians is pure fable. Well, maybe they were right all along. Maybe your experiences here have been only one of those little quirks in space-time which the Patrol tries to eliminate."

"I see," said Denison slowly.

"You were at Astyages's court pretty often when you were his vassal, I suppose. Okay, you guide me. We want the old guy himself, preferably alone at night."

"Sixteen years was a long time," said Denison.

"Hm?"

"If you're trying to change the past anyway, why use me at this point? Come get me when I'd been Cyrus only one year, long enough to be familiar with Ecbatana but—"

"Sorry, no. I don't dare. We're steering close enough to the wind as is. Lord knows what a secondary loop in the world lines could lead to. Even if we got away with it, the Patrol would send us both to the exile planet for taking that kind of chance."

"Well...yes. I see your point."

"Also," said Everard, "you're not a suicidal type. Would you actually want the you of this instant never to have existed? Think for a minute precisely what that implies."

He completed his settings. The man behind him shuddered. "Mithras!" said Denison. "You're right. Let's not talk about it."

"Here goes, then." Everard threw the main switch.

He hung over a walled city on an unfamiliar plain. Though this was also a moonlit night, the city was only a black huddle to his eyes. He reached into the saddlebags. "Here," he said. "Let's put on these costumes. I had the boys in the Middle Mohenjodaro office fix 'em up to my specs. Their situation is such that they often need this type of disguise for themselves."

Air whistled darkly as the hopper slanted earthward. Denison reached an arm past Everard to point. "That's the palace. The royal bedchamber is over on the east side..."

It was a heavier, less graceful building than its Persian successor in Pasargadae. Everard glimpsed a pair of winged bulls, white in an autumnal garden, left over from the Assyrians. He saw that the windows before him were too narrow for entrance, swore, and aimed at the nearest doorway. A pair of mounted sentries looked up, saw what was coming, and shrieked. Their horses reared, throwing them. Everard's machine splintered the door. One more miracle wasn't going to affect history, especially when such things were believed in as devoutly as vitamin pills at home, and possibly with more reason. Lamps guided him down a corridor where slaves and guards squalled their terror. At the royal bedroom he drew his sword and knocked with the pommel. "Take over, Keith," he said. "You know the Median version of Aryan."

"Open, Astyages!" roared Denison. "Open to the messengers of Ahuramazda!"

Somewhat to Everard's surprise, the man within obeyed. Astyages was as brave as most of his people. But when the king—a thickset, hardfaced person in early middle age—saw two beings, luminously robed, halos around their heads and fountaining wings of light on their back seated on an iron throne in midair, he fell prostrate.

Everard heard Denison thunder in the best tent-meeting style, using a dialect he could barely follow:

"O infamous vessel of iniquity, heaven's anger is upon you! Do you believe that your least thought, though it skulk in the darkness which begot it, was ever hidden from the Day's Eye? Do you believe that almighty Ahuramazda would permit a deed so foul as you plot..."

Everard didn't listen. He strayed into his own thoughts: Harpagus was probably somewhere in this very city, full of his youth and unridden as yet by guilt. Now he would never bear that burden. He would never lay a child upon the mountain and lean on his spear as it cried and shivered and finally became still. He would revolt in the future, for his own reasons, and become the Chiliarch of Cyrus, but he would not die in his enemy's arms in a haunted forest; and a certain Persian, whose name Everard did not know, would also be spared a Greek sword and a slow falling into emptiness.

Yet the memory of two men whom I killed is *printed on my brain cells; there is a thin white scar on my leg; Keith Denison* is *forty-seven years old and has learned to think like a king.*

"...Know, Astyages, that this child Cyrus is favored of heaven. And heaven is merciful: you have been warned that if you stain your soul with his innocent blood, the sin can never be washed away. Leave Cyrus to grow up in Anshan, or burn forever with Ahriman! Mithras has spoken!"

Astyages groveled, beating his head on the floor.

"Let's go," said Denison in English.

Everard hopped to Persian hills, thirty-six years futureward. Moonlight fell upon cedars near a road and a stream. It was cold, and a wolf howled.

He landed the scooter, got off and began to remove his costume. Denison's bearded face came out of the mask with strangeness written upon it. "I wonder," he said. His voice was nearly lost in the silence under the mountains. "I wonder if we didn't throw too much of a scare into Astyages. History does record that he gave Cyrus a three-year fight when the Persians revolted."

"We can always go back to the outbreak of the war and provide a vision encouraging him to resist," said Everard, straggling to be matter-of-fact; for there were ghosts around him. "But I don't believe that'll be necessary. He'll keep hands off the prince, but when a vassal rebels, well, he'll be mad enough to discount what by then will seem like a dream. Also, his own nobles, Median vested interests, would hardly allow him to give in. But let's check up. Doesn't the King lead a procession at the winter solstice festival?"

"Yeah. Let's go. Quickly."

And the sunlight burned around them, high above Pasargadae. They left their machine hidden and walked down on foot, two travelers among many streaming in to celebrate the Birthday of Mithras. On the way, they inquired what had happened, explaining that they had been long abroad. The answers satisfied them, even in small details which Denison's memories recorded but the chronicles hadn't mentioned.

At last they stood under a frosty-blue sky, among thousands of people, and salaamed when Cyrus the Great King rode past with his chief courtiers Kobad, Croesus, and Harpagus, and the pride and pomp and priesthood of Persia followed.

"He's younger than I was," whispered Denison. "He would be, I guess. And a little smaller...different face entirely, isn't it?...but he'll do."

"Want to stay for the fun?" asked Everard.

Denison drew his cloak around him. The air was bitter. "No," he said. "Let's go back. It's been a long time. Even if it never happened."

"Uh-huh." Everard seemed more grim than a victorious rescuer should be. "It never happened."

-10-

Keith Denison left the elevator of a building in New York. He was vaguely surprised that he had not remembered what it looked like. He couldn't even recall his apartment number, but had to check with the directory. Details, details. He tried to stop trembling.

Cynthia opened the door as he reached it. "Keith," she said, almost wonderingly.

He could find no other words than: "Manse warned you about me, didn't he? He said he would."

"Yes. It doesn't matter. I didn't realize your looks would have changed that much. But it doesn't matter. Oh, my darling!"

She drew him inside, closed the door and crept into his arms.

He looked around the place. He had forgotten how cramped it was. And he had never liked her taste in decoration, though he had yielded to her.

The habit of giving in to a woman, even of asking her opinion, was one he'd have to learn all over again. It wouldn't be easy.

She raised a wet face for his kiss. Was *that* how she looked? But he didn't remember—he didn't. After all that time, he had only remembered she was little and blond. He had lived with her a few months; Cassandane had called him her morning star and given him thee children and waited to do his will for fourteen years.

"Oh, Keith, welcome home," said the high small voice.

Home! he thought. *God!*

Midsummer Song

In silver-blue, the dew lies bright.
        The midsummer night
            Is abrim with light.
Come take each other by the hand,
        For music has wakened
            All over the land.
Go gladly up and gladly down.
        The dancing flies outward like laughter
From blossomfield to mountain crown.
        Rejoice in the joy that comes after!

The music sparkles fleet and sweet.
        She sways there before him
            On eager feet,
So lithe and blithe, and garlanded
        With roses and starshine
            Around her dear head.
Go gladly up and gladly down.
        The dancing flies outward like laughter
From blossomfield to mountain crown.
Rejoice in the joy that comes after!

He spurns the turf that once he paced.
        His arms throw a glowing
            Around her waist,
And whirled across the world, she sees
        Him light as the wind and
            More tall than the trees.
Go gladly up and gladly down.
        The dancing flies outward like laughter
From blossomfield to mountain crown.
Rejoice in the joy that comes after!

The peak grows gold, the east grows white,
        A breeze pipes the end
            Of the summer night,
And wide across a widespread land
        The dancers turn homeward with
            Hand laid in hand.
Go gladly up and gladly down.
        The dancing flies outward like laughter
From blossomfield to mountain crown.
Rejoice in the joy that comes after!

Christa McAuliffe

Where do we come from, students? We don't know—
Some hunters following the wet moraines
On windy heathlands where the ice had been
In search of reindeer? Odysseus himself
Was only beating homeward from his war,
And Hanno saw the sun impossibly
To northward while he groped out routes of trade.
Prince Henry dreamed a way to India—
And so Columbus; but a whole new world
Arose between him and the Asian wealth:
A world where ancient hopes could be reborn.
Then Galileo, being curious,
Looked up and found new worlds beyond the world.
There is another dream that drives us forth
Than hope of profit. Students, call the roll
Of Amerigo, Cook, Scott, Amundsen,
And many more who sought beyond the edge
Where stars go disappearing—but who knows
What profit there may come, of human joy
And human freedom, from the things we find?
We go to seek. And, students, as we die
We leave the heritage of search to you.

Brake

In that hour, when he came off watch, Captain Peter Banning did not go directly to his cabin. He felt a wish for uninhibited humor, such as this bleak age could not bring to life (except maybe in the clan gatherings of Venus—but Venus was *too* raw), and remembered that Luke Devon had a Shakespeare. It was a long time since Banning had last read *The Taming of the Shrew.* He would drop in and borrow the volume, possibly have a small drink and a chinfest. The Planetary Engineer was unusually worth talking to.

So it was that he stepped out of the companionway into A-deck corridor and saw Devon backed up against the wall at gun point.

Banning had not stayed alive as long as this—a good deal longer than he admitted—through unnecessary heroics. He slid back, flattened himself against the aluminum side of the stairwell, and stretched his ears. Very gently, one hand removed the stubby pipe from his teeth and slipped it into a pocket of his tunic, to smolder itself out. The fumes might give him away to a sensitive nose, and he was unarmed.

Devon spoke softly, with rage chained in his throat: "The devil damn thee black, thou cream-faced loon!"

"Not so hasty," advised the other person. It was the Minerals Authority representatives, Serge Andreyev, a large hairy man who dressed and talked too loudly. "I do not wish to kill you. This is just a needler in my hand. But I have also a gun for blowing out brains—if required."

His English bore its usual accent, but the tone had changed utterly. It was not the timbre of an irritating extrovert; there was no particular melodrama intended; Andreyev was making a cool statement of fact.

"It is unfortunate for me that you recognized me through all the surgical changes," he went on. "It is still more unfortunate for you that I was armed. Now we shall bargain."

"Perhaps." Devon had grown calmer. Banning could visualize him, backed up against the wall, hands in the air: a tall man, cat-lithe under the austere stiffness of his Order, close-cropped yellow hair and ice-blue eyes, and a prow of nose jutting from the bony face. *I wouldn't much like to have that hombre on my tail,* reflected Banning.

"Perhaps," repeated Devon. "Has it occurred to you, though, that a steward, a deck-hand...anyone...may be along at any moment?"

"Just so. Into my cabin. There we shall talk some more."

"But it *is* infernally awkward for you," said Devon. "'Is it a world to hide virtues in?—or prisoners, for that matter? Here we are, beyond Mars, with another two weeks before we reach Jupiter. There are a good fifteen people aboard, passengers and crew—not much, perhaps, for a ship as big as the *Thunderbolt*, but enough to search her pretty thoroughly if anyone disappears. You can't just cram me out any convenient air lock, you know, not without getting the keys from an officer. Neither can you keep me locked away without inquiries as to why I don't show up for meals...I assure you, if you haven't noticed, my appetite is notorious. Therefore, dear old chap—"

"We will settle this later," snapped Andreyev. "Quickly, now, go to my cabin. I shall be behind. If necessary, I will needle you and drag you there."

Devon was playing for time, thought Banning. If the tableau of gunman and captive remained much longer in the passageway, someone was bound to come by and—*As a matter of fact, son, someone already has.*

The captain slipped a hand into his pouch. He had a number of coins: not that they'd be any use on Ganymede, but he didn't want to reenter Union territory without beer cash. He selected several of nearly uniform size and tucked them as a stack into his fist. It was a very old stunt.

Then, with the quick precision of a hunter—which he had been now and then, among other things—he glided from the companionway. Andreyev had just turned his back, marching Devon up the hall toward Cabin 5. Peter Banning's weighted fist smote him at the base of the skull.

Devon whirled, a tiger in gray. Banning eased Andreyev to the floor with one hand; the other took the stun pistol, not especially aimed at the Engineer nor especially aimed away from him. "Take it easy, friend," he murmured.

"You...oh!" Devon eased, muscle by muscle. A slow grin crossed his face. "For this relief, much thanks."

"What's going on here?" asked the captain.

There was a moment of stillness. Only the ship spoke, with a whisper of ventilators. The sound might almost have belonged to that night of cold stars through which she hurled.

"Well?" said Banning impatiently.

Devon stood for an instant longer, as if taking his measure. The captain was a stocky man of medium height, with faintly grizzled black hair clipped short on a long head. His face was broad, it bore high cheekbones, and its dark-white skin had a somehow ageless look: deep trenches from wide nose to big mouth, crow's-feet around the bony-ridged gray eyes, otherwise smooth as a child's. He did not wear the trim blue jacket and white trousers of the Fireball Line but favored a Venusian-style beret and kilt, Arabian carpet slippers, a disreputable old green tunic of possibly Martian origin.

"I don't know," said the Planetary Engineer at last. "He just pulled that gun on me."

"Sorry, I heard a bit of the talk between you. Now come clean. I'm responsible for this ship, and I want to know what's going on."

"So do I," said Devon grimly. "I'm not really trying to stall you, skipper—not much, anyway." He stooped over Andreyev and searched the huddled body. "Ah, yes, here's that other gun he spoke of, the lethal one."

"Give me that!" Banning snatched it. The metal was cold and heavy in his grasp. It came to him with a faint shock that he himself and his entire crew had nothing more dangerous between them than some knives and monkey wrenches. A spaceship was not a Spanish caravel, her crew had no reason to arm against pirates or mutiny or—

Or did they?

"Go find a steward," snapped Banning. "Come back here with him. Mr. Andreyev goes in irons for the rest of the trip."

"Irons?" Under the cowl of his gray tunic, Devon's brows went up.

"Chains...restraint...hell, we'll lock him away. I've got a bad habit of using archaisms. Now, jump!"

The Engineer went quickly down the hall. Banning lounged back, twirling the gun by its trigger guard, and watched him go.

Where had he seen the fellow before?

He searched a cluttered memory for a tall blond man who was athlete, technician, Shakespearean enthusiast, and amateur painter in oils. Perhaps it was only someone he had read about, with a portrait; there was so much history—Wait. The Rostomily brotherhood. Of course. But that was three centuries ago!

Presumably someone, somewhere, had kept a few cells in storage, after that corps of exogenetic twins had finally made their secret open, disbanded, and mingled their superior genes in the common human lifestream. And then, perhaps thirty years ago, the Engineers had quietly grown such a child in a tank. Maybe a lot of them. Also anything could happen in that secret castle on the rim of Archimedes Crater, and the Solar System none the wiser till the project exploded in man's collective face.

The brotherhood had been a trump card of the early Un-men, in the days when world government was frail and embattled. A revived brotherhood must be of comparable importance to the Order. But for what purpose? The Engineers, quasi-military, almost religious, were supposed to be above politics; they were supposed to serve all men, an independent force whose only war was against the inanimate cosmos.

Banning felt a chill. With the civilization-splitting tension that existed on Earth and was daily wrung one notch higher, he could imagine what hidden struggles took place between the many factions. It wasn't all psychodynamics, telecampaigning or parliamentary maneuver: the Humanist episode had scarred Earth's soul, and now there were sometimes knives in the night.

Somehow an aspect of those battles had focused on his ship.

He took out his pipe, rekindled it, and puffed hard. Andreyev stirred, with a retch and a rattle in his throat.

There was a light footfall in the corridor. Banning looked up. He would have cursed the interruption had anyone but Cleonie Rogers appeared. As it was, he made the forgotten gesture of raising his cap.

"Oh!" Her hand went to her mouth. For an instant she looked frightened, then came forward in a way he liked: the more so as she had been consistently annoyed by Andreyev's loud attempts to flirt. "Oh, is he hurt? Can I help?"

"Better stand back, m'lady," advised Banning. She saw the stunner in his hand and the automatic in his waistband. Her lips parted in the large-eyed, snub-nosed face. With the yellow hair that fell softly down to bare shoulders, with a wholly feminine topless shimmergown and a whisper of cosmetics, she was a small walking anachronism.

"What happened?" A shaken courage rallied in her. It was well done, thought the man, considering that she was a child of wealth, never done a day's work in her life, bound for the Jovian Republic as an actual live tourist.

"That's what I'd kind of like to know," he told her. "This character here pulled an equalizer—a gun, I mean—on Engineer Devon. Then I came along and sapped him."

He saw her stiffen. Even aboard the *Thunderbolt*, which was not one of the inner-planet luxury liners but a freighter whose few passengers—except her—were bound for Ganymede on business...even here there were dimly lit corners and piped music and the majesty of the stars. Banning had noticed how much she and Devon had been together. Therefore he said kindly: "Oh, Luke wasn't hurt. I sent him for help. Must say it's taking him one hell of a time, too. Did the stewards crawl into the fire chamber for a nap?"

She smiled uncertainly. "What do you think the trouble is, Captain? Did Mr. Andreyev, ah—"

"Slip a cog?" Banning scowled. In his preoccupation he forgot that the rising incidence of nonsanity on Earth made the subject unfit for general conversation. "I doubt it. He came aboard with these toys, remember. I wonder, though. Now that the topic has come up, we do have a rum lot of passengers."

Devon was legitimate enough, his mind continued: a genuine Engineer, nursemaiding the terraforming equipment which was the *Thunderbolt's* prime cargo, the great machines which the Order would use to make Europa habitable.

And Cleonie must be an authentic tourist. (Since he regarded her as a woman, which he did not the crop-headed, tight-lipped, sad-clad creature that was today's typical Western Terrestrial female, Banning thought of her by her first name.) On the other, hand—

Andreyev was not a simple Union bureaucrat, sent to negotiate a trade agreement; or, if he was, he was also much more, and how about the big fellow, Robert Falken, allegedly a nucleonic technie offered a job on Callisto? He didn't say much at table, kept to himself, but Banning knew a hard, tough man when he saw one. And Morgan Gentry, astronaut, who said the Republic had hired him to pilot inter-satellite shuttles—undoubtedly a trained spaceman, but what was he besides that? And the exchange professor of advanced symbolics, dome-healed little Gomez, was he really bound for a position at the new University of X?

The girl's voice interrupted his reverie: "Captain Banning...what *could* be the matter with the passengers? They're all Westerners, aren't they?"

He could still be shocked, just a little bit every now and then. He hesitated a second before realizing that she had spoken not in ill will but from blank naiveté. "What has that got to do with it?" he said. "You don't really think, do you, Miss, that the conflict on Earth is a simple question of Oriental Kali worshipers versus a puritanical protechnological Occident?" He paused for breath, then plowed on: "Why, the Kali people are only one branch of the Ramakrishian Eclectics, and there are plenty of Asians who stand by population control and Technic civilization—I have a couple in my own crew—and there are Americans who worship the Destroyer as fervently as any Ganges River farmer—and the Husseinite Moslems are closer to you, Miss Rogers, than you are to the New Christendom—"

He broke off, shaking his head. It was too big to be neatly summarized, the schism which threatened to rip Earth apart. He might have said it boiled down to the fact that technology had failed to solve problems which must be solved; but he didn't want to phrase it thus, because it would sound antiscientific, and he wasn't.

Thank all kindly gods that there were men on other planets now! The harvest of all the patient centuries since Galileo would not be entirely lost, whatever happened to Earth.

Andreyev pulled himself up till he rested on his hands, head dangling between his shoulders. He groaned.

"I wonder how much of that is put on," mused Banning. "I did a well-calibrated job of slugging him. He shouldn't be too badly concussed." He gave Cleonie a beady look. "Maybe we ought to haul him into a cabin at that. Don't want to rattle any other cash customers, do we? Where are they all, anyway?"

"*I'm* not sure. I just left my cabin—" She stopped.

Someone came running from aft. The curvature of the hall, which was wrapped around the inner skin of the ship, made it impossible to see more than about forty meters. Banning shifted his gun, warily.

It was the large square-faced man, Falken, who burst into view. "Captain!" he shouted. The metal that enclosed all of them gave his tone a faint, unhuman resonance. "Captain, what happened?"

"How do you *know* about it, son?"

"A...eh...Engineer Devon—" Falken jogged to a halt; a meter away. "He told me—"

"Told you? Well, did he now?" Banning's gray gaze narrowed. Suddenly the needler in his hand leaped up and found an aim. "Hold it. Hold it there, pardner, and reach."

Falken flushed red. "What the ruination do you mean?"

"I mean that if you even look like you're going after a gun, I'll put you to sleep," said Banning. "Then if it turns out you only intended to offer me a peanut butter sandwich, I'll beg your humble pardon. But something sure smells here."

Falken backed away. "All right, all right, I'll go," he snarled. "I just wanted to help."

Cleonie screamed.

As Andreyev's burly form tackled him by the ankles and he went down, Banning knew a moment of rage at himself. He had been civilized too long…inexcusably careless of him—'Sbones and teeth!

He hit the deck with the other man on top. The red face glared murder. Andreyev yanked at the gun in Banning's kilt with one hand, his other grabbed the arm holding the stun pistol.

Banning brought his hard forehead up, into Andreyev's mouth. The fellow screamed. His fingers released the stunner. At that moment Falken joined the fight, snatching the sleep weapon before Banning could get it into action.

The skipper reached up with an efficiently unsportsmanlike thumb. He had not quite gouged out Andreyev's eye when the man bellowed and tried to scramble free. Banning rolled away. Falken fired at him. An anesthetic dart broke near Banning's nose, and he caught a whiff of vapor.

For a moment, while the universe waltzed around him, Banning accomplished nothing more than to reel to his feet. Falken sidestepped the weeping Andreyev, shoved the captain back against the wall, and yanked the automatic from his waistband. Cleonie came from behind and threw her arms around Falken's neck.

He shouted, bent his back, and tossed her from him. But it had been enough of a distraction. Banning aimed a kick for the solar plexus. Both guns went on a spin from Falken's hands.

Banning's sole had encountered hard muscle. Falken recovered fast enough to make a jump for the nearest weapon. Banning put a large foot on it. "Oh, no, you don't," he growled.

Falken sprang at him. It was not the first time Banning had been in a party which got rough, and he did not waste energy on fisticuffs. His hand snapped forward, open, the edge of a horny palm driving into Falken's larynx. There was a snapping noise.

Falken fell backward, over Andreyev, who still whimpered and dabbed at his injured eye. Banning stooped for the gun.

A bullet smashed down the corridor, ricocheted, and whined around his ears. Gentry came into view, with the drop on him.

"Oh, oh," said Banning. "School's out." He scooped up Cleonie and scampered back into the companionway.

Up the stairwell! His weight lessened with every jump as he got closer to the ship's axis of spin.

Passing C-deck, he collided with Charles Wayne. The young second mate had obviously been yanked from sleep by the racket. He was pulling on his gold-collared blue uniform jacket as he entered the companionway. "Follow me!" puffed Banning.

Gentry appeared at the foot of the stairs. The automatic in his grasp found an aim on the captain's stomach. "Stay there!" he rapped. "Raise your hands!"

Banning threw himself and Cleonie backward, into C-deck corridor. The bullet snapped viciously past Wayne's head. "Come on, I told you!" gasped Banning. "Get her to the bridge!"

Wayne looked altogether bewildered, but any spaceman learns to react fast. He slung the girl over his shoulder and dashed down the hall toward an alternate stairwell. Banning followed. He heard Gentry's shoes clang on metal, up the steps after him. As he ran, he groped after his pipe lighter, got it out, and thumbed the switch.

There were rails and stanchions along the wall, for use in null-gravity. Aided by his lessened weight, Banning swarmed ape fashion up the nearest and waved his flame beneath a small circle in the ceiling.

Then down again, toward the stair! Gentry burst into the hall and fired. Coriolis force deflected the bullet, it fanned the captain's cheek. The next one would be more carefully aimed.

The ceiling thermocouple reacted to heat, flashed a signal, and put the C-deck fire extinguisher system into action with a lather of plastifoam. Gentry's second shot flew off to nowhere. Thereafter he struggled with the stuff while Banning scampered up the stairs.

The bridge was a bubble in the ship's nose, precisely centered on the axis of rotation. There was virtually no weight, only a wilderness of gleaming consoles and the great viewscreen ablaze with its simulacrum of the sky.

Cleonie hung on to a stanchion, torn and shaken by the wretchedness of sudden, unaccustomed free fall. Tetsuo Tokugawa, the first mate, whose watch this was, floated next to her, offering an antidizzy pill. Wayne crouched by the door, wild-eyed. "What's going on, sir?" he croaked.

"I'm curious to know myself," panted Banning. "But it's all hell let out for noon."

Tokugawa gave him a despairing look. "Can you stuff this pill down her throat, skipper?" he begged. "I've seen people toss their dinner in null-gee."

"Uh, yeah, it is rather urgent." Banning hooked a knee around a stanchion, took the girl's head in one hand, and administered the medicine veterinary fashion. Meanwhile he clipped forth his story.

Tokugawa whistled. "What the destruction is this?" he said. "Mutiny?"

"If passengers can mutiny…neat point of law, that. Be quiet." Banning cocked his head and listened. There was no sound from the passages beyond the open door. He closed and bolted it.

Wayne looked sick. He wasn't a bad young fellow, thought the captain, but he was brought up in the puritan reaction of today's Western peoples. He was less afraid of danger, now, than stunned by a kick to his sense of propriety. Tokugawa was more reliable, being Lunar City bred, with all the Lunar colonist's cat-footed cosmopolitanism.

"What are we going to do?" rasped the second mate. "Find out things," grunted Banning. He soared across to the intercom cabinet, entered it, and flicked switches. The first thing he wanted was information about the ship. If that failed them, it would be a long walk home.

The *Thunderbolt* was a steelloy spheroid, flattened along the axis of the drive-tubes whose skeletal structure jutted like an ancient oil derrick from the stern. She was a big ship: her major diameter more than three hundred meters; she was a powerful ship: not required to drift along a Hohmann ellipse, but moving at a speed which took her on a hyperbolic orbit—from Earth Station Prime to the Jovian System in less than a month! But she had her limitations.

She was not intended to enter an atmosphere, but orbited and let shuttle-boats bring or remove her cargo. This was less because of the great mass of her double hull—that wasn't too important, when you put atomic nuclei to work for you—than because of the design itself. To build up her fantastic velocities, she must spurt out ions at nearly the speed of light: which required immensely long accelerating tubes, open to the vacuum of space. They would arc over and burn out if air surrounded the charged rings.

She carried no lifeboat. If you abandon ship at hyperbolic speeds, a small craft doesn't have engine enough to decelerate you before running out of reaction mass. Here, in the big cold darkness beyond Mars, there was no escaping this vessel.

Banning tuned in the screen before him. It gave two-way visual contact between a few key points, in case of emergency. "And if this ain't an emergency," he muttered, "it'll do till one comes along."

First, the biotic plant, armored at the heart of the ship. He breathed a gusty sigh. No one had tampered with that—air and water were still being renewed.

Next, the control gyros. The screen showed him their housing, like the pillars of some heathen temple. In the free fall at the ship's axis, a dead man drifted past them. The slow air currents turned him over and over. When his gaping face nudged the screen pickup, Banning recognized Tietjens, one of the two stewards. He had been shot through the head, and there was a grisly little cloud of red and gray floating around him.

Banning's lips grew thin. "I was supposed to look after you," he mumbled. "I'm sorry, Joppe."

He switched to the engine room. His view was directed toward the main control board, also in the axial null-gee state. The face that looked back at him, framed by the tall machines, belonged to Professor Gomez.

Banning sucked in a breath. "What are you doing there?" he said.

"Oh…it's you, Captain. I rather expected you to peer in. "The little man shoved himself forward with a groundlubber's awkwardness, but he was calm, not spacesick at all. "Quite a job you did on Falken. He's dead."

"Too bad you weren't in on that party," said Banning. "How are the other boys? Mine, I mean."

"The red-haired man—he was on watch here when I came—I am afraid I found it necessary to terminate him."

"Tietjens and O'Farrell," said Banning, very slowly. "Just shot down, huh? Who else?"

"No one, yet. It's your fault, Captain. You precipitated this affair before we were ready; we had to act in haste. Our original plan did not involve harming any person." The shriveled face grew thoughtful. "We have them all prisoners, except for you there on the bridge. I advise you to surrender peacefully."

"What's the big idea?" growled Banning. "What do you want?"

"We are taking over this ship."

"Are you crazy? Do you know what sort of job it is to handle her—do you know how much kinetic energy she's got, right now?"

"It is unfortunate that Falken died," said Gomez tonelessly. "He was to have been our engineer. But I daresay Andreyev can take his place, with some help from me—I know a bit about nucleonic controls. Gentry, of course, is a trained astrogator."

"But who are you?" shouted Banning. He had the eerie feeling that the whole world had gone gibbering insane around him. "What are you doing this for?"

"It is not essential for you to know that," said Gomez. "If you surrender now, you will receive good treatment and be released as soon as possible. Otherwise we shall probably have to shoot you. Remember, we have all the guns."

Banning told him what he could do with the guns and cut the circuit. Switching on the public-address mike, he barked a summary of the situation for the benefit of any crewmen who might be at liberty. Then, spinning out of the booth, he told the others in a few harsh words how it stood.

Cleonie's face had gotten back a little color. Now, between the floating gold locks of hair, it was again drained of blood. But he admired the game way she asked him: "What can we do?"

"Depends on the situation, m'lady," he replied. "We don't know for sure...let's see, another steward, two engineers, and a deck-hand...we don't know if all four of the crewmen still alive are prisoners or not. I'm afraid, though, that they really are."

"Luke," she whispered. "You sent him off—"

Banning nodded. Even in this moment, he read an anguish in her eyes and knew pity for her. "I'm afraid Luke has been clobbered," he said. "Not permanently, though, I hope."

Wayne's gaze was blank and lost. "But what are they *doing?"* he stammered. "Are they...ps-ps-psychotic?"

"No such luck," said Banning. "This was a pretty well-laid plan. At the proper time, they'd have pulled guns on us and locked us away—or maybe shot us. Luke happened to...I don't know what, but it alarmed Andreyev, who stuck him up. Then I horned in. I sent Luke after help. Not suspecting the other passengers, he must have told Tietjens in the presence of another member of this gang. So poor old Joppe got shot, but apparently Luke was just herded off. Then the whole gang was alerted, and Gomez went to take over the engine room while Falken and Gentry came after me." He nodded heavily. "A fast, smooth, operation, in spite of our having thrown 'em off balance. No, they're sane, for all practical purposes."

He waited a moment, gathering his thoughts, then:

"The remaining four crewmen would all have been in their quarters, off duty. The situation as she now stands depends on whether Gentry broke off from chasing me in time to surprise them in that one place. I wish I'd gotten on the mike faster."

Suddenly he grinned. "Tetsuo," he rapped, "stop the ship's rotation. Pronto!"

The mate blinked, then laughed—a short rough bark in his gullet—and leaped for the controls. "Hang on!" said Banning.

"What...what do you plan to do, sir?" asked Wayne.

"Put this whole tub into null-gee. It'll equalize matters a bit."

"I don't understand."

"No, you've never seen a weightless free-for-all, have you? Too bad. There's an art to it. A trained man with his hands can make a monkey of a groundlubber with a gun."

It was hard to tell whether Wayne was more deeply shocked at the mutiny or at learning that his captain had actually been in vulgar brawls. "Cheer up, son," said Banning. "You, too Cleonie. You both look like vulcanized oatmeal."

There was a brief thrumming. The tangential jets blew a puff of chemical vapor and brought the spin of the ship to a halt. For a moment, the astro screen went crazy, still compensating for a rotation which had ceased, then the cold image of the constellations steadied.

"O.K.," said Banning. "We've got to move fast. Tetsuo, come, with me. Charlie, Cleonie, guard the bridge. Lock the door behind us, and don't open it for anyone whose voice you find unmusical. If our boys do show up, tell 'em to wait here."

"Where are you going?" breathed the girl shakenly.

"Out to kill a few people," said Banning with undiminished good cheer.

He led the way, in a long soaring glide through the door. "Up" and "down" had become meaningless; there was only this maze of halls, rooms, and stairwells. His skin prickled with the thought that an armed man might be waiting in any cross-corridor. The silence of the ship drew his nerves taut as wires. He pulled himself along by the rails, hand over hand, accelerating till the doorways blurred past him.

The galley was on B-deck, just "above" passenger country. When Banning opened the door, an unfastened kettle drifted out and gonged on his head. A rack held the usual kitchen assortment of knives. He stuck a few in his waistband, giving the two longest to himself and Tokugawa. "Now I don't feel so nude," he remarked.

"What's next?" whispered the mate.

"If our lads are being kept prisoner, it's probably in crew territory. Let's try—

The spacemen's own cabins were on this level; they did not require the full Earth-value of spin-gravity given the passengers on A-deck. Banning slipped with a caution that rose exponentially toward the area he always thought of as the forecastle.

He need not have been quite so careful. Andreyev waited with a pistol outside a cabin door, Andreyev had been unprepared for a sudden change to no-weight. His misery was not active, but it showed.

Banning launched himself.

Andreyev's abused senses reacted slowly. He looked around, saw the hurtling form, and yelled. Almost instinctively, he whipped his gun about and fired. It was nearly pointblank, but he missed. He could not help missing when the recoil sent him flying backward with plenty of english.

He struck the farther wall, scrabbled wildly, bounced off it, and pinwheeled to the ceiling. Banning grinned, changed course with a thrust of leg against floor, and closed in. Andreyev fired again. It was a bomb-burst roar in the narrow space. The bullet tore Banning's sleeve. Recoil jammed Andreyev against the ceiling. As he rebounded, it was onto his enemy's knife.

The captain smiled sleepily, grabbed Andreyev's tunic with his free hand, and completed the job.

Tokugawa dodged a rush of blood. He looked sick. "What did you do that for?" he choked.

"Tietjens and O'Farrell," said Banning. The archaic greenish light faded from his eyes, and he added in a flat tone: "Let's get that door open."

Fists were hammering on it. The thin metal dented beneath the blows but held firm. "Stand aside!" yelled Tokugawa. "I'm going to shoot the lock off—can't find the key, no time—" He picked Andreyev's gun from the air, put the muzzle to the barrier, and fired. He was also thrown back by reaction but knew how to control such forces.

Luke Devon flung the door open. The Engineer looked as bleak as Banning had ever known a man to be. Behind him crowded the others, Nielsen, Bahadur, Castro, Vladimirovitch. Packing five men into a cubbyhole meant for one had in itself been a pretty good way to immobilize them.

Their voices surfed around the captain. "Shut up!" he bawled. "We got work to do!"

"Who else is involved in this?" demanded Devon. "Gentry killed Tietjens and took me prisoner...herded all of us in here, with Andreyev to help...but who else is there to fight?"

"Gentry and Gomez," said Banning. "Falken is dog's meat. We still hold the bridge and we outnumber 'em now—but they've got the engine room *and* all the guns but one." He passed out knives. "Let's get out of here. We've made enough racket to wake the Old Martians. I don't want Gentry to come pot-hunting."

The men streamed behind him as he dove along another stairwell, toward the bowels of the ship. He wanted to post a guard over the gyros and biotics. But he had not gotten to them when the spiteful crack of an automatic toned between metal walls.

His hands closed on the rail, slamming him to a halt that skinned his palms. "Hold it," he said, very softly. "That could only have come from the bridge."

If we can shoot a door open, I reckon Gentry can, too.

There was only one approach to the bridge, a short passageway on which several companionways converged. To either side of this corridor were the captain's and mate's cabins; at the far end was the bridge entrance.

Banning came whizzing out of a stairwell. He didn't stop, but glided on into the one opposite. A bullet smashed where he had been.

His brain held the glimpsed image: the door open, Gentry braced in it with his feet on one jamb and his back against the door. That way, he could cover Wayne and Cleonie—if they were still alive—and the approach as well. The recoil of his fire wouldn't bother him at all.

Banning's followers milled about like the debris of a ship burst open. He waited till Gentry's voice reached out:

"So you have all your men back, Captain...and therefore a gun, I presume? Nice work. But stay where you are. I'll shoot the first head that pokes around a corner. I know how to use a gun in null-gee, and I've got Wayne and Rogers for hostages. Want to parley?"

Banning stole a glimpse at Devon. The Engineer's nostrils were pinched and bloodless. It was he who answered:

"What are you after?"

"I think you know, Luke," said Gentry.

"Yes," said Devon. "I believe I do."

"Then you're also aware that anything goes. I won't hesitate to shoot Rogers—or dive the ship into the sun before the Guard gets its claws on us! It would be better if you gave up."

There was another stillness. The breathing of his men, of himself, sounded hoarse in Banning's ears. Little drops of sweat pearled off their skin, glistened in the fluorotube light, and danced away On air currents.

He cocked a brow at Devon. The Engineer nodded. "It's correct enough, skipper," he said. "We're up against fanatics."

"We could rush him," hissed Banning. "Lose a man or two, maybe, but—"

"No," said Devon. "There's Cleonie to think about." A curious mask of peace dropped over his bony face. "Let me talk to him. Maybe we can arrange something. You be ready to act as...as indicated."

He said, aloud, that he would parley. "Good," grunted Gentry. "Come out slow, and hang on to the rail with both your hands where I can see them." Devon's long legs moved out of Banning's view. "That's close enough. Stop." *He must still be three or four meters from the door,* thought the captain, and moved up to the corner of the stairwell.

It came to him, with a sudden chill, what Devon must be planning. The Rostomily clan had always been that sort. His scalp prickled, but he dared not speak. All he could do was take a few knives from the nearest men.

"Luke." That was Cleonie's voice, a whisper from the bridge. "Luke, be careful."

"Oh, yes." The Engineer laughed. It had an oddly tender note.

"Just what happened to kick off this landslide, anyway?" asked Gentry.

" 'Thou hast the most unsavory similes,' " said Devon.

"What?"

The roar which followed must have jerked all of Gentry's remaining attention to him as Devon launched himself into space.

The gun crashed. Banning heard the bullet smack home. Devon's body turned end over end, tumbling backward down the hall.

Banning was already around the corner. He did not fire at Gentry; it would have taken a whole fatal second to brace himself properly against a wall.

He threw knives.

The recoil was almost negligible; his body twisted back and forth as his arms moved, but he was used to that. It took only a wink to stick four blades in Gentry.

The spaceman screamed, hawked blood, and scrabbled after the gun that had slipped from his fingers. Tokugawa came flying, hit him with one shoulder. They thudded to the floor. The mate wrapped his legs about Gentry's and administered an expert foul blow to the neck.

Cleonie struggled from the bridge toward Devon. Banning was already there, holding the gray form between his knees while he examined the wound. The girl bumped into them. *"How is he?"* Banning had heard that raw tone, half shriek, often and often before this day—when women saw the blood of their men.

He nodded. "Could be worse, I reckon. The slug seems to've hit a rib and stopped. Shock knocked him out, but well, a bullet never does as much harm in free fall, the target bounces away from it easier." He swatted at the little red globules in the air. "Damn!"

Wayne emerged, green-faced. "This man…shot the door open when we wouldn't let him in," he rattled. "We hadn't any weapon…he threatened Miss Rogers—"

"O.K., never mind the breast-beating. Next time remember to stand beside the door and grab when the enemy comes through. Now, I assume you have the medical skills required for your certificate. Get Luke to sick bay and patch him up. Nielsen, help Mr. Wayne. Gentry still alive?"

"He won't be if he doesn't get some first aid quick," said Tokugawa. "You gashed him good." He whistled in awe. "Don't you ever simply *stun* your enemies, boss?"

"Take him along too, Mr. Wayne, but Devon gets priority. Bahadur, break out the vacuum sweeper and get this blood sucked up before it fouls everything. Tetsuo…uh, Mr. Tokugawa, go watch the after bulkhead in case Gomez tries to break out Vladimirovitch, tag along with him. Castro, stick around here."

"Can I help?" asked Cleonie. Her lips struggled for firmness.

"Go to sick bay," nodded Banning. "Maybe they can use you."

He darted into the bridge and checked controls. Everything was still off—good. Gomez couldn't start the engines without rigging a bypass circuit. However, he had plenty of ancillary machines, generators and pumps and whatnot, at his disposal down there. The captain entered the intercom cabinet and switched on the engine room screen.

Gomez's pinched face had taken on a stiffened wildness. "For your information, friend," said Banning, "we just mopped up Andreyev and Gentry. That leaves you alone. Come on out of there, the show's over."

"No," said Gomez. His voice was dull, abnormally calm. It gave Banning a creepy sensation.

"Don't you believe me? I can haul the bodies here if you want."

"Oh, yes, I will take your word." Gomez's mouth twisted. "Then perhaps you will do me the same honor. It is still you who must surrender to me."

Banning waited for a long few seconds.

"I am here in the engine room," said Gomez. "I am alone. I have locked the outer doors: emergency seal, you'll have to burn your way through, and that takes hours. There will be plenty of time for me to disable the propulsion system."

Banning was not a timid man, but his palms were suddenly wet, and he fumbled a thick dry tongue before he could shape words: "You'd die, too."

"I am quite prepared for that."

"But you wouldn't have accomplished anything! You'd just have wrecked the ship and killed several people."

"I would have kept this affair from being reported to the Union," said Gomez. "The very fact of our attempt is more of a hint than we can afford to let the Guard have."

"What are you doing all this *for?"* howled the captain.

The face in the screen grew altogether unhuman. It was a face Banning knew—millennia of slaughterhouse history knew it—the face of embodied Purpose.

"It is not necessary for you to be told the details," clipped Gomez. "However, perhaps you will understand that the present government's spineless toleration of the Kali menace in the East and the moral decay in the West has to be ended if civilization is to survive."

"I see," said Banning, as gently as if he spoke in the presence of a ticking bomb. "And since toleration is built into Union law—"

"Exactly. I do not say anything against the Uniters. But times have changed. If Fourre were alive today, he would agree that action is necessary."

"It's always convenient to use a dead man for a character witness, isn't it?"

"What?"

"Never mind." Banning nodded to himself. "Don't do anything radical yet, Gomez. I'll have to think about this."

"I shall give you exactly one hour," said the desiccated voice. "Thereafter I shall begin work. I am not an engineer myself, but I think I can disable something—I have studied a trifle about nucleonics. You may call me when you are ready to surrender. At the first suspicion of misbehavior, I will, of course, wreck the propulsion system immediately."

Gomez turned away.

Banning sat for a while, his mind curiously empty. Then he shoved across to the control board, alerted the crew and started the rotation again. You might as well have some weight.

"Keep an eye on the screen," he said as, he left the main pilot chair. "Call me on the intercom if anything develops. I'll be in sick bay."

"Sir?" Castro gaped at him.

"Appropriate spot," said Banning. "Velocity is equivalent to temperature, isn't it? If so, then we all have a fever which is quite likely to kill us?"

* * * *

Devon lay stretched and stripped on the operating table. Wayne had just removed the bullet with surgical pincers. Now he clamped the wound and began stitching. Nielsen was controlling the sterilizers, both UV and sonic, while Cleonie stood by with bowl and sponges. They all looked up, as if from a dream, when Banning entered. The tools of surgery might be developed today to a point where this was an operation simple enough for a spaceman's meditechnic training; but there was a man on the table who might have died, and only slowly did their minds break away from his heartbeat.

"How is he?" asked the captain.

"Not too bad, sir, considering." Given this job, urgent and specific, Wayne was competent enough; he spoke steadily. "I daresay he presented his chest on purpose when he attacked, knowing the bones had a good chance of acting as armor. There's a broken rib and some torn muscle, of course, but nothing that won't heal."

"Gentry?"

"Conked out five minutes ago, sir," said Nielsen. "I stuck him in the icebox. Maybe they've got revivification equipment on Ganymede."

"Wouldn't make much difference," said Banning. "The forebrain would be too far gone by the time we arrived—no personality survival to speak of." He shuddered a little. Clean death was one thing; this was another matter, one which he had never quite gotten used to. "Luke, though," he went on quickly, "can he stand being brought to consciousness? Right away?"

"No!" Almost, Cleonie lifted her basin to brain him.

"Shut up." He turned his back on her. "It'd be a poor kindness to let him sleep comfy now and starve to death later, maybe, out beyond Pluto. Well, Mr. Wayne?"

"Hm-m-m...I don't like it, sir. But if you say so, I guess I can manage it. Local anesthesia for the wound and a shot of mild stimulant; oxygen and neoplasma, just in case—Yes, I don't imagine a few minutes' conversation would hurt him permanently."

"Good. Carry on." Banning fumbled after his pipe, remembered that he had dropped it somewhere in all the hallabaloo, and swore.

"What did you say?" asked Nielsen.

"Never mind," said Banning. True, women were supposed to be treated like men these days, but he had old-fashioned ideas. It was useful to know a few earthy languages unfamiliar to anyone else.

Cleonie laid a hand on his arm. "Captain," she said. Her eyes were shadowed, with weariness and with—compassion? "Captain, is it necessary to wake him? He's been hurt so much—for our sakes."

"He may have the only information to save our lives," answered Banning patiently.

The intercom cleared its throat: "Sir...Castro on bridge—he's unbolting the main mass-tank access port."

Wayne turned white as he labored. He understood. Banning nodded. "I thought so. Did you ask him what he was up to? He promised us an hour."

"Yes, sir. He said we'd get it, too, but…but he wanted to be ready, in case—"

"Smart boy. It'll take him awhile to get to the flush valves; they're quite well locked away and shielded. Then the pump has to have time. We might have burned our way in to him by then."

"Maybe we should do it, sir. Now!"

"Maybe. It'd be a race between his wrenches and our torches. I'll let you know. Stand by."

Banning turned back to Devon, gnawing his lip. The Engineer was stirring to wakefulness. As he watched, the captain saw the eyes blink palely open, saw color creep into the face and the mouth tighten behind the transparent oxygen mask.

Cleonie moved toward the table. "Luke—"

Devon smiled at her, a sudden human warmth in this cold room of machines. Gently, Banning shoved her aside. "You'll get your innings later, girl," he said. Bending over the Engineer: "Hello, buster. You're going to be O.K. Can you tell me some things in a hell of a hurry?"

"I can try—" It was the merest flutter of air. "Tell me—"

Banning began to talk. Devon lay back, breathing deeply and making some curious gestures with his hands. He'd had Tighe System training, then—total integration—good! He *would* be able to hang on to his consciousness, even call up new strength from hidden cellular reserves.

"We clobbered all the gang except Gomez, who seems, to be the kingpin. He's holed up in the engine room, threatens to wreck us all unless we surrender to him inside an hour. Does he mean it?"

"Yes. Oh, yes." Devon nodded faintly.

"Who is this outfit? What do they want?"

"Fanatic group…quasi-religious…powerful, large membership furnishes plenty of money…but the real operations are secret, a few men—"

"I think I know who you mean. The Western Reformists, huh?"

Devon nodded again. The pulse that flickered in his throat seemed to strengthen.

Banning spent a bleak moment of review. In recent years, he had stayed off Earth as much as possible; when there, he had not troubled himself with political details, for he recognized all the signs of a civilization going under. It had seemed more worthwhile to give his attention to the Venusian ranch he had bought, against the day of genocide and the night of ignorance and tyranny to follow. However, he did understand that the antitechnic Oriental cult of Kali had created its own opposite pole in the West. And the prim grim Reformists might well try to forestall their enemies by a coup.

"Sort of like the Nazis versus the Communists, back in Germany in the 1920s," he muttered.

"The who?" said Nielsen.

"No matter. It's six of one and half a dozen of the other. Let me see, Luke." Banning took a turn around the room. "In order to overthrow constitutional government and impose their will on Earth, the Reformists would have to kill quite a few hundred millions of people, especially in Asia. That means nuclear bombardment, preferably from space. Am I right?"

"Yes—" said Devon. His voice gained resonance as he went on. "They have a base, somewhere in the asteroid belt. They hope to build it up to a fortress, with a fleet of ships, arsenal, military corps...the works. It's a very long-range thing, of course, but the public aspect of their party is going to need lots of time anyway, to condition enough citizens toward the idea of—Well. At present their base doesn't amount to much. They can't just buy ships, the registry would give them away...they have to build...they need at least one supply ship, secretly owned and operated, before they can start serious work at all."

"And we're elected," said Devon. "Yeah. I can even see why. Not only is this a fast ship with a large capacity, but our present cargo, the terraforming stuff, would be valuable to them in itself...Uh-huh. Their idea was to take over this clunk, bring her in to their base—and the *Thunderbolt* becomes another ship which just plain vanished mysteriously."

Devon nodded.

"I scarcely imagine they'd have kept us alive, under the circumstances," went on Banning.

"No."

"How do you know all this?"

"The Order...We stay out of politics...officially...but we have our Intelligence arm and use it quietly." So that was why he'd been reluctant to explain Andreyev's actions! "We knew, in a general way, what the situation was. Of course, we didn't know *this* ship, on this particular voyage, was slated for capture."

"That's fairly obvious. You recognized Andreyev."

"Yes. Former Engineer, under another name—expelled for...good reasons. Surgical changes made, but the overall gestalt bothered me. All of a sudden, I thought I knew who he was. Like a meddling fool, I tried a key word on him. Yes, he reacted, by pulling a gun on me! Later on—again, like an idiot—I didn't think Gentry might be his partner, so I told Tietjens what had happened while Gentry was there." Devon sighed. "Old Rostomily would disown me."

"You weren't trained for secret service work, yourself," said Banning. "All right, Luke. One more question. Gomez wants us to surrender to him. I presume this means we'll let ourselves be locked away except for one or two who slow down the ship while he holds a gun on 'em. After we've decelerated to a point where a boat from the Reformist asteroid can match velocities, he'll radio and—Hell! What I'm getting at is, would our lives be spared afterward?"

"I doubt it," said the Engineer.

"Oh my darling—" As he closed his eyes, Cleonie came to his side. Their hands groped together.

Banning swung away. "Thanks, Luke," he said. "I didn't know if I had the right to risk lives for the sake of this ship, but now I see there's no risk at all. We haven't got a thing to lose. Cleonie, can you take care of our boy here?"

"Yes," she whispered, enormous-eyed. "If there's no emergency."

"There shouldn't be. They fabricated him out of teflon and rattlesnake leather. O.K., then, you be his nurse. You might also whomp up some coffee and sandwiches. The rest of the crew meet me at the repair equipment lockers, aft section...no, you stay put, Castro. We're going to burn our way in to friend Gomez."

"But he...he'll dump the reaction mass!" gasped Wayne.

"Maybe we can get at him before he gets at the tanks," said Banning. "A man might try."

"No—look, sir. I know how long it takes to operate the main flush system. Even allowing for Gomez being alone and untrained, he can do it before we can get through the after bulkhead. We haven't a chance that way!"

"What do you recommend, Mr. Wayne?" asked Banning slowly.

"That we give in to him, sir."

"And be shot down out of hand when his pals board the ship?"

"No, sir. There'll be seven of us to one of Gomez before that happens. We have a faint hope of being able to jump him—"

"A very faint hope indeed," said Banning. "He's no amateur. And if we don't succeed, not only will we die, but that gang of hellhounds will have gotten the start it wants. Whereas, if we burn through to Gomez but fail to stop him disabling the ship...well, it'll only be us who die, now. Not a hundred million people twenty or thirty years from now."

Is this the truth? Do you really believe one man can delay the Norns? What is your choice, Captain? By legal definition, you are omnipotent and omniscient while the ship is under way. What shall be done, Oh god of the ship?

Banning groaned. *Per Jovem,* it was too much to ask of a man!

And then he stiffened.

"What is it, sir?" Nielsen looked alarmed.

"By Jupiter," said Banning. "Well, by Jupiter!"

"What?"

"Never mind. Come on. We're going to smoke Gomez out of there!"

The last, stubborn metal glared white, ran molten down the gouge already carved, and froze in gobbets. Bahadur shut off the electric torch, shoved the mask away from his dark turbanned face, and said: "All right, sir."

Banning stepped carefully over the heavy torch cables. His gang had attacked the bulkhead from a point near the skin of the ship, for the sake of both surprise and weight. "How's the situation inside?" he asked the air.

The intercom replied from the bridge, where Castro huddled over the telescreen that sowed him Gomez at work. "Pump still going, sir. I guess he really means business."

"We've got this much luck," said Banning, "that he isn't an engineer himself. You'd have those tanks flushed out half an hour ago."

He stood for another instant, gathering strength and will. His mind pawed over the facts again.

The outer plates of the ship would stop a fair-sized meteor, even at hyperbolic relative velocity: it would explode into vapor, leaving a miniature Moon-crater. Anything which might happen to break through that would lose energy to the self-sealer between the hulls; at last it would encounter the inner skin, which could stand well over a hundred atmospheres of pressure by itself. It was not a common accident for a modern spaceship to be punctured.

But the after bulkhead was meant to contain stray radiation, or even a minor explosion, if the nuclear energies which drove the ship should get out of hand. It was scarcely weaker than the double hull. The torches had required hours to carve a hole in it. There would have been little or no saving of time by cutting through the great double door at the axis of the ship, which Gomez had locked; nor did Banning want to injure massive pieces of precision machinery. The mere bulkhead would be a lot easier to repair afterward—if there was an afterward.

Darkness yawned before him. He hefted the gun in his hand. "All right, Vladimirovitch, let's go," he said. "If we're not back in ten minutes, remember, let Wayne and Bahadur follow."

He had overruled Tokugawa's anguished protests and ordered the first mate to stay behind under all circumstances. The Lunarite alone had the piloting skill to pull off the crazy stunt which was their final hope. He and Nielsen were making a racket at the other end of the bulkhead, a diversion for Gomez's benefit.

Banning slipped through the hole. It was pitchy beyond, a small outer room where no one had turned on the lights. He wondered if Gomez waited just beyond the door with a bullet for the first belly to come through.

He'd find out pretty quick.

The door, which led into the main control chamber, was a thin piece of metal. Rotation made it lie above Banning's head. He scampered up the ladder. His hand closed on the catch, he turned it with an enormous caution—flung the door open and jumped through.

The fluoros made a relentless blaze of light. Near the middle of that steel cave, floating before an opened panel, he saw Gomez. So the hell-bound Roundhead hadn't heard them breaking in!

He did now. He whirled; clumsily, and scrabbled for the gun in his belt. Banning fired. His bullet missed, wailed and gonged around the great chamber. Gomez shot back. Recoil tore him from the stanchion he held, sent him drifting toward the wall.

Banning scrambled in pursuit, over the spidery network of ladders and handholds. His weight dropped with each leap closer to the axis; he fought down the characteristic Coriolis vertigo. Gomez spiraled away from him, struck a control chair, clawed himself to a stop, and crouched in it.

Banning grew aware of the emergency pump. It throbbed and sang in the metal stillness around him, and every surge meant lost mass...like the red spurting from the slashed artery. The flush system was rarely used—only if the reaction mass got contaminated, or for some such reason. Gomez had found a *new* reason, thought Banning grimly. To lose a ship and murder a crew.

"Turn that thing off, Vlad," he said between his teeth.

"Stay where you are!" screamed Gomez. "I'll shoot! I will!"

"Get going!" roared the captain.

Vladimirovitch hauled himself toward the cutoff switch. Gomez flipped his pistol to full automatic and began firing.

He didn't hit anything of value in the few seconds granted him. In a ship rotating in free fall, the pattern of forces operating on a bullet is so complicated that practical ballistics must be learned all over again. But that hose of lead was bound to kill someone, by sheer chance and ricochet, unless—

Banning clutched himself to a rod, aimed, and fired.

On the second shot, Gomez jerked. The pistol jarred from his hand, he slumped back into the chair and lay still.

Banning hurried toward him. It would be worthwhile taking Gomez alive, to interrogate and—No. As he reached the man, he saw the life draining out of him. A shot through the heart is not invariably fatal, but this time it was.

The pump clashed to silence.

Banning whirled about. "Well?" His shout was raw. "How much did we lose?"

"Quite a bit, sir." Vladimirovitch squinted at the gauges. His words came out jerkily. "Too much, I'm afraid."

Banning went to join him, leaving Gomez to die alone.

They met in the dining saloon: seven hale men, an invalid, and a woman. For a moment they could only stare at the death in each other's eyes.

"Break out the Scotch, Nielsen," said Banning at last. He took forth his pipe and began loading it. A grin creased his mouth. "If your faces get any longer, people, you'll be tripping over your own jawbones."

Cleonie, seated at the head of the couch on which Devon lay, ruffled the Engineer's hair. Her gaze was blind with sorrow. "Do you expect us to be happy, after all that killing?" she asked.

"We were lucky," shrugged Banning. "We lost two good men, yes. But all the ungodly are dead."

"That's not so good a thing," said Devon. "I'd like to have them narcoed, find out where their asteroid is and—" He paused. "Wait. Gentry's still in the freeze, isn't he? If he was revived at Ganymede, maybe his brain wouldn't be too deteriorated for a deep-memory probe; at least."

"Nix," said Banning. "The stiffs are all to be jettisoned. We've got to lighten ship. If your Order's Intelligence men—or the Guard's, for that matter—are any good, they'll be able to trace back people like our late playfellows and rope in their buddies."

Cleonie shivered. "Please!"

"Sorry." Banning lit his pipe and took a long drag. "It is kind of morbid, isn't it? O.K. then, let's concentrate on the problem of survival. The question is how to use the inadequate amount of reaction mass left in the tanks."

"I'm afraid I don't quite understand," said the girl.

She looked more puzzled than frightened. Banning liked her all the more for that. Devon was a lucky thus-and-so, if they lived...though she deserved better than an Engineer, always skiting through space and pledged to contract no formal marriage till he retired from field service.

"It's simple enough," he told her. "We're on a hyperbolic orbit. That means we're moving with a speed greater than escape velocity for the Solar System. If we don't slow down quite a bit, we'll just keep on going; and no matter how we ration it, there's only a few weeks' worth of food aboard and no suspended-animation stuff."

"Can't we radio for help?"

"We're out of our own radio range to anywhere."

"But won't they miss us—send high-acceleration ships after us? They can compute our orbit, can't they?"

"Not that closely. Too much error creeps in when the path gets as monstrous long as ours would be before we could possibly be overhauled. It'd be remarkable if the Guard ship came as close to us as five million kilometers, which is no use at all." Banning wagged his pipestem at her "It's up to us alone. We have a velocity of some hundreds of kilometers per second to kill. We don't have reaction mass enough to do it."

Nielsen came in with bottles and glasses. He went around doing the honors while Devon said: "Excuse me, Captain, I assume this has occurred to you, but after all, it's momentum which is the significant quantity, not speed *per se.* If we jettison everything which isn't absolutely essential, cargo, furnishings, even the inner walls and floors—"

"Tet and I figured on that," answered Banning. "You remember just now I said we had to lighten ship. We even assumed stripping off the outer hull and taking a chance on meteors. It's quite feasible, you know. Spacehips are designed to come apart fairly easily under the right tools, for replacement work, so if we all sweat at it, I think we can finish peeling her down by the time we have to start decelerating."

Wayne looked at the whiskey bottle. He didn't drink; it wasn't considered quite the thing in today's West. But his face grew tighter and tighter, till suddenly he reached out and grabbed the bottle and tilted it to his mouth.

When he was through choking, he said hoarsely: "All right, sir. Why don't you tell them? We still can't lose enough speed."

"I was coming to that," said Banning.

Devon's hand closed on the girl's. "What are the figures?" he asked in a level tone.

"Well," said Banning, "we can enter the Jovian System if we like, but then we'll find ourselves fuelless with a velocity of about fifty kilometers per second relative to the planet."

The Engineer whistled.

"Must we do that, though?" inquired Bahadur. "I mean, sir, well, if we can decelerate that much, can't we get into an elliptic orbit about the sun?"

" 'Fraid not. Fifty k.p.s. is still a lot more than solar escape velocity for that region of space."

"But look, sir. If I remember rightly, Jupiter's own escape velocity is well *over* fifty k.p.s. That means the planet itself will be giving us all that speed. If we didn't come near it, we should have mass enough left to throw ourselves into a cometary—"

"Smart boy," said Banning. He blew smoke in the air and hoisted his glass. "We computed that one, too. You're quite right, we can get into a cometary. The very best cometary we can manage will take a few years to bring us back into radio range of anyone—and of course space is so big we'd never be found on such an unpredictable orbit, unless we hollered for help and were heard."

"*Years,*" whispered Cleonie.

The terror which rose in her, then, was not the simple fear of death. It was the sudden understanding of just how big and old this universe which she had so blithely inhabited really was. Banning, who had seen it before, waited sympathetically.

After a minute she straightened herself and met his eyes. "All right, Captain," she said. "Continue the arithmetic lesson. Why can't we simply ask the Jovians to pick us up as we approach their system?"

"You knew there was a catch, eh?" murmured Banning. "It's elementary. The Republic is poor and backward. Their only spacecraft are obsolete intersatellite shuttles, which can't come anywhere near a fifty k.p.s. velocity."

"And we've no means of losing speed, down to something they can match." Wayne dropped his face into his hands.

"I didn't call you here for a weeping contest," said Banning. "We do have one means. It might or might not work—it's never been tried—but Tetsuo here is one hell of a good pilot. He's done some of the cutest braking ellipses you ever saw in your life."

That made them sit up. But Devon shook his head, wryly. "It won't work," he said. "Even after the alleged terraforming, Ganymede hasn't enough atmosphere to—"

"Jupiter has all kinds of atmosphere," said Banning.

The silence that fell was thunderous.

"No," said Wayne at last. He spoke quickly, out of bloodless lips. "It could only work by a fluke. We would lose speed, yes, if friction didn't burn us up... finally, on one of those passes, we'd emerge with a sensible linear velocity. But a broken shell like this ship will be after we lighten her—an atmosphere as thick. and turbulent as Jupiter's—there wouldn't be enough control. We'd never know precisely what orbit we were going to have on emergence. By the time we'd computed what path it really was and let the Jovians know and their antiquated boats had reached it...we'd be back in Jupiter's air on the next spiral!"

"And the upshot would be to crash," said Devon. "Hydrogen and helium at one hundred and forty degrees Absolute. Not very bteathable."

"Oh, we'd have spattered on the surface before we had to try breathing that stuff," said Vladimirovitch sarcastically.

"No, we wouldn't either," said Bahadur. "Our inner hull can stand perhaps two hundred atmospheres' pressure. But Jupiter goes up to the tens of thousands. We would be squashed flat long before we reached the surface."

Banning lifted his brows. "You know a better 'ole?" he challenged.

"What?" Wayne blinked at him.

"Know anything which gives us a better chance?"

"Yes, I do." The young face stiffened. "Let's get into that cometary about the sun. When we don't report in, there'll be Guard ships hunting for us. We have a very small chance of being found. But the chance of being picked up by the Jovians, while doing those crazy dives, is infinitesimal!"

"It doesn't look good either way, does it?" said Cleonie. A sad little smile crossed her lips. "But I'd rather be killed at once, crushed in a single blow, than… watch all of us shrivel and die, one by one—or draw lots for who's to be eaten next. I'd rather go out like a human being."

"Same here," nodded Devon.

"Not I!" Wayne stood up. "Captain, I won't have it. You've no right to…to take the smaller chance, the greater hazard, deliberately, just because it offers a quicker death. No!"

Banning slapped the table with a cannon-crack noise. "Congratulations on getting your master's certificate, Mr. Wayne," he growled. "Now sit down."

"No, by the Eternal! I demand—"

"Sit down!"

Wayne sat. "As a matter of fact," continued Banning mildly, "I agree that the chance of the Jovians rescuing us is negligible. But I think we have a chance to help ourselves.

"I think maybe we can do what nobody has ever tried before—enter Jovian sky and live to brag about it."

From afar, as they rushed to their destiny, Jupiter had a splendor which no other planet, perhaps not the sun itself, could match. From a cold great star to an amber disk to a swollen shield with storm—the sight caught your heart.

But then you fought it. You got so close that the shield became a cauldron and ate you down.

The figures spoke a bleak word: the escape velocity of Jupiter is about fifty-nine kilometers per second. The *Thunderbolt* had about fifty-two, relative. If she had simply whizzed by the planet, its gravitation would have slowed her again, and eventually she would have fallen back into it with a speed that would vaporize her. There was no possibility of the creaking old boats of the satellite colonists getting close to her at any point of such an orbit; they would have needed far more advance warning than a short-range radio could give them.

Instead, Tokugawa used the last reaction mass to aim at the outer fringes of atmosphere.

The first pass was almost soundless. Only a thin screaming noise, a sense of heat radiated in human faces, a weak tug of deceleration, told how the ship clove air. Then she was out into vacuum again, curving on a long narrow ellipse.

Banning worked his radio, swearing at the Doppler effect. He got the band of Ganymede at last. Beside him, Tokugawa and Wayne peered into the viewscreen, reading stars and moons, while the computer jabbered out an orbit.

"Hello. Hello. Are you there?"

The voice hissed weakly from X Spaceport: "Heh, *Thun'erbolt.* Central Astro Control, Ganymede. Harris speakin'. Got y'r path?"

"To a rough approximation," said Banning. "We'd need several more readings to get it exactly, of course. Stand by to record." He took the tape from the computer and read off the figures.

"We've three boats in y' area," said Harris. "They'll try t' find y'. G' luck."

"Thanks," said Banning. "We could use some."

Tokugawa's small deft fingers completed another calculation. "We'll strike atmosphere again in about fifty hours, skipper," he reported. "That gives the demolition gang plenty of time to work."

Banning twisted his head around. There was no rear wall now to stop his eyes. Except for the central section, with its vital equipment, little enough remained between the bridge and the after bulkhead. Torches had slashed, wrenches had turned, air locks had spewed out jagged temporary moons for days. The ship had become a hollow shell and a web of bracing.

He felt like a murderer.

Across the diameter of the great spheroid, he saw Devon floating free, ordering the crew into spacesuits. As long as they were in null-gee, the Engineer made an excellent foreman, broken rib and all.

His party was going out to cut loose reactor, fire chamber, ion tubes, everything aft. Now that the last mass was expended and nothing remained to drive the ship but the impersonal forces of celestial mechanics, the engines were so much junk whose weight could kill them. Never mind the generators—there was enough energy stored in the capacitor bank to keep the shell lighted and warmed for weeks. If the Jovians didn't catch them in space, they might need those weeks, too.

Banning sighed. Since men first steered a scraped-out log or a wicker basket to sea, it has been an agony for a captain to lose his ship.

He remembered a submarine once, long ago—it still hurt him to recall, though it hadn't been his fault. Of course, he'd gotten the idea which might save all their lives now because he knew a trifle about submarines...or should the Montgolfiers get the credit, or Archimedes?

Cleonie floated toward him. She had gotten quite deft in free fall during the time before deceleration in which they orbited toward Jupiter, when spin had been canceled to speed the work of jettisoning. "May I bother you?" she asked.

"Of course." Banning took out his pipe. She cheered him up. "Though the presence of a beautiful girl is not a bother. By definition."

She smiled, wearily, and brushed a strand of loose hair from her eyes. It made a halo about her worn face. "I feel so useless," she said.

"Nonsense. Keep the meals coming, and you're plenty of use. Tietjens and Nielsen were awful belly robbers."

"I wondered—" A flush crossed her cheeks. "I do so want to understand Luke's work."

"Sure." Banning opened his tobacco pouch and began stuffing the pipe, not an easy thing to do in free fall. "What's the question ?"

"Only...we hit the air going so fast—faster than meteors usually hit Earth, wasn't it? Why didn't we burn up?"

"Meteors don't exactly burn. They volatilize. All we did was skim some very thin air. We didn't convert enough velocity into heat to worry about. A lot of what we did convert was carried away by the air itself."

"But still—I've never heard of braking ellipses being used when the speed is as high as ours."

Banning clicked his lighter, held it "above" the bowl, and drew hard. "In actual fact," he said, "I don't think it could be done in Earth or Venus atmosphere. But Jupiter has about ten times the gravitational potential, therefore the air thins out with height correspondingly more slowly. In other words, we've got a deeper layer of thin air to brake us. It's all right. We'll have to make quite a few passes—we'll be at this for days, if we aren't rescued—but it can be done."

He got his pipe started. There was a trick to smoking in free fall. The air-circulating blowers, which kept you from smothering in your own breath, didn't much help as small an object as a pipe. But he needed this comfort. Badly.

Many hours later, using orbital figures modified by further observation, a shuttleboat from Ganymede came near enough to locate the *Thunderbolt* on radar. After maneuvering around so much, it didn't have reaction mass enough to match velocities. For about a second it passed so close that Devon's crew, working out on the hull, could see it—as if they were the damned in hell watching one of the elect fly past.

The shuttleboat radioed for a vessel with fuller tanks. One came. It zeroed in—and decelerated like a startled mustang. The *Thunderbolt* had already fallen deeper into the enormous Jovian gravity field than the boat's engines could rise.

The drifting ship vanished from sight, into the great face of the planet. High clouds veiled it from telescopes—clouds of free radicals, such as could not have existed for a moment under humanly endurable conditions. Jupiter is more alien than men can really imagine.

Her orbit on reemergence was not so very much different. But the boats which had almost reached her had been forced to move elsewhere; they could not simply hang there, in that intense a field. So the *Thunderbolt* made another long, lonesome pass. By the time it was over, Ganymede was in the unfavorable position, and Callisto had never been in a good one. Therefore the ship entered Jupiter's atmosphere for a third time, unattended.

On the next emergence into vacuum, her orbit had shortened and skewed considerably. The rate at which air drag operated was increasing; each plunge went deeper beneath the poison clouds, each swung through clear space took less time. However, there was hope. The Ganymedeans were finally organizing themselves. They computed an excellent estimate of what the fourth free orbit would be and planted well-fueled boats strategically close at the right times.

Only—the *Thunderbolt* did not come anywhere near the predicted path.

It was pure bad luck. Devon's crew, working whenever the ship was in a vacuum, had almost cut away the after section. This last plunge into stiffening air resistance finished the job. Forces of drag and reaction, a shape suddenly altered, whipped the *Thunderbolt* wildly through the stratosphere. She broke free at last, on a drastically different orbit.

But then, it had been unusual good luck which brought the Jovians so close to her in the first place. Probabilities were merely reasserting themselves.

The radio said in a weak, fading voice: "Missed y' 'gain. Do' know 'f we c'n come near, nex' time. Y'r period's gettin' very short."

"Maybe you shouldn't risk it." Banning sighed. He had hoped for more, but if the gods had decided his ship was to plunge irretrievably into Jupiter, he had to accept the fact.

"We'll be all right, I reckon."

Outside, the air roared hollowly. Pressures incomparably greater than those in Earth's deepest oceans waited below.

On his final pass into any approximation of clear space—the stars were already hazed—Banning radioed: "This will be the last message, except for a ten-minute signal on the same band when we come to rest. Assuming we're alive! We've got to save capacitors. It'll be some time before help arrives. When it does, call me. I'll respond if we've survived, and thereafter emit a steady tone by which we can be located. Is that clear?"

"Clear. I read y'. Luck, spaceman...over an' out."

Watching the mists thicken in the viewscreen, Banning added figures in his head for the hundredth time.

His schedule called for him to report at Phobos in fifteen days. When he didn't, the Guard would send a high-acceleration ship to find out what had gone wrong. Allow a few days for that. Another week for it to return to Mars with a report of the facts. Mars would call Luna on the radio beam—that, at least, would be quick—and the Guard, or possibly the Engineers; would go to work at once.

The Engineers had ships meant to enter atmosphere: powerful, but slow. Such a vessel could be carried piggyback by a fast ion-drive craft of the Guard. Modifications could be made en route. But the trip would still require a couple of weeks, pessimistically reckoned.

Say, then, six weeks maximum until help arrived. Certainly no less than four, no matter what speeds could be developed by these latest models.

Well, the *Thunderbolt* had supplies and energy for more than six weeks. That long a time under two-plus gees was not going to be fun, though gravanol injections would prevent physiological damage. And the winds were going to buffet them around. That should be endurable, though; they'd be above the region of vertical currents, in what you might call the Jovian stratosphere—

A red fog passed before the screen.

Luke Devon, strapped into a chair like everyone else, called across the empty, ship: "If I'd only known this was going to happen—what a chance for research! I do have a few instruments, but it'll be crude as hell."

"Personally," said Banning, "I saved out a deck of cards and some poker chips. But I hardly think you'll have much time for research—in Jovian atmospherics, anyway."

He could imagine Cleonie blushing. He was sorry to embarrass her, he really did like that girl, but the ragged laugh he got from the others was worth it. While men could laugh, especially at jokes as bad as his, they could endure.

Down and down the ship went. Once, caught in a savage gust, she turned over. If everything hadn't been fastened down, there could have been an awful mess. The distribution of mass was such that the hulk would always right itself, but...yes, reflected Banning, they'd all have to wear some kind of harness attached to the interior braces. It could be improvised.

The wind that boomed beyond the hull faded its organ note, just a trifle.

"We're slowing down," said Tokugawa.

And later, looking up from the radaltimeter: "We've stopped."

"End of the line." Banning stretched. He felt bone-crushingly tired. "Nothing much we can do now. Let's all strap into our bunks and sleep for a week."

His Jovian weight dragged at him. But they were all alive. And the ship might be hollowed out, but she still held food and drink, tools and materials, games and books—what was needed to keep them sane as well as breathing in the time they must wait.

His calculations were verified. A hollow steelloy shell, three hundred odd meters in diameter, could carry more than a hundred thousand tons, besides its own mass, and still have a net specific gravity of less than 0.03. Now the Jovian air has an average molecular weight of about 3.3, so after due allowance for temperature and a few other items, the result was derived that at such a thickness its pressure is an endurable one hundred atmospheres.

Like an old drop in a densitometer, like a free balloon over eighteenth-century France, like a small defiant bubble in the sky, the *Thunderbolt* floated.

Jennifer's Song

A sailor fares a lonely way.
His lass is lonely too.
She yearns horizonward by day,
Where there is only blue,
Or only gulls are winging white,
Like sails across the sky.
She hears alone, alone at night
The wind's "Ahoy!" go by.

The sun will come, the sun will go,
The year will have no rest,
The blood will ebb, the blood will flow
Within the maiden's breast,
Till springtime blows from oversea
To gust against the shore,
And spindrift green across a tree
Says he'll come back once more.

He will return, he will return,
She knows it in her soul,
As surely as the stars must quern
About the constant pole.
The masts will rise above the rim
Where heaven meets the sea
And beckon her to welcome him,
At last, at last set free.

And when she's standing breast to breast
Against her mariner,
She'll speak of how this day is blest
That brought him home to her
And tell herself it is no use
In all their little world

Science Fiction and Science: The Hardness of Hard Science Fiction

Once a lawyer, a doctor, an engineer, and a politician were arguing as to whose profession as the oldest.

Said the lawyer: "Adam and Eve couldn't have lived in the Garden of Eden without some rules, and in fact the Bible tells us that God told them what to do and not do. So law came first."

"Oh, no," objected the doctor. "Before then, God created Eve from Adam's rib—a surgical procedure."

"But earlier still," the engineer maintained, "God brought order out of chaos, obviously an engineering job."

"Ah," said the politician, "and who do you think made the chaos?"

—In like manner, students of science fiction disagree about which kind of it is primary, whether in point of chronological appearance, importance, or whatever. As I remarked in the opening essay of this series, I think that's a mere quibble over definitions. If, say, we co-opt Homer or Lucian as the original science fiction writer, then the Marvelous Voyage is the most ancient theme in our field. If we date everything from *Frankenstein,* as Brian Aldiss does, then the Prometheus motif is (or, if you prefer, the Mad Scientist, or the Android, or the Things Man Was Never Meant to Know, or more seriously, the conflict between man and his works). Several other historical schemes exist for the birth and development of science fiction, as well as countless attempts to define what it is. I have opined that the questions thereby raised are of the sort which have no real answers, and therefore no real significance.

Still, since I am supposed to discuss the field, it seems wise to begin with a part which is indubitably important and, what's more, unequivocally belongs to it. That is the kind which nowadays often bears the name "hard" science fiction.

The term came from the late James Blish, who afterward declared that it soon acquired a meaning he hadn't intended at all. This is doubly ironic, because even in its current sense it does not refer to anything clearly delimited or unambiguously definable.

I am going to use it for stories firmly based on known scientific facts and to a considerable extent (though seldom exclusively) devoted to exploring possible consequences of these. Later I will have to qualify that usage. I'll offer a few examples and counterexamples. and touch on ways in which the former can be constructed. As for their philosophical implications, hard science stories would appear to bear the most intimate relationship to science itself and thus be a commentary of sorts upon it. We'll find that appearances are somewhat deceiving.

Let's start with Verne. There may have been a little hard science fiction before him, but his work is surely the prime source and, to this day, the archetype of the school. True, it was by no means the sole kind of yarn he spun. In fact, most of his are straight adventure stories laid on contemporary Earth. *Around the World in Eighty Days* is, at best, borderline. It describes something which could have been done at the time had anybody wanted to take the trouble; the one "scientific" point in it concerns the International Date Line, which had already been established. At the opposite end of the spectrum, such stories as *Journey to the Center of the Earth* and *Hector Servadac* are outright tall tales. Verne protested Wells' cavalier attitude toward scientific plausibility, but he adopted it himself when a notion was otherwise attractive.

Twenty Thousand Leagues Under the Sea comes close to being a hundred-percent hard science novel, but isn't quite. The author's descriptions of the deep are accurate, for their day, as well as loving. However, in themselves they hold no extrapolations, unless we count the ruins of Atlantis or an educated guess about the nature of the polar sea. The submarine and its ancillary equipment are described in detail which is carefully thought out and genuinely extrapolative. However, *pace* Walt Disney, they involve no atomic energy. Doubtless because he recognized the practical problems of refueling, Verne cleverly avoided saying what the ultimate power source of the *Nautilus* was. We may as well lay another bit of folklore to rest; he did not "invent" the periscope in this book, which never mentions any such thing.

Still, it represents a remarkable exercise of the disciplined imagination. *From the Earth to the Moon* and its sequel are absolutely hard science fiction. I did once think the author had fudged a couple of items. When his characters are launched into space by a cannon, the acceleration should have crushed them to jelly and air resistance destroyed their capsule. Then I happened to mention this to Robert Heinlein, and he pointed out to me that in Verne's era it was quite unknown what the effects of those factors would be.

A science fiction writer can't be expected to see where real science would go. Such an ability would make him a prophet with supernatural powers. Thus, the *Venus Equilateral* stories of the late 1940's had interplanetary communications engineers using vacuum tubes and slide rules. There was no way for the author, George O. Smith, to predict the transistor that has made these things obsolete, for it wasn't even a theoretical possibility at the time. His writing gave its special pleasure—and still does on rereading—precisely because he made his imagination work strictly from known facts (at least in the initial parts of this series).

Early in the twentieth century, Konstantin Tsiolkovsky published a novel about a space program which remains a dazzling example of extrapolation. It also fails to include a lot, such as the vital role of computers. Nevertheless, one way or another, most of what it describes has now come to pass or soon will, because he reasoned out that that was how the development would have to go. The book would have been more influential on science fiction—in the West, at any rate—had it not appeared in Russia and had it not been clumsy as a novel, a thinly disguised treatise.

After Hugo Gernsback founded the world's first science fiction magazine, he loved to print stories of this kind, loaded with ponderous lectures. I would, though, like to state that his own famous *Ralph 124C41+* is not hard science fiction as often alleged. Aside from a vague forecast of radar, the elaborate technology in it does not rise solidly—usually does not rise at all—from solid knowledge, but consists mostly of words, mostly coined on the spot.

We can go into the modern era and mention Lester del Rey's "Nerves," which described an atomic power plant well before Alamogordo, plus the medical problems that might arise and the response to these[1]; or Heinlein's *Have Spacesuit, Will Travel* and *Starship Troopers,* which went into close detail about spacesuits, on which the author once worked; or Frank Herbert's *Under Pressure* (also known as *The Dragon in the Sea),* which harked back to Verne by carrying submarine development into our future and whose suggestion of a method of undersea transport has since been tried out; or Arthur C. Clarke's *Prelude to Space* and *A Fall of Moondust,* whose meticulousness is not spoiled by reality having turned out to be different; or—The list might continue for a while.

I'll break it off, arbitrarily but for a good reason. The fact is that hitherto we have been considering fiction about technology rather than about science.

Granted, there is no clear boundary here either. Not only do technological developments spring from scientific, but *vice versa.* Work on atomic energy or spacecraft has involved studying certain fundamental properties of matter; but it takes engineering to build a particle accelerator, whereas spacecraft have helped give us basic information about the universe. In modern medicine, work in disciplines such as biochemistry is almost simultaneous with clinical application of what is learned; the results of that provide additional data which further the "pure" research.

Still, however closely they cooperate, the astronomer and the astronaut, the mathematician and the computer programmer, the archeologist and the hydraulics engineer (an actual case in Israel) are not identical. They differ not simply in the details of their endeavors, but in their general orientations. Theodore Sturgeon has called science fiction "knowledge fiction." Even nowadays, much science is devoted to gathering knowledge for its own sake. A school of writing exists, as accuracy-conscious as the one we've been considering, which reflects this attitude.

It appears to be slightly younger than the technological kind. Wells' story "The Star" is an early example—what might happen if a large astronomical body wandered into the Solar System? "The Land Ironclads" shows that Wells could

1 It was later expanded to novel length, but that was postwar.

write hard technology fiction when he wanted to. "The Star" proves the same for hard *science* fiction.

About the same time appeared, in France, J. -H. Rosny aînés *La Guerre du Feu (The Fire War),* an epical novel of prehistoric man. That theme may be hackneyed now, but then it was not; the author was drawing on findings newly made. He put them into human—or, we might say, phenomenological—terms. He showed what the paleolithic world, which science knew only through tools and bones and so on, might have felt like. This is no different in principle from what a modern writer does who tries to show us what it's probably like on Mars or possibly like on a planet of 61 Cygni.

John Taine in *Before the Dawn* and, more recently, L. Sprague de Camp in "A Gun for Dinosaur," gave us vivid accounts of the Mesozoic era, as correct as possible, with the gaps in available information filled in by speculative but careful reasoning. To be sure, both stories necessarily used ideas of the time travel sort in order to bring the scene before humans or bring humans onto the scene, so they are not totally hard science. Fredric Brown's lovely little "Starvation" perhaps is, being told from a dinosaur's viewpoint, but this can't be done very often.

Developments in biology have given ideas to writers who took care to stay accurate as regards known facts and to be conservative, no matter how imaginative, in their extrapolations from these. That is, of course they went beyond the facts, but did not contradict them nor bring in anything basically different. Aldous Huxley's *Brave New World* forecast exogenesis, which is now experimental, and hypnopedia—which did not turn out to be feasible, but the author could not have known that. In 1942, Heinlein's *Beyond This Horizon* described control of heredity in some detail and showed that it would not be an unmixed blessing—which is what the 1976 conference at Asilomar was about. Ursula K. Le Guin's "Nine Lives" and, more sketchily, *The Left Hand of Darkness* include plausible biological developments and their consequences. Again, one could multiply examples.

By and large, though, hard biology has been just a single element in most stories which contain it. Their emphasis has been on psychology or sociology, no doubt because the life sciences strike close to home. We must turn spaceward to find many cases where the science is what the narrative is primarily about.

Though Stanley Weinbaum did not confine himself to hard science copy, in his tragically short career he was a brilliant pioneer of it. "A Martian Odyssey" and its sequel "Valley of Dreams" depict a Mars which—unlike that of Burroughs or Buck Rogers, or later of Bradbury—could well have existed, as far as astronomers of the time were able to tell. More significantly, Weinbaum was aware that differences from Earth have effects ranging from the spectacular to the subtle, as we are learning today from our space program. His various interplanetary tales amount to delighted exploration of the possibilities.

In modern times, Herbert's *Dune* trilogy sprang from the author's close study of sandy environments such as beaches and deserts. He went on into ecology and anthropology until he had fashioned a wonderfully complete world. When we read these books, we have been there. Granted, some readers have taken technical exception to some parts of them; for instance, would the ecology really work as described, under the given circumstances? However, this playing of what Hal Clement calls the Game—in which readers try to catch writers in errors of fact or logic—is among the special joys of this kind of literature. Larry Niven's *Ringworld* has been a subject of the same kind of debate. This would not have happened were it not such a fascinating blend of reason and imagination.

Clement is the grand master of hard science fiction. His most famous work, *Mission of Gravity,* is an adventure with an extraterrestrial setting, but mainly an intellectual odyssey. The enormous world of Mesklin, its weird shape and variable gravity, its chill beneath two dim red suns, the life it has brought forth and the many different climes it provides for that life, physics, chemistry, biology, oceanography, navigation, everything is considered and brought together into a seamless web, as nearly as a mortal may do so. No better job of worldbuilding has ever come forth, nor ever likely will, unless by the author himself.

He is not infallible; indeed, he, a modest man, would be the last to make that claim. At the time it was first published, *Mission of Gravity* drew a few criticisms of the sort I've described. Subsequently, Pioneer flybys of Jupiter and closer analyses of the behavior of the star 61 Cygni suggest that a planet the size of Mesklin may be red-hot or may not occur at all in that system. Changes in scientific ideas are the doom of hard science stories: though I say "may" above in order to emphasize that the case against Mesklin is by no means proven as yet.

I must confess to being caught out myself upon occasion. For instance, once I had a scene in which a certain wine, the best in the house, was being drunk, and a French reader wrote to protest: "Ah, no, no *monsieur,* for that wine, that was a very bad year!" Another Frenchman, a prehistorian, objected to a scene in a story laid in Cro-Magnon times, which mentioned a sabertoothed tiger; he pointed out that, while the sabertooth still flourished in America, it was then extinct in Europe, and added, "It seems that long-toothed carnivores always survive later in America." I could go on at length, but will conclude in a more sober vein by citing *We Have Fed Our Sea* (also known as *The Enemy Stars).* It was intended as hard science fiction, but even when I was writing, a few things which I thought might be true had, in the opinion of most physicists, been disproven.

Still, the book provides a handy example, because one of the hard elements in it was technological; I devoted some effort to roughing out a design for the spaceship. This illustrates the fact that science and technology are no more separable in fiction than they are in real life.

Nor are they jointly separable from the rest of what people do. As a case in point of that, let me spend words on another novel of my own, *The People of the Wind*—not because it's the best in any sense, but because it includes both hard and "soft" components—and, mainly, because it's mine, so that I won't risk misrepresenting somebody else. *Mutatis mutandis,* let it stand for any number of works by others.

The genesis is as complicated as the genesis of most things. For long I'd wanted to do a tale about humans and nonhumans living together on the same world and the hybrid society that would result. However, it was vague in my mind, no real story there.

Then I happened to be in New York and had lunch with John Campbell, the last time we ever met. Though he was in considerable pain from arthritis, his mind was as luminous as always. In the course of talk I raised a question: If reptiles evolved from amphibians, and mammals from reptiles, what might evolve from mammals? He replied that that's us, that intelligence was the next development. I insisted: Suppose intelligence had not arisen, what then? At once Campbell suggested a forced-draft air intake, which ought to give enormous cursive ability.

Thinking about this afterward, I saw that it would also enable a larger creature to fly than has ever been the case upon Earth. Years before, I'd imagined winged sophonts, but that was on a planet with much denser atmosphere. The possibility of them under more or less familiar conditions remained a challenge of the hard-science kind. After all, they'd have to be fairly massive, in order to include sufficient brains, and this meant considerable wing loading. Where would the energy come from to power such an animal? Campbell had answered that question, without knowing that he did.

Things were at this indefinite stage when my wife and colleague Karen Anderson and I chanced to be traveling through Alsace, came to Belfort, and learned how gallantly that city had withstood German siege in the Franco-Prussian War although the Alsatians are ethnically more German than French. In consequence, Bismarck, who was no fool, let Belfort remain in French enclave after he had annexed the rest of Alsace to his empire.

Here was the story structure I had been wanting, to bring the interactions of two races into high relief; and those winged beings were the kind of aliens I needed, because it was clear that they'd differ from humans in basic ways, yet might have enough in common with us for a close relationship. A while after returning home, I got busy.

First came the matter of designing planets. Although the plot required worlds where humans could live unaided, mere copies of Earth with a few geographical names changed and a few "rabbitoids" and "dandelionoids" in the landscape are unsatisfying. Then what could some plausible differences be? It does seem that our globe is what it is because of being delicately balanced in a narrow radiation zone, as well as because of many other factors—

—so take a star of a reasonable type, not quite the same as that of Sol; put your planet in orbit around it at such a mean distance that you'll get the right mean temperature; this will determine the length of the year, which, along with axial tilt and orbital eccentricity, determines a great deal else; if the planet itself has a certain mass and density, and any satellites it possesses have these-and-those characteristics, then other consequences are likely... The design process involves a fair amount of mathematics and a larger amount of *chutzpah.*[2]

Less exact, therefore in a way more intriguing, was the construction of winged nonhumans. Just for openers, what would they use for hands? My earlier flyers

2 I have described it at length in "The Creation of Imaginary Worlds: The World Builder's Handbook and Pocket Companion," in *Science Fiction, Today and Tomorrow*, Reginald Bretnor ed. (Harper & Row 1974)

had been six-limbed, but this now struck me as a copout, though conceivably such beings do live here and there in the universe. All Terrestrial vertebrates have four limbs, no more. If one pair are wings and one pair legs, what can serve as arms with tool-wielding hands?

Well, Karen keeps a parrot, which often uses a foot in an eerily handlike way. However, it must stand meanwhile upon the other foot, and I felt pretty sure that two hands would be necessary for the making of early tools (bearing in mind that sophonts are the products of a long evolution, if they are not artificial creations). Could the aliens use their wings for support on the ground, thereby liberating both feet? I found justification for this idea in a South American bird called the hoactzin. Juveniles have claws on their wings, which they use for crawling around in trees until they are ready to fly. A similar feature might be retained and developed in the adult (though it is not in the hoactzin, but lost), even as the juvenile ape characteristics of large head and relative hairlessness are retained and developed in man. In fact, our opposable thumb is elaborated from a primitive arrangement of the digits which occurs in most of the higher animals only at a fetal stage.

Presumably the wings of my race, in flight, could drive a sort of bellows to operate Campbell's supercharger...Of course, oxygen uptake in our blood is already pretty high, so they'd need something other than hemoglobin; but you wouldn't expect the biochemistry to be identical anyway...

I found it necessary to plan this creature from the skeleton outward. Drawings are still in my files, but it's as well that no photographs were taken of me moving around on the floor, elbows to carpet, to get a notion of how the wings must be articulated. Meanwhile I was thinking further about the chemistry. A supercharged being would have tremendous energy requirements; therefore it was probably carnivorous and, oh, yes, very territorial...

The rest is in the book, implicitly or explicitly. I have gone into these details to show how the mind of one hard science fiction writer worked upon one occasion. I cannot speak for others, though it would be most interesting if they did for themselves.

Now *The People of the Wind* is not absolutely hard, because it includes things like faster-than-light travel and gravity control which do not lie within the purview of present-day science. Even *Mission of Gravity* employs the first of these, and says that the second may result from research on Mesklin. Thus boundaries blur, as always, and by degrees we move into further-out kinds of stories. These days, science itself is getting far out—all of which is proper material for the next essay.

The Burning Bridge

The message was an electronic shout, the most powerful and tightly-beamed shortwave transmission which men could generate, directed with all the precision which mathematics and engineering could offer. Nevertheless that pencil must scrawl broadly over the sky, and for a long time, merely hoping to write on its target. For when distances are measured in lightweeks, the smallest errors grow monstrous.

As it happened, the attempt was successful. Communications Officer Anastas Mardikian had assembled his receiver after acceleration ceased—a big thing, surrounding the flagship *Ranger* like a spiderweb trapping a fly—and had kept it hopefully tuned over a wide band. The radio beam swept through, ghostly faint from dispersion, wave length doubled by Doppler effect, ragged with cosmic noise. An elaborate system of filters and amplifiers could make it no more than barely intelligible.

But that was enough.

Mardikian burst onto the bridge. He was young, and the months had not yet devoured the glory of his first deep-space voyage. "Sir!" he yelled. "A message…I just played back the recorder…from Earth!"

Fleet Captain Joshua Coffin started. That movement, in weightlessness, spun him off the deck. He stopped himself with a practiced hand, stiffened, and rapped back: "If you haven't yet learned regulations, a week of solitary confinement may give you a chance to study them."

"I...but, sir—" The other man retreated. His uniform made a loose rainbow splash across metal and plastic. Coffin alone, of all the fleet's company, held to the black garments of a space service long extinct.

"But, sir," said Mardikian. His voice seemed to have fallen off a high cliff. "Word from Earth!"

"Only the duty officer may enter the bridge without permission," Coffin reminded him. "If you had anything urgent to tell, there is an intercom."

"I thought—" choked Mardikian. He paused, then came to the free-fall equivalent of attention. Anger glittered in his eyes, "Sorry, sir."

Coffin hung quiet a while, looking at the dark young man in the brilliant clothes. *Forget it,* he said to himself. *Times are another. You went once to e Eridani, and almost ninety years had passed when you returned. Earth was like a foreign planet. This is as good as spacemen get to be nowadays, careless, superstitions, jabbering among each other in languages I don't understand. Thank God there are any recruits at all, and hope He will let there continue to be a few for what remains of your life.*

The duty officer, Hallmyer, was tall and blond and born in Lancashire; but he watched the other two with Asian eyes. No one spoke, though Mardikian breathed heavily. Stars filled the bow viewport, crowding a huge night.

Coffin sighed. "Very well," he said. "I'll let it pass this time."

After all, he reflected, a message from Earth was an event. Radio had, indeed, gone between Sol and Alpha Centauri, but that was with very special equipment. To pinpoint a handful of ships, moving at half the speed of light, and to do it so well that the comparatively small receiver Mardikian had erected would pick up the beam—Yes, the boy had some excuse for gladness.

"What was the signal?" Coffin inquired.

He expected it would only be routine, a test, so that engineers a lifetime hence could ask the returning fleet whether their transmission had registered. (If there were any engineers by then, on an Earth sinking into poverty and mysticism.)

Instead, Mardikian blurted: "Old Svoboda is dead. The new Psychologics Commissioner is Thomas...Thomson...that part didn't record clearly...anyway, he must be sympathetic to the Constitutionalists. He's rescinded the educational decree—promised more consideration to provincial mores. Come hear for yourself, sir!"

Despite himself, Coffin whistled. "But that's why the e Eridani colony was being founded," he said. His words fell flat and silly into silence.

Hallmyer said, with the alien hiss in his English that Coffin hated, for it was like the Serpent in a once noble garden:

"Apparently the colony has no more reason to be started. But how shall we consult with three thousand would-be pioneers lying in deep-sleep?"

"Shall we?" Coffin did not know why-not yet-but he felt his brain move with the speed of fear. "We've undertaken to deliver them to Rustum. In the absence of definite orders from Earth, are we even allowed to consider a change of plans... since a general vote can't be taken? Better avoid possible trouble and not even mention—" He broke off. Mardikian's face had become a mask of dismay.

"But, sir!" bleated the Com officer.

A chill rose up in Coffin. "You have already told," he said.

"Yes," whispered Mardikian. "I met Coenrad de Smet, he had come over to this ship for some repair parts, and...I never thought—"

"Exactly!" growled Coffin.

The fleet numbered fifteen, more than half the interstellar ships humankind possessed. But Earth's overlords had been as anxious to get rid of the Constitutionalists (the most stubborn ones, at least; the stay-at-homes were *ipso facto* less likely to be troublesome) as that science-minded, liberty-minded group of archaists were to escape being forcibly absorbed by modern society. Rustum, e Eridani

II, was six parsecs away, forty-one years of travel, and barely habitable: but the only possible world yet discovered. A successful colony would be prestigious, and could do no harm; its failure would dispose of a thorn in the official ribs. Tying up fifteen ships for eight decades was all right too. Exploration was a dwindling activity, which interested fewer men each generation.

So Earth's government co-operated fully. It even provided speeches and music when the colonists embarked for the orbiting fleet. After which, Coffin thought, the government had doubtless grinned to itself and thanked its various heathen gods that that was over with.

"Only now," he muttered, "it isn't."

He free-sat in the *Ranger's* general room, a tall, bony, faintly grizzled Yankee and waited. The austerity of the wails was broken by a few pictures. Coffin had wanted to leave them bare—since no one else would care for a view of the church where his father had preached, a hundred years ago, or be interested in a model of that catboat the boy Joshua had sailed on a bay which glittered in summers now forgotten—but even the theoretically absolute power of a fleet captain had its limits. At least the men nowadays were not making this room obscene with naked women. Though in all honesty, he wasn't sure he wouldn't rather have that than... brush-strokes on rice paper, the suggestion of a tree, and a classic ideogram. He did not understand the new generations.

The *Ranger* skipper, Nils Kivi, was like a breath of home: a small dapper Finn who had traveled with Coffin on the first e Eridani trip. They were not exactly friends, an admiral has no intimates, but they had been young in the same decade.

Actually, thought Coffin, *most of us spacemen are anachronisms. I could talk to Goldstein or Yamato or Pereira, to quite a few on this voyage, and not meet blank surprise when I mentioned a dead actor or hummed a dead song. But of course, they are all in unaging deepsleep now. We'll stand our one-year watches in turn, and be put back in the coldvats, and have no chance to talk till journey's end.*

"It may prove to be fun," mused Kivi.

"What?" asked Coffin.

"To walk around High America again, and fish in the Emperor River, and dig up our old camp," said Kivi. "We had some fine times on Rustum, along with all the work and danger."

Coffin was startled, that his own thoughts should have been so closely followed. "Yes," he agreed, remembering strange wild dawns on the Cleft edge, "that was a pretty good five years."

Kivi sighed. "Different this time," he said. "Now that I think about it, I am not sure I do want to go back. We had so much hope then—we were discoverers, walking where men had never even laid eyes before. Now the colonists will be the hopeful ones. We are just their transportation."

Coffin shrugged. "We must take what is given us, and be thankful."

"This time," said Kivi, "I will constantly worry: suppose I come home again and find my job abolished? No more space travel at all. If that happens, I refuse to be thankful."

Forgive him, Coffin asked his God. *It is cruel to watch the foundation of your life being gnawed away.*

Kivi's eyes lit up, the briefest flicker. "Of course," he said, "if we really do cancel this trip, and go straight back, we may not arrive too late. We may still find a few expeditions to new stars being organized, and get on their rosters."

Coffin tautened. Again he was unsure why he felt an emotion: now, anger. "I shall permit no disloyalty for the purpose for which we are engaged," he clipped.

"Oh, come off it," said Kivi. "Be rational. I don't know your reason for undertaking this wretched cruise. You had rank enough to turn down the assignment; no one else did. But you still want to explore as badly as I. If Earth didn't care about us, they would not have bothered to invite us back. Let us seize the opportunity while it lasts." He intercepted a reply by glancing at the wall chrono. "Time for our conference." He flicked the intership switch.

A panel came to life, dividing into fourteen sections, one for each accompanying vessel. One or two faces peered from each. The craft which bore only supplies and sleeping crewmen were represented by their captains. Those which had colonists also revealed a civilian spokesman.

Coffin studied every small image in turn. The spacemen he knew, they all belonged to the Society and even those born long after him had much in common. There was a necessary minimum discipline of mind and body, and the underlying dream for which all else had been traded: new horizons under new suns. Not that spacemen indulged in such poetics; they had too much work to do.

The colonists were something else. Coffin shared things with them—predominantly North American background, scientific habit of thought, distrust of all governments. But few Constitutionalists had any religion; those who did were Romish, Jewish, Buddhist, or otherwise alien to him. All were tainted with the self-indulgence of this era: they had written into their covenant that only physical necessity could justify moralizing legislation, and that free speech was limited only by personal libel. Coffin thought sometimes he would be glad to see the last of them.

"Are you all prepared?" he began.

"Very well, let's get down to business. It's unfortunate the Com officer gossiped so loosely. He stirred up a hornet's nest." Coffin saw that few understood the idiom. "He made discontent which threatens this whole project, and which we must now deal with."

Coenrad de Smet, colonist aboard the *Scout,* smiled in an irritating way he had. "You would simply have concealed the fact?" he asked.

"It would have made matters easier," said Coffin stiffly.

"In other words," said de Smet, "you know better what we might want than we do ourselves. That, sir, is the kind of arrogance we hoped to escape. No man has the right to suppress any information bearing on public affairs."

A low voice, with a touch of laughter, said through a hood: "And you accuse Captain Coffin of preaching!"

The New Englander's eyes were drawn to her. Not that he could see through the shapeless gown and mask, such as hid all the waking women; but he had met Teresa Zeleny on Earth. Hearing her now was somehow like remembering Indian summer on a wooded hilltop, a century ago.

An involuntary smile quirked his lips. "Thank you," he said. "Do you, Mr. de Smet, know—what the sleeping colonists might want? Have you any right to decide for *them?* And yet we can't wake them, even the adults, to vote. There simply isn't room; if nothing else, the air regenerators couldn't supply that much oxygen. That's why I felt it best to tell no one, until we were actually at Rustum. Then those who wished could return with the fleet, I suppose."

"We could rouse them a few at a time, let them vote, and put them back to sleep," suggested Teresa Zeleny.

"It would take weeks," said Coffin. "You, of all people, should know metabolism isn't lightly stopped, or easily restored."

"If you could see my face," she said, again with a chuckle, "I would grimace amen. I'm so sick of tending inert human flesh that...well, I'm glad they're only women and girls, because if I also had to massage and inject men I'd take a vow of chastity!"

Coffin blushed, cursed himself for blushing, and hoped she couldn't see it over the telecircuit. He noticed Kivi grin.

Kivi provided the merciful interruption. "Your few-at-a-time proposal is pointless anyhow," he said. "In the course of those weeks we would pass the critical date."

"What's that?" asked a young girl's voice.

"You don't know?" said Coffin, surprised.

"Let it pass for now," broke in Teresa. Once again, as several times before, Coffin admired her decisiveness. She cut through nonsense with a man's speed and a woman's practicality. "Take our word for it, June, if we don't turn about within two months, we'll do better to go on to Rustum. So, voting is out. We could wake a few sleepers, but those already conscious are really as adequate a statistical sample."

Coffin nodded. She spoke for five women on her ship, who stood a year-watch caring for two hundred ninety-five asleep. The one hundred twenty who would not be restimulated for such duty during the voyage, were children. The proportion on the other nine colonist-laden vessels was similar; the crew totaled one thousand six hundred twenty, with forty-five up and about at all times. Whether the die was cast by less than two per cent, or by four or five per cent, was hardly significant.

"Let's recollect exactly what the message was," said Coffin. "The educational decree which directly threatened your Constitutionalist way of life has been withdrawn. You're no worse off now than formerly—and no better, though there's a hint of further concessions in the future. You're invited home again. That's all. We have not picked up any other transmissions. It seems very little data on which to base so large a decision."

"It's an even bigger one, to continue," said de Smet. He leaned forward, a bulky man, until he filled his little screen. Hardness rang in his tones. "We were able people, economically rather well off. I daresay Earth already misses our services, especially in technological fields. Your own report makes Rustum out a grim place; many of us would die there. Why should we not turn home?"

"Home," whispered someone.

The word filled a sudden quietness, like water filling a cup, until quietness brimmed over with it. Coffin sat listening to the voice of his ship, generators, ventilators, regulators, and he began to hear a beat frequency which was *Home, home, home.*

Only his home was gone. His father's church was torn down for an Oriental temple, and the woods where October had burned were cleared for another tentacle of city, and the bay was enclosed to make a plankton farm. For him, only a spaceship remained, and the somehow cold hope of heaven.

A very young man said, almost to himself: "I left a girl back there."

"I had a little sub," said another. "I used to poke around the Great Barrier Reef, skindiving out the air lock or loafing on the surface. You wouldn't believe how blue the waves could be. They tell me on Rustum you can't come down off the mountain tops."

"But we'd have the whole planet to ourselves," said Teresa Zeleny.

One with a gentle scholar's face answered: "That may be precisely the trouble, my dear. Three thousand of us, counting children, totally isolated from the human mainstream. Can we hope to build a civilization? Or even maintain one?"

"Your problem, pop," said the officer beside him dryly, "is that there are no medieval manuscripts on Rustum."

"I admit it," said the scholar. "I thought it more important my children grow up able to use their minds. But if it turns out they can do so on Earth—How much chance will the first generations on Rustum have to sit down and really think, anyway?"

"Would there even be a next generation on Rustum?"

"One and a quarter gravities—I can feel it now."

"Synthetics, year after year of synthetics and hydroponics, till we can establish an ecology. I had steak on Earth, once in a while."

"My mother couldn't come. Too frail. But she's paid for a hundred years of deepsleep, all she could afford...just in case I do return."

"I designed skyhouses. They won't build anything on Rustum much better than sod huts, in my lifetime."

"Do you remember moonlight on the Grand Canyon?"

"Do you remember Beethoven's Ninth in the Federal Concert Hall?"

"Do you remember that funny little Midlevel bar, where we all drank beer and sang *Lieder?*"

"Do you remember?"

"Do you remember?"

* * * *

Teresa Zeleny shouted across their voices: "In Anker's name! What are you thinking about? If you care so little, you should never have embarked in the first place!"

It brought back the silence, not all at once but piece by piece, until Coffin could pound the table and call for order. He looked straight at her hidden eyes and said: "Thank you, Miss Zeleny, I was expecting tears to be uncorked any moment."

One of the *girls* snuffled behind her mask.

Charles Lochaber, speaking for the *Courier* colonists, nodded. "Aye, 'tis a blow to our purpose. I am not so sairtain I myself would vote to continue, did I feel the message was to be trusted."

"What?" De Smet's square head jerked up from between his shoulders.

Lochaber grinned without much humor. "The government has been getting more arbitrary each year," he said. "They were ready enough to let us go, aye. But they may regret it now—not because we could ever be any active threat, but because we will be a subversive example, up there in Earth's sky, Or just because we will *be.* Mind ye, I know not for sairtain; but 'tis possible they decided we are safer dead, and this is to trick us back. 'Twould be characteristic dictatorship behavior."

"Of all the fantastic—" gasped an indignant female voice.

Teresa broke in: "Not as wild as you might think, dear. I have read a little history, and I don't mean that censored pap which passes for it nowadays. But there's another possibility, which I think is just as alarming. That message may be perfectly honest and sincere. But will it still be true when we get back? Remember how long that will take! And even if we could return overnight, to an Earth which welcomed us home, what guarantee would there be that our children, or our grandchildren, won't suffer the same troubles as us, without the same chance to break free?"

"Ye vote, then, to carry on?" asked Lochaber.

Pride answered: "Of course."

"Good lass, I too."

Kivi raised his hand. Coffin recognized him, and the spaceman said: "I am not sure the crew ought not to have a voice in this also."

"What?" De Smet grew red. He gobbled for a moment before he could get out: "Do you seriously think you could elect us to settle on that annex of hell—and then come home to Earth yourselves?"

"As a matter of fact," said Kivi, smiling, "I suspect the crew would prefer to return at once. I know I would, Seven years may make a crucial difference."

"If a colony is planted, though," said Coffin, "it might provide the very inspiration which space travel needs to survive."

"Hm-m-m. Perhaps. I shall have to think about that."

"I hope you realize," said the very young man with ornate sarcasm, "that every second we sit here arguing takes us one hundred fifty thousand kilometers farther from home."

"Dinna fash yourself," said Lochaber. "Whatever we do, that girl of yours will be an auld carline before you reach Earth."

De Smet was still choking at Kivi: "You lousy little ferryman, if you think you can make pawns of us—"

And Kivi stretched his lips in anger and growled, "If you do not watch your language, you clodhugger, I will come over there and stuff you down your own throat."

"Order!" yelled Coffin. "Order!"

Teresa echoed him: "Please...for all our lives' sake...don't you know where we are? You've got a few centimeters of wall between you and zero! Please, whatever we do, we can't fight or we'll never see any planet again!"

But she did not say it weeping, or as a beggary. It was almost a mother's voice—strange, in an unmarried woman—and it quieted the male snarling more than Coffin's shouts.

The fleet captain said finally: "That will do. You're all too worked up to think. Debate is adjourned sixteen hours. Discuss the problem with your shipmates, get some sleep, and report the consensus at the next meeting."

"Sixteen hours?" yelped someone. "Do you know how much return time that adds?"

"You heard me," said Coffin. "Anybody who wants to argue may do so from the brig. Dismissed!"

He snapped off the switch.

Kivi, temper eased, gave him a slow confidential grin. "That heavy-father act works nearly every time, no?"

Coffin pushed from the table. "I'm going out," he said. His voice sounded harsh to him, a stranger's. "Carry on."

He had never felt so alone before, not even the night his father died. *O God, who spake unto Moses in the wilderness, reveal now thy will.* But God was silent, and Coffin turned blindly to the only other help he could think of.

Space armored, he paused a moment in the air lock before continuing. He had been an astronaut for twenty-five years—for a century if you added time in the vats—but he could still not look upon naked creation without fear.

An infinite blackness flashed: stars beyond stars, to the bright ghost-road of the Milky Way and on out to other galaxies and flocks of galaxies, until the light which a telescope might now register had been born before the Earth. Looking from his air-lock cave, past the radio web and the other ships, Coffin felt himself drown in enormousness, coldness, and total silence—though he knew that this vacuum burned and roared with man-destroying energies, roiled like currents of gas and dust more massive than planets and travailed with the birth of new suns—and he said to himself the most dreadful of names, *I am that I am,* and sweat formed chilly little globules under his arms.

This much a man could see within the Solar System. Traveling at half light-speed stretched the human mind still further, till often it ripped across and another lunatic was shoved into deepsleep. For aberration redrew the sky, crowding stars toward the bows, so that the ships plunged toward a cloud of Doppler hell-blue. The constellations lay thinly abeam, you looked out upon the dark. Aft, Sol was still the brightest object in heaven, but it had gained a sullen red tinge, as if already grown old, as if the prodigal would return from far places to find his home buried under ice.

What is man that thou art mindful of him? The line gave its accustomed comfort; for, after all, the Sun-maker had also wrought this flesh, atom by atom, and at the very least would think it worthy of hell. Coffin had never understood how his atheist colleagues endured free space.

Well—

He took aim at the next hull and fired his little spring-powered crossbow. A light line unreeled behind the magnetic bolt. He tested its security with habitual care, pulled himself along until he reached the companion ship, yanked the bolt loose and fired again, and so on from hull to slowly orbiting hull, until he reached the *Pioneer.*

Its awkward ugly shape was like a protective wall against the stars. Coffin drew himself past the ion tubes, now cold. Their skeletal structure seemed impossibly frail to have hurled forth peeled atoms at one half c. Mass tanks bulked around the vessel; allowing for deceleration, plus a small margin, the mass ratio was about nine to one. Months would be required at Rustum to refine enough reaction material for the home voyage. Meanwhile such of the crew as were not thus engaged would help the colony get established—

If it ever did!

Coffin reached the forward air lock and pressed the "doorbell." The outer valve opened for him, and he cycled through. First Officer Karamchand met him and helped him doff armor. The other man on duty found an excuse to approach and listen; for monotony was as corrosive out here as distance and strangeness.

"Ah, sir. What brings you over?"

Coffin braced himself. Embarrassment roughened his tone: "I want to see Miss Zeleny."

"Of course—But why come yourself? I mean, the telecircuit—"

"In person!" barked Coffin.

"What?" escaped the crewman. He propelled himself backward in terror of a wigging. Coffin ignored it.

"Emergency," he snapped. "Please intercom her and arrange for a private discussion."

"Why…why…yes, sir. At once. Will you wait here...I mean...yes, sir!" Karamchand shot down the corridor.

Coffin felt a sour smile on his own lips. He could understand if they got confused. His own law about the women had been like steel, and now he violated it himself.

The trouble was, he thought, no one knew if it was even required. Until now there had been few enough women crossing space, and they only within the Solar System, on segregated ships. There was no background of interstellar experience. It seemed reasonable, though, that a man on his year-watch should not be asked to tend deepsleeping female colonists. (Or vice versa!) The idea revolted Coffin personally; but for once the psychotechs had agreed with him. And, of course, waking men and women, freely intermingling, were potentially even more explosive. Haremlike seclusion appeared the only answer; and husband and wife were not to be awake at the same time.

Bad enough to see women veiled when there was a telecircuit conference. (Or did the masks make matters still worse, by challenging the imagination? Who knew?) Best seal off the living quarters and cold-vat sections of the craft which bore them. Crewmen standing watches on those particular ships had better return to their own vessels to sleep and eat.

Coffin braced his muscles. *The rule wouldn't apply if a large meteor struck,* he reminded himself. *What has come up is more dangerous than that. So never mind what anyone thinks.*

Karamchand returned to salute him and say breathlessly: "Miss Zeleny will see you, captain. This way, if you please."

"Thanks." Coffin followed to the main bulkhead.The women had its doorkey. Now the door stood ajar. Coffin pushed himself through so hard that he overshot and caromed off the farther wall.

Teresa laughed. She closed the door and locked it. "Just to make them feel safe out there," she said. "Poor well-meaning men! Welcome, captain."

He turned about, almost dreading the instant. Her tall form was decent in baggy coveralls, but she had dropped the mask. She was not pretty, he supposed: broad-faced, square-jawed, verging on spinsterhood. But he had liked her way of smiling.

"I—" He found no words.

"Follow me." She led him down a short passage, hand-over-hand along the null-gee rungs. "I've warned the other girls to stay away. You needn't fear being shocked." At the end of the hall was a little partitioned-off room. Few enough personal goods could be taken along, but she had made this place hers, a painting, a battered Shakespeare, the works of Anker, a microplayer. Her tapes ran to Bach, late Beethoven and Strauss music which could be studied endlessly. She took hold of a stanchion and nodded, all at once grown serious.

"What do you want to ask me, captain?"

Coffin secured himself by the crook of an arm and stared at his hands. The fingers strained against each other. "I wish I could give you a clear reply," he said, very low and with difficulty. "You see, I've never met anything like this before. If it involved only men, I guess I could handle the problem. But there are women along, and children."

"And you want a female viewpoint. You're wiser than I had realized. But why me?"

He forced himself to meet her eyes. "You appear the most sensible of the women awake."

"Really!" She laughed. "I appreciate the compliment, but must you deliver it in that parade-ground voice, and glare at me to boot? Relax, captain." She cocked her head, studying him. Then: "Several of the girls don't get this business of the critical point. I tried to explain, but I was only an R.N. at home, and I'm afraid I muddled it rather. Could you put it in words of one and a half syllables?"

"Do you mean the equal-time point?"

"The Point of No Return, some of them call it."

"Nonsense! It's only—Well, look at it this way. We accelerated from Sol at one gravity. We dare not apply more acceleration, even though we could, because so many articles aboard have been lightly built to save mass—the coldvats, for example. They'd collapse under their own weight, and the persons within would die, if we went as much as one-point-five gee. Very well. It took us about one hundred eighty days to reach maximum velocity. In the course of that period, we covered not quite one-and-a-half light-months. We will now go free for almost forty years. At the end of that time, we'll decelerate at one gee for some one hundred eighty days, covering an additional light-month and a half, and enter the e Eridani System with low relative speed. Our star-to-star orbit was plotted with care, but of course the errors add up to many Astronomical Units; furthermore, we have to maneuver, put our ships in orbit about Rustum, send ferry craft back and forth. So we carry a reaction-mass reserve which allows us a total velocity change of about one thousand kilometers per second after journey's end.

"Now imagine we had changed our minds immediately after reaching full speed. We'd still have to decelerate in order to return. So we'd be almost a quarter light-year from Sol, a year after departure, before achieving relative rest. Then, to come back three light-months at one thousand K.P.S. takes roughly seventy-two years. But the whole round trip as originally scheduled, with a one-year layover at Rustum, runs just about eighty-three years!

"Obviously there's some point in time beyond which we can actually get home quicker by staying with the original plan. This date lies after eight months of free fall, or not quite fourteen months from departure. We're only a couple of months from the critical moment right now; if we start back at once, we'll still have been gone from Earth for about seventy-six years. Each day we wait adds months to the return trip. No wonder there's impatience!"

"And the relativity clock paradox makes it worse," Teresa said.

"Well, not too much," Coffin decided. "The tau factor is 0.87. Shipboard time during eighty years of free fall amounts to about seventy years; so far the difference isn't significant. And anyhow, we'll all spend most of the time in deep-sleep. What they're afraid of, the ones who want to go back, is that the Earth they knew will have slipped away from them."

She nodded. "Can't they understand it already has?" she said.

It was like a blade stabbed into Coffin. Though he could not see why that should be: surely he, of all men, knew how relentlessly time flowed. He had already come back once, to an Earth scarcely recognizable. The Society had been a kind of fixed point, but even it had changed; and he—like Kivi, like all of them—was now haunted by the fear of returning again and not finding any other spacemen whatsoever.

But when she spoke it—

"Maybe they're afraid to understand," he said,.

"You keep surprising me, captain," said Teresa with a hint of her smile. "You actually show a bit of human sympathy."

And, thought a far-off part of Coffin, *you showed enough to put me at ease by getting me to lecture you with safe impersonal figures.* But he didn't mind. The fact was that now he could free-sit, face to face, alone, and talk to her like a friend.

"Since we could only save about seven years by giving up at once," he said, "I admit I'm puzzled why so many people are so anxious about it. Couldn't we go on as planned and decide things at Rustum?"

"I think not," said Teresa, "You see, nobody in his right mind wants to be a pioneer. To explore, yes; to settle rich new country with known and limited hazards, yes; but not to risk his children, his whole racial future, on a wild gamble. This group was driven into space by a conflict which just couldn't be settled at home. If that conflict has ended—"

"But…you and Lochaber…you pointed out that it had *not* ended. That at best this is a breathing spell."

"Still, they'd like to believe otherwise, wouldn't they? I mean, at least believe they have a fighting chance on Earth."

"All right," said Coffin. "But it looks a safe bet, that there are a number of deepsleepers who'd agree with you, who'd think their chances are actually better on Rustum. Why can't we take them there first? It seems only fair."

"Uh-uh." Her hair was short, but it floated in loose waves when she shook her head, and light rippled mahogany across it. "You've been there and I haven't, but I've studied your reports. A handful couldn't survive. Three thousand is none too many. It will have to be unanimous, whatever is decided."

"I was trying to avoid that conclusion," he said wearily, "but if you agree—Well, can't we settle the argument at Rustum, after they've looked the place over?"

"No. And I'll tell you why, captain," she said. "I know Coenrad de Smet well, and one or two others. Good men...don't get me wrong…but born politicians, intuitive rather than logical thinkers. They believe, quite honestly, it's best to go back. And, of course, the timid and lazy and selfish ones will support them. They don't want to risk having Rustum there, a whole new world for the taking—and the vote to go against them. I've seen plenty of your photographs, captain. They were so beautiful, some of them, that I can hardly wait for the reality, I know—and so does de Smet—High America is a magnificent place, Room, freedom, unpoisoned air. We'll remember all that we hated on Earth and that isn't on Rustum; we'll reflect much more soberly how long a time will have passed before we could possibly get back, and what a gamble we'd be taking on finding a tolerable situation there. The extra quarter gee won't seem so bad till it's time for heavy manual labor; the alien biochemistry won't bother us much till we have to stop eating rations and start trying to farm; the isolation won't really be felt till your spaceships have departed and we're all the humanity there is for more than twenty lightyears.

"No...de Smet won't risk it. He might get caught up in the glamour himself!"

Coffin murmured thoughtfully: "After only a few days of deceleration, there won't be enough reaction mass to do anything but continue home."

"De Smet knows that, too," said Teresa. "Captain, you can make a hard decision and stick to it. That's why you have your job. But maybe you forget how few people can—how most of us pray someone will come along and tell us what to do. Even under severe pressure, the decision to go to Rustum was difficult. Now that there's a chance to undo it, go back to being safe and comfortable—but still a real risk that by the time we get home, Earth will no longer be safe *or* comfortable—we've been forced to decide all over again. It's agony, captain! De Smet is a strong man, in his way. He'll compel us to do the irrevocable, as soon as possible, just because it will make a final commitment. Once we've turned far enough back, it'll be out of our hands and we can stop thinking."

He regarded her with a sort of wonder. "But you look calm enough," he said.

"I made my decision back on Earth," she answered. "I've seen no reason to change it."

"What do the women think?" he asked, leaping back to safely denumerable things.

"Most want to give up, of course." She said it with a mildness which softened the judgment. "Few of them really wanted to come in the first place, They did so only because their men insisted. Women are much too practical to care about a philosophy, or a frontier, or anything except their families."

"Do you?" he challenged her.

She shrugged ruefully. "I've no family, captain. At the same time, I suppose…a sense of humor…kept me from sublimating it into a Cause of any kind." Counterattacking: "Why do you care what we do, captain?"

"Why?" He was taken aback, and found himself stammering, "Why…. because…I'm in charge—"

"Oh, yes. But isn't it more than that? You spent years on Earth lecturing about Rustum and its colonization. I think it must be a deep symbol to you. Don't worry, I won't go analytic. I happen to think, myself, that this colony is enormously important, objectively speaking, I mean. If our race muffs this chance, we may never get another. But you and I wouldn't care about that, not really, unless it was personally important too. Would we? Why did you accept this thankless job, commanding a colonial fleet? It can't be an itch to explore. Rustum's already been visited once, and you'll have precious little time to carry on any further studies. You could have been off to some star where men have never traveled at all. Do you see, captain? You're not a bit more cold-blooded about this than I. You *want* that colony planted."

She stopped, laughed, and color went across her face. "Oh, dear, I do chatter, don't I? Pardon me, Let's get back to business."

"I think," said Coffin, slowly and jaggedly, "I'm beginning to realize what's involved."

She settled back and listened.

He bent a leg around a stanchion to hold his lean black frame in place and beat one fist softly into the palm of another. "Yes, it is an emotional issue," he said, the words carving the thoughts to shape. "Logic has nothing to do with it. There are some who want so badly to go to Rustum and be free, or whatever they hope to be there, that they'll dice with their lives for the privilege—and their wives' and children's lives. Others went reluctantly, against their own survival instincts, and now that they think they see a way of retreat, something they can justify to themselves, they'll fight any man who tries to bar it. Yes. It's a ghastly situation.

"One way or another, the decision has got to be made soon. And the facts can't be hidden. Every deep-sleeper must be wakened and nursed to health by someone now conscious. The word will pass, year after year, always to a different combination of spacemen and colonists, with always a proportion who're furious about what was decided while they slept. No, furious is too weak a word. Onward or backward, whichever way we go, we've struck at the emotional roots of people. And interstellar space can break the calmest men. How long before just the wrong percentage of malcontents, weaklings, and shaky sanities goes on duty? What's going to happen then?"

He sucked in an uneven breath. "I'm sorry," he faltered. "I should not—"

"Blow off steam? Why not?" she asked calmly. "Would it be better to keep on being the iron man, till one day you put a pistol to your head?"

"You see," he said in his misery, "I'm *responsible.* Men and women...all the little children—But I'll be in deepsleep, I'd go crazy if I tried to stay awake the whole voyage; the organism can't take it. I'll be asleep, and there'll be nothing I can do, but these ships were given into my care!"

He began to shiver. She took both his hands. Neither of them spoke for a long while.

When he left the *Pioneer,* Coffin felt oddly hollow, as if he had opened his chest and pulled out heart and lungs. But his mind functioned with machine precision. For that he was grateful to Teresa: she had helped him discover what the facts were. It was a brutal knowledge, but without such understanding the expedition might well be doomed.

Or might it? Dispassionately, now, Coffin estimated chances. Either they went on to Rustum or they turned back; in either case, the present likelihood of survival was—fifty-fifty? Well, you couldn't gauge it in percentages. Doubtless more safety lay in turning back. But even there the odds were such that no sane man would willingly gamble. Certainly the skipper had no right to take the hazard, if he could avoid it by any means.

But what means were there?

As he hauled himself toward the *Ranger,* Coffin watched the receiver web grow in his eyes, till it snared a distorted Milky Way. It seemed very frail to have carried so much hell. And, indeed, it would have to be dismantled before deceleration. No trick to sabotage the thing. *If only I had known!*

Or if someone on Earth, the villain or well-meaning fool or whatever he was who wrote that first message...if only he would send another. "Ignore preceding. Educational decree still in force...Or something. But no. Such things didn't happen. A man had to make his own luck, in an angry world.

Coffin sighed and clamped bootsoles to his flagship's air lock.

Mardikian helped him through. When he removed his hoarfrosted space helmet, Coffin saw how the boy's mouth quivered. A few hours had put years on Mardikian.

He was in medical whites. Unnecessarily, to break the silence with any inane remark, Coffin said: "Going on vat duty, I see."

"Yes, sir." A mutter. "My turn." The armor made a lot of noise while they stowed it. "We'll need some more ethanol soon, captain," blurted Mardikian desperately.

"What for?" grumbled Coffin. He had often wished the stuff were not indispensable. He alone had the key to its barrel. Some masters allowed a small liquor ration on voyage, and said Coffin was only disguising prejudice in claiming it added risk. ("What the devil *can* happen in interstellar orbit? The only reason anyone stays conscious at all is, the machinery to care properly for sleepers would mass more than the extra supplies do. You can issue the grog when a man comes off watch, can't you? Oh, never mind, never mind! I'm just grateful I don't ship under you!")

"Gammagen fixative…and so on...sir," stumbled Mardikian. "Mr. Hallmyer will...make the requisition as usual."

"All right." Coffin faced his radio man, captured the fearful eyes and would not let them go. "Have there been any further communications?" he snapped.

"From Earth? No. No, sir. I...I wouldn't really expect it...we're about at the… the...the limit of reception now. It's almost a miracle, sir, I suppose, that we picked up the first. Of course, we might get another—" Mardikian's voice trailed off.

Coffin continued to stare. At last: "They've been giving you a hard time, haven't they?"

"What?"

"The ones like Lochaber, who want to go on. They wish you'd had the sense to keep your mouth shut, at least till you consulted me. And then others, like de Smet, have said the opposite. Even over telecircuit, it's no fun being a storm center, is it?"

"No, sir—"

Coffin turned away. Why torment the fellow more? This thing had happened, that was all. And the fewer who realized the danger, and were thereby put under still greater strain, the less that danger would be.

"Avoid such disputes," said Coffin. "Most especially, don't brood over those which do arise. That's just begging for a nervous breakdown—out here. Carry on."

Mardikian gulped and went aft. Coffin drifted athwartships. The vessel thrummed around him.

He was not on watch, and had no desire to share the bridge with whoever was. He should eat something, but the idea was nauseating; he should try to sleep, but that would be useless. How long had he been with Teresa, while she cleared his mind and gave him what comfort she had to offer? A couple of hours. In fourteen hours or less, he must confront the spokesmen of crew and colonists. And meanwhile the fleet seethed.

On Earth, he thought wearily, a choice between going on and turning back would not have drawn men so close to insanity, even if the time elements had been the same. But Earth was long domesticated. Maybe, centuries ago, when a few wind-powered hulks wallowed forth upon hugeness, unsure whether they might sail off the world's edge—maybe then there had been comparable dilemmas. Yes...hadn't Columbus' men come near mutiny? Even unknown, though, and monster-peopled by superstition, Earth had not been as cruel an environment as space; nor had a caravel been as unnatural as a spaceship. Minds could never have disintegrated as quickly in midocean as between the stars.

Coffin grew aware, startled, that he had wandered to the radio shack.

He entered. It was a mere cubbyhole, one wall occupied by gleaming electronic controls, the rest full of racked equipment, tools, testers, spare parts, half-assembled units for this and that special purpose. The fleet did not absolutely need a Com officer—any spaceman could do the minimal jobs, and any officer had intensive electronics training—but Mardikian was a good, conscientious, useful technician.

His trouble was, perhaps, only that he was human.

Coffin pulled himself to the main receiver. A tape whirred slowly between spools, preserving what the web gathered. Coffin looked at a clipboard. Mardikian had written half an hour ago: "Nothing received. Tape wiped and reset, 1530 hr." Maybe since then—? Coffin flipped a switch. A scanner went quickly through the recording, found only cosmic noise—none of the orderliness which would have meant code or speech—and informed the man.

Now if it had just—

Coffin grew rigid. He floated among the mechanisms for a long time, blank-eyed as they, and alone the quick harsh breath showed him to be alive.

O God, help me do that which is right.

But what is right?

I should wrestle with Thy angel until I knew. But there is no time. Lord, be not wroth with me because I have no time.

Anguish ebbed. Coffin got busy.

Decision would be reached at the meeting, fourteen hours hence. A message which was to make a substantial difference ought to be received before then. But not very much before; nor too late, eleventh-hour-reprieve style, either.

But first, what should its wording be? Coffin didn't have to look up the last one. It was branded on his brain. An invitation to return and talk matters over. But necessarily short, compact, with minimum redundancy: which meant an increased danger of misinterpretation.

He braced himself before the typer and began to compose, struck out his first words and started again, and again and again. It had to be exactly right. A mere cancellation of the previous message wouldn't do after all. Too pat. And a suspicion, brooded on during a year-watch, could be as deadly as an outright sense of betrayal. So...

Since fleet now approaching equal-time point, quick action necessary. Colonization plans abandoned. Expedition ordered, repeat ordered to return to Earth. Education decree already rescinded (a man back home wouldn't be certain the first beam had made contact) *and appeals for further concessions will be permitted through proper channels. Constitutionalists reminded that their first duty is to put their skills at disposal of society.*

Would that serve? Coffin read it over. It didn't contradict the first one; it only changed a suggestion to a command, as if someone were growing more frantic by the hour. (And a picture of near-chaos in government wasn't attractive, was it?) The bit about "proper channels" underlined that speech was not free on Earth, and that the bureaucracy could restore the school decree any time it wished. The pompous last sentence ought to irritate men who had turned their backs on the thing which Terrestrial society was becoming.

Maybe it could be improved, though—Coffin resumed work.

When he ripped out his last version, he was astonished to note that two hours had passed. Already? The ship seemed very quiet. Too quiet. He grew feverishly aware that anyone might break in on him at any time.

The tape could run for a day but was usually checked and wiped every six or eight hours. Coffin decided to put his words on it at a spot corresponding to seven hours hence. Mardikian would have come off vat duty, but probably be asleep; he wouldn't play back until shortly before the council meeting.

Coffin turned to a small auxiliary recorder. He had to tape his voice through a circuit which would alter it beyond recognition. And, of course, the whole thing had to be blurred, had to fade and come back, had to be full of squeals and buzzes and the crackling talk of the stars. No easy job to blend all those elements, in null-gee at that. Coffin lost himself in the task. He dared not do otherwise, for then he would be alone with himself.

Plug in this modulator, add an oscillation—Let's see, where's that slide rule, what quantities do you want for—

"What are you doing?"

Coffin twisted about. Fingers clamped on his heart.

Mardikian floated in the doorway, looking dazed and afraid as he saw who the intruder was. "What's wrong, sir?" he asked.

"You're on watch," breathed Coffin.

"Tea break, sir, and I thought I'd check and—" The boy pushed himself into the shack. Coffin saw him framed in meters and transformer banks, like some futuristic saint. But sweat glistened on the dark young face, broke free and drifted in tiny spheroids toward the ventilator.

"Get out of here," said Coffin thickly. And then: "No! I don't mean that! Stay where you are!"

"But—" Almost, the captain could read a mind: *If the old man has gone space-dizzy, name of fate, what's to become of us all?* "Yes, sir."

Coffin licked sandy lips. "It's O.K.," he said. "You surprised me, our nerves are on edge. That's why I hollered."

"S-s-sorry, sir."

"Anyone else around?"

"No, sir. All on duty or—" *I shouldn't have told him that!* Coffin read. *Now he knows I'm alone with him!*

"It's O.K., son," repeated the captain. But his voice came out like a buzz saw cutting through bone. I had a little project here I was, uh, playing with, and... uh—"

"Yes, sir. Of course." *Humor him till I can get away. Then see Mr. Kivi. Let him take the responsibility. I don't want it! I don't want to be the skipper, with nobody between me and the sky. It's too much. It'll crack a man wide open.*

Mardikian's trapped eyes circled the little room. They fell on the typer, and the drafts which Coffin had not yet destroyed.

Silence closed in.

"Well," said Coffin at last. "Now you know."

"Yes, sir." Mardikian could scarcely be heard.

"I'm going to fake this onto the receiver tape."

"B-b...Yes, sir." *Humor him!* Mardikian was drawn bowstring tight, his nostrils flared by terror.

"You see," rasped Coffin, "it has to look genuine. This ought to get their backs up. They'll be more united on colonizing Rustum than they ever were before. At the same time, I can resist them, claim I have my orders to turn about and don't want to get into trouble. Finally, of course, I'll let myself be talked into continuing, however reluctantly. So no one will suspect me of...fraud."

Mardikian's lips moved soundlessly. He was close to hysteria, Coffin saw.

"It's unavoidable," the captain said, and cursed himself for the roughness in his tone. Though maybe no orator could persuade this boy. What did he know of psychic breaking stress, who had never been tried to his own limit? "We'll have to keep the secret, you and I, or—" No, what was the use? Within Mardikian's small experience, it was so much more natural to believe that one man, Coffin, had gone awry, than to understand a month-by-month rotting of the human soul under loneliness and frustration.

"Yes, sir," Mardikian husked. "Of course, sir."

Even if he meant that, Coffin thought, *he might talk in his sleep. Or I might; but the admiral, alone of all the fleet, has a completely private room.*

He racked his tools, most carefully, and faced about. Mardikian shoved away, bulging-eyed. "No," whispered Mardikian. "No. Please."

He opened his mouth to scream, but he didn't get time. Coffin chopped him on the neck. As he doubled up, Coffin gripped him with legs and one hand, balled the other fist, and hit him often in the solar plexus.

Mardikian rolled in the air like a drowned man.

Swiftly, then, Coffin towed him down the corridor, to the pharmacy room. He unlocked the alcohol barrel, tapped a hypo, diluted it with enough water, and injected. Lucky the fleet didn't carry a real psychiatrist; if you broke, you went into deepsleep and weren't revived till you got home again to the clinics.

Coffin dragged the boy to a point near the air lock. Then he shouted. Hallmyer came from the bridge. "He started raving and attacked me," panted the captain. "I had to knock him out."

Mardikian was revived for a checkup, but since he only mumbled incoherently, he was given a sedative. Two men began processing him for the vat. Coffin said he would make sure that the Com officer hadn't damaged any equipment. He went back to the shack.

Teresa Zeleny met him. She did not speak, but led him to her room again.

"Well," he said, strangling on it, "so we're continuing to Rustum, by unanimous vote. Aren't you happy?"

"I was," she said quietly, "till now, when I see that you aren't. I hardly think you're worried about legal trouble on Earth; you have authority to ignore orders if the situation warrants. So what is the matter?"

He stared beyond her. "I shouldn't have come here at all," he said. "But I had to talk with someone, and only you might understand. Will you bear with me a few minutes? I won't bother you again."

"Not till Rustum." Her smile was a gesture of compassion. "And it's no bother." After waiting a bit: "What did you want to say?"

He told her, in short savage words.

She grew a little pale. "The kid was actually dead drunk, and they didn't know it when they processed him?" she said. "That's a grave risk. He might not live."

"I know," said Coffin, and covered his eyes.

Her hand fell on his shoulder. "I suppose you've done the only possible thing," she said with much gentleness. "Or, if there was a better way, you didn't have time to think of it."

He said through his fingers, while his head turned away from her: "If you don't tell on me, and I know you won't, then you're violating your own principles, too: total information, free discussion and decision. Aren't you?"

She sighed. "I imagine so. But don't all principles have their limits? How libertarian, or kind...how human can you be, out here?"

"I shouldn't have told you."

"I'm glad you did."

Then, briskly, as if she, too, fled something, the woman said: "The truth is bound to come out when your fleet returns to Earth, so we'll need to work out a defense for you. Or is necessity enough?"

"It doesn't matter." He raised his head, and now he could again speak steadily. "I don't figure to skulk more than I must. Let them say what they will, eight decades from now. I'll already have been judged."

"What?" She retreated a little, perhaps to see the gaunt form better. "You don't mean you'll stay on Rustum? But it isn't necessary!"

"A liar...quite likely a murderer...I am not worthy to be the master of a ship." His voice cracked over. "And maybe, after all, there isn't going to be any more space travel to come home to."

He jerked free of her and went through the door. She stared after him. She had better let him out; no, the key had been left in the bulkhead lock. She had no excuse to follow.

You aren't alone, Joshua, she wanted to call. *Every one of us is beside you. Time is the bridge that always burns behind us.*

Veleda Speaks

Hear me and heed ye, highborn and lowborn,
still in your strength or stumbling graveyard,
doomed to death and dreeing the weird
boldly or badly. I bid ye hearken.
When life is lost, alone is left
for yourself and your sons, what is said of you.
Doughty deeds shall never die,
But in minds of men remain forever—
night and nothingness for the names of cravens!
No good the gods will give to traitors,
nor aught but anger unto the slothful.
Who fears to fight will lose his freedom,
will cringe and crawl to get moldy crusts,
his children chafing in chains and shame.
Hauled into whoredom, helplessly,
his women weep. These woes are his.
Better a brand should burn his home
While he, the hero, harvests foemen
till he falls defiant and fares on skyward.

Hoofs in heaven heavily ring.
Lightning leaps, blazing lances.
All the earth resounds with anger.
Seas in surges smite the shores.
Now will Nerha naught more suffer.
Wraithful she rides to bring down Rome,
the war gods with her, the wolves and ravens.

SCIENCE FICTION AND HISTORY

The work of Gregory Benford is always interesting. His essay "Pandering and Evasions" *(Amazing Stories,* January 1988) is no exception, and not merely because it says a couple of nice things about me. It seems to call for a response—not a rebuttal, because I have no quarrel with it, but a little further exploration of one topic he brings up in passing.

Rightly deploring the unimaginative and unconvincing social backgrounds of too many science-fiction stories, he mentions "the unexamined assumption that liberal Capitalism (or, more rarely, state socialism) will form the backdrop of societies centuries from now...Worse, there are even semi-feudal regimes invoked in high-tech societies...Similarly, writers who sing of empire had better examine their assumptions. The solar system is a vast place, with radically different environments. Does the reflexive analogy to the old European empires, with their imperial fleets and rural colonies of docile natives, make any sense?"

Excellent points. However, they deserve closer examination. To what extent can we reasonably model the future on the present or the past? Of course, events never repeat themselves exactly, and it is debatable to what extent classes of events do, but this is at the very least a legitimate debate. What kinds of change in the human condition are reversible and what kinds are not? Does it or doesn't it make sense to imagine future Caesars, future Jeffersons and Bolivars, future Carnegies, and so on?

I don't believe anybody has any sure answers. Certainly I don't. Still, we can look at the record and make a few suggestions, for whatever they may be worth.

Let's begin with the record of science fiction itself. Quite a few stories suppose that developments to come will resemble developments that have already occurred, and some of these stories are by well-regarded, rather cerebral writers. We might hark back to Robert Heinlein's old "future history" series, which has raw colonialism, including indentured labor, appear on the planets and religious dictatorship arise at home. Soon afterward came Murray Leinster's classic "First Contact," wherein the characters take for granted that the aliens they encounter could be murderous bandits or imperialists. In recent years, Jerry Pournelle has described wars, revolutions, and empires among the stars (and so have I). Contrastingly, Larry Niven depicts a solar system under the governance of the United Nations. At first glance this may look different from anything hitherto, but in fact the society is quite Western; and the ideal of the UN as a peace-keeping force antedates the organization itself. Isaac Asimov's Foundation saga has a Galactic Empire develop. Perhaps this takes place peacefully, though little is said about that; in any case, eventually the state displays all the traditional trappings of despotism, and decays along the same lines as Rome did. We could go on at length, but these examples ought to suffice.

Some stories have indeed shown future societies unlike any of the past. Among them is "The Heart of the Serpent," by the late Soviet writer Ivan Efremov. He wrote it explicitly as a response to "First Contact." In it, humans and aliens also meet in deep space, but good will and mutual trust are immediate because any civilization that has developed to the point of making interstellar voyages must necessarily have evolved beyond warlikeness or banditry. In a letter to me, Efremov opined that either humankind will soon cross that threshold or else it will destroy itself, so he figured he might as well make the optimistic assumption. Other writers in the Eastern bloc generally do likewise, although several include ironies and dilemmas in their work.

The question is, How likely are we to undergo basic changes, for better or worse? *Can* we? Certain of the writers who reply "yes" have given us fascinating imagined futures to think about—to name only three, Benford himself, Greg Bear, and William Gibson. Time may prove them correct in principle. I simply wish to argue that in our present state of ignorance, "no" and "maybe" are answers just as intellectually respectable. The single thing I feel sure of is that nobody has foreseen or will foresee the real future; whatever comes to pass, we are bound to be surprised.

To make my case, I shall have to show that recurrence of institutions and patterns of events is not absurd. This is already implicit in the better stories that employ that assumption. Benford mentions Niven and Pournelle's *Oath of Fealty*, in which neo-feudalism is a logical consequence of high-tech. But let me now step out of science fiction and look at the matter from a wider perspective.

We live in an era of many revolutions. Are any of them irreversible? For example, what will be the effect of nuclear weapons on war? They have definitely failed to abolish it. Have they, though, made all-out, life-and-death strife between the great powers, in the manner of World War Two, impossible? If not, will such a conflict terminate civilization, or will it end in a negotiated peace of exhaustion, or will it have a clear winner? While the last of these propositions is highly unfashionable in the West, it is not unthinkable, being a keystone of Soviet military doctrine.

Even if no nuclear wars are ever fought on Earth, conceivably they will be waged in space, perhaps fairly often, with the victors then controlling the "high ground" and able to dictate terms. This situation bears resemblances to wars between city-states in Renaissance Italy, which were usually carried on by mercenaries. Disunited and without effective citizen forces, the peninsula became the booty of foreigners, such as the French and Spanish. We can imagine the United States and the Soviet Union, neglecting their strength on Earth in favor of their space weapons, suddenly threatened by a vast, modernized Chinese army. The details would make for an interesting, if melodramatic story.

Mind you, I do not say this will ever happen or that it ever can. I simply offer it as one supposable analogue of past history.

For the past gives us our only real clues to the future. The present is too small a slice of time, a mere interface between what has been and what will be. Although nearly all primitive societies are, today, extinct or dying, we should include the findings of anthropology in our historical studies. They help show us how various and unpredictable our species is.

After all, the high-tech West comprises a scanty fraction of Earth's population and occupies rather little of the acreage. While Benford declares, with much justice, that "thinking about a future that is urban, diverse, technology-driven, and packed with ambiguities" is "what SF is about," the majority of mankind still lives in rural environments, under conditions that have changed only superficially from the early Iron Age or the late Stone Age. Its institutions and ways of thinking haven't altered a great deal either. When change has occurred, the consequences have more often been catastrophic than benign; see any slum, urban or rural, anywhere on our planet. Adoption of modern technology has not usually gone together with Americanization.

Therefore it seems unrealistic to take for granted that the high-tech minority will engulf the backward majority. Maybe; or maybe the present gap between them will widen until we almost have two separate species; or maybe high-tech will founder.

Let's assume that it will survive. The alternatives are so depressing. Moreover, survival does look probable. How far will it develop, though? Could it regress for reasons internal to itself?

One hopes not. These days it is chic among Western intellectuals to sneer at "technofixes." Nevertheless, technofixes are what have largely given us our civilization, or our very humanity. They began with hominids taming fire and making the first crude tools. They went on through agriculture, with everything that that brought about in the way of cities, literacy, and (alas) government. I need hardly describe what the subsequent technofixes of medicine and scientific instrumentation have meant to the human spirit.

On the whole, technological revolutions have been irreversible. This is true even when their immediate effects have been bad. A case in point is early agriculture. Without romanticizing the life of hunter-gatherers, we must admit—archaeology and anthropology have shown—that it was easier, more free and less subject to famine and disease than the life of a peasant in the ancient riparian kingdoms. However, agricultural societies could support denser populations and muster far more for hence they either swamped the hunters or the latter took up a similar way of life. (This is an oversimplification, of course, but basically right. Where the environment was more favorable, as in Europe, farmers lived better than in the original civilizations.)

There was never any large-scale reversion. Occasionally and locally, societies collapsed and people went back to a rude existence. Examples include Greece after the fall of Mycenaean civilization and the Guatemala-Yucatan area after the decline of the Mayas. Yet everything that had been learned continued to be practiced elsewhere. No important art has ever been lost, nor has any minor one been for any significant length of time.

On this analogy, we can expect that high-tech will not disappear, short of a planetwide catastrophe. If such destruction does occur, probably the knowledge will be preserved here and there, and will be put back to work after new societies have become secure and wealthy enough. (The knowledge of how to build good roads and bridges did not vanish when Rome fell, it simply lay in abeyance for a thousand years or so.) To be sure, those societies will doubtless be quite different from the old, and confront different conditions. For instance, they will have inherited a world poorer in natural resources than it once was, and be forced to adjust their technologies to that—something I looked into in *Orion Shall Rise* and other stories.

But I see nothing inevitable about high-tech spreading to all humanity or continuing indefinitely to get higher and higher. Indeed, the latter seems quite unlikely. Growth curves characteristically have an S shape; they rise sharply for a while, then taper off toward a plateau. The potential for continued advance may remain, but economic and other social factors prevent its realization. Some major developments have actually been aborted.

An example is Chinese seafaring. Under the Ming Dynasty, expeditions went throughout Southeast and South Asia, crossed the Indian Ocean, and rounded the southern tip of Africa. The imperial bureaucrats then called a halt, ordered the demolition of every deep-water ship, and forbade anyone to leave the empire on pain of death. It has been pointed out that this was not altogether a bit of witless reaction. The voyages had just been for purposes of prestige; enormously costly, they returned no profit.

Meanwhile the Europeans, who did stand to gain, were sailing eastward from the Cape of Good Hope and westward across the Atlantic...The parallels to our space program are a little chilling.

Despite the obstacles, it is possible that everyone will eventually come into the high-tech fold. Corresponding things have happened before. Again, the most obvious example is civilization itself. This was invented in the Old World only once or twice; archaeologists disagree whether the Indus Valley peoples got the idea independently or it spread from the Mesopotamians. In either case, the complex of agriculture, cities, centralized government, etc., gradually diffused almost everywhere south of the Arctic and north of the Sahara Desert, plus, to some extent, Africa farther on. A similar thing happened in the New World, though less completely because the European invasion interrupted it. Here, civilization definitely did have two distinct origins, in Central and South America.

Nevertheless, look what widely divergent forms it took among the assorted nations. Directly or indirectly, Egyptians, Phoenicians, Medes, Persians, Greeks, and more all learned from the Mesopotamians, but none of them much resembled the latter nor each other. The Far East saw cultures still more foreign arise.

The Scientific Revolution began in southern Europe, the Industrial Revolution in northern Europe. By now they have affected the whole world. Most countries have sought to industrialize, with varying degrees of success, and several have contributed outstanding scientists. Yet beneath the shared machinery and shared conventions, how alike are they?

As a fairly trivial but perhaps amusing example, when I was in Brazil the people I met, besides being charming, were highly educated and cultured, splendid specimens of Western civilization; and Brazil is an important country. Now one would think that punctuality is essential to the smooth running of modern society. But that's an Anglo notion. I soon learned that when a Brazilian said he'd meet me at 9 A.M., he meant sometime before noon; and presently I learned to relax and accept this. Nothing terrible happened.

More seriously, in our century we have seen Russia and China make gigantic efforts to catch up technologically, with impressive results. However, they have not thereby become more like us. They are adapting the new instrumentalities to their societies, rather than the other way around. In a subtler fashion, the same is true of countries such as Japan. There we see people in Western clothes using Western equipment under capitalism and parliamentary democracy—but their own versions, uniquely Japanese beneath the facade.

I do not by any means decry this. It would be tragic for humankind to lose its diversity; our future would then look like an anthill. I simply point out that science fiction is presumptuous and unimaginative when it extrapolates solely from Western, usually American civilization of the late twentieth century. Dominant influences in the future may well come from elsewhere and be, from our present-day point of view, archaic—for example, Japanese paternalism or Islamic zealotry.

It seems equally possible that elements from our own past will return to claim us. While technological revolutions, which do have social consequences, may well be irreversible, social characteristics not immediately related to technology have always been labile. This brings us to the politics of the future.

Some philosophers of history have maintained that it moves, or tends very strongly to move, through cycles; if events do not repeat, classes of events do. Arnold Toynbee is the best-known of these thinkers. We can identify similarities between the natures and fates of, say, the Egyptian Middle Kingdom, the Chinese Han Dynasty, the Roman Empire, and several others. They cannot be purely coincidental. But it is a matter of interpretation how close the similarities actually are, and a matter of theory what causes them. "The ineluctable logic of events" is a sonorous phrase and gives rise to considerable thought, but it is scarcely comparable to Newton's laws of motion. Still, I'd call it a legitimate starting point for a science-fiction story; *vide,* again, Asimov.

Its implication is that we will make the same old mistakes over and over again, with the same old consequences, though at the time these will always be called new and progressive. As I have remarked elsewhere, the lessons of history aren't really hard to learn; the trouble is that hardly anybody wants to learn them. Rudyard Kipling's poem "The Gods of the Copybook Headings" says this about as well as it has ever been said.

To give illustrations from the present day would be to go into political polemics, which is not my purpose here. Suffice it to say that much is going on that looks quite familiar. The world has repeatedly seen the rise and fall of many analogous institutions and ideals.

Americans naturally tend to think the future in terms of republican government and democratic ethos. Yet theirs, the oldest continuously existing republic on Earth, has barely passed its two hundredth birthday. Republics have generally been short-lived and democracies (which are not the same thing) still more so. At the moment democracy seems to be in a position, worldwide, like that of monarchy in nineteenth-century Europe; almost everybody goes through the motions of it, but in most cases this is a pious fiction and the structure is moribund. Many science-fiction stories have depicted it as giving way, in fact if not in name, to the dictatorship of corporate capitalism. In practice, though, private organizations exist on sufferance of the state, and the real dictator is always the man who controls the armed forces and the police. At most, large corporations may be junior partners of government—very junior and this is possible in just a few countries. Other outfits, such as unions, could as well fill the role, and churches have sometimes been coequal or senior.

Freedom has always been rare and fragile, perhaps because most people don't value it much. Institutions are more likely than not to revert to primitive forms. For example, chattel slavery was essentially abolished in the course of the nineteenth century, but in the twentieth, Nazis and Communists brought back forced labor on an enormously larger scale.

Equality and official compassion are more commonly associated with powerful government than with liberty. Thus, it was not the Roman Republic but the Roman Empire that gave slaves some protection from the grossest forms of abuse. The Empire also saw women, at least in the upper classes, accorded rights and respect comparable to those men enjoyed. There was a feminist movement similar to today's. We know what became of it and of other reformist hopes.

There was, too, a rising tide of superstition, general belief in everything from astrology to necromancy. In other words, Rome had its own New Age. Eventually the Christian Church took over, and disorganized credulity yielded to organized religion. Perhaps our fundamentalists will play such a part in the future.

The prospect of strong-arm rule, social immobility, racism, sexism, and blind faith is as unpleasant to me as it is to you. I do not say it will come to pass. I merely say that it can, and that stories that depict it are not necessarily by authors who lack imagination.

Nor is it necessarily simpleminded to anticipate no new orderings of society, different in kind from any that have gone before. Though often proclaimed, this advent hasn't happened yet, in thousands of years. Instead, we have gotten changes rung on the same half-dozen or so themes. For example, in many Bronze Age societies and in Peru of the Incas, the economy was not based on exchange as we understand it. Everything that was produced, beyond the simple necessities of life for the commoners who produced it, went to the god-king. He then handed the goods out as he saw fit. Today a less extreme version of this is known as income redistribution in the United States, socialism abroad; and far from being a quantum leap of progress, true communism would amount to the old thing itself.

Granted, countless details of tribalism, monarchy, hierocracy, hierocracy, democracy, etc., have varied throughout history, and so has the overall mix. For instance, universal literacy has had a significant influence on political arrangements and processes—though it can as readily strengthen the bonds of the state on the individual as it can set him free. In such interaction of factors lies the possibility of many stories.

Agreed, the future will be no simple replay of the past, and some scenarios will never be seen again. They doubtless include the interplanetary Wild West long beloved of science fiction. We won't get the asteroid prospector poking around in his spaceship like the Sierra prospector with his burro. Even if spacecraft become cheap enough, as Eric Drexler's work on nanotechnology suggests may happen, they will be too powerful, too potentially destructive, for us to let just anybody have them. Meanwhile, there will surely be developments unprecedented in history, unforeseen by us all—though science-fiction writers can have fun trying.

Yes, I do expect changes in the future, as radical as were wrought by fire or agriculture or literacy or the scientific method, transforming humanity as profoundly as they did. I think these changes will spring from science and technology, not from anyone's great new blueprint for utopia. It is conceivable that eventually they will bring about a social order that does not carry the seeds of its own destruction. Be that as it may, the outlook is not hopeless. Good societies have in fact flourished now and then, for a while. They can again in times to come.

Yet if we are to have any real control over our tomorrows, we must learn the lessons of our yesterdays. We need to do that even if all we want is to write believable science fiction.

Suggested Reading

A few nonfiction works, chosen almost randomly out of many, which take up some of the matters touched upon in this essay or in the stories that it mentions, are listed below.

Gordon Childe, *The Dawn of European Civilization,* sixth ed.; Alfred A. Knopf, New York 1958.

_______ , *Man Makes Himself;* New American Library, New York 1951.

Eric Drexler, *Engines of Creation;* Doubleday, New York 1986.

Sidney Hook, *The Paradoxes of Freedom;* University of California Press, Berkeley, California 1970.

Bertrand de Jouvenel, *On Power;* Viking Press, New York 1948.

H. J. Muller, *The Loom of History;* Harper & Bros., New York 1958.

_______ , *The Uses of the Past;* Oxford University Press, New York 1952.

Lewis Mumford, *Technics and Civilization;* Harcourt, Brace, New York 1934.

Amaury de Riencourt, *Sex and Power in History;* David McKay, New York 1947.

Arnold J. Toynbee, *A Study of History,* one-volume ed.; Oxford University Press, New York 1947.

A World Called Maanerek

The glider followed the slope of Kettleback Fell, caught an updraft rising from Brann's Dale and swung toward a blued-silver sky of twilit clouds. Above the cold white brawl of Skara River there lay a chill hazy air mass which sucked it down again.

Vilyan's hands were briefly frantic on the controls. Then he had crossed the river and was once more upborne, until presently he went above the timberline.

"We are close now, oath-brother," he said. "Best you make ready."

Torrek nodded, left his seat and crawled down the narrow length of the fuselage. He felt the light fabric, oiled cloth drawn tight on a frame of hollow canes, shiver to his touch. It was very silent; somehow, the great booming winds did not penetrate.

Reaching the little trapdoor, he peered through its glass inset, down at a savage barrenness streaked with snowfields. He tested his arrangements—the coiled rope knotted to a crossbar, the three knives sheathed at his waist, the net which bound his long yellow hair to keep it from his eyes. Otherwise he wore only a loincloth, for he dared weigh no more than he must on this lethal errand.

He was a big and supple young man, with a harsh bony cast to his face that made him an alien among the handsome people of Dumethdin. And the name they had given him, Torrek, meant more than simply "stranger"—it hinted at a degree of monstrousness, for he alone of all folk under the Rings could not even guess at his parentage. Nevertheless, Clan and Lodge emblems were tattooed on his face.

"There's the nest!" Sweat leaped out on Vilyan's forehead, pearling the blue symbol etched there, the sign of Sea Bear Lodge in which he found sworn brotherhood with Torrek. His hands jerked, a bare trifle, on the sticks, and the glider shuddered.

They had climbed high, until now they were slipping along that gaunt dark mountaintop called the Skara Man's Hat. On a windy crag overlooking three thousand feet of cold sky, there was raised an enormous, disorderly heap of branches, welded with the decay of centuries into one fortress mass. As far back as tradition remembered, krakas had nested here.

Certain Elders, far down in Diupa, thought it an unholy work to slay the kraka, for she had been there so long, and her mothers and grandmothers before her, reaving the valleys below. If the kraka sat no longer on the Skara Man's Hat, menace brooding over Fenga Fjord, there would be an emptiness in the sky.

Folk whose livestock and small children had been carried up to these unclimbable heights thought otherwise.

Vilyan's dark reckless face split in a sudden grinning tautness. "There she comes herself, oath-brother!"

"Good," grunted Torrek.

"May Ellevil and the Moon Lady ward you—"

"Hold her steady now," Torrek interrupted harshly.

One who did not know him might have been offended at such surliness, even when death beat upwind to meet him, but in Diupa they thought they understood their changeling. You could not look for ease, or mirth, or even much courtesy, from one whose life had been so hideously uprooted. His brain, they thought, must still be plowed with the scars of memory torn loose, five years ago.

Therefore Vilyan only nodded. But when Torrek had left the glider and Vilyan was bringing it back toward the fisher town—for he could not hover in this home of the warring winds—he sang the Long Faring Song for those who have gone away to battle and are not likely to return.

Torrek opened the little door, threw out the rope and slid down its length. One of his daggers was gripped between his teeth.

For long, ghastly minutes, he swung like a bell clapper, more than a mile above the fjord. Now he could hear the wind, a huge hollow roaring through the blue dusk. Its force streamed him ahead at the rope's end.

The challenge of the kraka cut through to him. She came threshing upward from her nest, blind with murder, for at this time of year she had young in the nest and that thing of stiff wings dared fly over them! Almost, she hurled herself straight at the glider—her mother had thus crashed one, a man's lifetime ago. But then, as Torrek had planned, she saw him dangling like bait on a fish hook, and she veered and plunged toward him.

The man felt a final tightening of nerve and muscle. His eyes seemed to gain an ultimate clarity, his ears to be whetted until they heard the crashing of Smoky Falls where Skara plunged down the Steeps, time to slow until the onrushing kraka poised in midair and he could count the stripes on her tawny hide after each giant wingbeat. But he was not afraid. In a bare five years of remembered life, there is small time to learn the habits called fear.

Then the kraka struck.

She was a little smaller than he, discounting the thirty-foot span of leathery wings and the long rudder-shaped tail. But her four feet ended in talons which had been known to split men at one blow and her muzzle held saber teeth. Few people, hanging one-handed from a cord, could have kept from pitching downward to escape.

Torrek drew himself up, at the last instant, into a ball. As the winged thunderbolt shot below him, he let go. His legs closed around the lean belly, his left arm around the neck, and his right hand thrust a dagger into her throat.

She screamed.

For a few wild seconds, she threshed and bucked and writhed in the air, seeking to hurl him off. His knife was torn from his grasp and sparkled meteoric downward. He needed both arms and every draining drop of strength to keep his place.

Then his weight became too much for her and they slid down the wind toward the sterile slopes. Her wings, flailing the sky, slowed that fall somewhat, turned it into a long glide...and meanwhile Torrek had drawn another knife and was slashing methodically at her vitals.

He felt no pity for this most splendid of animals—there were too many small bones up on Skara Man's Hat. But he had a moment in which to think that she was brave.

And a moment, incredibly high in the air, to look over the misty woods and the green depths of Brann's Dale, across Smoky Falls and the narrow fields that men had plowed between the cliffs and the fjord, to Diupa town.

More: he could see across Fenga Fjord to Holstok and the White River Delta, a low rich land fair for the harvest. He could see the narrow end of the bay and follow its windings northward between sheer rock to the mouth. There, where the Roost foamed with an incoming tide, lay those guardian islands called the Merry Men; and Torrek thought he could even see the grim walls of Ness, the fort on Big Ulli which watched lest the beast-helmeted pirates of Illeneth descend again on Dumethdin.

But now the kraka was weakening, her blood spattering the blue twilight air, and as her wings beat less frantically, her fall became the faster. Clench-jawed, Torrek thought she would have her revenge by painting his flesh on the Steeps of Skara next to her own.

Then, with a wobbling convulsion, she staggered eastward again, and the updraft from the warmer plowed fields gave her a final helping hand, and it was the fjord into which she plunged.

Torrek dived from her just before she struck. He split the water with a force that drove him down and down into greenish depths until his eardrums popped their protest and a coraloid spear raked his flank. When he had finally struggled back to the surface, his lungs seemed ready to explode. It was a long time before his gasping ceased.

The kraka floated not far away, upborne by her enormous wings—dead. And the early lamps of Diupa glimmered within easy distance.

"Well, old girl," panted Torrek, "that was friendly of you. Now wait here and be so good as not to let the ollenbors find you and clean your bones—I want that striped hide!"

He strode out for the town, wearily at first, but his strength came back with the swiftness he knew to be abnormal. Sometimes, alone with his own truncated soul at night, Torrek wondered if he were human...or what?

There were canoes putting out from the pier. His landing had been dimly espied by the townsfolk. Lean outriggered shapes clove murmurous waves, a hundred paddles struck the water in unison, and the colored paper lanterns hung at the stem posts were like seeking eyes.

"Ohoyohoa!" A conch lowed after the cry, and the brass throb of gongs took up an underlying rhythm. *"Ohoyohoa!* May the sea give you up, O my beloved! May the sea surrender you living, *ohoyohoa!"*

"Here I am!" called Torrek unceremoniously.

The nearest boat veered. Muscular hands drew him up and soon the conches and gongs and voices roared victory.

By the time the fleet had come back, dragging the slain kraka and bearing Torrek on a captain's dais, the Diupa people had all swarmed to the dock.

Masked and feather-cloaked, shaking their rattles and their weapons—crossbows, axes, warmattocks, halberds, blowpipes—the young men of Sea Bear Lodge danced out the pride he had given them. Grave in their embroidered robes of scarlet and blue, his adoptive Clan Elders waited under glowing lanterns. Between the long, low, airy houses, of painted oilcloth and carved wood panels and peaked shingle roofs, the children and the maidens strewed flowers for him.

Even the humblest farmers, artisans, fishermen, with no more finery than a bast loincloth and a feather headdress, lifted their tridents and shouted his honor when he stepped among them.

High over the mountains, the thin evening clouds broke apart. The sun was down, though it would not be dark for hours yet, here in the warm latitudes of the World Called Maanerek. But the sky showed an infinite clear blue, with two of the moons riding high, nearly full. And enormous to the south lifted the rainbow arch of the Rings, most holy bridge.

It was the usual thing that the clouds of the long warm day—forty hours while the sun strode over the Islands—should disperse as evening cooled toward night. Yet Torrek, with the fjord's chill kiss still tingling on his skin, imagined that all kindly Rymfar must be with him, to draw the curtain from the sky just as he stepped ashore to his people.

His people. Now, for the first time, he felt a thawing in himself. These lithe, dark, high-cheeked folk had made him their own, when they found him speechless and helpless in the fields, had taught him with the same patient kindliness they showed their children, had forgiven him the blunders and breaches inevitable to one not raised from birth in their ways.

In return, he had sailed in their canoes—yes, fished and hunted and plowed the fields, had fought in their lines when the robbers of Illeneth forced the Roost and entered Dumethdin.

And the folk had given him rank according to his growing abilities, so that now he rated Pilot.

But he had still been the waif. He had not truly bought back his life from them...until today.

"Drink," said Elder Yensa, banding him the ancient silver Cup of Council.

Torrek went to one knee and drained the thin spiced wine.

"Let your name be written on the scroll of Harpooners," said Scribe Glamm, "and when next the Fleet goes forth after the sea snakes, may you wield a goodly spear and be rewarded with the share due to your work."

Torrek bowed. "I am unworthy, Reverend Uncle," he said.

In fact, he knew very well he deserved the elevated rank, he had expected to gain it, if he lived. Now—

He straightened and his eyes went to the young women, respectfully waiting on the edge of lantern light.

Sonna saw him and looked down. A slow flush crept up her cheeks. She lowered her head until the long dark garlanded hair hid the small face from him.

"Reverend Uncle," said Torrek, bowing to the gray man of Korath Clan who watched him from shrewd eyes, "a Harpooner is of rank sufficient to speak as friends with the child of a Captain. Is it not so?"

"It is so," agreed Baelg.

"Then have I your consent to go into the mountains with your daughter Sonna?"

"If she is willing, that is my will," said Baelg. A grin twitched his short beard. "And I believe she is. But you must rest yourself first."

"I will rest in the mountains, Reverend Uncle."

"A mighty man indeed!" said Baelg, while the young men flashed teeth in admiration. "Go, then, and if the will of you two be later for marriage, I shall not look askance."

Silently Torrek bowed to the Elders, to the Scribe, to the Councilors of Diupa and the Viceroy of the King of Dumethdin. Sonna fell behind him, matching his long strides. In a few minutes, they were beyond the town, on a road which wound through fields up into the mountains.

"I could have stayed for the feasting, Sonna, if you wished," he said awkwardly. "Perhaps I was too hasty."

"You were not too hasty for me," she answered with an enormous gentleness. "I have been waiting a long time for this night."

The road became a narrow trail winding upward between great cool fronds, under soughing leaves. There was a damp green smell in the air and a rushing noise of waterfalls. Here many caves were found, and a young man and woman could lie in their shelter on beds of gathered blossoms, eating wild fruits and splitting the hard-shelled skalli nuts, through all the long light night of the World Called Maanerek

As their trail, a ledge which tumbled down through a deepening purple twilight, led them briefly out of the forest, Torrek and Sonna saw the Inner Moon rise and go hurtling across the sky. There were four outer moons visible now among the few soft stars, as well as the shuddering bands of the Rings, and they built sharded bridges of light on Fenga Fjord and across the ocean beyond.

Distantly, inaudibly from here, a lacy curtain of white spray broke around the Merry Men, as one of the tidal bores which guarded Dumethdin and challenged her sailors came roaring in through the Roost.

Sonna sighed and took his arm. "Wait a little," she said quietly. "I have never seen it so beautiful before."

A curious, angry emotion stirred in Torrek. He stood stiff and savored the bitterness of it until he knew what it was: a resentful jealousy of others who had trod this path with her.

But that was a crazy, ugly thing to feel, he told himself in bewilderment—considering a woman, an unwed girl who had pledged herself to no man as yet, to be property: to rage when she acted like a free human creature, as he might rightly rage at someone who used his personal flensing tools!

He bit off the insane feeling and spat it out, but the after-taste remained, a gray doubt of himself.

Who am I?

"There is grief in you, Torrek," murmured Sonna.

"It is nothing," he answered.

Why am I?

"No...I can feel it in you.

Your arm became suddenly like wood." Her fingers stroked down its muscled length, tickling the gold hairs which also set him off from the brown smooth men of Dumethdin. "It is not right that you should know grief."

"Let us choose a cave," he said in a voice that grated like a hull on a rocky reef.

"No, wait, Torrek." She searched his moonlit face with dark oblique eyes. "I will not spend a night with rage and sorrow up here...not beside you."

He felt a dizziness. In spite of Baelg's words, it had been too much to hope that Sonna would ever—

"Ever wed a nameless man," he mumbled without thinking.

She smiled, a smile of victory, but stepped past the main issue to say: "Not nameless. You are fully adopted, Torrek. You know that. And after today's work—"

"It is not enough," he said in returning despair. "I will always be the one without roots, the torrek whom they found in the plowed fields five years ago, speechless, kinless, memoryless. I might be a child of hill trolls, for all I will ever know!"

"Or a child of the Rymfar," said Sonna, "or of the black Flitters they tell of among the mountain tribes. What of it? You are yourself and only yourself."

He was shocked. The idea of a human existing as a single creature, self-sufficient, part of no Clan or Lodge or Nation, and with no need to be a part, was unheard-of. Sonna was a woodswitch to voice it!

And then, as if a bolt had clicked home, he understood the rightness of the idea. It was not that he lost his wistfulness—he would always long for a blood kinship that had been denied him—but his lonely status was no longer a monstrosity. He was different, yes, even crippled in a way, but he was not unnatural.

For another slow moment, he stood wondering why Sonna's carelessly tossed-off words, whose implications she could not really have grasped, should so bite into him. It was almost as if she had touched and awakened a memory of—

"No more!" he exclaimed, laughing aloud. "The night is not so long that we can stand here wasting it."

"No," breathed Sonna demurely. Her hand stole into his.

There came a humming in the sky.

Briefly, Torrek was puzzled. Then as the noise grew, and he heard the whine of sundered air behind it, the hair stood up along his back.

He had only brought his remaining knife for weapon. It jumped into his hand. He shoved Sonna roughly against the cliff wall and stood in front of her, peering upward. Moonlight dazzled him.

The black shape crossed the Rings and slid down an invisible wire, and one end of the wire was pegged to him. It came too fast for thought, too fast for a dash back into the woods. Torrek had not yet grasped the size of the thing, twice the length of a longboat, when it halted by the ledge.

It hung there and speared him.

No other word—he was *held,* pressed against the cliff by a rubbery force he could not see. When he roared and hurled all the weight and strength he owned against that net, it threw him back onto Sonna with a fury that knocked a gasp from her.

"Torrek," she whispered. Her hands groped at his waist, blindly in the pitiless unreal moonlight. "Torrek, do you know—"

He did not. He had no memory of this lean, dully black fish shape...and yet it did not quite seem a thing from nightmare, not quite the vengeful ghost of the kraka. Somehow, he could accept it, as he might accept a new and deadly kind of animal.

"It's not a glider," he said through clenched jaws. "No wings. But it's been forged or cast—metal."

"The Flitters." Her voice shook.

He gave it some thought, standing there pinned in the racking earthquake of his own heart. The Flitters were a tale, a rumor, a recent mumble among the inland barbarians. This had been seen, that had happened, strange flyings and curiously dressed men…

A circular door opened in the flank of the—ship? Beyond it was a similar one which also opened. A metal gangway protruded, tongue-fashion, to the ledge.

Torrek could not see inside, but the light that spilled forth was hellishly brilliant. It so stunned his eyes that those who walked over the gangway became no more than shadows.

When they reached him and stood staring, he could see a little better. They were big men, with something of himself in their features and coloring. But they were wrapped from boots to neck in drab one-piece garments and they wore massive round helmets.

Behind him, Sonna whimpered.

The men talked to each other. It was a language Torrek had not heard, a choppy unmusical tongue, but there was no great excitement in the tones. These men were doing a routine job.

Through a haze of anger, Torrek saw them reach some kind of decision—it seemed to involve Sonna rather than him—and go to work. They cast supple cords into the unseen force-mesh, nooses that closed on him and were drawn taut until he was trussed up like a wooly for slaughter.

One of them waved an arm in signal. Torrek fell to the rock as the force died away. Sonna sprang past him, spitting her fury. A man grinned, side-stepped her rush and grabbed an arm, which he forced behind her back. She went to her knees with a cry and was quickly bound.

"What are they doing?" she cried in alarm. "Torrek, beloved, what do they want?"

"I don't know," he said.

He was slowly overcoming his own helpless wrath, forcing it to the ground as if it were his opponent in a wrestling match. A great chill watchfulness rose in its place.

"O my dearest—" wept Sonna.

It cracked across Torrek's heart. He mumbled some meaningless comfort or other. Inwardly, he thought of knives for these grinning, chattering bandits in hideous clothes. He thought of hanging their heads in Diupa's smokehouse.

Sonna writhed and tried to bite when they picked her up and took her inside the ship. It earned her nothing but a stunning cuff. Torrek conserved his strength, watching the metal bleakness through which he was borne.

Lashed in a chair, he had a view of the sky and the Steeps through a kind of—no, not window, nor telescope—image-maker? He focused on that, ignoring the alienness of furnishings around him. Even when the ship rose noiselessly into the sky, and the highest peaks fell out of sight, and Sonna's courage broke in a raw scream, Torrek remained watching the view.

But when the stars harshened and came forth in their hundreds, when the great bowl of the world turned into a ringed shield dazzling against darkness, and Sonna clenched her eyes and would not look...he had an eerie sense of homecoming.

Almost, he *knew* the monster mother ship would be waiting there and would draw this little boat into herself.

Was it only the speculations of Diupa's philosophers, or did he remember as a fact that the World Called Maanerek was merely a single one of uncountably many?

He shivered at a ghostly thought, a thin frightened wisp of—recollection?—of how cruel and alien those worlds could be.

Torrek whirled, in the narrowness of the cell where they had caged him. One hand snatched for his knife. When he remembered it was gone, his teeth clicked together, as if closing in a throat.

Sonna caught his arm. "No," she said.

He came back to humanness like one awakening from a dream. The carnivore light faded as he looked down at her.

"What?" he asked vaguely.

"It is no use to fight them," she said. "Not till we know more."

He nodded stiffly, as if his neckbones creaked. Then he held her in his arms and glared at the men who were opening the door.

The younger one raised a weapon. At least Torrek supposed it was a weapon, shaped like a very small blowgun, but grasped in a single fist. This person, or troll, or whatever he was, seemed healthier than his fellows: his skin had a normal weatherbeaten look, not the dead paleness of the others, and he moved with a muscular assurance. He was almost as big as Torrek, with the same yellow hair cropped short, but with a beak of a nose and a rigid set to his lips.

He spoke. It was a heavily accented version of the Naesevis tongue, the common mercantile language of the Islands. Torrek was not expert in it himself, though so wealthy a nation as Dumethdin naturally attracted many traders, but it was near enough kin to that spoken along Fenga Fjord for him to use.

"Best you do not attack me.

This *gun*—this weapon shoots a—it can put you to sleep instantly. Awaking from such a sleep is painful."

Torrek spat on the floor.

"You do understand me, do you not?"

"Yes," said Torrek, "I understand you." The pronoun he chose was insulting, but the stranger did not seem to know the difference.

"Good. I am Coan Smit. This man beside me is the learned Frain Horlam."

The other was little and old, with thin gray hair and blinking watery eyes. Like Coan Smit, he wore a plain greenish coverall, but lacked the young man's insignia.

"What do you call yourself?" Smit asked.

"I am Torrek, a Harpooner of Diupa, adopted to the Bua Clan and an oath-brother in full standing of Sea Bear Lodge, pledged to the King of Dumethdin."

It was another insult: anyone who knew Naesevis should have been familiar enough with the symbology of the Islands to read Torrek's allegiances off his tattoos. Once more, it made no impression.

Not at all offended, Smit grinned briefly and said something to Frain Horlam, who nodded with a curious eagerness. Then, turning back to his prisoners, Smit went on in a careful tone: "Thank you. I want you to understand, Torrek, that we are your friends. We are in fact, your *people,* and you are about to be given back your rightful heritage."

As from an immense distance Torrek heard Sonna's indrawn gasp. He himself felt no great shock. The knowledge had been growing within him since that sky-boat came through darkness to grip him fast. In part, it was that he looked like these folk. But in a deeper part, lying beyond all words, this was something he simply knew.

It was a cold and poisoned knowledge.

"Well, what have you to say further?" he demanded curtly.

"If you will come with us, we will take you to a place where it can better be explained."

"I will do so, provided this woman come with me."

"No, it is best she stay. There would be too much trouble; even without her, it will be hard enough to make things clear to you."

"Let it be so, my dear one," mumbled Sonna. There was a beaten weariness about her. She had seen and suffered too much in too short a time.

Torrek saw how the unhumanly stiff manner of Coan Smit, a manner of metal, broke open as his eyes drifted down the girl where she stood. Almost, then, Torrek seized Smit in the grip of a wrestler, to crack his spine across a knee.

He choked back his rage and the icy wariness that replaced it was so unlike Dumethdin's warm folk—it branded him so sharply as one of this witch-race—that he slumped and grew saddened.

"Let us go," he said.

As he followed Horlam down a glaring bare corridor, with Smit and Smit's weapon at his back, he turned over his last glimpse of Sonna; a small figure at the barred door, all alone in a cage.

It was not to a room where he could look out on the arrogant stars and the cool ringed shield which was his home that they took him. Their walking ended down in the guts of the ship, in a great chamber which was a flashing, blinking, quivering, humming wilderness of philosophic apparatus.

"Sit down, Torrek," invited Smit.

The Diupa man crouched back from the chair, for it was an ugly thing of wires, instruments and shackles.

"On the floor, perhaps—not in that," he answered.

"You will sit in that chair," Smit told him, hefting his weapon "and permit yourself to be bound into it. Whether you do so freely or let me knock you out with this gun is your affair."

Torrek snarled at him. Smit was standing too far, too ready, for a leap. Therefore Torrek yielded. As Horlam closed the steel bands which locked him by wrists, waist and ankles to the chair, his lips moved, invoking the nine evils on Coan Smit.

Horlam lowered a grid of wires and less comprehensible things onto Torrek's head and began adjusting it in various ways. Smit pulled up a chair for himself, sheathed his gun and crossed his legs.

"Well," he said, "this will take a little time—to adjust the *circuits,* I mean—so I may as well tell you what you wish to know." He grinned wryly. "It is hard to figure where to begin. Some nations of men understand that the world is a round ball spinning about the sun and that the stars are other suns. I do not know if in your country—"

"I have heard such tales," grunted Torrek.

Till now, the imaginings of Diupa's learned men had not seemed very plausible to him. But now he knew—beyond all reason, without needing as proof the fact of this ship—that Smit spoke the truth. But why did he know it so surely?

"Very well, then," said Smit. "It is a great distance from sun to sun, greater than men can truly understand. And there are more suns than have ever been fully counted. Nevertheless, men learned how to cross such distances in ships like this, overcoming the barriers of space, time, heat, cold, weightlessness, airlessness. Spreading from one world, very long ago, they strewed their seed on thousands of other worlds.

"Then the Empire went down in wreck and men forgot," Smit continued. "On *planets* like yours, far removed from the old centers of civilization, thinly populated at the time of the disaster—on such worlds, hardly a memory remains of the Empire and its fall."

Torrek shivered. It was not alone the weirdness of the tale, but this sense of having been told it once before, in some forgotten dream.

He said slowly: "There are legends concerning those who existed Before the Rymfar."

Smit nodded. "Of course. Not all knowledge was lost. On some worlds, a kind of civilization survived. But only slowly, through numberless agonies, has it struggled back. The Empire has not yet been rebuilt; there are many separate nations of planets. Most of the *Galaxy* is still an unexplored wilderness—But I am talking beside the point.

"All right. This is a scout ship of a certain nation, your nation, which lies an enormous distance away. We have been cruising through this region of space for a number of years, mapping, studying...preparing the ground, in a way. Five years ago, we discovered your planet and tested a new procedure.

"You are Korul Wanen, an officer of this ship. Your memories—all your memories of your entire life—were stripped from you. You were left to be picked up by the Island folk. Now we are taking you back."

Smit turned and waved an imperious arm at one of the gray-robed men who stole meekly about, serving the switches and dials of the great machine. He let Torrek sit there with sweat spurting out on the skin, while he gave an order. Then he faced back, grinning.

"You don't like it, do you, Korul Wanen?" he said.

"It's a lie!" croaked Torrek.

"How could you have found me if—"

"A good question: But I fear it will not disprove my assertions. You see, a small *radiating*—signaling unit, drawing its power from your own body, was implanted in a bone of yours, before you were put down. We could locate you from many miles away."

"But no one would be so stupid!" roared Torrek. "I might have died! The folk you say you left me with might have been cannibals and eaten me! What then could you possibly have gained?"

"Nothing," said Smit. "But neither would we have lost anything—except one expendable unit of the crew."

There was a certain avidness in Smit's pale eyes. He was not telling this because there was any special need to, Torrek saw. He was telling it because he wanted to watch his prisoner squirm.

Torrek stiffened. It was hard to remain calm, when his heart beat so heavily and his mouth was so dry.

Why, he thought, in a remote, astonished part of his brain, *I am afraid! This is what it feels like!*

The gray-robed person came back with a black cylinder the size of a man's forearm and gave it to Smit, who handled it as one handles heavy objects.

He smiled at Torrek. "In here," he said, "is the ghost of Korul Wanen."

Torrek clamped lips together. He would not ask!

"He will live again in his own body," said Smit. "But first, of course, Torrek must be rubbed out."

That drew a howl. "No!"

"Yes," said Smit eagerly.

He passed the cylinder to Horlam, who fitted it into the machine next to another one.

"You might turn over your memories one last time, Torrek. They will soon be nothing but a scribing in a tube."

Torrek struggled, uselessly, until he thought his muscles would burst. If they but would, he prayed in anguish, if he could only know clean death!

As the dizziness and the darkness closed in on him, the machine screaming inside his head until he felt it must rack his brain apart, he saw Smit lean closer to peer at him. The last thing of which Torrek the Harpooner had awareness was Smit's look of enjoyment.

Korul Wanen

He hefted the cylinder.

"Five years!" he murmured.

"Oh, it could hold several centuries' worth of experience, my boy," said Dr. Frain Horlam. "When you use individual molecules to store information—"

Wanen looked up from the cylinder, across the desk to the aging psychologist. He was not certain how to act. On the one hand, the old fellow was a non-Cadre civilian; as such, he rated scant respect from a lieutenant in the Astro service. On the other hand, Horlam was in charge of the major scientific undertaking of this expedition, and on an exploratory trip, such work was subordinate only to the gathering of militechnic data.

Therefore Wanen said with a carefully noncommittal courtesy: "The theory of this never was explained to me. As long as you only wish me to make conversation, with no subject assigned, perhaps you would be kind enough to instruct me."

Horlam's gray head lifted. "In a rough way, if you like," he said. He leaned back and took out a cigar. "Smoke?"

"No!" Wanen collected himself. "You know I am an Academy man and therefore conditioned against vice."

"Why?" Horlam tossed the question off so casually, between puffs on his own cigar, that Wanen answered without thinking:

"In order to serve the Hegemony and the Cadre which guides it more efficiently—" He jarred to a halt. "You're deliberately baiting me!"

"If you say so."

"These are not joking matters. Don't make me report you."

"This ship is a starvish long way from home," said Horlam, with no obvious relevance. "Seven years now since we left. Nobody back there knows where we are—we didn't know ourselves just where we were going. The stars have changed position so much that the old Imperial astro data are no use at all, and space is so big, and there are so many stars—if we don't come back, it will be hundreds of years, probably, before another Hegemony ship chances to come exploring around this way again."

Wanen's uneasy puzzlement grew. It might only be the lingering strangeness of his experience. He had wanted to report for duty as soon as he awoke in the sick-bay cot, but they had made him rest for a while and then sent him to Horlam's office. An informal talk was to probe his restored self and make certain he was once again fit to serve. But this was *too* informal!

"Why do you say these things?" Wanen asked in a very low, controlled voice. "They're platitudes, but your tone...somehow, it all borders on deviationism."

"For which I could be given anything on the scale of corrections, from a reprimand, up through death, to lobotomy or memory erasure—eh?" Horlam smiled around his cigar. "Never mind, boy. You must also know that there aren't any secret police aboard to whom I could be reported. The reason I'm saying all this is that there are certain things I must tell you. I want to cushion the shock. This is your first deep-space voyage, isn't it?"

"Yes."

"And you only had two years of it. Then you were mindblanked and deposited on that planet. The rest of us have been batting around this part of the Galaxy for five years more. Things change under such conditions. There has to be a certain adjustment—a loosening of discipline, a letdown of idealism. You'll see it for yourself. Don't be unduly shocked. The Cadre knows the phenomenon well, allows for it."

Wanen realized suddenly that this was why deep-space men never returned to the home worlds of the Hegemony. When you had made your first really long voyage, you were never allowed closer to the Inner Stars than a year's journey; your home became the great naval bases. You knew this in advance, and were told it was a matter of quarantine, and accepted the sacrifice as a small offering to make for the Cadre.

Now he saw that the disease he might conceivably be carrying, against which the people of the Inner Stars must forever be protected, was not a physical one.

"Very well," he said, smiling his relief. "I understand."

"Glad to hear it," said Horlam. "Makes things that much easier."

Wanen laid the cylinder on the desk. "But we were discussing this, were we not?"

"Uh, yes. I was explaining the fundamental idea." Horlam drew a breath and set forth on a lecture. "Memory patterns, including the unconscious habit patterns, are taken to be synaptic pathways 'grooved' into the nervous system—if I may speak very loosely. The personality at any instant is a function of basic heredity, physical constitution health, diet and so on—and the accumulated total of these synaptic paths. Now the paths, being physical, can be scanned, and, of course, whatever is scanned can be recorded.

"Inside this cylinder is a complex protein whose molecules are selectively distorted to record the scanned data. But that's detail. Whatever can be scanned can also be selectively heterodyned, canceled, rubbed out—call it what you like—leaving the adult body a memoryless, mindless hulk. But such a body relearns with astonishing speed; it becomes a new, wholly functioning personality in less than a year.

"If these new memories, such as those you acquired in the past five years, are scanned and canceled, the recording of the old ones can be 'played back,' so to speak—reimposed on your nervous system. And thus Lieutenant Korul Wanen returns to life."

The young man scowled. "I know all that," he protested. "You explained it to me yourself when I got this assignment...but perhaps you've forgotten. After all, to you it happened five years ago. What I was interested in now were the more technical details: the type of signal used, for instance."

"I can't tell you much," said Horlam regretfully.

"Classified? I'm sorry I asked."

"It's not that classified. No, first is the fact that you would have to learn three new sciences for me to make sense to you. Second, it's an ancient Imperial technique, totally lost during the Dark Ages. An exploratory ship found a wrecked machine and a set of handbooks in the ruins of a city on Balgut IV, about thirty years ago. Slowly and painfully, the research unit to which I belong has rebuilt the psychalyzer, as we call it, and learned a few things about it. But we're still mostly groping in the dark."

"This record here—" Wanen nodded at the cylinder, which stood on the desk like some crude idol—"you intend to study it, I imagine?"

"Yes, but as an electronic phenomenon, not as a set of memories *per* se, which it could only become by being reimposed on a living brain, which I suspect could only be your brain. But with our apparatus, we can make a point-by-point comparison of this record with the record we have of yourself as Wanen—run statistical analyses and so on. I'm especially interested in trying to find out precisely what patterns in the recording correspond to the learned elements of personality.

"This was a totally new kind of experiment, you understand. Never before has the same body experienced two totally different cultures. Now we can really separate out the significant factors. Give my computers—and me—a few years to chew all the data and I may actually begin to know something about the human brain. Yes, you've performed a real service to science."

"I hope it is also a service to the Hegemony," said Wanen.

"Oh, it is. Consider what might be done about deviationism. At present, the psychalyzer can only wipe out the total memory of a non-loyal unit. The process of reeducation from the ground up is slow and costly; lobotomy and reduction to low civilian rank is a waste of good human potential. If we knew how, deviant tendencies could be corrected much more neatly, without sacrificing the deviant's skills and experience. In fact, perhaps conditioning could be made so thorough that no one would be physically able to have non-loyal thoughts."

It was such a splendid vision that Wanen jumped to his feet and blurted: "Thank you! Thank you for letting me serve!"

Horlam knocked the ash off his cigar and nodded in a slow, somehow old fashion. "You're all right," he said in a dry voice. "You may report for duty."

Coan Smit had changed in five years. He was no longer quite the steel-hard, steel-proud Academy youngster who had forever left the Inner Stars in order to serve them more fully.

Wanen grew only slowly aware of it, in the course of hours when they stood watch by the Number Five boat launcher, as they had done so many times before. Smit was still deft, crisp, neat. If his face had darkened, that was an honorable badge, given him by the sun and wind of the ringed planet. Wanen himself, after all, was even more deeply tanned, and added thereto was a barbarian tattoo.

But Smit was not *absolutely* Academy; the creases in his uniform were merely knife-edged, his boots did not blind the eye. He stood properly straight, but without actually straining his muscles. He walked with the regulation pace, but was there the faintest hint of a swagger?

When they were finally relieved, Smit yawned in a most un-Astro fashion. "Good to see you again, Lieutenant," he said.

"Thank you, Lieutenant," said Wanen formally.

"Let's get a cup of coffee. I want to talk to you."

Their hard heels clacked on metal as they went down the passage toward the junior officers' wardroom. Wanen found himself noticing the enlisted men he passed. They had grown sloppier than the officers, not outrageously so, but it was there; and when they saluted his insignia, he sensed an air of cringing.

Many punishments must have been ordered aboard the *Seeker* in the last five years: sweatbox, nerve-pulsing and worse. But that should not have been necessary...or should it?

Wanen sighed in confusion. They raised you from birth to serve—his mind recited the comforting Hierarchy: *The unit which is called I serves the unit called the Ship, which serves the Fleet, which is an arm of the almighty Hegemony and of the Cadre that guides us all toward the New Empire; there are no other loyalties.*

You were bred and raised for one purpose only, like all units below Cadre level. Your particular purpose was to serve in the Outer Fleet. And that, of course, was right and good; but it was a narrow education that did not prepare you for the sudden impact of strangeness.

For two years, while the *Seeker* hurtled through unmapped hundreds of parsecs, he had seen a little of the otherness which is deep space—just a little. Then five years dropped from his life and here he was again, in a ship which for half a decade had had the cold wild otherness seeping through her armor and—

They entered the small wardroom. No one else was present. Smit dialed for coffee and, when it came, sat cradling the hot cup in his hands for a while, as if he were chilled.

"I saw you, of course, a good many hours ago," he said finally. "But you wouldn't remember that. You were still Torrek then."

"Torrek?" Wanen raised his brows inquiringly.

"That was your name, you said. Oh, you were a proper savage, I can tell you!" Smit chuckled. "Beautifully easy to bait, too. I hope you don't—*Hey!*"

Wanen yanked himself back barely in time. His hands were still crooked claws. He looked at them numbly and it came to him that they had curved to fit a man's throat.

"What are you *doing*?" gasped Smit.

"I don't know." Wanen sat down again heavily and stared before him. "All of a sudden, a derangement. I wanted to kill you."

"Hm." Smit recovered with the rapidity of disciplined nerves. He sat a little farther away, but his face grew calm again. After a moment, he said in a thoughtful tone: "Some underlying disturbance—yes, I suppose that's it. A residual effect of the transformation you've undergone." He shrugged. "Well, why not? This is a new kind of experiment. You'd best see Horlam again, but I don't imagine it's anything too serious."

"Yes." Wanen stood up.

"Not now, you idiot! Relax. Drink your coffee. I want to discuss matters with you. It's important to our whole mission."

That brought Wanen back into his chair. "Proceed," he said. If his heart still shivered, he kept it under control.

"I hope the doctors can get that ugly tattoo off your face," complained Smit. "It bothers everybody."

"It's no worse than combat scars," said Wanen huffily.

"Oh, yes, it is. It stands for something different—something none of us want to be reminded of." Smit glowered into his coffee for a little while longer before resuming: "You recall that we found only two inhabited planets, both of them the usual wretched, uninteresting places, before coming on Ring here. That's the nickname the crew have given it: Ring. It's important and exciting enough to rate a pet name.

"You must also remember that our preliminary scoutings showed it to be an unusually fertile planet with a human population which had lost all traces of Empire civilization—but had, on the other hand, built up a rich variety of cultures for themselves. The highest society, technologically speaking, is in the Islands, the big subtropical archipelago. They're just on the verge of printing and chemical explosives, and could easily come up with a scientific-industrial revolution. That's the people we dropped you among."

"Yes," said Wanen. "I remember seeing it from the air. They told me that was the place—" His voice ran on, almost as if another mind were musing aloud. "There was a deep fjord, and towns along it, and mountains with long valleys like green fingers reaching down to the water and—No, I'm not sure," He rubbed his eyes. "Did I see clouds floating under a high peak? There was something about a peak, like victory. No, I can't recall."

He grew aware that Smit was regarding him oddly, but the sense of exaltation remained within him.

"Continue," Wanen said. "You were bringing me up to date."

"Yes. I was. Well, then, we left Ring and for nearly five years more we've been prowling this part of the spiral arm."

"What did you find?"

"Planets. Some with people on them. Nothing to compare with Ring. About six months ago, therefore, we came back. I and some others went down on ethnic survey in the Island region. I suppose you've heard something about the techniques. Kidnap a native, use accelerine and hypnosis to get the language and basic cultural information from him in a hurry, then dispose of him and go out yourself. Claim to be a foreigner from some other country. It works pretty well with societies that know there are other nations 'beyond the horizon,' but don't know exactly what they're like."

"What's a Boats man doing in ethnic survey?"

"You're Boats, too, Lieutenant."

"That's different. There were certain physical qualifications needed for the experiment, to give the blanked man a chance of survival, and training was, of course, irrelevant. But you—"

A bleakness crossed Smit's face. "We're short of ethnic specialists," he said, "and war boats aren't needed hereabouts. I had to fill in. So did a number of others."

"High casualties elsewhere?"

"Yes."

"But—from primitives?" Wanen was startled. "I thought they weren't even supposed to know there were observers among them—let alone get unnecessarily antagonized—let alone kill our men with—with spears!"

"All those things happened," said Smit grimly. "The loss of quality—competence, adjustedness, efficiency, even loyalty—the decay of the entire crew was incredible. In the case of the ethnic men, it was disastrous. See here, Lieutenant—half the casualties among survey terms were due to our having to shoot the men ourselves for radical deviationism."

Wanen sat as if struck on the head. "No," he whispered.

Smit bared his teeth. It was not a smile, nor quite a snarl. "Yes. I've felt the tendencies in myself. What did you expect? Seven years of metal walls and celibacy!"

"But we have Antisex. We have loyalty rallies—"

"Mere suppression of overt symptoms. Frustration continues to build up underneath, until it breaks loose in sheer destruction and negativism. Even a lifetime's conditioning can't survive that kind of pressure."

"But this can't be the first time—"

"Of course not. It always happens on a really long voyage. When the first troubles arose, the captain explained the phenomenon to all us officers."

"Well, then!" Wanen leaned back, sighing his relief. "So there must be a procedure in the Classified Manuals."

"There is," agreed Smit. "After casualties due to such causes exceed a certain percentage, the ship is to find a backward planet. A certain small area is to be occupied. Built-up aggressions may then be freely vented on its men and children. Antisex is discontinued and the local women made generally available."

Wanen felt a curious, sick reluctance within himself. He couldn't understand it. Even from an altruistic viewpoint, such measures were for the good of the barbarians, too, since the procedure was obviously essential to the expansion of the Hegemony and the Hegemony would come at last to include all mankind everywhere in the Galaxy.

Nevertheless, he could hardly get the words out: "So Ring has been picked?"

"No," said Smit. "The tension release I spoke of took place months ago, on the last planet we stopped at."

A second's inexplicable relief was followed by a new tightness of soul. "Then why are we still here?"

"Problems! A dilemma!"

Smit shoved his empty cup away, got up and started pacing the floor. It was not the act of an Academy man, taught never to show uncertainty to the world.

"You see, the Classified Manuals further recommend that a ship return to base immediately after such release has been effected. Otherwise—well, just consider the ordinary insignificant little enlisted man, the faceless unit among hundreds of other interchangeable units. For a few weeks, he has been a conqueror, killing, whipping, flaying, burning, raping, drinking himself stupid every night. Resuming ship discipline and Antisex isn't easy. In fact, if he isn't pointed back toward normal surroundings at once, the Cadre alone knows what deviationism can arise."

Wanen said, "Having recovered me, why don't we go home?"

"We've got to occupy Ring," said Smit shakily. "Not for the—the previous purpose. For militechnic reasons."

"What? But I thought this was only a survey."

"Oh, it is. Or was. But look. The average backslid planet is a pretty miserable affair. It's just naturally so hostile to human life that when the Empire broke up and all the artificial gadgets and props were destroyed, or rusted away, civilization went to maximum entropy in an obscene hurry. On most planets, Man simply became extinct. In the cases where adaptation was possible, the normal outcome was savagery.

"Ring, though, is a world where men can really feel at home. They've flourished! There are millions of them and they include some extremely able, sophisticated races. It's almost as good a conquest as a unified planet with full industrial culture.

"And remember, Lieutenant, we have mortal enemies. The Republic, the Libertarian League, the Royal Brotherhood, the High Earls of Morlan—there are a dozen other civilizations spreading into space, each with its own idea of what the New Empire should be like. We don't dare let one of their scouts stumble on Ring. Whoever garrisons it first has got possession of it, at this distance from all naval bases."

"Easy now!" said Wanen. "What are the odds of their finding Ring? A hundred billion stars in the Galaxy and this one to find among them all."

"And the GO stars are always investigated first," Smit said, "and they're not too common in this spiral arm, and we *know* there are League ships mapping it, too. It's a finite chance, certainly—I know that—but one we dare not take. We *must* plant a garrison down there; it's in the Manuals. Then we head back to base, report our find and have a task force sent which can take over the entire planet, fortify it properly, civilize the inhabitants, and so on.

"But it'll take us nearly two years to get home—a year to organize the task force, probably—two more years to come back—

"Five years! Can we trust a garrison for five years?"

Horlam began unclipping the electrodes from Wanen's head and body. His lips were pursed and he frowned, thinking.

"Well?" exclaimed Wanen. Only after half a minute of silence did he realize how un-Astro it had been for him to reveal emotion before a non-Cadre civilian. *What was wrong with him?*

"Well," said Horlam presently, "according to every known encephalographic and neurographic technique, you have no surviving memories of your stay on Ring."

"Are you certain?" insisted Wanen. "There must be something to account for—for—Look here." He forced the words out, one by one. "On my way to your office, I looked out at the planet. I have never seen anything so beautiful in my life. I loved it as I ought to love only the Cadre. I had to run from there before the tears came." He felt pain in his hands and unclenched them; the nails had bitten into the palms. "Something·about the experience must have changed me. I'm *deviant*."

"See here," said Horlam patiently, "it's my specialty, not yours, to know what memory is. It's a permanent alteration of protoplasm as the result of a stimulus. The memory patterns are all in the brain, except for a few habits which are synaptic patterns in the nerves proper. Well, I've just run a comparison of the Wanen record we have, your cylinder, with the Wanen record in your own nervous system. This is an absolutely objective process, a tracing out of electronic patterns of flow, resistance—it makes an electronic map of your entire nervous system."

He finished releasing the younger man, sat down on a corner of his workbench and took out a cigar. "The difference between the two patterns, my friend, is insignificant—a few additional traces caused by your experiences since your normal personality was reimposed. You've been telling yourself an old-time ghost story, with lingering traces of your Torrek memories in place of the ghost. Now forget it. I assure you that there are no such traces."

"But then what's making me have these fits?" Wanen felt himself almost cringing back.

"I'm not certain," shrugged Horlam. "I told you psychalysis is still a half-science fumbling in the dark. But at least I've proved your trouble is nothing very basic to yourself.

"Tentatively, my diagnosis is minor glandular upset. You've spent five years on an alien planet, eating its home-grown food. Perfectly good, nourishing food for a man, but there are doubtless subtle biochemical differences—hormone traces, vitaminlike compounds, and so on. Your body adapted. Now it's having a little difficulty readapting to ship rations. The slight chemical imbalance is expressing itself as irrational surges of emotion."

Wanen nodded. His tension began to ease. Chemical neuroses were not unheard of in this service, and easily correctible. "If I'm not actually deviating toward non-loyalty—"

"Not enough to matter," drawled Horlam. "These glandular-digestive hoo-raws do sometimes express themselves queerly. For instance, this desire to kill Lieutenant Smit that you mentioned, or your feeling toward Ring the attitudes appropriate only to the Cadre. And—let's see, have you had dreams the last night or two?"

Wanen shuddered. "Nightmares. I saw my own crewmates being killed—atro-ciously."

"An obvious expression of resentment toward them—toward the entire Hege-mony culture," said Horlam casually. When Wanen jerked, half leaping to his feet, the psychologist laughed. "Take it easy there, son. You're not non-loyal and nobody is going to shoot you. It happens all the time and doesn't mean a thing."

He got his cigar going. "After all, Man evolved as a creature of forests and open air and—intimacy, shall we say? A family animal. Our civilization forbids all this, locks us indoors with machines, selects our mates for us, whom we seldom see, and takes our children away to raise in creches. Naturally our instincts revolt. The good unit will not deny that he has bestial instincts—rather, he will accept the fact and use his strength to overcome them."

Wanen found the slow voice relaxing. He even began to feel warm. "I see," he answered. "Thank you. What treatment do you plan?"

"None, unless your symptoms get worse. And I expect they'll improve by themselves. Now you're dismissed. The exec wants you to report to him for spe-cial assignment."

It was curious, the thick pounding of his heart as he walked toward the door. The austerity of the ship, blank hallways and neat little cubicles, eternal white glare of fluorescents, gave the mind nothing to seize. It was thrown back on its own sick fantasies.

Wanen rehearsed his orders—any escape from the chaos and the sullen feel-ing of rebellion that lay coiled in his skull. The trouble was, his orders were so indefinite. In Astro, you were necessarily encouraged to think for yourself to some extent. Even an enlisted man was no use on a spaceship if the critical facul-ties were electrically burned out of his brain, as was done for the lower ranks of civilians in childhood. But this was too much latitude for a plain lieutenant of Boats. What was he supposed to *do*?

"This young woman who was picked up with you. She was the first of a series of prisoners we intend to take, to furnish more detailed information about the country. But she's proven too savage, even dangerous, to be of help. All that's been accomplished is to teach her the Cadric language by psychalysis, under accelerine. What information we have about her people suggests that none we might capture is likely to be of much greater value to us. However, since she was accompanying you, Lieutenant, she may be more cooperative if she is left alone with you. Persuade her to assist us.

"Our ground-fighting forces are not so large nor so well equipped that we could easily hold an island against the determined opposition of the archipelago nations—especially since deviationism is anticipated among the garrison, which may culminate in open mutiny if there is a strong enemy to whom the mutineers could desert afterward. Therefore it will be necessary, if we are to occupy even one island, that we exterminate all natives throughout the archipelago. The information she can furnish would be of value in conducting such an operation efficiently."

"The Intelligence men—did they try coercion, sir?"

"On the woman? Of course. She stood nerve-pulsing till she fainted, so that's no help. The so-called truth drugs disorganize the mind too much; we need systematic information. We could try mutilation, or the threat of it, but I doubt if it would work either; her culture seems to set a high value on intransigence. Either you persuade her, Lieutenant, or we discard her completely and fish for other prisoners."

"Yes, sir. But if it is permitted me to ask, why should we attack the Islands at all? There must be more backward areas, even desert regions, which could more easily be occupied."

"No doubt. But it so happens that the Islands are the only part of Ring which have been studied in any detail. That is because the ethnic officers were naturally most interested in the planet's most advanced culture. Now we do not have enough ethnic or cartographic specialists left to map any other region soon enough."

"I see. Thank you, sir."

"Service to the Cadre! Dismissed."

"Service to the Cadre!"

Wanen halted at the door. He was, he realized with a cold shock, afraid of what lay beyond.

Then, mumbling a curse, he palmed the lock. It opened for his prints and he went through. The door clashed shut behind him.

She sprang from her bunk and stood for a moment without stirring, as if frozen. And yet, he thought dizzily, the lines of her were fleetness itself. He had never in all his, memory seen so wild and lovely a creature as the one which poised in the steel bareness of this little cell.

(Yes, he had—as Torrek. But Torrek had been peeled from him, like a skin taken off living flesh.)

She wept and ran to his arms.

As he held her, he felt again the sensation which had risen in him when Ring swam across the stars. Only it was a deeper thing this time, a knife twisting inside him and a summer's breeze in his hair, trumpeted victory and a long blue twilight where they two walked alone. Almost, he carried her to the bunk—

But only almost.

He remembered in barest time that there was a spyscope mounted somewhere. It brought him back to a sense of his duty, but with the heaviness of a world oppressing him.

She babbled endearments in a language he did not know, until at last he put a hand under her chin and tilted her face up toward his (where had he learned the gesture?) and said with an overwhelming tenderness: "Speak Cadric. I have forgotten."

"Oh—" She drew a little away from him. His arms would not release her, not entirely, but he saw terror in her eyes.

"It's all right," he said. "It's only that I have forgotten what happened on—in the Islands. You see, I have been returned to my people."

"*Your* people!" She said it slowly. The unfamiliar language was stiff on her lips.

"Yes." He let her go and stared at the floor, feeling obscurely ashamed. She did not run from him, but there was no place to run to. He plowed ahead: "I regret any inconveniences you may have suffered, but it was necessary. We've come for the good of all mankind."

"It—may be." She eased a trifle and whispered: "But you have forgotten everything indeed, Torrek. They have shorn your mind like your hair?"

"I don't even know your name any more," he said wryly.

"Even—I am Sonna, Baelg's daughter." A slow flush crossed her cheeks. "We were going into the mountains together."

He remembered acutely that he had not yet been issued his Antisex tablets. But it was hard to define his feelings toward the girl. She was more than a means of relieving tension; more, even, than a co-procreator of loyal units.

Surely his trouble went deeper than Horlam admitted!

"Don't you remember how you killed the kraka?" she asked him wonderingly. Her fists drew together. "It was unfair to take that from you!"

"It's all right," he said. "After all, I have regained so much more. I remember my—well, my first indoctrination, instead of—oh, say, my first fishing trip—Never mind! You simply wouldn't understand."

'What is your name now?" she asked.

"Korul Wanen."

"I shall always think of you as Torrek." She sat down on the bunk, smiling unhappily. "Come, join me, at least, and tell me about your people."

He did. It was mostly an astronomy lesson, with a sketch of history since the Empire died and a lecture on the New Empire of the future. He spoke in a most dry, uninspired tone and looked straight before him.

"Yes," she said finally, "it is a glorious vision, to make all men brothers again. I think Dumethdin will be pleased to make an alliance with you."

"An alliance?" he stumbled.

"That's not just what—what we had in mind."

"No? What then?"

Being trained only to guide spaceships, and in combat to operate one of the small boats which guarded a major formation, Wanen proceeded to tell her.

She grew altogether still.

"It is, of course, for the best," he said.

She stood up. "Get out."

"What? But I was explaining—"

"I know I cannot kill you. But get out before I dirty my hands by trying!"

"See here—your own self-interest—loyalty to the Cadre is expected of *all* humans—"

She did something then which told him how alien her homeland was and he himself had been. She sat down, cross-legged, and ignored him. She erased him from her private universe of perceptions. He realized only slowly what she was doing; afterward, he wondered why he understood at all. He had never heard of such a thing before, except in his canceled Torrek incarnation.

But when it penetrated his mind, he turned and ran from her, shaking with fear.

"You have been an idiot," said Coan Smit. They sat alone in the wardroom, after coming off Boats watch once again.

"How was I to know?" asked Wanen miserably. He stared at his cup without really seeing it. "Diplomacy isn't my field. I'm not an ethnic man, for Cadre's sake! The exec himself said he could not reprimand me."

"I can. An Academy man isn't some stupid civilian—we're not only allowed versatility, it's expected of us. You've let down the Academy, Wanen."

"Shut up!" The emotion within Wanen exploded in a roar. "Shut up or I'll wring your neck!"

"Lieutenant!" Smit sprang erect. "Your behavior is deviant."

"For your information," said Wanen between his teeth, "my rank is equal to yours. I'm going to file a criticism of your language."

"And *I* am going to file a suspicion of deviationism," Smit retorted. "Horlam is another idiot. He should have turned you inside out. Just because your trouble isn't due to lingering memory traces doesn't prove that you have no trouble."

"I am also physiologically and biochemically checked out," snapped Wanen. "Any imbalance is a question of micro quantities. When were you last investigated? And what business is it of yours, anyway?"

"'Anyone's business is everyone's business."

Wanen had heard the slogan often enough. He had cited it himself now and then, in a past which seemed impossibly remote. But all at once it tasted like brass in his mouth. He hunched over his coffee cup, smoldering.

"We're too far from home," said Smit, more gently. "If we don't return, it may be centuries before a Hegemony ship comes this way again. An enemy scout may find Ring meanwhile. *Anything* might happen. Better to dispose of you on suspicion than risk our entire operation."

"Yes," said Wanen automatically. "That's the obvious solution."

"Not that I really think that'll be necessary." Smit was fairly bedewed with good-fellowship now. He came around the table and laid a brotherly hand on the other man's shoulder. "Actually, I myself believe your trouble is just some trivial thing. A few shots of hormone, perhaps some conditioning, and you should be as good as new. Or—wait. Now that I come to think of it, you've gone a full seven years without tension release!"

"I was on Ring," mumbled Wanen. "I was a man of—what did she call it?—a man of Dumethdin. We didn't need to do such things."

"No doubt. But now you've forgotten. Hm." Smit paused.

Looking up, Wanen saw him thoughtfully rubbing his chin and realized with an illogical resentment that the fellow was trying to be helpful.

"I have an idea," Smit went on."It'll have to be approved, of course, but I don't see why it shouldn't be. And if all you need is release, this will certainly provide it."

"What will?"

"This girl, the one we captured. Since she just won't cooperate and a total reconditioning isn't worthwhile, I understand that she'll be lobotomized and turned over to the enlisted men for a few days. Now if you were allowed to watch the operation and then have her first and throw her out of the airlock yourself when she's no use any more—why, it should be as good as a six months' furlough!"

Wanen sat very still. After Smit had gone out, he remained in his position, crouched over the wardroom table. His heartbeat had slowed so much that he could no longer feel or hear it. Once, vaguely and indifferently, he wondered if he were dead.

Then he realized that he was insane.

The Boats watch was changed every four hours, with the same men taking it every fourth time around. Between such duties, one ate, slept, studied, participated in loyalty demonstrations—but there was also a certain amount of time to oneself, at least on the officer level. The young men played ball in the gym, or gambled in the wardroom, or perhaps they sat and talked.

At any rate, there would be nothing suspicious about an off-duty lieutenant walking through almost any part of the ship.

Wanen was counting on that. There was a curious peace within him. He knew he was mad. In view of Horlam's exhaustive tests and their uniformly negative results, it was the only possible explanation. The strain of changing personalities clearly had cracked his mind open. He was crazy, and he expected to be killed somewhere along the way, and it didn't matter greatly. Nevertheless, he took no unnecessary chances.

He forged his squadron commander's name to a Special Orders slip and presented Lieutenant Rosnin with it when that conscientious young man went on Boats watch.

"Full combat lading for Seventeen, including fusion missiles?" Rosnin's brows went up. "What's going on?"

"Classified," said Wanen briskly. "Don't you see this is a Special form?"

Rosnin might have wondered why any junior officer should be entrusted with Classified orders and, simultaneously, present the directive in so casual a fashion.

But he was not a man of great curiosity, nor given to annoying his superiors with questions. Wanen had remembered that from the outbound voyage and counted on it.

"It shall be done. Service to the Cadre!"

"Service to the Cadre."

Wanen wheeled and marched to the issue room, where he checked out a Mark IV sidearm with an extra clip of explosive bullets. Normal ship routine would force him to account for his action in about six hours, when a higher-up looked over the day's requisitions. But Wanen didn't expect to be around that much longer.

He had to walk fast now, being already late for his appointment. He was depending on the fact that never before in all history had a properly conditioned unit gone deviant to the point of treason without first showing overt symptoms. He himself was at present considered merely to be under tension. But too fast a gait might attract attention.

No matter. To entropy with it. Korul Wanen was already a dead man on leave.

He came to sickbay and was passed by the armed guard. The damned ship swarmed with guards, he thought irritably—guards, paper work, anything that might keep a man too busy to think.

Well—

Frain Horlam waited, surgically gowned, in the operating room. There were two husky meditechs to assist.

The old man looked coldly at Wanen. "I never knew anybody to be late for tension release," he said.

"I was busy," snapped Wanen. "Get on with it."

Horlam switched on the sterilizers. One of the techs went out. He brought in Sonna, strapped to a wheeled cot. Her eyes were blank with a terror she could not choke off, but when she saw Wanen, she spat.

"Is the spyscope turned on?" he asked.

"Not to my knowledge, said Horlam in an acid tone. "Everyone else is too busy right now. It's you who needs a thrill."

"I only wondered."

"While we sterilize the surroundings—it wouldn't do to have her get sick, would it?—you will probably enjoy explaining what is about to be done to her," said Horlam. He did not look at Wanen; he washed his hands over and over again, with exaggerated care. "Also, of course, we must take the hair off her head before we open the skull. That should, provoke an interesting reaction all by itself. Most primitive women are quite proud of their hair."

"Stop that," said Wanen.

"I'm only outlining the pleasures you have in store," Horlam explained, his voice rusty. "We can do the operation under local anesthesia, so that she'll be conscious through most of it. Naturally, once she's been made docile, you'll have to wait a few days for her to heal up enough—" He broke off.

"Go on, Lieutenant." One of the meditechs said it urgently. His eyes were very bright, fixed on the girl. "Go on, tell it to her like the doctor says."

"Well," suggested, Wanen, "both of you fellows come stand here beside her. There, that's right."

Sonna stared up at him. He could imagine her thoughts, he told himself emptily. She would be wishing she could faint, wishing she could die, but there was too much life in her. Torrek must have had such wishes, right at the end, before they peeled him off Wanen and locked him in a black cylinder.

Wanen walked up behind the techs, laying a hand on the shoulder of each. "I suppose you boys are getting some release, too."

"Yes, *sir*!"

"Good." Wanen's hands slid upward, palming their heads. Then the muscles which had wrestled the kraka smashed their skulls together.

They went down like stones, but he kicked them deftly behind the ears, to make sure. Mostly his attention was on Horlam. He yanked the gun from beneath his coverall and turned its staring eye on the old man.

"Don't move," he said. "Take it easy or I'll kill you."

Horlam's face drained of blood. "What are you doing?" he gasped.

"I am going to break out of here. Yes, I am deviant. I am also non-loyal, obstructionist and homicidal. My greatest wish is to shoot my own dear shipmates one at a time. Please don't make me start on you. Gently now—very gently—keep your hands and feet in plain sight. Come up here and let the girl go."

For a minute, he thought that Sonna had indeed fainted. But when Horlam had unstrapped her, she wavered to her feet.

"Torrek," she whispered. "Torrek, *elskling.*"

"I am going to take you home, Sanna," he told her.

There was a curious expression on Horlam's thin face. The shock had passed; mostly, now, he looked interested.

"Do you really hope to get away with this?" he asked.

"No," said Wanen.

"Hitherto, this sort of thing has been a clinical impossibility. By all objective tests, you were functioning within the limits of normality—"

"Shut up. Get a surgical gown and mask for the girl. Help her put them on... Very well. Now, Horlam, you go first out the door."

The clumsy disguise did not get them past the sentry outside. It did slow his comprehension a little bit—long enough for Wanen to shoot him down as he grabbed for his rifle.

Thereafter, they ran.

Twice it was necessary to kill men who got in the way. By the time Wanen and Sonna had reached Boat Seventeen, the whole ship was one great clamor of sirens and shouts and hurrying feet.

His explosive bullets mopped up the guard by the launching robot. But as he was setting it to eject the boat, he saw Coan Smit burst from a side passage. Wanen fired once and missed. Then Smit made a dive, tackled him by the ankles, and his gun went flying.

"Go through that door, Sonna!" Wanen ordered.

Smit's hands groped after his vulnerable spots, in the standard Academy infighting technique. Wanen blocked him with the same automatic procedure. But then, somehow, Wanen's arms and legs were going through motions unknown to any civilized folk. He broke Smit's back across his knee.

A spatter of bullets rang down the hall. Wanen got up, threw the launcher lock switch open and followed Sonna.

The boat's combat-ready motors roared as he shoved up the main bar. He vaulted into the pilot chair and grabbed for the controls. Sonna crouched behind him, cramped, bruised, and screaming a call that was somehow familiar to him.

Boat Seventeen leaped from the mother ship and hurled starlight back from her flanks.

"They'll hunt us down—" It was an unexpected groan in Wanen's ears.

"No, they won't!" he said roughly. "I thought of that, too."

He slammed a lever. The fusion missiles leaped from their tubes.

"Cover your eyes!" he shouted, and accelerated brutally to escape.

When the soundless explosion was over, only an incandescent gas cloud remained. It glowed for a moment, unbearably bright, before it expanded and cooled. Darkness gulped it down.

Wanen pointed his boat toward the beautiful ringed planet.

He began to weep.

Sonna reached across the narrow cockpit. There was alarm in the gesture. Horlam stopped her.

"No," he said gently. "Let him get it out. He's just denied his entire lifetime."

She sank back. Through the transparent canopy, the swelling lambent planet tangled its many-colored luminance in her hair.

"Why are you here, old man?" she breathed. "You could have dropped behind easily enough as we fled. You did not know he meant to destroy the ship."

"I might have guessed," said Horlam dryly. "Or—let us say that I have been a trifle deviationist myself for a good many years, and when the opportunity came—It was my task to detect emerging humanness in men and uproot it. But there is a very ancient saying which asks, "Who shall watch the watchmen?"

Ever so faintly, Sonna's fingers brushed the blond head which lay shuddering before her. "Has Torrek come back?"

"Not in the way you hope," said Horlam. "The open, overt memories of Torrek—the deeds done, words spoken, things seen—I'm afraid they went forever with the ship. But there is another kind of memory. Our theories don't allow for it—but then Hegemony science is almost as narrow and mechanical as Hegemony life. You can't, after all, separate the brain and nerves from the rest of the body: from muscles, veins, viscera, skin, blood and lungs and bones. The living organism is a wholeness.

"Apparently your way of life, down there in the Islands, is a biologically sound one. It suits Man's deepest instincts, as ours does not. Therefore, five years of it made a deeper impression on our boy here than the twenty-odd years of slogans and exercises before that. When we brought him back, the psychalyzer wiped out the memories, yes. I even thought it had removed the habits.

"But it didn't touch the *true* habits—those deep reactions, perhaps on an actual cellular level, which we call emotional patterns. Wanen could forget that he had been an Islander. He could not forget what it meant to be an Islander—pride, freedom, decency—whatever it *does* mean. His body remembered that for him!"

Horlam smiled. "I was not without slight suspicions of this," he finished, "but I was already deviationist enough not to report it. I was curious to see what would develop. Now I know and I'm not sorry."

The girl leaned over the seat and rubbed her cheek against Wanen's. He lifted his head and wiped his eyes, pathetically like a child.

"What are we going to do now?" she asked.

"Return to your country—our country," Wanen said with a gathering strength. "Warn them. We have a long time yet to make ourselves ready, invent our own science and build our own ships and find our own allies among the stars—my knowledge and Horlam's will help with the first beginnings, but it will take many lifetimes to finish. It's a good work for a man."

"Oh, Torrek, my poor hurt Torrek—everything you have forgotten!"

"I remembered what was important, didn't I?" He twisted around to face her. "The rest I can learn over again. Will you teach me?"

THE PIRATE

We guard the great Pact; but the young generations, the folk of the star frontier, so often do not understand.

They avail themselves of our ordinary work. *(Ship* Harpsong *of Nerthus, out of Highsky for David's Landing, is long overdue…Please forecast the competition which a cybernation venture on Oasis would probably face after the older firms elsewhere learned that a market had been established…Bandits reported… How shall we deal with this wholly strange race of beings we have come upon?)* But then we step in their own paths and say, "Thou shalt not." And suddenly we are the Cordys, the enemy.

The case of the slain world named Good Luck is typical. Now that the Service is ready, after a generation, to let the truth be known, I can tell you about Trevelyan Micah, Murdoch Juan Smokesmith, red Faustina, and the rest, that you may judge the rights or wrongs for yourself.

In those days Trevelyan spent his furloughs on Earth. He said its quiet, its intellectuality, were downright refreshing, and he could get all the rowdiness he wanted elsewhere. But of course his custom put him at the nerve center of the Service, insofar as an organization operating across a fraction of the galaxy can have one. He got a larger picture than most of his colleagues of how it fared with the Pact. This made him more effective. He was a dedicated man.

I suspect he also wanted to renew his humanity at the wellspring of humankind, he who spent most of his life amidst otherness. Thus he was strengthened in his will to be a faithful guardian.

Not that he was a prig. He was large and dark, with aquiline features and hard aquamarine eyes. But his smile was ready, his humor was dry, his tunic and culottes were always in the latest mode, he enjoyed every aspect of life.

When the machine summoned him to the Good Luck affair, he had been living for a while at Laugerie Haute, which is in the middle of the steep, green, altogether beautiful Dordogne country. His girl of the moment had a stone house that was built in the Middle Ages against an overhanging cliff. Its interior renovation did not change its exterior ancientness, which made it seem a part of the hills or they a part of it. But in front grew bushes, covering a site excavated centuries ago, where flint-working reindeer hunters lived for millennia while the glacier covered North Europe. And daily overhead through the bright sky glided a spear that was the Greenland-Algeria carrier; and at night, across the stars where men now traveled, moved sparks that were spaceships lifting out of Earth's shadow. In few other parts of the planet could you be more fully in the oneness of time.

"You don't have to go, not yet," Braganza Diane said, a little desperately because she cared for him and our trumpeter blows too many "Farewells" each year.

" 'Fraid I do," he said. "The computer didn't ring me up for fun. In fact, it's a notoriously sober-sided machine." When she didn't answer his grin, he explained: "The data banks show I'm the only person available who's dealt with, uh, a certain individual before. He's a slippery beast, with sharp teeth, and experience might make the critical quantum of difference."

"It better!" She curbed the tears that could have caused him to think her immature and bent her lips upward. "You will add...the rest of this leave...to your next, and spend it with me. Won't you?"

"I'd love to," he said, carefully making no promises. He kissed her, where they stood in the hay scent of summer. They went back to the house for a while.

After he packed his kit and phoned good-bye to some neighbors—landholders, friendly folk whose ancestors had dwelt here for generations beyond counting—she flew him to Aerogare Bordeaux. Thence he took a carrier to Port Nevada. The computer had briefed him so well that he could go straight to work, and he wanted to catch Murdoch Juan at ease if possible.

His timing was good. Sunset was slanting across western North America and turning the mountains purple when he arrived. The city walled him off from that serenity as he entered. It shouldered big square buildings above streets in which traffic clamored; the growl of machines perpetually underlay the shrill of voices; frantically flickering signs drowned out the stars; humans and nonhumans hustled, jostled, chiseled, brawled, clashed, stole, evangelized, grew rich, grew poor, came, went, and were forgotten; beneath a tawdry front was that heedless vigor which the cargo ships bring from their homes to enclaves like this. Trevelyan allowed himself a brief *"Phew!"* when the stinks rolled around him.

He knew this town, on a hundred different worlds. He knew how to make inquiries of chance-met drinking companions. Eventually he found one of Murdoch's crew who could tell him where the boss was this evening. It turned out to be no dive, with the smoke of a dozen drugs stinging the eyes, but the discreet and expensive Altair House.

There a headwaiter, live though extraterrestrial, would not conduct him to his man. Captain Murdoch had requested privacy for a conference. Captain Murdoch was entitled to—Trevelyan showed his identification. It gave him no legal prerogative; but a while ago the Service had forestalled a war on the headwaiter's native planet.

Upstairs, he chimed for admittance to the room. He had been told that Captain Murdoch's dinner guest had left, seemingly well pleased, while Captain Murdoch and his female companion stayed behind with a fresh order of champagne, vigorator, and other aids to celebration. "Come in, come in!" boomed the remembered hearty voice. The door dilated and Trevelyan trod through.

"Huh? I thought you were...Sunblaze! You again!" Murdoch surged to his feet. Briefly he stood motionless, among drapes and paintings, sparkling glassware, drift of music and incense. Then, tiger softly, he came around the table to a fist's reach of Trevelyan.

He was as tall, and broader in the shoulders. His features were rugged, deeply weathered, blond hair and a sweeping blond moustache. His clothes were too colorful to be stylish on Earth, but he wore them with such panache that you didn't notice.

The woman remained seated. She was as vivid in her way as he in his, superbly formed, the classicism of her face brought to life by the nearly Asian cheekbones; and she owned the rare combination of pure white skin and fox-red hair. Yet she was no toy. When she saw Murdoch thus taken aback, Trevelyan read shock upon her. It was followed by unflinching enmity.

He bowed to her. "Forgive me if I intrude," he said.

Murdoch relaxed in a gust of laughter. "Oh, sure, sure, Mike, you're forgiven. If you don't stay too mugthundering long." He clapped hands on the agent's shoulders. "How've you been, anyway? How many years since last?"

"Five or six." Trevelyan tried to smile back. "I'm sorry to bother you, but I understand you're shipping out day after tomorrow, which no doubt means you'll be busy for the prior twenty-four hours."

"Right, buck," Murdoch said. "This here tonight is our lift-off party. However, it began with business—lining up a financial backer for later on—so it may as well continue that way a few microseconds." The tone stayed genial, but the gaze was pale and very steady. "Got to be business, don't it? You didn't track me down just to wish an old sparring partner a bonny voyage."

"Not really," Trevelyan admitted.

Murdoch took his arm and led him to the table. "Well, sit yourself and have a glug with us. Faustina, meet Trevelyan Micah of the Stellar Union Coordination Service."

"Juan has spoken of you," the woman said distantly.

Trevelyan eased into a chair. His muscles relaxed, one by one, that his brain might be undistracted in the coming duel. "I hope he used language suitable to a lady," he said.

"I'm from New Mars," she snapped. "We don't have time for sex distinctions in our manners."

I might have guessed, he thought. There aren't as many unclaimed planets habitable by man as is popularly believed; so the marginal ones get settled too. He could imagine scarring poverty in her background, and Murdoch Juan as the great merry beloved knight who took her from it and would bear her on his saddlebow to the castle he meant to conquer for them.

"I did my duty as I saw it, which happened to conflict with Captain Murdoch's rights as he saw them," Trevelyan said.

"I was making a fortune off fur and lumber on Vanaheim," the other man said.

"And disrupting the ecology of a continent," Trevelyan replied.

"You didn't have to come in and talk them into changing the laws on me," Murdoch said without rancor. He raised a glass from the water carafe and filled it with champagne. "Hope you don't mind this being used first by a financier."

"No. Thank you." Trevelyan accepted.

"And then, when he was honorably engaged as a mercenary—" Faustina's tone held venom.

"Bringing modern weapons in against primitives who were no menace," Trevelyan said. "That's universally illegal. Almost as illegal as dispossessing autochthons or prior colonists."

"Does your precious Union actually claim jurisdiction over the entire cosmos?"

"Ease off, Faustina," Murdoch said.

"The Union is not a government, although many governments support it," Trevelyan said to the woman. "This galaxy alone is too big for any power to control. But we do claim the right to prevent matters from getting out of hand, as far as we're able. That includes wrongdoing by our own citizens anywhere."

"The Cordys never jailed me," Murdoch said. They only scuppered my operation. I got away in time and left no usable evidence. No hard feelings." He raised his glass. Unwillingly, Trevelyan clinked rims with him and drank. "In fact," Murdoch added, "I'm grateful to you, friend. You showed me the error of my ways. Now I've organized a thing that'll not only make me rich, but so respectable that nobody can belch in my presence without a permit."

Faustina ignited a cigarette and smoked in hard puffs.

"I've been asked to verify that," Trevelyan said.

"Why, everything's open and honest," Murdoch said. "You know it already. I got me a ship, never mind how, and went exploring out Eridanus way. I found a planet, uninhabited but colonizable, and filed for a discoverer's patent. The Service inspection team verified that Good Luck, as I'm calling it, is an awfully exploitable world. Here I am on Earth, collecting men and equipment for the preliminary work of making a defined area safe for humans. You remember"—his manner grew deliberately patronizing—"check for dangerous organisms and substances in the environment, establish the weather and seismic patterns, et cetera. When we're finished, I'll advertise my real estate and my ferry service to it. For the duration of my patent, I can set the terms of immigration, within limits. Most discoverers just charge a fee. But I aim to supply everything—transportation there, a functioning physical community built in advance, whatever people need to make a good start. That's why I've been discussing financial backing."

"Your approach has been tried," Trevelyan warned, "but never paid off. The cost per capita of a prefabricated settlement is more than the average would-be immigrant can afford. So he stays home, and puff goes the profit. Eventually, the entrepreneur is glad to sell out for a millo on the credit."

"Not this one," Murdoch said. "I'll be charging irresistibly little—about half what it'd cost 'em to buy unimproved land and make their own homes and highways and such out of local materials. They'll come." He tossed off the rest of his glass and refilled it. "But why are you curious, you Cordys? I haven't told you anything that isn't on file. If you wanted to snoop, why didn't you come see me earlier?"

"Because we have too much else on file," Trevelyan said bitterly. "Our computer didn't get around to correlating certain facts until yesterday. We're trying to keep the galaxy livable, but it's too much for us, too diverse—"

"Good!" Faustina said.

He gave her a grave look. "Be careful, my lady," he said, "or one day a piece of that diversity may kill you."

Murdoch scowled. "That'll do." he said. "I've been nice, but this is my evening out with my girl and you're obviously on a fishing expedition. You haven't got a thing against me, legally, have you? Get out."

Trevelyan tensed where he sat. "Or goodnight, if you prefer," Murdoch said in friendlier wise.

Trevelyan rose, bowed, murmured the polite formulas, and left. Inwardly he felt cold. There had been more than a gloat in his enemy's manner; there had been the expectation of revenge.

It looks as if I'd better take direct action, he thought.

The *Campesino* cleared from orbit, ran out of the Solar System on gravs, and went into hyperdrive in the usual fashion. She was a long-range cruiser with boats and gear for a variety of conditions. Aboard were Murdoch, Faustina, half a dozen spacemen and a score of technicians.

The Service speedster *Genji* followed, manned by Trevelyan and that being whose humanly unpronounceable name was believed to mean something like Smokesmith. To shadow another vessel is more art than science and more witchcraft than either. *Campesino* could easily be tracked while in the normal mode—by amplified sight, thermal radiation, radar, neutrinos from the power plant. But once she went over to the tachyon mode, only a weak emission of superlight particles was available. And Murdoch also had detectors, surely kept wide open.

With skill and luck, *Genji* could stay at the effective edge of the field she was observing, while it masked her own. For this to be possible, however, she must be much smaller as well as much faster than the other craft. Therefore nothing more formidable could be used. She did have a blast cannon, a couple of heavy slugthrowers, and several one-meter dirigible missiles with low-yield nuclear warheads. But Trevelyan would have been surprised if Murdoch's people didn't build huskier weapons en route.

He sat for hours at the conn, staring into the jeweled blackness of its star simulacrum, while the ship murmured around him and the subliminal beat of drive energies wove into his bones. At last he said, "I think we've done it." He pointed to the instruments. A hunter's exultation lifted within him. "They are definitely sheering off the Eridanus course."

"They may have become aware of us, or they may do so later, and attack," replied the flat artificial voice of Smokesmith.

"We take that chance," Trevelyan agreed. "I can't quite believe it of Murdoch, though. He plays rough, but I don't know about any cold-blooded murders he's done."

"Our information concerning his world line is fragmentary, and zero about its future segment. Furthermore, available data indicate that his companions are quite unintegrate."

"Hm-m-m, yes, hard cases, none Earth-born, several nonhumans from raptor cultures among them. That was one fact which alerted us."

"What else? We departed too hurriedly for me to obtain entire background, I being ignorant of the biological and social nuances among your species."

Trevelyan considered his shipmate. Chief Rodionov had had to assign the first and presumably best agent he could, and there were never many nonhumans at Australia Center. Homo sapiens is a wolfish creature; two of him can end with ripping each other apart, on an indefinitely long voyage in as cramped a shell as this. But even when our agents have gentler instincts, we try to make up teams out of diverse breeds. The members must be compatible in their physical requirements but, preferably, different enough in psychologies and abilities that they form a whole which is more than its parts,

The trouble was, Trevelyan had never before encountered a being from the planet men called Reardon's. He had heard of them, but space is too full of life for us to remember it all, let alone meet it.

Smokesmith's barrellike body stood about one hundred forty centimeters high on four stumpy, clawfooted legs. Four tentacles ringed the top of it each ending in three boneless fingers whose grip was astonishing. The head was more like a clump of fleshy blue petals than anything else; patterns upon them were the outward signs of sense organs, though Trevelyan didn't know how these worked. Withal, Smokesmith was handsome in his (?) fashion. Indeed, the mother-of-pearl iridescence on his rugose torso was lovely to watch.

The man decided on a straightforward approach. "Well," he said, "the fact that Murdoch is involved was in itself suspicious. He probably came to Earth to outfit, rather than some colonial world where he isn't known, because he wouldn't attract attention."

"I should extrapolate otherwise, when few commercial ventures originate on Earth."

"But the average Terrestrial hasn't got the average colonist's lively interest in such matters. The port cities are mostly ignored by the rest of the planet, a regrettable necessity to be kept within proper bounds. Then too, Murdoch would have a better chance of getting substantial but close-mouthed—uh, that means secretive—money help on Earth, which is still the primary banker of the human species. And finally, though it's true that Service reports from everywhere go to the molecular file at Center...that fact makes the data flow so huge that Murdoch might well have completed his business and departed before the continuous search-and-correlation noticed him."

"What was smelled, then, to excite suspicion? I do not hypothesize that the initial stimulus was the composition of his crew."

"No. We checked that out later. Nor did the economics of his project look especially interesting. Doubtless his ready-built community will be a wretched clutter of hovels; but *caveat emptor,* he'll be within the law, and word will soon get around not to buy from him.

"No, the real anomaly is the equipment he ordered. The report on this Good Luck of his is complete enough that you can fairly well predict what a ground-preparation gang will need. The planet's smaller than Earth, relatively cold and arid, relatively thin atmosphere. But it has a magnetic field and a weak sun; hence the radiation background is low."

"What is required would depend on what race is to colonize."

"Sure. Murdoch will sell to humans. Not Earth humans, naturally. Colonial ones, from all over. We won't be able to monitor every embarkation and debarkation, any except a tiny fraction. Not when we are as few as we are, with so much else to do. And local authorities won't care. They'll be too glad to get rid of excess population. Besides, most colonials are anarchic oriented; they won't stand for official inquiries into their business." Trevelyan blinked in surprise. "What started me off on that?"

"Conceivably an element of your mentation has sensed a thought."

"If so, it's a hunch too faint to identify. Well. Why doesn't he have waterfinding gear with him, drills and explosives to start forming lakes, that kind of stuff? Why does he have a full line of radiation spotters and protective suits? The biological laboratory he's assembled isn't right for Good Luck either; it's meant to study life forms a lot more terrestroid. I could go on, but you get the idea."

"And now he has changed course." Smokesmith considered the indicators with whatever he used to see. "A geodesic, which will bring him in the direction of Scorpius."

"Huh? You don't have to ask the computer? Trouble is, no law says he must go to his announced destination, or tell us why he didn't." Trevelyan smiled with shut lips. "Nor does any law say we can't tail along."

A keening broke from Smokesmith, made not with his vocoder but with his own tympani. It wavered up and down the scale; a brief shakenness in his nerves told Trevelyan it entered the subsonic. Odors rolled upon the air, pungencies like blood and burnt sulfur and others men do not know.

"Good Cosmos, what're you doing?" he exclaimed.

"It is an old communication of my infraculture. Of whetted winds, frost, a mountain that is a torch, beneath iron moons, a broken night, and the will to pursue that which has poison fangs...Enough."

Five hundred and twenty-eight light-years from Sol, the sky ahead suddenly blazed.

Trevelyan had been meditating upon his philosophy. That, and reading, and listening to music tapes, and tinkering with handicrafts, and physical exercises, had been his refuge from the weary weeks. Smokesmith was a decent being in his way, but too alien for games or conversation. When asked how he passed the time, with no apparent motion save of his endlessly interweaving arms, he replied: "I make my alternate life. Your language lacks the necessary concepts."

The blossoming of what had been merely another, slowly waxing, blue star, jerked Trevelyan to alertness. He sat up, clenched hands on chair arms, and stared at the simulacrum until his vision seemed to drown in those glittering dark. depths. The star climbed in brilliance even as he watched, for *Genji* passed the wave front of the initial explosion and entered that which had come later. It dominated the whole sky before Trevelyan could shout:

"Supernova!"

And still it flamed higher, until its one searing point gave fifty times the light that full Luna does to Earth, ten million times the light of the next most luminous—and nearby—sun. Although the screens throttled down that terrible whiteness, Trevelyan could not look close to it, and his vision was fogged with shining spots for minutes after the glimpse he had first gotten.

Smokesmith's claws clicked on the deck of the conn section as the Reardonite entered. Trevelyan caught a hackle-raising whiff from him and knew he was equally awed. Perhaps his expressionless phrasing was a defense:

"Yes, a supernova of Type II, if the theoretical accounts I have witnessed are correct. They are estimated to occur at the rate of one every fifty-odd years in the galaxy. The remnants of some have been investigated, but to date no outburst has been observed within the range of recorded explorations."

"We've gone beyond that range already," the man whispered. He shook himself. "Is Murdoch headed toward it?"

"Approximately. No change in course."

"Can't be coincidence. He must have traveled far, looking for game the Cordys wouldn't take from him, and—" Roughly: "Let's get some readings."

Instruments, astrophysical files carried on every Service vessel, and computation produced a few answers. The star was about one hundred fifty parsecs away, which meant it had died five centuries ago. It had been a blue giant, with a mass of some ten Sols, an intrinsic luminosity of perhaps fifty thousand; but the Scorpian clouds had hidden it from early Terrestrial astronomers, and modern scientists were as yet too busy to come this far afield.

So wild a burning could not go on for many million years. Instabilities built up until the great star shattered itself. At the peak of its explosion, it flooded forth energy equal to the output of the rest of the galaxy.

That could last for no more than days, of course. Racing down the lightyears, Trevelyan saw the lurid splendor fade. A mistiness began to grow, a nebula born of escaped gases, rich in new nuclei of the heavier elements, destined at last to enter into the formation of new suns and planets. Instruments picked out the core of the star: whitely shining, fiercer still in the X-ray spectrum, lethal to come near. But it collapsed rapidly beneath its own monstrous gravitation, to the size of a dwarf, a Jupiter, an Earth. At the end of megayears it would be so dense that nothing, not even light, could leave; and it would have vanished.

Trevelyan said with bleak anger: "He didn't report it. The information that's already been lost as the wave front swelled—"

"Shall we return at once?" the Reardonite asked.

"Well...no, I suppose not. If we let Murdoch go, Cosmos knows what deviltry might happen. There'll be other supernovas, but a dead sentience doesn't come back."

"We have a strong indication of his goal."

"What?" Trevelyan set down the pipe he had been nervously loading.

"Examine the photomultiplier screen, and next these." Finger-tendrils snaked across dial faces. "The star to which I point is an ordinary G3 sun within a hundred light-years of the supernova. Proper motions show that it was somewhat closer at the time of the eruption. Our study object is on an unmistakable intercept track. It is plausible that this is meant to terminate there."

"But—No!" Trevelyan protested. "What can he want?"

"The dosage received by any planet of the lesser sun, through the cosmic rays given off by the larger at its maximum, was in the thousands of roentgens, delivered in a period of days. Atmosphere and magnetic field would have provided some shielding, but the effect must nonetheless have been biologically catastrophic. Presumably, though, most lower forms of life would survive, especially vegetable and marine species. A new ecological balance would soon be struck, doubtless unstable and plagued by a high mutation rate but converging upon stability. Probably the infall of radionuclides, concentrated in certain areas by natural processes, would make caution advisable to the present time. But on the whole, this hypothetical planet could now be salubrious for your race or mine, if it otherwise resembles our homes sufficiently. I might add that it has been conjectured that accidents of this sort were responsible for periods of massive extinction on numerous worlds, including your own home sphere."

Trevelyan scarcely heard the flat words. All at once he was confronting horror.

When the yellow sun was a disk, too lightful for bare eyes but softly winged with corona and zodiacal glow in a step down screen: then the supernova nebula, thirty parsecs off, was only an irregular blur, a few minutes across, among the constellations opposite, as if a bit of the Milky Way had drifted free. One had trouble imagining how it had raged in these skies four hundred years ago. Nor did interplanetary space any longer have an unusual background count; nor did the seven attendant worlds that *Genji's* cameras identified seem in any way extraordinary.

That was a false impression, Trevelyan knew. Every world is a wilderness of uncountably many uniquenesses. But the third one out, on which his attention focused, resembled Earth.

He was confined to optical means of study. Beams and probes might be detected aboard *Campesino.* Murdoch had gone out of hyper into normal mode several millions of kilometers back. His shadowers necessarily followed suit. Then—lest he spot their neutrino emission, as they were now tracking him by his—they stopped the fusion generators and orbited free at their considerable distance, drawing power from the accumulators.

"The study object is in the final phase of approach to atmosphere of the terrestroid planet," Smokesmith announced.

"I'm scarcely surprised," Trevelyan answered. He looked up from his meters and notes. "Apparently it is as terrestroid as any you'll ever find, too. Air, irradiation, size, mass as gotten from the satellites—nearly identical. Those are two small, fairly close-in moons, by the way; so the tide patterns must be complicated, but the oceans will be kept from stagnation. Twenty-eight-hour spin, twelve-degree tilt. Mean temperature a touch higher than Earth's, no polar caps, somewhat less land area...an interglacial macroclimate, I'd guess. In short, aside from pockets of left-over radioactivity, idyllic."

"And possible ecological difficulties," the Reardonite said.

Trevelyan winced. "Damn, did you have to remind me?" He left off peering, leaned back in his chair, held his chin and scowled. "Question is, what do we do about Murdoch? He doesn't seem to have committed any violation except failure to register a discovery. And we probably couldn't prove this isn't his own first time here, that he didn't come this way on impulse. Besides, the offense is trivial."

"Do methods not exist of compelling humans to speak truth?"

"Yes. Electronic brainphasing. Quite harmless. But our species has rules against involuntary self-incrimination. So it's mainly used to prove the honesty of prosecution witnesses. And as I said, I've no case against him."

"Need we do more than report back? Authorized expeditions could then be dispatched."

"'Back' is a mighty long ways. What might he do here meanwhile? Of course ...hm-m-m...if Murdoch doesn't suspect we're on to him, he may proceed leisurely with his preparations, giving us a chance to—"

"The study object has ceased to emit."

"What?" Trevelyan surged from his chair. He abraded his arm on his companion's integument, so fast did he brush by to look for himself. The indications were subtle, because the normal neutrino count is always high. But this tracer included a computer which identified engine sign amidst noise and put its volume on a single dial. That needle had fallen to zero.

Chilled, Trevelyan said: "He's going down on accumulators and aerodynamics. By the time we come in range for a different tracking method, he can be wherever on the surface."

Smokesmith's tone was unchanging, but an acrid odor jetted from him and the petals of his face stirred. "Apparently he does not fear detection from the ground. We observe no trace of atomic energy, hence doubtless no one capable of locating it. The probability is that he desires to remove us and none else from his trail."

"Yeh." Trevelyan began to pace, back and forth between the caging hulkheads. "We half expected he'd tag us somewhere along the line, when I'd already put him on the *qui vive* in Port Nevada. But why's he telling us unequivocally that he has?"

"In my race, messages are always intended as vectors on the world line of the percipient."

"In mine, too, sort of." Trevelyan's strides lengthened. "What does Murdoch hope to get us to do by thumbing his nose at us? We have two alternatives. We can go straight back, or we can land first for a closer look."

"The latter would not add significantly to the interval before we can have returned."

"That's the black deuce of it, my friend. The very nearest Service base where we could originate any kind of investigatory expedition is Lir, I suppose, if they aren't still too busy with the Storm Queen affair. There are frontier planets closer than that, full of men who'll gladly swarm here for a chance of striking it rich. And if they can also do the Cordys one in the eye, why, fine."

"Furthermore," Smokesmith pointed out, "we have no clear proof that anything is involved sufficiently important to justify a long-range mission. The supernova, yes. That is a scientific treasure. But here we have merely a seemingly uninhabited planet. Why should a base commander who does not know Murdoch's past—especially a nonhuman base commander who cannot ingest its significance—assume he has an unlawful purpose? Will he not expect Murdoch to request an inspection team, that a patent of discovery may be issued?"

Trevelyan nodded. "We are scattered so thinly, we who guard the great Pact. Often we must pass by tracks that may well lead toward a hidden evil, because we *know* about another beast elsewhere. Or we learn of something that was wrong at the beginning and should have been stopped, but whose amendment now would be a worse wrong. We have Nerthus, for example, always before us: a human colony founded and flourishing, then learning that native intelligent life did exist. We are fortunate that in that case the interests of the two species are reconcilable, with endless difficulty."

"Does Murdoch wish us to return in alarm bearing data inadequate to provoke prompt official action?" Smokesmith queried. "That seems plausible. Coming as he lately did from the Union's Scorpian march, he must be better informed than we about current situations there. Thus, he might know we can get no help at Lir."

"We can…we can even commandeer civilian ships and personnel—if yonder planet has sentient beings on it. Clear and present danger of territorial conquest. Or Murdoch might simply be plundering them."

"It is improbable that such are alive."

"True. If dead—"

Trevelyan stopped. He looked long outward. Unmagnified, the world was a point of light, a clear and lovely blue. But close in would be mapless immensity. The other crew would have had ample chance to conceal their vessel. They could be anywhere, preparing anything. They surely outnumbered and outgunned him. He hated to imagine big, bluff Murdoch Juan as planning murder. On the other hand, Faustina might, and she had had this entire voyage in which to be the only human female…

Resolution crystallized. "We're going in," he said.

* * * *

They approached slowly, both to observe in detail and to make certain preparations. Circling in the fringes of atmosphere, they confirmed the thing they had guessed at.

This had been a peopled world. The people had been slain.

Were there survivors, there would be evidence of them. Civilization might well have gone under in mass death, panic, anarchy, and famine after crops perished in fields now brushland or desert. But savage descendants of a city-building race would live in villages. *Genji's* sensors would register their very campfires. Besides, it was more reasonable that some comeback would have been made, however weak. For the sleet of cosmic radiation harmed no buildings, no tools or machines, no books—little, indeed, except what was alive.

Gazing into a viewscreen, where clouds parted briefly to show high towers by a lake, Trevelyan said, "Populous, which means they had efficient agriculture and transportation, at least in their most advanced regions. I can identify railway lines and the traces of roads. Early industrial, I'd guess, combustion engines, possible limited use of electricity...But they had more aesthetic sense, or something, than most cultures at that technological level. They kept beauty around them." He hauled his thoughts away from what that implied. If he did not stay impersonal, he must weep.

"Did they succumb to radiation effects alone?" Smokesmith wondered. He appeared to have no trouble maintaining detachment. But then, he did not feel humanlike emotions, as Trevelyan judged the dead beings had. "Shelter was available."

"Maybe they didn't know about radioactivity. Or maybe the escapers were too few, too scattered, too badly mutated. Anyhow, they're gone—Hold!"

Trevelyan's hands danced over the board. *Genji* swung about, backtracked, and came to hover.

Atmosphere blurred the magnified view, but beams, detectors, and computer analysis helped. A town stood on an island in a wide river. Thus, despite the bridges that soared from bank to bank, it was not thickly begrown by vegetation. What had entered was largely cleared away; recent work, the rawness identifiable. The job had been done by machines, a couple of which stood openly in a central plaza. Trevelyan couldn't spot details, but never doubted they were Earth-made robotic types. Several buildings had been blasted, either as too ruinous or as being in the way, and the rubble shoved aside. He got no indications of current activity, but strong electronic resonance suggested that a modern power network was partly completed.

"Murdoch," Trevelyan said like a curse.

"Can you obtain indications of his ship?" the Reardonite asked.

"No. When he detected us approaching, he must have moved her, and screened as well as camouflaged the hull. Maybe he hoped we wouldn't chance to notice what he's been up to, or maybe this is another gibe. Certainly he must've gotten busy here the instant he landed, after choosing the site on his first visit."

Trevelyan put the speedster back into orbit. For a while the conn held only a humming silence. The planet filled half the sky with clouds, seas, sunrises and sunsets; the other half was stars.

"No autochthons left," Smokesmith mused at last. "Their relics are of limited scientific interest. Will this be adjudged grounds for sending armed craft, that are badly needed elsewhere, to make him stop?"

"Supposing it is—that's uncertain, as you say, but supposing it is—*can* they stop him?" Trevelyan seized the controls again. The power hum deepened. "Prepare for descent."

He chose a city near the edge of morning, that he might have a long daylight. A mole jutted from its waterfront into an emerald-and-sapphire bay. Sonic beams declared it to be of reinforced concrete, as firm as the day it was dedicated. He landed there, and presently walked forth. A grav sled would have taken him faster and easier, but part of his aim was to get to know somewhat about those who were departed. His ship, all systems on standby, fell behind him like a coppery cenotaph.

He didn't worry about the safety of the environment. Murdoch had proven that for him. What had still to be learned was mere detail: for instance, what imported crops would do well?

Any number, Trevelyan felt sure. It was a rich and generous planet. No doubt it had been more so before the catastrophe, but it remained wonderful enough, and nature was fast healing the wounds.

The bay glittered and chuckled between golden-green hills. At its entrance began an ocean; coming down, he had identified fantastically big shoals of marine plants and animals. No birds rode the wind that rumpled his hair. Most, perhaps all vertebrates were extinct. But lower forms had survived the disaster. Insects, or their equivalent, swarmed on delicate wings that often threw back the sunlight in rainbows. Silvery forms leaped from the water. The wind smelled of salt, iodine, and life.

Overhead wandered some clouds, blue-shadowed in a dazzlingly blue heaven. At this season, the supernova was aloft by day, invisible. Disaster, Trevelyan thought with a shudder. How little had Earth's ancient astrologers known of how terrible a word they were shaping!

But the day was sunny, cool, and peaceful. He walked shoreward, looking.

The watercraft had sunk or drifted free of their rotted lines. However, the shallower water inshore was so clear that he could see a few where they lay, somewhat preserved. The gracious outlines of the sailboats did not astonish him; that demand was imposed by natural law. But his eyes stung to think that the dead had loved sloops and yawls as much as he did. And they had put bronze figureheads on many, whose green-corroded remnants hinted at flowers, wings, flames, anything fair and free. A large ship had drifted aground. It had been iron-hulled and, judging from the stacks, steam-propelled. But it, no, she had also been designed to look like a dancer on the waves.

He neared the quay. A row of wooden warehouses (?) was partly moldered away, partly buried under vines. Nevertheless he could make out how roofs once swept in high curves that the doorways matched. A rusting machine, probably a crane, was decorated at the end of its lifting arm with a merry animal face.

He stood for some while before an arch at the head of the mole. Here the dwellers had represented themselves.

Their art was not photographic. It had a swing of line and mass that woke a pulse in Trevelyan, it was not quite like anything he had ever seen before. But the bipeds with their long slim six-fingered hands, long necks and long-beaked heads, came through to him as if still alive. He almost thought he could hear their stone cloaks flap in the wind.

Walking further into the city, he began to find their bones.

Carrion eaters had seldom or never disturbed them. Dust blew in, settled on pavement, became soil; seeds followed, struck frail roots that gradually crumbled brick and concrete; bushes and vines grew over that first carpet and up the walls; those kinds of trees that survived extended their range into the domains of trees that had not, and beyond that into farm and town. But the invasion was slow. The wilderness had all the time in the world. It was in full occupation of the shoreward edges of this city, and reducing the next line, but as yet just a few forerunners and—Trevelyan thought with a hurtful smile—sappers had won this near the waterfront.

The buildings of granite, marble, and masonry rose tall, washed by rain and sunlight, little damaged by weather, only occasional creepers blurring their outlines. Like the relief sculpture on their walls, they leaped and soared, not as man-built skyscrapers do but in that peculiar rhythm which made their heights seem to fly. They were colonnaded, balustrated, many-windowed, and kept some of the coloring that once softened their austerity.

Trevelyan wondered at the absence of parks or gardens. His observations from altitude had suggested a deep-reaching love of landscape and care for it. And floral motifs were about the commonest decorations. Well, the dwellers had not been human; it would take long to get some insight into what their race psyche might have been. Maybe they enjoyed the contrast of art and openness. If this place was typical, every city was a delight to live in. At some economic sacrifice, the dwellers had avoided filling their air and water with noise, dirt, and poison. To be sure, they were lucky that no heating was required. But as far as Trevelyan had been able to ascertain, industrial plants were widely scattered outside urban limits, connected by railways. There were no automobiles, though that was probably within the technological capabilities. Instead, he found the depictions, and some bones, of large quadrupeds that served like horses; he also identified the hulks of what appeared to have been public vehicles with primitive electric motors. It was hard to tell after four hundred years, but he at least got the impression that, while theirs was a productive and prosperous civilization, the dwellers had not created overly much trash either. They could have foreseen the problem and taken steps. He'd like to know.

Not that they were saints. He came upon statues and dimmed murals which showed combat. Twice, above inscriptions he would never interpret, he saw a being dressed in rags bursting chains off himself; no doubt somebody put those chains on in the first place. But most often he found imagery which he read as of affection, gentleness, work, teaching, discovery, or the sheer splendor of being alive.

He entered courtyards, walked past dried pools and fountains, on into the buildings. Few had elevators, which was suggestive since the culture could have supplied them. He noted that the shafts of the wide circular staircases would easily accommodate grav lifts. The murals indoors were scarcely faded; their vividness took some of the grief off him. Nevertheless, and although he was not superstitious or even especially religious, he knocked on the first door he came to.

Every door was sliding or folding, none bore locks or latches, which again implied unusual traits. The majority of apartments had been deserted. Cloth had decayed, metal tarnished, plaster cracked, and dust fallen centimeters thick. But the furnishings remained usable by humans, who were formed quite like the dwellers. Clean and patch up; restore the water supply; make do with the airily-shaped oil lanterns, if need be, and a campstove since the original owners didn't seem to have cooked anything; throw padding over chairs, divans, beds, intricately grained floors: and you would be altogether comfortable. Soon power would become available, and you could change the place around until it was ideal.

Early in the game, though, you'd better get rid of those pictures, papers, enigmatic tools, and shelvesful of books. They could be disturbing to live with.

As the hours passed, Trevelyan did find skeletons in a few apartments. Either these individuals had died by surprise, like those he infrequently noticed in the streets, or they desired privacy for their final day. One lay in a kind of chaise longue, with a book upon what had been the lap. Twice he found small skeletons covered by a large one. Did the mother understand that death was coming from the sky? Yes, she could see it up there, a point of radiance too brilliant to look near, surrounded by the auroras it invoked in this atmosphere. Probably she knew that death was everywhere. But she was driven by the instinct of Niobe.

When he discovered the ossuary, Trevelyan decided there must be several, and this was how the average dweller had elected to go. It was in a large hall—theater? auditorium? temple? The most susceptible must already have died, and radiation sickness be upon the rest. In man it approaches its terminus with nausea, vomiting, hair coming out, internal bleeding, blood from the orifices and eyes, strengthlessness, fever, and delirium. Doubtless it was similar for the dwellers.

Outside were the remnants of several improvised coal furnaces. Their pipes fed into the sealed hall, carbon monoxide generators. Bones and rusted weapons nearby suggested the operators had finished their task and then themselves. The door was the single tightly fastened one Trevelyan had encountered, but being wooden it yielded to his boot in a cloud of punk. Beyond lay the skeletons of adults, hundreds of them, and many more young, and toys, games, cups, banners, musical instruments—*I don't know what they did at that party,* Trevelyan thought, *but if we humans had the same guts, we'd tell the children that Carnival came early this year.*

He walked back out into the bright quiet. Something like a butterfly went past, though its wings were fairer than anything evolved on Earth. Being a little of an antiquarian, he said aloud: "The Lord giveth and the Lord taketh away; I will not bless the name of the Lord. But I will remember. Oh, yes, I will remember."

He had not gone much further toward the middle of town when he heard a thunder rumble. Looking up past the towertops, he saw the great shining form of *Campesino* descend. She came between him and the sun and covered him with her shadow.

Reflexively, he took shelter in a doorway. One hand dropped to his pistol. With a sour grin at himself, he activated the tiny radio transceiver in his tunic pocket. On the standard band, he heard Murdoch's voice: "Cordy ahoy! Respond!"

The empty speedster made no reply. A drone and a quivering went through the air as *Campesino* balanced on her gravs.

"You!" Murdoch barked. "We picked up your tachyons halfway to here. We followed you down by your neutrinos. Don't try bluffing us about having a friend in reserve. You're alone, and we've got a cyclic blast zeroed in, and I want to speak with you."

More silence in the receivers. Trevelyan felt the sweat on his ribs, under his arms, and smelled it. He could not foretell what would happen. At best, he had sketched behavior patterns Murdoch might adopt and responses he might make. His plan amounted to creating a situation where he could improvise—whether successfully or not.

A barely distinguishable background growl: "No one inside, I'd guess. Exploring the city?"

"Could be," Murdoch said. "Odd they'd leave their boat unguarded."

"A trap?"

"Well—maybe. Don't seem Cordy style, but maybe we better keep clear."

Trevelyan did in fact wish *Campesino* to set down elsewhere, making *Genji* less of a hostage. He decided to push matters, trod forth and shot a flash from his gun into the air. It crackled. Ozone touched his nostrils.

"Look! Below! You, do you read us?"

Trevelyan saw no sense in giving away the fact that he could listen. He might gain some slight advantage thereby; and Cosmos knew, with that metal stormcloud hanging above him, he needed whatever help he could get. He waved and jogged off toward the city center, where he had noticed a plaza from above.

After a conference he couldn't make out, the others did what he would have done in their place. *Campesino* opened a hatch and discharged a grav sled with a man or two aboard. Not carrying missiles, she could give them no effective armament. But they would hover near *Genji* and cry warning of anything suspicious. The ship herself dropped behind the towers. When she landed, the ground trembled and echoes boomed slowly from wall to wall.

Trevelyan switched off his radio speaker, turned on the transmitter, and hastened his trot. Once he accidentally kicked a skull. It rolled aside with a dry clatter. *I'm sorry,* he thought to it. That being not altogether alien to him had felt this street underfoot, sunwarmth reflected off cataractlike facades, muscle movement, heartbeat, breath. The city had lived around the being, with friends, loves, traffic, music, pleasure...did the race laugh? *I may be joining you soon,* he added, and scorned himself for the juvenilism.

He emerged not on a square but a golden rectangle. Grassy growth was thrusting up and apart those blocks which had paved it, but the rains of four centuries had not quite washed out the grooves worn by generations of feet. The enclosing buildings were lower here. Their lines bespoke tranquility rather than excitement, though three of them held the fragments of dazzling stained-glass windows. Numerous skeletons lay prostrated before one. *Campesino* rose brutal from the plaza center.

Several men and not-men waited, guns at the ready. They were a hard-looking gang. Murdoch stood at ease, Faustina tensed beside him. Both wore black coveralls with silver ornamentation. Her hair glowed in the light. Trevelyan approached at a reduced pace, hands well away from his pistol.

"Mike!" the adventurer bawled. He threw back his head in laughter that made his moustaches vibrate. "Why the chaos didn't I expect you'd be the one?"

"Who else with you?" Faustina said.

Trevelyan shrugged. "Who with you?" he countered.

"You've seen our roster," Murdoch said. "I figured you'd refuse to board, afraid we'd grab you, so I came out." He jerked a thumb at the sheer hull behind. "Got a full complement inside at alert stations."

Trevelyan achieved a smile. "What makes you expect trouble, Juan?" he asked in his mildest voice.

Murdoch blinked. "Why...you dogged us clear from Earth—"

"No, think," Trevelyan said. "Space is free. The Coordination Service investigates where it can, but forbids violence to its agents except under extreme necessity. You know that as well as I do."

The guards around shifted stance, muttered among themselves, flicked eyes from side to side. Trevelyan virtually felt the unease in them.

"For example," he drawled, "You're breaking the law here, first by not reporting a discovery—"

"We've only just made it!" Faustina said. Red stained the white cheekbones. Her fists were clenched. He studied her for a moment, thinking with compassion: *She's afraid I'll take away her glory—her chance to rake in money until she can lose the fear of being poor that was ground into her,* and with caution: *In an aggressive human personality, fear begets ruthlessness.*

"Please let me finish," he said. "I'm not interested in lodging charges, nor would my superiors be. The offense probably occurs hundreds of times a year, and seldom matters. Out of necessity, the Service operates on the old principle that the law should not concern itself with trifles."

She stepped back, breathing hard, lips pulled away from teeth, but plainly bemused. Murdoch's massive features had grown immobile. "Continue," he said.

"You've committed a more important breach of law by tampering with and destroying material of scientific value." Trevelyan kept his tone amiable and a faint smile on his mouth. "I refer to that island city. But the planet is such an archaeological and biological Golconda that we'll overlook your indiscretion, we'll put it down to an amateur's forgivable enthusiasm, in exchange for the service you've done to civilization by bringing this world to our knowledge. You'll remember an agent like me has authority to issue pardons in minor cases. I'll write you one today, if you wish, and recommend you for next year's Polaris Medal into the bargain."

He offered his hand. "Stop worrying," he said. "Let's have a drink and go home together."

Murdoch did not take the hand. The big man stood for a while, staring, and the silence of the dead grew and grew. He broke it with a whisper: "Are you serious?"

Trevelyan dropped pretense. He said in a hardened voice, while his nerves felt the surrounding guns: "It's an honest offer. You, already have Good Luck to make your living off. Be content with that."

"Good Luck?" Faustina cried. She swept one arm in a taloned arc. "You idiot! *This* is Good Luck!"

"I kept hoping it wasn't," Trevelyan said low.

"What do you figure I had in mind?" Murdoch demanded.

"Obvious," Trevelyan sighed. "Here was your real discovery. But how to exploit it? You couldn't get a patent, because the Union would forbid colonization until the scientists finished their researches. Considering the distance, and the shortage of personnel, and the vast amount there is to study, that would take at least a hundred years, probably longer. In fact, the odds are we'd put a secrecy seal on the coordinates for a decade or two, to keep unqualified visitors away until a big enough enterprise got started and the scientists could do their own guarding."

"Scientists!" Faustina nearly shrieked.

"What a means to a fortune, though!" the coordinator said. "You could offer an utterly desirable home, complete with every facility for hundreds of millions of people, at a price the ordinary colonial can afford. You stood to become one of the wealthiest humans that ever lived.

"Well, you went looking for a world we wouldn't disallow. What you turned up isn't particularly good. But it's no worse than some which have been settled, and at least doesn't have a population already squeezing its meager resources. People would buy your real estate there, if the preliminary work had been done for them and the cost was not beyond their means.

"Some you actually would take to the marginal planet—say when an agent like me happened to be around. You'd lose money on them. But it wouldn't matter, because most would be shipped here, where entire cities cost you practically nothing. They'd write home. Your ships would carry the overjoyed mail, maybe censoring it a wee bit to keep us Cordys from getting wind of your enterprise too soon. Not that we'd be likely to, when we're run off our feet with urgent cases, and when few people on those thousands of entire worlds give us any active cooperation. You could carry on for a number of years, I'm sure, before the discrepancies got so glaring that we investigated."

"What'd you do after you learned?" Murdoch asked.

"Nothing," Trevelyan said. "How could we displace tens of thousands, maybe millions of men, women, and children, who'd come in good faith, started a good new life, put down roots, begun bringing forth a new generation? It'd be a political impossibility, a moral one, maybe a physical one. They'd fight for their homes, and we couldn't bomb them, could we?

"You personally would be subject to—in theory, confiscation of your properties and imprisonment of your body. In practice, you'd have put both where we couldn't touch them without more effort and killing than it was worth. You'd have rigged the colonial government and its constitution early in the game to make you something like the Founding Father president of Good Luck. They'd fight for you, too. So, rather than violate its own prohibition on conquest—for the sake of scientific and aesthetic values that'd already been ruined—the Union would accept what you'd done to it."

Trevelyan closed his mouth. He felt hoarse and tired and wanted a smoke, but didn't dare reach for his pipe under those guns.

Murdoch nodded. "You read me good." He chuckled. "Thanks for the Founding Father title. I hadn't thought of that. Sounds like what I need."

"I can't allow it, you know," Trevelyan said.

"Why not?" Murdoch grew curiously earnest. "What's here, really? A worldful of bones. I'm sorry it happened, but dead's dead. And they were, well, one more race among millions. What can we learn from them that matters? Oh, I suppose you can hope for a new technique or art form or whatever, that'll revolutionize civilization. But you prob'ly understand better than me how small that chance is. Meanwhile, yonder we've got people who're alive, and hurting, now."

"The planet will be opened for settlement, region by region, in due course."

"How long is due course? How many'll die during it, that could've lived happier?"

"Emigrants are always replaced at home by fresh births. In the long run, the exact time of migration makes no difference."

"Forget the long run and think about flesh and blood."

Trevelyan's anger broke his control. "Don't hand me that guff, Murdoch," he snapped. "You're about as altruistic as a blast cannon."

"And you," Faustina spat, "you're a machine. I look forward to killing you—dismantling you!"

"Wait, wait, there," Murdoch said. "Ease off and let's talk sane."

He regarded the ground for a moment before he straightened, faced Trevelyan squarely, and said: "I'll tell you how it lies. When we knew we were being dogged, we decided to lead you on, because once the supernova got reported, this sector would be swarmed and somebody else might find our Good Luck.

"You could've skitted for home without landing. If you'd done that, we'd've made for the nearest human planets to here. We'd've rallied a lot of men, transported 'em free, gotten well dug in before you could raise any action at headquarters. It might've been enough to stop you from doing anything."

"I assumed that was your plan," Trevelyan said. "On my way back, I'll visit every Scorpian world and announce, without specifying location too closely, that this planet is interdicted to preserve cultural values. To come here then, knowingly, will justify and require violence by the Service. We do have to maintain the precedent."

"What makes you think you're going back?" asked Faustina. She grinned with hatred.

"Ease off," Murdoch repeated. To Trevelyan: "I did hope you'd land, like you have. Waved a large red flag at you, didn't I? You see, I knew you must have less beef than my ship. Now I've got you."

"What will you do with me?" the coordinator replied.

"Well, uh, I'll admit some of my mates got a little, uh, vehement," Murdoch said. "But I don't see any point in killing you. I sure don't want to. You're not a bad osco, Mike, for a Cordy. And they can't have any idea on Earth which way we headed. I'm not about to return there; I've done my credit arranging. If they ask me about you later on, why, I never had any notion you were trying to follow me. You must've come to grief somehow, and I'm awful sorry. Maybe I'll use your boat to fake some clues."

His mask of bashfulness fell away. He beamed. "Tell you what, Mike," he said. "Let's find you a nice island out in mid-ocean. We'll leave you tools and supplies and show you what's safe to eat. You Cordys are supposed to be philosophers. You should be glad of a few years for thinking. If you want, I'll try to get you a woman. And soon's I can, I'll flit you to our spaceport we'll've built. How's that for a fair proposition?"

Trevelyan savored the breath he drew, the light he saw, the will rising within him like a physical tide. "Let me be sure I understand you," he said. "Do you seriously intend to maroon me in order that I won't report the facts of this case?"

"Too good for you," Faustina said. "But if Juan's that tender-spirited, yes."

"Do you realize that this involves grave violations of personal integrity?" Trevelyan asked. "Do you realize that it involves direct interference with an officer of the Union in the performance of his duty?"

Murdoch flushed. "Your duty!"

"I demand you let me go back to my spacecraft and depart unmolested," Trevelyan said.

Faustina snickered.

"You will not?" Trevelyan asked.

He waited. A breeze whispered.

"Very well," he said. "I can now testify under brainphasing that you are guilty of attempted crimes sufficient to justify your arrest. Will you come quietly with me?"

"Have you lost your orbit?" Murdoch exclaimed.

"Since you resist arrest in addition," Trevelyan said, "the necessity of applying force becomes incontestable."

The guards jabbered, swore, and brought their weapons to bear. Faustina hissed. Murdoch's hand streaked to his own pistol.

Trevelyan ostentatiously folded his arms and said: "If my Service does not respect your rights, civilization is worthless. But civilization has rights of its own. I admit I led your thoughts away from my partner"—he heard a gasp and an oath—"but that scarcely constitutes entrapment. He's under a roof in this city, on an accumulator-powered grav sled, along with several nuclear missiles. Through a miniradio in my pocket, he's been listening to our conversation. If you don't surrender yourselves, he'll destroy you."

He paid scant attention to the uproar of the guards. His focus was entirely on their leaders.

Murdoch yanked a transceiver from his jacket to speak an order.

"Give them a demonstration, Smokesmith," Trevelyan said.

No one saw the torpedo rise. It went too fast. Momentarily the sky was bedazzled with hell-colored flame. Concussion smote, not unduly hard from that altitude, but it shook men where they stood and bellowed in their ears. The bones before the temple shuddered.

"A bit close," Trevelyan said. He was aware that his own body quivered and went dry in the mouth. A remote part of him decided this was an unintegrate reaction and he needed more training. Speech and reasoning mind, though, were steel cold. "We may want antirad shots. I think you'll agree, Juan, the next can drop right here. Afterward my Reardonite friend won't have trouble picking off your watchmen."

"You'll be dead, too," Murdoch groaned.

"I don't want to be," Trevelyan said, "but rather more is at stake than what I want."

Faustina whipped around behind Murdoch. She snatched his gun from the holster, flung herself forward and rammed the muzzle into Trevelyan's belly. "Oof" he choked. *I don't exactly cut a heroic figure, do I?* flashed through him. *But the beings here only had what dignity they could make for themselves, after heaven's meaningless anger fell on them.*

"I'll kill you myself!" she raved. He knew tricks for knocking the weapon aside and taking it from her. But others were trained on him.

He met her eyes, from which the tears went flooding, and said: "If you do, why should my partner not destroy you?"

Murdoch wrenched the gun from her. She raked at his face. He knocked her down. Panting, sweat a-river on his skin, he said: "What do you want?"

"If you know something about Reardonites," Trevelyan said, and saw that Murdoch did, "you realize it won't bother Smokesmith to annihilate me along with you. But he agrees it's undesirable. So is the destruction of this beautiful plaza. Let's compromise."

"I asked what do you want, you devil?"

"Safe conduct back to my vessel. Smokesmith will monitor me by radio. Your ship will stay put. At the first sign of any ill faith whatsoever, he shoots. At worst, you see, he must eliminate both ships and hope this world gets rediscovered by someone who'll respect it. Once aloft, I'll quickly drop down again and pick him up, too quickly for you to rise. At that point you'll be helpless, but have no fears. With a head start and a faster craft, I'll be on the frontier planets before you, issuing prohibitions. No one's going to follow you when he knows it'll bring warships down on him. I suggest you find a place and lie low."

Murdoch beat fist into palm, again and again. For a minute he looked old and hollowed out.

Then his mirth awoke. "You win this 'un too, Mike," he said. "I'll escort you to your boat personal. Here." He offered his pistol. Trevelyan accepted it.

Faustina sat up. A bruise was spreading on her slim jaw where her lover's fist had smitten. She looked at them both, through tears and matted locks, and was no longer anything except a bewildered beaten child.

"Why?" she pleaded. "Why can't we have a patent—when w-w-we found the supernova for you? You'd do this—wreck everything for two, three hundred s-s-specialists...and their *curiosity?"*

Trevelyan hunkered down before her. He took both her hands in one of his. The other pointed around, ending at the temple. "No," he said most gently. "For these. Have they no rights? That someone shall come to know them, and they won't be lost from us."

But she did not understand. We guard the great Pact, which is the heart of civilization, of society, and ultimately of life itself: the unspoken Pact between the living, the dead, and the unborn, that to the best of poor mortal abilities they shall all be kept one in the oneness of time. Without it, nothing would have meaning and it may be that nothing would survive. But the young generations so often do not understand.

To Build a World

-1-

Suddenly the plain exploded. A pillar of steam shot skyward, bone-white against darkness and the stars, tinged red with incandescent drops of metal. Steel chunks from the drill rig whizzed out of the boiling and roaring, struck the ground and skittered murderously across kilometers. They sounded like bees, heard through thunder. Cracks opened around the well, broadened to meters-wide ravines as they ran outward. The hole stretched itself into a crater and spat ash and boulders. Then the rush of steam was hidden in smoke and dust that whirled up from the shuddering surface.

Don Sevigny had thrown himself prone when the convulsion began. He clung in blindness to rock, felt it heave against his belly and heard the shrapnel that had once been machinery go past. There was a taste of blood in his mouth *Poy,* his mind stammered, *Erich, they were right on the spot!*

What went wrong?

The explosions ended. Great hollow echoes rolled back from the cliffs of the Caucasus, toned away and were lost in the growl and seethe of the newborn volcano. The ground still quivered, but the first dreadful seasick roll was over. Sevigny jumped to his feet. Dust roiled around his helmet, he was cut off from his men, from Earth and Moon, alone in a night that clamored.

"Report!" he yelled. "By the numbers!"

Names trickled in; one, Aarons, two, Bergsma, three, Branch, four...nobody, Erich Decker was mute...five, Gourmont, six—"

"—Twelve," said R'ku's vocalizer.

Youkhannan finished with twenty. The whole crew was accounted for but Decker and Leong.

The haze was leaving Sevigny's vision as the mineral flour settled. Bit by bit he made out the scene, the gray plain chopped off two kilometers away by the brutal upsurge of the Caucasus, the stars that glittered above those peaks, the scattered shapes of men and equipment. He turned to see the eruption and looked straight at Earth, not much above the near southern horizon. It was waning toward half phase, but the white-banded blue brilliance was still such that for a moment he was again blind.

The dazzle departed in ragged after-images. He saw a black geyser gushing from the riven soil. At five hundred meters it spread mushroom-like. By then it was pale azure in the Earthglow—an umbrella of ice crystals condensing at 75 degrees below Celsius zero. The cloud was not large; it melted at the edges, scattered by the thin, swift wind that blew steadily east toward the sun.

There was no time to be afraid. Two men had been caught near the blast. They might still be alive. Lava would soon come out of that hole.

Sevigny plunged after the nearest moontrac. "Three of you help me!" he called. "Maybe we can hook Poy and Erich out of there."

Even under Lunar gravity, it was an awkward scramble in his airsuit to reach the high mounted cab. He leaned panting over the control board for several seconds before he realized that not one man or Martian had joined him.

Huh?

The canopy was raised, the cab exposed to a wintry heaven. Camp had been established some time ago. Given inflated domes, covered with Lunar dust against the heat and radiation that would come at sunrise, there was no need to maintain vehicles at pressure or keep their screen generators in operation. Sevigny had only to lean over the edge to shout, "What's ailing you? I want three helpers!"

Some heartbeats passed when only the volcano spoke. Then Branch replied, his sound amplifier tuned to maximum, as if in extra defiance: "Are you out of your brain? Those jims are dead!"

"Maybe not," Sevigny barked. "We'll find out."

"And kill four more? That thing's going to spit molten rock any minute."

For a moment Sevigny failed to understand. The situation just didn't make logic. It was like being caught in a dream.

His gauntlets closed on the cab rim so hard that the thermowires in them creaked. "You—" All at once he found the word that would express his feelings. "You *Earthlings!'*

"By God, boss, you're right!" Aarons came over the plain in kangaroo bounds. Dust puffed where his boots struck. One by one, some others began to follow. Sevigny could only identify them, through the long shadows, by the phosphorescent numbers on their chests.

"Youkhannan and Nakajima!" he rapped. "You're closest. The rest of you get our stuff to a safe distance." Anger lifted a fresh and he finished with a chosen insult: "R'ku, you're in charge."

"Very well," The Martian had not stirred. Now his gaunt shape got into motion—a few jumps that no human could have matched, a sweeping overview, and a series of cool orders.

I don't blame him for not volunteering, Sevigny thought. *He'd be no use, the minute that much water hit his skin; and Martians don't go in for romantic gestures. The rest, though—I didn't take them for crawlguts!*

But then it struck him that Earthlings did not, after all, have clan bonds like Cythereans, as the Venus colonials had taken to calling themselves. For that matter, if he'd simply been one of the crew, he might also have hesitated to risk his neck for somebody with whom he had swapped no oaths. As boss, of course, he was in a different situation.

Aarons, Youkhannan and Nakajima reached the flat bed of the trac and grabbed the cargo kingposts for support. Sevigny threw himself into the pilot's seat and gunned the right engines. Electric power surged from the accumulators massed below. The vehicle turned until its blunt nose pointed at the geyser. Sevigny cut in the left engines. Eight huge, soft-tired wheels rolled forward.

A crevasse had opened in the ground between. Sevigny didn't pause to gauge distances. After a year on the Moon, his eyes were well trained. He threw a switch at a moment which he felt with his bones rather than his intellect was correct. Two metal arms lifted the portable bridge off the trac bed, carried it over the cab and laid it down precisely as the trac arrived at the verge. Wheels trundled across, with a boom and a rattle that resounded dimly through the cataract noise of the volcano. When weight was off the bridge, the arms swung it back into place.

Wind-whipped ash drove across the view. Sevigny heard it click against his faceplate. The trac lurched over tumbled stones, wallowed in new-formed mud. He leaned forward, straining to see, while his hands and feet wrestled with the machine. There—He steered for the dim bulk on the crater's edge, reached it and braked to a halt.

Half buried in wet cinders. the other trac lay broken on its side. A section of pipe had been coughed from the well and rammed through the hoist engine block. Close by was the drill rig's force unit, grotesquely canted, the casing scarred by energetic debris. He saw no human figures. The wind squealed faintly through the volcano roar.

He turned his amplifier to max and asked, "Anybody see either of them?"

"No, sir." Youkhannan's voice was only identifiable in the Iraqi accent. "Likely they were pitched downslope and buried."

"Grab shovels and go look," Sevigny commanded. "I'll scratch around here."

He ignored the ladder, vaulted over the canopy edge and fell with maddening slowness. Heat gusted from the crater to bite through his airsuit's insulation. The thermostatic units switched over to cooloff; their pump-throb went in time with his pulse. He stumbled through black shards that grated underfoot and slipped beneath his soles.

Wait! Under the cab of the wreck...a boot projected! Sevigny knelt and dug with his hands, dog fashion. Sweat was sharp in his nostrils, painful in his eyes, clammy in his undergarment. Somewhere far off a stranger cursed without cease and another stranger remembered how Mount Victory loomed over green Carl's Lake, beautiful and irrelevant on Venus. The brawling around him deepened, there came a fresh moonquake and cinders shot forth to turn the murk nearly absolute.

Sevigny freed both legs, rose and heaved. The breath was harsh and dry in his throat. Almost at the end of his endurance, the body came loose with a suddenness that tumbled him on his rear. He crawled back, unclipped his flashlight, squatted and squinted through the ash rain. It was Leong. Air oozed in a vapor cloud from a rip in the man's suit, but some bubbles of blood on the lips behind the faceplate still seemed to move. Sevigny got him in his arms, pulled himself erect and lurched toward his own vehicle.

With a deliberate and terrible drumfire, the first magma spilled from the hole. Sevigny dragged Leong onto the trac bed, laid him down and fumbled with a patch from the kit at his belt. The teakettle stream came to an end. On shaking legs, Sevigny rose to switch on the floodlamp above the cab. *Should'a done this before. How else can the boys find me? I'm beaten stupid!* Now he could again make out the force unit, through the mineral rain and swirling primordial dust. On a half animal impulse, he activated the crane that extended from the left kingpost. It swung out, hovered above the two-meter steel cube, dipped and grappled. He raised it. The trac swayed beneath such a weight. Metal sang in the cables.

The lava was very close now, a dully glowing glacier. Sevigny got into the cab. "Nakajima!" he cried uselessly against the reverberations. "Youkhannan! Aarons! Get back here, for everything's sake!" Momentarily he—rather, his clansman's reflexes—debated the ethics of abandoning them. They should be able to reach safety on foot...No. Someone had to tend to Leong, or he might be dead before he reached the camp wagon.

A blackened shape came out of the whirl, and another and another. They hadn't found Erich, then. *Well, we did what we could.* Sevigny gunned the engines. He barely waited for his gang to climb aboard before he engaged the transmission.

"One of you get Poy here and treat him," he said. "The rest hang on!"

He dared not go full speed on this terrain, though the Mare Serenitatis might open beneath him at any time. And what a hell of a name that was, he thought in the back of his head. So lost was he in his driving that he didn't notice what went on around him. When he emerged from the smoke into clear vision, onto safe and stable rock, he was actually surprised to find the canopy dogged down and the air tanks opened to make full pressure.

He glanced behind. Leong's airsuit had been peeled off. The man sprawled on the rear seat, eyes still closed, breath fast and shallow. Aarons knelt beside him, helmet and gloves removed. The lean hooked face dripped sweat down onto the blood which trickled from Leong's nostrils.

"Well?" Sevigny asked

"Decompression, of course," Aarons said in an exhausted monotone. "Probably shock, concussion, maybe a fracture or two." He opened the medikit, got a hypodermic needle and filled it from an ampoule. "I'll give him 20 cc. of ADR to play safe, but looks like you got him in time. Where was he?"

"By his own trac. I imagine he hit something when it was knocked over, and therefore simply slid down. Erich got thrown a distance."

Aarons looked back at the pillar of smoke and the slow flood of fire. He shivered. "No use hunting any more for him." After a silence: "I'm glad you made us come along, boss, even if we didn't have much luck."

Sevigny grunted.

The four remaining vehicles—camp and service wagons, 'dozer and scoop—were close now, boxlike shapes on the plain with the men huddled around. R'ku stood a little apart. His long thin legs were crouched as if to leap, but folded arms and lowered abdomen bespoke repose. Earthlight shimmered off the metal-blue hide. His unhuman head seemed crowned with stars.

As Sevigny pulled alongside the camp wagon, which held bunks and some sickbay equipment, the Martian stirred. A single spring brought him to the trac. Seen thus in flight, the mantis-like form was no longer stiff or grotesque, but fluid elegance, an abstract statue cast in mercury. When he landed, his head was level was Sevigny's; and the cab seat was 150 centimeters off the ground.

R'ku's stare had long stopped bothering the Cytherean; it had merely been that those big turquoise eyes were made so unlike a man's, and never blinked. The narrow insectoidal face had always seemed more handsome than otherwise. At present it was largely hidden by the air helmet. Lunar atmosphere had by now gotten so thick that Martians didn't require suits, but the composition remained wrong. Not enough nitrogen to breathe, poisonous methane and ammonia; and while they needed small amounts of water as men need vitamins, there was too much of the vapor around these days for their metabolisms to handle.

"What success did you have?" R'ku inquired. His words penetrated the glasolite canopy with the expected flatness. Sevigny sometimes wondered if the Martians' reputation for unemotionality was due to no more than the fact that they must use mechanical vocalizers to make humanly recognizable sounds. On the other hand, they seldom showed excitement in their behavior...

"We saved Leong," he answered. "Have 'em snake a tube from the wagon for him."

R'ku gestured. Four men got busy. They avoided looking in Sevigny's direction.

"You brought back the force unit," R'ku observed.

"Yeah. Maybe that's what caused the trouble. We'll take it on to GHQ. There's nothing more we can do here. And Poy has to get to a hospital."

"He is salvageable, then?"

"I hope so." With an idiotic desire for conversation: "What'd you do if he wasn't?"

"I understand that your custom is burial."

"On Mars, I mean."

"That would depend upon what culture was involved. We of the Great Confederation would dry and powder the body and scatter it on the winds. But in Illach they would process it to fuel their Biological Engine; K'nea would use it for animal fodder; Hs'ach—"

"Never mind." The man sagged in his seat. Weariness rose and hit him like a fist.

He had not felt so alone since first he arrived at Port Kepler. Then he was a bright young terraform engineer, with no more than three standard years' experience in the Drylands to justify a job offer from the Luna Corporation. Since then he'd been too busy learning the tricks of this world's trade, working his way up until he headed a deeptap gang, losing himself in riotous furloughs at Paradise, to think widely. But how little the clans of Venus knew about the rest of the universe, under their clouded sky—how isolated they were!

A man lay dead under molten stone because *his* well had erupted.

He shook himself. "Move along, you sons," he said harshly. "Get that tube connected."

-2-

The Buffalo laid his cigar in an old-fashioned ashtray and said, "Hi, there. You're Sevigny? I thought at first you were the wrath of God."

"I feel like its results," Sevigny mumbled.

The Buffalo laughed. "Well, come on in, ease your freight. Bring your black friend, too. I'm kind of curious about him."

Sevigny blinked, started a little out of his lassitude. "You mean Oscar? But how did you know—"

"I got a visual to the outer office." The Buffalo pointed at a small screen set in his intercom box. "I like to see who my secretary is telling I'm in conference." Small eyes darted slyly toward the visitor. "I also got an auditory to her. Earplug set; that's how come all my girls wear their hair long. In case I decide I'm not in conference. Besides," he added thoughtfully, "I like long hair on women."

Sevigny felt himself under closer observation than he would have believed possible. Automatically he bristled, and one hand edged the least bit nearer his sidearm. A man did not pay that kind of heed to another man on Venus unless a fight was brewing. He remembered he was on Luna. But he still had the pride of his clan to maintain.

"As you wish," he snapped, and turned on his heel with calculated insolence. The frosted glass on the door said:

BRUNO NORRIS
CHIEF OF OPERATIONS

It opened for him and he stuck his head out and whistled. Oscar jumped from the chair on which he had been grooming himself and darted inside, up to Sevigny's shoulder in one low-gravity spring.

The secretary gave him a surprised look, which lingered. He was not handsome: a big, rawboned young man with jutting nose and chin, blue eyes under shaggy fair brows, sandy hair not as well combed as it might be. But the sun had browned him, and he walked like a soldier. Long tunic with clan insignia, bare knees and buskins marked him out too, among the Russian blouses and bell-bottomed trousers currently fashionable on Earth.

He returned the girl's look with interest, in both senses of the word. The Buffalo's fame for choosing spectacular female help had turned out to be quite justified.

A little regretfully, but also a little more cheerful; he let the door close and faced around again. The gray-thatched, kettel-bellied giant behind the desk waved at a chair. "Squat yourself. Cigar?"

"No, thanks. I don't smoke." Sevigny took the edge of the seat.

"What's the matter, you want to live forever? Well, how about a drink? I estimate the sun just went over the yardarm. But let's see." The chief activated a full-wall viewscreen.

It scanned the surface, rather than the underground warren which Port Kepler mostly was. In the direction of the harsh morning sun, the crater floor lay almost untouched, naked rock reaching toward the stark ringwall. Elsewhere, though, entry turrets, radars, control towers, solar cell banks, rail lines, the whole clutter of man had overrun the landscape. Earth was a wan half disc in a deep-blue sky where a few tentative clouds drifted.

Crow's feet meshed in a broad ruddy visage. "Um-m-m," the Buffalo said, "reckon we'll have to lower the yardarm a trifle. *Selah.*" He reached into a drawer for a bottle of brandy and tumblers, into another, refrigerated drawer for ice and soda.

"I don't know, Mr. Norris." Sevigny hesitated. "This is a serious matter—"

"Good lord, man! Have you no redeeming vices?"

"Oh...all right. Thanks." A nearly involuntary smile tugged at the corner of the Cytherean's mouth.

Liquid gurgled forth. Oscar sat up, curious. Silky midnight fur tickled Sevigny's neck.

"Here's to our noble selves." The Buffalo tossed off half a glass in a gulp and resumed puffing on his cigar. "I give up. What is that beastie?"

"A dirrel. They're kind of one-man animals, so I had to bring him with me." That still looked frivolous. "Everyone, almost, keeps a dirrel in the Shaws, my home country. It'd be too easy to get lost in the wilderness without something for a guide that can climb the tallest trees. And then they're good at finding game."

"I thought Venus was mainly desert yet."

"Some regions were ripe for ecology as soon as the water had precipitated. Native organic matter in the soil. When life was introduced, it multiplied explosively."

"M-m...yeah, I remember now. That's probably the source of a lot of your clan feuds, hey? Squabbles over land that didn't need so much work before it could be settled. What species did the geneticists makes your pet from?"

Sevigny shrugged. "I don't know. Some rodent. They bred to a mass of seven or eight kilos, hands of a sort, and a pretty good brain. Oscar can communicate with me—a little, in a special language." He rubbed the large, sharp-nosed head between the ears. Oscar arched his back and elevated his magnificent plume of tail.

"Oh. Sure. I see. His ancestors—but *no importe.* This is a pleasure, meeting you," said the Buffalo. "I wish I could get back out in the field myself. Those crews are apt to be weird and wonderful mixtures. I recall one Nigerian—"

The tension which had been departing returned to Sevigny. He sat straight again and said roughly, "I'm sure your time is valuable, Mr. Norris. What did you want to see me about?"

"That accident—Now hold on, son. Not so defensive, if you please. By all accounts, you did just fine. I know it was pretty much of a shock, your first job as crew chief going sour that way. But you handled matters better'n a lot of veterans would have. What I'd like is your own story of what happened. From the beginning."

"You have my report."

"Pretend I haven't read it. Pretend I don't even know deep-tap procedure. I'll tell you why later on, but right now go ahead and talk."

Sevigny scowled. He didn't know what to make of this first encounter with his ultimate boss. *Okay,* he thought, *blame yourself for the consequences.*

"We reached Mare Serenitatis Site Four at sunset, as per schedule," he bit off. "While the drill rig was being erected and started, the rest of the crew made camp. Everything seemed normal until circa 1800 hours of the second day past midnight. We cleared ground and dug channels for the expected outflow of liquid, according to the maps drawn by Survey. At the time of the accident, a work shift was ending. Decker and Leong were at the well, about to change the cutter. The eruption caught them. We managed to rescue Leong—he's recovering nicely now—but couldn't find Decker before the lava forced us back. We struck camp and proceeded directly here. R'ku, the Martian on the team, stayed behind to observe. His last radio report to me was the well had collapsed and outflow ceased. I told him to return. He ought to arrive at Little Mars shortly."

As he spoke he had a vision of that tall strange figure, imperturbably watching the volcano die, then loading what meager gear he needed on his thorax and soaring off across barrenness, into Lunar day. That was hot enough and bright enough to kill a man who wasn't careful, the atmospheric blanket was still too thin to moderate the climate as much as Earth's is moderated. But the Martians never suffered, though temperature rocketed beyond anything they had ever known at home. It was one reason the Corporation paid them so well... Somehow, the picture was an eldritch and lonely one.

Sevigny's attention switched back to immediacies as the Buffalo asked, "In your opinion, what caused the accident?"

"Probably failure of the force unit. Survey had warned us, on the basis of sonic probes, that there was a layer of allotropic ice at the depth we were reaching then. Without counter-pressure in the bore, the stuff exploded into the lower density form, and the released energy vaporized it. That left a cavity through which molten rock further down could rise."

"Sounds reasonable. You did damn well to snatch that unit away."

"Have your technies learned anything from it?"

"I've had a lab report," the Buffalo nodded. "There was crystallization in the Terence head. It broke apart under stress."

"What?" Sevigny started so violently that Oscar almost fell off. The dirrel chattered an indignant remark and clung tighter with his small half-human fingers.

"But...how did any such thing get by inspection at the manufacturer's?" Sevigny choked.

The Buffalo's fist clenched on his desktop. "That," he said, "is what I'd like to know."

He leaned over and refilled both tumblers. "Son," he continued, "we got troubles. That's why I wanted to see you and listen to you. To size you up. This isn't the first accident the project ought not to have had."

"But—" Sevigny realized he was gaping and drew his lips shut.

"I've QT'd them fairly well," said the chief. "Can't go on doing that, though, if the farce proceeds. Oh, there's been a semi-plausible explanation every time. But the upshot is that I'm not sure any longer who the devil I can trust."

He sighed; then his gaze nailed the younger man and he asked, "How much do you know about the political background of this undertaking?"

"Why...uh...the Corporation's an international venture, chartered under the Commonwealth, with the different governments holding most of the stock." Sevigny hunted through memories. "That's about all I know," he admitted lamely.

"Guess I needn't've expected more. Where you come from, the clan is the economic as well as the political unit; and with so little to trade thus far, Venus doesn't have a lot of contact with Earth. Never mind. I'll try to fill you in."

The Buffalo stubbed out his cigar and lit a fresh one. He didn't speak until several noisy puffs had gotten it well burning.

"We're in a funny situation nowadays," he said. "People haven't quite realized it yet, but the era of stability has begun to end. (Hey, ain't that a lousy hunk of rhetoric?) Our hyper-ballyhooed world order was really a peace of exhaustion, following the global wars and their aftermath. Problems weren't so much solved as swept under the carpet, while the leading countries proceeded with their glorious conquest of space. Now the human race is getting restless again. The fact that nobody resisted much when you Cythereans declared your independence is considered a textbook example of how Man Has Matured and such-like brain grease. Actually, though, if you'll excuse me saying it, the significant fact was not that you got away with breaking loose, but that you got the idea in the first place. Since then, more cracks have appeared in the system.

"Well—" He filled his mouth and blew rings. "You needn't look so alarmed. I'm not about to read you my Lecture Number 27-B, Theory and Practice of Declinesmanship. What matters is that the project of terraforming Luna had enemies from the start. Setting up the Corporation was a necessary dodge. We'd never've swung it as a straightforward public enterprise."

Sevigny took a long and badly wanted swallow from his tumbler. "I don't understand," he said. "Why, the Venus project was far bigger and less directly rewarding—"

The Buffalo shook his massive head. "Nuh-uh, son. The cost was relative peanuts in your case, even with spaceships as crude and expensive as they were then. Those algae only had to be seeded. Oh, sure, when they'd finished their job, a hellful of work remained. Still does, after all this time. But...it can be done piecemeal, by private outfits. There's the origin of your clans. And then, too, Venus is quite a ways off. A morning and evening star, no more. It doesn't hang overhead; it doesn't rise big as a pumpkin over anyone's personal hills, to keep him reminded.

"You'd be surprised how much purely sentimental opposition there was to changing the looks of the dear old Moon. How many older people who remember have stayed resentful to this day. And also, when a world hasn't got an atmosphere to start with...well, you should hear our cost accountants squeal every time the latest budget is presented. Mainly, though, there are interests on Earth with their own sound, cold-blooded reasons for not wanting this to go through."

Unnoticed by himself, Sevigny's hand dropped to the butt of his gun. "Are you implying sabotage, Mr. Norris?"

"I don't know. I really don't. Still a series of major setbacks for us would make very nice political ammunition, don't you think?"

Sevigny shook his head. "Sorry, but *I* should think Earth is committed. I mean, uh, with the enormous investment already made—that can't simply be written off. Can it?"

"One of our own best talking points," the Buffalo agreed. "Please don't think I'm being paranoid. Just because everybody picks on me...I only thought I'd mention the general background, and ask you to read a few books and articles I'll list. They're kind of interesting in their own right regardless."

"Frankly, what little I know of politics bores me like an auger."

"Which shows how little you know about politics, son. It's the only game in town. I do wish you'd study up a bit before you go to Earth."

"What?"

"Would you pick his jaw off the floor, please, Oscar?" The Buffalo grinned. "Sure. After what you did at Site Four, you rate a vacation. Need one, too. Human nerves don't unstretch overnight, and that was a rough cob for you."

"But I hadn't planned—"

"Eh? You didn't mean to drop in when your contract expires, at least? See the green hills of Earth, the ocean Columbus sailed, Westminster Abbey, the Taj Mahal, the Brisbane Follies?"

"No. Why spend a lot of money on tourism when what I want is heavy reclamation equipment to use at home?"

"If you'd let me show you some pictures from the Follies, you'd know why. But no matter." The Buffalo jabbed his cigar in Sevigny's direction. "You'll go at Corporation expense, and we aren't gonna look too squinch-eyed at your accounts."

He grew serious. "I can't leave right now, with everything there is to do," he explained. "And as I told you, I'm no longer sure who I can trust. But you're outside these fractions, you're a bright boy, Presumably a tough fighting man, and the Treaty of Toronto gives you the right to bear arms anywhere. All I want you to do is convoy that force unit you rescued to World Safety Corps headquarters, and then ride their tails to make certain there's a thorough investigation. That crystallized metal looks mighty like sabotage to me. A heavy dose of radiation 'ud cause it, and how could that happen by chance? I could ask the Corps to send someone here, but the evidence would have to go Earthside anyway. And without one of my boys riding along. Not that I don't think the Corps is honest—however—if the news is simply that I've sent an engineer to discuss possible changes in machine design, then no one will be tempted to try some fancy stunt. You'll have an easy trip, a couple of weeks layover, a chance to wash some of that damned Swede-faced seriousness out of your system and serve the project better than you could here. How's about it?"

-3-

"Oh!" exclaimed the girl. "I beg your pardon."

Sevigny held stiff the arm against which she had stumbled until she regained balance. Her floor-length gown and curl-toed silver shoes were made to throw anybody.

So were their contents. She was bronze brunette, with spectacular half-Oriental features, and the decollete dress fitted her like another skin. He had spent several seconds after he stepped out of his room, admiring her as she undulated down the hall. "Quite okay," he said. "In fact—frankly, a pleasure."

She laughed. The synthodiamond necklace sparkled no more brightly than her teeth. "I didn't know a wild Cytherean warrior could turn so pretty a compliment."

In spite of what the Buffalo had said, Sevigny had a normal capacity for fun. But to maintain his clan's good name, he responded, "Is that what they believe on Earth? Not true, my lady. We work hard and don't fight except when we have to."

"Poof." She wrinkled her nose."There goes another illusion. Did you arrive today? I'm sure I would have noticed otherwise."

"Yes, on the Lunar packet."

"The Moon?" She widened an incredible pair of eyes. "Then you must be connected with the terraforming." He nodded. "But this is wonderful. How long will you be here?"

"Only till tomorrow, my lady. I've business elsewhere."

He had intended to go directly from Pacific Spacedrome to Paris. But for some reason no transplanetary flight was available for days which could accommodate the ponderous engine he had in charge. Swearing, he had gotten a surface boat to Honolulu and arranged a private charter. Now the crate rested in a hotel storeroom and he had a loose evening.

It didn't worry him. A few dollars to the service captain had let him leave Oscar on guard. The dirrel was quite able to chatter an alarm into a short-range sender, in the unlikely event that something suspicious happened; and the receiver lay in Sevigny's tunic pocket. He hadn't told the quarantine inspector about that piece of equipment. It might be illegal—and he didn't intend to do without it.

"Damn," said the girl. She frowned, charmingly. Then: "Please don't think I'm forward. The mores on Venus are probably different from here. But...are you busy tonight?"

"No. I was about to have dinner." Sevigny's pulse quickened. "Is there a chance of your joining me, my lady?"

"More than a chance, thank you. I know this looks like rushing matters, but you see, the whole interplanetary situation fascinates me. One hears so many arguments and, oh, there are documentaries on TriV and so forth, but all second hand. This is my first encounter with someone who's actually lived it."

Sevigny managed to harness his delight and say in an academic tone, "That's surprising. I thought you upper level people knew everybody."

Her lashes fluttered. "I'm not upper level, if you mean the ten or twenty per cent who keep civilization running. My father has money, yes, but he got it in entertainment." She laughed anew. "So I've a date with a man whose name I don't even know. I'm Maura Soemantri—born in Djakarta, educated in Chicago, and here for the surfriding."

"Donald Sevigny, Clan Woodman of the Shaws, at your service." He made a formal bow.

Her hand rested lightly in his before she said, "I was supposed to eat at the Kamehameha tonight with my club. Nobody will be mad if I don't show, but I'd better call to tell them. 'Scuse. I'll be right back."

With conscious pleasure, Sevigny watched her walk off. He had grown used to Earth weight faster than expected, but had forgotten how much it added to the female gait.

The analytical part of him considered ways and means. She could prove expensive. Still, he had a goodly piece of cash on him, and had been told to indulge himself. a bit...Why not? He hadn't relished the idea of a solitary evening. Now, with luck, he might have company till his jet took off tomorrow. Judging by how gracefully she moved, she hadn't tripped against him by accident.

Maura returned in a few minutes. She took his arm and they strolled to an elevator. "I suppose I ought to decide where we're bound," he said, "but as a complete stranger—"

"Don't worry about clothes," she said. "On Earth a uniform is correct any place, from the Imperial Saturn to a Subchicago pot min. And that outfit of yours is really a uniform, right? I like the Moon Room here myself. The view is gorgeous."

"Quite," he said, looking downward.

At the top of the elevator's range, they were met by an expertly obsequious headwaiter and conducted to a table next the glasolite dome. Sevigny had stopped being surprised at the amount of live service in an automated society. What else was the bulk of the population able to do? He was also getting used to being stared at. The stares were discreet here, and largely veiled by dimness, but he knew he was a conspicuous object.

Seated, he turned eyes away from the shadowed people, and caught his breath.

Left and right at the foot of the Goldwater's soaring skyscraper, Honolulu stretched further than he could see, a galactic sprawl of light, ruby, old gold, topaz, emerald, turquoise, sapphire, amethyst, flashing and glistening across night-purple hills. Southward the ocean sheened beneath a sky crowded with softened stars, and a lowering second quarter Moon turned the Waikiki surf to what he guessed a snowstorm must be.

Maura regarded him gravely. "Yes," she said, "old Earth is beautiful, isn't she?"

"Here, at least," he answered.

"M-m-m...all right, I daresay you've seen pictures and statistics. Most of the planet has become rather awful. Too many people, too little opportunity. Your ancestors were right in going to Venus. But will you ever make it over into this?"

"Some day." He thought, with an uninvited pang, of forests that roared in the wind, leaves that gleamed with raindrops, and a wild bull shaking his horns against nacreous heaven. "Here and there, in its own way, it already is—no, not the same. Can't be. But we've got *room.*"

He pointed at Luna. Atmosphere fuzzed its edge, made the dark part glimmer and the bright part shine as men had never seen it before. "You Earth people, though, will have the same thing, yonder, in not too many more decades," he said.

"Do you really believe that?"

"Why, of course. The Lunar area equals a fourth of Earth's land surface—"

Cocktails arrived. Maura smiled and clinked glasses. "I'm afraid you're an idealist, Don. But welcome nevertheless."

The martini was cold and pungent on his tongue. He studied the menu with little comprehension. "I must admit our eating habits are barbaric on Venus," he surrendered, "and the Corporation is more interested in nourishing our bodies than our souls. What do you suggest?"

"By Sol, a man who doesn't have to pretend masculinity! Let me see...Whale teriyaki looks good. With that we'd probably want consomme Mexique, filet of mahimahi, tossed salad—and may I be greedy and have ice cream with that wonderful Martian herb sauce for dessert?"

"Uh, champagne's right, isn't it?" He selected one by the simple criterion of price and gave his order.

Appetizers were set down. Pate de foie gras, smoked oysters, marinated artichokes and thousand-year eggs were separate adventures for Sevigny. "A whole dimension of living," he exulted. "How can I thank you for programming me?"

"Show me around your planet in exchange—if I can ever promote a ticket there."

"You must. Frontiers don't happen often in history. The Moon's more accessible, true. But it won't have breathable air for a long time."

"If ever."

He gave her a puzzled look. "Why are you do doubtful?"

"Oh...one hears so many things. Like, well, doesn't Earth's magnetic field shield us from a lot of radiation? And the Moon hasn't got any to speak of."

"Nor Venus, much. Given enough atmosphere, that doesn't matter. Our atmosphere amounts to a good bit more than yours."

"But the Moon's so small! How can it hold onto gases?"

"Loss to space isn't that fast. They won't have to worry about it for an estimated half million years. As for atmospheric shielding, the Moon actually has an advantage over Earth. So low a gravitational field makes a correspondingly lower gradient. A surface pressure equal to three-fourths of Earth sea level, which is what's planned, means that there will be a measurable concentration at altitudes which correspond to open space here. Charged particles won't penetrate deep, and actinic rays will be absorbed."

"I've heard, though, that there isn't enough gas to be had."

"The selenologists swear there is. Not as such, naturally. As buried ice, water of crystallization, carbon, nitrogen and sulfur compounds released when minerals—and the organics left over from the original nebula—break down. What we're doing, actually, is using deep wells and atomic bombs to start vulcanism. The same process that gave all the smaller planets their atmospheres. Only we're going to tickle Luna so much that everything will happen several orders of magnitude faster than it did in nature."

"But suppose your figures are wrong?"

"That's been thought of. It won't be hard to deflect some comets into collision orbits, if necessary, and they're mostly big balls of frozen gas." Sevigny chuckled. "One way or another, the final stages ought to be quite a show—from this safe, comfortable distance!"

"And what will you have when you're finished?" she argued. "Poisons?"

She can't be that ignorant. Can she? Must simply be making conversation. Letting me show off my *male knowledge. Fine.*

"Venus didn't have anything else," he reminded her. "Nitrogen, carbon dioxide, and a certain amount of water in the clouds. But the photosynthesizing algae grew exponentially once they'd been seeded in the upper atmosphere. They released oxygen; then they kept sinking to lower levels where it was so hot they decomposed into carbon and water. The greenhouse effect dropped off until temperatures went below a hundred; and for ten years it rained without pause. Given liquid water, the Urey process operated, raw rock consumed still more CO_2 and at last there was air that men could breathe." He sipped from his glass. "Solar protons and ultraviolet radiation helped also, especially in breaking down hydrogen compounds. In other words, a weak magnetic field is an asset to the terraformer."

"Do you plan the same thing for Luna, then?"

"What else? Different in many details, of course. Luna isn't identical with Venus or ancient Earth. Right now the air we've already given it is a lot like Mars'. Radiation's been releasing oxygen from water; the free hydrogen goes up and the free oxygen promptly attacks methane, ammonia and hydrogen sulfide. This yields carbon dioxide, free nitrogen, sulfites and more water to split. But once the atmosphere is thick enough—anyhow that part is quite well understood, what has to be done. Far more so than the present stage of operations." He thought of Decker, buried under the ruins of his own, Don Sevigny's, well, and his fingers tightened on the stem of his glass.

"What's wrong?" she asked.

"Nothing." He drank. "I was reminded of an accident we had recently. Rather not talk about that."

There was a slight bustle as pair of men were shown to a table close by. Sevigny couldn't help gawking. They were in ordinary clothes, but if the pictures in the school anthropology text hadn't lied, one was an Arab and one from India—He recollected his manners. Besides, Maura was prettier.

"I hear rumors about your having trouble," she was saying. "That could get many people angry, the ones who claim the project has already cost more than it's worth."

"I can't understand that attitude," he said, and congratulated himself on how neatly he could dodge the question of accident rates. "Seems to me a whole new world is worth a billion times any conceivable price you'll have to pay."

"How many people will get any use out of that world? That's becoming a political issue too. They say only the rich will be able to live there."

"Pure demagoguery, my lady. The Corporation charter"—Sevigny was glad now that his chief had made him read it before departure—"says that one fourth of the Moon is reserved for recreational purposes, and that there's to be adequate housing at decent prices for all residents. Who'll make a sizeable number, you realize. The Moon has rich mineral resources. Once it's habitable, those will really be exploited."

He began to plagiarize other literature that had been given him: "Also, the project develops sciences and technologies which'll be useful elsewhere. As an example of international cooperation, it strengthens the Commonwealth. The fact that a great deal of the Moon will be left in woods and meadows is important; Earth has very little greenscape any more. And...not altogether pleasant to think about...but nuclear weapons do exist and times of trouble may come back again. The more worlds colonized, the better the race's chances of lasting."

"You've convinced me," she said merrily, "and here comes the soup. So let's talk about other things. Like yourself."

"You're a more interesting subject...Maura."

"Very well. We'll take turns!"

Clan culture discouraged individual boasting, but Sevigny found it remarkably easy to glamorize himself. He didn't even need to embroider his reminiscences much. She had never hunted, camped in a forest or a desert, trucked fish to a new ocean, built a dam, fought a battle—And then he found that he had never gone submarining or seen an opera or been to—

"Ti'ki!"

The wine glass dropped from his hand and shattered.

"Don," Maura cried low, "what's the matter?"

He snatched the vibrating little box from his pocket and laid it to his ear. "*R-r-rik-ik-ik, ti'ki, ti'ki, ch!*

Oscar the dirrel had no words for a great concrete chamber five levels below ground, or a ramp leading out, or a truck with a hoist. But it had to be that. *Men come, four men come, machine, fright, chase Oscar, thing-Oscar-watch go, Don, come, ti'ki, ki, ki!*

Sevigny was half out of the room before Maura screamed.

The headwaiter, a blurred shape, a hand to shake off, "Can I help you, sir?"

"No! Emergency!" The engineer burst from among the tables and plunged to the elevator.

It wasn't there. He stabbed the button again and again, while Oscar chittered fear and rage from the overhead pipes where he crouched.

Maura reached him. He saw her across a quivering immenseness, hardly felt her hands drag at him. The tears didn't register either. "Don, Don, what's wrong? Are you banzai? Please come back—"

The elevator door opened. He moved her aside. "I may be back in a while," he got out.

Another shape brushed past her. The man was slender, chocolate-skinned, full lips curved very slightly upward. "May I?" he said, and entered the cage.

Sevigny recognized the Indian from the table near his. He tried to thrust him out, and grasped air. The man had dodged like bird. "Emergency," Sevigny snarled once more.

"Perhaps I can help," said the Indian blandly.

No time to waste on him. Sevigny punched for subfive. The door closed on Maura. Her face had lost its strickenness.

Weight decreased. "May I suggest notifying the hotel detective?" the Indian said.

Jarred from his haste, Sevigny made himself think about that. It hadn't occurred to him; the clans took care of their own. "Will you do so?" he asked. "And the, uh, city police. There's a theft being committed in sub-501." He took his gun from the holster. "I'll get out and see what I can do. You go straight back to the lobby and holler for troops."

"Is the matter worth such a risk to yourself?"

A man of Clan Woodman was entrusted with that crate. "Yes."

"As you will. If you wonder, sir, why I left my own dinner to accompany you, may I present myself as a physician." The narrow dark head bent in a slight bow. "Dr. Krishnamurti Lal Gupta of Benares, at your service. I was afraid you might have been taken ill."

Rik-ik-chik-ri-ch, Don, come, fast come, screamed the box that Sevigny held.

He stuck it back into his pocket. The elevator slowed. *Sub-5* flashed onto the indicator panel. "Stand by to raise her," Sevigny said. The door glided open. He sprang into a bare, gray, coldly lit corridor.

Something stung him between the shoulders. He whirled with a curse. Gupta stood in the cage, a tiny flat pistol in one hand. He was still smiling. Sevigny's. world dissolved in surf and darkness...He tried to raise his gun and couldn't. Its clatter when it hit the floor reached him as a remote and tiny thud. His knees gave way and he fell on top of it. Then he ceased to be.

-4-

Awareness was first of the same countenance, hovering above him with the same friend-expression. He struggled to sit up and Gupta stepped back. This time he held a hypodermic needle.

Crazily through the fogs Sevigny remembered Aarons bent over Leong while the volcano drowned Decker. Because someone had bombarded the keystone of a machine with X-rays...Rage rose in him, so strong that it had a taste. Adrenalin joined the counter-drug in his bloodstream. Strength and senses rushed forth. He bounded to his feet.

"Stop right there," said a man across the room. He was the Arab who had been with Gupta. His eyes were the most intent that Sevigny had ever seen. The gun in his hand reined the Cytherean to a halt.

"That's better," said the third man. He was sumptuously clad, in gold and scarlet that contrasted with Gupta's white simplicity and the gunman's somberness; at the end of middle age, he was bald, wattled and potgutted. But his jaw was like a ram and he spoke in a young voice. "*Mama mia!* When did a person come out from under a sleepy jolt this damn fast, Kreesho?"

"Rarely, Mr. Baccioco," said Gupta. "But he is both strong and excited. Please relax, clansman. We have no intention of harming you."

A door opened. Maura came through. Sevigny paid more immediate attention to Oscar, who zoomed past her, went up his tunic in one streak, hugged him around the neck and unburdened his own soul so noisily that nothing else could be heard at that moment.

Sevigny got the dirrel quieted down at length, with much stroking and reassuring. Most of him, meanwhile, studied the surroundings. He was in a rich man's room, which seemed to be part of a suite. He couldn't identify the pictures which glowed from the walls, but they were likeliest totirepros of medieval European masters. The windows were blanked out, and no sound penetrated from beyond. A clock said 2345.

Maura had settled into a relaxer. Her gown was changed for slacks and blouse. The effect remained explosive. She smoked a cigarette in short hard puffs and did not return Sevigny's protracted stare.

Gupta sat quite at ease on a couch upholstered in what Sevigny thought must be genuine leather; cheap on Venus, but he'd been told that an Earthman might go through life without seeing any. The older man. Baccioco, prowled back and forth, hands tightly clasped behind his back. The Arab waited in a corner, weapon now pointed at the floor but eyes never leaving Sevigny.

"Well, are his fears allayed, the little fellow?" Gupta said. "Fine, fine. You will. I hope, Clansman Sevigny, take his presence as earnest of our good intentions. When you were brought unconscious into the storeroom and laid in the truck—what else could we do?—your pet stormed down from his hiding place and fell upon you. I was forced to anesthetize him too, his distress was so noisy, but had not the heart to leave him behind."

"Thanks for that," Sevigny said curtly.

"Please do not be too discomfited at your present situation—"

"Mainly I'm disgusted. With myself." Sevigny stared so long at Maura that she had to turn her face to him. "I walked right into the oldest trap in the universe, didn't I?" He spat at her feet.

"Maron!" Baccioco gestured indignantly. "Is that a decent way to behave? Watch yourself!"

"We must make allowances, sir," Gupta soothed him.

Maura bit her lip. "We never meant to hurt you. Don," she said in a flat voice. "I was only supposed to keep you busy till the thing had been removed. And as long afterward as possible. I wish it had gone that way. I was honestly enjoying your company."

"How did you learn?" the Arab demanded.

"Shut up, Rashid," Baccioco said.

"Well, it is a question we meant to ask," Gupta said. "Do you mind telling us, clansman?"

They don't know Oscar can talk to me. That might be a *hole card. Barely might.* Sevigny held his face rigid and shrugged. "I put a scanner among the overhead pipes, connected to a microcaster. You doubtless found the receiver in my tunic."

Baccioco studied him. Silence grew, under the white fluorescents, among the thick red drapes, until the slither when Rashid shuffled his feet was startlingly loud. A whiff of Maura's cigarette drifted to Sevigny, acrid when he remembered the perfume earlier. Without his gun he felt naked, lopsided; and Oscar's warm weight on his shoulder was not much comradeship.

"Well," Baccioco said, "that sounds reasonable. I will have a man search for your scanner tomorrow, to make quite certain. As for now, though, here we are, no? You don't want to be here and we don't want to have you here. What to do?"

"I suggest we all begin by reducing our tensions," Gupta said in his mild fashion. "Maura, would you be so good as to fetch coffee? Or would anyone prefer something stronger?"

There was no reply. The girl rose and left the room. Her head drooped a little.

"Do be seated, gentlemen," Gupta went on. Baccioco snorted but threw himself into an armchair. After a moment, Sevigny took another. Rashid remained standing in his corner.

"We should show our guest the courtesy of further identifying ourselves," Gupta said. "Signor Baccioco is—"

"No!" the Italian broke in.

"Yes," Gupta responded. "Please consider. If Clansman Sevigny remembers your name at all, or even your appearance, he need only ask the first alert person he meets in order to be told that Ercole Baccioco is chairman of the board of Eureclam S. A. You must not be so modest about your reputation, sir...Having inevitably revealed that much, I trust I can do no harm in describing our friend

Rashid Gamal ibn Ayith as a representative, in our little organization, of the Fatimite Brotherhood. As for myself, I am actually a physician, but may have gained a small prominence through my activity in the Conservationist party of my native land."

A corporation head, a politician and some kind of religious fanatic. The girl, I suppose, a hireling, like those workers who removed the force unit. What are they doing together tonight? As Sevigny's muscles tautened, Oscar bristled on his lap. He stroked the dirrel into calm. Oscar had to remain very, very inconspicuous.

"The matter must be important, to bring people like you here," he said slowly.

"Critical indeed," Gupta nodded. "It was essential for us to obtain possession of that engine." *Then they knew I was bringing it to Earth. So there's a spy in the Buffalo's top staff. He could have sent a coded radiogram without attracting much notice; that's common enough. Still, if we get a chance to check the Comcenter records*—"Through various connections, we arranged that you would be delayed in Honolulu overnight." *Thunder and fury, how many tentacles have they got?* "But believe me, I beg you, there was no idea of involving you otherwise. That was pure misfortune."

"Why did you want the unit?" Sevigny asked.

No one replied. Maura came in with cups on a tray. She went among the men, lingering briefly by Sevigny. He took his cup without regarding her. Rashid refused his. She sat down again.

"This is ridiculous," Baccioco grumbled. "Far past my bedtime, and here I sit talking with a...an outplanet savage."

"Not the least ridiculous, sir," Gupta said, "and in many respects the Cytherean culture is preferable to any on modern Earth." He took an appreciative sip. "Ah! Do notice the coffee, clansman. Hawaiian kona is one of the glories of this planet...Information for information. If you will tell us what you know and surmise, we shall reciprocate. Gladly. We want you to understand that our motives are altruistic. Who knows, you may even enlist in our cause."

"Can we believe him?" Rashid growled.

"What do you have against me?" Sevigny flung at him.

The gun lifted a few centimeters. "You defile God's work!"

"As you may readily learn by watching a few newscasts, the Fatimite Brotherhood takes a fundamentalist view of terraforming," Gupta said. "A change in the appearance of the Moon is especially distressing. Little can be done to reverse the process, but it should not be allowed to go any further."

"And you?" Sevigny asked, turning to the doctor.

Gupta uttered a small laugh. "Now, now. Pray do not look for vast, complicated motivations. Such things occur only on the TriV. The Conservationist Party of India, like its counterparts in numerous other countries, maintains quite openly that the Luna Corporation is wasting enormous, badly needed resources on a utopian scheme that, if realized at all, will make no difference to Earth for decades."

"Isn't your own government a major stockholder?"

"True. The Vishnuists unfortunately command a parliamentary majority." Lightness left the voice and the big dark eyes turned incandescent. "City dwellers! They have not been out in the hinterlands, have not watched children starve because soil is exhausted and water tables are emptied and raw materials too costly for chemosynthesis. *There* is the place to begin reclamation!" He finished his cup in one draught. His hand shook.

"And...hm." Sevigny rested his gaze on Baccioco. "Eureclam S. A., chartered and equipped, no doubt, for work on Earth only. There'll be plenty of fat contracts to make the deserts fertile and so forth, if the Moon job is abandoned. "Hey?"

Baccioco reddened. "The question is not of money but of sound policy."

"So you say. But look, you must realize that in the long run the Moon'll payoff ten times what Earth can."

"Too long a run," Gupta said. "It will dehumanize us to plan in such terms."

"I told you, Don, there is a political fight going on." Maura could barely be heard.

"Which your side is losing," Sevigny pounced.

"What makes you think so?" Baccioco retorted angrily.

"Otherwise you wouldn't have to resort to sabotage."

"That is a most serious accusation," Gupta said.

"Why else did you steal that force unit?" Sevigny challenged. "You couldn't afford to let me bring evidence of your work to the Safety Corps. An investigation would blow your gang open."

Gupta spread his hands. "I cannot tell you everything," he said, "and hence cannot at this moment refute your statement however false it be. I will swear by anything you wish that you would not have missed our engine, had all gone well. But come now, I offered information for information. Your turn, clansman"

"What the devil have I got to tell you? I was only an errand boy."

"You had numerous confidential talks with Mr. Bruno Norris. How much hard data does he possess? How much does he surmise?"

Sevigny leaned back and grinned at them. Inside, hatred made a cold lump in his stomach. Erich Decker, a man under command of a woodman, had been murdered by agents of these.

Rashid took a step forward. "You will talk," he said. "There are ways."

"Please." Gupta lifted a palm. "Nothing violent. Means have a sorry habit of affecting ends."

"There has been too much kitten play," Baccioco declared. "He will most certainly talk."

Okay, we might as *well bring it out in the open.* "I'm bound to talk when you let me go, am I not?" Sevigny said. The hatred left scant room for fear, but the blood thrummed in his veins. "That fairly well proves you won't let me go—alive at any rate. So what have I to gain by helping you?"

In the return of the stillness, where Baccioco's breath rattled with rheum, he thought: *Maybe they always intended to kidnap me. The theft of my evidence would itself be evidence—No, wait. If I'd not burst in on them, they could have substituted another force unit, also damaged but in a way that'd look like ordinary failure, that'd give no clues to the Safety Corps labs...That must be it. So Gupta wasn't lying when he said I'd never have missed my engine. But now I can tell what's happened, under truth drug, and an investigation will start regardless.*

If I can get away whole, that is.

Maura lit another cigarette. Her free hand clenched.

Gupta leaned forward, elbows on knees, fingers bridged, and peered amiably at Sevigny. "Clansman," he said, "we serve a humane cause. But we are determined that it shall prevail. No one will wonder at your disappearance for days. The message to Corps headquarters in Paris that you were coming never left the Moon. Mr. Norris will not expect to hear from you until there is something definite to report. Meanwhile, as you doubtless know, there are certain potent psychopharmaceutical which will elicit information even from unwilling subjects. There is also a treatment to remove memories. And...I am a medical man."

He paused. "The experience of being interrogated under drugs is admittedly unpleasant," he said. "Memory removal involves a grave risk of removing too much. Moreover, at best you would be found in the gutter, apparently at the end of a monumental debauch, in the course of which you had lost the object entrusted to you. It would do credit to neither yourself nor your clan.

"You are a foreigner, owing no duty to any organization on Earth. If you consider the matter objectively, you will surely, as a reasonable man, see that justice lies with us. Not to mention the prospect of substantial material reward. Think well."

He stood up. "The hour is late," he said. "We are all tired. Please accept our hospitality for the night. I will discuss the subject with you again tomorrow. Through that door, if you will be so kind."

Now!

Sevigny slid a hand under Oscar. He poked with a hard thumb. The dirrel hopped to his hind legs and chattered out a protest.

"What ails him this time?" asked Baccioco surly.

"Too much excitement. Let me cool him off," Sevigny said. He began murmuring.

"You remember, your pet is a hostage too," Baccioco said. "Nasty things could happen to him."

"Tk-tk quee ch-rik, k-k-k ti-oo—" Oscar crouched like a cat. Sevigny picked him up in one arm and rose. Rashid glided near, gun aimed at the Cytherean's breast.

"You will rest sounder if you take a sleeping tablet," Gupta smiled. "I shall come along to your room and give you one."

"Better than chains, huh?" Sevigny looked around at Maura. Damn, but she was a dish! "Good night; my lady."

"Good night," she whispered.

Rashid passed Sevigny, two meters away, to get behind him.

"Ki-ik!"

Oscar leaped. Sevigny went to one knee. But the bullet did not fly where he had been. It cracked into the floor. Oscar had already landed on Rashid's wrist.

The Arab cursed and struck. Oscar sank teeth into his hand. Rashid yelled. Sevigny charged across the distance between. Gupta clawed at him. Sevigny's left fist met the Indian's face. Gupta lurched aside. Sevigny kicked Rashid in the larynx. The Arab fell in a heap. The gun clattered free. Sevigny scooped it up and jumped back out of reach."

"Okay," he panted, "stay where you are!"

Maura screamed. "Be still!" Sevigny told her. He didn't know if there was anyone else in this apartment. Slowly, he moved to the wall until he covered every approach.

"*Tu porco*—" Baccioco was aiding Gupta to rise. Blood dripped heavily from the doctor's mouth. Oscar joined Sevigny and gibbered at the whole world. His fur stood on end.

Rashid got to hands and knees. He stayed there a second or two, fighting for breath. Then he climbed to unsteady feet.

Gupta shook his head. The daze cleared from his eyes. "What do you plan to do?" he mumbled through puffed lips.

"Call the police," Sevigny told him. "Where's your phone?"

Rashid pulled a knife from inside his blouse and moved toward the Cytherean. He made mewing sounds and his eyes were crazy. Maura's mouth opened again where she huddled in her relaxer.

"Stop or I'll shoot," Sevigny said to the Arab.

"He won't stop," Gupta said.

"You will have to kill him."

Rashid edged closer. He held the knife in an expert underhand grip. His tread wobbled, but—

"For that matter," Gupta said, "I intend to make a break for help. I recommend that Miss Soemantri and Signor Baccioco do the same. Since you do not know where the alarm buttons are that will summon others, you will have to shoot the three of us. The American police do not look kindly upon homicide. You may have some difficulty in proving self-defense."

Sevigny moved crabwise along the wall until he was near a footstool. He snatched it with his free hand and threw it at Rashid. The Arab fell as the object hit him in the abdomen, staggered erect again and resumed his weak, relentless advance.

"All right!" Sevigny yelped. He passed his hand above the plate of what seemed to be the main door. It opened for him and he saw a corridor beyond, an elevator waiting not far down.

"If that lunatic chases me I will shoot," he said. "I'll try only to disable him." He backed through the door with Oscar and let it close. The other entrances he could see along the short length of the hall were on the same side, probably every one leading back into the suite. He retreated fast.

-5-

Fifty floors down, the elevator let him out into a lobby, small and empty despite its polished marble. "Blastula," he muttered, "I'd hoped this was a hotel." But no. You couldn't get away with as much in a hotel as you could in a soundproofed apartment. Baccioco probably maintained a number of those, around the planet. Sevigny debated whether to borrow someone's phone here. If he left this exit unwatched, his enemies could get away before the police arrived.

On the other hand, if he hung around they might well find some way to recapture him. And as for their escape, come to think of it, men as prominent as Baccioco and—he supposed—Gupta couldn't disappear. Rashid didn't matter, was little more than a tool. And he found himself hoping a bit that Maura would go free.

Oscar made comforting noises on his shoulder.

He walked out onto the street. It was wide and softly lit, lined with tall residential buildings. An occasional car went by, the whisper of its air cushion blending with the warm breeze that rustled in palm fronds. He was high above the ocean, which he glimpsed at the edge of the city glitter beneath. The Moon was no longer in sight, but he made out a few stars.

Where was the nearest public phone? He chose an eastward course arbitrarily and began striding. His buskins thudded; the slight jar and the sense of kinesthesia helped shake a little tightness out of him. But his skin was still wet, his stink sharp against a background of jasmine. his nerves still taut.

At the end of the block a pedestrian belt lifted him over the street. From the top of its arc he spied some glowsigns to the north, and headed that way. Before long he reached a cluster of shops. They were closed for the night, but even in his hurry he lost a few seconds gaping at their display windows. Was that much luxury possible on an Earth that everyone called impoverished? *Wait. Remember your history classes. Inordinate wealth for a few has always gone along with inordinate want for the many. Because the many no longer have the economic strength to resist—*

That recalled him to his purpose. There was a booth at the corner. He went in, fumbled for a half dollar and dropped the coin in the slot. The screen lit. He needed a minute to figure out how the system worked. On Venus and Luna they used radio for distance calls, intercoms when indoors. Finally he punched the button marked Directory and spelled out POLICE on the alphabet keys. A set of station numbers appeared. He dialed.

A face and a pair of uniformed shoulder came to view. "Honolulu Central. Can I help you?"

"I want to, report a theft and a kidnapping," Sevigny said. It felt odd not to be telling his troubles to a clan elder.

The voice and eyes sharpened. "Where are you?"

Sevigny peered out at the signs and read them off. "I don't know where the nearest station would be. I'm a stranger here."

"Name, please?" The man droned through a maddening series of questions. "Very well," he ended, "stay where you are and we'll dispatch a patrol."

Sevigny fretted for a time which seemed a deal longer than it was. When two dark teardrop shapes halted by the curb his heart slugged.

A large sergeant with an unexpectedly amiable brown face got out of one. "You the party sent for us?" he asked. Sevigny nodded. The officer took a minitaper from the pouch at his belt and thumbed the switch. "Tell me about it."

Sevigny went through the account in as few words as possible. When he spoke Baccioco's name, the policeman pursed his lips in a soundless whistle. At the conclusion he turned to the car he had come from and said "What you make of this, Bradford?"

"Damfino," said the indistinct shape within, "but sounds creaky to me."

"You're serious, Mr. Sevigny?"

"I sure as hell am," the Cytherean rasped. "And I suggest, instead of a lot of silly questions, you arrest them before they take off."

"Well, we can't do that on your bare word unless you make a formal complaint. Want to come down to the station with us? I ought to warn you, you being outplanet, if this isn't the truth you're in bad trouble."

"I'll confirm what I said under drugs, damn you!"

"Hey, hey, take it easy. I'm not calling you a liar. The boys in the other car will go talk to these people and follow them if they leave. So let's us be on our way." The officer opened the rear door and gestured at Sevigny to enter first. The plainclothesman in front fed instructions to the pilot and the car got moving.

Turning around, the detective gave Sevigny a hard look. "Maybe your side is fighting back, huh?" he said.

"What do you mean?" With an effort, the engineer kept his hand away from the gun at his hip.

"Making up stories to discredit the people who're campaigning against the Luna Corporation. Everybody knows President Edwards has been trying to get the Commonwealth Council to revoke its charter; and this is an election year, here in the States. A nice ripe scandal could toss Edwards out and shoo Hernandez in—and *he* wants to sink more American money into Corporation stock."

Oscar sensed hostility, fluffed out his tail and clicked his teeth together.

"Whoa, there, Bradford," said the officer in back. "You're letting your prejudices run away with you." He turned to Sevigny. "Me, I think this work on the Moon is the greatest thing that's happened since Maui's time. My grandchildren'll have elbow room like my grandfather used to talk about. Uh, my name's Kealoha, John Kealoha."

Sevigny shook the big hand. "Glad to meet you," he said. "I'd begun to wonder if anybody on Earth wanted us to succeed."

"Sure. Anybody who can see past the end of his own snout. Why else would the opposition have to turn criminal?"

"That story's plain fantastic," Bradford said. "I'd like to interrogate you, Sevigny. Alone."

The Cytherean's jaws closed. He'd taken more than he would have imagined possible without drawing a weapon. "Any time!"

"Slack off, you two," Kealoha urged. "Bradford, he said he'd take babble juice. Let the doc quiz him."

A waiting silence fell. Eventually the car stopped before precinct headquarters. The building was dwarfed by the apartment houses around, but thickly formed in concrete, doubtless a relic of the Unrest years. Mass aberration could come back again, Sevigny thought. And it would—if Earth's population didn't find some outlet. Not that the *Moon* would relieve crowding here, to any noticeable degree. But a place for temporary escape—

As they debarked, Bradford grasped the engineer's arm. "Come along, you," he ordered: and let go with a yell. Sevigny had cracked the blade of a hand across his wrist.

"You—"

Kealoha shoved his bulk between them. "None o' that," he rumbled. "You had no call to hustle him, Bradford. And you, Sevigny, don't ever resist an officer. Not ever."

"Even when I'm in the right?" The Cytherean was so astonished that half the anger drained from him. It flowed back and his mouth twisted. "Judas! I can't get off Earth too fast."

Under Bradford's glower, he entered the building. A lieutenant of police, evidently in charge at night, waited by the sergeant at the desk. "Sevigny?"

The curious, pale-checked tension of him registered only faintly through the engineer's emotions. "Yes. I want to file some charges."

"Well, that takes time. We have to get hold of a judge, you know, before you can swear out a warrant."

Bradford's expression froze. Kealoha's mouth fell open. The lieutenant frowned at him and made a slight negative gesture. Behind his desk, the other sergeant sat as if cast in metal.

"I'll make the call right away," the lieutenant said. "Meanwhile, turn your gun over to us."

Sevigny shook his head. "No. I have the right, by interplanetary agreement."

"And we have regulations. Do you want our help or don't you?"

A sense of being caught in some purposeless machine overwhelmed Sevigny. Without a word, he laid Rashid's pistol on the desk. It hadn't fitted his holster very well anyway. He sagged into a chair and stared across the bleak, harshly lit room, at nothing. Bradford grinned. Kealoha seemed puzzled and distressed.

The lieutenant went behind the desk and dialed. "MacEwen speaking, twelfth precinct station," he said. "Sevigny's here." He cut the circuit before there was a reply, came back and extended his hand with a smile. "The judge is on his way," he said. "Glad to meet you, clansman."

Something strange...But all Earth was an abyss of otherness. Sevigny shook hands unenthusiastically. "Did you alert him in advance, then?" he asked.

"Yes." MacEwen sat down, offered a pack of cigarettes, and took one for himself. "The, um, the situation was peculiar. We didn't know whether it'd be best to take you here or to main headquarters. So we asked Judge Hughes to stand by."

"Lieutenant—" Kealoha began.

"Shut up," MacEwen said. His voice was quiet but edged. Turning to Sevigny: "This is as odd a case as I ever heard about. You mustn't blame us for being careful."

"Too damn careful!" A little life returned to the Cytherean. He sat straight. "I don't know anything about police methods, but what are you idling here for? That force unit is important evidence of...sabotage, murder, conspiracy. Why haven't you got a crew, a squad, whatever you call 'em, at the Hotel Goldwater this minute, finding out how the devil those men got in with their truck and loaded a piece of goods registered to me?"

"Don't worry, clansman, MacEwen said. "There've been calls burning the lines throughout Honolulu." He hesitated. "And beyond. But don't you see, this is an international case. If your story is true, some mighty important foreigners are involved. It may be too big for us, may need the Safety Corps."

"So call them. They must have a local office."

"Please, clansman. I promise you we've gotten things under way. You'll have to be patient. While you wait for...for the judge, suppose you report what happened to you."

"I already have. Twice."

"That must've been pretty brief, though. You were in a hurry. We'll need to know everything you can recall. Best to put it on tape now, while it's fresh in your mind." MacEwen went back to a shelf for a recorder. "Sergeant Kealoha, how about getting us some coffee?"

"You're not even going to put him in an interrogation room?" the policeman asked incredulously.

"Get. That. Coffee. Sergeant."

Kealoha went out. He looked defeated. MacEwen started the recorder. "Go ahead, clansman," he invited. "Start as far back as possible."

Sevigny yielded. "That would be on the Moon," he sighed. "I was in charge of a deeptap gang—

"—so we went to dinner and talked. Not about anything significant." It hurt even to tell this much. "Suddenly—

"—a needle gun. I passed out!" Kealoha, who had been standing close by, refilled Sevigny's cup.

"— he claimed—"

The door opened. Two men in unobtrusive clothes entered. They were both young and hard-featured. "Excuse me," MacEwen blurted, jumping to his feet. The fifth successive cigarette smoldered between his fingers. "Are you the Federals?"

"Yes." One of them flashed a badge. The other nodded at Sevigny, who crouched forward in his chair. "That him?"

"Right." MacEwen stepped aside. There was awe in his expression.

The two men walked quickly over to the engineer. "Donald Sevigny," one said, not a question but a statement which didn't wait for reply. "We're from the Federal Police Agency of the United States."

"So?" Sevigny rose, balanced on the ends of his feet. He sensed a wrongness; his skin prickled. Oscar poised humpbacked on his shoulder, tail flicking from side to side. Kealoha, MacEwen and the desk sergeant grew altogether motionless. Bradford grinned afresh where he sat. For a space the silence was broken only by the remote drone of a freightcraft lumbering overhead.

"You are under arrest, Come along."

"What?" In spite of every premonition, the words struck like lightning. Sevigny took a backward step. His right hand grabbed for the gun that was no longer there, his left lifted as if to plead. "Are you all crazy on Earth?"

"Come along, I said." A needler seemed to appear from nowhere in the first man's fingers.

"Wait a minute!" Kealoha bellowed.

"Be quiet, sergeant," MacEwen ordered.

Huge and blue in his uniform, the policeman stood his ground. "You've already took too much advantage of him being ignorant! He's got a right to know the charge. I can't let you make an improper arrest."

"Conspiracy to violate the sovereignty retained by the United States government under the Commonwealth," clipped the second man.

"Nothing doing." Kealoha shook his head. "Too vague. I know that much law. What's he supposed to have done?"

"Go to quarters, sergeant, or I'll bust you," MacEwen said. "Damn it, these are *Federal* officers! Take him away, gentlemen."

Conspiracy indeed, it tolled through the thudding in Sevigny's skull. *Baccioco and Company got on the phone the minute I left. They must have partners in Washington. The President himself is antilunar. Word went back, the city police were to keep me for these—*

The second agent took a pair of handcuffs from his pocket. "You Cythereans have a reputation for violence," he said. "Hold out your wrists."

"God damn you, no!" Three generations of pride sent Sevigny recoiling. "Not on a clansman!"

The first man aimed his needler.

Oscar the dirrel knew only that his boss was threatened. He shrieked and launched himself. The anesthetic dart flew wide. Oscar swarmed up the agent's blouse and went after the eyes. The other man whipped his handcuffs across the animal's nose, got hold of the tail and hurled him to the floor. Bradford left his chair, pistol out. It coughed twice. Blood violently spurted.

"K-ti," said the ragged thing which had once been Oscar, and died.

There was no time for thought, caution, anything but revenge. Sevigny leaped. His right fist buried itself in the solar plexus of the first Federal. He could feel the shock, distantly and impersonally, in his shoulderblade. The agent sank to his knees, retching. Sevigny twirled. The other one's needler was out. Sevigny's foot lashed. The weapon arced across the room. Sevigny moved in, grabbed collar and belt, and threw the man against Bradford. Both went down as their bodies convulsively met.

"Stop!" Kealoha shouted. His own gun barked. A star rayed out in the wall where the bullet smote.

"Shoot to hit, you idiot!" Bradford rolled free and scrabbled for his pistol.

Sevigny went out the door. He was a dead man if he stayed. Kealoha was not far behind. The officer's shots whanged right and left. He stopped in the entrance, blocking it.

"Get out of the way!" Bradford screamed.

Kealoha stood where he was and fired at the night. Sevigny ran into the street. Lamps glared everywhere—No, that building across from him, surrounded by garden, tall stands of bamboo, and he was a hunter from the Shaws—He fled toward darkness.

-6-

Flat on the ground, beneath a rose hedge that raked at him, he watched two policemen go a meter past his nose. Their footfalls vibrated through the damp grass and their flashlights made bobbing spears in the murk. When they were beyond him, he started to crawl.

The grounds opened on another street. He peered from the shadow shelter of a hedge. Cars whirred by against shimmering store fronts, but he saw no pedestrians. He had to get out of this district fast, before a cordon was established. In spite of having spent a year under Lunar gravity, he could doubtless outrun any urbanite: but he could not outrun a needle or a bullet.

A vacant taxi came cruising by. He sprang out and waved. For a ghastly moment he thought its scanner had missed him. It stopped and he tumbled inside. The robot voice of a central monitor asked, "Where do you wish to go?"

"Head for the harbor," he panted. That area should be safely distant from here, though the safety wouldn't last. The machine purred into motion. A police car wailed and Sevigny huddled low: But they didn't think to stop his vehicle for a search. That would soon occur to them. His one lonely asset was a habit of swift action.

The avenues, seen on the edge of vision, took on a flickering quality as the taxi gained speed. He had already used this kind of transportation, from the dock to his hotel—God of time, scarcely twelve hours ago!—and knew how it worked. He fed money to the phone and punched for information on automats. Comparison of addresses with the posted city map give him the location of one near the waterfront. He told the monitor to send him there, sat back and tried to rest.

The first rage and grief were past. Poor loyal Oscar had come a long way to die; but it was up to him to use the dirrel's last gift. He wondered, briefly, if he could have escaped without that stimulus of berserkergang. Consciousness might never have gotten so reckless. But now the fighting man's reflexes had taken him as far as they could; only brain would keep him free.

There was no use arguing with himself whether he should have done what he did. His act probably was right. The more he considered the behavior of the Federals, the less aboveboard it looked. Once in custody, he would most likely not have been taken to a nice public jail and allowed to call for legal help. He didn't relish guessing what would have happened instead. But no difference that. The fact was, he had resisted arrest, assaulted law officers and made himself a fugitive who could be shot on sight by the most honest of constables.

He stared out at the city. It was so gigantic, so inhuman, that he must choke down panic. What to do now, where to hide, whom to trust, anywhere on the turning planet?

One step at a *time,* he scolded. That reminded him, in his friendlessness, of his old drillmaster in war school; of parade grounds dusty in the hot gray light of day, enchanted through Venus' long, aurora-lit night; horseplay in barracks, the clean oil smell of weapons, maneuvers and marches and companionship in bivouac; and he calmed himself with the chant that had gone over so many kilometers. *Left, right! Left, right! It's seventeen marches to water, it's twenty-eight further to beer. But when we come toddling to Helltown, the hellgirls will see us and cheer. Left, right! Left, right—*

The taxi stopped. He gave it thirty dollars, took his change and went quickly out when the door unlocked for him. He'd need transportation again soon, but best not use this one. Though his image was wiped by the monitor as soon as it ascertained everything was in order, the record would remain that a fare had been picked up close in space-time to the escape episode. The cab droned off to seek other trade, leaving him alone in a satisfactorily asleep neighborhood.

A depressing one, though. The darkened tenements that lifted around him, blocking off world and all but a string of sky, were not tumbledown like many he had seen pictures of. This was no slum, must in fact be a lower middle class district. But they were uglier and less personal than Lunar domes, the spacing of windows bespoke the crampedness of apartments, and there hung a faint stench in the air of too many bodies too close together.

Yes...Earth needed a living Moon.

As Sevigny had hoped, there was no watchman in the automat—everything must be equipped with alarms that went directly to the nearest police station—and no other customer at this hour. Compared to the one in Port Kepler, the place was stupefying. He zigzagged around for minutes before locating the tailor booth. Once inside, he took off his clothes and activated the measurers. From the fabric samples he chose something cheap and dark blue, from the styles the one which seemed most conservative. The price appeared on a screen, he stuffed in money, machines hummed, a door opened in the wall and a parcel slid forth. He donned the new outfit, wrapped his clan garments and—not without a sense of guilt—pitched them down the first waste chute he came upon.

Now I won't be quite so easy to find.

He wasn't hungry, but he felt the beginnings of weakness and his hands trembled. A drug vendor displayed more brands of pills than he had known existed. Its battered appearance suggested that it saw a lot of use. He chose a stimulant combined with a mild euphoriac, and tapped himself a cup of coffee at the lunch dispenser to play with while the pill took effect.

And while he groped for a plan.

Once beyond American territory, I should be safe. If the Federals then want me on their damned charges, they'll have to apply to the World Safety Corps. And they aren't likely to do that; it'd provoke too many questions. So I shouldn't have anything to fear except assassins. Scornfully: If what I've met is a fair sample, that's nothing to fret a clansman.

Worry returned. *How am I going to get away, though? I haven't got the price of a flier, even if I dared try to buy one. Every outgoing common carrier will be under surveillance. Give a robot at headquarters my description, hook a motion analyzer into the circuit to watch for characteristics like walk and gesture which've been well documented by the socio-anthropologists, then feed in continuous data from scanners at every ticket office and embarkation point—I can't possibly disguise myself well enough.*

He could try to reach the local Corps office...No. If it had not itself been corrupted, it would be staked out in anticipation of just such an attempt. At least, he had better not assume otherwise. Suppose he phoned and asked for an escort there—That was out too. The Commonwealth's peace officers had, he remembered from reading, no authority to keep a man wanted on a strictly local warrant. And it would take too long to convince them that this was an international problem. The most he could hope to do was get them interested, and an eventual investigation started. Meanwhile he would have been taken off by the Federals, who served desperate masters.

The same argument applied even more strongly to the Luna Corporation's Honolulu agents.

The whole planet wasn't hunting him. He must hang onto that fact, must remember powerful men like Norris and humble ones like Kealoha. If he could get in touch with those who were influential, there would be lawyers, publicity, political and financial pressure on his behalf. Only, who? It had to be someone in town to begin with, and he didn't know anyone. Besides, you didn't simply buzz a vip, you hacked your way through an abatis of underlings. And during that time the police closed in. The Buffalo was easily accessible to him, and could perhaps tell him where to take cover, but he hadn't the cash for a message to the Moon over a pay phone.

Sanctuary, breathing space, a man of some importance who could act for him—

Wait!

Sevigny's breath quickened. He dashed to a call booth, punched for the directory and spelled out CONSULATES.

So few of their people visited Earth that the Cytherean clans kept nothing more than a joint embassy in Paris. But Mars did a considerable amount of trade, especially since the Lunar project began, and the Great Confederation of Y had long agreed, for a fee, that its local representatives would look after any Cytherean problems that arose. Also, the Martians had extraterritoriality!

There was only one Outplanet listing. "Mars." Sevigny scratched his head in wonder. Every major society maintained its own diplomats, he knew, not only an ambassador to the Commonwealth but a minister to each important nation... Well, evidently a mere city consulate was different. Y and Illach and Hs'ach and the rest could save money there by employing a single person together.

Sevigny consulted Public Data and learned that in this case the person wasn't even Martian by race. Again, though, it made sense. Why build an expensive dome and supply expensive sealed cars and antiweight drugs for an agent who doubtless worked part time and on largely routine business?

The Who's Who file informed him that Oleg N. Volhontseff had been born fifty-eight years ago in the Ga'ea'm region of K'nea, child of a biologist in the scientific colony; had received his elementary education there, taken degrees at Moscow and Brasilia, returned to Mars as a xenologist and only in the last few years retired to work on his books. An impressive catalogue of scholarly publications marched over the phone screen...why, wait, Volhontseff was the man who had translated the T'hu-Rayi. He must think as much like a Martian as was possible for a human brain, no wonder he'd never married!

"Better and better," Sevigny exulted, sent for a cab and left. He didn't think the pill alone had put bounce back into his stride.

-7-

Volhontseff's office was at home in the hills above the university. The neighborhood was lawns, bowers, individual houses of some architectural distinction. To a Cytherean it felt crowded; nevertheless, on today's Earth this must be a wealthy district. Half-time consular pay couldn't be much, nor the royalties from monographs on things like Illachi fosterbirth practices. Had the man inherited a private fortune?

Sevigny glided from the cab into the darkness under a tree and stood for a while straining his senses. Nothing moved but leaves in the breeze, under a velvety dark sky embroidered with constellations. A window spilled yellow light onto Volhontseff's yard. *Good, I was afraid I'd have to wake him.* Sevigny walked up a graveled path, that scrunched louder than he liked, to the front door. As he mounted the porch, he heard the bell peal. For the benefit of the viewer screen he tried to look harmless.

The door opened. A small man in a brown robe glared at him from disconcertingly bright green eyes, set in a nutcracker face beneath a high hairless skull. "Well, sir?" Volhontseff crackled.

"I'm sorry to bother you so late—" Sevigny began.

"I should hope so! I always do my writing at night. Had half a mind not to answer. Who are you and what do you want?"

"May I come in?"

"Not without stating your business."

"I'm Donald Sevigny of Clan Woodman on Venus—"

"Yes, yes, your accent is obvious. No one but a Shawdweller treats English diphthongs thus. Why are you not in national costume?"

"Well, I—Oh, hell. I claim sanctuary. Frisk me for weapons if you like."

Volhontseff didn't so much as blink. "Sanctuary from whom?"

"Enemies of the Luna Corporation," Sevigny snapped, exasperated, "and you know how important that's become to the Martian economy. This is your affair as well as mine."

"Indeed? The project has enabled Martians to earn outplanet exchange for their societies, and of course, once Lunar mining starts in earnest, they will be able to buy minerals cheaper there than from the asteroids. But otherwise—well." Volhontseff's irritation seemed to vanish. Suddenly he had no expression, and his voice was robotic, "Come in and let us discuss the matter."

He led the way down a corridor wainscoted in genuine oak, where eerily carved staffs hung as ornaments, to a study walled with books. "Sit down." He waved at a deep antique armchair. For himself he took a seat behind a desk cluttered with papers and library apparatus, lit a cigarette without offering one, leaned back and watched Sevigny through a blue cloud. So proceed with your story," he directed.

As the Cytherean stumbled through it, Volhontseff began to show animation again. Now and then he nodded, a few times he interrupted with tightly perceptive questions. At the end he sat for some while before stating, with a scowl:

"This puts me in an awkward position. I am not an American national, you realize and do not wish to have my residence permit revoked. The climate here is too good for aging bones that grew under Martian gravity. And my references, my collections—no, moving them would be quite unfeasible. So I must not exceed my legal prerogatives; and those are limited."

Sevigny slammed a fist on the desk top. "What the devil do you mean?" he exploded. "You're the Martian consul! You have extraterritorial jurisdiction."

"Only over Martians, and that only because it is manifestly impossible to apply human legal concepts to them. Cythereans—hm, they are supposed to lack special privilege except for what was granted by the Treaty of Toronto. On the other hand, perhaps one could argue that my authority extends to everyone whom I represent, regardless of affiliation. I do not know and in fact I do not know if the question has ever arisen in court!"

Hope hatched in Sevigny and chirped. "Well," he said, "that's a talking point. You can refuse to hand me over till you get a top-level decision. What we need is delay and publicity. The enemy can't survive that."

Volhontseff gave him a narrow look. "Young man," he murmured, "for a colonial you are developing a remarkable shrewdness. Very well. I must have the support, or at least the involvement, of an important organization. But I can get in direct touch with the Martian ambassador—"

"Which one?"

"What?"

"All of them? Might be best."

Volhontseff stubbed out his cigarette and made a production of igniting the next. "I must think about that," he said. "Intersocietal relations on Mars are complicated. They don't have wars, but rivalries aren't the less real for being subtle."

"Oh, well, something else is equally important," Sevigny said. "To get a message to my boss on Luna, Bruno Norris at Port Kepler. He'll have reliable contacts in the Commonwealth hierarchy." He showed teeth in a dog's grin. "Those poor, bought Feds won't know what blasted them."

Volhontseff drummed nervously on his desk. "They do raise a problem, however," he said. "Whether or not they acted lawfully, they were still officers and you are guilty of resisting them. If I do not notify them at once of your presence, then I will have been harboring a fugitive from justice. Yet if I do notify them, they may forcibly remove you before the influences on our side can be brought to bear, and tell me to appeal to the courts."

And what can a dead man, "shot in a second attempt to escape," prove? Sevigny thought grimly. *Volhontseff here has nothing but my unsupported word to go on. The Buffalo can try to raise a stink, and maybe in time he'll get the Safety Corps interested. But meanwhile the antilunar faction will have been alerted, will have had a chance to cover its tracks, to cry that it's being smeared by the dirty opposition—yes. I'm afraid that if the police arrest me now I won't see another Moonrise.*

"So they're not going to," he said aloud.

"Eh?" Volhontseff said. His air of calculation had gone, as mercurially as his previous moods; he looked very much an old professor, helpless against the savageries that lived outside his books.

"You'll postpone telling the locals I'm here until you've raised every possible ally and they've had time to act," Sevigny informed him.

"But—"

Sevigny rose, loomed over the small shape before him, lifted one fist and said: "I'm threatening you, understand? I'm bigger than you. I smooth talked my way into this house, and now you have no choice but to do as I want. That clears you legally, correct?"

"Well—well—"

The Cytherean tapped the phone on the desk. "Start calling, friend."

Volhontseff looked away and gradually, as he sat rubbing his chin, Sevigny saw decision crystallize. *How much like R'ku he* is, the engineer thought; and that returned him for a minute to Luna and his work; and Oscar's wistful ghost was there. He blinked away tears and barked, "You heard me."

"Yes. I was thinking." The mask came down on Volhontseff's countenance. "About certain difficulties. Calls can be monitored. And we don't know how many spies the enemy has planted in key positions. If a call from the Moon was never sent, how can you be sure that one will ever be received?"

Sevigny teetered back on his heels. "That's right. But damn the universe, we can't do nothing."

"No. I have an idea. Let me simply get in touch with the K'nean Embassy. The hour must be about noon in Paris, the office is open and that circuit includes a scrambler. I will give them the facts and request them to transmit messages elsewhere. You are quite correct about Mars' vital interest in the terraforming work. And on so high a level, they can make direct contact with the others."

"Hm." Sevigny pondered. It sounded good. "Okay. But what about me?"

Volhontseff made a parched chuckle. "You stay here and do not allow me outside. I am in your power, remember."

His fingers danced across the lock on a drawer. It opened and he took out a notebook and riffled through the pages. "Here we are. The unlisted number of the ambassador's private office." At once he closed the book and started dialing. Sevigny moved around the desk to stand at his back.

The screen brightened with the image of a room strangely furnished. A long, squatting figure swung luminous eyes toward the phone. Volhontseff unhooked a vocalizer attachment and began talking.

Sevigny jerked it from his hand. "None of that. I don't understand any Martian language."

"You must trust me," Volhontseff said.

"As far as necessary. No further. Sorry."

Impassive, the ambassador waited.

Volhontseffs narrow shoulders lifted and fell. "No difference, I suppose. Ah... Nyo, we shall use English, if you please. The matter is urgent and critical. Kindly record. I have here an employee of the Luna Corporation with a rather unusual story to relate."

"Proceed," said the transformed voice.

Once again Sevigny went through his narration. At the end, Volhontseff said, "This must be transmitted to the following persons in strictest confidence: the head of the World Safety Corps, the president of the Corporation, the Cytherean ambassador and Mr. Bruno Norris, operations manager in Port Kepler."

The chitinous Martian visage had not stirred. It could not. "Yes," Nyo said, "I grasp your meaning."

Volhontseff hunched forward and said in the most intense tone Sevigny had yet heard from him: "You realize that no time can be lost. My guest and I will remain here, but the situation is obviously unstable. Can you dispatch a diplomatic flier for him? You must have a pair of reliable humans available to man it and fetch him to safety."

Nyo reflected for a while, during which Sevigny's pulse grew loud. "Yes," the Martian said, "I believe that can be done. We will assign someone near you if possible, *exempli gratia* from the San Francisco consulate, so that they can land at your house before dawn. Stand by."

The screen blanked.

Volhontseff put another cigarette between his yellowed fingers. *I just hope he gets his cancer shots regularly,* Sevigny thought.

"Excellent," the small man said. "I expect you need not wait long. Two or three hours, perhaps. Ah...do you suppose that my part in this affair can be—hushed down, is that the idiom? It would simplify matters. But let me prepare a bed for you."

Sevigny shook his head. "No, thanks. I'm strung too tight. Besides, I don't dare sleep."

"As you wish."

"If you want to rack out, though—"

"Not in the least. Come, we shall have breakfast." Volhontseff got to his feet and tugged at Sevigny's arm.

"I'm not hungry."

"I am. You shall watch me eat and possibly gain appetite. Afterward you will no doubt be interested to see some of my Martian relics."

"Take my mind off my troubles, anyway." Sevigny's gaze traveled around the room and lighted on a piece of sculptured crystal on a bookshelf. "What's that?"

"From Illach. Nothing of great value."

"But lovely." The engineer went over to have a closer look.

"Come, I say!" Volhontseff jittered near the door.

Sevigny turned around. A tingle went along his spine. "You're mighty anxious to get me out of here," he said low.

"I am hungry, I told you."

"Well, go eat...Why'd you call the K'neans in particular?"

"I did most of my field work in their area, as you can find out from my publications. I know them best. They are to be trusted."

"I think," Sevigny said experimentally, through a tightened gullet, "we ought to buzz the Cytherean Embassy ourselves, just to make sure."

Volhontseff became waspish. "Ridiculous. That is not only unnecessary now, it is unsafe. I have no scrambler connection to them."

"Why should any of your calls be tapped?" Sevigny retorted. "If the cops suspect I'm here, they'll come in person." He took a pair of giant steps back to the desk. "What are you up to?"

"Get away from my private papers!" Volhontseff yelled. He darted at the engineer, who shoved him staggering back.

"Retro yourself, jim," Sevigny said. "If I'm wrong, I'll apologize. But a hunted man can't take chances."

He picked up the notebook. Volhontseff snatched at it. Sevigny warded him off without effort. The consul turned and ran. Sevigny beat him to the door, closed it and growled, "Were you after a gun?"

Volhontseff recoiled. His chest rose and fell with breathing. Sevigny flipped through the pages. Names, addresses, phone numbers, in Cyrillic script but he knew Russian—

Ercole Baccioco leaped at him, and an Earthwide list of residences. One was the apartment building where he had been a prisoner.

-8-

"So." He stared at the little man's rigid figure. Sweat rolled from beneath his arms. Swiftly, then, he searched, and found Gupta entered. A local hotel had been pencilled under the Benares address.

He stuck the book in his pocket. "All right, Volhontseff," he said. The words fell like iron weights through the night silence. "You belong to the enemy too. And so must that Martian. Tell me about it."

Volhontseff retreated. Sevigny sprang, grabbed a skinny wrist and twisted until the other fell to his knees."You bully!" Volhontseff squalled.

"Not so loud," Sevigny said between his teeth. "Your saboteurs have killed men on Luna. One of them was under my command. I've also lost another friend tonight, and my own life is on the block. Do you expect me to play pattycake with you?"

Volhontseff squirmed and tried to bite. Sevigny cuffed him so that the bald head rocked. "Hold still and talk...quietly!"

A curse answered. Sevigny hesitated. Even now he didn't want to—His mind cometed through darkness, toward understanding.

"The outlines are obvious," he said, word by word, reasoning as he went on. "These different antilunar factions have gotten together. Certain members of them, that is. Probably not many, or men as big as Baccioco and Gupta needn't have dirtied their personal hands with me. The ordinary antilunar person doesn't know about the gang, of course, and'd be shocked if he learned. But religious nuts; those who want, fanatically, to reclaim the last open parts of Earth so as to fill them too with miserable trapped people; those who want contracts for that reclamation; and now K'nea.

"You're an agent of K'nea.

"They're slipping you money under the counter, so you can sit close to Pacific Spacedrome and watch events and exert your influence and help direct any foul play that seems indicated. K'nea is wealthy, one of the first-rank Martian societies. I wouldn't be surprised but what they're financing most of the gang's operations.

"And then there must be someone in the American government, so powerful he can order Federal police to arrest me on a trumped-up charge the moment his good friend Baccioco told him I'd gotten away. Who can probably arrange for me to be killed, or at least have my memory wiped. Who...yes, who must have gotten a warrant issued in the first place, to have my force unit removed. It had to look official, that removing, or there'd've been too much ruckus. But 'reasons of state' has always been the only excuse an overlord needed to order anything, as long as most people believe in the Holy State. Who is he?"

"Let me loose!" Volhontseff cried.

"With what I've now got to go on, my side can find out the answer. You might as well tell me. The President himself?"

"Nyet—"

"Who, then? Or we'll assume it is Edwards, and what'll that do in the election?"

Volhontseff crumpled. Sevigny had to hold him up. "Gilman," he whispered. "Secretary of Resources. Appointed by Edwards, yes, but...I swear he acts for himself!"

"Why? What motive? Same as Gupta? The United States has its problems, but I don't believe they're near as bad as India's...Ah! If the Lunar project is discontinued, there'll be more funds to spend at home. Gilman's bureaucracy will grow. He'll become even bigger than he is. Right?"

"I do not understand these Earthside motives." Volhontseff began to sob. "You are wild beasts, you humans! I only took the pay so I could finish my work. And K'nean policy is not evil, not evil."

"What does K'nea want?" Sevigny snapped the fingers of his free hand. "Never mind. I see for myself. The greatest hurdle the antilunars have to face is the investment already made in the Moon. No matter how much trouble and discredit they heap on us, Earth can scarcely afford to stop. But if K'nea suddenly offered to payoff the shareholders of a failing enterprise, lease the whole satellite and do what little more is necessary to make it over into a new Mars—sure! And that would make K'nea the most powerful society on the home planet by a light-year. They'd dominate their entire species."

"They must protect their philosophy," Volhontseff wept. "The Confederation and the Illachi are more alien to them than you can ever c-c-comprehend."

"Well, Mars will have to solve its own problems," Sevigny said coldly. He let Volhontseff slide to the floor and lie huddled while he paced, back and forth in the cage of the office.

His temples throbbed. Now, more than he had imagined, the information he had was beyond price. And it would be scrubbed out of his brain, by drugs and electric potentials or by death, before sunrise. Nyo's men were plainly supposed to land soon and invite him, unsuspicious, to board their flier. He wouldn't fall for that stunt. But they they need only tell the Federals where he was.

Volhontseff, trembling at his feet, must have a car. That offered escape. He could bind the consul and lay him on the floor with a rug thrown on top.

But a ground vehicle wouldn't get him off Oahu and as soon as the pursuit grasped what had happened they would check the registry and throw out their nets.

Shame hit him in midstride. He halted with an oath. What was he doing, a Woodman, worried about his own precious neck when he had contracted out his loyalty to the Corporation?

I'm no hero—Judas, I'm scared! But there'd be no returning home if I went coward. I can at least try to keep them from murdering my story.

Besides, I've got anyway a couple of hours before the flier arrives.

He flung himself into the chair at the desk and searched Volhontseff's private directory. En route, he was aware of surprise when his glance fell on Maura Soemantri's name. He'd assumed she was imported to beguile him and had used a pseudonym; but no, there she was with a town address. Well, the organization probably kept girls like her on the payroll in most major cities, to use on local politicians and such...The Cytherean Embassy wasn't noted. Why should it be, at that? The clans were apart from this power grapple. By the same token, though. their diplomatic office must be free of double agents.

He dialed Paris, got the number, and put the call through. An Earthified young man regarded him with shock. *I must look like a derailed hamburger,* Sevigny realized, *Dirty, bristly, unkempt, red-eyed, and not even the memory of a binge to show for it.* Curtly, he identified himself.

"Samuel Craik, Clan Duneland of Duneland," the young man said with elaborate formality. "At your service."

"Who's the highest ranking person I can talk to at once?"

Craik looked pained. "Really, clansman, when you aren't even in proper garb—"

"All right," Sevigny sighed. "You record my message. I warn you right off that you won't believe a word. But play it for your superiors. Have them check with the Luna Corporation office on the Moon. That's the main thing I ask you: pass the tape on to Bruno Norris in Port Kepler, and make bloody damn sure that he himself gets it." He drew a long breath and intoned: "This I lay on you for the right and honor of the clans of Venus."

Craik looked still more unhappy. *Oh, Lord, I'll bet that fop thinks the Word is a quaint barbarian custom,* Sevigny groaned to himself. He launched into the account.

"Clansman!" Craik protested after a few minutes."Do you feel well?"

"I told you you wouldn't believe me," Sevigny gritted. "Now hold still and let me finish."

The violence that churned in him suddenly spouted forth an idea. He gasped. Somehow he managed to keep talking while he thought with more and more excitement about it.

Why not? Secure Volhontseff out of sight and tell 'em he had to go on an errand. If there isn't a gun in the house, there must be some of those beautiful Martian dart knives. Nyo's agents won't know that I know their purpose. I can board the flier with them. Its diplomatic registry will pass it through national checkpoints without inspection. Once we're aloft, them not yet ready to take me and not expecting any trouble—

Laughter coughed silent in him. *A good honest fight, a clear track to Paris, and won't brother Craik be surprised when I walk in on him!*

"—changed clothes," his tongue formed, "and got to the consulate here—"

The door clicked shut again.

Sevigny was halfway there before he realized what had happened. Volhontseff! The withered little devil had crawled out when he wasn't looking!

The door was locked. He palmed the plate and it swung open with Inquisition slowness.The moment he could, he squeezed through; and tumbled flat on his belly. Volhontseff had laid half a dozen Martian staffs there for him to trip on.

The tiny shape was at the front entrance. "Stop!" Sevigny bawled. The door began to gape. Sevigny grabbed a staff and threw it like a spear. It shattered where Volhontseff had been a half second before. He scampered from sight, yammering louder than seemed possible.

No use chasing him. He must already have awakened his neighbors. The police would arrive in minutes.

Sevigny hurried back to the phone. "What's gone wrong now?" Craik asked superciliously.

"Record this!" Sevigny overran him. "I know these are conspiring—Nyo, the K'nean ambassador; Ercole Baccioco of Eureclam; Krishnamurti Lal Gupta of

Benares and the Indian Conservationist Party; Gilman, the United States Secretary of Resources; the Fatimite Brotherhood. They want—" He outlined the scheme. "In the name of God and honor, *get* them investigated!"

He snapped off the set and ran back through the house. Maybe his message would spread. And maybe it wouldn't. He had to stay free and make sure. Besides, he himself was the most important piece of evidence there was. Once repeated under truth drug, in the presence of so many Safety Corps officers that a majority were bound to be honest, his accusation was certain to start their machine.

First, though, I've got to start a *different machine. If time allows.*

A rear door led directly into the garage. Volhontseff's car was impressive to see. But Sevigny was interested only in getting at the prime circuit. No chance of finding the key before the cops showed. However, any Cytherean must needs have mechanical skills, and there were tools on a wall rack. He flung back the hood and fairly ripped the cover off the pilot. Hotwire here? No. Here? The engine awoke. He sat down behind the wheel and eased in power. The garage door opened.

He was steering manually now, and that was illegal in town. Any prowl car that passed near would fail to register an active pilot and take off after him. So he couldn't go many kilometers.

But away!

He backed out into the street precisely as a police vehicle rounded the corner. "Okay," he spat, "want to race?" The motor roared with energies.

Downhill he went in a shriek of wind and of pursuing siren, squealed around a corner, zigzagged up another twisting way as fast as he had once taken a gun car up a mountainside at the Battle of Jerry's Landing, swooped among the trees of a small park on his airblast—

It was unfair to pit a lifetime driver on pavements against a Cytherean. In minutes Sevigny moved alone, slowly and quietly, through the nighted tangletown.

But the ether was acrackle with calls, he knew, and every road would soon be blocked.

What about those mountains, humping high in the north against a sky that had begun ever so faintly to pale? Honolulu had sprawled far into them, but there should be brush-grown empty areas yet, where a man might skulk...No. He'd never make it. His auto had to be abandoned fast. In any event, whatever wild section remained couldn't be so large that a determined search with modern manhunting equipment wouldn't soon flush him out. Nor would he have any way of knowing what went on in the world.

Left, right! Left, right! drummed senselessly through his head. *Good soldiers can always find cover when enemies menace their life. Our loveable sergeant has said it. Take cover, my lads, with his wife. Left, right! Left, right! I know you're a man of Clan Woodman, I known you are gallant and true.* So *don't turn your back in our army; they'll give you the royallest —*

Sevigny slapped the Halt switch. He had half unconsciously been looking from side to side. When he saw what he wanted, dim in starlight, he recognized what it was. A garage stood open and empty. Some night owl was going to be surprised when he got home. With luck, that wouldn't be for hours; and meanwhile the hounds would cast about in vain for this car.

He slid it inside. For a space he slumped, and a tide of exhaustion rose in him. *Venus,* he thought, *morning star, even the tenecs of your desert have a place to lair. But you are forty million kilometers away. Goodby, Venus.*

And then the remembrance came to him, and he sat up with a strangled yell.

-9-

Pre-dawn light seeped through a window at the end of the tenth floor corridor. Sevigny stepped from the elevator and walked down its lushly carpeted length. On the way he noticed a mail slot. *Good, I won't have to wait till night to mail my letter. Any time that no one's around, I—we—can slip out.* Door No. 14 came into view. The directory in the lobby had given him that information.

Now for the tricky part. His walk had been long but uneventful. The police search was concentrated in the Manoa Road area, where there were roofs for a forester to hide on while men went beneath, gardens and byways for him to slip through. Afterward a city map taken from the auto had guided him on a route avoiding important streets. Doubtless an alarm would be broadcast with the morning news, his description and perhaps a drawing based on what those who knew him could tell. Or even a photograph, if Gupta had thought to take one while he lay unconscious. But to passersby in the last couple of hours he had only been a lone walker, belated or early as the case might be, nothing to take heed of. If afterward someone remembered him, little harm in a metropolis like this.

The next few minutes were what counted.

The automatic doorbell had been turned off for the night. He shoved the manual button. The chime sounded remote, not quite real. He hunched his shoulders and dropped his chin. With the help of the car mirror he had rubbed grime into his hair, brows and sprouting beard. That, a change of clothes and posture, a lowered face, a disguised voice, might get him past the viewer.

If not, he was done.

"Wha' you wan'?" The voice from the speaker was blurred with sleepiness. Fine.

Aloud, with the best Russian accent he could muster: "I am from Oleg Volhontseff. Please to let me in. I have a very fast message from him."

"Ah-yaw...urn...why di'n'e call?"

"He could not. I shall explain. It has to do with the Martian you know of, him from K'nea."

"Oh! One minute, please."

He gathered his muscles. So his guess was right. Volhontseff must have gotten in touch with Baccioco and Gupta by now, but not lesser agents like Rashid and the girl...

The door opened. He hurtled through. Maura's lips parted to scream. He got a hand over them, held her locked in a wrestler's grip and hissed, "Keep still or I'll snap your spine. I haven't much to lose, you know!"

The door closed. He guided her to a chair in the luxurious room, released her, but kept one hand on her neck, letting her feel its weight and hardness.

"Don," she shuddered.

"I don't want to hurt you," he said with entire honesty. "Cooperate and you'll be okay. I need a hiding place. Where better than with a member of the opposition?"

"You can't! It's not possible, you've got to go away!"

"Quiet down, I said. You must be able to see I can't leave. Your friends sicced the Federal police onto me the moment I'd gone. But as I hoped, they didn't wake you later to tell you I'd had a run-in with Volhontseff. No reason for them to do so. I used his name to establish my bona fides here." Sevigny let go of her, crossed to the door and shoved a heavy couch across. "There. You won't run loose as he did."

He turned around, wondering how wild his appearance was. "I repeat, I've no intention of hurting you," he said. "The most I'll do is tie and gag you while I sleep or am otherwise busy. I'm efficient at knots, by the way. I suppose you've got food in the kitchen to last the several days I'll need until this mess is straightened out. We'll stay inside, and I hope the TriV programs aren't too dull."

"No—" She saw her robe had come open, and gathered it with a calculatedly provocative movement. He was not unaffected, but had no urge to be fooled twice. "Don," she pleaded, "I can't stay here that long. I've got appointments."

"Call and cancel them. Say you're sick, or have to go out of town, or something. I'll stand by in easy reach."

"You wouldn't harm me if I got them to come here, would you? Not really."

He grinned. "Okay, my lady. A deterrent has to be credible, and clansmen don't attack women. But I plan to cobble together some weapons from whatever I can find around this place. If the enemy finds me, they'll have to force their way in, and I'll put up one Satan of a fight. There's an excellent chance you'll get caught in the fire. Is that believable?"

She swallowed and nodded.

"I don't need too long," he said. "We are going to venture out once, very briefly, in half an hour or so, to post a letter I'll write, addressed to my boss at his private apartment in Port Kepler. It should get on the returning packet tomorrow sunrise. If I know him, he won't need much time to swing into action." He paused. "And then, Maura. you may be damn glad I was here, to put in a word for you—or look the other way while you catch a jet to Djakarta

She considered him. A certain coolness descended on her. "Djakarta might be a good idea at that," she said, "because I was born Mary Stafford in Chicago." He choked. Cat-adaptable, she laughed. "Or maybe Venus, hm?"

"God help Venus," he muttered in awe.

She rose and said practically, "You must be starved. I'll fix breakfast. Afterward—"

Her gaze dwelt on him. "Frankly," she said, "the TriV programs *are* dull."

* * * *

"So I lay doggo till you appeared personally on the newscast to vouch that the charges against me had been dropped," Sevigny concluded.

"What was this person's name you were with?" the Buffalo asked.

"Never mind," Sevigny said. The Buffalo gave him a look, shrugged and remarked nothing but: "You seem to've had a tough time. I haven't often seen a man so pooped."

"It could've been worse," Sevigny answered dreamily.

The Buffalo blew out his cheeks in an enormous snort and wallowed back into the lounger. "Whoof, but I'll be glad to get back!" he said. "I'm far too old and fat for Earth weight. Fuel me, will you?"

"You must've been working pretty hard too," Sevigny sympathized. He opened the liquor cabinet and poured two drinks of Glenlivet. The Goldwater had seemed swank when he first got here, but that was before he was introduced to the Andromeda Suite.

"I've seen damned little on the news, though, about this whole business," he complained. "Isn't the investigation getting anywhere?"

"All kinds of places," the Buffalo replied. "But don't expect ultra-sensational revelations. Enough little fish will get netted to put a crimp in the gang. The big ones will mostly go free, as usual."

"Huh? But—

"Calm down and give me my booze. What did you think would happen? There are high-explosive international and interplanetary implications. A first-class scandal would raise too much partisanship, too many hard feelings. They'd fight back almighty mean if they got desperate: same as you did, if you recall. So—ah, thanks." The Buffalo drank deep, belched and wiped his mouth with the back of one hairy paw. "The Chinese had a proverb in their warlord era, that you should always leave your enemy a line of retreat. We'll do best not to pry too deep. Let some of those jims retire gracefully from public life. Let the rest know we're watching 'em close and they'd better reel in their horns. Make just one or two stiff examples of secondary figures, to show we mean business. Who're your candidates for that? Eenie, meenie, minie, moe."

"But the others'll try again!" Sevigny protested.

"Some of 'em might. I sort of doubt it—they're likelier to jump on your bandwagon. But they might. We're forewarned now, though, thanks largely to you. We didn't know, before, how strong and piratish the antlunar coalition was. Hah! Wait till they see ours!"

"What?" Sevigny nearly dropped his tumbler.

"Of course. Remember, we still have to keep down the honest antilunars, who had nothing to do with the gang. But there's a bucketful of organizations with a vested interest in Moon development. Like the various national political parties who voted to establish the Corporation while they were in office. Like different bureaucrats—space commissioners, for instance. Like the companies which stand to make a profit when Lunar exploitation really gets going. Like the Great Confederation of Y. Like, maybe, a few million plain, ordinary people that daydream about some uncluttered place to go. We had an active lobby in the beginning, to start the project. But then we let it fall apart. Now we'll build a new one, stronger than ever, since the work is in fact well under way. We'll propagandize, and get our personal boys elected, and pressure their colleagues, and logroll, and drop a tiny bribe here and there where that'll do some good, and—" the Buffalo laughed, earthquake style—"all in all, the other coalition ain't gonna have a marshmallow's chance on Mercury!"

Sevigny went to the window and stared downward. The street below crawled with dwarfed traffic. '"I suppose you know best," he said in weariness. "Me, I only want to get back to work."

"That's what I was talking about, son," the Buffalo boomed. "Fitting you and me into our proper slots. Hey, don't look so bitter. If your chin dropped a centimeter more we could use it for a 'dozer blade. As soon as the Corps gets through with you and you've had a rest—I know a place in Canada, sho'nuff forest preserve, set aside for billionaires and you—back you go to the air mines. Now drink up and let's go eat!"

Sevigny found himself grinning. The tumblers clinked together.

Say It with Flowers

Whiskey Johnny was eighteen hours out of Sam's when her radar registered another ship. There was no doubt about that. A natural object, a meteorite or asteroid tumbling through the Belt, even a comet falling inward from near-infinity, could never have had such a vector as the computer printed out. And the vessel could hardly be anything but North American: hostile.

The pilot uttered expert obscenities. They bounced around his ears, in the tiny, thrumming cockpit where he sat. He punched for distance and velocity at closest approach, as if the keys under his fingers were noses in a barroom battle The answer was unpleasantly small. However, that assumed that he himself continued acceleration. If he went free...yes, better. The enemy craft—a big one, the radar said—was itself under power, so it would gain speed with respect to him...

To reduce his detectability, he cut the Emetts and throttled his nuclear generator down to a minimum. The scoopship yielded to the pull of the sun, shrunken and brilliant to starboard. Her path did not curve much. She had already built up enough velocity to swing in a flat hyperbola that would take her out of the Solar System were it not modified. But she was, now, in free fall.

So was her pilot, since he had shut off the internal field generators. He floated in his seat harness, in a quiet so deep and sudden that he heard the blood beat through his own veins. A fan came on automatically, to keep fresh air moving past him, but that whirr only emphasized the silence. He peered out the inertrans canopy as if to see the patrolling warship from Earth. Of course he couldn't, at those distances. Stars crowded the blackness, unwinking and winter-cold; the Milky Way girdled the universe with diamond dust; Jupiter blazed enormous, not many astronomical units to port.

No asteroids were visible to the naked eye. Those clustered in the vicinity of Sam's lay far behind. Pallas, where *Whiskey Johnny* was bound, lay hours ahead, even at the high acceleration of which a scoopship was capable. As for the rest of the Belt—well, there are thousands of worldlets, millions of meteorites, but space is huge and they spread thinly.

The pilot fished a cigar from his breast pocket. Presently the cockpit air was as thick as that of Venus, and nearly as poisonous. He didn't mind. He had spent half of his forty Earth-years digging and building on raw rocks where only the tough could hope to survive. His face was so craggy that the assorted scars looked natural. Half open, his frayed old Long John revealed a chest like a barrel; through the hair showed an enormous tattoo in enormously bad taste, a comet which was also a flag. The naked woman who danced on his right biceps was probably in worse taste yet. His left forearm was shaven, which indicated that the design of roses and lilies inked into its skin was very recent. Some people never grow up.

He puffed hard. It was a strain, waiting. He tried to think of matters more pleasant than the war. Like, say, that bender he went on back at Sam's, shortly before he started on this mission. Trouble was, the wingding had been too good. Several girls...yeah...and then afterward Billy Kirk showed up with a bottle in either fist...and then everything was blank, until he woke with volcanoes in his head and those silly posies on his arm. *Why* had he elected that design?

Well, there'd be a doctor at Pallas who could take it off for him. And plenty of booze and wild, wild women. The colonists had fleet enough to defend their capital and its supply lines. Otherwise they could only hold strong points like Sam's. But they were scattered through millions of kilometers, on hundreds of asteroids; their ships were manned with deadly skill; little by little, they wore down their one-time masters. Meanwhile, on Earth, their diplomats intrigued in various capitals. Other nations would bring pressure to bear on North America. Eventually the Republic would be free to shape its own destiny.

The pilot didn't think in any such high-flown terms. He'd just gotten sick and tired of being taxed to support a bureaucracy which seemed interested only in regulating his life for him.

The radio buzzed. A call on the universal band.

"Huh!" he growled. "I'm on to that stunt, buster. You broadcast, and I turn up my receiver, and you detect that." He went on to suggest, in some detail, what the American could do with his 'caster.

Although—wait! The signal was coming in much too strong. Either the warship had gotten close, or it was sending a maser beam. Sweat prickled forth on his skin. He got busy with his instruments.

Both cases were true. The ship had locked a beam onto his vessel and it was coming about to make rendezvous.

So its sky-sweeping radars had picked him up after all, and never lost him again.

No choice, after that, but to answer. He flipped a switch. "Scoopship *Whiskey Johnny* receiving call," he said in a flat basso.

"NASS *Chicago* transmittin'. Prepare to match velocities."

"What the double blue hell is this? I'm minding my own business."

"I doubt that," drawled the Texan voice. "You're from Sam's for Pallas. Don't bother denyin' it. We got plenty good data on your path. So you're a courier."

"You're out of your ever-loving mind," said the asterite, in rather more pungent language.

"What else would you be, son, in a small fast boat like that? Listen. don't try to get rid of your dispatches. We're near enough to register anything you pitch out the air lock. As of this minute, you're a prisoner of war and subject to discipline."

Kirk warned me about narcoquizzes. And if I keep on claiming to be a civilian, I could be shot as a spy.

"Identify yourself," said the voice.

"Lieutenant Robert Flowers, Space Force of the Asteroid Republic," the pilot snapped.

Briefly, furiously, he considered making a run for it. He could out-accelerate a capital ship by several gees. Probably he could evade a missile. But no. The warhead needn't burst very close for radiation to kill him. Or a laser gun might track him and gnaw through to his engine. Flowers cursed some more and donned the battered officer's cap which put him legally in uniform.

"Well, you rebels call it a republic," said the Texan. "O.K., punch these here instructions into your autopilot. And then you might as well relax. You'll be locked away for quite a spell, I reckon."

The cruiser was a great ovoid, dully agleam in the harsh spatial sunlight. Rifles poked dinosaurian from their turrets, missile launchers gaped like moths. The scoopship edged inward, dwarfed.

"Cease drive," came the order. They weren't taking chances on a suicide plunge.

"Smelly" Flowers obeyed. He stuck a fresh cigar between his teeth and got up a good head of steam.

A geegee beam reeled him in. A boat hatch opened. He felt the slight shock and heard the clang as *Whiskey Johnny* entered a cradle. Now steel enclosed him. Air whistled back to the compartment. Four bluejackets appeared, and motioned him out. He slid back the canopy, which he had already unsealed, and jumped down. Smoke gushed from his mouth, into the nearest face. The man gasped and staggered.

"All right, funny boy," said the ensign in charge. "Give me that."

"Huh?" cried Flowers. "Can't a joe even have a smoke?"

"Not if I say he can't." The ensign yanked the cigar from the prisoner's lips, threw it to the deck and ground it under his heel. "Frisk him, Justus. Iwasaki, get his dispatches."

Flowers submitted. *I could take all these pups in a rough-and-tumble, and Judas, I'd love to,* he thought. *But their sidearms are a bit much.*

Iwasaki, in the cockpit, lifted a small steel tube. "Would this be it, sir?"

"I suppose so. Toss." The ensign caught it. "Commander Ulstad will know. But search the whole craft and report anything unusual. You others come with me."

They went unspeaking down long bleak corridors. The crewmen they passed stared at Flowers—for the most part, without the ensign's hostility. This had been a gentlemen's war, on the whole, and the asterite cause had its sympathizers in North America. After all, the colonists were American, too, and the rebellion was for the sake of that individual freedom to which lip service was still paid at home.

Probably the ensign was impatient to get back to his girl.

A murmur went through the metal, a slight shiver was added to the steady one gee of the interior field. The ship was under weigh again, returning to its patrol orbit.

At the end of the walk, Flowers was urged through a door. He found himself in a small office. It was furnished with proper naval austerity, but a few scenic views of Earth were pasted on the bulkheads, and the desk bore pictures of wife and children. The man behind was lean, erect, gray at the temples, his long face reasonably kind.

However, onto this cabin there opened an interrogation lab.

The ensign saluted. "Reporting with prisoner, sir. He had this aboard his boat."

"Let me see." Commander Ulstad—must be him, and he must be Intelligence—reached for the tube. He unscrewed the cap and shook out a scroll of shiny plastic. Spreading it on his desk, he looked for a moment at the blank surface.

"Yes, evidently his dispatches," he murmured. "Magnetic, what else?" He rose and went into his laboratory. Flowers saw him thread the scroll into a scanner. The machine clicked to itself. A screen flickered with shifting dots, lines, curves.

Flowers knew, in a general way, how the system worked: analogously to an old-fashioned tape recording. The visual pattern of the message was encoded in a series of magnetic pulses which imposed a corresponding pattern on iron particles embedded in the plastic. Of course, for military purposes you first enciphered the message and then put a scrambler in the recording circuit. The result couldn't even be seen, let alone cleared, without a descrambler in the playback.

Ulstad frowned and made adjustments. Realization jarred through Flowers: *He expects to project the thing. Blast, and befoul! Somehow they've learned our scrambler patterns.*

The officer tried several other settings. Nonsensical images gibed at him. Flowers sank into a chair. A slow, happy grin spread across his mouth. So the Republic had gotten wise and adopted a new code, huh? Gr-r-reat!

"Well." Ulstad returned. Excitement barely tinged his voice. "We seem to have caught a rather big fish." He punched the intercom. "Commander Ulstad here. Get me Captain Thomas."

He sat down and held forth a pack of cigarettes. "Would you like a smoke, Lieutenant Flowers?" he invited.

The asterite leered at the ensign, who stood in the doorway with his guards. "How about that, chum?" he said, and accepted. "Thanks."

Ulstad turned on a recorder. "You understand I have to ask you some questions," he said. "Please state your correct name, rank, and serial number."

"Robert Henry Flowers, Space Force lieutenant, number…uh, I never can remember the mucking thing." He read it off his ID bracelet. That was one more bit of junk he meant to throw into a sunbound orbit, when the war was over and he could be his own man again.

Ulstad smiled. "You don't look like anyone named Flowers," he remarked.

"Yeah, I know. That's how come I've got this busted nose and such. You should'a seen those other bums, though. I don't take being razzed."

"You won't be. I have every intention of treating you with the respect due a commissioned officer." The intercom buzzed. "Excuse me."

The cruiser's captain spoke out of it. "Yes, Commander, what do you want?"

"About this courier we just captured, sir," Ulstad told him, "I can't read his dispatches. That means the enemy has changed the scrambler code again, and no doubt the ciphers as well."

"So?"

"So in the first place, sir, the enemy probably realizes that we have cracked his last set of codes. He doesn't change them often or lightly, when word about new arrangements has to be sent over lines of communication as long as his. Therefore, our own GHQ has to know: Then second, this particular message must be delivered for analysis as fast as possible. I respectfully suggest that we shoot a speedster off to Luna Base at once."

"Um-m-m," grunted the captain. "Don't like that. Too many asterite frigates skulking around."

"Well, then, we'd better make rendezvous with a ship able to defend herself, and send the message by her."

"We've mighty few ships to spare, Commander." The captain paused. "But this is important. I'll contact CINCOBELT when our position allows, and they'll see what can be done."

"Thank you, sir. Over and out." Ulstad turned off the intercom.

His gaze went to Flowers, who had gone rigid, and he nodded. "Yes," he said, "we have computers at Luna Base which can discover any scrambler pattern and then go on to break any cipher. Not too easily, I confess. You have some fiendishly clever people in your code section. But the machines can always grind out the answer, by sheer electronic patience."

Flowers recollected some remarks overheard when he reported for briefing. He hadn't paid much attention. But…yeah, asterite Intelligence must suspect the truth. There had been comings and goings of late, couriers bringing secret word from Pallas to Sam's as well as to other Republican centers. Only the higher-ups knew what that word amounted to. A warning?

His bemusement vanished in a puff of indignation. Space was too vast for the North Americans to blockade very effectively those places too well-armed to capture. Most boats got through. Why did *his* have to be among the unlucky ones?

"I suppose you have no idea what message you were conveying," said Ulstad conversationally.

"Think I'd tell you if I did?" bristled Flowers.

"Yes, under drugs and brain stimulation," said Ulstad.

"Well, I don't know!"

"We'll find out."

"You rust-eaten mutant—"

"Please." Ulstad waved back one of the guards, who had taken a forward step with anger on his face. His own tone stayed mild. "The process doesn't hurt or do any damage. We're fighting this war by the Geneva convention, the same as you people are. But still, we consider it the suppression of an insurrection: which gives us the right to use police procedures. Your interrogators do likewise to our boys, without that legality."

Flowers finished his cigarette and flipped the butt into a disposal. "You can stuff those quibbles," he said. "Get on with your dirty work so I can get out of here."

"What's your hurry, Lieutenant? You'll be aboard the *Chicago* for a number of hours, till we can arrange your transfer to a supply ship. And it will only be going to Vesta, where you'll sit out the war in a prison camp. Dull place. We'll do our best to make you happy, on this ship. Cool your motors. Enjoy our hospitality. Would you like some coffee?"

Flowers swallowed his rage. Doubtless Ulstad was trying to disarm him, but the fellow seemed decent at heart. "Druther have booze," he said.

"Sorry. Me, too, but regulations." Ulstad crossed his legs and leaned back in his chair. "Let's get acquainted. I'm always interested to meet a colonist. You weren't born out here, were you?"

Flowers had no wish to spill military information; not that he had much. But by gabbing a little while, he postponed the humiliation of narco. Besides—"Brooklyn," he said. "Moved to space at eighteen. Uh, my parents are still alive. You wouldn't know about them, would you?"

"'Fraid not. I'm from Wisconsin myself. Your folks must be all right, though. The government doesn't discriminate against anyone who happens to have rebel kinfolk, as long as they keep their own noses clean." Ulstad kindled another cigarette. "Really, we're not the monsters your more overheated propagandists claim. In fact, our society is a good deal more benevolent than yours."

"Yeah. So benevolent that I felt smothered, every visit I made back home."

"De gustibus non disputandum est, which personally I translate as 'There is no disputing that Gus is in the east.' You weren't a Jupiter diver in civilian life, I am sure of that."

"No, a rockjack. Construction gang superintendent, if you must know. We only use scoopships for messenger boats because they're fast. Their regular pilots are too good for that kind of job. Do better at captaining warcraft."

"How well I realize that," Ulstad sighed. "I wonder, though, why you don't send more stuff directly by maser."

Flowers clammed up.

Ulstad grinned. "All right, I'll tell you," he said. "First, our side has too good a chance of intercepting a beam; and evidently your Intelligence suspects we can break your cryptograms. A courier flits away from the ecliptic plane and probably makes a safe trip. Second, if we really can use your own ciphers, and you rely too much on radio, we could send misleading messages to your commanders." He shrugged. "Of course, the courier system ties up boats that might be put to better use elsewhere. But then, it ties up a lot of our fleet on patrol duty, so honors are even."

"Not quite," Flowers snapped. "Especially after the last battle."

"The engagement near Sam's you mean? I take it you were there?"

"I sure was, chum."

"In what capacity?" drawled Ulstad.

Flowers crammed on a deceleration vector. "Never mind. It's enough that you took a licking."

"We'd at least like to know what happened to those of our ships which never reported back. Were all of them utterly destroyed?"

"I suppose so."

Ulstad leaned across the desk. "Even if you weren't told officially, you may have heard something." His smile was wistful. "I'm interested for private reasons. A nephew on the *Vega.*"

"Sorry. I can't help you, though."

"We'll find out about that."

"Go ahead!"

"Very well, Lieutenant." Ulstad rose. "If you please?"

Flowers tensed himself. His entire being rebelled. But he stole a glance behind, and saw that the ensign would be only too glad to use force. Like, say a pistol barrel against the prisoner's head.

Flowers got to his feet. "Look me up after the war," he invited. "I know some back alleys where the cops won't interfere."

"I might at that," said the ensign.

"Control yourself, young man," said Ulstad. He led the way into the lab. "If you will lie down on this couch, Lieutenant—"

The anesthetic shot took rapid hold and Flowers spiraled into a darkness full of voices.

Afterward he lay with closed eyes, letting will and strength creep back. He must be recovering faster than was usual, because he heard Ulstad say, as if across a black gulf:

"Nothing to speak of. He's what he claims to be, a big dumb rockjack who ordinarily commands an engineer group. I suppose they dispatched him precisely because he doesn't have any worthwhile information. And I hope the poor devil doesn't go stir crazy in prison camp, with so few inner resources."

"What'll we do with him now, sir?"

"Oh, lock him in a spare cabin. How long will he be on your hands?"

"I checked that, sir. We'll make contact with the transport in five hours."

"He'll only need one meal from us, then. Inform the cook. Regular mess time is O.K., three hours hence." Ulstad chuckled. "Maybe I do him an injustice, calling him an ignorant boor. His cussing under dope was sheer poetry!"

Save for a bunk, the cabin was bare. Tiny, comfortless, atremble with the energies of the ship, it surrounded Flowers like a robot womb. That was his first thought as he struggled back to consciousness.

Then, through the racking stutter of a pulse run wild, he knew that hands lifted his head off the deck. He gasped for breath. Sweat drenched his coverall, chill and stinking. Fear reflexes turned the universe into horror. Through blurred vision, he looked up at the bluejacket who squatted to cradle his head.

"Flip that intercom, Pete!" the North American was saying. "Get hold of the doc. Fast!"

Flowers tried to speak, but could only rattle past the soreness in his throat.

The other guard, invisible to him, reported: "The prisoner, sir. We heard him call out and then fall. He was unconscious when we opened the door. Come to in a couple of minutes, but he's cold to touch and got a heartbeat like to bust his ribs."

"Possibly cardiac," said the intercom. "Carry him to sickbay. I'll be there."

Flowers tried to relax in the arms of the young men and bring his too rapid breathing under control. That wasn't easy. When they laid him on an examination bench, amidst goblin-eyed instruments, he must force his spine to unarch.

The medical officer was a chubby man who poked him with deft fingers while reeling off, "Chest pains? Shortness of breath? Ever had any seizures before?" He signaled an orderly to attach electrodes.

"No. No. I ache all over, but—"

"Cardiogram normal, aside from the tachycardia," the doctor read off the printouts. "Encephalogram…hm-m-m, hard to tell, not epileptiform, probably just extreme agitation. Neurogram shows low-level pain activity. Take a blood sample, Collins." He ran his palms more thoroughly over abdomen, chest, and throat. "My God," he muttered, "where did you get those tattoos?" His gaze sharpened. "Redness here, under the chin. Sore?"

"Uh-huh," whispered Flowers.

"What happened to you?"

"I dunno. Started feeling bad. Blacked out."

A chemical analyzer burped and extruded a strip of paper. The orderly ripped it off. "Blood pH quite high, sir," he read. "Everything else negative."

"Well—" The doctor rubbed his chin. "We can't do more except take an X-ray. A warcraft isn't equipped like a clinic." He nodded at Flowers. "Don't worry. You'll transfer to the other ship in half an hour or so, and I understand she's going almost directly to Vesta. The camp there has adequate facilities. Though you look a little better already."

"What…might this…'a been?" Flowers managed to ask.

"My guess," said the doctor, "is an allergic reaction to something you ate. That can overstimulate the vagus nerve and produce these other symptoms. You asterites never see a good many Terrestrial foods, and this navy prides itself on its menus. I'll find out what went into your dinner, including seasonings, and give you a list. Avoid those things, till the culprit has been identified, and you may have no more trouble."

Flowers lay back while they X-rayed him. That was negative, too. The doctor said he could stay where he was, under guard, 'til transfer time. He stared at the overhead and concentrated on getting well.

The *Chicago* slid into orbit and halted her Emetts. The doctor came back with his list. "You appear to be in much better shape," he said. "Got some color, and your breath and pulse are nearly normal. Think you can walk?"

"I'll try." Flowers sat up. Slowly he swung his legs off the bench, put feet to deck, and raised himself. He staggered. Leaning on the bench, head hung low, he mumbled, "I get dizzy."

"O.K., we'll take you on a stretcher," said one of his guards. "Captain's orders are to get you out fast so this ship can proceed to where she belongs."

Flowers would have enjoyed the ride had there not been such a tension gathering in him.

At the air lock where they went, two sidearmed men from the transport waited. "What the hell?" exclaimed the right-hand man.

A bearer related the situation. The newcomer made a spitting noise. "You're mighty tender with a rebel," he said.

"Oh, ease off, Joe," said his companion. "They're not bad fellows. Hell, after we've beaten some sense into their thick heads, I've half a mind to quit the service and come live in the Belt myself."

Joe spoke a bad word, but took his end of the stretcher. They passed through a jointube, into the boat. As Flowers had expected, this was merely a gig, with a single cabin where the pilot sat in the forward end. You don't bring full-size ships together if you can avoid it: too ticklish an operation. The freighter lay several kilometers off; he glimpsed its bulky shape through a port, among the constellations.

His new guards put his stretcher down in the aisle between the seats, dogged the air lock, and retracted the jointube. The pilot tickled his controls and the boat slid smoothly away from the *Chicago.* The bluejackets returned to sit on either side of their prisoner.

"How you feel?" asked the man who had sympathized.

"Like a court-martialed kitten," Flowers whispered.

The man laughed. His companion still looked sour.

"I'd like to try sitting, though, if you'll help me," Flowers went on.

"Sure you ought to?"

"Well, I might be able to board your ship under my own power, but I'd better practice first."

"O.K. Gimme a hand, Joe."

Both guards bent close to the lying man. Flowers laid an arm across either pair of shoulders. They raised him.

His hands slid to the backs of their necks. His gorilla arms cracked the two skulls together.

They lurched, stunned, blood running from their scalps. Flowers snatched the nearest pistol from its holster and sprang into the aisle.

"Hands up or I shoot," he rapped.

To the pilot: "Cut the drive. Now. Get out o' that chair."

Oaths ionized the atmosphere. He grinned. "I'm a desperate man," he said. "As soon kill you as look at you. Maybe rather. Git!"

The pilot got. Flowers approached him in the aisle. His hands were aloft, his belly exposed. Flowers' unoccupied fist rocketed forward to the solar plexus. As the pilot doubled, Flowers hooked him in the jaw. He fell.

The man called Joe reached for his gun. He was slow about it, and Flowers clopped him. With some regret, the asterite gave the same treatment to the other man, who had been nice to him. Before consciousness could return, he trussed all three with their belts and shirts and harnessed them in chairs.

The radio buzzer sounded hysterical. Flowers vaulted to the pilot board and clicked the receiver switch. "What's going on there?" bawled a voice.

"Listen," Flowers said. "This is the asterite. I've got your men prisoners. They're not hurt to speak of. But I'm bound home. You can stop me, sure—by destroying this boat. That'll cost you three North American lives, because I'm not issuing any spacesuits. It don't seem like much of a bargain. Better just say good riddance to me."

Words squawked. Flowers used the time to swing the gig around and apply a vector in the general direction of Pallas. Later he would calculate an exact path; right now he wanted nothing more intensely than distance between himself and the guns of the *Chicago.*

His victims awoke. He made them speak, to prove to their buddies they were alive. Cruiser and freighter dwindled beyond naked-eye vision. Stars blazed everywhere about.

Ulstad's tones leaped over the kilometers, cool and almost amused. "I'm not sure we ought to let a man of your capabilities escape, Lieutenant. My fault. I took you for a stupid laborer. I should have remembered, stupid people don't survive in space."

Flowers gulped. "I'm no prize, Commander. But you got three good men here. I'm sorry I had to be rough with them, and I'll treat them as decent as I can."

"How did you manage this caper?"

"Tell you after the war."

Ulstad actually laughed. "Very well," he said: "Seeing that we have no alternative except to fire on our own men, Captain Thomas has decided to let you go. After all, we have your dispatch, which is the important thing. I'm unmilitary to say this, but...good luck."

"Same to you," Flowers husked. He broke the beam and concentrated on driving the boat.

The revolutionaries were so short of manpower that quite a few women held high rank. Colonel Adler of Intelligence was among them. In uniform, her hair cut short, she didn't much suggest the opera star who had once dazzled the capitals of Earth. But her tunic couldn't flatten out every curve, and Flowers was in some respects a very suggestible man

He leaned back in the swivel chair, flourished his cigar, and tried to be modest. "Faking sickness was easy," he said. "I counted time till I knew the transfer boat 'ud be along pretty soon."

"How did you count?" she asked.

"Oh, I sang songs in my head. I'd timed that years ago. Often useful to know how long, say 'The Ballad of Eskimo Nell' takes—Well, never mind that, ma'm. Anyhow, then I started hyperventilating, Do that a while and you get the doggonedest symptoms. When my body chemistry was way off kilter, I let out a yell, then pressed my carotid arteries till I passed out."

"That took courage," she murmured, "when fear is part of the syndrome."

"You said it, I didn't. Of course, I couldn't be sure I'd get away with anything. The doc could've spotted the cause. However, since they took me for an ignorant nank, he never thought I could be faking it. Naturally, I recovered my strength fast, and didn't let on. I kind of hoped I'd have a chance to do something, because they'd be off guard with a sick man. But, sure, I had luck with me."

Colonel Adler drummed fingers on her desk and glanced out the viewplate. Pallas Town bustled under a dark, starry sky. The geegee fields gave Earth weight and held atmosphere, but it was a thin atmosphere and, space glittered through, cold and huge. She turned back to Flowers. "Why did you proceed here?" she asked. "Sam's was closer."

"Uh, well, I figured GHQ should know as soon as possible about those codebusting machines of the enemy's."

"GHQ already did, as your interrogator believed. In any event, the information could have been sent from Sam's, along with a duplicate of your original dispatch."

Flowers reddened. He had expected to be treated like a hero. "So I made a mistake. I'm no professional. "

She smiled. "Perhaps you did not err after all, Lieutenant. But come, let's get the quizzing over with. Then I'll authorize some furlough time for you. You've earned it."

Flowers nearly swallowed his cigar. "Quiz? You mean narco?"

She nodded. "An examination in depth."

"Whatever *for?*"

"SOP in cases like this. If nothing else, we have to be sure the enemy hasn't begun on that dirty trick of implanting posthypnotic suggestions. I'll handle the job myself, and anything personal which might come out will never get past me."

"You? Huh? I mean…look, I'll go along with this if I've got to, but not with a lady!"

The colonel chuckled. "I'm older and I've seen more of the universe than you might think. You won't outrage any propriety of mine. Now come with me. That's an order."

When he woke, he found her regarding him most thoughtfully. Her cheeks were a bit flushed.

"Whuzzamattuh?" he mumbled.

"I made a discovery," she said. "I can be shocked."

Anger whipped him to full consciousness. He sat up and growled, "My private life's my own. Isn't that one of the ideas we're supposed to be fighting for? Now with your permission, ma'm, I'll get out of here."

"Please." She fluttered hands at him. Also eyelashes. "I didn't think I could be shocked any more. It was a delightful surprise. You mentioned some fascinating—Well, Smelly, I mean to say, I get off at 1800 hours and I do have some civilian clothes and if you'd like to meet me somewhere..."

Trade boomed after independence was won. and Pallas, boomed loudest. Each time he visited the place—which was often, since his construction business required him to see people there—Flowers thought it had doubled in population and noisiness. But one little bar near the space docks remained unchanged. You could sit in a booth, under a stereo mural of Saturn, and have an honest beer and an uninterrupted talk.

"I see you changed tattoos," Ulstad remarked.

Flowers glanced at his left forearm, bare in an incadescent sports shirt, and grunted. "Yeah. That one. Very soon after I escaped from you, in fact. A dame I was going with for a while said she didn't like the design. I didn't either, so I had it removed. I, uh, this is a kind of sentimental thing to say, but I had reasons for substituting this eagle. Symbol of friendship with the mother country and all that sort of engine spew, huh?"

"Yes. I'm glad you feel that way," Ulstad took a swallow of Tuborg. "Glad I could finally get hold of you, too, and learn how you did get away from us. What a yarn!"

Flowers grinned. "I didn't know the whole story till after the war."

Ulstad pricked up his ears. "Go on."

"This is no secret any longer, or I wouldn't've been told yet. But the message I was carrying—you never did decipher it, did you?"

"No. We finally decided it was a blind, wasting much too much valuable computer time."

"Kee-rect. A pure random pattern. Quite a few of our couriers carried similar ones for a while. It was a safe bet that at least one man would get captured and so confuse you. I happened to be the man."

Ulstad frowned. "Seems like poor strategy. You couldn't spare that many ships for a single trick."

"Oh, no. 'Course not. But you see, messages were being sent anyway."

"What? How in the name of—"

Flowers drained his beer and bellowed for another. While he waited, he produced a cigar. "That tattoo on my arm," he said. "I only knew I'd gotten blind drunk. Figured I must've ordered the damn thing put on and never remembered afterward. Actually, my booze had been mickeyed.

"The message was important. They did capture the *Vega* in the battle off Sam's, you know. And maybe by now you also know they locked onto her code books. Pallas had to be told what your ciphers were, but we couldn't risk a maser beam being intercepted."

"Certainly not." Ulstad grimaced.

"It took several disasters before we realized what must have happened."

"That code was in my tattoo," Flowers said. "There're thousands of punctures in any such picture. For some of 'em you can use a needle with a special dye—standard color, nothing different except for a few iron atoms—to write anything you please. Put the arm under a scanner while I'm anesthetized and can't blab, and there you are."

The beer arrived and he drained half the tankard. "I really needn't have bothered escaping, I suppose," he mused. "Our high command would've gotten me included in the next prisoner exchange. Still, I did get the information to HQ faster, and saved myself a bad time."

Ulstad whistled. After a while, with a touch of malice, he said: "Remember I told you I had a nephew on the *Vega?* Not true. I was only trying to soften you up a bit."

Flowers started. Then he guffawed and raising his draught. "You know," he said, "I could use a man like you in my business."

"Might be fun at that," said Ulstad. The tankards touched.

My Object All Sublime

We met in line of business. Michaels' firm wanted to start a subdivision on the far side of Evanston and discovered that I held title to some of the most promising acreage. They made me a good offer, but I was stubborn; they raised it and I stayed stubborn; finally the boss himself looked me up. He wasn't entirely what I'd expected. Aggressive, of course, but in so polite a way that it didn't offend, his manners so urbane you rarely noticed his lack of formal education. Which lack he was remedying quite fast, anyhow, via night classes and extension courses as well as omnivorous reading.

We went out for a drink while we talked the matter over. He led me to a bar that had little of Chicago about it: quiet, shabby, no jukebox, no television, a bookshelf and several chess sets, but none of the freaks and phonies who usually infest such places. Besides ourselves, there were only half a dozen customers—a professor-emeritus type among the books, some people arguing politics with a degree of factual relevancy, a young man debating with the bartender whether Bartok was more original than Schoenberg or vice versa. Michaels and I found a corner table and some Danish beer.

I explained that I didn't care about money one way or another, but objected to bulldozing some rather good-looking countryside in order to erect still another chrome-plated slum. Michaels stuffed his pipe before answering. He was a lean, erect man, long-chinned and Roman-nosed, his hair grizzled, his eyes dark and luminous. "Didn't my representative explain?" he said. "We aren't planning a row of identical split-level sties. We have six basic designs in mind, with variations, to be located in a pattern…so."

He took out pencil and paper and began to sketch. As he talked, his accent thickened, but the fluency remained. And he made his own case better than anyone had done for him. Like it or not, he said, this was the middle twentieth century and mass production was here to stay. A community need not be less attractive for being ready-made, could in fact gain an artistic unity. He proceeded to show me how.

He didn't press me too hard, and conversation wandered.

"Delightful spot, this," I remarked. "How'd you find it?"

He shrugged. "I often prowl about, especially at night. Exploring."

"Isn't that rather dangerous?"

"Not in comparison," he said with a touch of grimness.

"Uh...I gather you weren't born over here?"

"No. I didn't arrive in the United States until 1946. What they called a DP, a displaced person. I became Thad Michaels because I got tired of spelling out Tadeusz Michalowski. Nor did I want any part of old-country sentimentalism; I'm a zealous assimilationist."

Otherwise he seldom talked much about himself. Later I got some details of his early rise in business, from admiring and envious competitors. Some of them didn't yet believe it was possible to sell a house with radiant heating for less than twenty thousand dollars and show a profit. Michaels had found ways to make it possible. Not bad for a penniless immigrant.

I checked up and found he'd been admitted on a special visa, in consideration of services rendered the U. S. Army in the last stages of the European war. Those services had taken nerve as well as quick-wittedness.

Meanwhile our acquaintance developed. I sold him the land he wanted, but we continued to see each other, sometimes in the tavern, sometimes at my bachelor apartment, most often in his lakeshore penthouse. He had a stunning blonde wife and a couple of bright, well-mannered boys. Nonetheless he was a lonely man, and I fulfilled his need for friendship.

A year or so after we first met, he told me the story.

I'd been invited over for Thanksgiving dinner. Afterward we sat around and talked. And talked. And talked. When we had ranged from the chances of an upset in the next city election to the chances of other planets following the same general course of history as our own, Amalie excused herself and went to bed. This was long past midnight. Michaels and I kept on talking. I had not seen him so excited before. It was as if that last subject, or some particular word, had opened a door for him. Finally he got up, refilled our whisky glasses with a motion not altogether steady, and walked across the living room (noiseless on that deep green carpet) to the picture window.

The night was clear and sharp. We overlooked the city, streaks and webs and coils of glittering color, ruby, amethyst, emerald, topaz, and the dark sheet of Lake Michigan; almost it seemed we could glimpse endless white plains beyond. But overhead arched the sky, crystal black, where the Great Bear stood on his tail and Orion went striding along the Milky Way. I had not often seen so big and frosty a view.

"After all," he said, "I know what I'm talking about."

I stirred, deep in my armchair. The fire on the hearth spat tiny blue flames. Besides this, only one shaded lamp lit the room, so that the star swarms had also been visible to me when I passed by the window earlier. I gibed a little. "Personally?"

He glanced back toward me. His face was stiff. "What would you say if I answered yes?"

I sipped my drink. King's Ransom is a noble and comforting brew, most especially when the Earth itself seems to tone with a deepening chill. "I'd suppose you had your reasons and wait to see what they were."

He grinned. one-sidedly. "Oh, well, I'm from this planet too," he said. "And yet—yet the sky is so wide and strange, don't you think the strangeness would affect men who went there? Wouldn't it seep into them, so they carried it back in their bones, and Earth was never quite the same afterward?"

"Go on. You know I like fantasies."

He stared outward, and then back again, and suddenly he tossed off his drink. The violent gesture was unlike him. But so had his hesitation been.

He said in a harsh tone, with all the former accent: "Okay, then, I shall tell you a fantasy. It is a story for winter, though, a cold story, that you are best advised not to take so serious."

I drew on the excellent cigar he had given me and waited in the silence he needed.

He paced a few times back and forth before the window, eyes to the floor, until he filled his glass anew and sat down near me. He didn't look at me but at a picture on the wall, a somber, unintelligible thing which no one else liked. He seemed to get strength from it, for he began talking, fast and softly.

"Once upon a time, a very, very long time in the future, there was a civilization. I shall not describe it to you, for that would not be possible. Could you go back to the time of the Egyptian pyramid builders and tell them about this city below us? I don't mean they wouldn't believe you; of course they wouldn't, but that hardly matters. I mean they would not understand. Nothing you said could make sense to them. And the way people work and think and believe would be less comprehensible than those lights and towers and machines. Not so? If I spoke to you of people in the future living among great blinding energies, and of genetic changelings, and imaginary wars, and talking stones, and a certain blind hunter, you might feel anything at all, but you would not understand.

"So I ask you only to imagine how many thousands of times this planet has circled the sun, how deeply buried and forgotten we are; and then also to imagine that this other civilization thinks in patterns so foreign that it has ignored every limitation of logic and natural law, to discover means of traveling in time. So, while the ordinary dweller in that age (I can't exactly call him a citizen, or anything else for which we have a word, because it would be too misleading), the average educated dweller, knows in a vague, uninterested way that millennia ago some semi-savages were the first to split the atom—only one or two men have actually been here, walked among us, studied and mapped us and returned with a file of information for the central brain, if I may call it by such a name. No one else is concerned with us, any more than you are concerned with early Mesopotamian archeology. You see?"

He dropped his gaze to the tumbler in his hand and held it there, as if the whisky were an oracular pool. The silence grew. At last I said, "Very well. For the sake of the story, I'll accept the premise. I imagine time travelers would be unnoticeable. They'd have techniques of disguise and so on. Wouldn't want to change their own past."

"Oh, no danger of that," he said. "It's only that they couldn't learn much if they went around insisting they were from the future. Just imagine."

I chuckled.

Michaels gave me a shadowed look. "Apart from the scientific," he said, "can you guess what use there might be for time travel?"

"Well," I suggested, "trade in objects of art or natural resources. Go back to the dinosaur age and dig up iron before man appeared to strip the richest mines."

He shook his head. "Think again. They'd only want a limited number of Minoan statuettes, Ming vases, or Third World Hegemony dwarfs, chiefly for their museums. If 'museum' isn't too inaccurate a word. I tell you, they are not like us. As for natural resources, they're beyond the point of needing any; they make their own."

He paused, as if before a final plunge. Then: "What was this penal colony the French abandoned?"

"Devil's Island?"

"Yes, that was it. Can you imagine a better revenge on a condemned criminal than to maroon him in the past?"

"Why, I should think they'd be above any concept of revenge, or even of deterrence by horrible examples. Even in this century, we're aware that that doesn't work."

"Are you sure?" he asked quietly. "Side by side with the growth of today's enlightened penology, haven't we a corresponding growth of crime itself? You were wondering, some time ago, how I dared walk the night streets alone. Furthermore, punishment is a catharsis of society as a whole. Up in the future they'd tell you that public hangings did reduce the crime rate, which would otherwise have been still higher. Somewhat more important, these spectacles made possible the eighteenth century birth of real humanitarianism." He raised a sardonic brow. "Or so they claim in the future. It doesn't matter whether they are right, or merely rationalizing a degraded element in their own civilization. All you need assume is that they do send their very worst criminals back into the past."

"Rather rough on the past," I said.

"No, not really. For a number of reasons, including the fact that everything they cause to happen has already happened...Damn! English isn't built for talking about these paradoxes. Mainly, though, you must remember that they don't waste all this effort on ordinary miscreants. One has to be a very rare criminal to deserve exile in time. And the worst crime in the world depends on the particular year of the world's history. Murder, brigandage, treason, heresy, narcotics peddling, slaving, patriotism, the whole catalogue, all have rated capital punishment in some epochs, and been lightly regarded in others, and positively commended in still others. Think back and see if I'm not right."

I regarded him for a while, observing how deep the lines were in his face and recalling that at his age he shouldn't be so gray. "Very well," I said. "Agreed. But would not a man from the future, possessing all its knowledge—"

He set his glass down with audible force. "*What* knowledge?" he rapped. "Use your brains! Imagine yourself left naked and alone in Babylon. How much Babylonian language or history do you know? Who's the present king, how much longer will he reign, who'll succeed him? What are the laws and customs you must obey? You remember that eventually the Assyrians or the Persians or someone will conquer Babylon and there'll be hell to pay. But when? How? Is the current war a mere border skirmish or an all-out struggle? If the latter, is Babylon going to win? If not, what peace terms will be imposed? Why, there wouldn't be twenty men today who could answer those questions without looking up the answers in a book. And you're not one of them; nor have you been given a book."

"I think," I said slowly, "I'd head for the nearest temple, once I'd picked up enough of the language. I'd tell the priest I could make…oh…fireworks—"

He laughed, with small merriment. "How? You're in Babylon, remember. Where do you find sulfur and saltpeter? If you can get across to the priest what you want, and somehow persuade him to obtain the stuff for you, how do you compound a powder that'll actually go off instead of just fizzing? For your information, that's quite an art. Hell, you couldn't even get a berth as a deckhand. You'd be lucky if you ended up scrubbing floors. A slave in the fields is a likelier career. Isn't it?"

The fire sank low.

"All right," I conceded. "True."

"They pick the era with care, you know." He looked back toward the window. Seen from our chairs, reflection on the glass blotted out the stars, so that we were only aware of the night itself.

"When a man is sentenced to banishment," he said, "all the experts confer, pointing out what the periods of their specialties would be like for this particular individual. You can see how a squeamish, intellectual type, dropped into Homeric Greece, would find it a living nightmare, whereas a rowdy type might get along fairly well—might even end up as a respected warrior. If the rowdy was not the blackest of criminals, they might actually leave him near the hall of Agamemnon, condemning him to no more than danger, discomfort, and homesickness.

"Oh, God," he whispered. "The homesickness!"

So much darkness rose in him as he spoke that I sought to steady him with a dry remark: "They must immunize the convict to every ancient disease. Otherwise this'd only be an elaborate death sentence."

His eyes focused on me again.

"Yes," he said. "And of course the longevity serum is still active in his veins. That's all, however. He's dropped in an unfrequented spot after dark, the machine vanishes, he's cut off for the rest of his life. All he knows is that they've chosen an era for him with...such characteristics...that they expect the punishment will fit his crime."

Stillness fell once more upon us, until the clock on the mantel became the loudest thing in the world, as if all other sound had frozen to death outside. I glanced at its dial. The night was old; soon the east would be turning pale.

When I looked back, he was still watching me, disconcertingly intent. "What was your crime?" I asked.

He didn't seem taken aback, only said wearily, "What does it matter? I told you the crimes of one age are the heroisms of another. If my attempt had succeeded, the centuries to come would have adored my name. But I failed."

"A lot of people must have got hurt," I said. "A whole world must have hated you."

"Well, yes," he said. And after a minute: "This is a fantasy I'm telling you, of course. To pass the time."

"I'm playing along with you," I smiled.

His tension eased a trifle. He leaned back, his legs stretched across that glorious carpet. "So. Given as much of the fantasy as I've related, how did you deduce the extent of my alleged guilt?"

"Your past life. When and where were you left?"

He said, in as bleak a voice as I've ever heard, "Near Warsaw, in August, 1939."

"I don't imagine you care to talk about the war years."

"No, I don't."

However, he went on when enough defiance had accumulated: "My enemies blundered. The confusion following the German attack gave me a chance to escape from police custody before I could be stuck in a concentration camp. Gradually I learned what the situation was. Of course, I couldn't predict anything. I still can't; only specialists know, or care, what happened in the twentieth century. But by the time I'd become a Polish conscript in the German forces, I realized this was the losing side. So I slipped across to the Americans, told them what I'd observed, became a scout for them. Risky—but if I'd stopped a bullet, what the hell? I didn't; and I ended up with plenty of sponsors to get me over here; and the rest of the story is conventional."

My cigar had gone out. I relit it, for Michaels' cigars were not to be taken casually. He had them especially flown from Amsterdam.

"The alien corn," I said.

"What?"

"You know. Ruth in exile. She wasn't badly treated, but she stood weeping for her homeland."

"No, I don't know that story."

"It's in the Bible."

"Ah, yes. I really must read the Bible sometime." His mood was changing by the moment, toward the assurance I had first encountered. He swallowed his whisky with a gesture almost debonair. His expression was alert and confident.

"Yes," he said, "that aspect was pretty bad. Not so much the physical conditions of life. You've doubtless gone camping and noticed how soon you stop missing hot running water, electric lights, all the gadgets that their manufacturers assure us are absolute necessities. I'd be glad of a gravity reducer or a cell stimulater if I had one, but I get along fine without. The homesickness, though, that's what eats you. Little things you never noticed, some particular food, they way people walk, the games played, the small-talk topics. Even the constellations. They're different in the future. The sun has traveled that far in its galactic orbit.

"But, voluntary or forced, people have always been emigrating. We're all descended from those who could stand the shock. I adapted."

A scowl crossed his brows. "I wouldn't go back now even if I were given a free pardon," he said, "the way those traitors are running things."

I finished my own drink, tasting it with my whole tongue and palate, for it was a marvelous whisky, and listened to him with only half an ear. "You like it here?"

"Yes," he said. "By now I do. I'm over the emotional hump. Being so busy the first few years just staying alive, and then so busy establishing myself after I came to this country, that helped. I never had much time for self-pity. Now my business interests me more and more, a fascinating game, and pleasantly free of extreme penalties for wrong moves. I've discovered qualities here that the future has lost...I'll bet you have no idea how exotic this city is. Think. At this moment, within five miles of us, there's a soldier on guard at an atomic laboratory, a bum freezing in a doorway, an orgy in a millionaire's apartment, a priest making ready for sunrise rites, a merchant from Araby, a spy from Muscovy, a ship from the Indies..."

His excitement softened. He looked from the window and the night, inward, toward the bedrooms. "And my wife and kids," he finished, most gently. "No, I wouldn't go back, no matter what happened."

I took a final breath of my cigar. "You *have* done rather well."

Liberated from his gray mood, he grinned at me. "You know, I think you believe that yarn."

"Oh, I do." I stubbed out the cigar, rose, and stretched. "The hour is late. We'd better be going."

He didn't notice at once. When he did, he came out of his chair like a big cat. *"We?"*

"Of course." I drew a nerve gun from my pocket. He stopped in his tracks. "This sort of thing isn't left to chance. We check up. Come along, now."

The blood drained from his face. "No." he mouthed, "no, no, no, you can't, it isn't fair, not to Amalie, the children—"

"That," I told him, "is part of the punishment."

I left him in Damascus, the year before Tamerlane sacked it.

Innocent At Large

The visiphone chimed when Peri had just gotten into her dinner gown. She peeled it off again and slipped on a casual bathrobe: a wisp of translucence which had set the president of Antarctic Enterprise—or had it been the chairman of the board?—back several thousand dollars. Then she pulled a lock of lion-colored hair down over one eye, checked with a mirror, rumpled it a tiny bit more and wrapped the robe loosely on top and tight around the hips.

After all, some of the men who knew her private number were important.

She undulated to the phone and pressed its Accept. "Hello-o, there," she said automatically. "So sorry to keep you waiting. I was just taking a bath and—Oh. It's you."

Gus Doran's prawnlike eyes popped at her. "Holy Success," he whispered in awe. "You sure the wires can carry that much voltage?"

"Well, hurry up with whatever it is," snapped Peri. "I got a date tonight."

"I'll say you do! With a Martian!"

Peri narrowed her silver-blue gaze and looked icily at him. "You must have heard wrong, Gus. He's the heir apparent of Indonesia, Inc., that's who, and if you called up to ask for a piece of him, you can just blank right out again. I saw him first!"

Doran's thin sharp face grinned. "You break that date, Peri. Put it off or something. I got this Martian for you, see?"

"So? Since when has all Mars had as much spending money as one big-time marijuana rancher? Not to mention the heir ap—"

"Sure, sure. But how much are those boys going to spend on any girl, even a high-level type like you? Listen, I need you just for tonight, see? This Martian is strictly from gone. He is here on official business, but he is a yokel and I do mean hayseed. Like he asked me what the Christmas decorations in all the stores were! And here is the solar nexus of it, Peri, kid."

Doran leaned forward as if to climb out of the screen. "He has got a hundred million dollars expense money, and they are not going to audit his accounts at home. One hundred million good green certificates, legal tender anywhere in the United Protectorates. And he has about as much backbone as a piece of steak alga. Kid, if I did not happen to have experience otherwise with a small nephew, I would say this will be like taking candy from a baby."

Peri's peaches-and-cream countenance began to resemble peaches and cream left overnight on Pluto. "Badger?" she asked.

"Sure. You and Sam Wendt handle the routine. I will take the go-between angle, so he will think of me as still his friend, because I have other plans for him too. But if we can't shake a million out of him for this one night's work, there is something akilter. And your share of a million is three hundred thirty-three—"

"Is five hundred thousand flat," said Peri. "Too bad I just got an awful headache and can't see Mr. Sastro tonight. Where you at, Gus?"

The gravity was not as hard to take as Peter Matheny had expected. Three generations on Mars might lengthen the legs and expand the chest a trifle, but the genes had come from Earth and the organism readjusts. What set him gasping was the air. It weighed like a ton of wool and had apparently sopped up half the Atlantic Ocean. Ears trained to listen through the Martian atmosphere shuddered from the racket conducted by Earth's. The passport official seemed to bellow at him.

"Pardon me for asking this. The United Protectorates welcome all visitors to Earth and I assure you, sir, an ordinary five-year visa provokes no questions. But since you came on an official courier boat of your planet, Mr. Matheny, regulations force me to ask your business."

"Well—recruiting."

The official patted his comfortable stomach, iridescent in neolon, and chuckled patronizingly. "I am afraid, sir, you won't find many people who wish to leave. They wouldn't be able to see the Teamsters Hour on Mars, would they?"

"Oh, we don't expect immigration," said Matheny shyly. He was a fairly young man, but small, with a dark-thatched, snub-nosed, gray-eyed head that seemed too large for his slender body. "We learned long ago that no one is interested any more in giving up even second-class citizenship on Earth to live in the Republic. But we only wanted to hire—uh, I mean engage—an, an advisor. We're not businessmen. We know our export trade hasn't a chance among all your corporations unless we get some—a five-year contract...?"

He heard his words trailing off idiotically, and swore at himself.

"Well, good luck." The official's tone was skeptical. He stamped the passport and handed it back. "There, now, you are free to travel anywhere in the Protectorates. But I would advise you to leave the capital and get into the sticks—um, I mean the provinces. I am sure there must be tolerably competent sales executives in Russia or Congolese Belgium or such regions. Frankly, sir, I do not believe you can attract anyone out of Newer York."

"Thanks," said Matheny, "but, you see, I—we need—that is...Oh, well. Thanks. Good-by."

He backed out of the office.

A dropshaft deposited him on a walkway. The crowd, a rainbow of men in pajamas and robes, women in Neo-Sino dresses and goldleaf hats, swept him against the rail. For a moment, squashed to the wire, he stared a hundred feet down at the river of automobiles. *Phobos!* he thought wildly. *If the barrier gives, I'll be sliced in two by a dorsal fin before I hit the pavement!*

The August twilight wrapped him in heat and stickiness. He could see neither stars nor even moon through the city's blaze. The forest of multi-colored towers, cataracting half a mile skyward across more acreage than his eyes reached, was impressive and all that, but—he used to stroll out in the rock garden behind his cottage and smoke a pipe in company with Orion. On summer evenings, that is, when the temperature wasn't too far below zero.

Why did they tap me for this job? he asked himself in a surge of homesickness. *What the hell is the Martian Embassy here for?*

He, Peter Matheny, was no more than a peaceful professor of sociodynamics at Devil's Kettle University. Of course, he had advised his government before now—in fact, the Red Ankh Society had been his idea—but still he was at ease only with his books and his chess and his mineral collection, a faculty poker party on Tenthday night and an occasional trip to Swindletown—

My God, thought Matheny, *here I am, one solitary outlander in the greatest commercial empire the human race has ever seen, and I'm supposed to find my planet a con man!*

He began walking, disconsolately, at random. His lizardskin shirt and black culottes drew glances, but derisive ones: their cut was forty years out of date. He should find himself a hotel, he thought drearily, but he wasn't tired; the spaceport would pneumo his baggage to him whenever he did check in. The few Martians who had been to Earth had gone into ecstasies over the automation which put any service you could name on a twenty-four-hour basis. But it would be a long time before Mars had such machines. If ever.

The city roared at him.

He fumbled after his pipe. *Of course,* he told himself, *that's why the Embassy can't act. I may find it advisable to go outside the law. Please, sir, where can I contact the underworld?*

He wished gambling were legal on Earth. The Constitution of the Martian Republic forbade sumptuary and moral legislation; quite apart from the rambunctious individualism which that document formulated, the article was a practical necessity. Life was bleak enough on the deserts, without being denied the pleasure of trying to bottom-deal some friend who was happily trying to mark the cards. Matheny would have found a few spins of roulette soothing: it was always an intellectual challenge to work out the system by which the management operated a wheel. But more, he would have been among people he understood.

The frightful thing about the Earthman was, the way he seemed to exist only in organized masses. A gypsy snake oil peddler, plodding his syrtosaur wagon across Martian sands, just didn't have a prayer against, say, the Grant, Harding & Adams Public Relations Agency.

Matheny puffed smoke and looked around. His feet ached from the weight on them. Where could a man sit down? It was hard to make out any individual sign through all that flimmering neon. His eye fell on one that was distinguished by relative austerity.

THE CHURCH OF CHOICE
Enter, Play, Pray

That would do. He took an upward slideramp through several hundred feet of altitude, stepped past an aurora curtain, and found himself in a marble lobby next to an inspirational newsstand.

"Ah, brother, welcome," said a red-haired usherette in demure black leotards. "The peace that passeth all understanding be with you. The restaurant is right up those stairs."

"I—I'm not hungry," stammered Matheny. "I just wanted to sit in—"

"To your left, sir."

The Martian crossed the lobby. His pipe went out in the breeze from an animated angel. Organ music sighed through an open doorway. The series of rooms beyond was dim, Gothic, interminable.

"Get your chips right here, sir," said the girl in the booth.

"Hm?" said Matheny.

She explained. He bought a few hundred-dollar tokens, dropped a fifty-buck coin down a slot marked CONTRIBUTIONS, and sipped the martini he got back while he strolled around studying the games. He stopped, frowned. Bingo? No, he didn't want to bother learning something new. He decided that the roulette wheels were either honest or too deep for him. He'd have to relax with a crap game instead.

He had been standing at the table for some time before the rest of the congregation really noticed him. Then it was with awe. The first few passes he had made were unsuccessful. Earth gravity threw him off. But when he got the rhythm of it, he tossed a row of sevens. It was a customary form of challenge on Mars. Here, though, they simply pushed chips toward him. He missed a throw, as anyone would at home: simple courtesy. The next time around, he threw for a seven just to get the feel. He got a seven. The dice had not been substituted on him.

"I say!" he exclaimed. He looked up into eyes and eyes, all around the green table. "I'm sorry. I guess I don't know your rules."

"You did all right, brother," said a middle-aged lady with an obviously surgical bodice.

"But—I mean—when do we start actually *playing?* What happened to the cocked dice?"

The lady drew herself up and jutted an indignant prow at him. "Sir! This is a church!"

"Oh—I see—excuse me, I, I, I—" Matheny backed out of the crowd, shuddering. He looked around for some place to hide his burning ears.

"You forgot your chips, pal," said a voice.

"Oh. Thanks. Thanks ever so much. I, I, that is—" Matheny cursed his knotting tongue. *Damn it, just because they're so much more sophisticated than I, do I have to talk like a leaky boiler?*

The helpful Earthman was not tall. He was dark and chisel-faced and sleekly pomaded, dapper in blue pajamas with a red zigzag, a sleighbell cloak and curly-toed slippers.

"You're from Mars, aren't you?" he asked in the friendliest tone Matheny had yet heard.

"Yes. Yes, I am. M-my name's Peter Matheny. I, I—" He stuck out his hand to shake and chips rolled over the floor. "Damn! Oh, excuse me, I forgot this was a church. Never mind the chips. No, please. I just want to g-g-get the hell out of here."

"Good idea. How about a drink? I know a bar downshaft."

Matheny sighed. "A drink is what I need the very most."

"My name's Doran. Gus Doran. Call me Gus."

They walked back to the deaconette's booth and Matheny cashed what remained of his winnings.

"I don't want to—I mean if you're busy tonight, Mr. Doran—"

"Nah. I am not doing one thing in particular. Besides, I have never met a Martian. I am very interested."

"There aren't many of us on Earth," agreed Matheny. "Just a small embassy staff and an occasional like me."

"I should think you would do a lot of traveling here. The old mother planet and so on."

"We can't afford it," said Matheny. "What with gravitation and distance, such voyages are much too expensive for us to make them for pleasure. Not to mention our dollar shortage." As they entered the shaft, he added wistfully: "You Earth people have that kind of money, at least in your more prosperous brackets. Why don't you send a few tourists to us?"

"I always wanted to," said Doran. "I would like to see the what they call City of Time, and so on. As a matter of fact, I have given my girl one of those Old Martian rings last Ike's Birthday and she was just gazoo about it. A jewel dug out of the City of Time, like, made a million years ago by a, uh, extinct race...I tell you, she *appreciated* me for it!" He winked and nudged.

"Oh," said Matheny.

He felt a certain guilt. Doran was too pleasant a little man to deserve—

"Of course," Matheny said ritually, "I agree with all the archeologists it's a crime to sell such scientifically priceless artifacts, but what can we do? We must live, and the tourist trade is almost nonexistent."

"Trouble with it is, I hear Mars is not so comfortable," said Doran. "I mean, do not get me wrong, I don't want to insult you or anything, but people come back saying you have given the planet just barely enough air to keep a man alive. And there are no cities, just little towns and villages and ranches out in the bush. I mean you are being pioneers and making a new nation and all that, but people paying half a megabuck for their ticket expect some comfort and, uh, you know."

"I do know," said Matheny. "But we're poor—a handful of people trying to make a world of dust and sand and scrub thorn into fields and woods and seas. We can't do it without substantial help from Earth, equipment and supplies—which can only be paid for in Earth dollars—and we can't export enough to Earth to earn those dollars."

By that time, they were entering the Paul Bunyan Knotty Pine Bar & Grill, on the 73rd Level. Matheny's jaw clanked down.

"Whassa matter?" asked Doran.

"Ain't you ever seen a ecdysiastic technician before?"

"Uh, yes, but—well, not in a 3-D image under ten magnifications."

Matheny followed Doran past a sign announcing that this show was for purely artistic purposes, into a booth. There a soundproof curtain reduced the noise level enough so they could talk in normal voices.

"What'll you have?" asked Doran. "It's on me."

"Oh, I couldn't let you. I mean—"

"Nonsense. Welcome to Earth! Care for a thyle and vermouth?"

Matheny shuddered. "Good Lord, no!"

"Huh? But they make thyle right on Mars, don't they?"

"Yes. And it all goes to Earth and sells at 2000 dollars a fifth. But you don't think we'd *drink* it, do you? I mean—well, I imagine it doesn't absolutely *ruin* vermouth. But we don't see those Earthside commercials about how sophisticated people like it so much."

"Well, I'll be a socialist creeper!" Doran's face split in a grin. "You know, all my life I've hated the stuff and never dared admit it!" He raised a hand. "Don't worry, I won't blabbo. But I am wondering, if you control the thyle industry and sell all those relics at fancy prices, why do you call yourselves poor?"

"Because we are," said Matheny. "By the time the shipping costs have been paid on a bottle, and the Earth wholesaler and jobber and sales engineer and so on, down to the retailer, have taken their percentage, and the advertising agency has been paid, and about fifty separate Earth taxes—there's very little profit going back to the distillery on Mars. The same principle is what's strangling us on everything. Old Martian artifacts aren't really rare, for instance, but freight charges and the middlemen here put them out of the mass market."

"Have you not got some other business?"

"Well, we do sell a lot of color slides, postcards, baggage labels and so on to people who like to act cosmopolitan, and I understand our travel posters are quite popular as wall decoration. But all that has to be printed on Earth, and the printer and distributor keep most of the money. We've sold some books and show tapes, of course, but only one has been really successful—*I Was a Slave Girl on Mars.*

"Our most prominent novelist was co-opted to ghostwrite that one. Again, though, local income taxes took most of the money; authors never have been protected the way a businessman is. We do make a high percentage of profit on those little certificates you see around—you know, the title deeds to one square inch of Mars—but expressed absolutely, in dollars, it doesn't amount to much when we start shopping for bulldozers and thermonuclear power plants."

"How about postage stamps?" inquired Doran. "Philately is a big business, I have heard."

"It was our mainstay," admitted Matheny, "but it's been overworked. Martian stamps are a drug on the market. What we'd like to operate is a sweepstakes, but the anti-gambling laws on Earth forbid that."

Doran whistled. "I got to give your people credit for enterprise, anyway!" He fingered his mustache. "Uh, pardon me, but have you tried to, well, attract capital from Earth?"

"Of course," said Matheny bitterly. "We offer the most liberal concessions in the Solar System. Any little mining company or transport firm or—or anybody who—wanted to come and actually invest a few dollars in Mars why, we'd probably give him the President's daughter as security. No, the Minister of Ecology has a better-looking one. But who's interested? We haven't a thing that Earth hasn't got more of. We're only the descendants of a few scientists, a few political malcontents, oddballs who happen to prefer elbow room and a bill of liberties to the incorporated state—what could General Nucleonics hope to get from Mars?"

"I see. Well, what are you having to drink?"

"Beer," said Matheny without hesitation.

"Huh? Look, pal, this is on me."

"The only beer on Mars comes forty million miles, with interplanetary freight charges tacked on," said Matheny. "Heineken's!"

Doran shrugged, dialed the dispenser and fed it coins.

"This is a real interesting talk, Pete," he said. "You are being very frank with me. I like a man that is frank."

Matheny shrugged. "I haven't told you anything that isn't known to every economist."

Of course I haven't. I've not so much as mentioned the Red Ankh, for instance. But, in principle, I have told him the truth, told him of our need; for even the secret operations do not yield us enough.

The beer arrived. Matheny engulfed himself in it. Doran sipped at a whiskey sour and unobtrusively set another full bottle in front of the Martian.

"Ahhh!" said Matheny. "Bless you, my friend."

"A pleasure."

"But now you must let me buy you one."

"That is not necessary. After all," said Doran with great tact, "with the situation as you have been describing—"

"Oh, we're not *that* poor! My expense allowance assumes I will entertain quite a bit."

Doran's brows lifted a few minutes of arc. "You're here on business, then?"

"Yes. I told you we haven't any tourists. I was sent to hire a business manager for the Martian export trade."

"What's wrong with your own people? I mean, Pete, it is not your fault there are so many rackets—uh, taxes—and middlemen and agencies and et cetera. That is just the way Earth is set up these days."

Matheny's finger stabbed in the general direction of Doran's pajama top. "Exactly. And who set it up that way? Earthmen. We Martians are babes in the desert. What chance do we have to earn dollars on the scale we need them, in competition with corporations which could buy and sell our whole planet before breakfast? Why, we couldn't afford three seconds of commercial time on a Lullaby Pillow 'cast. What we need, what we have to hire, is an executive who knows Earth, who's an Earthman himself. Let him tell us what will appeal to your people, and how to dodge the tax bite and—and—well, you see how it goes, that sort of, uh, thing."

Matheny felt his eloquence running down and grabbed for the second bottle of beer.

"But where do I start?" he asked plaintively, for his loneliness smote him anew. "I'm just a college professor at home. How would I even get to see—"

"It might be arranged," said Doran in a thoughtful tone. "It just might. How much could you pay this fellow"?"

"A hundred megabucks a year, if he'll sign a five-year contract. That's Earth years, mind you."

"I'm sorry to tell you this, Pete," said Doran, "but while that is not bad money, it is not what a high-powered sales scientist gets in Newer York. Plus his retirement benefits, which he would lose if he quit where he is now at. And I am sure he would not want to settle on Mars permanently."

"I could offer a certain amount of, uh, lagniappe," said Matheny. "That is, well, I can draw up to a hundred megabucks myself for, uh, expenses and, well… let me buy you a drink!"

Doran's black eyes frogged at him. "You might at that," said the Earthman very softly. "Yes, you might at that."

Matheny found himself warming. Gus Doran was a thentic bobber. A hell of a swell chap. He explained modestly that he was a free-lance business consultant and it was barely possible that he could arrange some contacts…

"No, no, no commission, all done in the interest of interplanetary friendship…well, anyhow, let's not talk business now. If you have got to stick to beer, Pete, make it a chaser to akvavit. What is akvavit? Well, I will just take and show you."

A hell of a good bloke. He knew some very funny stories, too, and he laughed at Matheny's, though they were probably too rustic for a big-city taste like his.

"What I really want," said Matheny, "what I really want—mean what Mars really needs, get me?—is a confidence man."

"A what?"

"The best and slickest one on Earth, to operate a world-size con game for us and make us some *real* money."

"Con man? Oh. A slipstring."

"A con by any other name," said Matheny, pouring down an akvavit.

Doran squinted through cigarette smoke. "You are interesting me strangely, my friend. Say on."

"No." Matheny realized his head was a bit smoky. The walls of the booth seemed odd, somehow. They were just leatheroid walls, but they had an odd quality.

"No, sorry, Gus," he said. "I spoke too much."

"Okay. Forget it. I do not like a man that pries. But look, let's bomb out of here, how about it? Go have a little fun."

"By all means." Matheny disposed of his last beer. "I could use some gaiety."

"You have come to the right town then. But let us get you a hotel room first and some more up-to-date clothes."

"Allez," said Matheny. "If I don't mean *allons,* or maybe *alors.*"

The drop down to cab-ramp level and the short ride afterward sobered him; the room rate at the Jupiter-Astoria sobered him still more.

Oh, well, he thought, *if I succeed in this job, no one at home will quibble.*

And the chamber to which he and Doran were shown was spectacular enough, with a pneumo direct to the bar and a full-wall transparency to show the vertical incandescence of the towers.

"Whoof!" Matheny sat down. The chair slithered sensuously about his contours. He jumped. "What the dusty hell—Oh." He tried to grin, but his face burned. "I see."

"That is a sexy type of furniture, all right," agreed Doran. He lowered himself into another chair, cocked his feet on the 3-D and waved a cigarette. "Which speaking of, what say we get some girls? It is not too late to catch them at home. A date here will usually start around 2100 hours earliest."

"What?"

"You know. Dames. Like a certain blonde warhead with twin radar and swivel mounting, and she just loves exotics. Such as you."

"Me?" Matheny heard his voice climb to a schoolboy squeak. "Me? Exotic? Why, I'm just a little college professor. I g-g-g, that is—" His tongue got stuck on his palate. He pulled it loose and moistened uncertain lips.

"You are from Mars. Okay? So you fought bushcats barehanded in an abandoned canal."

"What's a bushcat? And we don't have canals. The evaporation rate—"

"Look, Pete," said Doran patiently. "She don't have to know that, does she?"

"Well—well, no. I guess not. No."

"Let's order you some clothes on the pneumo,'" said Doran. "I recommend you buy from Schwartzherz. Everybody knows he is expensive."

While Matheny jittered about, shaving and showering and struggling with his new raiment, Duran kept him supplied with akvavit and beer.

"You said one thing, Pete," Doran remarked. "About needing a slipstring. A con man, you would call it."

"Forget that. Please. I spoke out of turn."

"Well, you see, maybe a man like that is just what Mars does need. And maybe I have got a few contacts."

"What?" Matheny gaped out of the bathroom.

Doran cupped his hands around a fresh cigarette, not looking at him. "I am not that man," he said frankly. "But in my line I get a lot of contacts, and not all of them go topside. See what I mean? Like if, say, you wanted somebody terminated and could pay for it, I could not do it. I would not want to know anything about it. But I could tell you a phone number."

He shrugged and gave the Martian a sidelong glance. "Sure, you may not be interested. But if you are, well, Pete, I was not born yesterday. I got tolerance. Like the book says, if you want to get ahead, you have got to think positively."

Matheny hesitated. If only he hadn't taken that last shot! It made him want to say yes, immediately, without reservations. And therefore maybe he became overcautious.

They had instructed him on Mars to take chances if he must.

"I could tell you a thing or two that might give you a better idea," he said slowly. "But it would have to be under security."

"Okay by me. Room service can send us up an oath box right now."

"What? But—but—" Matheny hung onto himself and tried to believe that he had landed on Earth less than six hours ago.

In the end, he did call room service and the machine was trundled in. Doran swallowed the pill and donned the conditioner helmet without an instant's hesitation.

"I shall never reveal to any person unauthorized by yourself whatever you may tell me under security, now or at any other time," he recited. Then, cheerfully: "And that formula, Pete, happens to be the honest-to-zebra truth."

"I know." Matheny stared, embarrassed, at the carpet. "I'm sorry to—to—I mean of course I trust you, but—"

"Forget it. I take a hundred security oaths a year, in my line of work. Maybe I can help you. I like you, Pete, damn if I don't. And, sure, I might stand to get an agent's cut, if I arrange—Go ahead, boy, go ahead." Doran crossed his legs and leaned back.

"Oh, it's simple enough," said Matheny. "It's only that we already are operating con games."

"On Mars, you mean?"

"Yes. There never were any Old Martians. We erected the ruins fifty years ago for the Billingsworth Expedition to find. We've been manufacturing relics ever since."

"*Huh?* Well, why, but—"

"In this case, it helps to be at the far end of an interplanetary haul," said Matheny. "Not many Terrestrial archeologists get to Mars and they depend on our people to—Well, anyhow—"

"I will be clopped! Good for you!"

Doran blew up in laughter. "That is one thing I would never spill, even without security. I told you about my girl friend, didn't I?"

"Yes, and that calls to mind the Little Girl," said Matheny apologetically. "She was another official project."

"Who?"

"Remember Junie O'Brien? The little golden-haired girl on Mars, a mathematical prodigy, but dying of an incurable disease? She collected Earth coins."

"Oh, that. Sure, I remember Hey! You didn't!"

"Yes. We made about a billion dollars on that one."

"I will be double damned. You know, Pete, I sent her a hundred-buck piece myself. Say, how is Junie O'Brien?"

"Oh, fine. Under a different name, she's now our finance minister." Matheny stared out the wall, his hands twisting nervously behind his back. "There were no lies involved. She really does have a fatal disease. So do you and I. Every day we grow older."

"Uh!" exclaimed Doran.

"And then the Red Ankh Society. You must have seen or heard their ads. 'What mysterious knowledge did the Old Martians possess? What was the secret wisdom of the Ancient Aliens? Now the incredibly powerful semantics of the Red Ankh (not a religious organization) is available to a select few—' That's our largest dollar-earning enterprise."

He would have liked to say it was his suggestion originally, but it would have been too presumptuous. He was talking to an Earthman, who had heard everything already.

Doran whistled.

"That's about all, so far," confessed Matheny. "Perhaps a con is our only hope. I've been wondering, maybe we could organize a Martian bucket shop, handling Martian securities, but—well, I don't know."

"I think—" Doran removed the helmet and stood up.

"Yes?" Matheny faced around, shivering with his own tension.

"I may be able to find the man you want," said Doran. "I just may. It will take a few days and might get a little expensive."

"You mean…Mr. Doran—Gus—you could actually—"

"I cannot promise anything yet except that I will try. Now you finish dressing. I will be down in the bar. And I will call up this girl I know. We deserve a celebration!"

Peri was tall. Peri was slim. Peri smoldered when she walked and exploded when she stretched. Her apartment was ivory and ebony, her sea-green dress was poured on, and the Neo-Sino mode had obviously been engineered to her personal specifications.

She waved twelve inches of jade cigarette holder, lifted her glass and murmured throatily: "To you, Pete. To Mars."

"I, I, I," stammered Matheny. He raised his own glass. It slopped over. "Oh, damn! I mean…gosh, I'm so sorry, I—"

"No harm done. You aren't used to our gravity yet." Peri extended a flawless leg out of her slit skirt and turned it about on the couch, presumably in search of a more comfortable position. "And it must seem terribly cramped here on Earth, Pete," she continued. "After roaming the desert, hunting, sleeping under the twin moons. Two moons! Why, what girl could resist that?"

"Uh, well, as a matter of fact, the moons are barely visible," floundered Matheny.

"Must you spoil my dreams?" she said. "When I think of Mars, the frontier, where men are still men, why, my breast swells with emotion."

"Uh, yes." Matheny gulped. "Swell. Yes."

She leaned closer to his chair. "Now that I've got you, don't think you'll get away," she smiled. "A live Martian, trapped!"

Doran looked at his watch. "Well," he said, "I have got to get up tomorrow, so I had better run along now."

"Ta-ta," said Peri. Matheny rose. She pulled him down beside her. "Oh, no, you don't, Mars lad. I'm not through with you yet!"

"But, but, but," said Matheny.

Doran chuckled. "I'll meet you on the Terrace at fourteen hundred hours tomorrow," he said. "Have fun, Pete."

The door closed on him.

Peri slithered toward her guest. He felt a nudge and looked down. She had not actually touched him with her hands. "Gus is a good squiff," she said, "but I wondered if he'd ever go."

"Why, why…what do you mean?" croaked Matheny.

"Haven't you guessed?"

She kissed him. It was rather like being caught in a nuclear turbine with soft blades.

Matheny, said Matheny, *you represent your planet.*

Matheny, said Matheny, *shut up.*

Time passed.

"Have another drink," said Peri, "while I slip into something more comfortable."

Her idea of comfort was modest in one sense of the word: a nightdress or something, like a breath of smoke, and a seat on Matheny's lap.

"If you kiss me like that just once more," she breathed, "I'll forget I'm a nice girl."

Matheny kissed her like that. The door crashed open. A large man stood there, breathing heavily. "What are you doing with my wife?" he bawled.

"Sam!" screamed Peri. "I thought you were in Australia!"

"And he said he might settle out of court," finished Matheny. He stared in a numb fashion at his beer. "He'll come to my hotel room this afternoon. What am I going to do?"

"It is a great shame," said Doran. "I never thought…You know, he told everybody he would be gone on business for weeks yet. Pete, I am more sorry than I can express."

"If he thinks I'll pay his miserable blackmail," bristled Matheny, "he can take his head and stick—"

Doran shook his own. "I am sorry, Pete, but I would pay if I was you. He does have a case. It is too bad he just happened to be carrying that loaded camera, but he is a photographer and our laws on Earth are pretty strict about unlicensed correspondents. You could be very heavily fined as well as deported, plus all the civil-damage claims and the publicity. It would ruin your mission and even make trouble for the next man Mars sent."

"But," stuttered Matheny, "b-but it's a badger game!"

"Look," said Doran. He leaned over the table and gripped the Martian's shoulder. "I am your friend, see? I feel real bad this happened. In a way, it is my fault and I want to help you. So let me go talk to Sam Wendt. I will cool him off if I can. I will talk down his figure. It will still cost you, Pete, but you can pad your expense account, can't you? So we will both come see you today. That way there will be two people on your side, you and me, and Sam will not throw his weight around so much. You pay up in cash and it will be the end of the affair. I will see to that, pal!"

Matheny stared at the small dapper man. His aloneness came to him like a blow in the stomach. *Et tu, Brute,* he thought.

He bit his lip. "Thanks, Gus," he said. "You are a real friend."

Sam blocked the doorway with his shoulders as he entered the room. Doran followed like a diminutive tug pushing a very large liner. They closed the door. Matheny stood up, avoiding Sam's glare.

"Okay, louse," said Sam. "You got a better pal here than you deserve, but he ain't managed to talk me into settling for nothing."

"Let me get this—I mean well," said Matheny. "Look, sir, you claim that I, I mean that your wife and I were, uh, well, we weren't. I was only visiting—"

"Stow it, stow it." Sam towered over the Martian. "Shoot it to the Moon. You had your fun. It'll cost you. One million dollars."

"*One mil*—But—but—Gus," wailed Matheny, "this is out of all reason! I thought you said—"

Doran shrugged. "I am sorry, Pete. I could not get him any farther down. He started asking fifty. You better pay him."

"No!" Matheny scuttled behind a chair. "No, look here! I, Peter Matheny of the Martian Republic, declare you are blackmailing me!"

"I'm asking compensation for damages," growled Sam. "Hand it over or I'll go talk to a lawyer. That ain't blackmail. You got your choice, don't you?"

Matheny wilted. "Yes."

"A megabuck isn't so bad, Pete," soothed Doran. "I personally will see that you earn it back in—"

"Oh, never mind." Tears stood in Matheny's eyes. "You win." He took out his checkbook.

"None of that," rapped Sam. "Cash. Now."

"But you claimed this was a legitimate—"

"You heard me."

"Well—could I have a receipt?" begged Matheny.

Sam grinned.

"I just thought I'd ask," said Matheny. He opened a drawer and counted out one hundred ten-kilobuck bills. "There! And, and, and I hope you choke on it!"

Sam stuffed the money in a pocket and lumbered out.

Doran lingered. "Look here, Pete," he said, "I will make this up to you. Honest. All you have got to do is trust me."

"Sure." Matheny slumped on the bed. "Not your fault. Let me alone for a while, will you?"

"Listen, I will come back in a few hours and buy you the best dinner in all the Protectorates and—"

"Sure," said Matheny. "Sure."

Doran left, closing the door with great gentleness.

* * * *

He returned at 1730, entered, and stopped dead. The floor space was half taken up by a screen and a film projector.

"What happened, Pete?" he asked uncertainly.

Matheny smiled. "I took some tourist movies," he said. "Self-developing soundtrack film. Sit down and I'll show you."

"Well, thanks, but I am not so much for home movies."

"It won't take long. Please."

Doran shrugged, found a chair and took out a cigarette. "You seem pretty well cheered up now," he remarked. "That is a spirit I like to see. You have got to have faith."

"I'm thinking of a sideline business in live photography," said the Martian. "Get back my losses of today, you know."

"Well, now, Pete, I like your spirit, like I say. But if you are really interested in making some of that old baroom, and I think you are, then listen—"

"I'll sell prints to people for home viewing," went on Matheny. "I'd like your opinion of this first effort."

He dimmed the transparency and started the projector. The screen sprang into colored motion. Sam Wendt blocked the doorway with his shoulders.

"Who knows, I might even sell you one of the several prints I made today," said Matheny.

"Okay, louse," said Sam.

"Life is hard on Mars," commented Matheny in an idle tone, "and we're an individualistic culture. The result is pretty fierce competition, though on a person-to-person rather than organizational basis. All friendly enough, but—Oh, by the way, how do you like our Martian camera technology? I wore this one inside my buttonhole."

Doran in the screen shrugged and said: "I am sorry, Pete." Doran in the chair stubbed out his cigarette, very carefully, and asked, "How much do you want for that film?"

"Would a megabuck be a fair price?" inquired Matheny.

"Uh...huh."

"Of course, I am hoping Sam will want a copy too."

Doran swallowed. "Yeah. Yes, I think I can talk him into it."

"Good." Matheny stopped the projector. He sat down on the edge of the table, swinging one leg, and lit his pipe. Its bowl glowed in the dimness like the eye of a small demon. "By the way," he said irrelevantly, "if you check the newscast tapes, you'll find I was runner-up in last year's all-Martian pistol contest. It's a tough contest to win. There are no bad shots on Mars—survival of the fittest, you know."

Doran wet his lips. "Uh, no hard feelings. No, none at all. But say, in case you are, well, you know, looking for a slipstring, what I came here for was to tell you I have located the very guy you want. Only he is in jail right now, see, and it will cost—"

"Oh, no!" groaned Matheny. "Not the Syrtis Prospector! Kids are taught that swindle in kindergarten."

Doran bowed his head. "We call it the Spanish Prisoner here," he said. He got up. "I will send the price of those films around in the morning."

"You'll call your bank and have the cash pneumoed here tonight," said Matheny. "Also Sam's share. I daresay he can pay you back."

"No harm in trying, was there?" asked Doran humbly.

"None at all." Matheny chuckled. "In fact, I'm grateful to you. You helped me solve my major problem."

"Huh? I did what? How?"

"I'll have to investigate further, but I'm sure my hunch will be confirmed. You see, we Martians have stood in awe of Earthmen. And since for a long time there's been very little contact between the two planets except the purely official, impersonal sort, there's been nothing to disabuse us. It's certainly true that our organizations can't compete with yours, because your whole society is based on organizations. But now, by the same token, I wonder if your individuals can match ours. Ever hear of the Third Moon? No? The whipsaw play? The aqueduct squeeze? Good Lord, can't you even load a derrel set?"

Matheny licked his chops. "So there's our Martian export to Earth. Martian con men. I tell you this under security, of course not that anyone would believe you, till our boys walk home with the shirt off the Terrestrial back."

He waved an imperious pipestem. "Hurry up and pay me, please. I've a date tonight with Peri. I just called her up and explained the situation and she really *does* seem to like Martians."

Route Song of the Winged Folk

Light that leaps from a sun still sunken
hails the hunter at hover,
washes his wings in molten morning,
startles the stars to cover.
Blue is the bell of hollow heaven,
rung by a risen blowing.
Wide lie woodlands and mountain meadows,
great and green with their growing.
    But—look oh, look!—
    a red ray struck
    through tattered mist.
    A broadhorn buck
    stands traitor-kissed.
    The talons crook.
Tilt through tumult of wakened wind-noise
whining, whickering, whirly;
slip down a slantwise course of currents.
Ha, but the hunt comes early!
Poise on the pinions, take the target
there in the then of swooping—
Thrust on through by a wind-wild wingbeat,
stark the stabber comes stooping.
    The buck may pose
    for one short breath
    before it runs
    from whistling death.
    The hammer stuns.
    The talons close.

Broad and bright is the nearing noontide.
Drawn to dreamily drowsing,
shut-eyed in shade he sits now, sated,
Suddenly sounds his rousing.
Cool as the kiss of a ghost, then gusty,
rinsed by the rainfall after,
breezes brawl, and their forest fleetness
lives in leafage like laughter.

Among the trees
the branches shout
and groan and throw
themselves about.
It's time to go.
The talons ease.

Beat from boughs up to row through rainstreams.
Thickly thutters the thunder.
Hailwinds harried by lash of lightning
roar as they rise from under.
Blind in the black of clawing cloudbanks,
wins he his way, through slowly,
breaks their barrier, soars in sunlight.
High is heaven and holy.

The glow slants gold
caressingly
across and through
immensity
of silent blue.
The talons fold.

The Corkscrew of Space

"It is the very essence of being human that Man should ever long for new horizons, onward, upward striving. When Man ceases to hunger for the frontier, he will no longer be Man. They say Columbus was looking for a new trade route for spices from the Orient. What nonsense! As if the divine discontent could be reduced to an investment of the Grocery Guild! And likewise, on that memorable day whose centenary we are now observing, that unforgettable day when Man broke the last shackles of space and time, it was the holy fire which burned in that dauntless pioneer—" Speech by Hon. J. Farnsworth Willisgate, Martian Representative, in United Nations Assembly, 14 May 2247.

Everybody in Syrtis turned out when the Fleet arrived, and those who could traveled from as far as Yellowpeak and Whatsit for the occasion. A fair sprang up overnight, tents and booths sprawling over dusty miles, carnivals, migratory shows both live and recorded, noise and bustle and cheer. The alcohol plants and the fun houses did a rush business and you couldn't get a hotel room for love, money or good sweet water. Some folk even had to break the law and camp in the ruins, the long extinct native race sheltering a new, non-furry breed of Martian.

Laslos Magarac threaded past the crowd till he got to the spaceport fence. He had an impulse to pay a dollar to one of the telescope concessionaires for a look at the fifty great ships orbiting around the planet, but decided against it—the line was too long. After all, twice a local year was about once an Earth-year, so it was a capitalized Event—but the shuttle boats blasting down, sheeting flame through clouds of kicked-up red dust, were spectacular enough.

There was one arriving now, descending on a tail of fire some four miles away—which put it almost on the horizon. It was a bright gleam against the dark-blue sky, under the shrunken sun. As he watched, it entered its cradle and was wheeled off toward the waiting electrotrucks. Unloading began immediately; the trucks gulped packages and scurried like beetles toward the warehouses. Mail, merchandise, tools and luxuries—it was like a friendly greeting from old Earth.

Another line of vehicles was chuffing toward an empty shuttle with boxed and baled Martian goods, mostly drybean extract with a scattering of jewels, hopper pelts and prehistoric relics. The Fleet had to work fast, deliver its cargo and get loaded and start home again in a few days.

Magarac found a place in the post office line and resigned himself to waiting an hour. He was a somewhat dehydrated-looking man with a gaunt ugly face and dry black hair. The coverall which protected him from the late-afternoon chill was the standard Martian garment, but as a well-to-do planter, he bore an expensive cloak patterned like a rainbow.

"Ah...impatient, I see, my friend."

Magarac turned around. Oliver Latourelle had joined the queue behind him. The physicist was a well-nourished man with a plump, sharp-nosed face, watery blue eyes and bushy white hair fringing an egg-shaped skull. "Is it that you await mail from a fair one back on Earth?"

"Not any more," said Magarac gloomily. "Three Mars-years was too long to wait."

Latourelle clicked his tongue in sympathy. "The old tale, no? You are going to Mars to raise drybeans and make a fortune. But it takes long to become rich, even in the Dominion, and meanwhile the radio beams are too public and first-class mail is ten dollars an ounce."

"I'm doing okay," said Magarac defensively. "On Mars, that is. The trouble is that passage home would eat up half my money," He didn't like to discuss his personal affairs, but when there are barely 10,000 people on an entire planet, privacy hardly exists.

"Be consoled," advised Latourelle. "I speak as a man of experience. No one ever died of a broken heart. That organ is capable of miraculously rapid self-repair. The secret is to give it time to do so."

"Oh, I'm long over that business," said Magarac. "What I'm anxious to find out is how synthetic chemistry is progressing on Earth."

"So? I realize that to operate a plantation here requires a good scientific background, but are you so vitally interested that you cannot wait until your mail is delivered?"

"I am," said Magarac. "And so is all Mars, whether they know it or not. Eighty per cent of our industry is based on the dry bean. It won't grow anywhere else, and they're finding new medicinal uses for the extract every year.

"But figure it out for yourself. Freight rates being what they are, the stuff costs fifty dollars an ounce by the time the Earth doctor gets it. Every chemical firm you can name has a team trying to synthesize the basic molecule. One day soon, they're going to do it and then the drybean planters are finished. I'm watching the technical journals so I can sell out in time."

"And what will you do then, with the Dominion broke?"

"God only knows."

"And I thank Him I was born to be a research physicist, and I thank the Rockefeller Foundation for so generously subsidizing my work," said Latourelle. "Though with all respect to this excellent planet of yours, my friend, it seems a long and dry three years ahead until I can return to France." He had arrived with the Fleet before last, but even if he finished ahead of schedule, he would have to wait his turn for passage.

"What d'you have to be here for, anyway?" asked Magarac. He had gotten quite friendly with Latourelle, but knew little of the man's highly specialized project.

"I am studying magnetism. Mars, you see, does not have a core like Earth, but is of uniform composition. Apparently that accounts for its peculiar magnetic field...Yet in what way? I think it is an effect of relativistic wave mechanics. I have developed a most beautiful theory of Riemannian folds in a multiply connected space. Now I am checking the magnetic data to see if my theory will hold—you pardon the expression—water."

"And so what's your hurry to get your mail?" Magarac chuckled. "A gorgeous dame of your own?"

"No. Not that I am too old even now, I assure you, but I have more sense than to expect a delectable woman to wait five Earth-years for my return. I shall simply start afresh. No, no, my friend, it is that I have been extravagant with myself. Well, say rather that I am supplying a necessity. If you would care to visit my house tonight for a little private discussion—?"

And Latourelle would say nothing more. With elaborate silence, he picked up a large wooden case at the desk, and Margarac's last sight of him was a small suspicious figure hugging the box to his chest and stumping off toward Syrtis.

The news, no doubt, was good for humanity at large, but it would hit Mars heavily. Magarac had been an engineer on Earth, with added experience in chemistry, and could read between the lines. M'Kato announced cautiously that he thought he had the structural formula of protenzase. If he was right, they, would be synthesizing it in another year. Quite probably, the next Fleet would not be accepting drybean extract.

Magarac slouched gloomily away from the lights and music and swirl of the fair. What the devil was a man to do?

So far, the history of Mars had been economic history. The first colony had been planted to mine the rich uranium beds of the Aetheria. To save freight, it had had to be made self-sufficient; and, since this was not Periclean Greece, it had had to include women. Children resulted and dry bean culture provided a new source of income...so good a source that Mars stopped shipping uranium and used it instead to break down iron oxides and produce a breathable atmosphere.

Now they were the Dominion, with junior status in the UN, and talked big about gaining full self-government.

But when their economy was kicked in the stomach—

Magarac found Solis Avenue deserted. Only a few early returnees like himself, and the puritan isolationists who had not gone to the fair at all, were in town. He walked along the street between the flat-roofed stone houses of a rainless, timberless world. Overhead glittered a night of splendid stars, but he missed the Moon. Phobos and Deimos weren't worth writing home about.

He sighed and took out a cigarette and winced as he lit it. Synthetic tobacco, synthetic alcohol, synthetic steaks...God! Maybe he ought to throw in his hand and go back to Earth.

Only he liked it here. There was room in the deserts and the equatorial moors. A man was still a man, not a number. You worked with your hands and brain, for yourself, and making a time-gnawed sandstone waste blossom green was more satisfying than punching a clock in an Earthside factory. He wanted to get married and fill his ranch house with kids and raise them up proud of being Martians and Magaracs.

He turned a corner and emerged on Matsuoko Plaza. The thin air carried sound so poorly that he was almost on the rally before he realized.

It was the man himself, ranting from the balcony of Barsoom House. Magarac had to admit the demagogue had personality—a thick-set, dynamic type, with a fierce head that he was always tossing dramatically back, a voice which was organ and trumpet and bass drum. What the planter did not like was the words, or the crowd, or the greenshirted goons stationed around the square.

"—And I say to you, it was hard work, hard work and obedience which made the glorious vision of our grandfathers into the reality you see about you, which transformed a planetwide desolation into a world of men! It was thrift and sobriety. Yes, let me say it was intolerance—intolerance of vice, of drink, of laziness and rebelliousness against constituted authority, which made us what we now are.

"Then let us be intolerant! These self-styled democrats, these Earth-lovers, with their hell-brewed liquor and their loose women and their hair-splitting Bill of Rights designed only to thwart the Will of the People, will ruin us if they can. It is we who Believe who must save the destiny of Mars—"

Magarac shrank into a dark corner. The mob numbered almost a hundred men, shoving and yelling in an ugly mood, and Magarac was no friend of Blalock's Freeman Party. As an assemblyman of Syrtis District, he had often spoken publicly against him.

Freeman! Haw! And all the horses laughed. And all the horses' donkeys laughed. It was the old story, the would-be dictator, appealing to that queer, deep streak of masochistic puritanism in the Martian culture. The first colonists had needed such traits, to nerve them for their heartbreaking job.

But now—good Lord! Wasn't it about time Mars became civilized?

How it happened, Magarac was never sure. One minute, Blalock was talking himself beserk and the crowd was crying amen; the next minute, they were across the plaza, tearing Cassidy's Bar & Grill apart.

Cassidy was the most inoffensive little man in the Solar System, who often apologized for the rotgut he had to sell and the prices he had to charge. Martian beer was just barely preferable to none at all, though it cost as much as champagne would on Earth, and Cassidy operated a friendly neighborhood pub where men could shed the grinding sameness of desert reclamation in a few hours of conviviality. Magarac not only liked the place and its owner, but figured they were important to keeping the town sane.

When he saw glass splinter as two six-foot bruisers tossed Cassidy through his own window, and when he saw the whole investment smashed and running out in the street, Laslos Magarac decided that if Blalock had intimidated the police, the skunk ought to be shown there was still one man left in Syrtis.

A man, by God!

He ran across the square and started swinging.

Latourelle opened the door and stood uncertainly. "But what happened to you, my friend? You look like one of the old Martian ruins."

"Just a ruined Martian." Magarac lurched into the house and headed for the bathroom.

"Use the whole week's water ration if you desire," said Latourelle anxiously. "Me, I am not drinking water any more."

He hovered about trying to be helpful while Magarac got washed and patched. Apart from a missing tooth, the damage was only skin deep and a glass of analgesite took away the pain. It was with a sigh almost of contentment that Magarac finally stretched out in a battered easy chair.

Latourelle's house consisted of three rooms: bath, living-dining-sleeping, and a laboratory. The lab took up most of the space. But with his genius for being comfortable, the Frenchman had made his home a place of cheer.

"When the assembly meets next week, they're going to get an earful," said Magarac. "Not that it'll do any good. Blalock's bullies have everybody else cowed. But you shoulda seen the other guy." He smiled dreamily, with bruised and swelling lips. "Four of 'em was one too many for me, but they won't forget me in a hurry."

"I take it, then, you had the run-in with the Freemen?"

"They were busting up Cassidy's tavern. I dragged him away and called a doctor. He'll be all right."

"Barbarians! Have they no consideration for others?"

"Not the Freemen. They want to march around in fancy uniforms and so they figure everybody else ought to want the same." Magarac scowled and lighted a cigarette. His fingers shook a little. "Ollie, Mars is really sick."

"It must be, if this sort of thing is proceeding unhindered."

"We're out of touch with history. What can we do but stagnate, when you have to work a lifetime to save up enough money for one vacation on Earth? Blalock would be laughed out of town back there. But here he's a big frog because the whole planet is such a small puddle. And life is so grim at best that the shoddy excitement he can offer appeals to the young men."

Magarac spoke fast, with the feverish loquacity of weariness. "We have to live ascetically because of economics. So, sooner or later, we're going to rationalize that fact and turn ascetism from an unpleasant necessity to a shining virtue." He puffed hard, seeking comfort from the vile fake tobacco. "When that happens, Mars will no longer be fit to live on."

"It is not now, I fear," said Latourelle.

"Sure, it still is, because we have hope. We can work and hope to improve the place. But if Blalock gets into power, there won't even be that hope."

"These things, they come and go," said Latourelle fatalistically. "The beast will have his day and then be forgotten."

"Not when the bottom is going to be knocked out of our economy—which will happen pretty soon. Then everybody will be desperate enough to try the old panacea, the Almighty State." Magarac's face twisted. "And we could do so much, Ollie, if we had the chance! We have minerals, we have space for agriculture... and Earth is getting so overcrowded, someday it'll be desperate for food. But the damned cost of shipping! The time it takes! If we had a fast, cheap method of space travel, we could shuck this lopsided drybean economy, build up diversified industries, turn Mars into an Eden."

"One cannot very well argue with a gravitational potential difference," shrugged Latourelle.

"No, but a rocket is such a slow and wasteful way to overcome it." Magarac looked wistful. "And if we had something better, we'd be in close touch with Earth. We'd have a living culture to nourish us—books, music, art, everything Man needs to be more than just a two-legged belly."

"Well, be of good heart, my friend. In another fifty or a hundred years such a method will be available."

"Hm?" Magarac looked up through two black eyes. "What d'you mean?"

"Did you not know? *Bien*, I suppose not; you are no theoretical physicist. But if my concept of warped space is valid, then it should be entirely possible to—well, yes, to bring a spaceship directly from the surface of Mars to the surface of Earth, or vice versa, in the wink of an eye, at negligible cost. The ship would follow a geodesic through the appropriate fold in space—"

Magarac jumped to his feet. "You don't mean it!"

"But I do," Latourelle beamed. "There, is not that consolation to you?"

"No," said Magarac bleakly. "Fifty years will be too late. Mars will have been ruined in a decade." He leaned over and gripped Latourelle's shoulders. "D'you think you can build such a ship now?"

"What do you think I am? A sorcerer?"

"I know you're a Nobel Prize winner, a genuine genius and—"

"And an old tired man who will in a few years return to his beloved valley of the Dordogne and sit on a vine-covered terrace and sip a glass of Medoc. Shall we say a Pouillac?" Latourelle smiled wistfully. "I cannot produce miracles to order."

"You've done it, blast you! That neutron recycler of yours—"

"That was to prove a point which interested me. My heart goes out to you, but up here—" Latourelle tapped his gleaming forehead—"up here is a selfish animal, the subconscious mind, which must first be given an all-important motive before it will work. And as I am only to be on Mars three more years, I have no such motive."

Magarac slumped back in his chair. "Yeah...yeah, I guess so."

"Come on to Earth," urged Latourelle. "Come to France and I will show you how to live. You poor Martians must wolf your tasteless synthetics and gulp your miserable beer and try to persuade yourselves you are still human. It is no wonder that prohibitionism is growing. This Blalock now, if he could ever taste a properly prepared mousse of shad roe, with a Barsac—no, let us say a Puligny Montrachet—ah, he would realize that there are higher values than his own ambition and that the goodness of God is a more alive thing than the cold charity of the State."

Magarac braced himself. He liked Latourelle, but the old fellow was a bore on this one topic.

"I have given some thought to my first menu," went on the physicist raptly. "I cannot now specify the vintages, for I have lost touch, but give me time when I return, give me time. We will begin, of course, with a light dry sherry. There are those who maintain the virtues of vermouth as an *aperitif*, but not just before a meal, if you please. After the appetizers and the clear soup, there will be the fish and the white Burgundy, of which I spoke."

He was almost crooning now. "With the *tournedos*, we will serve Bordeaux... Chateau Lafite, I believe, if there has been a good year. With the salad, which must naturally be based on that great American contribution, the *calavo*, one might argue the merits of a Chateau Cheval Blanc, a Clos Fortet or an Haut Brion, but I think—"

Magarac nodded. He jerked to wakefulness when Latourelle stopped and regarded him with a hurt expression.

After a moment, the Frenchman looked contrite. "But of course! Forgive me! Here you have been in battle, righteous battle but a lost cause, and I sit droning on about joys out of your reach. I promised you a surprise, did I not? Well, a surprise you shall have, one to lighten your soul and renew your manhood. I have been saving it, denying it even to myself till you should come, for shared pleasures are best. But now—wait!"

He sprang to his feet and went over to a cabinet and opened it. Bottles glistened within, row on row of them, slender bottles with labels of gentle witchcraft.

Magarac felt his jaw clank down. He pulled it up again with an effort.

Latourelle laughed boyishly and rubbed his hands. "Is it not a noble sight? Is it not a vision for the gods? I assure you, this hope is all that has sustained me in my time on Mars."

"My God!" stammered Magarac. "It must have cost a fortune!"

"It did, it did indeed. Luckily, I have a fortune—or had." Latourelle broke out two slim glasses and a corkscrew. "You see, it has hitherto been impossible to export liquors to other planets. Quite apart from the cost, the prolonged high acceleration and then the free fall, they ruin it. Even crossing an ocean, a good wine is sadly bruised. Crossing space, it simply dies; one might as well drink Martian beer."

"Um...yes, I've heard of that. Colloidal particles agglomerate and obscure chemical reactions take place. Even whisky won't survive the trip." Magarac approached the cabinet reverently. "But this—"

"This is a new process. The last fleet brought me a letter announcing success and I hastened to order a case of assorted wines, It will not be much, but it will help keep me sane until the next shipment can arrive."

Latourelle extracted a bottle and held it up to the light. "The process, it involves a tasteless, harmless additive which stabilizes both the colloids and the chemistry. The finest Chambertin-Clos has been flown through an Atlantic hurricane and served that same night in New York with no slightest injury done to it."

The cork popped out with a flourish. "Now, my old friend, we drink the first wine to cross interplanetary space!"

The living red stream sparkled into the glasses. Silently, as if performing a holy rite, the two men raised their drinks and sipped.

Latourelle went white. *"Nom de diable!* Pure vinegar!"

That dauntless pioneer, the Immortal Oliver Latourelle! At a time of crisis, when the fair planet of Mars faced ruin and dictatorship, it was he and his great associate Laslos Magarac, later to become Premier of the Dominion and first President of a fully independent nation—it was those two men. driven by the need to expand humanity's frontiers to the very stars, who created the space-warp ship.

"Think of it, gentlemen! In one month, Latourelle had worked out the principles of such a vessel.

"In two more months, he had equipped an old ship, the piously renamed St. Emilion, *with a warp engine and had crossed to Earth in a few microseconds. It was only a token cargo he brought back to Mars, a case of wine, doubtless to symbolize the achievements of his own fair country, but he had proved it could be done. That simple case of wine foreshadowed the argosies which now ply between a thousand suns.*

"And it was the great Latourelle's first words when he emerged from his ship on his return from Earth and staggered across the sands of Mars—surely too overcome by emotion to walk straight—it was his words which have become the official motto of the Martian Republic and will live forever in Martian hearts as a flaming symbol of human genius:

"A votre santé!"

A Little Knowledge

They found the planet during the first Grand Survey. An expedition to it was organized very soon after the report appeared; for this looked like an impossibility.

It orbited its G9 sun at an average distance of some three astronomical units, thus receiving about one-eighteenth the radiation Earth gets. Under such a condition (and others, e.g., the magnetic field strength which was present) a subjovian ought to have formed; and indeed it had fifteen times the terrestrial mass. But—that mass was concentrated in a solid globe. The atmosphere was only half again as dense as on man's home, and breathable by him.

"Where 'ave h'all the H'atoms gone?" became the standing joke of the research team. Big worlds are supposed to keep enough of their primordial hydrogen and helium to completely dominate the chemistry. Paradox, as it was unofficially christened, did retain some of the latter gas, to a total of eight percent of its air. This posed certain technical problems which had to be solved before anyone dared land. However, land the men must; the puzzle they confronted was so delightfully baffling.

A nearly circular ocean basin suggested an answer which studies of its bottom seemed to confirm. Paradox had begun existence as a fairly standard specimen, complete with four moons. But the largest of these, probably a captured asteroid, had had an eccentric orbit. At last perturbation brought it into the upper atmosphere, which at that time extended beyond Roche's limit. Shock waves, repeated each time one of these ever-deeper grazings was made, blew vast quantities of gas off into space: especially the lighter molecules. Breakup of the moon hastened this process and made it more violent, by presenting more solid surface. Thus at the final crash, most of those meteoroids fell as one body, to form that gigantic astrobleme. Perhaps metallic atoms, thermally ripped free of their ores and splashed as an incandescent fog across half the planet, locked onto the bulk of what hydrogen was left, if any was.

Be that as it may, Paradox now had only a mixture of what had hitherto been comparatively insignificant impurities, carbon dioxide, water vapor, methane, ammonia, and other materials. In short, except for a small amount of helium, it had become rather like the young Earth. It got less heat and light, but the greenhouse effect kept most of its water liquid. Life evolved, went into the photosynthesis business, and turned the air into the oxynitrogen common on terrestrials.

The helium had certain interesting biological effects. These were not studied in detail. After all, with the hyperdrive opening endless wonders to them, spacefarers tended to choose the most obviously glamorous. Paradox lay a hundred parsecs from Sol. Thousands upon thousands of worlds were more easily reached; many were more pleasant and less dangerous to walk on. The expedition departed and had no successors.

First it called briefly at a neighboring star, on one of whose planets were intelligent beings that had developed a promising set of civilizations. But, again, quite a few such lay closer to home.

The era of scientific expansion was followed by the era of commercial aggrandizement. Merchant adventurers began to appear in the sector. They ignored Paradox, which had nothing to make a profit on, but investigated the inhabited globe in the nearby system. In the language dominant there at the time, it was called something like Trillia, which thus became its name in League Latin. The speakers of that language were undergoing their equivalent of the First Industrial Revolution, and eager to leap into the modern age.

Unfortunately, they had little to offer that was in demand elsewhere. And even in the spacious terms of the Polesotechnic League, they lived at the far end of a long haul. Their charming arts and crafts made Trillia marginally worth a visit, on those rare occasions when a trader was on such a route that the detour wasn't great. Besides, it was as well to keep an eye on the natives. Lacking the means to buy the important gadgets of Technic society, they had set about developing these for themselves.

Bryce Harker pushed through flowering vines which covered an otherwise doorless entrance. They rustled back into place behind him, smelling like allspice, trapping gold-yellow sunlight in their leaves. That light also slanted through ogive windows in a curving wall, to glow off the grain of the wooden floor. Furniture was sparse: a few stools, a low table bearing an intricately faceted piece of rock crystal. By Trillian standards the ceiling was high; but Harker, who was of average human size, must stoop.

Witweet bounced from an inner room, laid down the book of poems he had been reading, and piped, "Why, be welcome, dear boy-oo-oo-ooh!"

He looked down the muzzle of a blaster.

The man showed teeth. "Stay right where you are," he commanded. The vocalizer on his breast rendered the sounds he made into soprano cadenzas and arpeggios, the speech of Lenidel. It could do nothing about his vocabulary and grammar. His knowledge did include the fact that, by omitting all honorifics and circumlocutions without apology, he was uttering a deadly insult.

That was the effect he wanted—deadliness.

"My, my, my dear good friend from the revered Solar Commonwealth," Witweet stammered, "is this a, a jest too subtle for a mere pilot like myself to comprehend? I will gladly laugh if you wish, and then we, we shall enjoy tea and cakes.

I have genuine Lapsang Soochong tea from Earth, and have just found the most darling recipe for sweet cakes—"

"Quiet!" Harker rapped. His glance flickered to the windows. Outside, flower colors exploded beneath reddish tree trunks; small bright wings went fluttering past; The Waterfall That Rings Like Glass Bells could be heard in the distance. Annanna was akin to most cities of Lenidel, the principal nation on Trillia, in being spread through an immensity of forest and parkscape. Nevertheless, Annanna had a couple of million population, who kept busy. Three aircraft were crossing heaven. At any moment, a pedestrian or cyclist might come along The Pathway Of The Beautiful Blossoms And The Bridge That Arches Like A Note Of Music, and wonder why two humans stood tense outside number 1337.

Witweet regarded the man's skinsuit and boots, the pack on his shoulders, the tightly drawn sharp features behind the weapon. Tears blurred the blue of Witweet's great eyes. "I fear you are engaged in some desperate undertaking which distorts the natural goodness that, I feel certain, still inheres," he quavered. "May I beg the honor of being graciously let help you relieve whatever your distress may be?"

Harker squinted back at the Trillian. *How much do we really know about his breed, anyway? Damned nonhuman thing—Though I never resented his existence till now*—His pulse knocked, his skin was wet and stank, his mouth was dry and cottony-tasting.

Yet his prisoner looked altogether helpless. Witweet was an erect biped; but his tubby frame reached to barely a meter, from the padded feet to the big, scalloped ears. The two arms were broomstick thin, the four fingers on either hand suggested straws. The head was practically spherical, bearing a pug muzzle, moist black nose, tiny mouth, quivering whiskers, upward-slanting tufty brows. That, the tail, and the fluffy silver-gray fur which covered the whole skin, had made Olafsson remark that the only danger to be expected from this race was that eventually their cuteness would become unendurable.

Witweet had nothing upon him except an ornately embroidered kimono and a sash tied in a pink bow. He surely owned no weapons, and probably wouldn't know what to do with any. The Trillians were omnivores, but did not seem to have gone through a hunting stage in their evolution. They had never fought wars, and personal violence was limited to an infrequent scuffle.

Still, Harker thought, *they've shown the guts to push into deep space. I daresay even an unarmed policeman—Courtesy Monitor—could use his vehicle against us, like by ramming.*

Hurry!

"Listen," he said. "Listen carefully. You've heard that most intelligent species have members who don't mind using brute force, outright killing, for other ends than self-defense. Haven't you?"

Witweet waved his tail in assent. "Truly I am baffled by that statement, concerning as it does races whose achievements are of incomparable magnificence. However, not only my poor mind, but those of our most eminent thinkers have been engaged in fruitless endeavors to—"

"Dog your hatch!" The vocalizer made meaningless noises and Harker realized he had shouted in Anglic. He went back to Lenidellian-equivalent. "I don't propose to waste time. My partners and I did not come here to trade as we announced. We came to get a Trillian spaceship. The project is important enough that we'll kill if we must. Make trouble, and I'll blast you to greasy ash. It won't bother me. And you aren't the only possible pilot we can work through, so don't imagine you can block us by sacrificing yourself. I admit you are our best prospect. Obey, cooperate fully, and you'll live. We'll have no reason to destroy you." He paused. "We may even send you home with a good piece of money. We'll be able to afford that."

The bottling of his fur might have made Witweet impressive to another Trillian. To Harker, he became a ball of fuzz in a kimono, an agitated tail and a sound of coloratura anguish. "But this is insanity...if I may say that to a respected guest...One of *our* awkward, lumbering, fragile, unreliable prototype ships—when you came in a vessel representing centuries of advancement—? Why, why, why, in the name of multiple sacredness, why?"

"I'll tell you later," the man said. "You're due for a routine supply trip to, uh, Gwinsai Base, starting tomorrow, right? You'll board this afternoon, to make final inspection and settle in. We're coming along. You'd be leaving in about an hour's time. Your things must already be packed. I didn't cultivate your friendship for nothing, you see! Now, walk slowly ahead of me, bring your luggage back here and open it so I can make sure what you've got. Then we're on our way."

Witweet stared into the blaster. A shudder went through him. His fur collapsed. Tail dragging, he turned toward the inner rooms.

Stocky Leo Dolgorov and ash-blond Einar Olafsson gusted simultaneous oaths of relief when their leader and his prisoner came out onto the path. "What took you that time?" the first demanded. "Were you having a nap?"

"Nah, he entered one of their bowing, scraping, and unction-smearing contests." Olafsson's grin held scant mirth.

"Trouble?" Harker asked.

"N-no...three, four passersby stopped to talk—we told them the story and they went on," Dolgorov said. Harker nodded. He'd put a good deal of thought into that excuse for his guards' standing around—that they were about to pay a social call on Witweet but were waiting until the pilot's special friend Harker had made him a gift. A lie must be plausible, and the Trillian mind was not human.

"We sure hung on the hook, though." Olafsson started as a bicyclist came around a bend in the path and fluted a string of complimentary greetings.

Dwarfed beneath the men, Witweet made reply. No gun was pointed at him now, but one rested in each of the holsters near his brain. (Harker and companions had striven to convince everybody that the bearing of arms was a peaceful but highly symbolic custom in *their* part of Technic society, that without their weapons they would feel more indecent than a shaven Trillian.) As far as Harker's wire-taut attention registered, Witweet's answer was routine. But probably some forlornness crept into the overtones, for the neighbor stopped.

"Do you feel quite radiantly well, dear boy?" he asked.

"Indeed I do, honored Pwiddy, and thank you in my prettiest thoughts for your ever-sweet consideration," the pilot replied. "I...well, these good visitors from the starfaring culture of splendor have been describing some of their experiences—oh, I simply must relate them to you later, dear boy!—and naturally, since I am about to embark on another trip, I have been made pensive by this." Hands, tail, whiskers gesticulated. *Meaning what?* wondered Harker in a chill; and clamping jaws together: *Well, you knew you'd have to take risks to win a kingdom.* "Forgive me, I pray you of your overflowing generosity, that I rush off after such curt words. But I have promises to keep, and considerable distances to go before I sleep."

"Understood." Pwiddy spent a mere five minutes bidding farewell all around before he pedaled off. Meanwhile several others passed by. However, since no well-mannered person would interrupt a conversation even to make salute, they created no problem.

"Let's go." It grated in Dolgorov's throat.

Behind the little witch-hatted house was a pergola wherein rested Witweet's personal flitter. It was large and flashy—large enough for three humans to squeeze into the back—which fact had become an element in Harker's plan. The car that the men had used during their stay on Trillia, they abandoned. It was unmistakably an off-planet vehicle.

"Get started!" Dolgorov cuffed at Witweet.

Olafsson caught his arm and snapped: "Control your emotions! Want to tear his head off?"

Hunched over the dashboard, Witweet squeezed his eyes shut and shivered till Harker prodded him. "Pull out of that funk," the man said.

"I...I beg your pardon. The brutality so appalled me—" Witweet flinched from their laughter. His fingers gripped levers and twisted knobs. Here was no steering by gestures in a light-field, let alone simply speaking an order to an autopilot. The overloaded flitter crawled skyward. Harker detected a flutter in its grav unit, but decided nothing was likely to fail before they reached the spaceport. And after that, nothing would matter except getting off this planet.

Not that it was a bad place, he reflected. Almost Earthlike in size, gravity, air, deliciously edible life forms—an Earth that no longer was and perhaps never had been, wide horizons and big skies, caressed by light and rain. Looking out, he saw woodlands in a thousand hues of green, meadows, river-gleam, an occasional dollhouse dwelling, grainfields ripening tawny and the soft gaudiness of a flower ranch. Ahead lifted The Mountain Which Presides Over Moonrise In Lenidel, a snowpeak pure as Fuji's. The sun, yellower than Sol, turned it and a few clouds into gold.

A gentle world for a gentle people. Too gentle.

Too bad. For them.

Besides, after six months of it, three city-bred men were about ready to climb screaming out of their skulls. Harker drew forth a cigarette, inhaled it into lighting and filled his lungs with harshness. *I'd almost welcome a fight,* he thought savagely.

But none happened. Half a year of hard, patient study paid richly off. It helped that the Trillians were—well, you couldn't say lax about security, because the need for it had never occurred to them. Witweet radioed to the portmaster as he approached, was informed that everything looked okay, and took his flitter straight through an open cargo lock into a hold of the ship he was to pilot.

The port was like nothing in Technic civilization, unless on the remotest, least visited of outposts. After all, the Trillians had gone in a bare fifty years from propeller-driven aircraft to interstellar spaceships. Such concentration on research and development had necessarily been at the expense of production and exploitation. What few vessels they had were still mostly experimental. The scientific bases they had established on planets of next-door stars needed no more than three or four freighters for their maintenance.

Thus a couple of buildings and a ground-control tower bounded a stretch of ferrocrete on a high, chilly plateau; and that was Trillia's spaceport. Two ships were in. One was being serviced, half its hull plates removed and furry shapes swarming over the emptiness within. The other, assigned to Witweet, stood on landing jacks at the far end of the field. Shaped like a fat torpedo, decorated in floral designs of pink and baby blue, it was as big as a Dromond-class hauler. Yet its payload was under a thousand tons. The primitive systems for drive, control, and life support took up that much room.

"I wish you a just too, too delightful voyage," said the portmaster's voice from the radio. "Would you honor me by accepting an invitation to dinner? My wife has, if I may boast, discovered remarkable culinary attributes of certain sea weeds brought back from Gwinsai; and for my part, dear boy, I would be so interested to hear your opinion of a new verse form with which I am currently experimenting."

"No…I thank you, no, impossible, I beg indulgence—" It was hard to tell whether the unevenness of Witweet's response came from terror or from the tobacco smoke that had kept him coughing. He almost flung his vehicle into the spaceship.

Clearance granted, *The Serenity of the Estimable Philosopher Ittypu* lifted into a dawn sky. When Trillia was a dwindling cloud-marbled sapphire among the stars, Harker let out a breath. "We can relax now."

"Where?" Olafsson grumbled. The single cabin barely allowed three humans to crowd together. They'd have to take turns sleeping in the hall that ran aft to the engine room. And their voyage was going to be long. Top pseudovelocity under the snail-powered hyperdrive of this craft would be less than one lightyear per day.

"Oh, we can admire the darling murals," Dolgorov fleered. He kicked an intricately painted bulkhead.

Witweet, crouched miserable at the control board, flinched. "I beg you, dear, kind sir, do not scuff the artwork," he said.

"Why should you care?" Dolgorov asked. "You won't be keeping this junkheap."

Witweet wrung his hands. "Defacement is still very wicked. Perhaps the consignee will appreciate my patterns? I spent such a time on them, trying to get every teensiest detail correct."

"Is that why your freighters have a single person aboard?" Olafsson laughed. "Always seemed reckless to me, not taking a backup pilot at least. But I suppose two Trillians would get into so fierce an argument about the interior decor that they'd each stalk off in an absolute snit."

"Why, no," said Witweet, a trifle calmer. "We keep personnel down to one because more are not really needed. Piloting between stars is automatic, and the crewbeing is trained in servicing functions. Should he suffer harm en route, the ship will put itself into orbit around the destination planet and can be boarded by others. An extra would thus uselessly occupy space which is often needed for passengers. I am surprised that you, sir, who have set a powerful intellect to prolonged consideration of our astronautical practices, should not have been aware—"

"I was, I was!" Olafsson threw up his hands as far as the overhead permitted. "Ask a rhetorical question and get an oratorical answer."

"May I, in turn, humbly request enlightenment as to your reason for...sequestering...a spacecraft ludicrously inadequate by every standards of your oh, so sophisticated society?"

"You may." Harker's spirits bubbled from relief of tension. They'd pulled it off. They really had. He sat down—the deck was padded and perfumed—and started a cigarette. Through his bones beat the throb of the gravity drive: energy wasted by a clumsy system. The weight it made underfoot fluctuated slightly in a rhythm that felt wavelike.

"I suppose we may as well call ourselves criminals," he said; the Lenidellian word he must use had milder connotations. "There are people back home who wouldn't leave us alive if they knew who'd done certain things. But we never got rich off them. Now we will."

He had no need for recapitulating except the need to gloat: "You know we came to Trillia half a standard year ago, on a League ship that was paying a short visit to buy art. We had goods of our own to barter with, and announced we were going to settle down for a while and look into the possibility of establishing a permanent trading post with a regular shuttle service to some of the Technic planets. That's what the captain of the ship thought too. He advised us against it, said it couldn't pay and we'd simply be stuck on Trillia till the next League vessel chanced by, which wouldn't likely be for more than a year. But when we insisted, and gave him passage money, he shrugged," as did Harker.

"You have told me this," Witweet said. "I thrilled to the ecstasy of what I believed was your friendship."

"Well, I did enjoy your company," Harker smiled. "You're not a bad little osco. Mainly, though, we concentrated on you because we'd learned you qualified for our uses—a regular freighter pilot, a bachelor so we needn't fuss with a family, a chatterer who could be pumped for any information we wanted. Seems we gauged well."

"We better have," Dolgorov said gloomily. "Those trade goods cost us everything we could scratch together. I took a steady job for two years, and lived like a lama, to get my share."

"And now we'll be living like fakirs," said Olafsson. "But afterward—afterward!"

"Evidently your whole aim was to acquire a Trillian ship," Witweet said. "My bemusement at this endures."

"We don't actually want the ship as such, except for demonstration purposes," Harker said. "What we want is the plans, the design. Between the vessel itself, and the service manuals aboard, we have that in effect."

Witweet's ears quivered. "Do you mean to publish the data for scientific interest? Surely, to beings whose ancestors went on to better models centuries ago—if, indeed, they ever burdened themselves with something this crude—surely the interest is nil. Unless…you think many will pay to see, in order to enjoy mirth at the spectacle of our fumbling efforts?" He spread his arms. "Why, you could have bought complete specifications most cheaply; or, indeed, had you requested of me, I would have been bubbly-happy to obtain a set and make you a gift." On a note of timid hope: "Thus you see, dear boy, drastic action is quite unnecessary. Let us return. I will state you remained aboard by mistake—"

Olafsson guffawed. Dolgorov said, "Not even your authorities can be that sloppy-thinking." Harker ground out his cigarette on the deck, which made the pilot wince, and explained at leisured length:

"We want this ship precisely because it's primitive. Your people weren't in the electronic era when the first human explorers contacted you. They, or some later visitors, brought you texts on physics. Then your bright lads had the theory of such things as gravity control and hyperdrive. But the engineering practice was something else again.

"You didn't have plans for a starship. When you finally got an opportunity to inquire, you found that the idealistic period of Technic civilization was over and you must deal with hardheaded entrepreneurs. And the price was set way beyond what your whole planet could hope to save in League currency. That was just the price for diagrams, not to speak of an actual vessel. I don't know if you are personally aware of the fact—it's no secret—but this is League policy. The member companies are bound by an agreement.

"They won't prevent anyone from entering space on his own. But take your case on Trillia. You had learned in a general way about, oh, transistors, for instance. But that did not set you up to manufacture them. An entire industrial complex is needed for that and for the million other necessary items. To design and build one, with the inevitable mistakes en route, would take decades at a minimum, and would involve regimenting your entire species and living in poverty because every bit of capital has to be reinvested. Well, you Trillians were too sensible to pay that price. You'd proceed more gradually. Yet at the same time, your scientists, all your more adventurous types were burning to get out into space.

"I agree your decision about that was intelligent too. You saw you couldn't go directly from your earliest hydrocarbon-fuelled engines to a modern starship—to a completely integrated system of thermonuclear powerplant, initiative-grade navigation and engineering computers, full-cycle life support, the whole works, using solid-state circuits, molecular-level and nuclear-level transitions, force-fields instead of moving parts—an *organism*, more energy than matter. No, you wouldn't be able to build that for generations, probably.

"But you could go ahead and develop huge, clumsy, but workable fission-power units. You could use vacuum tubes, glass rectifiers, kilometers of wire, to generate and regulate the necessary forces. You could store data on tape if not in single molecules, retrieve with a cathode-ray scanner if not with a quantum-field pulse, compute with miniaturized gas-filled units that react in microseconds if not with photon interplays that take a nanosecond.

"You're like islanders who had nothing better than canoes till someone happened by in a nuclear-powered submarine. They couldn't copy that, but they might invent a reciprocating steam engine turning a screw—they might attach an airpipe so it could submerge—and it wouldn't impress the outsiders, but it would cross the ocean too, at its own pace; and it would overawe any neighboring tribes."

He stopped for breath.

"I see," Witweet murmured slowly. His tail switched back and forth. "You can sell our designs to sophonts in a proto-industrial stage of technological development. The idea comes from an excellent brain. But why could you not simply buy the plans for resale elsewhere?"

"The damned busybody League," Dolgorov spat.

"The fact is," Olafsson said, "spacecraft—of advanced type—have been sold to, ah, less advanced peoples in the past. Some of those weren't near industrialization, they were Iron Age barbarians, whose only thought was plundering and conquering. They could do that, given ships which are practically self-piloting, self-maintaining, self-everything. It's cost a good many lives and heavy material losses on border planets. But at least none of the barbarians have been able to duplicate the craft thus far. Hunt every pirate and warlord down, and that ends the problem. Or so the League hopes. It's banned any more such trades."

He cleared his throat. "I don't refer to races like the Trillians, who're obviously capable of reaching the stars by themselves and unlikely to be a menace when they do," he said. "You're free to buy anything you can pay for. The price of certain things is set astronomical mainly to keep you from beginning overnight to compete with the old-established outfits. They prefer a gradual phasing-in of newcomers, so they can adjust.

"But aggressive, warlike cultures, that'd not be interested in reaching a peaceful accommodation—they're something else again. There's a total prohibition on supplying their sort with anything that might lead to them getting off their planets in less than centuries. If League agents catch you at it, they don't fool around with rehabilitation like a regular government. They shoot you."

Harker grimaced. "I saw once on a telescreen interview," he remarked, "Old Nick van Rijn said he wouldn't shoot those kinds of offenders. He'd hang them. A rope is reusable."

"And this ship can be copied," Witweet breathed. "A low industrial technology, lower than ours, could tool up to produce a modified design, in a comparatively short time, if guided by a few engineers from the core civilization."

"I trained as an engineer," Harker said. "Likewise Leo; and Einar spent several years on a planet where one royal family has grandiose ambitions."

"But the horror you would unleash!" wailed the Trillian. He stared into their stoniness. "You would never dare go home," he said.

"Don't want to anyway," Harker answered. "Power, wealth, yes, and everything those will buy—we'll have more than we can use up in our lifetimes, at the court of the Militants. Fun, too." He smiled. "A challenge, you know, to build a space navy from zero. I expect to enjoy my work."

"Will not the, the, the Polesotechnic League...take measures?"

"That's why we must operate as we have done. They'd learn about a sale of plans, and then they wouldn't stop till they'd found and suppressed our project. But a non-Technic ship that never reported in won't interest them. Our destination is well outside their sphere of normal operations. They needn't discover any hint of what's going on—till an interstellar empire too big for them to break is there. Meanwhile, as we gain resources, we'll have been modernizing our industry and fleet."

"It's all arranged," Olafsson said. "The day we show up in the land of the Militants, bringing the ship we described to them, we'll become princes."

"Kings, later," Dolgorov added. "Behave accordingly, you xeno. We don't need you much. I'd soon as not boot you through an airlock."

Witweet spent minutes just shuddering.

The *Serenity*, etc. moved on away from Trillia's golden sun. It had to reach a weaker gravitational field than a human craft would have needed, before its hyperdrive would function.

Harker spent part of that period being shown around, top to bottom and end to end. He'd toured a sister ship before, but hadn't dared ask for demonstrations as thorough as he now demanded. "I want to know this monstrosity we've got, inside out," he said while personally tearing down and rebuilding a cumbersome oxygen renewer. He could do this because most equipment was paired, against the expectation of eventual in-flight down time.

In a hold, among cases of supplies for the research team on Gwinsai, he was surprised to recognize a lean cylindroid, one hundred twenty centimeters long. "But here's a Solar-built courier!" he exclaimed.

Witweet made eager gestures of agreement. He'd been falling over himself to oblige his captors. "For messages in case of emergency, magnificent sir," he babbled. "A hyperdrive unit, an autopilot, a radio to call at journey's end till someone comes and retrieves the enclosed letter—"

"I know, I know. But why not build your own?"

"Well, if you will deign to reflect upon the matter, you will realize that anything we could build would be too slow and unreliable to afford very probable help. Especially since it is most unlikely that, at any given time, another spaceship would be ready to depart Trillia on the instant. Therefore this courier is set, as you can see if you wish to examine the program, to go a considerably greater distance—though nevertheless not taking long, your human constructions being superlatively fast—to the planet called, ah, Oasis…an Anglic word meaning a lovely, cool, refreshing haven, am I correct?"

Harker nodded impatiently. "Yes, one of the League companies does keep a small base there."

"We have arranged that they will send aid if requested. At a price, to be sure. However, for our poor economy, as ridiculous a hulk as this is still a heavy investment, worth insuring."

"I see. I didn't know you bought such gadgets—not that there'd be a pegged price on them; they don't matter any more than spices or medical equipment. Of course, I couldn't find out every detail in advance, especially not things you people take so for granted that you didn't think to mention them." On impulse, Harker patted the round head. "You know, Witweet, I guess I do like you. I will see you're rewarded for your help."

"Passage home will suffice," the Trillian said quietly, "though I do not know how I can face my kinfolk after having been the instrument of death and ruin for millions of innocents."

"Then don't go home," Harker suggested. "We can't release you for years in any case, to blab our scheme and our coordinates. But we could smuggle in whatever and whoever you wanted, same as for ourselves."

The head rose beneath his palm as the slight form straightened. "Very well," Witweet declared.

That fast? jarred through Harker. *He is nonhuman, yes, but*—The wondering was dissipated by the continuing voice:

"Actually, dear boy, I must disabuse you. We did not buy our couriers, we salvaged them."

"What? Where?"

"Have you heard of a planet named, by its human discoverers, Paradox?"

Harker searched his memory. Before leaving Earth he had consulted every record he could find about this entire stellar neighborhood. Poorly known though it was to men, there had been a huge mass of data—suns, worlds…"I think so," he said. "Big, isn't it? With, uh, a freaky atmosphere."

"Yes." Witweet spoke rapidly. "It gave the original impetus to Technic exploration of our vicinity. But later the men departed. In recent years, when we ourselves became able to pay visits, we found their abandoned camp. A great deal of gear had been left behind, presumably because it was designed for Paradox only and would be of no use elsewhere, hence not worth hauling back. Among these machines we came upon a few couriers. I suppose they had been overlooked. Your civilization can afford profligacy, if I may use that term in due respectfulness."

He crouched, as if expecting a blow. His eyes glittered in the gloom of the hold.

"Hm." Harker frowned. "I suppose by now you've stripped the place."

"Well, no." Witweet brushed nervously at his rising fur. "Like the men, we saw no use in, for example, tractors designed for a gravity of two-point-eight terrestrial. They can operate well and cheaply on Paradox, since their fuel is crude oil, of which an abundant supply exists near the campsite. But we already had electric-celled grav motors, however archaic they are by your standards. And we do not need weapons like those we found, presumably for protection against animals. We certainly have no intention of colonizing Paradox!"

"Hm." The human waved, as if to brush off the chattering voice. "Hm." He slouched off, hands in pockets, pondering.

In the time that followed, he consulted the navigator's bible. His reading knowledge of Lenidellian was fair. The entry for Paradox was as laconic as it would have been in a Technic reference; despite the limited range of their operations, the Trillians had already encountered too many worlds to allow flowery descriptions. Star type and coordinates, orbital elements, mass density, atmospheric composition, temperature ranges, and the usual rest were listed. There was no notation about habitability, but none was needed. The original explorers hadn't been poisoned or come down with disease; Trillian metabolism was similar to theirs.

The gravity field was not too strong for this ship to make landing and, later, ascent. Weather shouldn't pose any hazards, given reasonable care in choosing one's path; that was a weakly energized environment. Besides, the vessel was meant for planetfalls, and Witweet was a skilled pilot in his fashion…

Harker discussed the idea with Olafsson and Dolgorov. "It won't take but a few days," he said, "and we might pick up something really good. You know I've not been too happy about the Militants' prospects of building an ample industrial base fast enough to suit us. Well, a few machines like this, simple things they can easily copy but designed by good engineers…could make a big difference."

"They're probably rustheaps," Dolgorov snorted. "That was long ago."

"No, durable alloys were available then," Olafsson said. "I like the notion intrinsically, Bryce. I don't like the thought of our tame xeno taking us down. He might crash us on purpose."

"That sniveling faggot?" Dolgorov gibed. He jerked his head backward at Witweet, who sat enormous-eyed in the pilot chair listening to a language he did not understand. "By accident, maybe, seeing how scared he is!"

"It's a risk we take at journey's end," Harker reminded them. "Not a real risk. The ship has some ingenious failsafes built in. Anyhow, I intend to stand over him the whole way down. If he does a single thing wrong, I'll kill him. The controls aren't made for me, but I can get us aloft again, and afterward we can re-rig."

Olafsson nodded. "Seems worth a try," he said. "What can we lose except a little time and sweat?"

* * * *

Paradox rolled enormous in the viewscreen, a darkling world, the sky-band along its sunrise horizon redder than Earth's, polar caps and winter snowfields gashed by the teeth of mountains, tropical forest and pampas a yellow-brown fading into raw deserts on one side and chopped off on another side by the furious surf of an ocean where three moons fought their tidal wars. The sun was distance-dwarfed, more dull in hue than Sol, nevertheless too bright to look near. Elsewhere, stars filled illimitable blackness.

It was very quiet aboard, save for the mutter of power plant and ventilators, the breathing of men, their restless shuffling about in the cramped cabin. The air was blued and fouled by cigarette smoke; Witweet would have fled into the corridor, but they made him stay, clutching a perfume-dripping kerchief to his nose.

Harker straightened from the observation screen. Even at full magnification, the rudimentary electro-optical system gave little except blurriness. But he'd practiced on it, while orbiting a satellite, till he felt he could read those wavering traces.

"Campsite and machinery, all right," he said. "No details. Brush has covered everything. When were your people here last, Witweet?"

"Several years back," the Trillian wheezed. "Evidently vegetation grows apace. Do you agree on the safety of a landing?"

"Yes. We may snap a few branches, as well as flatten a lot of shrubs, but we'll back down slowly, the last hundred meters, and we'll keep the radar, sonar, and gravar sweeps going." Harker glanced at his men. "Next thing is to compute our descent pattern," he said. "But first I want to spell out again, point by point, exactly what each of us is to do under exactly what circumstances. I don't aim to take chances."

"Oh, no," Witweet squeaked. "I beg you, dear boy, I beg you the prettiest I can, please don't."

After the tension of transit, landing was an anticlimax. All at once the engine fell silent. A wind whistled around the hull. Viewscreens showed low, thick-boled trees; fronded brownish leaves; tawny undergrowth; shadowy glimpses of metal objects beneath vines and amidst tall, whipping stalks. The sun stood at late afternoon in a sky almost purple.

Witweet checked the indicators while Harker studied them over his head. "Air breathable, of course," the pilot said, "which frees us of the handicap of having to wear smelly old spacesuits. We should bleed it in gradually, since the pressure is greater than ours at present and we don't want earaches, do we? Temperature—" He shivered delicately. "Be certain you are wrapped up snug before you venture outside."

"You're venturing first," Harker informed him.

"What? Oo-ooh, my good, sweet, darling friend, no, please, no! It is *cold* out there, scarcely above freezing. And once on the ground, no gravity generator to help, why, weight will be tripled. What could I possibly, possibly do? No, let me stay inside, keep the home fires burning—I mean keep the thermostat at a cozy temperature and, yes, I will make you the nicest pot of tea—"

"If you don't stop fluttering and do what you're told, I'll tear your head off," Dolgorov said. "Guess what I'll use your skin for."

"Let's get cracking," Olafsson said. "I don't want to stay in this Helheim any longer than you."

They opened a hatch the least bit. While Paradoxian air seeped in, they dressed as warmly as might be, except for Harker. He intended to stand by the controls for the first investigatory period. The entering gases added a whine to the wind-noise. Their helium content made speech and other sounds higher pitched, not quite natural; and this would have to be endured for the rest of the journey, since the ship had insufficient reserve tanks to flush out the new atmosphere. A breath of cold got by the heaters, and a rank smell of alien growth.

But you could get used to hearing funny, Harker thought. And the native life might stink, but it was harmless. You couldn't eat it and be nourished, but neither could its germs live off your body. If heavy weapons had been needed here, they were far more likely against large, blundering herbivores than against local tigers.

That didn't mean they couldn't be used in war.

Trembling, eyes squinched half-shut, tail wrapped around his muzzle, the rest of him bundled in four layers of kimono, Witweet crept to the personnel lock. Its outer valve swung wide. The gangway went down. Harker grinned to see the dwarf-ish shape descend, step by step under the sudden harsh hauling of the planet.

"Sure you can move around in that pull?" he asked his companions.

"Sure," Dolgorov grunted. "An extra hundred-fifty kilos? I can backpack more than that, and then it's less well distributed."

"Stay cautious, though. Too damned easy to fall and break bones."

"I'd worry more about the cardiovascular system," Olafsson said. "One can stand three gees a while, but not for a very long while. Fluid begins seeping out of the cell walls, the heart feels the strain too much—and we've no gravanol along as the first expedition must have had."

"We'll only be here a few days at most," Harker said, "with plenty of chances to rest inboard."

"Right," Olafsson agreed. "Forward!"

Gripping his blaster, he shuffled onto the gangway. Dolgorov followed. Below, Witweet huddled. Harker looked out at bleakness, felt the wind slap his face with chill, and was glad he could stay behind. Later he must take his turn outdoors, but for now he could enjoy warmth, decent weight—

The world reached up and grabbed him. Off balance, he fell to the deck. His left hand struck first, pain gushed, he saw the wrist and arm splinter. He screamed. The sound came weak as well as shrill, out of a breast laboring against thrice the heaviness it should have had. At the same time, the lights in the ship went out.

Witweet perched on a boulder. His back was straight in spite of the drag on him, which made his robes hang stiff as if carved on an idol of some minor god of justice. His tail, erect, blew jauntily in the bitter sunset wind; the colors of his garments were bold against murk that rose in the forest around the dead spacecraft.

He looked into the guns of three men, and into the terror that had taken them behind the eyes; and Witweet laughed.

"Put those toys away before you hurt yourselves," he said, using no circumlocutions or honorifics.

"You bastard, you swine, you filthy treacherous xeno, I'll kill you," Dolgorov groaned. "Slowly."

"First you must catch me," Witweet answered. "By virtue of being small, I have a larger surface-to-volume ratio than you. My bones, my muscles, my veins and capillaries and cell membranes suffer less force per square centimeter than do yours. I can move faster than you, here. I can survive longer."

"You can't outrun a blaster bolt," Olafsson said.

"No. You can kill me with that—a quick, clean death which does not frighten me. Really, because we of Lenidel observe certain customs of courtesy, use certain turns of speech—because our males in particular are encouraged to develop esthetic interests and compassion—does that mean we are cowardly or effeminate?" The Trillian clicked his tongue. "If you supposed so, you committed an elementary logical fallacy which our philosophers name the does-not-follow."

"Why shouldn't we kill you?"

"That is inadvisable. You see, your only hope is quick rescue by a League ship. The courier can operate here, being a solid-state device. It can reach Oasis and summon a vessel which, itself of similar construction, can also land on Paradox and take off again…in time. This would be impossible for a Trillian craft. Even if one were ready to leave, I doubt the Astronautical Senate would permit the pilot to risk descent.

"Well, rescuers will naturally ask questions. I cannot imagine any story which you three men, alone, might concoct that would stand up under the subsequent, inevitable investigation. On the other hand, I can explain to the League's agents that you were only coming along to look into trade possibilities and that we were trapped on Paradox by a faulty autopilot which threw us into a descent curve. I can do this in *detail*, which you could not if you killed me. They will return us all to Trillia, where there is no death penalty."

Witweet smoothed his wind-ruffled whiskers. "The alternative," he finished, "is to die where you are, in a most unpleasant fashion."

Harker's splinted arm gestured back the incoherent Dolgorov. He set an example by holstering his own gun. "I…guess we're outsmarted," he said, word by foul-tasting word. "But what happened? Why's the ship inoperable?"

"Helium in the atmosphere," Witweet explained calmly. "The monatomic helium molecule is ooh-how-small. It diffuses through almost every material. Vacuum tubes, glass rectifiers, electronic switches dependent on pure gases, any such device soon becomes poisoned. You, who were used to a technology that had long left this kind of thing behind, did not know the fact, and it did not occur to you as a possibility. We Trillians are, of course, rather acutely aware of the problem. I am the first who ever set foot on Paradox. You should have noted that my courier is a present-day model."

"I see," Olafsson mumbled.

"The sooner we get our message off, the better," Witweet said. "By the way, I assume you are not so foolish as to contemplate the piratical takeover of a vessel of the Polesotechnic League."

"Oh, no!" said they, including Dolgorov, and the other two blasters were sheathed.

"One thing, though," Harker said. A part of him wondered if the pain in him was responsible for his own abnormal self-possession. Counterirritant against dismay? Would he weep after it wore off? "You bargain for your life by promising to have ours spared. How do we know we want your terms? What'll they do to us on Trillia?"

"Entertain no fears," Witweet assured him. "We are not vindictive, as I have heard some species are; nor have we any officious concept of 'rehabilitation.' Wrongdoers are required to make amends to the fullest extent possible. You three have cost my people a valuable ship and whatever cargo cannot be salvaged. You must have technological knowledge to convey, of equal worth. The working conditions will not be intolerable. Probably you can make restitution and win release before you reach old age.

"Now, come, get busy. First we dispatch that courier, then we prepare what is necessary for our survival until rescue."

He hopped down from the rock, which none of them would have been able to do unscathed, and approached them through gathering cold twilight with the stride of a conqueror.

MARQUE AND REPRISAL

-1-

Le roi a fait battre tambour,
Le roi a fait battre tambour—

Gunnar Heim halted in midstride. A while he stood, turning his head in search of the voice that had risen out of the dark.

Pour voir toutes ces dames.
Et la premiere qu'il a vue—

It was some distance off, almost lost in the background of machine rumble to landward of the docks. But only one man was likely to be making his mock with that sinister old ballad, in San Francisco on this night.

Lut a ravi son ame.
Rataplan! Rataplan! Rataplan-plan-plan-plan!

Heim started after the sound. He could still move fast and softly when he wanted to. In a moment his ears picked up the ring and snarl of a guitar played in anger.

Rataplan! Rataplan! Rataplan-plan-plan-plan!

Warehouses bulked black on his right. At this hour not very long before dawn, the city had dimmed; there was only a reddish haze above the roofs, and the remote luminous leap of the palace towers on Nob Hill. To the left a cargo submarine lay like a sleek moon-scaled dragon, but no longshore robots or men were at work around it. The bay was ebony and a shimmer of glade. Kilometers distant, the hills on the eastern shore made a wall besprinkled with artificial stars. The real stars were wan, and so was the defense satellite that climbed rapidly into view—as if all suns had withdrawn from a planet gone strengthless. Luna stood at half phase near the zenith. He could not see the light-spot of Apollo City on the dark side, through the damp autumn air.

> *"Marquis, dis moi, la connais tu?*
> *Marquis, dis moi, la connais tu?*
> *Quelle est cette jolie dame?"*
> *Et le marquis a répondu:*
> *"Sire Roi, c'est ma femme."*
> *Rataplan! Rataplan! Rataplan-plan-plan-plan!*
> *Rataplan! Rataplan! Rataplan-plan-plan-plan!*

Heim rounded a shed by the pier and saw the minstrel. He sat on a bollard, looking out across the water, a man more small and shabby than expected. His fingers leaped across the twelve strings as if attacking an enemy, and the moon gleamed off tears on his face.

Heim paused in the shadow of the wall. He ought not to interrupt. They had related, in the Spaceman's Rest, that the buck was drunk and wild. "And when he'd spent his last millo, he wanted to sing for booze," the bartender said. "I told him we didn't want none of that here. He said he'd sung his way through a dozen planets and what was wrong with Earth that nobody wanted to listen to him. I said the strip show was coming on the 3V in a minute and that's what the customers wanted, not any of his foreign stuff. So he yelled about singing to the stars or some such pothead notion. I told him go ahead, get out before I threw him out. And out he went. That was about an hour ago. Friend of yours?"

"Maybe," Heim said.

"Uh, you might go look for him then. He could get into trouble. Somebody might go for an expensive gutbucket like he was hauling."

Heim nodded and tossed off his beer. The Welfare section of any large city was bad to be alone in after nightfall. Even the police of Western countries made little effort to control those whom the machines had displaced before birth. They settled for containing that fury and futility in its own district, well away from the homes of people who had skills the world needed. On his walk-abouts through the subculture of the irrelevant men, Heim carried a stun pistol. He had had use for it on occasion.

They knew him locally, though. He had told them he was a retired spaceman—anything nearer the truth would have been unwise—and before long he was accepted as a genial drinking or gambling companion, less odd than many of the floaters who drifted in and out of their indifferent purview. He waved at several acquaintances, some feral and some surrendered to hopelessness, and left the bar.

Since the minstrel had probably headed for the Embarcadero, Heim did too. His stride lengthened as he went. At first there had been no sense of mission about finding the fellow. It had merely been an excuse to go on yet another slumming trip. But the implications grew in his mind.

And now that his search was ended, the song caught at him and he felt his pulse accelerate. This stranger might indeed have the truth about that which had happened among yonder constellations.

> *—La reine a fait faire un bouquet*
> *De belles fleurs de lyse.*
> *Et la senteur de ce bouquet*
> *A fait mourir marquise.*

As the older tale, also of tyranny, treachery, and death, crashed to its end, Heim reached a decision.

> *Rataplan! Rataplan! Rataplan-plan-plan-plan!*
> *Rataplan! Rataplan! Rataplan-plan-plan-plan!*

Silence followed, except for the lapping of water and the ceaseless throb of that engine which was the city. Heim trod forth.

"Good evening," he said.

The minstrel jerked where he sat, drew a ragged breath, and twisted about. Heim spread his hands, smiling. "I'm harmless," he said. "Was just admiring your performance. Mind if I join you?"

The other wiped at his eyes, furiously. Then the thin sharp face steadied into a considering look. Gunnar Heim was not one you met unperturbed, in such an area. He was nigh two meters tall, with breadth to match. His features were blunt and plain, an old scar zigzagging across the brow, under reddish-brown hair that in this forty-sixth year of his age was peppered with gray. But he was decently clad, in the high-collared tunic and the trousers tucked into soft half-boots that were the current mode. The hood of his cloak was thrown back. His weapon did not show.

"Well—" The minstrel made a spastic shrug. "This is a public place." His English was fluent, but bore a heavier accent than his French.

Heim took a flat bottle of whisky from his pocket. "Will you drink with me, sir?"

The minstrel snatched it. After the first swallow he gusted, "Ahhh!" Presently: "Forgive my bad manners. I needed that." He raised the flask. *"Isten éltesse,"* he toasted, drank again, and passed it back.

"Skaal." Heim took a gulp and settled himself on the wharf next to the bollard. What he had already drunk buzzed in him, together with a rising excitement. It was an effort to stay relaxed.

The minstrel came down to sit beside him. "You are not American, then?" he asked. His tone wavered a bit; he was obviously trying to make unemotional conversation while the tears dried on his high cheekbones.

"I am, by naturalization," Heim said. "My parents were Norwegian. But I was born on Gea, Tau Ceti II."

"What?" The hoped-for eagerness sprang into the singer's countenance. He sat up straight. "You are a spaceman?"

"Navy, till about fifteen years ago. Gunnar Heim is my name."

"I...Endre Vadász." The agile fingers disappeared in Heim's handshake. "Hungarian, but I have spent the last decade off Earth."

"Yes, I know," Heim said with care. "I saw you on a news program recently."

Vadász's lips writhed. He spat off the dock.

"You didn't get a chance to say much during the interview," Heim angled.

"No. They were cautious to mute me. 'So you are a musician, Mr. Vadász. You have worked your way by any means that came to hand, from star to star, bearing the songs of Mother Earth to the colonists and the non-humans. *Isn't* that interesting!'" The guitar cried out under a stroke.

"And you wanted to tell about New Europe, and they kept steering you from the subject. I wondered why."

"The word had come to them. From your precious American authorities, under pressure from the big brave World Federation. It was too late to cancel my announced appearance, but I was to be gagged." Vadász threw back his head and laughed, a coyote bark under the moon. "Am I paranoid? Do I claim I am being persecuted? Yes. But what if the conspiracy against me is real? Then does my sanity or lunacy make any difference?"

"M-m-m." Heim rubbed his chin and throttled back the emotions within himself. He was not an impetuous man. "How can you be sure?"

"Quinn admitted it, when I reproached him afterward. He said he had been told the station might lose its license if it, ah, lent itself to allegations which might embarrass the Federation in this difficult time. Not that I was too surprised. I had had talks with officials, both civil and military, since arriving on Earth. The kindest thing any one of them said was that I must be mistaken. But they had seen my proofs. They knew."

"Did you try the French? They'd be more likely to do something, I should think."

"Yes. In Paris I got no further than an assistant undersecretary. He was frightened of my story and would not refer me to anyone higher who might believe. I went on to Budapest, where I have kin. My father arranged for me to see the foreign minister himself. He was at least honest with me. New Europe was no concern of Hungary, which could in any event not go against the whole Federation. I left his office and walked for many hours. Finally I sat down in the dark by the Freedom Memorial. I looked at Imre Nagy's face, and it was only cold bronze. I looked at the figures of the martyrs, dying at his feet, and knew why no one will listen to me. So I got very drunk." Vadász reached for the bottle. "I have been drunk most of the time since."

Now we ask him! It flared in Heim. His voice would not remain calm any longer; but Vadász didn't notice. "Your story, I gather from what bits and pieces have leaked past this unofficial official censorship—your story is that the people are not dead on New Europe. Right?"

"Right, sir. They fled into the mountains, every one of them."

"The Haute Garance," Heim nodded. He had all he could do merely to nod. "Good guerrilla country. Lots of cover, most never mapped, and you can live off the land."

"You have been there!" Vadász set the bottle down and stared.

"Pretty often, while in the Navy. It was a favorite spot to put in for overhaul and planet leave. And then I spent four months in a stretch on New Europe by myself, recovering from this." Heim touched the mark on his forehead.

Vadász peered close through the dappled moonlight. "Did the Aleriona do that to you?"

"No. This was over twenty years ago. I bought it while we were putting down the Hindu-German trouble on Lilith, which you're probably too young to remember. The skirmishes with Alerion didn't begin till later." Heim spoke absently. For this moment the drive and ferocity in him were overlaid by—

Red roofs and steep narrow streets of Bonne Chance, winding down along the River Carsac to the Bale des Pecheurs, which lay purple and silver to the world's edge. Lazy days, drinking Pernod in a sidewalk cafe and lapping up the ruddy sunshine as a cat laps milk. When he got better, hunting trips into the highlands with Jacques Boussard and Toto Astier...good bucks, open of heart and hand, a little crazy as young men ought to be. Madelon—

He shook himself and asked roughly, "Do you know who is, or was, in charge?"

"A Colonel de Vigny of the planetary constabulary. He assumed command after the *mairie* was bombed, and organized the evacuation."

"Not old Robert de Vigny? My God! I knew him." Heim's fist clenched on the concrete. "Yes, in that case the war is still going on."

"It cannot last," Vadász mumbled. "Given time, the Aleriona will hunt everyone down."

"I know the Aleriona too," Heim said. He drew a long breath and looked at the stars. Not toward the sun Aurore. Across a hundred and fifty light-years, it would be lost to his eyes; and it lay in the Phoenix anyway, walled off from him by the heavy curve of Earth. But he could not look straight at the minstrel while he asked, "Did you meet one Madelon Dubois? That'd be her maiden name. I expect she's long married."

"No." Vadász's drink-slurred voice became instantly clear and gentle. "I am sorry, but I did not."

"Well—" Heim forced a shrug. "The chances were way against it. There's supposed to be half a million people on New Europe. Were the...the casualties heavy?"

"I heard that Coeur d'Yvonne, down in Pays d'Or, was struck by a hydrogen missile. Otherwise—no, I do not believe so. The fighting was mostly in space, when the Aleriona fleet disposed of the few Federation Navy ships that happened to be near. Afterward they landed in force, but in uninhabited areas at first, so that except for a couple of raids with nothing worse than lasers and chemical bombs, the other towns had time to evacuate. They had been called on to surrender, of course, but de Vigny refused and so many went off with him that the rest came too."

Damn it, I have got *to keep this impersonal. At least till I know more.* "How did you escape? The newscasts that mentioned you when you first arrived were vague about it. Deliberately, I suppose."

Vadász made the bottle gurgle. "I was there when the attack came," he said, thickly again. "The French commandeered a merchant vessel and sent it after help, but it was destroyed when scarcely above the atmosphere. There was also a miner in from Naqsa." He got the non-human pronunciation nearly right "You may know that lately there has been an agreement, the Naqsans may dig in Terre du Sud for a royalty. So far off, they had seen nothing, knew nothing, and cloud cover above Garance would keep them ignorant After a radio discussion, the Aleriona commander let them go, I daresay not wanting to antagonize two races at once. Of course, the ship was not allowed to take passengers. But I had earlier flitted down for a visit and won the captain's fancy—that a human should be interested in *his* songs, and even learn a few—so he smuggled me aboard and kept me hidden from the Aleriona inspectors. De Vigny thought I could carry his message—hee, hee!" Vadász's laugh was close to hysteria. Fresh tears ran out of his eyes. "From Naqsa I had to, what you call, bum my way. It took time. And was all, all for nothing."

He laid the guitar across his knees, strummed, and sang low:

> *Adieu, ma mie, adieu, mon coeur,*
> *Adieu, ma mie, adieu, mon coeur,*
> *Adieu, mon espirance—*

Heim took the bottle, then abruptly set it down so hard that it clanked. He jumped to his feet and began pacing. His shadow wove back and forth across the minstrel, his cloak fluttered against the moonlight on the water.

"Nej, ved fanden!" he exploded.

"Eh?" Vadász blinked up at him.

"Look, do you say you have proof?"

"Yes. I have offered to testify under drugs. And de Vigny gave me letters, photographs, a whole microfilm packet with every bit of information he could scrape together. But no one on Earth will admit it is genuine. Few will even look at it."

"I will," Heim said. The blood roared in his ears.

"Good. Good. Right here, the package is." Vadász fumbled in his soiled tunic.

"No, wait till later. I'll take your word for now. It fits in with every other scrap of fact I've come across."

"So I have convinced one man," Vadász said bitterly.

"More than that." Heim drew a long breath. "Look, friend, with due respect for you—and I respect anyone who's had the guts to go out and make his own kind of life—I'm not a raggedy-ass self-appointed troubadour. I'm boss and chief owner of Heimdal."

"The nuclear motor makers?" Vadász shook his head, muzzily. "No. *Non. Nein. Nyet.* You would never be here. I have seen your motors as far from home as the Rigel Domain."

"Uh-huh. Damn good motors, aren't they? When I decided to settle on Earth, I studied the possibilities. Navy officers who've resigned their commissions and don't want to go into the merchant fleet have much too good a chance of ending down among the unemployables. But I saw that whoever was first to introduce the two-phase control system the Aleriona invented would lock gravs on the human market and half the non-human ones. And...I'd been there when Tech Intelligence dissected an Aleriona ship we captured in the set-to off Achernar. My father-in-law was willing to stake me. So today I'm—oh, not one of the financial giants. But I have ample money.

"Also, I've kept in touch with my Academy classmates. Some of them are admirals by now. They'll pay attention to my ideas. And I'm a pretty good contributor to the Libertarian Party, which means that Twyman will listen to me too. He'd better!"

"No." The dark tousled head moved from side to side, still drooping. "This cannot be. I cannot have found someone."

"Brother, you have." Heim slammed a fist into his palm with a revolver noise. A part of him wondered, briefly, at his own joy. Was it kindled by this confirmation that they were not dead on New Europe? Or the chance that he, Gunnar Heim, might personally short-circuit Alerion the damned? Or simply and suddenly a purpose, after five years without Connie? He realized now the emptiness of those years.

No matter. The glory mounted and mounted.

He bent down, scooped up the bottle with one hand and Vadász with the other. *"Skaal!"* he shouted to Orion the Hunter, and drank a draught that made the smaller man gape. "Whoo-oo! Come along, Endre. I know places where, we can celebrate this as noisily as we damn please. We shall sing songs and tell tales and drink the moon down and the sun up and then shall go to work. Right?"

"Y-yes—" Still dazed, Vadász tucked his guitar under an arm and wobbled in Heim's wake. The bottle was not quite empty when Heim began "The Blue Landsknechts," a song as full of doom and hell as he was. Vadász hung the guitar from his neck and chorded. After that they got together on "La Marseillaise," and "Die Beiden Grenadiere," and "Skipper Bullard," and about that time they had collected a fine bunch of roughneck companions, and all in all it turned out to be quite an evening.

-2-

1700 hours in San Francisco was 2000 in Washington, but Harold Twyman, senior senator from California and majority leader of United States representatives in the Parliament of the World Federation, was a busy man whose secretary could not arrange a sealed-call appointment any earlier on such short notice as Heim had given. However, that suited the latter quite well. It gave him time to recover from the previous night without excessive use of drugs, delegate the most pressing business at the Heimdal plant to the appropriate men, and study Vadász's evidence. The Magyar was still asleep in a guest room. His body had a lot of abuse to repair.

Shortly before 1700 Heim decided he was sufficiently familiar with the material Robert de Vigny had assembled. He clicked off the viewer, rubbed his eyes, and sighed. An assortment of aches still nibbled at him. Once—Lord, it didn't seem very long ago!—he could have weathered twenty times the bout he'd just been through, and made love to three or four girls, and been ready to ship out next morning. *I'm at the awkward age,* he thought wryly. *Too young for antisenescence treatment to make any difference, too old for—what? Nothing, by Satan! I simply sit too much these days. Let me get away for a bit and this paunch I'm developing will melt off.* He sucked in his stomach, reached for a pipe, and stuffed the bowl with unnecessary violence.

Why not take a vacation? he thought. Go into the woods and hunt; he had a standing invitation to use Ian McVeigh's game preserve in British Columbia. Or sail his catamaran to Hawaii. Or order out his interplanetary yacht, climb the Lunar Alps, tramp the Martian hills; Earth was so stinking cluttered. Or even book an interstellar passage. He hadn't seen his birthplace on Gea since his parents sent him back to Stavanger to get a proper education. Afterward there had been Greenland Academy, and the Deepspace Fleet, and Earth again, always too much to do.

Sharply before him the memory rose: Tau Ceti a ball of red gold in the sky; mountains coming down to the sea as they did in Norway, but the oceans of Gea were warm and green and haunted him with odors that had no human name; the Sindabans that were his boyhood playmates, laughing just like him as they all ran to the water and piled into a pirogue, raised the wingsail and leaped before the wind; campfire on the island, where flames sprang forth to pick daoda fronds and the slim furry bodies of his friends out of a night that sang; chants and drums and portentous ceremonies; and—and—*No.* Heim struck a light to his tobacco and puffed hard. *I was twelve years old when I left. And now Far and Mor are dead, and my Sindabans grown into an adulthood which humans are still trying to understand. I'd only find an isolated little scientific base, no different from two score that I've seen elsewhere. Time is a one-way lane.*

Besides—his gaze dropped to the micros on his desk—*there's work to do here.*

Footfalls clattered outside the study. Glad of any distraction, Heim rose and walked after them. He ended in the living room. His daughter had come home and flopped herself in a lounger.

"Hi, Lisa," he said. "How was school?"

"Yechy." She scowled and stuck out her tongue. "Old Espinosa said I gotta do my composition over again."

"Spelling, eh? Well, if you'd only buckle down and learn—"

"Worse'n correcting spelling. Though why they make such a fuss about that, *me* don't know! He says the semantics are upwhacked. Old pickleface!"

Heim leaned against the wall and wagged his pipe stem at her. " 'Semantics' is a singular, young'un. Your grammar's no better *than* your orthography. Also, trying to write, or talk, or think without knowing semantic principles is like trying to dance before you can walk. I'm afraid my sympathies are with Mr. Espinosa."

"But Dad!" she wailed. "You don't *realize!* I'd have to do the whole paper again from *go!"*

"Of course."

"I *can't!"* Her eyes, which were blue like his own—otherwise she was coming to look heartbreakingly like Connie—clouded up for a squall. "I got a date with *Dick*—Oh!" One hand went to her mouth.

"Dick? You mean Richard Woldberg?" Lisa shook her head wildly. "The blaze you don't," Heim growled. "I've told you damn often enough you're not to see that lout."

"Oh, Dad! J-j-just because—"

"I know. High spirits. I call it malicious mischief and a judge that Woldberg Senior bought, and I say any girl who associates with that crowd is going to get in trouble. Nothing so mild as pregnancy, either." Heim realized he was shouting. He put on his court-martial manner and rapped: "Simply making that date was not only disobedience but disloyalty. You went behind my back. Very well, you're confined to quarters for a week whenever you're not in school. And I expect to see your composition tomorrow, written right."

"I hate you!" Lisa screamed. She flung out of the lounger and ran. For a second the bright dress, slender body, and soft brown hair were before Heim's gaze, then she was gone. He heard her kick the door of her room, as if to make it open for her the faster.

What else could I do? he cried after her, but of course there was no reply. He prowled the long room, roared at a maid who dared come in with a question, and stalked forth to stand on the terrace among the roses, glaring across San Francisco.

The city lay cool and hazed under a lowering sun. From here, on Telegraph Hill, his view ranged widely over spires and elways, shining water and garden islands. That was why he had picked this suite, after Connie died in that senseless flyer smash and the Mendocino County house got too big and still. In the past year or so Lisa had begun to whine about the address being unfashionable. But the hell with her.

No. It was only that fourteen was a difficult age. It had to be only that. And without a mother—He probably should have remarried, for Lisa's sake. There'd been no lack of opportunity. But at most the affairs had ended as...affairs... because none of the women were Connie. Or even Madelon. Unless you counted Jocelyn Lawrie, but she was hopelessly lost in her damned peace movement and anyway—Still, he could well be making every mistake in the catalogue, trying to raise Lisa by himself. Whatever had become of the small dimpled person to whom he was the center of the universe?

He glanced at his watch and swore. Past time to call Twyman.

Back in the study he had a wait while the secretary contacted her boss and sealed the circuit. He couldn't sit; he paced the room, fingering his books, his desk computer, his souvenirs of the lancer to whose command he had risen. Hard had it been to give up *Star Fox.* For a year after his marriage, he'd remained in the Navy. But that wouldn't work out, wasn't fair to Connie. He stroked a hand across her picture, without daring to animate it right now. *Not hard after all, sweetheart. Well worth everything.*

The phone chimed and the secretary said, "The senator is on the line, sir." Her image gave way to Twyman's distinguished gray head. Heim sat down, on the edge of the chair.

"Hello, Gunnar," Twyman said. "How's everything?"

"Comme ci, comme ça," Heim answered. "A little more *ci* than *ça,* I think. How's with you?"

"Rushed damn near to escape velocity. The Aleriona crisis, you know."

"Uh-huh. That's what I wanted to talk about"

Twyman looked alarmed. "I can't say much."

"Why not?"

"Well…well, there really isn't much to say yet. Their delegation has only been here for about three weeks, you remember, so no formal discussions have commenced. Diplomacy between different species is always like that. Such a fantastic lot of spadework to do, information exchange, semantic and xenological and even epistemological studies to make, before the two sides can be halfway sure they're talking about the same subjects."

"Harry," said Heim, "I know as well as you do that's a string of guff. The informal conferences are going on right along. When Parliament meets with the Aleriona, you boys on the inside will have everything rigged in advance. Arguments marshaled, votes lined up, nothing left to do but pull the switch and let the machine ratify the decision you've already made."

"Well, ah, you can't expect, say, the Kenyan Empire representatives to understand something so complex—"

Heim rekindled his pipe. "What are you going to do, anyhow?" he asked.

"Sorry, I can't tell you."

"Why not? Isn't the Federation a 'democracy of states'? Doesn't its Constitution guarantee free access to information?"

"You'll have as much information as you want," Twyman snapped, "when we start to operate on an official basis."

"That'll be too late." Heim sighed. "Never mind. I can add two and two. You're going to let Alerion have New Europe, aren't you?"

"I can't—"

"You needn't. The indications are everywhere. Heads of state assuring their people there's no reason to panic, we're not going to have a war. Politicians and commentators denouncing the 'extremists.' Suppression of any evidence that there might be excellent reason to go to war."

Twyman bristled. "What do you mean?"

"I've met Endre Vadász," Heim said.

"Who?—oh, yes. That adventurer who claims—Look, Gunnar, there is some danger of war. I'm not denying that. France especially is up in arms, demonstrations, riots, mobs actually tearing down the Federation flag and trampling on it. We'll have our hands full as is, without letting some skizzy like him inflame passions worse."

"He's not a skizzy. Also, Alerion's whole past record bears him out. Ask any Navy man."

"Precisely." Twyman's voice grew urgent. "As we move into their sphere of interest, inevitably there've been more and more clashes. And can you blame them? They were cruising the Phoenix region when men were still huddled in caves. It's theirs."

"New Europe isn't. Men discovered and colonized it."

"I know, I know. There are so many stars—The trouble is, we've been greedy. We've gone too far, too fast."

"There are a lot of stars," Heim agreed, "but not an awful lot of planets where men can live. We need 'em."

"So does Alerion."

"Ja? What use is a people-type world to them? And even on their own kind of planet, why didn't they ever colonize on anything like our scale, till we came along?"

"Response to our challenge," Twyman said. "What would you do if an alien culture started grabbing planetary systems as near to Sol as Aurore is to The Eith?" He leaned back. "Oh, don't get me wrong. The Aleriona are no saints. They've sometimes been fiends, by our standards. But we have to inhabit the same cosmos with them. War is unthinkable."

"Why?" drawled Heim.

"What? Gunnar, are you out of your brain? Haven't you read any history? Looked at the craters? Understood how close a call the Nuclear Exchange was?"

"So close a call that ever since the human race has been irrational on the subject," Heim said, "But I've seen some objective analyses. And even you must admit that the Exchange and its aftermath rid us of those ideological governments."

"An interstellar war could rid us of Earth!"

"Twaddle. A planet with space defenses like ours can't be attacked from space by any fleet now in existence. Every beam would be attenuated, every missile intercepted, every ship clobbered."

"That didn't work for New Europe," Twyman said. He was getting angry.

"No, of course not. New Europe didn't have any space fortresses or home fleet. Nothing but a few lancers and pursuers that happened to be in the vicinity—when Alerion's armada came."

"Don't be ridiculous, Gunnar. The affair was simply another clash, one that got out of hand."

"So the Aleriona say," Heim murmured. "If that's the truth, how come none, not one, of our vessels escaped?"

Twyman ignored him. "We'll never be sure who fired the first shot. But we can be sure the Aleriona wouldn't have missiled New Europe if our commander hadn't tried to pull his ships down into atmosphere for a toadhole maneuver. What other conceivable reason was there?"

If New Europe really was missiled, Heim thought. *But it wasn't.*

The senator checked indignation, sat silent for a bit, and went on almost mildly. "The whole episode illustrates how intolerable the situation has become, how matters are bound to escalate if we don't halt while we still can. And what do we want to fight for? A few wretched planets? We need only let Alerion's traditional sphere alone, and the rest of the galaxy is open to us. Fight for revenge? Well, you can't laugh off half a million dead human beings, but the fact remains that they are dead. I don't want to send any more lives after theirs."

"Okay," Heim said with equal quietness. "What do you figure to do?"

Twyman studied him before answering: "You're my friend as well as a political backstop. I can trust you to keep your mouth shut. And to support me, I think, once you know. Do I have your promise?"

"Of secrecy...well...yes. Support? That depends. Say on."

"The details are still being threshed out. But in general, Alerion offers us an indemnity for New Europe. A very sizable one. They'll also buy out our other interests in the Phoenix. The exact terms have yet to be settled—obviously they can't pay in one lump—but the prospect looks good. With us out of their sphere, they'll recognize a similar one for humans around Sol, and keep away. But we aren't building any walls, you understand. We'll exchange ambassadors and cultural missions. A trade treaty will be negotiated in due time.

"There. Does that satisfy you?"

Heim looked into the eyes of a man he had once believed honest with himself, and said: "No."

"Why not?" Twyman asked most softly.

"From a long-range viewpoint, your scheme ignores the nature of Alerion. They aren't going to respect our sphere any longer than it takes them to consolidate the one you want to make them a present of. And I do mean a present—because until a trade treaty is agreed on, which I predict will be never, how can we spend any of that valuta they so generously pay over?"

"Gunnar, I know friends of yours have died at Aleriona hands. But it's given you a persecution complex."

"Trouble is, Harry," Heim stole from Vadász, "the persecution happens to be real. You're the one living in a dream. You're so obsessed with avoiding war that you've forgotten every other consideration. Including honor."

"What do you mean by that?" Twyman demanded.

"New Europe was not missiled. The colonists are not dead. They've taken to the hills and are waiting for us to come help them."

"That isn't so!"

"I have the proof right here on my desk."

"You mean the documents that—that tramp forged?"

"They aren't forgeries. It can be proved. Signatures, fingerprints, photographs, the very isotope ratios in film made on New Europe. Harry, I never thought you'd sell out half a million human beings."

"I deny that I am doing so," Twyman said glacially. "You're a fanatic, *Mister* Heim, that's all. Even if it were true what you say...how do you propose to rescue anyone from a planet occupied and space-guarded? But it isn't true. I've spoken to survivors whom the Aleriona brought here. You must have seen them yourself on 3V. They witnessed the bombardment."

"Hm. You recall where they were from?"

"The Coeur d'Yvonne area. Everything else was wiped clean."

"So the Aleriona say," Heim retorted. "And doubtless the survivors believe it too. Any who didn't would've been weeded out during interrogation. I say that Coeur d'Yvonne was the only place hit by a nuke. I say further that we can fight if we must, and win. A space war only; I'm not talking the nonsense about 'attacking impregnable Alerion' which your tame commentators keep putting into the mouths of us 'extremists,' and Earth is every bit as impregnable. I say further that if we move fast, with our full strength, we probably won't have to fight. Alerion will crawfish. She isn't strong enough to take us on...yet. I say further and finally that if we let down those people out there who're trusting us, we'll deserve everything that Alerion will eventually do to us." He tamped his smoldering pipe. "That's my word, Senator."

Twyman said, trembling: "Then my word, Heim, is that we've outgrown your kind of sabertooth militarism and I'm not going to let us be dragged back to that level. If you're blaze enough to quote what I've told you here in confidence, I'll destroy you. You'll be in the Welfare district, or correction, within a year."

"Oh, no," Heim said. "I keep my oaths. The public facts can speak for themselves. I need only point them out."

"Go ahead, if you want to waste your money and reputation. You'll be as big a laughingstock as the rest of the warhawk crowd."

Taken aback, Heim grimaced. In the past weeks, after the news of New Europe, he had seen what mass media did to those who spoke as he was now speaking. Those who were influential, that is, and therefore worth tearing down. Ordinary unpolitical people didn't matter. The pundits simply announced that World Opinion Demanded Peace. Having listened to a good many men, from engineers and physicists to spacehands and mechanics, voice their personal feelings, Heim doubted if world opinion was being correctly reported. But he couldn't see any way to prove that.

Conduct a poll, maybe? No. At best, the result would frighten some professors, who would be quick to assert that it was based on faulty statistics, and a number of their students, who would organize parades to denounce Heim the Monster.

Propaganda? Politicking? A Paul Revere Society?...Heim shook his head, blindly, and slumped.

Twyman's face softened. "I'm sorry about this, Gunnar," he said. "I'm still your friend, you know. Regardless of where your next campaign donation goes. Call on me any time." He hesitated, decided merely to add "Good-by," and switched off.

Heim reached into his desk for a bottle he kept there. As he took it forth, his gaze crossed the model of *Star Fox* which his crew had given him when he retired. It was cast in steel, retrieved from that Aleriona battlewagon into which the lancer put an atomic torpedo at Achernar.

I wonder if the Aleriona make trophies of our wrecks.

Hm. Odd. I never thought about it before. We know so little of them. Heim put his feet on the desk and tilted the bottle to his lips. *Why don't I corner one of their delegation and ask?*

And then he choked on his drink and spluttered; his feet thumped to the floor, and he never noticed. The thought had been too startling. *Why not?*

-3-

The ceiling glowed with the simulated light of a red dwarf sun, which lay like blood on leaves and vines and slowly writhing flowers. A bank of Terrestrial room instruments—phone, 3V, computer, vocascribe, infotrieve, service cubicle, environmental control board—stood in one corner of the jungle with a harsh incongruity. The silence was as deep as the purple shadows. Unmoving, Cynbe waited.

The decompression chamber finished its cycle and Gunnar Heim stepped out. Thin dry atmosphere raked his throat. Even so, the fragrances overwhelmed him. He could not tell which of them—sweet, acrid, pungent, musky—came from which of the plants growing from wall to wall, reaching to the ceiling and arching down again in a rush of steel-blue leaves, exploding in banks of tawny, crimson, black, and violet blossoms. The reduced gravity seemed to give a lightness to his head as well as his frame. Feathery turf felt like rubber underfoot. The place was tropically warm; he sensed the infrared baking his skin.

He stopped and peered about. Gradually his eyes adjusted to the ember illumination. They were slower to see details of shapes so foreign to Earth.

"Imbiac dystra?" he called uncertainly. "My lord?" His voice was muffled in that tenuous air.

Cynbe ru Taren, Intellect Master of the Garden of War, fleet admiral, and military specialist of the Grand Commission of Negotiators, trod out from beneath his trees. "Well are you come, sir," he sang. "Understand you, then, the High Speech?"

Heim made the bowing Aleriona salute of a ranking individual to a different-but-equal. "No, my lord, I regret. Only a few phrases. It's a difficult language for any of my race to learn."

Cynbe's beautiful voice ranged a musical scale never invented by men. "Wish you a seat, Captain Heim? I can dial for refreshment."

"No, thank you," the human said, because he didn't care to lose whatever psychological advantage his height gave him, nor drink the wine of an enemy. Inwardly he was startled. *Captain* Heim? How much did Cynbe know?

There would have been ample time to make inquiries, in the couple of days since this audience was requested. But one couldn't guess how interested an Aleriona overlord was in a mere individual. Very possibly Heim's wish had been granted at Harold Twyman's urging, and for no other reason. The senator was a strong believer in the value of discussion between opponents. *Any discussion. We may go down, but at least we'll go down talking.*

"I trust your trip hither was a pleasant one?" Cynbe cantillated.

"Oh...all right, my lord, if, uh, one doesn't mind traveling with sealed eyelids after being thoroughly searched."

"Regrettable is this necessity to keep the whereabouts of our delegation secret," Cynbe agreed. "But your fanatics—" The last word was a tone-and-a-half glissando carrying more scorn than Heim would have believed possible.

"Yes." The man braced himself. "In your civilization, the populace is better... controlled." *I haven't quite the nerve to say "domesticated" but I hope he gets my meaning.*

Cynbe's laughter ran like springtime rain. "You are a marksman, Captain." He advanced with a movement that made cats look clumsy. "Would your desire be to walk my forest as we discuss? You are maychance not enrolled with the few humans who set ever a foot upon Alerion."

"No, my lord, I'm sorry to say I haven't had the pleasure. Yet."

Cynbe halted. For a moment, in the darkling light, they regarded each other. And Heim could only think how fair the Aleriona was.

The long-legged, slightly forward-leaning body, 150 centimeters tall, its chest as deep and waist as spare as a greyhound's, the counterbalancing tail never quite at rest, he admired in abstraction. How the sleek silvery fur sparkled with tiny points of light; how surely the three long toes of either digitigrade foot took possession of the ground; how graciously the arms gestured; how proudly the slim neck lifted. The humans were rare who could have dressed like Cynbe, in a one-piece garment of metallic mesh, trimmed at throat and wrists and ankles with polished copper. It revealed too much.

The head, though, was disturbing. For the fur ended at the throat, and Cynbe's face-marble-hued, eyes enormous below arching brows, nose small, lips vividly red, wide cheekbones and narrow chin—could almost have been a woman's. Not quite: there were differences of detail, and the perfection was inhuman. Down past the pointed ears, along the back and halfway to the end of the tail, rushed a mane of hair, thick, silken fine, the color of honey and gold. A man who looked overly long at that face risked forgetting the body.

And the brain, Heim reminded himself.

A blink of nictitating membrane dimmed briefly the emerald of Cynbe's long-lashed feline eyes. Then he smiled, continued his advance, laid a hand on Heim's arm. Three double-jointed fingers and a thumb closed in a gentle grip. "Come," the Aleriona invited.

Heim went along, into the murk under the trees. "My lord," he said in a harshened tone, "I don't want to waste your time. Let's talk business."

"Be our doings as you choose, Captain." Cynbe's free hand stroked across a phosphorescent branch.

"I'm here on behalf of the New Europeans."

"For the mourned dead? We have repatriated the living, and indemnified they shall be."

"I mean those left alive on the planet. Which is nearly all of them."

"Ah-h-h-h," Cynbe breathed.

"Senator Twyman must have warned you I'd bring the subject up."

"Truth. Yet assured he the allegation is unbelieved."

"Most of his side don't dare believe it. Those who do, don't dare admit it."

"Such accusations could imperil indeed the peace negotiations." Heim wasn't sure how much sardonicism lay in the remark. He stumbled on something unseen, cursed, and was glad to emerge from the bosket, onto a little patch of lawn starred with flowers. Ahead rose the inner wall, where some hundred books were shelved, not only the tall narrow folios of Alerion but a good many ancient-looking Terrestrial ones. Heim couldn't make out the titles. Nor could he see far past the archway into the next room of the suite; but somewhere a fountain was plashing.

He stopped, faced the other squarely, and said: "I have proof that New Europe was not scrubbed clean of men—in fact, they retreated into the mountains and are continuing resistance to your occupation force. The evidence is in a safe place"—*Goodness, aren't we melodramatic?*—"and I was planning to publicize it. Which would, as you say, be awkward for your conference."

He was rather desperately hoping that the Aleriona didn't know the facts of life on Earth well enough to understand how forlorn his threat was. Cynbe gave him no clue. There was only an imperturbable upward quirk of mouth, and: "Seeming is that you have decided upon another course, Captain."

"That depends on you," Heim answered. "If you'll repatriate those people also, I'll give you the evidence and say no more."

Cynbe turned to play with a vine. It curled about his hand and reached its blossoms toward his face. "Captain," he sang presently, "you are no fool. Let us assume your belief is truth. We shall speak of a folk in wrath under the mountain peaks. How shall they be made come to our ships?"

"They're fighting because they expect help. If representatives of the French government told them to return here, they would. The parley can be arranged by radio."

"But the entity France, now, would it so cooperate?"

"It'd have no choice. You know even better than I, a majority of the Federation doesn't want to fight over New Europe. About the only thing that could provoke such a war is the plight of the settlers. Let them come back unharmed and...and you'll have your damned conquest."

"Conceivable that is." Light rippled red down Cynbe's locks when he nodded. His gaze remained with the blooms. "But afterward?" he crooned. "Afterward?"

"I know," Heim said. "The New Europeans would be living proof you lied—not only about them, but about the entire battle. Proof that things didn't happen because someone got trigger happy, but because you planned your attack." He swallowed a nasty taste. "Well, read Terrestrial history, my lord. You'll find we humans don't take these matters as seriously as we might. Lies are considered a normal part of diplomacy, and a few ships lost, a few men killed, are all in the day's work. If anything, this concession of yours will strengthen the peace party. 'Look,' they'll say, 'Alerion isn't so bad, you can do business with Alerion, our policies saved those lives and avoided an expensive war.' Unquote."

Now the muliebrile face did turn about, and for a while the eyes lay luminous upon Heim. He felt his pulse grow thick. The sound of the fountain seemed to dwindle and the hot red dusk to close in.

"Captain," Cynbe sang, almost too low to hear, "The Eith is an ancient sun. The Aleriona have been civilized for beyond a million of your years. We sought not far-flung empire, that would crack an order old and stable; but our Wanderers ranged and our Intellects pondered. Maychance we are wiser in the manifold ways of destiny than some heedless newcomer. Maychance we have read your own inwardness more deeply than have you yourselves."

" 'Afterward' did I say. The word carries another freight when echoed through a million of years. My regard was to no gain for a decade, a generation, a century. I speak beyond

"Between these walls, let truth be what you have claimed. Then let truth also be that Alerion cannot hithersend five hundred thousand of individuals to leaven their race with anger.

"Had they yielded, the case were otherwise. We would have told Earth this battle was one more incident than tolerable and now we must have our own sphere where no aliens fare. But any of your colonists enwished to stay might do so, did they become subject to Alerion. We would offer inspection, that Earth might be sure they were not oppressed. For such little enclaves are significanceless; and Alerion has ways to integrate them into civilization; ways slow, as you look upon time, ways subtle, ways quite, quite certain.

"The colonists yielded not, I say between these walls. Even could we capture them alive, in so much wilderness—and we cannot—even then could they not become subject to Alerion. Not as prisoners, forever dangerous, forever an incitement that Earth deliver them. Yet if the entity France commanded them home: in their nerves, that were betrayal of folk who had not surrendered, and they must strive for a Federation government of males more brave. I look in the future and I see how they shame the others of you—yes, yes, Captain, such intangibles make your history, you are that kind of animal. Truth, there would not be war to gain back Europe Neuve. Those bones grow dry before leaders as I speak of come to power. But when the next debatable issue arises—ah-h-h."

So there is to be a next issue, Heim thought. *Not that he's told me anything I hadn't already guessed. I wonder, though, when the second crisis is scheduled. Maybe not in my lifetime. But surely in Lisa's.*

His voice came out flat and remote, as if someone else spoke: "Then you're not going to admit the colonists are alive. What will you do? Hunt them down piecemeal?"

"I command space fleets, Captain, not groundlings." Astonishingly, Cynbe's lashes fluttered and he looked down at his hands. The fingers twined together. "I have said more than needful, to you alone. But then, I am not Old Aleriona. My type was bred after the ships began their comings from Earth. And...I was at Achernar." He raised his eyes. "*Star Fox* captain, as Earth's men do, will you clasp my hand farewell?"

"No," said Heim. He turned on his heel and walked toward the compression chamber.

-4-

His escort of Peace Control troopers unsealed his eyes and let him off the official flyer at Port Johnson in Delaware. They'd taken longer on whatever circuitous route they followed than he had expected. There was barely time to make his appointment with Coquelin. He hurried to the beltway headed for the civilian garages, elbowed aboard through the usual crowd, and found he must stand the whole distance.

Fury had faded during the hours he sat blind, exchanging banalities with the earnest young officer of his guards ("Weather Reg really muffed the last hurricane, don't you think?"..."Yes, too bad about New Europe, but still, we've outgrown things like imperialism and revenge, haven't we? Anyhow, the galaxy is big."..."I sure envy you, the, way you've traveled in space. We get around in this job, of course, but seems like the places and people on Earth get more alike every year.") or thinking his own thoughts. He hadn't really expected to accomplish anything with the Aleriona. The attempt was nothing but a duty.

Grayness remained in him. *I don't see what I can do in Paris either.*

A shabby man, unnecessarily aggressive, pushed him. He controlled his temper with an effort—he hated crowds—and refrained from pushing back. You couldn't blame the poor devil for being hostile to one whose good clothes revealed him a member of the technoaristocracy.

That's why we've got to move into space, he told himself for the thousandth time. *Room. A chance to get out of this horrible huddle on Earth, walk free, be our own men, try out new ways to live, work, think, create, wonder. There was more happiness on New Europe, divided among half a million people, than these ten billion could even imagine.*

What is it in them—fear? inertia? despair? plain old ignorance?—makes them swallow that crock about how the rest of the universe is open to us?

Because it was a crock. Habitable planets aren't that common. And most of those that exist have intelligent natives; a good many of the rest have already been colonized by others. Heim did not want his race forced to the nearly ultimate immorality of taking someone else's real estate away.

Though more was involved in the Phoenix affair. A loss of nerve; throughout history, yielding to an unjustifiable demand for the sake of a few more years of peace has been the first step on a long downward road. An admission of the essentially vicious principle of "interest spheres"; there should not be any boundaries in space. And, to be sure, appalling fatuity: a blank refusal to read the record which proved Alerion's intentions toward Earth, a positive eagerness to give the enemy the time and resources he needed to prepare for his next encroachment.

But what can a man do?

Heim claimed his flyer at the garage and fretted while TrafCon stalled about sending him aloft. Quite a time passed before the pattern of vehicle movement released him. He went on manual for a while, to have the satisfaction of personally getting away. The gravitrons in this Moonraker were custom-built, with power to lift him far into the stratosphere. Otherwise the flyer was nothing special; he was fairly indifferent to creature comforts. He set the autopilot for Orly, took a long hot bath, got some whale from the freezer and made himself a 'burger for lunch, and bunked out for a couple of hours.

The clock woke him with the "Light Cavalry Overture" and handed him a mug of coffee. He changed into fresh clothes—somewhat formal, gold on the collar and down the pants—while the flyer slanted in for a landing. Momentarily he debated whether to go armed, for he would be carrying Vadász's package. But no, that might start more argument than it was worth. If he failed here too, he doubted if there would be any further use for New Europe's appeal. No action would be possible, except to get roaring drunk and afterward consider emigration to an especially remote planet.

Entering the *Douane* office, he showed his ID and got a thirty-day permit. France, being less crowded than most countries, was rather stuffy about letting people in. But this official was balm and unguents from the moment he saw Heim's name. "Ah, yes, yes, monsieur, we 'ave been told to expect ce pleasure of your company. A car is waiting for you. Does monsieur 'ave any baggage 'e wishes carried? No? *Bien,* cis way, please, and 'ave a mos' pleasant visit."

Quite a contrast with what Endre Vadász must have experienced. But he was only a musician of genius. Gunnar Heim headed a well-known manufacturing concern and was son-in-law to Curt Wingate, who sat on the board of General Nucleonics. If Gunnar Heim requested a private interview with Michel Coquelin, minister of extraterrestrial affairs and head of French representatives in the World Parliament, why, of course, of course.

Even so, he had crowded his schedule. Twyman had leaned backward to oblige him about seeing Cynbe; nevertheless, the peacemongers were fairly sure to have agents keeping tabs on him, and if he didn't move fast they might find ways to head him off.

The car entered Paris by ground. Blue dusk was deepening into night. The trees along the boulevards had turned their leaves, red and yellow splashed against Baron Haussmann's stately old walls or scrittling among the legs of pretty girls as they walked with their men. The outdoor cafes had little custom at this season. Heim was as glad of that. Paris could have made him remember too many things.

The car stopped at the Quai d'Orsay and let him out. He heard the Seine lap darkly against its embankment, under the thin chill wind. Otherwise the district was quiet, with scant traffic, the whirr of the city machines nearly lost. But skyglow hid the stars.

Gendarmes stood guard. Their faces were tense above the flapping capes. All France was tensed and bitter, one heard. Heim was conducted down long corridors where not a few people were working late, to Coquelin's office.

The minister laid aside a stack of papers and rose to greet him. "How do you do," he said. The tone was weary but the English flawless. That was luck; Heim's

French had gotten creaky over the years. Coquelin gestured at a worn, comfortable old-style chair by his desk. "Please be seated. Would you like a cigar?"

"No, thanks, I'm a pipe man." Heim took his out

"I too." Coquelin's face meshed in crow's feet and calipers when he smiled; he sat down and began to load a still more disreputable briar. He was short but powerfully built, square of countenance, bald of dome, with very steady brown eyes. "Well, Mr. Heim, what can I do for you?"

"Uh...it concerns New Europe."

"I thought so." The smile died.

"In my opinion—" Heim decided he was being pompous.

"M. Coquelin," he said, "I believe Earth ought to do whatever is necessary to get New Europe back."

Coquelin's look went over his guest's features, centimeter by centimeter, while he started his pipe. "Thank you for that," he said at length. "We have felt lonely in France."

"I have some material here that might help."

The least intake of breath went through Coquelin's teeth. "Proceed, if you please."

He sat altogether expressionless, smoking, never glancing away, while Heim talked. Only once did he interrupt: "Cynbe? Ah, yes, I have met him. The one they have quartered at—No, best I not say. Officially I am not supposed to know. Go on."

In the end he opened the packet, slipped a few films into the viewer on his desk, read, and nodded. The stillness quivered near breaking point Heim puffed volcano-like, stared out the window into darkness, shifted his bulk so the chair groaned, and listened to his own heartbeat

Finally Coquelin muttered, "There have been rumors about this." After another silence: "I shall see that you and Vadász join the Légion d'Honneur. Whatever happens."

"What will?" Heim asked. His jaws ached with being clamped together.

Coquelin shrugged. "Nothing, probably," he said, dull-voiced. "They are determined to buy what they call peace."

"Oh. Yes, you'd know. So I can tell you I also know the plan."

"That Alerion shall have Europe Neuve? Good, we can speak freely. I am naturally honor bound not to reveal what is being decided until my fellow committeemen agree, and it would be a futile act with disastrous political consequences if I broke that promise. So I am most glad to have an outside listener." Coquelin passed a hand across his eyes. "But there is little we can say, no?"

"There's plenty!" Heim exclaimed. "Come the formal meeting, you can show this stuff to Parliament, with scientific proof it's genuine. You can ask them how anyone can hope to get re-elected after selling out so many human beings."

"Yes, yes." Coquelin stared at his pipe bowl, where the fire waxed and waned, waxed and waned. "And some will say I lie. That my evidence is forged and my scientists are bribed. Others will say alas, this is terrible, but—half a million people? Why, a few missiles striking population centers on Earth could kill twenty times that many, a hundred times; and we had no right to be in the Phoenix; and nothing matters except to make friends with Alerion, for otherwise we must look for decades of war; so we can only weep for our people out there, we cannot help them." His grin was dreadful to see. "I daresay a monument will be raised to them. Martyrs in the cause of peace."

"But this is ridiculous! Earth can't be attacked. Or if it can, then so can Alerion, and they won't provoke that when we have twice their strength. A single flotilla right now could drive them out of the Auroran System."

"Half the Navy has been recalled for home defense. The other half is out in the Marches, keeping watch on the Aleriona fleet, which is also maneuvering there. Even some of the admirals I have consulted do not wish to spare a flotilla for Aurore. For as you must know, monsieur, the numbers available on either side are not large, when a single nuclear-armed vessel has so much destructive capability."

"So we do nothing?" Heim grated. "Why, at the moment even one ship could—could make serious trouble for the enemy. They can't have any great strength at Aurore as yet. But give them a year or two and they'll make New Europe as unattackable as Earth."

"I know." Coquelin swiveled around, rested his elbows oh his desk, and let his head sink between his shoulders. "I shall argue. But...tonight I feel old, Mr. Heim."

"My God, sir! If the Federation won't act, how about France by herself?"

"Impossible. We cannot even negotiate as a single country with any extraterrestrial power, under the Constitution. We are not allowed any armed force, any machine of war, above the police level. Such is reserved for the Peace Control Authority."

"Yes, yes, yes—"

"In fact—" Coquelin glanced up. A muscle twitched in one cheek. "Now that I think about what you have brought me, these documents, I do not know if I should make them public."

"What?"

"Consider. France is furious enough. Let the whole truth be known, including the betrayal, and I dare not predict what might happen. It could well end with Peace Control troops occupying us. And, yes, that would hurt the Federation itself, even more than France. One must put loyalty to the Federation above anything else. Earth is too small for national sovereignty. Nuclear weapons are too powerful."

Heim looked at the bent head, and the rage in him seemed about to tear him apart. "I'd like to go out myself!" he shouted.

"This would be piracy," Coquelin sighed.

"No...wait, wait, wait." The thought flamed into being. Heim sprang to his feet. "Privateers. Once upon a time there were privately owned warships."

"Eh, you have read a little history, I see." Some life came back to Coquelin. He sat straighter and watched the huge, restless figure with eyes again alert. "But I have read more. Privateering was outlawed in the nineteenth century. Even countries not signatory to that pact observed the prohibition, until it came to be regarded as a part of international law. Admitted, the Federal Constitution does not mention so archaic a matter. Still—"

"Exactly!" Heim roared; or was it the demon that had come to birth in his skull?

"No, no, flout the law and the Peace Control forces arrive. I am too old and tired, me, to stand trial before the World Court. To say nothing of the practical difficulties. France cannot declare war by herself. France cannot produce nuclear weapons." Coquelin uttered a small sad chuckle. "I am a lawyer by past profession. If there were a, you say loophole?—I could perhaps squirm through. But here—"

Word by word, Heim said: "I can get hold of the weapons."

Coquelin leaped in his seat. *"Qu'est-ce que vous dites?"*

"Off Earth. I know a place. Don't you see—Alerion has to put space defenses in orbit around New Europe, or she can't hold it against any determined attack." Heim was leaning on the desk now, nose to nose with the other, talking like a machine gun. "New Europe has only a limited industry. So the Aleriona will have to bring most of the stuff from home. A long supply line. One commerce raider—what'd that do to their bargaining position? What'd it do for our own poor buffaloed people? *One ship!"*

"But I have told you—"

"You told me it was physically and legally impossible. I can prove the physical possibility. And you said you were a lawyer."

Coquelin rose too, went to the window, and stared long out across the Seine. Heim's pace quivered the floor. His brain whirled with plans, data, angers, hopes; he had not been so seized by a power since he bestrode his bridge at Alpha Eridani.

And then Coquelin turned about. His whisper filled the silence: *"Peut-etre—"* and he went to the desk and began punching keys on an infotrieve.

"What are you after?" Heim demanded.

"Details of the time before quite every country had joined the Federation. The Moslem League did not recognize that it had any right as a whole to deal with them. So during the troubles, the Authority was charged with protecting Federation interests in Africa." Coquelin gave himself entirely to his work. Once, though, he met Heim's eyes. His own danced in his head. *"Mille remercîments, man frère,"* he said. "It may be for no more than this night, but you have given me back my youth."

-5-

Endre Vadász took the lid off the kettle, inhaled a sumptuous odor, gave the contents a stir, and re-covered them. "Almost done, this," he said. "I had better make the salad. Have you the materials ready?"

Lisa Heim blushed. "I...I'm afraid I'm not so good at slicing cucumbers and stuff," she said.

"Poof to that." Vadász scooped the disorderly pile of greens into a bowl. "For a cadet, you do very well...Find me the seasonings, will you? One must needs be an engineer to operate this damned machine shop you call a kitchen...As I was saying, small one, when I so rudely interrupted myself, we shall yet win you to your cook and bottle washer (j.g.) rating. Charge, a boar's head erased with an apple gules in its mouth, field barry of six vert and or. That's for cabbage and clotted cream."

Lisa giggled and hopped onto the table, where she swung her legs and watched Vadász with embarrassing warmth. He had only tried to be good company to his host's daughter while her father was away. He gave the herbs and spices more attention than was really necessary.

"My mother taught me a Spanish saying," he remarked, "that it takes four men to make a salad: a spendthrift for the oil, a philosopher for the seasonings, a miser for the vinegar, and a madman for the tossing."

Lisa giggled again. "You're cute."

"Er—here we go." Vadász got to work, singing.

There was a rich man and he lived in Jerusalem.
Glory, hallelujah, hi-ro-de-rung!
He wore a top hat and his clothes were very spruce-iung.
Glory, hallelujah, hi-ro-de-rung!
Hi-ro-de-rung! Hi-ro-de-rung!
Skinna-ma-rinky doodle doo, skinna-ma-rinky doodle doo,
Glory, hallelujah, hi-ro-de-rung!

"Is that a real old song too?" Lisa asked when he paused for breath. He nodded. "I just love your songs," she said.

"Now outside his gate there sat a human wreckiung," Vadász continued hastily.

Glory, hallelujah, hi-ro-de-rung!
He wore a bowler hat in a ring around his neckiung.
Glory, hallelujah, hi-ro-de-rung!

Lisa grabbed a skillet and spoon to beat out time as she joined him in the chorus.

Hi-ro-de-rung! Hi-ro-de-rung!
Skinna-ma-rinky doodle doo, skinna-ma-rinky doodle doo,
Glory, hallelujah, hi-ro-de-rung!

Now the poor man asked for a piece of bread and cheese-iung.
Glory, hallelujah, hi-ro-de-rung!
The rich man said, "I'll send for the police-iung"
Glory, hallelujah, hi-ro-de-rung!

"Hi-ro-de-rung! Hi-ro-de-rung!" chimed in a bull basso. Gunnar Heim stormed through the door.

"Skinna-ma-rinky doodle doo, skinna-ma-rinky doodle doo ("Daddy!" "Gunnar!").

"Glory, hallelujah, hi-ro-de-rung!" He snatched Lisa off the table, tossed her nearly to the ceiling, caught her, and began to whirl her around the floor. Vadász went merrily on. Helm took the chorus while he stamped out a measure with the girl, who squealed.

> *Now the poor man died and his soul went to Heaviung.*
> *Glory, hallelujah, hi-ro-de-rung!*
> *He danced with the angels till a quarter past eleviung.*
> *Glory, hallelujah, hi-ro-de-rung!*
> *Hi-ro-de-rungl Hi-ro-de-rung!*
> *Skinna-ma-rinky doodle doo, skinna-ma-rinky doodle doo,*
> *Glory, hallelujah, hi-ro-de-rung!*

"Oh, Daddy!" Lisa collapsed in a laughing fit.

"Welcome home," Vadász said. "You timed yourself well."

"What's going on here, anyway?" Heim inquired. "Where are the servants? Why put a camp stove in a perfectly good kitchen?"

"Because machines are competent enough cooks but will never be chefs," Vadász said. "I promised your daughter a goulash, not one of those lyophilized glue-stews but a genuine handmade *Gulyás* and sneeze-with-joy in the spices."

"Oh. Fine. Only I'd better get me—"

"Nothing. A Hungarian never sets the table with less than twice as much. You may, if you wish, contribute some red wine. So, once more, welcome home, and it is good to see you in this humor."

"With reason." Heim rubbed his great hands and smiled like a happy tiger. "Yes, indeedy."

"What have you done, Daddy?" Lisa asked.

"'Fraid I can't tell you, *jente min.* Not for a while." He saw the first symptoms of mutiny, chucked her under the chin, and said, "It's for your own protection."

She stamped her foot. "I'm not a child, you know!"

"Come, now; come, now," interrupted Vadász. "Let us not spoil the mood. Lisa, will you set a third place? We are eating in the high style, Gunnar, in your sunroom."

"Sure," she sighed. "If I can have the general intercom on, vid and audio both. Can I, please, Daddy?"

Heim chuckled, stepped out to the central control panel, and unlocked the switch that made it possible to activate any pickup in the apartment from any other room. Vadász's voice drifted after him:

> *Now the rich man died and he didn't fare so welliung.*
> *Glory, hallelujah, hi-ro-de-rung!*
> *He couldn't go to Heaven so he had to go to Helliung.*
> *Glory, hallelujah—*

and on to the end.

When Heim came back, he remarked in an undertone, because she'd be watching and listening, "Lisa doesn't want to miss a second of you, eh?"

The finely molded face turned doleful. "Gunnar, I didn't mean—"

"Oh, for crying in the beer!" Heim slapped Vadász on the back. "You can't imagine how much I'd rather have her in orbit around you than some of that adolescent trash. Everything seems to be turning sunward for me."

The Magyar brightened. "I trust," he said, "this means you have found a particularly foul way to goosh our friends of Alerion."

"Shh!" Heim jerked a thumb at the intercom screen. "Let's see, what wine should I dial for your main course?"

"Hey, ha, this is quite a list. Are you running a hotel?"

"No, to be honest, my wife tried to educate me in wines but never got far. I like the stuff but haven't much of a palate. So except when there's company, I stay with beer and whisky."

Lisa appeared in the screen. She laughed and sang,

> *Now the Devil said, "This is no hoteliung."*
> *Glory, hallelujah, hi-ro-de-rung!*
> *"This is just a plain and ordinary helliung."*
> *Glory, hallelujah, hi-ro-de-rung!*

Vadász put thumb to nose and waggled his fingers. She stuck out her tongue. They both grinned, neither so broadly as Heim.

And supper was a meal with more cheer, more sense of being home, than any he could remember since Connie died. Afterward he could not recall what was said—banter, mostly—it had not been real talk but a kind of embracement.

Lisa put the dishes in the service cubicle and retired demurely to bed; she even kissed her father. Heim and Vadász went downramp to the study. He closed the door, took Scotch from a cabinet, ice and soda from a coldbox, poured, and raised his own glass.

Vadász's clinked against it. "And a voice valedictory..." the minstrel toasted. "Who is for Victory? Who is for Liberty? Who goes home?"

"I'll drink to that," said Heim, and did, deeply. "Where's it from?"

"One G. K. Chesterton, a couple of centuries ago. You have not heard of him? Ah, well, they no longer care for such unsophisticated things on Earth. Only in the colonies are men so naive as to think victories are possible."

"Maybe we can make 'em change their minds here, too." Heim sat down and reached for a pipe.

"Well," Vadász said, in a cool tone but with a kind of shiver through his slim form, "now we come to business. What has happened, these last several days while I fretted about idle?"

"I'll begin from the beginning," Heim said. He felt no compunction about revealing what Twyman had admitted, since this listener could be trusted. His acquaintance with Vadász, though brief, had been somewhat intense.

The Magyar wasn't surprised anyway. "I knew they had no intention to get New Europe back when none would hear me."

"I found a buck who would," Heim said, and went on with his account. As he finished, Vadász's jaw fell with a nearly audible clank.

"A privateer, Gunnar? Are you serious?"

"Absodamnlutely. So's Coquelin, and several more we talked with." Heim's mirth had dissolved. He drew hard on his pipe, streamed the smoke out through dilated nostrils, and said:

"Here's the situation. One commerce raider in the Phoenix can make trouble out of all proportion to its capabilities. Besides disrupting schedules and plans, it ties up any number of warships, which either have to go hunt for it or else run convoy. As a result, the Aleriona force confronting ours in the Marches will be reduced below parity. So if then Earth gets tough, both in space and at the negotiations table—we shouldn't have to get very tough, you see, nothing so drastic that the peacemongers can scream too loud—one big naval push, while that raider is out there gobbling Aleriona ships—We can make them disgorge New Europe. Also give *us* some concessions for a change."

"It may be. It may be." Vadasz remained sober. "But how can you get a fighting craft?"

"Buy one and refit it. As for weapons, I'm going to dispatch a couple of trusty men soon, in a company speedster, to Staurn—you know the place?"

"I know of it. Ah-ha!" Vadasz snapped his fingers. His eyes began to glitter.

"Yep. That's where our ship will finish refitting. Then off for the Auroran System."

"But...will you not make yourself a pirate in the view of the law?"

"That's something which Coquelin is still working on. He says he thinks there may be a way to make everything legal and, at the same time, ram a spike right up the exhaust of Twyman and his giveaway gang. But it's a complicated problem. If the ship does have to fly the Jolly Roger, then Coquelin feels reasonably sure France has the right to try the crew, convict them, and pardon them. Of course, the boys might then have to stay in French territory, or leave Earth altogether for a colony—but they'll be millionaires, and New Europe would certainly give them a glorious reception."

Heim blew a smoke ring. "I haven't time to worry about that," he continued. "I'll simply have to bull ahead and take my chances on getting arrested. Because you'll understand how Coquelin and his allies in the French government—or in any government, because not every nation on Earth has gone hollowbelly—well, under the Constitution, no country can make warlike preparations. If we did get help from some official, that'd end every possibility of legalizing the operation. We'd better not even recruit our men from a single country, or from France at all.

"So it depends on me. I've got to find the ship, buy her, outfit her, supply her, sign on crew, and get her off into space—all inside of two months, because that's when the formal talks between Parliament and the Aleriona delegation are scheduled to begin." He made a rueful face. "I'm going to forget what sleep's like."

"The crew—" Vadász frowned. "A pretty problem, that. How many?"

"About a hundred, I'd say. Far more than needful, but the only way we can finance this venture is to take prizes, which means we'll need prize crews. Also... there may be casualties."

"I see. Wanted, a hundred skilled, reliable spacemen, Navy experience preferred, for the wildest gamble since Argilus went courting of Witch Helena. Where do you find them?...Hm, hm, I may know a place or two to look."

"I do myself. We can't recruit openly for a raider, you realize. If our true purpose isn't kept secret to the last millisecond, we'll be in the calaboose so fast that Einstein's ghost will return to haunt us. But I think, in the course of what look like ordinary psych tests, I think we can probe attitudes and find out who can be trusted with the truth. Those are the ones we'll hire."

"First catch your rabbit," Vadász said. "I mean find a psychologist who can be trusted!"

"Uh-huh. I'll get Wingate, my father-in-law, to co-opt one. He's a shrewd old rascal with tentacles everywhere, and if you think you and I are staticked about Alerion, you should listen to him for a while." Heim squinted at the model of *Star Fox,* shining across the room. "I don't believe ordinary crewmen will be too hard to find. When the Navy appropriation was cut, three years ago, a good many fellows found themselves thumb-twiddling on planet duty and resigned in disgust. We can locate those who came to Earth. But we may have trouble about a captain and a chief engineer. People with such qualifications don't drift free."

"Captain? What do you mean, Gunnar? You'll be captain."

"No." Heim's head wove heavily back and forth. A good deal of his bounce left him. "I'm afraid not. I want to—God, how I want to!—but, well, I've got to be sensible. Spaceships aren't cheap. Neither are supplies, and especially not weapons. My estimates tell me I'll have to liquidate all my available assets and probably hock everything else, to get that warship. Without me to tend the store, under those conditions, Heimdal might well fail. Lord knows there are enough competitors who'll do everything they can to make it fail. And Heimdal, well, that's something Connie and I built—her father staked us, but she worked the office end herself while I bossed the shop, those first few tough years. Heimdal's the only thing I've got to leave my daughter."

"I see." Vadász spoke with compassion. "Also, she has no mother. You should not risk she lose her father too."

Heim nodded.

"You will forgive me, though, if I go?" Vadász said.

"Oh, *ja, ja,* Endre, I'd be a swine to hold you back. You'll even have officer rank: chief steward, which means mainly that you oversee the cooking. And you'll bring me back some songs, won't you?"

Vadász could not speak. He looked at his friend, chained to possessions and power, and there ran through his head:

Now the moral of the story is riches are no jok-iung.
Glory, hallelujah, hi-ro-de-rung!

We'll all go to Heaven, for we all are stony broke-iung.
Glory, hallelujah, hi-ro-de-rungt

But the rhythm got into his blood, and he realized what Heim had done and what it meant, leaped to his feet, and capered around the study shouting his victorious music aloud till the walls echoed,

Hi-ro-de-rung! Hi-ro-de-rung!
Skinna-ma-rinky doodle doo, skinna-ma-rinky doodle doo,
Glory, hallelujah, hi-ro-de-rung!

-6-

From WORLDWEEK:

31 October

Gunnar Heim, principal of the American firm Heimdal Motors, has purchased the starship Pass of Balmaha from British Minerals, Ltd. The transaction astonished shipping circles by its speed. Heim made a cash offer that was too good to turn down, but insisted on immediate occupancy.

He has announced that he plans to send an expedition in search of new worlds to colonize. "We seem to have lost out in the Phoenix," he told 3V interviewer John Phillips. "Frankly, I am shocked and disgusted that no action has been taken in response to Alerion's attack on New Europe. But I can't do much about it except try to find us some new place—which I hope we'll have the nerve to defend."

As large and powerful as a naval cruiser, Glasgow-built Pass of Balmaha was originally intended to prospect for ores. But no deposits were found sufficiently rich to pay the cost of interstellar shipment when the Solar System still has workable mines. The ship has therefore been in Earth orbit for the past four years. Sir Henry Sherwin, chairman of the board of British Minerals, told Phillips, "We're overjoyed to get rid of that white elephant, but I must confess I feel a bit guilty about it."

7 November

U.S. Senator Harold Twyman (Libn., Calif.), high-ranking member of the Federal pre-formal negotiations team conferring with the delegation from Alerion, issued a statement Thursday denying rumors of a planned sell-out of New Europe.

"Certainly we are already talking business with them," he said. "And that, by the way, is a slow and difficult process. The Aleriona are alien to us, biologically and culturally. In the past we have had far too little contact with them, and far too much of what we did have was hostile. You don't get understanding out of a battle. Some of the finest xenologists on Earth are working day and night, trying to acquire a knowledge in depth that we should have gotten three decades ago.

"But we do know that the Aleriona share some things with mankind. They too are rational beings. They too wish to live. Their ancient civilization, which achieved a million years of stability, can teach us a great deal. And no doubt we can teach them something. Neither can do this, however, until we break the vicious circle of distrust, competition, fight, and retaliation.

"That's why the Deepspace Fleet has been ordered not to fire except in self-defense. That's why we aren't crowding the government of Alerion—if it *is* anything like what we understand by a government—to get out of the Auroran System. That's why we are taking our time with the honorable delegation: who, remember, came to us on Alerion's own initiative.

"Under the Constitution, only Parliament as a whole is empowered to negotiate with non-human states. Certainly the Executive Committee will observe this law. But you can't expect a body as large, diverse, and busy as Parliament to do the spadework in a case so intricate. Its duly appointed representatives were given that duty. We hope in a few more weeks to have a complete draft treaty ready for submission. At that time we shall be prepared to meet every conceivable objection to it. Meanwhile, however, it would be too great a handicap for us to operate in a glare of publicity.

"But we do not, repeat not, plan to betray any vital interest of the human race. Negotiation is a mutual process. We shall have to give a little as well as take a little. The Aleriona realize this too, perhaps better than some members of our own young and arrogant species. I am confident that, in the last analysis, all men of good will are going to agree that we have opened a new and hopeful era of cosmic history. The people of New Europe have not died in vain."

14 November

Retired Vice Admiral Piet van Rinnekom, 68, was set upon by about twenty men as he neared his house in Amsterdam on Monday evening, and badly beaten. When the police arrived, the assailants fled shouting taunts of "Warmonger!" They appeared to be of mixed nationality. Van Rinnekom has been an outspoken opponent of what he describes as "appeasement of Alerion," and is the author of the so-called Manhood Petition, whose backers are trying to gather one billion signatures in favor of Earth using force, if necessary, to regain New Europe. Most sociologists consider this sheer lunacy.

His condition is listed as serious.

At his Chicago office, Dr. Jonas Yore, founder and president of World Militants for Peace, issued the following statement: "Naturally this organization regrets the incident and hopes for Admiral van Rinnekom's recovery. But let us be honest. He has only gotten a taste of the very violence he advocated. The issue before us is one of life and death. WMP stands for life. Unhappily, a great many uninformed people have let their emotions run away with them and are crying for blood with no thought of the consequences. WMP exists to fight this tendency, to fight for sanity, to give atavism its deathblow, by any means required. We make no threats. But let the militarists beware."

21 November

Last Tuesday mankind throughout the Solar System watched an unprecedented event. Cynbe ru Taren, a member of the Aleriona delegation to Earth, appeared on an official 3V broadcast and answered questions put to him by Crown Prince Umberto of Italy, who represented the World Federation.

The questions were selected from an estimated forty million sent in by people around the globe, with Cynbe choosing a dozen from the final list. As he remarked, with a grim humor he displayed throughout the interview, "Thirteen bears for you an unhappy freight. It numbered either that one who betrayed or that one who was slain."

In general, he repeated statements already made about the New Europe tragedy. How did it happen? "Our ships were on maneuvers. Near Aurore did they pass, for Alerion recognizes no other claim of sovereignty in the Phoenix. Maychance the Terrestrial chief believed this was attack, for truth is we had many. When fired on, we made response, with more than he may have awaited. His remnants entered atmosphere for an outflank with radiation protection. That it might save itself, our closest detachment launched weapons of multiple megatonnage. Grief, the settled fringe of that continent they named Pays d'Espoir was lineally beneath. At orbital height the warheads kindled a firestorm. Terrible it ran, from end to end of that coast. When we could land, we found none alive, and but few in the southern region, where also a missile struck. Those we have hither brought, with our own mourning. Yet their Thirteenth-the-Betrayer was that captain who took them not into account when he plunged."

Why does Alerion now keep possession? "Naught but woe came ever from this intermingling. Time and again have humans ordered us from planets we discovered thousands of years agone, whose peace is now broken with machines and alien feet. And truth, we have often felt need to forbid places, even force them evacuated of the first few men. Races that knew us long grow latterly hostile to us, unrestful by what men have told and sold them. Resources we need are taken away. From such has come tension, which unseldom bursts in battle. Long past is that hour we should have ended it."

Why doesn't Alerion let an inspection team from Earth visit New Europe? "As we understand the symbolism of your culture, this were an admission of weakness and wrongness. Too, we cannot hazard espionage, or yet a suicide mission with nuclear bombs ensmuggled. I say never your Parliament would such plot, but you have individuals who are otherwise, some in high command. Maychance later, when faith has been achieved..."

28 November

The Aleriona Craze, already well established in North America, gained so much momentum from delegate Cynbe ru Taren's recent 3V appearance that in the past week it has swept like a meteorite through the upper-class teenagers of most countries. Quite a few in Welfare have caught the fever too. Now girls blessed with naturally blonde long hair flaunt it past their sisters waiting in line to buy wigs and metal mesh jerkins—like their brothers. No disciplinary measure by parents or teachers seems able to stop the kids warbling every word they utter. You need ear seals not to be assaulted by the minor-key caterwaulings of "Alerion, Alerion" from radio, juke, and taper. The slithering Aleriona Ramble has driven even the Wiggle off the dance floors. On Friday the city of Los Angeles put an educational program on the big screen at La Brea Park, a rebroadcast of the historic interview; and police fought three hours to halt a riot by five thousand screaming high-schoolers.

In an effort to learn whether this is a mere fad or a somewhat hysterical expression of the world's sincere desire for peace, our reporters talked with typical youngsters around the globe. Some quotes:

Lucy Thomas, 16, Minneapolis: "I'm just in hyperbolic orbit about him. I play the show back even when I'm asleep. Those eyes—they freeze you and melt you at the same time. Yee-ee!"

Pedro Fraga, 17, Buenos Aires: "They can't be male. I won't believe they are."

Machiko Ichikawa, 15, Tokyo: "The Samurai would have understood them. So much beauty, so much valor."

Simon Mbulu, 18, Nairobi: "Of course, they frighten me. But that is part of the wonder."

In Paris, Georges de Roussy, 17, threatened surlily: "I don't know what's gotten into those young camels. But I'll tell you this. Anybody *we* saw in that costume would get her wig cut off, and her own hair with it."

No comment was available from the still hidden delegates.

5 December

Lisa Heim, 14, daughter of manufacturer and would-be exploration entrepreneur Gunnar Heim of San Francisco, disappeared Wednesday. Efforts to trace her have so far been unsuccessful, and police fear she may have been kidnapped. Her father has posted a reward of one million American dollars for "anything that helps get her back. I'll go higher than this in ransom if I have to," he added.

-7-

Uthg-a-K'thaq twisted his face downward as far as he could, which wasn't much, and pointed his four chemosensor tendrils directly at Heim. In this position the third eye on top of his head was visible to the man, aft of the blowhole. But it was the front eyes, on either side of those fleshy feelers, that swiveled their gray stare against him. A grunt emerged from the lipless gape of a mouth: "So war, you say. We 'rom Naqsa know lit-tle ow war."

Heim stepped back, for to a human nose the creature's breath stank of swamp. Even so, he must look upward; Uthg-a-K'thaq loomed eighteen centimeters over him. He wondered fleetingly if that was why there was so much prejudice against Naqsans.

The usual explanation was their over-all appearance. Uthg-a-K'thaq suggested a dolphin, of bilious green-spotted yellow, that had turned its tail into a pair of short fluke-footed legs. Lumps projecting under the blunt head acted as shoulders for arms that were incongruously anthropoid, if you overlooked their size and the swimming-membranes that ran from elbows to pelvis. Except for a purse hung from that narrowing in the body which indicated a sort of neck, he was naked, and grossly male. It wasn't non-humanness as such that offended men, said the psychologists, rather those aspects which were parallel but different, like a dirty joke on *Homo sapiens.* Smell, slobbering, belching, the sexual pattern—

But mainly they're also space travelers, prospectors, colonizers, freight carriers, merchants, who've given us stiff competition, Heim thought cynically.

That had never bothered him. The Naqsans were shrewd but on the average more ethical than men. Nor did he mind their looks; indeed, they were handsome if you considered them functionally. And their private lives were their own business. The fact remained, though, most humans would resent even having a Naqsan in the same ship, let alone serving under him. And...Dave Penoyer would be a competent captain, he had made lieutenant commander before he quit the

Navy, but Heim wasn't sure he could be firm enough if trouble of that nasty sort broke out.

He dismissed worry and said, "Right. This is actually a raiding cruise. Are you still interested?"

"Yes. Hawe you worgotten that horriwle den you wound me in?"

Heim had not. Tracking rumors to their source, he had ended in a part of New York Welfare that appalled even him. A Naqsan stranded on Earth was virtually helpless. Uthg-a-K'thaq had shipped as technical adviser on a vessel from the planet that men called Caliban, whose most advanced tribe had decided to get into the space game. Entering the Solar System, the inexperienced skipper collided with an asteroid and totaled his craft. Survivors were brought to Earth by the Navy, and the Calibanites sent home; but there was no direct trade with Naqsa and, in view of the crisis in the Phoenix where his world also lay, no hurry to repatriate Uthg-a-K'thaq. *Damnation, instead of fooling with those Aleriona bastards, Parliament ought to be working out a distressed-spaceman covenant.*

Bluntly, Heim said, "We haven't any way of testing your mind in depth as we can for our own sort. I've got to trust your promise to keep quiet. I suppose you know that if you pass this information on, you'll probably get enough of a reward to buy a ride home."

Uthg-a-K'thaq burbled in his blowhole. Heim wasn't sure whether it represented laughter or indignation. "You hawe my word. Also, I am wothered awout Alerion. Good to strike at them. And, *suq,* will there not we loot to share?"

"Okay. You're hereby our chief engineer." *Because the ship has got to leave soon, and you're the only one I could get who knows how to repair a Mach Principle drive.* "Now about details—"

A maid's voice said over the intercom, which was set for one-way only: "Mail, sir."

Heim's heart shuddered, as it daily did. "Excuse me," he said. "I'll be back. Make yourself comfortable."

Uthg-a-K'thaq hissed something and settled his glabrous bulk on the study couch. Heim jogged out.

Vadasz sat in the living room, bottle to hand. He hadn't spoken much or sung a note in the past few days. The house was grown tomb silent. At first many came; police, friends, Curt Wingate and Harold Twyman arrived at the same hour and clasped hands; of everyone Heim knew well only Jocelyn Lawrie had remained unheard from. That was all a blur in his memory; he had continued preparations for the ship because there was nothing else to do, and he scarcely noticed when the visits stopped. Drugs kept him going. This morning he had observed his own gauntness in an optex with faint surprise—and complete indifference.

"Surely the same null," Vadász mumbled.

Heim snatched the stack of envelopes off the table. A flat package lay on the bottom. He ripped the plastic off. Lisa's face looked forth. His hands began to shake so badly that he had trouble punching the animator button. The lips that were Connie's opened.

"Daddy," said the small voice. "Endre. I'm okay. I mean, they haven't hurt me. A woman stopped me when I was about to get on the elway home. She said her bra magnet had come loose and would I please help her fix it I didn't think anybody upper-class was dangerous. She was dressed nice and talked nice and had a car there and everything. We got in the car and blanked the bubble. Then she shot me with a stunner. I woke up here. I don't know where it is, a suite of rooms, the windows are always blanked. Two women are staying with me. They aren't mean, they just won't let me go. They say it's for peace. Please do what they want." Her flat speech indicated she was doped with antiphobic. But suddenly herself broke through. "I'm so lonesome!" she cried, and the tears came.

The strip ended. After a long while Heim grew aware that Vadász was urging him to read a note that had also been in the package. He managed to focus on the typescript.

> Mr. Heim:
>
> For weeks you have lent your name and influence to the militarists. You have actually paid for advertisements making the false and inflammatory claim that there are survivors at large on New Europe. Now we have obtained information which suggests you may be plotting still more radical ways to disrupt the peace negotiations.
>
> If this is true, mankind cannot allow it. For the sake of humanity, we cannot take the chance that it might be true.
>
> Your daughter will be kept as a hostage for your good behavior until the treaty with Alerion has been concluded, and for as long thereafter as seems wise. If meanwhile you publicly admit you lied about New Europe, and do nothing else, she will be returned.
>
> Needless to say, you are not to inform the police of this message. The peace movement has so many loyal supporters in so many places that we will know if you do. In that event, we will be forced to punish you through the girl. If on the other hand you behave yourself, you to receive occasional word from her.
>
> Yours for peace and sanity.

He had to read three or four times before it registered.

"San Francisco meter," Vadász said. He crumpled the plastic and hurled it at the wall. "Not that that means anything."

"Gud i himlen." Heim stumbled to a lounger, fell down, and sat staring into the unspeakable. "Why don't they go straight after me?"

"They have done so," Vadász answered.

"Personally!"

"You would be a risky target for violence. A young and trusting girl is easier."

Heim had a feeling that he was about to weep. But his eyes remained two coals in his skull. "What can we do?" he whispered.

"I don't know," Vadász said like a robot. "So much depends on who they are. Obviously not anyone official. A government need only arrest you on some excuse."

"The Militants, then. Jonas Yore." Heim rose and walked toward the exit.

"Where are you going?" Vadász grabbed his arm. It was like trying to halt a landslip.

"For a gun," Heim said, "and on to Chicago."

"No. Hold. Stop, you damned fool! What could you do except provoke them into killing her?"

Heim swayed and stood.

"Yore may or may not know about this," Vadász said. "Certainly no one has definite information about your plans, or they would simply tip the Peace Control. The kidnappers could be in the lunatic fringe of the Militants. Emotions are running so high. And that sort must needs be dramatic, attack people in the street, steal your daughter, strut their dirty little egos—yes, Earth has many like them in the upper classes too, crazed with uselessness. Any cause will do. 'Peace' is merely the fashionable one."

Heim returned to the bottle. He poured himself a drink, slopping much. *Lisa is alive,* he told himself. *Lisa is alive, Lisa is alive.* He tossed the liquor down his gullet. "How long will she be?" he screamed.

"Hey?"

"She's with fanatics. They'll still hate me, whatever happens. And they'll be afraid she can identify them. Endre, help me!"

"We have some time," Vadász snapped. "Use it for something better than hysterics."

The glow in Heim's stomach spread outward. *I've been responsible for lives before,* he thought, and the old reflexes of command awoke. *You construct a games theoretical matrix and choose the course with smallest negative payoff.* His brain began to move. "Thanks, Endre," he said.

"Could they be bluffing about spies in the police?" Vadász wondered.

"I don't know, but the chance looks too big to take."

"Then...we cancel the expedition, renounce what we have said about New Europe, and hope?"

"That may be the only thing to do." It whirred in Heim's head. "Though I do believe it's wrong also, even to get Lisa home."

"What is left? To hit back? How? Maybe private detectives could search—"

"Over a whole planet? Oh, we can try them, but—No, I was fighting a fog till I got the idea of the raider, and now I'm back in the fog and I've got to get out again. Something definite, that they won't know about before too late. You were right, there's no sense in threatening Yore. Or even appealing to him, I guess. What matters to them is their cause. If we could go after *it—"*

Heim bellowed. Vadász almost got knocked over in the big man's rush to the phone. "What in blue hell, Gunnar?"

Heim unlocked a drawer and took out his private directory. It now included the unlisted number and code of Michel Coquelin's sealed circuit. And 0930 in California was—what? 1730?—in Paris. His fingers stabbed the buttons.

A confidential secretary appeared in the screen. *"Bureau de—oh, M. Heim."*

"Donnez-vous moi M. le Minister tout de suite, s'il vous plaît." Despite the circumstances, Vadász winced at what Heim thought was French.

The secretary peered at the visage confronting him, sucked down a breath, and punched. Coquelin's weary features

"Gunnar! What is this? News of your girl?"

Heim told him. Coquelin turned gray. "Oh, no," he said. He had children of his own.

"Uh-huh," Heim said. "I see only one plausible way out. My crew's assembled now, a tough bunch of boys. And you know where Cynbe is."

"Are you crazy?" Coquelin stammered.

"Give me the details: location, how to get in, disposition of guards and alarms," Heim said. "I'll take it from there. If we fail, I won't implicate you. I'll save Lisa, or try to save her, by giving the kidnappers a choice: that I either cast discredit on them and their movement by spilling the whole cargo; or I get her back, tell the world I lied, and show remorse by killing myself. We can arrange matters so they know I'll go through with it."

"I cannot—I—"

"This is rough on you, Michel, I know," Heim said. "But if you can't help me, well, then I'm tied. I'll have to do exactly what they want. And half a million will die on New Europe."

Coquelin wet his lips, stiffened his back, and asked: "Suppose I tell you, Gunnar. What happens?"

-8-

"Space yacht *Flutterby,* GB-327-RP, beaming Georgetown, Ascension Island. We are in distress. Come in, Georgetown. Come in, Georgetown."

The whistle of cloven air lifted toward a roar. Heat billowed through the forward shield. The bridge viewports seemed aflame and the radar screen had gone mad. Heim settled firmer into his harness and fought the pilot console.

"Garrison to *Flutterby.*" The British voice was barely audible as maser waves struggled through the ionized air enveloping that steel meteorite. "We read you. Come in, *Flutterby.*"

"Stand by for emergency landing," David Penoyer said. His yellow hair was plastered down with sweat. "Over."

"You can't land here. This island is temporarily restricted. Over." Static snarled around the words.

Engines sang aft. Force fields wove their four-dimensional dance through the gravitrons. The internal compensators held steady, there was no sense of that deceleration which made the hull groan; but swiftly the boat lost speed, until thermal effect ceased. In the ports a vision of furnaces gave way to the immense curve of the South Atlantic. Clouds were scattered woolly above its shiningness. The horizon line was a deep blue edging into space black.

"The deuce we can't," Penoyer said. "Over."

"What's wrong?" Reception was loud and clear this time.

"Something blew as we reached suborbital velocity. We've a hole in the tail and no steering pulses. Bloody little control from the main drive. I think we can set down on Ascension, but don't ask me where. Over."

"Ditch in the ocean and we'll send a boat. Over."

"Didn't you hear me, old chap? We're hulled. We'd sink like a stone. Might get out with spacesuits and life jackets, or might not. But however that goes, Lord Ponsonby won't be happy about losing a million pounds' worth of yacht. We've a legal right to save her if we can. Over."

"Well—hold on, I'll switch you to the captain's office—"

"Nix. No time. Don't worry. We won't risk crashing into Garrison. Our vector's aimed at the south side. We'll try for one of the plateaus. Will broadcast a signal for you to home on when we're down, which'll be in a few more ticks. Wish us luck. Over and out."

Penoyer snapped down the switch and turned to Heim. "Now we'd better be fast," he said above the thunders. "They'll scramble some armed flyers as soon as they don't hear from us."

Heim nodded. During those seconds of talk *Connie Girl* had shot the whole way. A wild dark landscape clawed up at her. His detectors registered metal and electricity, which must be at Cynbe's lair. Green Mountain lifted its misty head between him and the radars at Georgetown. He need no longer use only the main drive. *That* had been touch and go!

He cut the steering back in. The boat swerved through an arc that howled like a wolf. A tiny landing field carved from volcanic rock appeared in the viewports. He came down in a shattering blast of displaced air. Dust vomited skyward.

The jacks touched ground. He slapped the drive to Idle and threw off his harness. "Take over, Dave," he said, and pounded for the main airlock.

His score of men arrived with him, everyone spacesuited.

Their weapons gleamed in the overhead illumination. He cursed the safety seal that made the lock open with such sadistic slowness. Afternoon light slanted through. He led the way, jumped off the ramp before it had finished extruding, and crouched in the settling dust.

There were three buildings across the field, as Coquelin had said: a fifteen-man barracks, a vehicle shed, and an environmental dome. The four sentries outside the latter held their guns in a stupefied fashion, only approximately pointed at him. The two men on a mobile GTA missile carrier gaped. Georgetown HQ had naturally phoned them not to shoot if they detected a spacecraft. The rest of the guard were pouring from quarters.

Heim counted. Some weren't in sight yet...He lumbered toward them. "Emergency landing," he called. "I saw your field—"

The young man with Peace Control lieutenant's insignia, who must be in charge, looked dismayed. "But—" He stopped and fumbled at his collar.

Heim came near. "What's wrong?" he asked. "Why shouldn't I have used your field?"

That was a wicked question, he knew. Officially PCA didn't admit this place existed.

The Aleriona overlords who comprised the delegation could not be housed together. They never lived thus at home; to offer them less than total privacy would have been an insult, and perhaps risky of all their lives. So they must be scattered around Earth. Ascension was a good choice. Little was here nowadays except a small World Sea Police base. Comings and goings were thus discreet.

"Orders," the lieutenant said vaguely. He squinted at the argent spear of the yacht. "I say, you don't look damaged." You could fake a name and registry for *Connie Girl,* but not unsoundness. The last couple of men emerged from barracks. Heim raised his arm and pointed. "On her other side," he said. He chopped his hand down and clashed his faceplate shut.

Two men in the airlock stepped back. The gas cannon they had hidden poked its nose out. Under fifty atmospheres of pressure, the anesthetic aerosol boiled forth.

A sentry opened fire. Heim dove for dirt. A bullet splintered rock before his eyes. The yellow stream gushed overhead, rumbling. And now his crew were on their way, with stunners asnicker. No lethal weapons; he'd hang before he killed humans doing their duty. But this was an attack by men who had seen combat against men whose only job had been to prevent it. Death wasn't needed.

The short, savage fight ended. Heim rose and made for the dome. Zucconi and Lupowitz came behind, a ram slung between them on a gravity carrier. Around the field, *Connie Girl's* medical team started to check the fallen Peacemen and give what first aid was indicated.

"Here," said Heim into his suit radio. Zucconi and Lupowitz set down the ram and started the motor. Five hundred kilos of tool steel bashed the dome wall at sixty cycles. The narcotic fog clamored with that noise. The wall smashed open. Heim leaped through, into the red sun's light.

A dozen followed him. "He's somewhere in this mess," Heim said. "Scatter. We've got maybe three minutes before the cops arrive."

He burst into the jungle at random. Branches snapped, vines shrank away, flowers were crushed underfoot. A shadow flitted-Cynbe! Heim plunged.

A laser flame sizzled. Heim felt the heat, saw his combat breastplate vaporizing in coruscant fire. Then he was upon the Aleriona. He wrenched the gun loose. *Mustn't close in-he'd get burned on this hot metal.* Cynbe grinned with fury and whipped his tail around Heim's ankles. Heim fell, but still Cynbe hung on. His followers arrived, seized their quarry, and frogmarched away the Intellect Master of the Garden of War. Outside, Cynbe took a breath of vapor and went limp.

I hope the biomeds are right about this stuff's being harmless to him, Heim thought.

He ran onto the field and had no more time for thought. A couple of PCA flyers were in the sky. They stooped like hawks. Their guns pursued Heim's crew. He saw the line of explosions stitch toward him, heard the crackle and an overhead whistle through his helmet. "Open out!" he yelled. His throat was afire. Sweat soaked his undergarments. "Let 'em see who you're toting!" The flyers screamed about and climbed.

They'll try to disable my boat. If we can't get away fast—The ramp was ahead, hell-road steep. A squadron appeared over Green Mountain. Heim stopped at the bottom of the ramp. His men streamed past. Now Cynbe was aboard. Now everyone was. A flyer dove at him. He heard bullets sleet along the ramp at his heels.

Over the coaming! Someone dogged the lock. *Connie Girl* stood on her tail and struck for the sky. Heim lay where he was for some time.

Eventually he opened his helmet and went to the bridge. Space blazed with stars, but Earth was already swallowing them again. "We're headed back down, eh?" he asked.

"Right-o," Penoyer answered. The strain had left him, his boyish face was one vast grin. "Got clean away, above their ceiling and past their radar horizon before you could say fout."

Then a long curve above atmosphere, but swiftly, racing the moment when Peace Control's orbital detectors were alerted, and now toward the far side of the planet. It had been a smooth operation, boded well for the privateer. If they carried it the whole way through, that was.

Heim lockered his suit and got back steadiness from the routine of an intercom check with all stations. Everything was shipshape, barring some minor bullet pocks in the outer plates. When Lupowitz reported, "The prisoner's awake, sir," he felt no excitement, only a tidal flow of will. "Bring him to my cabin," he ordered. The boat crept downward through night. Timing had been important. The Russian Republic was as amiably inept about TrafCon as everything else, and you could land undetected after dark on the Siberian tundra if you were cautious. Heim felt the setdown as a slight quiver. When the engines ceased their purr, the silence grew monstrous.

Two armed men outside his cabin saluted in triumph. He went through and closed the door.

Cynbe stood near the bunk. Only his tailtip stirred, and his hair in the breeze from a ventilator. But when he recognized Heim, the beautiful face drew into a smile that was chilling to see. "Ah-h-h," he murmured.

Heim made the formal Aleriona salute. "*Imbiac,* forgive me," he said. "I am desperate."

"Truth must that be"—it trilled in his ears—"if you think thus to rouse war."

"No, I don't. How could I better disgrace my side of the argument? I just need your help."

The green eyes narrowed. "Strange is your way to ask, Captain."

"There wasn't any other. Listen. Matters have gotten so tense between the war and peace factions on Earth that violence is breaking out. Some days ago my daughter was stolen away. I got a message that if I didn't switch sides, she'd be killed."

"Grief. Yet what can I do?"

"Don't pretend to be sorry. If I backed down, you'd have a distinct gain, so there was no point in begging your assistance. Now, no matter what I myself do, I can't trust them to return her. I had to get a lever of my own. I bribed someone who knew where you were, recruited this gang of men, and—and now we'll phone the head of the organized appeasement agitators."

Cynbe's tail switched his heels. "Let us suppose I refuse," said the cool music.

"Then I'll kill you," Heim said without rancor. "I don't know if that scares you or not. But your delegation meets Parliament in another week. They'll be handicapped without their military expert. Nor are things likely to proceed smoothly, after such a stink as I can raise."

"Will you not terminate my existence in every case, Captain, that I never denounce you?"

"No. Cooperate and you'll go free. I simply want my daughter back. Why should I commit a murder that'll have the whole planet looking for the solution? They'd be certain to find me. The general type of this vessel is sufficient clue, since I've no alibi for the time of the kidnapping."

"Yet have you not said why I shall not accuse you."

Heim shrugged. "That'd be against your own interest. Too sordid a story would come out. A father driven wild by the irresponsible Peace Militants, and so forth. I'd produce my documents from New Europe in open court. I'd testify under neoscop what you admitted when last we talked. Oh, I'd fight dirty. Sentiment on Earth is delicately balanced. Something like my trial could well tip the scales."

Cynbe's eyes nictitated over. He stroked his chin with one slim hand.

"In fact," Heim said, "your best bet is to tell PCA you were taken by an unidentified bunch who wanted to sabotage the treaty. You persuaded them this was the worst thing they could do, from their own standpoint, and they let you go. Then insist that our own authorities hush the entire affair up. They will, if you say so, and gladly. A public scandal at this juncture would be most inconvenient." Still the Aleriona stood hooded in his own thoughts. "Cynbe," said Heim in his softest voice, "you do not understand humans. We're as alien to you as you are to us. So far you've juggled us pretty well. But throw in a new factor, and what are all your calculations worth?"

The eyes unveiled. "Upon you I see no weapon," Cynbe crooned. "If I aid you not, how will you kill me?"

Heim flexed his fingers. "With these hands."

Laughter belled forth. "*Star Fox* captain, let us seek the radiophone."

It was late morning in Chicago. Jonas Yore's Puritan face looked out of the screen with loathing. "What do you want, Heim?"

"You know about my girl being snatched?"

"No. I mean, I'm sorry for her if not for you, but how does it concern me? I have no information."

"I got word the kidnappers are skizzies in the peace faction. Wait, I don't accuse you of having any part in it. Every group has bolshes. But if you passed the word around quietly, personal calls to your entire membership list, directly or indirectly you'd get to them."

"See here, you rotten—"

"Turn on your recorder. This is important. I want to present Delegate Cynbe ru Taren." In spite of everything, Heim's heart came near bursting.

The Aleriona glided into pickup range. "My lord!" Yore gasped.

"In honor's name did Captain Heim appeal me-ward," Cynbe sang. "A bond is between us that we did battle once. Nor may my ancient race drink of shame. Is not yonder child returned, we must depart this planet and invoke that cleansing which is in open war. Thus do I command your help."

"M-m-my lord—I—Yes! At once!"

Heim switched off the set. The air whistled from his lungs and his knees shook. "Th-th-thanks," he stuttered. "Uh...uh...as soon as Vadász lets me know she's arrived, we'll take off. Deliver you near a town."

Cynbe watched him for a time before he asked: "Play you chess, Captain? Of Earth's every creation, there is the one finest. And well should I like that you not have her enminded a while."

"No, thanks," Heim said. "You'd win on fool's mate every time. I'd better see about getting our false identification removed."

He was glad of the winter cold outside.

They were almost through when Cynbe appeared in the airlock, etched black across its light. His tone soared: "Captain, be swift. The wandersinger calls from your home. She is again."

Heim didn't remember running to the phone. Afterward he noticed bruises on shin and shoulder. But he did lock the radio-room door.

Lisa looked at him. "Oh, Daddy!"

"Are you all right?" he cried. His hands reached out. The screen stopped them.

"Yes. They...they never hurt me. I got doped. When I woke up, we were parked here in town. They told me, take an elway from there. I was still dopey and didn't pay any attention—no number—Please hurry home."

"I'll—*ja*. Two, three hours."

The remnants of the drug left her more calm than him. "I think I know how it happened, Daddy. I'm awful sorry. That night you and Endre talked about your—you know—well, you'd forgot to turn off the general intercom switch. I listened from my room."

He remembered how slinky and mysterious she had acted in the following couple of weeks. He'd put that down to an attempt at impressing Vadász. Now the knowledge of his carelessness hit him in the belly.

"Don't," she asked. "I never told. Honest. Only when Dick and some other kids teased me 'cause I wouldn't go in for that stupid Aleriona stuff, I got mad and told them one human was worth a hundred of those crawlies and my father was going to prove it. I never said more. But I guess word got back to somebody, 'cause those women kept asking me what I'd meant. I told them I was just bragging. Even when they said they'd beat me, I told them it was just a brag, and I guess they believed that because they never did beat me. Please don't be too mad, Daddy."

"I'm not," he said harshly. "I'm more proud than I deserve. Now go to bed and rest. I'll be home as fast as I can."

"I missed you so much."

She switched off. Then Heim could weep.

Connie Girl purred aloft, and down again a kilometer outside Krasnoe. Heim escorted Cynbe to the ground. It was frozen, and rang underfoot. A few lights shone from outlying houses, dim compared to the winter stars.

"Here." Awkwardly, Heim proffered a heated cloak. "You'll want this."

"My thanks," blew from under the frost-cold locks. "When your authorities fetch me, I shall tell as you suggested. Wisest for Alerion is thus; and for I, who would not see you further hurt."

Heim stared at the thin snowcrust. It sparkled like Cynbe's fur. "I'm sorry about what I did," he mumbled. "It was no way to treat you."

"No more of anger in-dwells." Cynbe's song dropped low. "I knew not humans hold their young so dear. Well may you fare."

"Good-by." This time Gunnar Heim shook hands.

The boat took off afresh, found orbital height, and went toward Mojave Port along a standard trajectory. As far as the world was concerned, she had gone out to check on the loading of the star cruiser. Heim was surprised to note how calmly he could now wait to see his daughter again.

And when it'd be for such a short time, too. The ship must depart in a few more days, with him her captain.

That had to be, he saw. The evil had grown so mighty that he dared not challenge it with less than his whole strength: which was found among the stars, not on this sick Earth. Nor would he be worthy to be Lisa's father, if he sent men against that thing whose creatures had tried to devour her, and did not go himself.

She'd be safe in Wingate's care. As for the Heimdal company, it might or might not survive without him, but that really made no difference. Lisa's grandfather would provide for her, whatever happened. *And don't forget the chance of prize money!*

Laughter welled in Heim. *Maybe I'm rationalizing a selfish, atavistic desire to raise hell. Okay, what if I am? This is the way it's going to be.*

-9-

They had celebrated an early Christmas. The tree glittered forlorn in the living room. Outside, a surf of rain drove against the windows.

"It's so awful," Lisa said. "That there has to be war."

"There doesn't, pony," Heim answered. "In fact, that's what we're trying to prevent."

She regarded him in bewilderment

"If we don't stand up to Alerion," Heim said, "there'll be trouble and more trouble, worse each time, and we'll forever lose, until at last Earth is driven into a corner. And when it's cornered, the human race always does fight, with everything it's got. Planet against planet—that would be the real Ragnarok. What we have to do is show them right now that we aren't going to be pushed. Then we and they can talk business. Because space truly is big enough for everybody, as long as they respect each other's right to exist." He put on his cloak. "We'd better start."

They went downshaft in silence to the garage, and entered his flyer—himself, his daughter, her grandfather, two hard-looking men who must keep watch over her until this affair had been outlived, and Vadász. Out the doors they glided, and rose through storm. The hull shivered and resounded. But when they got into the upper lanes, blue stillness encompassed them, with clouds below like snow mountains.

Wingate lit a cigar and puffed, his nutcracker face squinched together. Finally he barked, "I hate these good-by waits, sitting around wishing you could think of something to say. Let's tune in Parliament."

"Not worth while," Heim replied. "They expect a full week of preliminary debate before they invite the Aleriona delegation. Every two-cent politician wants to make sure he's heard at least once."

"But according to the news yesterday, France came out near the top of the alphabetical draw. Coquelin will probably start to speak any minute."

"Hell—oh, go ahead." Heim was chiefly conscious of the slight form huddled between him and Vadász.

The time was not much later in Mexico City than here, but you couldn't tell that from inside the Capitol. The view swept across the Chamber of Council, faces and faces and faces, white, brown, black, amber, their eyes zeroed on the rostrum as the speaker for Finland stepped down. President Fazil knocked with his gavel; through that waiting quiet, the sound was like nails being driven into a coffin. Wingate, whose Spanish was not the best, dialed for English translation.

"—the honorable spokesman for France, M. Michel Coquelin."

Heim set the 'pilot and leaned back to watch. The square shape trudged down the aisle deliberately, almost scornfully, and took a stance at the lectern. The camera zoomed in on a countenance shockingly aged, but one which might have been cast in iron.

"Mr. President, distinguished delegates, ladies and gentlemen. I shall not detain you long at this point. The world knows the French feeling about New Europe. My country wishes to make her position entirely clear and to advance a certain argument. Since this is sure to precipitate considerable discussion, I request leave to defer my address until the other honorable spokesmen have finished theirs."

"You see?" Heim said. "He has to gain time for us to get clear. It was bad luck that France came on so early in the session, but he'll handle it."

"What's he going to say, anyhow, Daddy?" Lisa asked. "He *can't* let you be called pirates!"

Heim grinned. "You'll find out."

"Mr. President! Point of order." The camera wheeled around and closed in on Harold Twyman. He had jumped to his feet and looked angry. "In so grave a matter, a departure from precedence must be approved in the form of a motion."

Coquelin raised his brows. "I fail to see why there should be any objection to France yielding precedence," he said.

"Mr. President, distinguished members of this body," Twyman rapped, "the honorable spokesman for France has warned us that he intends a surprise. This is a time for serious discussion, not for debater's tricks. If we find ourselves forced to rebut an unexpected assertion, our meeting with the honorable delegates of Alerion may easily be postponed another week. There has already been too much delay. I insist that this chamber vote upon whether to let M. Coquelin play with us or not."

"Mr. President—" The Frenchman's retort was cut off. Fazil slammed his gavel and said:

"The chair finds the point well taken, if perhaps somewhat heatedly expressed. Does anyone wish to make a motion that the French statement be deferred until every other national spokesman has finished his remarks?"

"Oh, oh," Vadász muttered. "This does not look good."

Heim reached out and adjusted the 'pilot for top speed. The engine hum strengthened. Above it he heard a member of the Argentine group say, "I so move," and a Dutchman, "I second."

"It has been moved and seconded—"

"What if they don't let him?" Lisa wailed.

"Then we've got to go like bats out of Venus," Heim said.

Coquelin began to speak in favor of the motion. After a few minutes, Vadász clicked his tongue and said admiringly: "Never did I hear anything so long-winded. That man is an artist."

"Um," Wingate grunted. "He may antagonize 'em."

"Obviously," said Heim in a bleak tone, "he doesn't expect to win, no matter what."

Debate droned back and forth. The flyer left the storm behind and fled over a huge wrinkled landscape. Far to the east gleamed the Sierra peaks. *We could lose all that beauty someday,* Heim thought.

Mojave Field sprawled into view. He slanted down on the beam and saw *Connie Girl* poised in the open. Garaging, formalities of clearance, the long walk across concrete under a glaring sun—was the light what blinded him?

They stopped at the ramp. "Well," said Wingate gruffly, "you can't waste time. God ride with you, Son." He let the handclasp die.

Lisa came into Heim's arms. "Daddy, Daddy, I'm sorry, I c-c-can't help bawling."

"Blaze to that." He ruffled her hair and held her close against his chest. "We'll be back, you know. Rich and famous and a million stories to tell." He swallowed. "You...you've been...you are a good girl. I couldn't have asked for a finer girl. So long. Plain old *pa gensyn.*"

He gave her to Vadász, who embraced her very lightly and bestowed a kiss on the wet cheek. *"Isten veled,"* the Magyar said low. "I shall bring you home a song."

Hastily, then, they mounted the ramp, stood waving while it retracted, and saw the lock close before them.

"Thanks, Endre," Heim said. He turned on his heel. "Let's get cracking."

The yacht could have sprung straight into orbit. But better not show unseemly haste. Heim took her up according to the beams. The sky darkened and stars awoke, until blackness was a jewel box. Vadász fiddled with the com controls and eventually succeeded in getting a satellite relay from Mexico.

Debate on a procedural motion was not unlimited. The voting started before *Connie Girl* had made rendezvous. A roll call tolled overwhelming defeat.

"Mr. President," Coquelin's voice lifted from the 3V, blurred, small as an insect's, "this is a strange development. France had looked for the normal courtesies. Since I am required to make my country's basic policy statement today, I will. However, I note the time is near midday, and I warn the distinguished representatives that I shall be speaking at some length. Accordingly, I suggest that first we adjourn for lunch."

"The chair so rules," Fazil conceded. "This meeting will resume at 1400 hours sharp." His gavel clubbed down.

"An artist, I tell you," Vadász laughed.

"A couple hours isn't much time to get under way, with a crew new to the ship," Heim reminded him.

The great torpedo shape hove in sight and waxed as he closed until it filled his bow vision. As yet she was un-camouflaged, and sunlight lay furious on the stern assembly; drive units, Mach rings, boathouses, turrets, hatches cast long shadows on the metal flanks.

"Yacht *Connie Girl* calling cruiser *Fox II.* We are coming in. Please stand by. Over."

Wingate had argued about the change of cognomen. "I know what your old command meant to you, Gunnar," he said. "But you'll get enough people mad without taking the name of a Navy ship."

"I'm not, exactly," Heim said. "Last I heard, foxes were still in the public domain. Besides, I damn well figure to rub people's noses in what the Navy ought to be doing. What it wants to do, in fact."

Number Four boathouse stood open for him. He cradled the yacht—she was about the size of a regular auxiliary—and fretted while airpumps filled the shell. The corridors beyond were bustle and clangor. He'd had the men aboard for assignments and instruction, but nonetheless he wished terribly there had been time for a shakedown cruise.

First Officer Penoyer saluted on the bridge. "Welcome, sir." Until Dave greeted him so, he had not really remembered how alone the captain is. "Full roster present. Work proceeding. Estimated time of acceleration, 2300 hours GMT."

"Knock at least an hour off that," Heim said.

"Sir?"

"You heard me." Heim sat down and riffled through the manual of operations. "Here, for instance. The C.E. doesn't have to check out the internal field compensators again. If they fail, we'll accelerate at no more than one-point-five gee; once in free fall, we can stand weightlessness till they're fixed. Not that I expect any trouble in his department anyway. He's good. Have him proceed directly to tuning the pulse manifolds. The more carefully that job is done, the nearer Sol we can go FTL."

"Aye, aye, sir." With noticeable distaste, Penoyer flicked the intercom and spoke to Uthg-a-K'thaq. Heim continued his search for corners that might be cut.

And somehow, in some typically human left-handed fashion, the job was done. At 2145 klaxons hooted, orders echoed, atoms flamed in fusion generators, and gravitational forces laid hold of space. Slowly, smoothly, with a deep purr felt less within the ears than the bones, *Fox II* slipped her moorings to Earth and departed orbit.

Heim stood on the bridge and watched his world recede. Still she dominated heaven, vast and infinitely fair, clouds and seas and a sapphire rim of sky. He had observed the continents in their nights and days as he rounded her: Africa, whence man came; Asia, where first he was more than a savage; Europe, where he outgrew myth and measured the stars; Australia, long-sought dream; Antarctica of the heroes. But he was happy that his last sight as he drove starward was of America, where the law was first written that all men are free.

Doubts and fears, even homesickness, had fallen away. He was committed now, and joy dwelt within him.

"Stations report condition satisfactory," Penoyer announced after a while.

"Very good. Carry on." Heim found the intercom and called the steward's department. "Endre? D'you have things in hand so they can get along without you for a spell?...Okay, come onto the bridge. And bring your guitar. We'll want a song or two."

The Magyar's voice was troubled. "Captain, have you been listening to Parliament?"

"Uh...no. Too busy. Good Lord, they started fresh more than an hour ago, didn't they?"

"Yes. We're picking up the beam to Mars. I have watched and—well, they did not let Coquelin delay. He tried, with a long introductory speech, and the chair ruled he must keep to the point Then he tried to introduce the evidence about New Europe, and someone objected and they decided to vote on whether that was germane now. The roll is still being called, but already he has a majority against him."

"Oh-oh." Heim was not shaken, on this day when he commanded anew a ship for Earth. But the need for action stabbed through his nerves. "Mr. Penoyer," he directed, "signal for maximum acceleration and order all hands to emergency stations."

The mate gulped and obeyed. "Have Sparks shunt that debate to our 3V," Heim went on. "Mr. Vadász, please come to the bridge." His chuckle was flat. "Yes, bring your guitar."

"What's the problem, sir?" Penoyer asked in unease.

"You'll see," Heim replied. "France is about to throw a nuke into the whole machine. Our plan was to have *Fox* well away by then. Now we'll need luck as well as brains and beauty."

The screen flickered to fuzzy motion. Coquelin was nearly drowned out by the risen rumble of engines. Earth dwindled among the stars and Luna's pocked face grew nearer.

"—this assembly is determined to give my country not one centimeter. As you like, ladies and gentlemen. I wished to say this gradually, for the blow is heavy at best. Now you must hear me whether you are ready or not."

The camera zoomed so close that Coquelin's visage filled the screen. That was a lousy trick, Heim thought. But, if he wasn't letting his own prejudices hoodwink him, this time it didn't work. Instead of underscoring every blemish, warts, moles, hairs, wrinkles—the close-up showed anger and unbreakable strength. Heim believed himself confirmed when the view moved back after a minute, to make Coquelin another man shuffling papers on a lectern.

"Mr. President, honorable delegates—" The translation could only suggest how the voice shifted, became the dry detached recital of an attorney making a technical point. "The Federation was founded and still exists to end the tragic anarchy that prevailed among nations before, to bring them under a law that serves the good of all. Now law cannot endure without equal justice. The popularity of an argument must be irrelevant. Only the lawful cause may be admitted. In the name of France, I therefore advance the following points.

"1. The Constitution forbids each member nation to keep armed forces above the police level or to violate the territorial integrity of any other member nation in any way. To enforce this, the Peace Control Authority is vested with the sole military power. It may and must take such measures as are necessary to stop aggressive acts, including conspiracy to commit such acts. The individuals responsible must be arrested and brought to trial before the World Court.

"2. The naval branch of the Authority has been used beyond the Solar System, albeit only in relatively minor actions to suppress insurrection and riot or to protect the lives and property of humans on distant planets. By authorizing such action, and by negotiating agreements with various aliens, the Federation has *de facto* and *de jure* assumed the posture with respect to non-human societies that was traditional between governments on Earth prior to the Constitution. Hence Earth as a whole is a sovereign state with the lawful prerogative of self-defense.

"3. By attacking New Europe and subsequently occupying it, Alerion has committed an act of territorial aggression.

"4. If Alerion is not regarded as a sovereign state, negotiation of this dispute is legally impossible, and the Authority is required to take military measures against what can only be considered banditry."

A roar went through the hall. Fazil banged his desk. Coquelin waited, sardonicism playing over his mouth. When order had been restored, the spokesman of France said:

"Evidently this assembly does consider Alerion to be sovereign like Earth. So, to proceed—

"5. If Alerion is indeed a legitimate state, then by the preamble to the Constitution it belongs to the family of nations. Therefore it must be regarded as either (a) obliged to refrain from territorial aggression on pain of military sanctions, or (b) not so obliged, since it is not a member of the Federation.

"6. In case (a), Alerion is automatically subject to military sanctions by the Peace Control Authority. But in case (b), the Authority is also required, by the Constitution and by past precedent, to safeguard the interests of individual humans and of member states of the Federation. Note well, the *Authority* has that obligation. Not this honorable assembly, not the World Court, but the Peace Control Authority, whose action must under the circumstances be of a military nature.

"7. Accordingly, in either case an automatic state of war now exists between Alerion and the World Federation."

Chaos broke loose.

Vadász had come in. He watched the scene for a time, as hundreds stood booing or cheering or screaming to be recognized, before he murmured: "Is that not a weak point there?"

"No," said Heim. "Remember the Moslem League case. Also, I reread the Constitution, and it's quite clear. Of course, it helps that the thing was written before we'd met any non-humans comparable to us." He turned to the mate. "Radar reports?"

"Eh? Oh-oh, yes. A large craft about 10,000 kilometers starboard high, vector roughly like ours."

"Damn! That'd be one of the Navy units, pulled in to guard Earth. Well, we'll have to see what happens." Heim ignored the mob scene on the 3V, rested his eyes on the cold serenity of the Milky Way and thought that this, at least, would endure.

Somehow quiet was enforced. Coquelin waited until the silence had become deathly. He raised another typewritten sheet and resumed in the same parched tone:

"8. In the event of territorial aggression, member states of the Federation are required to give every appropriate assistance to the Peace Control Authority, in the name of the Federation.

"9. In the judgment of France, this imposes an inescapable duty to provide armed assistance to the colonists of New Europe. However, a member of the Federation is prohibited the manufacture or possession of nuclear weapons.

"10. There is no prohibition on individuals obtaining such weapons outside the Solar System for themselves, provided that they do not bring them back to the Solar System.

"11. Nor is there any prohibition on the unilateral authorization by a member state of the Federation of a *private* military expedition which so outfits itself. We grant that privateers were formerly required to be citizens of the country whose flag they flew, and that this might conflict with the national disarmament law. We grant also that eventually the issuance of letters of marque and reprisal was banned, by the Declaration of Paris in 1856. But while such treaties remain binding on their signatories, including France, they are not binding on the Federation as a whole, which is not a signatory and indeed has members such as the United States of America which never were signatories. And we have seen that the Federation is a sovereign state, possessing all rights and responsibilities not explicitly waived.

"12. Therefore the Federation has the unrestricted right to issue letters of marque and reprisal.

"13. Therefore, and in view of paragraphs 7, 8, and 9, France has the right and the duty to issue letters of marque and reprisal in the name of the Federation.

"France has done so."

The 3V shrieked—more faintly each minute, as *Fox II* accelerated outward and outward. When she lost the Mars beam and reception ended, the racket in the Capitol had not yet subsided.

Penoyer said, "Whew! What's next?"

"An interminable debate," Heim said. "Coquelin will fight for every comma. Meanwhile nothing can be done about jellyfishing to Alerion. Hopefully, the people with guts will see they aren't beaten at the outset, will rally round and—I don't know."

"But us?"

"Maybe we can escape before someone realizes who that French privateer must be. Not that they can legally stop us without an Admiralty warrant; and you know how long that takes to get. But a nuclear shell is kind of final, and whoever fires it will have powerful friends in court."

Vadász strummed his guitar and began to sing softly: *"Morgenrot, Morgenrot—"* Heim wondered what that was, until he remembered the old, old Austrian cavalry song:

Morning red, morning red,
Wilt thou shine upon me dead?
Soon the trumpets will be blowing,
Then must I to death be going,
I and many trusty friends!—

But it wasn't really sad, it had been chorused by troops of young merry men as they galloped with sunlight wild on banners and lances.

He laughed aloud. "Hey! An idea. There were exactly thirteen points in Coquelin's speech. I wonder if he did that on purpose?"

None answered, except the plangent strings. He gave himself to thoughts... Lisa, Connie, Madelon, Jocelyn...Earth and Moon lay far behind.

"PCA-SN *Neptune* to cruiser *Fox II.* Come in, *Fox II.*"

The voice rocketed them from their seats. "Judas," Penoyer whispered, "that's a blastship."

Heim checked the radar tapes. "The one paralleling us. She's gone to an interception course. And if they use English on us, when we've got a French registry, they know—" He bit his lip and settled before the com relay console. *"Fox II* to *Neptune,"* he said. "We read you. The master speaking. What's on your mind? Over."

"This is Rear Admiral Ching-Kuo, commanding *Neptune.* Cease acceleration and stand by to be boarded. Over."

Sickness fountained in Heim. "What do you mean?" he blustered. "We have clearance. Over."

"You are suspected of illegal intentions. You are ordered to return to Earth orbit. Over."

"Have you a warrant? Over."

"I will show you my authorization when I board, Captain. Over."

"That'll be too late, if you don't have any. Establish video contact and show me now. Otherwise I am not bound to obey. Over."

"Captain," said Ching-Kuo, "I have my orders. If you do not follow instructions, I shall be forced to fire on you. Over."

Heim's gaze flew among the stars. *No, no, no, not this! Another hour and we'd have been away! One hour!*

A flaring went through him. "You win, Admiral," he said; it sounded like a stranger talking. "Under protest, I yield. Give us time to compute a velocity-matching vector and we'll meet you. Over and out."

He slammed down the 'switch and opened the intercom to the engine room. "Captain to chief engineer," he said. "Are you there?"

"Indeed," Uthg-a-K'thaq belched. "All is satiswactory."

"No. Somebody's uncorked the bottle on hell. There's a blastship which says if we don't stop and surrender, he'll shoot. Prepare for Mach drive."

"Captain!" Penoyer yelled. "This deep in the sun's field?"

"If the sync is perfect, we can do it," Heim said. "If not...we're dead, no more. Uthg-a-K'thaq, do you believe we can?"

"Gwurru! What a thing to ask!"

"You overhauled those engines yourself," Heim said. "I trust you."

Vadász's guitar shouted at his back.

For a moment the intercom bore only the throb of machines. Then: "Cawtain, I am not God. Wut I think the chance is good for us. And I trust you."

Heim opened the general intercom. "Now hear this," he said; music raged around the words. "All hands stand by for Mach drive."

Penoyer clenched his fists. "Aye, aye, sir." The drone from aft rose until it was the noise of gales and great waters. Space twisted. Stars danced in the viewports.

Long ago, Ernst Mach of Austria *("Morgenrot, Morgenrot—")* had held the key. Nothing exists in isolation. Inertia has no meaning without an inertial frame of reference: which must be the entire universe. Einstein showed inertial and gravitational mass are the same. But as for the phenomena themselves—Gravitation is describable by equations of a warped space. Inertia is, then, an inductive effect of the cosmic gravitational field on mass. If your gravitrons can bend space, not the small amount needed for lift and thrust, but through a closed curve, your ship has no resistance to accelerative force. Theoretically, you can go as fast as you like. There are no more boundaries.

Neptune fired. The missile lagged by a million kilometers. Her captain yammered for instrument readings. Perhaps, oh, surely, surely, his prey had been torn apart by the forces generated with imperfect mesh of space curvatures here where the sun's power was still all-dominant. Nothing registered, no wreckage, no trace, except the howl of hydrogen atoms flung in bow wave and wake by a ship outpacing light. He dared not pursue.

Gunnar Heim straightened. One by one, he eased his muscles. "Well," he said, "we got away with it." The words were poor for the victory within him. Endre Vadász was doing better:

Glory, glory, hallelujah!
Glory, glory, hallelujah!
Glory, glory, hallelujah!
And we are outward bound!

Uncleftish Beholding

For most of its being, mankind did not know what things are made of, but could only guess. With the growth of worldken, we began to learn, and today we have a beholding of stuff and work that watching bears out, both in the workstead and in daily life.

The underlying kinds of stuff are the *firststuffs,* which link together in sundry ways to give rise to the rest. Formerly we knew of ninety-two firststuffs, from waterstuff, the lightest and barest, to ymirstuff, the heaviest. Now we have made more, such as aegirstuff and helstuff.

The firststuffs have their being as motes called *unclefts.* These are mighty small; one seedweight of waterstuff holds a tale of them like unto two followed by twenty-two naughts. Most unclefts link together to make what are called *bulkbits.* Thus, the waterstuff bulkbit bestands of two waterstuff unclefts, the sourstuff bulkbit of two sourstuff unclefts, and so on. (Some kinds, such as sunstuff, keep alone; others, such as iron, cling together in chills when in the fast standing; and there are yet more yokeways.) When unlike clefts link in a bulkbit, they make bindings. Thus, water is a binding of two waterstuff unclefts with one sourstuff uncleft, while a bulkbit of one of the forestuffs making up flesh may have a thousand or more unclefts of these two firststuffs together with coalstuff and chokestuff.

At first it was thought that the uncleft was a hard thing that could be split no further; hence the name. Now we know it is made up of lesser motes. There is a heavy *kernel* with a forward bernstonish lading, and around it one or more light motes with backward ladings. The least uncleft is that of everyday waterstuff. Its kernel is a lone forwardladen mote called a *firstbit.* Outside it is a backwardladen mote called a *bernstonebit.* The firstbit has a heaviness about 1840-fold that of the bernstonebit. Early worldken folk thought bernstonebits swing around the kernel like the Earth around the Sun, but now we understand they are more like waves or clouds.

In all other unclefts are found other motes as well, about as heavy as the firstbit but with no lading, known as neitherbits. We know a kind of waterstuff with one neitherbit in the kernel along with the firstbit; another kind has two neitherbits. Both kinds are seldom.

The next greatest firststuff is sunstuff, which has two firstbits and two bernstonebits. The everyday sort also has two neitherbits in the kernel. If there are more or less, the uncleft will soon break asunder. More about this later.

The third firststuff is stonestuff, with three firstbits, three bernstonebits, and its own share of neitherbits. And so it goes, on through such everyday stuffs as coalstuff (six firstbits) or iron (26) to ones more lately found. Ymirstuff (92) was the last until men began to make some higher still.

It is the bernstonebits that link, and so their tale fastsets how a firststuff behaves and what kinds of bulkbits it can help make. The worldken of this behaving, in all its manifold ways, is called *minglingken*. Minglingers have found that as the uncleftish tale of the firststuffs (that is, the tale of firststuffs in their kernels) waxes, after a while they begin to show ownships not unlike those of others that went before them. So, for a showdeal, stonestuff (3), headachestuff (11), potashstuff (19), redstuff (37), and bluegraystuff (55) can each link with only one uncleft of waterstuff, while coalstuff (6), sandstuff (14), germanstuff (22), tin (50), and lead (82) can each link with four. This is readily seen when all are set forth in what is called the *roundaround board of the firststuffs*.

When an uncleft or bulkbit wins one or more bernstonebits above its own, it takes on a backward lading. When it loses one or more, it takes on a forward lading. Such a mote is called a *farer,* for that the drag between unlike ladings flits it. When bernstonebits flit by themselves, it may be as a bolt of lightning, a spark off some faststanding chunk, or the everyday flow of bernstoneness through wires.

Coming back to the uncleft itself, the heavier it is, the more neitherbits as well as first bits in its kernel. Indeed, soon the tale of neitherbits is the greater. Unclefts with the same tale of firstbits but unlike tales of neitherbits are called *samesteads*. Thus, everyday sourstuff has eight neitherbits with its eight firstbits, but there are also kinds with five, six, seven, nine, ten, and eleven neitherbits. A samestead is known by the tale of both kernel motes, so that we have sourstuff-13, sourstuff-14, and so on, with sourstuff-16 being by far the mostfound. Having the same number of bernstonebits, the samesteads of a firststuff behave almost alike minglingly, They do show some unlikeness, outstandingly among the heavier ones, and these can be worked to sunder samesteads from each other.

Most samesteads of every firststuff are unabiding. Their kernels break up, each at its own speed. This speed is written as the *half-life*. which is how long it takes half of any deal of the same stead thus to shift itself. The doing is known as *lightrotting*. It may happen fast or slowly, and in any of sundry ways, offhanging on the makeup of the kernel. A kernel may spit out two firstbits with two neitherbits, that is, a sunstuff kernel, thus leaping two steads back in the roundaround board and four weights back in heaviness. It may give off a bernstonebit from a neitherbit, which thereby becomes a firstbit and thrusts the uncleft one stead up in the board while keeping the same weight. It may give off a *forwardbit*, which is a mote with the same weight as a bernstonebit but a forward lading, and thereby spring one stead down in the board while keeping the same weight. Often, too, a mote is given off with neither lading nor heaviness, called the *weeneitherbit*.

In much Iightrotting, a mote of light with most short wavelength comes out as well.

For although light oftenest behaves as a wave, it can be looked on as a mote, the lightbit. We have already said by the way that a mote of stuff can behave not only as a chunk, but as a wave. Down among the unclefts, things do not happen in steady flowings, but in leaps between bestandings that are forbidden. The knowledge-hunt of this is called *lump beholding.*

Nor are stuff and work unakin. Rather, they are groundwise the same, and one can be shifted into the other. The kinship between them is that work is like unto weight manifolded by the fourside of the haste of light.

By shooting motes into kernels, worldken folk have shifted samesteads of one firststuff into samesteads of another. Thus did they make ymirstuff into aegirstuff and helstuff, and they have afterward gone beyond these. The heavier firststuffs are all highly lightrottish and therefore are not found in the greenworld.

Some of the higher samesteads are *splitly.* That is, when a neitherbit strikes the kernel of one, as for a showdeal ymirstuff-235, it bursts into lesser kernels and free neitherbits; the latter can then split more ymirstuff-235. When this happens, weight shifts into work. It is not much of the whole, but nevertheless it is awesome.

With enough strength, lightweight unclefts can be made to togethermelt. In the Sun, through a row of strikings and lightrottings, four unclefts of waterstuff in this wise become one of sunstuff. Again some weight is lost as work, and again this is greatly big when set beside the work gotten from a minglingish doing such as fire.

Today we wield both kind of uncleftish doings in weapons, and kernelish splitting gives us heat and bernstoneness. We hope to do likewise with togethermelting, which would yield an unhemmed wellspring of work for mankindish goodgain.

Soothly we live in mighty years!

Besides his newbooks and truthbooks. the writer has forthshown in Likething Worldken Sagas/Worldken Truth, The Warehouse of Dreamishness and Worldken Sagas *and other roundaroundnesses.*

The Critique of Impure Reason

The robot entered so quietly, for all his bulk, that Felix Tunny didn't hear. Bent over his desk, the man was first aware of the intruder when a shadow came between him and the fluoroceil. Then a last footfall quivered the floor, a vibration that went through Tunny's chair and into his bones. He whirled, choking on a breath, and saw the blueblack shape like a cliff above him. Eight feet up, the robot's eyes glowed angry crimson in a faceless helmet of a head.

A voice like a great gong reverberated through the office:

"My, but you look silly."

"What the devil are you doing?" Tunny yelped.

"Wandering about," said Robot IZK-99 airily. "Hither and yon, yon and hither. Observing life. How deliciously right Brochet is!"

"Huh?" said Tunny. The fog of data, estimates, and increasingly frantic calculations was only slowly clearing from his head.

IZK-99 extended an enormous hand to exhibit a book.

Tunny read *The Straw and the Bean: a Novel of Modern Youth by Truman Brochet* on the front. The back of the dust jacket was occupied by a colorpic of the author, who had bangs and delicate lips. Deftly, the robot flipped the book open and read aloud:

> "Worms," she said. "that's what they are, worms, that's what we-uns all are, Billy Chile, worms that grew a spine an' a brain way back in the Obscene or the Messyzoic or whenever it was." Even in her sadnesses Ella Mae must always make her sad little jokes, which saddened me still more on this day of sad rain and dying magnolia blossoms. "We don't want them," she said. "Backbones an' brains, I mean, honey. They make us stiff an' topheavy, so we can't lie down no more an' be jus' nothin' ay-tall but worms."
>
> "Take off your clothes," I yawned.

"What has that got to do with anything?" Tunny asked.

"If you do not understand," said IZK-99 coldly, "there is no use in discussing it with you. I recommend that you read Arnold Roach's penetrating critical essay on this book. It appeared in the last issue of *Pierce, Arrow! The Magazine of Penetrating Criticism.* He devotes four pages to analyzing the various levels of meaning in that exchange between Ella Mae and Billy Chile."

"Ooh," Tunny moaned. "Isn't it enough I've got a hangover, a job collapsing under me because of you, and a fight with my girl, but you have to mention that rag?"

"How vulgar you are. It comes from watching stereovision." The robot sat down in a chair, which creaked alarmingly under his weight, crossed his legs and leafed through his book. The other hand lifted a rose to his chemosensor. "Exquisite," he murmured.

"You don't imagine I'd sink to reading what they call fiction these days, do you?" Tunny sneered, with a feeble hope of humiliating him into going to work. "Piddling little experiments in the technique of describing more and more complicated ways to feel sorry for yourself—what kind of entertainment is that for a man?"

"You simply do not appreciate the human condition," said the robot.

"Hah! Do you think you do, you conceited hunk of animated tin?"

"Yes, I believe so, thanks to my study of the authors, poets, and critics who devote their lives to the exploration and description of Man. Your Miss Forelle is a noble soul. Ever since I looked upon my first copy of that exquisitely sensitive literary quarterly she edits, I have failed to understand what she sees in you. To be sure," IZK-99 mused, "the relationship is not unlike that between the nun and the Diesel engine in *Regret for Two Doves.* but still...At any rate, if Miss Forelle has finally told you to go soak your censored head in expurgated wastes and then put the unprintable thing in an improbable place, I for one heartily approve."

Tunny, who was no mama's boy—he had worked his way through college as a whale herder and bossed construction gangs on Mars—was so appalled by the robot's language that he could only whisper, "She did not. She said nothing of the sort."

"I did not mean it literally," IZK-99 explained, "I was only quoting the renunciation scene in *Gently Come Twilight.* By Stichling, you know—almost as sensitive a writer as Brochet."

Tunny clenched fists and teeth and battled a wild desire to pull the robot apart, plate by plate and transistor by transistor. He couldn't, of course. He was a big blond young man with a homely, candid face; his shoulders strained his blouse and the legs coming out of his shorts were thickly muscular; but robots had steelloy frames and ultrapowered energizers. Besides, though his position as chief estimator gave him considerable authority in Planetary Developments, Inc., the company wouldn't let him destroy a machine which had cost several million dollars. Even when the machine blandly refused to work and spent its time loafing around the plant, reading, brooding, and denouncing the crass bourgeois mentality of the staff.

Slowly, Tunny mastered his temper. He'd recently thought of a new approach to the problem; might as well try it now. He leaned forward. "Look, Izaak," he said in the mildest tone he could manage, "have you ever considered that we need you? That the whole human race needs you?"

"The race needs love, to be sure," said the robot, "which I am prepared to offer; but I expect that the usual impossibility of communication will entangle us in the typical ironic loneliness."

"No, *no,* NO—um—that is, the human race needs those minerals that you can obtain for us. Earth's resources are dwindling. We can get most elements from the sea, but some are in such dilute concentration that it isn't economically feasible to extract them. In particular, there's rhenium. Absolutely vital in alloys and electronic parts that have to stand intense irradiation. It always was scarce, and now it's in such short supply that several key industries are in trouble. But on Mercury—"

"Spare me. I have heard all that *ad nauseam.* What importance have any such dead, impersonal, mass questions, contrasted to the suffering, isolated soul? No, it is useless to argue with me. My mind is made up. For the disastrous consequences of not being able to reach a firm decision, I refer you to the Freudian analyses of *Hamlet.*"

"If you're interested in individuals," Tunny said, "you might consider me. I'm almost an ancestor of yours, God help me. I was the one who first suggested commissioning a humanoid robot with independent intelligence for the Mercury project. This company's whole program for the next five years is based on having you go. If you don't, I'll be out on my ear. And jobs are none too easy to come by. How's that for a suffering, isolated soul?"

"You are not capable of suffering," said Izaak. "You are much too coarse. Now do leave me to my novel." His glowing eyes returned to the book. He continued sniffing the rose.

Tunny's own gaze went back to the be scribbled papers which littered his desk, the result of days spent trying to calculate some way out of the corner into which Planetary Developments, Inc. had painted itself. There wasn't any way that he could find. The investment in Izaak was too great for a relatively small outfit like this. If the robot didn't get to work, and soon, the company would be well and thoroughly up Dutchman's Creek.

In his desperation Tunny had even looked again into the hoary old idea of remote-controlled mining. No go—not on Mercury, where the nearby sun flooded every tele-device with enough heat and radiation to assure fifty percent chance of breakdown in twenty-four hours. It had been rare luck that the rhenium deposits were found at all, by a chemotrac sent from the underground base. To mine them, there must be a creature with senses, hands, and intelligence, present on the spot, to make decisions and repair machinery as the need arose. Not a human; no rad screen could long keep a man alive under that solar bombardment. The high-acceleration flight to base, and home again when their hitch was up, in heavily shielded and screened spaceships, gave the base personnel as much exposure as the Industrial Safety Board allowed per lifetime. The miner had to be a robot.

Only the robot refused the task. There was no way, either legal or practical, to make him take it against his will. Tunny laid a hand on his forehead. No wonder he'd worried himself close to the blowup point, until last night he quarreled with Jane and got hyperbolically drunk. Which had solved nothing.

The phone buzzed on his desk. He punched Accept. The face of William Barsch, executive vice-president, leaped into the screen, round, red, and raging.

"Tunny!" he bellowed.

"I-yi-yi!—I mean hello, sir." The engineer offered a weak smile.

"Don't hello me, you glue-brained idiot! When is that robot taking off?"

"Never," said Izaak. At his electronic reading speed, he had finished the novel and now rose from his chair to look over Tunny's shoulder.

"You're fired!" Barsch howled. "Both of you!"

"I hardly consider myself hired in the first place," Izaak said loftily. "Your economic threat holds no terrors. My energizer is charged for fifty years of normal use, after which I can finance a recharge by taking a temporary position. It would be interesting to go on the road at that," he went on thoughtfully, "like those people in that old book the Library of Congress reprostatted for me. Yes, one might indeed find satori in going, man, going, never mind where, never mind why—"

"You wouldn't find much nowadays," Tunny retorted. "Board a transcontinental tube at random, and where does it get you? Wherever its schedule says. The bums aren't seeking enlightenment, they're sitting around on their citizens' credit watching SteeVee." He wasn't paying much attention to his own words, being too occupied with wondering if Barsch was really serious this time.

"I gather as much," said Izaak, "although most contemporary novels and short stories employ more academic settings. What a decadent civilization this is: no poverty, no physical or mental disease, no wars, no revolutions, no beatniks!" His tone grew earnest. "Please understand me, gentlemen. I bear you no ill will. I despise you, of course, but in the most cordial fashion. It is not fear which keeps me on Earth—I am practically indestructible; not anticipated loneliness—I enjoy being unique; not any prospect of boredom in the usual sense-talent for the work you had in mind is engineered into me. No, it is the absolute insignificance of the job. Beyond the merely animal economic implications, rhenium has no meaning. Truman Brochet would never be aware the project was going on, let alone write a novel about it. Arnold Roach would not even mention it *en passant* in any critical essay on the state of the modern soul as reflected in the major modern novelists. Do you not see my position? Since I was manufactured, of necessity, with creative intelligence and a need to do my work right, I *must* do work I can respect."

"Such as what?' demanded Barsch.

"When I have read enough to feel that I understand the requirements of literary technique, I shall seek a position on the staff of some quarterly review. Or perhaps I shall teach. I may even try my hand at a subjectively oriented novel."

"Get out of this plant," Barsch ordered in a muted scream.

"Very well."

"No, wait!" cried Tunny. "Uh...Mr. Barsch didn't mean that. Stick around, Izaak. Go read a criticism or something."

"Thank you, I shall." The robot left the office, huge, gleaming, irresistible, and smelling his rose.

"Who do you think you are, you whelp, countermanding me?" Barsch snarled. "You're not only fired, I'll see to it that—"

"Please, sir," Tunny said. "I know this situation. I should. Been living with it for two weeks now, from its beginning. You may not realize that Izaak hasn't been outside this building since he was activated. Mostly he stays in a room assigned him. He gets his books and magazines and stuff by reprostat from the public libraries, or by pneumo from publishers and dealers. We have to pay him a salary, you know—he's legally a person—and he doesn't need to spend it on anything but reading matter."

"And you want to keep on giving him free rent and let him stroll around disrupting operations?"

"Well, at least he isn't picking up any further stimuli. At present we can predict his craziness. But let him walk loose in the city for a day or two, with a million totally new impressions blasting on his sensors, and God alone knows what conclusions he'll draw and how he'll react."

"Hm." Barsch's complexion lightened a bit. He gnawed his lip a while, then said in a more level voice: "Okay, Tunny, perhaps you aren't such a total incompetent. This mess may not be entirely your fault, or your girl friend's. Maybe I, or someone, should have issued a stricter directive about what he ought and ought not be exposed to for the first several days after activation."

You certainly should have, Tunny thought, but preserved a tactful silence.

"Nevertheless," Barsch scowled, "this fiasco is getting us in worse trouble every day. I've just come from lunch with Henry Lachs, the news magazine publisher. He told me that rumors about the situation have already begun to leak out. He'll sit on the story as long as he can, being a good friend of mine, but that won't be much longer. He can't let *Entropy* be scooped, and someone else is bound to get the story soon."

Well, sir, I realize we don't want to be a laughingstock—"

"Worse than that. You know why our competitors haven't planned to tackle that rhenium mine. We had the robot idea first and got the jump on them. Once somebody's actually digging ore, he can get the exclusive franchise. But if they learn what's happened to us...well, Space Metals already has a humanoid contracted for. Half built, in fact. They intended to use him on Callisto, but Mercury would pay a lot better."

Tunny nodded sickly.

Barsch's tone dropped to an ominous purr. "Any ideas yet on how to change that clanking horror's so-called mind?"

"He doesn't clank, sir:" Tunny corrected without forethought.

Barsch turned purple. "I don't give two squeals in hell whether he clanks or rattles or sings high soprano! I want results! I've got half our engineers busting their brains on the problem. But if you, yourself, personally, aren't the one who solves it, we're going to have a new chief estimator. Understand?" Before Tunny could explain that he understood much too well, the screen blanked.

*   *   *   *

He buried his face in his hands, but that didn't help either. The trouble was, he liked his job, in spite of drawbacks like Barsch. Also, while he wouldn't starve if he was fired, citizen's credit wasn't enough to support items he'd grown used to, such as a sailboat and a cabin in the Rockies, nor items he hoped to add to the list, such as Janet Forelle. Besides, he dreaded the chronic ennui of the unemployed.

He told himself to stop thinking and get busy on the conundrum—no, that wasn't what he meant either—Oh, fireballs! He was no use at this desk today. Especially remembering the angry words he and Janet had exchanged. He'd probably be no use anywhere until the quarrel was mended. At least a diplomatic mission would clear his head, possibly jolt his mind out of the rut in which it now wearily paced.

"Ooh," he said, visualizing his brain with a deep circular rut where there tramped a tiny replica of himself, bowed under a load of pig iron and shod with cleats. Hastily, he punched a button on his recep. "I've got to go out," he said. "Tell 'em I'll be back when."

The building hummed and murmured as he went down the hall. Open doorways showed offices, laboratories, control machines clicking away like Hottentots. Now and then he passed a human technie. Emerging on the fifth-story flange he took a dropshaft down to the third, where the northbound beltway ran. Gentle gusts blew upward in his face, for there was a gray February sky overhead and the municipal heating system had to radiate plenty of ergs. Lake Michigan, glimpsed through soaring gaily colored skyscrapers, looked the more cold by contrast. Tunny found a seat on the belt, ignoring the aimlessly riding mass of people around him, mostly unemployed. He stuffed his pipe and fumed smoke the whole distance to the University of Chicapolis.

Once there, he had to transfer several times and make his way through crowds younger, livelier, and more purposeful than those off campus. Education, he recalled reading, was the third largest industry in the world. He did read, whatever Izaak said—nonfiction, which retained a certain limited popularity; occasionally a novel, but none more recent than from fifty years ago. "I'm not prejudiced against what's being written nowadays," he had told Janet. "I just don't think it should be allowed to ride in the front ends of streetcars."

She missed his point, having a very limited acquaintance with mid-twentieth century American history. "If your attitude isn't due to prejudice, that's even worse," she said. "Then you are congenitally unable to perceive the nuances of modern reality."

"Bah! I earn my money working with the nuances of modern reality: systems analyses, stress curves, and spaceship orbits. That's what ails fiction these days, and poetry. There's nothing left to write about that the belleslettrists think is important. The only sociological problem of any magnitude is mass boredom, and you can't squeeze much plot or interest out of that. So the stuff gets too, too precious for words—and stinks."

"'Felix, you can't say that!"

"Can and do, sweetheart. Naturally, economics enters into the equation too. On the one hand, for the past hundred years movies, television, and now SteeVee have been crowding the printed word out of the public eye. (Hey, what a gorgeous metaphor!) Apart from some nonfiction magazines, publishing isn't a commercial enterprise any longer, And on the other hand, in a society as rich as ours, a limited amount of publishing remains feasible: endowed by universities or foundations or individual vanity or these authors' associations that have sprung up in the past decade. Only it doesn't try to be popular entertainment, it's abandoned that field entirely to SteeVee and become nothing but an academic mutual admiration society."

"Nonsense! Let me show you Scomber's critical essay on Tench. He simply tears the man to pieces."

"Yeah, I know. One-upmanship is part of the game too. The whole point is, though, that this mental inbreeding—no, not even that: mental—uh, I better skip *that* metaphor—anyhow, it never has and never will produce anything worth the time of a healthy human being."

"Oh, so I'm not a healthy human being?"

"I didn't mean that. You know I didn't. I only meant, well, you know...the great literature always was based on wide appeal, Sophocles, Shakespeare, Dickens, Mark Twain—"

But the fat was irretrievably in the fire. One thing led at high speed to another, until Tunny stormed out or was thrown out—he still wasn't sure which—and went to earth in the Whirling Comet Bar.

It wasn't that Janet was stuffy, he reminded himself as he approached the looming mass of the English building. She was cute as a kitten, shared his pleasure in sailboats and square dancing and low-life beer joints and most other things; also, she had brains, and their arguments were usually spirited but great mutual fun. They had dealt with less personal topics than last night's debate, though. Janet, a poet's daughter and a departmental secretary, took her magazine very seriously. He hadn't realized how seriously.

The beltway reached his goal. Tunny knocked out his pipe and stepped across the deceleration strips to the flange. The dropshaft lifted him to the fiftieth floor, where University publications had their offices. There was more human activity here than most places. Writing and editing remained people functions, however thoroughly automated printing and binding were. In spite of his purpose, Tunny walked slowly down the hall, observing with pleasure the earnest young coeds in their brief bright skirts and blouses. With less pleasure he noted the earnest young men. There wasn't much about them to suggest soldierly Aeschylus or roistering Marlowe or seagoing Melville or razzmatazz Mencken; they tended to be pale, long-haired, and ever so concerned with the symbolic import of a deliberately omitted comma.

The door marked *Pierce, Arrow!* opened for him and he entered a small shabby office heaped with papers, books, microspools, and unsold copies of the magazine. Janet sat the desk behind a manual typer and a stack of galleys. She was small herself, pert, extremely well engineered, with dark wavy hair that fell to her shoulders and big eyes the color of the Gulf Stream. Tunny paused and gulped. His heart began to knock.

"Hi," he said after a minute.

She looked up. "What—Felix!"

"I, uh, uh, I'm sorry about yesterday," he said.

"Oh, darling. Do you think I'm not? I was going to come to you." She did so, with results that were satisfactory to both parties concerned, however sickening they might have been to an outside observer.

After quite a long while, Tunny found himself in a chair with Janet on his lap. She snuggled against him. He stroked her hair and murmured thoughtfully: "Well, I suppose the trouble was, each suddenly realized how dead set on his own odd quirk the other one is. But we can live with the difference between us, huh?"

"Surely," Janet sighed. "And then, too, I didn't stop to think how worried you were, that robot and everything, and the whole miserable business my fault."

"Lord, no. How could you have predicted what'd happen? If anyone is responsible, I am. I took you there and could have warned you. But I didn't know either. Perhaps nobody would have known. Izaak's kind of robot isn't too well understood as yet. So few have been built, there's so little need for them."

"I still don't quite grasp the situation. Just because I talked to him for an hour or two—poor creature, he was so eager and enthusiastic—and then sent him some books and—"

"That's precisely it. Izaak had been activated only a few days before. Most of his knowledge was built right into him, so to speak, but there was also the matter of...well, psychological stabilization. Until the end of the indoctrination course, which is designed to fix his personality in the desired pattern, a humanoid robot is extremely susceptible to new impressions. Like a human baby. Or perhaps a closer analogy would be imprinting in some birds: present a fledgling with almost any object at a certain critical stage in its life, and it'll decide that object is its mother and follow the thing around everywhere. I never imagined, though, that modern literary criticism could affect a robot that way. It seemed so alien to everything he was made for. What I overlooked, I see now, was the fact that Izaak's fully humanoid. He isn't meant to be programmed, but has a free intelligence. Evidently freer than anyone suspected."

"Is there no way to cure him?"

"Not that I know of. His builders told me that trying to wipe the synapse patterns would ruin the whole brain. Besides, he doesn't want to be cured, and he has most of the legal rights of a citizen. We can't compel him."

"I do so wish I could do something. Can this really cost you your job?"

"'Fraid so. I'll fight to keep it, but—"

"Well," Janet said, "we'll still have my salary."

"Nothing doing. No wife is going to support me."

"Come, come. How medieval can a man get?"

"Plenty," he said. She tried to argue, but he stopped her in the most pleasant and effective manner. Some time went by. Eventually, with a small gasp, she looked at the clock.

"Heavens! I'm supposed to be at work this minute. I don't want to get myself fired, do I?" She bounced to her feet, a sight which slightly compensated for her departing his lap, smoothed her hair, kissed him again, and sped out the door.

Tunny remained seated. He didn't want to go anywhere, least of all home. Bachelor apartments were okay in their place, but after a certain point in a man's life they got damn cheerless. He fumbled out his pipe and started it again.

Janet was such a sweet kid, he thought. Bright, too. Her preoccupation with these latter-day word games actually did her credit; she wasn't content to stay in the dusty files of books written centuries ago, and word games were the only ones in town. Given a genuine literary milieu, she might well have accomplished great things, instead of fooling around with—what was the latest guff: Tunny got up and wandered over to her desk. He glanced at the galleys. Something by Arnold Roach.

> —the tense, almost fetally contracted structure of this story, exquisitely balanced in the ebb and flow of words forming and dissolving images like the interplay of ripples in water, marks an important new advance in the tradition of Arapaima as modified by the school of Barbel. Nevertheless it is necessary to make the assertion that a flawed tertiary symbolism exists in that the connotations of the primary word in the long quotation from Pollack which opens the third of the eleven cantos into which the story is divided, are not, as the author thinks, so much negative as—

"Yingle, yingle, yingle," Tunny muttered. "And they say engineers can't write decent English. If I couldn't do better than that with one cerebral hemisphere tied behind my back I'd—"

At which point he stopped cold and stared into space with a mountingly wild surmise. His jaw fell. So did his pipe. He didn't notice.

Five minutes later he exploded into action.

Four hours later, her secretarial stint through for the day, Janet returned to do some more proofreading. As the door opened, she reeled. The air was nearly unbreathable. Through a blue haze she could barely see her man grimy disheveled, smoking volcanically, hunched over her typer and slamming away at the keys.

"What off Earth!" she exclaimed.

"One more minute, sweetheart," Tunny said. Actually he spent 11.3 more minutes by the clock, agonizing over his last few sentences. Then he ripped the sheet out. threw it on a stack of others, and handed her the mess. "Read that."

"When my eyes have stopped smarting," Janet coughed. She had turned the air 'fresher on full blast and seated herself on the edge of a chair to wait. Despite her reply, she took the manuscript. But she read the several thousand words with a puzzlement that grew and grew. At the end, she laid the papers slowly down and asked, "Is this some kind of joke?"

"I hope not," said Tunny fervently.

"But—"

"Your next issue is due out when? In two weeks? Could you advance publication, and include this?"

"What? No, certainly I can't. That is, darling, I have to reject so many real pieces merely for lack of space, that it breaks my heart and...and I've got obligations to them, they trust me—"

"So." Tunny rubbed his chin. "What do you think of my essay? As a pure bit of writing."

"Oh...hm...well, it's clear and forceful, but naturally the technicalities of criticsm—"

"Okay. You revise it, working in the necessary poop. Also, choose a suitable collection of your better rejects, enough to make up a nice issue. Those characters will see print after all." While Janet stared with bewildered though lovely blue eyes, Tunny stabbed out numbers on the phone.

"Yes, I want to talk with Mr. Barsch. No, I don't give a neutrino whether he's in conference or not. You tell him Felix Tunny may have the answer to the robot problem...Hello, boss. Look, I've got an idea. Won't even cost very much. Can you get hold of a printing plant tonight? You know, someplace where they can run off a few copies of a small one-shot magazine?...Sure it's short notice. But didn't you say Henry Lachs is a friend of yours? Well, presume on his friendship—"

Having switched off, Tunny whirled about, grabbed Janet in his arms, and shouted, "Let's go!"

"Where?" she inquired, not unreasonably,

The pneumo went *whir-ping!* and tossed several items onto the mail shelf. IZK-99 finished reading *Neo-Babbitt: the Entrepreneur as Futility Symbol in Modern Literature* crossed his room with one stride, and went swiftly through the envelopes. The usual two or three crank letters and requests for autographs—any fully humanoid robot was news—plus a circular advertising metal polish and...wait... a magazine. Clipped to this was a note bearing the letterhead of the Mañana Literary Society. "—new authors' association...foundation-sponsored quarterly review...sample copies to a few persons of taste and discrimination whom we feel are potential subscribers..." The format had a limp dignity, with a plain cover reading:

p
i
p
e
t
t
e

Volume One
Number One

the journal of
analytical criticism

Excited and vastly flattered, IZK-99 read it on the spot in 148 seconds: so fast that he did a double take and stood for a time lost in astonishment. The magazine's contents had otherwise been standard stuff, but this one long article—Slowly, very carefully, he turned back to it and reread:

THUNDER BEYOND VENUS, by Charles Pilchard,
Wisdom Press (Newer York, 2026), 214 pp., UWF $6.50.
Reviewed by Pierre Hareng
Dept. of English, Miskatonic University

For many years I have been analyzing, dissecting, and evaluating with the best of them, and it has indeed been a noble work. Yet everything has its limits. There comes to each of us a bump, as Poorboy so poignantly says in *Not Soft Is the Rock.* Suddenly a new planet swims into our ken, a new world is opened, a new element is discovered and we stand with tools in our hands which are not merely inadequate to the task, but irrelevant. Like those fortunate readers who were there at the moment when Joyce invented the stream of consciousness, when Kafka plunged so gladly into the symbolism of absolute nightmare, when Faulkner delineated the artistic beauty of the humble corncob, when Durrell abolished the stream of consciousness, we too are suddenly crossing the threshold of revolution.

Charles Pilchard has not hitherto been heard from. The intimate details of his biography, the demonstration of the point-by-point relationship of these details to his work, will furnish material for generations of scholarship. Today, though, we are confronted with the event itself. For *Thunder Beyond Venus* is indeed an event which rocks the mind and, shakes the emotions and yet, at the same time, embodies a touch so sure, an artistry so consummate, that even Brochet has not painted a finer miniature.

The superficial skeleton is almost scornfully simple. It is, indeed, frankly traditional—the Quest motif in modern guise—dare I say that it could be made into a stereodrama? It is hard to imagine the sheer courage which was required to use so radical a form that many may find it incomprehensible. But in exactly this evocation of the great ghosts of Odysseus, King Arthur, and Don Juan, the author becomes immediately able to explore (implicitly; he is never crudely explicit) childhood with as much haunting delicacy as our most skilled specialists in this type of novel. Yet, unlike them, he is not confined to a child protagonist. Thus he achieves a feat of time-binding which for richness of symbolic overtones can well be matched against Betta's famous use of the stopped clock image in *The Old Man and the Umbrella.* As the hero himself cries, when trapped in that collapsing tunnel which is so much more than the obvious womb/tomb: "Okay, you stupid planet, you've got me pinched where it hurts. but by heaven: I've had more fun in life than you ever did. And I'll whip you yet!"

> The fact that he does then indeed overcome the deadly Venusian environment and goes on to destroy the pirate base and complete the project of making the atmosphere Earthlike (a scheme which an engineer friend tells me is at present being seriously contemplated) is. thus made infinitely more than a mechanical victory. It is a closing of the ring: the hero, who begins strong and virile and proud, returns to that condition at the end. The ironic overtones of this are clear enough, but the adroit use of such implements along the way as the pick which serves him variously as tool, weapon, and boathook when he and the heroine must cross the river of lava (to take only one random example from this treasure chest) add both an underscoring and a commentary which must be read repeatedly to be appreciated.

And on and on.

When he had finished, IZK -99 went back and perused the article a third time. Then he punched the phone. "Public library," said the woman in the screen.

Tunny entered the office of *Pierce, Arrowland* stood for a moment watching Janet as she slugged the typer. Her desk was loaded with papers, cigarette butts, and coffee equipment. Dark circles under her eyes bespoke exhaustion. But she plowed gamely on.

"Hi, sweetheart," he said.

"Oh...Felix." She raised her head and blinked. "Goodness, is it that late?"

"Yeah. Sorry I couldn't get here sooner. How're you doing?"

"All right—I guess—but darling, it's so dreadful."

"Really?" he came to her, stopped for a kiss, and picked up the reprostat page which she was adapting.

> The blaster pointed straight at Jon Dace's chest. Behind its gaping muzzle sneered the mushroom-white face and yellow slit-pupilled eyes of Hark Farkas. "Don't make a move, Earth pig!" the pirate hissed. Jon's broad shoulders stiffened. Fury seized him. His keen eyes flickered about, seeking a possible way out of this death trap—

"M-m-m, yeh, that is pretty ripe," Tunny admitted. "Where's it from? Oh, yes, I see. *Far Out Science Fiction,* May 1950. Couldn't you do any better than that?"

"Certainly. Some of those old pulp stories are quite good, if you take them on their own terms." Janet signaled the coffeemaker to pour two fresh cups. "But others, ugh! I needed a confrontation scene, though, and this was the first that came to hand. Time's too short to make a thorough search."

"What've you made of it?" Tunny read her manuscript:

> The gun opened a cerberoid mouth at him. Behind it, his enemy's face was white as silent snow, secret snow, where the eyes (those are pearls that were) reflected in miniature the sandstorm that hooted cougar-colored on the horizon.

* * * *

"Hey, not bad. 'Cougar-colored' I like that."

> There went a hissing: "Best keep stance, friend-stranger-brother whom I must send before me down the tunnel." Jon's shoulders stiffend. Slowly, he answered—

"Uh, sweetheart, honest, that cussing would make a bulldozer blush."

"How can you have intellectual content without four-letter words," Janet asked, puzzled.

Tunny shrugged. "No matter, I suppose. Time's too short, as you say, to polish this thing, and Izaak won't know the difference. Not after such a smorgasbord of authors and critics as he's been gobbling down...besides having so little experience of actual, as opposed to fictional, humans.

"Time's too short to *write* this thing," Janet corrected, her mouth quirking upward. "How did you ever find the stuff we're plagiarizing? I'd no idea any such school of fiction had ever existed."

"I knew about it vaguely, from mention in the nineteenth and twentieth-century books I've read. But to tell the truth, what I did in this case was ask the Library of Congress to search its microfiles for adventure-story publications of that era and 'stat me a million words' worth." Tunny sat down and reached for his coffee. "Whew, I'm bushed!"

"Hard day?" Janet said softly.

"Yeah. Keeping Izaak off my neck was the worst part."

"How did you stall him?"

"Oh, I had his phone tapped. He called the local library first. for a 'stat. When they didn't have the tape, he called a specialty shop that handles fiction among other things. But at that point I switched him over to a friend of mine, who pretended to be a clerk in the store. This guy told Izaak he'd call Newer York and order a bound copy from the publisher. Since then the poor devil has been chewing his fingernail, or would if a robot were able to, and faunching...mainly in my office."

"Think we can meet his expectations?"

"I dunno. My hope is that this enforced wait will make the prize seem still more valuable. Of course, some more reviews would help. Are you positive you won't run one in *Pierce?"*

"I told you, we're so short of space—"

"I talked to Barsch about that. He'll pay for the additional pages and printing."

"Hm-m-m...literary hoaxes do have an honorable tradition, don't they? But oh, dear—I just don't know."

"Barsch has gotten around Henry Lachs," Tunny insinuated. "There'll be a review in *Entropy.* You wouldn't want to be scooped by a lousy middlebrow news magazine, would you?"

Janet laughed. "All right, you win. Submit your article and I'll run it."

"I'll submit to you anytime," Tunny said. After a while: "Well, I feel better now. I'll take over here while you catch a nap. Let's see, what pickle did we leave our bold hero in?"

> This novel at once vigorous and perceptive...the most startling use of physical action to further the development that has been seen since Conrad, and it must be asserted that Conrad painted timidly in comparison to the huge, bold, brilliant, and yet minutely executed splashes on Pilchard's canvas...this seminal work, if one will pardon the expression...the metrical character of the whole, so subtle that the fact the book is a rigidly structured poem will escape many readers...
>
> —*Pierce, Arrow!*

Two hundred years ago, in the quiet, tree-shaded town of Amherst, Mass., spinster poetess Emily Dickinson (1830-86) wrote of the soul:

Unmoved, she notes the chariot's pausing
At her low gate;
Unmoved, an emperor is kneeling
Upon her mat.

In the brief poem of which these lines are a stanza, she expressed a sense of privacy and quiet independence which afterward vanished from the American scene as thoroughly as Amherst vanished into the Atlantic metropolitan complex.

It may seem strange to compare the shy, genteel lady of Puritan derivation to Charles Pilchard and his explosive, intensely controversial first novel. Yet the connection is there. The *Leitmotif*[1] of *Thunder Beyond Venus* is not the story itself. That story is unique enough, breathtakingly original in its use of physical struggle to depict the dark night of the soul. Some would say almost too breathtaking. Dazzled, the reader may fall to see the many underlying layers of meaning. But Emily Dickinson would understand the aloof, independent soul which animates hero Jon Dace.

Tall (6 ft. 3 1/2 in.), robust (225 lb.), balding Charles Pilchard, 38, himself a fanatical seeker of privacy, has written a master's thesis on Rimbaud but never taught. Instead he has lived for more than ten years on citizen's credit while developing his monumental work. (Cut of Charles Pilchard, captioned, "No charioteer he."] Twice married once divorced, he does not maintain a fixed residence but describes himself, like Jon, as "swimming around in the ocean called Man." He has probed deeply into the abysses of that ocean. Yet he has not emerged with the carping nega-

1 Borrowed from the operatic works of Richard Wagner (1813-83), Emily Dickinson's stormy German contemporary, this word has come to mean an underlying and recurrent theme. —Entropy

tivism of today's nay-sayers. For although he fully appreciates the human tragedy, Pilchard is in the end a triumphant yea-sayer...

The robot entered so noisily that Felix Tunny heard him halfway down the corridor. The engineer turned from his desk and waited. His fingers gripped his chair arms until the nails turned white.

"Hello, Izaak," he got out. "Haven't seen you for a couple of days."

"No," said the robot. "I have been in my room, thinking. And reading."

"Reading what?"

"*Thunder Beyond Venus,* of course. Over and over. Is anybody reading anything else?" One steel finger tapped the volume. "You have read it yourself, have you not?" Izaak asked on a challenging note.

"Well, you know how it goes," Tunny said. "Things are rather frantic around here, what with the company's plans being disrupted and so forth. I've been meaning to get around to it."

"Get around to it!" Izaak groaned. "I suppose eventually you will get around to noticing sunlight and the stars."

"Why, I thought you were above any such gross physical things," Tunny said. This was the payoff. His throat was so dry he could hardly talk.

Izaak didn't notice. "It has proven necessary to make a reevaluation," he said. "This book has opened my eyes as much as it has opened the eyes of the critics who first called my attention to its subtlety, its profundity, its universal significance and intensely individual analysis. Pilchard has written the book of our age, as Homer, Dante, and Tolstoy wrote the books of their own ages. He explores what is meaningful today as well as what is meaningful for all time."

"Bully for Pilchard."

"The conquest of space is, as the article in *pipette* showed also the conquest of self. The microcosm opens on the macrocosm, which reflects and re-reflects the observer. This is the first example of the type of book that will be written and discussed for the next hundred years."

"Could be."

"None but an utter oaf would respond to this achievement as tepidly as you," Izaak snapped. "I shall be glad to see the last of you."

"Y-y-you're going away? Where?" (Hang on, boy, countdown to zero!)

"Mercury. Please notify Barsch and have my spaceship made ready. I have no desire to delay so important an experience."

Tunny sagged in his chair. "By no means," he whispered. "Don't waste a minute."

"I make one condition, that for the entire period of my service you send to me with the cargo ships any other works by Pilchard that may appear, plus the quarterlies to which I subscribe and the other exemplars of the literary mode he has pioneered which I shall order on the basis of reviews I read. They must be transcribed to metal, you realize, because of the heat."

"Sure, sure. Glad to oblige."

"When I return," Izaak crooned, "I shall be so uniquely qualified to criticize the new novels that some college will doubtless give me a literary quarterly of my own."

He moved toward the door. "I must go arrange for *Thunder Beyond Venus* to be transcribed on steelloy," he said.

"Why not tablets of stone?" Tunny muttered.

"That is not a bad idea. Perhaps I shall." Izaak went out.

When he was safely gone, Tunny whooped. For a while he danced around his office like a peppered Indian, until he whirled on the phone. Call Barsch and tell him—No, to hell with Barsch. Janet deserved the good news first.

She shared his joy over the screens. Watching her, thinking of their future, brought a more serious mood on Tunny. "My conscience does hurt me a bit," he confessed. "It's going to be a blow to Izaak, out there on Mercury, when his brave new school of literature never appears."

"Don't be too certain about that," Janet said. "In fact—Well, I was going to call you today. We're in trouble again, I'm afraid. You know that office and clerk we hired to pretend to be Wisdom Press, in case Izaak tried to check up? She's going frantic. Calls are streaming in. Thousands of people already, furious because they can't find *Thunder Beyond Venus* anywhere. She's handed them a story about an accidental explosion in the warehouse, but—What can we do?"

"Oy." Tunny sat quiet for a space. His mind flew. "We did run off some extra copies, didn't we?" he said at length.

"Half a dozen or so. I gave one to Arnold Roach. He simply had to have it, after seeing the other articles. Now he's planning a rave review for *The Pacific Monthly,* with all sorts of sarcastic comments about how *Entropy* missed the whole point of the book. Several more critics I know have begged me at least to lend them my copy."

Tunny smote the desk with a large fist. "Only one way out of this," he decided. "Print up a million and stand by to print more. I don't just mean tapes for libraries, either. I mean regular, bound volumes."

"What?"

"I have a hunch that commercial fiction has been revived as of this week. Maybe our book is crude, but it does touch something real, something that people believe in their hearts is important. If I'm right, then there's going to be a spate of novels like this, and many will make a whopping profit, and some will even be genuinely good...Lord, Lord," Tunny said in awe. "We simply don't know our own strength, you and I."

"Let's get together,'" Janet suggested, "and find out."

Science and Creation

One of the less endearing—and more dangerous—features of the 20th century has been a worldwide tendency to substitute rhetoric for discourse. By now, reasoned debate is a rarity. There is seldom even any effort to understand an opposing point of view. Instead, a person attributes opinions or attitudes to the other fellow and proceeds to heap billingsgate upon him because of them, although they may not actually be what he means at all. Living near Berkeley, California, I have over the years watched this sort of thing develop in the academic community and its hangers-on, until I am inclined to agree with a fictional character of mine who remarked, "Sure, I'm anti-intellectual. I prefer people who think..."

Well, that may be just a little exaggerated, a hint of the same behavior I was condemning. It got your attention, though, didn't it? Let me try to make the rest of this essay an exercise in rationality.

I propose to discuss the "scientific creationism" which is so much in the current news. My conclusion will scarcely surprise you: that "scientific creationism" is a contradiction in terms. If that were all, there would be no point in stating it yet again. Why preach to the choir? However, it does seem to me that spokesmen for the scientific establishment have generally made their points poorly, because often they themselves don't quite realize what the concept of evolution signifies. Thus the argument we'll advance against creationism here will take a turn that may prove surprising, therefore enlightening to some readers. Indeed, it will be only the first step in a brief exploration of the philosophy of science.

We begin by forswearing invective. The creationists are *not* a bunch of yahoos. They are generally well-educated and well-mannered individuals, a number of them with excellent scientific credentials. (While I don't know just what James Irwin's views on evolution are, we all know he believes the Biblical story of Noah is substantially true, and led an expedition in search of the remains of the Ark—after having been on the moon!) Nor do most of them want to suppress any other doctrine. Socially and politically, they have several quite valid, important points to make. Secular humanism has in fact become the teaching of the public schools, to the exclusion of crucial parts of our heritage. The effects on culture are already sad, the implications for the future of liberty and even for national survival ominous. Would it really infringe anybody's constitutional rights if children were to learn something about the roots of their civilization?

But this does not mean they should learn things, at taxpayer expense, which simply are not true. By now, the scientific attitude and the body of discoveries to which it has led are themselves basic to society, and not merely Western society. "Scientific" creationism is not content to maintain that the universe is the work of God. It claims that this Earth is, at most, a few thousand years old, and that the species of living beings we know today came into being in their present forms. Of course, the First Amendment guarantees any American the right to believe and argue for that, and teach it privately. But the notion has no more claim on "equal time" in public education than do, say, astrology, psionics, or Marxism.

It is scarcely necessary here to repeat what has often been pointed out: that if the creationist assertion were true, then our astronomy, physics, chemistry, biology, and archaeology must be false. For example, evidence for geological ages includes matters as diverse as the well-established laws of radioactive decay and a cosmic red shift observed by familiar techniques of spectroscopy. Much has been made of certain unexplained anomalies in certain mineral formations—far too much. Science is always coming upon such phenomena, and needing time and effort to learn what brings them about. We don't yet understand ball lightning very well, either; but nobody says that, on this account, we should throw out our meteorology. Instead, what understanding we do have provides a context within which to seek explanations of countless details.

Thus the claim that our planet is less than a million years old, and has undergone no significant changes during its existence, is incompatible with science. At best, a person might declare that God created the universe recently, full of misleading clues to something quite different. Emotionally, I am inclined to think this is an insult to the Creator. In the famous words of Einstein. "The Lord is subtle, but He is not malicious." Logically, we need only note that the declaration is, by its nature, untestable, incapable of being disproven; therefore it is devoid of empirical meaning.

We might, though, find it worthwhile at this point to refute one statement frequently made by creationists, that the development of matter and life from primitive to complex forms would violate the second law of thermodynamics. Even some who have accepted evolution as a fact, such as the late Lecomte de Noüy, have maintained that it would have been statistically impossible without supernatural guidance. They should have known better.

Part of the problem arises because the second law is deceptively simple-looking but has profound and far-reaching implications. It can be expressed in confusingly many ways, and has been. In one of my college textbooks *(Physical Chemistry,* by Frank MacDougall, Macmillan, 1944) the phrasing of the law goes: "It is impossible to devise any mechanism or machine by means of which a quantity of heat can be converted into the equivalent amount of work without producing other changes in the state of some body or bodies concerned in the process." Another book *(Introduction to Theoretical Physics,* by Leigh Page, Van Nostrand. 1928) puts it as: "No self-acting engine can transfer heat from a body of lower temperature to one of higher temperature." Here a "self-acting engine" means, essentially, one which is isolated from outside influences and which takes its working substance through one or more complete cycles.

There are numerous other, equally valid versions of the same truth, but these two should be enough to show that we are dealing with something which is quite basic and not at all self-evident.

Not so incidentally, the first law of thermodynamics amounts to the law of the conservation of energy—that is that the total amount of energy in an isolated system can be neither increased nor decreased. While the only completely isolated system is the universe as a whole, in practice we can make arrangements which come very close to that condition.

Were it not for the first law, we could build perpetual motion machines of the first kind, as they are called, whose driving power comes from nowhere. Were it not for the second law, we could build perpetual motion machines of the second kind, which would draw their energy from anywhere. For instance, a motor at room temperature could be driven by the air molecules that happen to collide with its piston. The impossibility of this is not immediately obvious, which is why it was not established until the 19th century and is still overlooked in many science fiction stories.

Numerous people who understand the second law as a principle governing heat engines can get bewildered about the wider applications. These involve entropy, about which science fiction has also perpetrated a great deal of nonsense. Actually entropy is a measurable quantity. though you need calculus to describe it mathematically. In any thermodynamic process where an amount of heat Q is exchanged at a temperature T (which may vary throughout the volume and during the time in which things happen), the increase of entropy is equal to the integral of dQ/T.

Now "increase" can be negative, that is, represent a decrease. When something occurs thermodynamically in a system, entropy can and often does decrease somewhere. However, it increases elsewhere, and the second law states that the *total* gain in entropy is always positive. That is, whenever a change involving an energy transfer takes place in a system, entropy always is greater at the end of the process than it was in the beginning.

A "system" can be anything: an atom, a molecule. a machine, a living organism, a galaxy, the cosmos as a whole, anything. But we must consider the entire system, not just a selected part of it.

An increase in entropy corresponds to, or measures an increase in disorder. or a decrease in the orderliness of the system. Therefore, whenever something changes, we find there is less order afterward than there was before.

Here is a very rough example or analogy. Think of a house whose lady has brought it to absolutely perfect arrangement and cleanliness—not a single item of furniture out of place, not a speck of dirt or dust anywhere. Then her children come home from school and her husband home from the office, and the family starts using the place. Things *happen* in it. The immaculate condition doesn't last long, does it?

True, next morning the lady can restore her dwelling to its former orderliness. However, to do so she must expend energy, both her own and the energy of whatever appliances she uses, such as a vacuum cleaner. That energy comes from the conversion of food in her body—or fuel in an electric generator somewhere—into disorganized gases and masses. The house may become neat again. but the environment as a whole is more chaotic than it was.

This is not an argument against good housekeeping! It is simply a reminder that everything has its price.

The growth of life itself, and the maintenance of its exquisite complexity, is a wonderful example of order brought out of seeming chaos. Far too readily can we overlook the price paid, the net disorder. The solar energy which drives life was once tidily located in the sun. Its diffusion through the universe involves an enormous increase of disorder, of entropy. The profit that life makes along the way is minuscule by comparison.

In fact, even considered by themselves, biological processes require entropy increase. (The mean free energy does decrease, but that is an entirely different quantity.) We too are heat engines, subject to the same laws as all others.

The whole starry cosmos exemplifies the principle. There was no primordial chaos before the Big Bang—not really. Instead, everything was neatly concentrated in one location. Then it scattered, and is still scattering, a disorderliness far exceeding the structural order of galaxies, stars, planets, and life forms which have appeared in the course of the process.

Unfortunately, too few spokesmen for science grasp this themselves. Hence they are brought to incoherence by the specious claim that evolution is thermodynamically impossible. True, the refutation of that claim, even on the rudimentary level of this essay, might well drive away the popular audience whom the scientist wants to enlighten. Yet if the universe were any easier to describe than it is would it not be that much the less miraculous?

In a still more subtle way, it seems to me that advocates of evolution put themselves at an unnecessary disadvantage by underrating the concept for which they are arguing. Here we begin to touch on the nature of science itself.

Creationists generally talk of the "theory of evolution." Many who disagree with creationism reply that evolution is no such thing, but a fact. Thereby they fall into the same dogmatism as certain of their opponents, and become subject to the same refutation. After all, what is a "fact"? Nobody alive has ever met an Australopithecus or watched prokaryotic cells develop in the pre-Cambrian seas. It is a rather feeble retort that nobody has met Adam and Eve either, or watched the world coming into being by fiat.

In the last analysis, those of us who accept the idea of evolution do so because it is an inference, based on many different accumulated observations, which enables us to account for those data, fit them into a scheme that makes sense. The creationist can quite legitimately reply that this is what his beliefs do for him.

However, at this point in the history of science, it is a mistake to agree that evolution is a mere "theory." That concedes more to the creationist than he deserves.

What is a theory. anyway? To answer that question, we must take a look at the scientific method itself.

Now, a number of distinguished scientists have denied that there is any such thing, and I rather agree with them. That, though, would take us too far afield now. Let us just glance at the traditional paradigm, oversimplified though it is. The purpose will only be to make clear what we mean by certain words.

In this paradigm, scientists begin by making observations of nature, as exact as possible. Then somebody formulates a scheme which summarizes those observations, preferably in mathematical terms. That is because mathematics is the language *par excellence* of precision. Somebody else takes such a *description* and tries to explain it by a *hypothesis.* That is, this person proposes the existence of a mechanism or a relationship which would logically produce the observations themselves. A good hypothesis also yields *predictions;* it tells us what further observations we should try to make. If we make them, and the results fit the scheme well enough, then in due course the hypothesis gains the status of a *theory.* That is, we accept it as depicting, more or less correctly, some aspect of reality.

Later discoveries may prove irreconcilable with the theory. In that case, we have to discard it—or, at least, drastically modify it—and look for another.

The standard example comes from planetary astronomy. For untold millennia, observers had been gathering data about the motions of the heavenly bodies across the sky. This effort culminated, for the time being, in the magnificent work of Tycho Brahe in the 16th century. Meanwhile, of course, there had been many attempts to account for the data. The idea that everything revolves around Earth grew increasingly unlikely as information accumulated; the picture had to be made too complicated, with epicycles. As early as the 13th century, Alfonso X, king of Leon and Castile, remarked that if he had been present at the Creation, he could have given the Creator some good advice!

Eventually Nicholas Copernicus offered a much more satisfactory description, in which the sun was at the center. Galileo Galilei and others refined this system and added to it, Finally Johannes Kepler put it into elegant mathematical form, in his three laws of planetary motion.

Isaac Newton then accounted for those laws by his hypothesis of universal gravitation (even though he himself denied making hypotheses) together with his own three laws of the motion of all bodies, not just planets. Soon observation confirmed this so well that it became a basic theory in physics. By means of it, later generations discovered new planets and explained the behavior of distant stars.

There remained a few loose ends, such as a slow change in the orbit of Mercury. Early in the 20th century, Albert Einstein proposed a whole new theory, general relativity, which included Newtonian mechanics as a special case and which accounted for those anomalous phenomena.

Thus far the usual description of science in action. As said, it is much oversimplified, and in many instances is scarcely true at all. Still, if nothing else, it does help us give clear meaning to our words.

The important point here, though, is that even taken at face value it is incomplete. It omits a further stage of thought which is of primary importance.

Before going on to that, let us very sketchily review the history of the evolutionary concept. That way we can compare it to the development of astronomy. If nothing else, we will be reminding ourselves that the idea of evolution was not invented by a few subversives in the 19th century, but has a long and honorable past of its own.

By 1800 the concept was already in the air. There had been some speculation along those lines as far back as Classical times, if not before. During the Renaissance and after, men gradually realized that they were coming upon the petrified bones of beasts which no longer existed. Early in the 19th century, the great French naturalist Georges Cuvier advanced the hypothesis that more than one creation had occurred in the past: that life had appeared several times, to be wiped out by worldwide catastrophes, and that the account in the Bible refers only to the latest of these eras. Regardless of this deferral to religion, Cuvier was considered blasphemous by many. Once some of his students decided to throw a healthy scare into him. One of them costumed himself like the traditional Satan, entered the professor's home at night, woke him, and roared, "I am the Devil, and for your impiety I have come to eat you!" Cuvier looked him up and down and replied scornfully, "Hmf! Horns and hoofs. You can't. You're graminivorous."

His catastrophism was denied by a contemporary compatriot, Jean Baptiste Lamarck. A war hero at age sixteen, Lamarck later boldly maintained that living species, had developed from less specialized ancestors. However, he thought that the causes lay in environment and the actions of individual organisms. This was so unconvincing that few accepted it until the 20th century, when for a time a version of it became official dogma in the Soviet Union.

In 1830 the Englishman Charles Lyell published the first volume of his epoch-making *Principles of Geology,* in which he showed that the forces that had shaped Earth in the past were the same as those at work today. By then it was becoming clear that man had coexisted with many animals long vanished, and in 1836 the Dane Christian Thomsen laid the foundations of modem archaeology by his scheme of successive Stone, Bronze, and Iron Ages, with the Stone Age reaching extremely far back in time.

Public as well as scientific interest in prehistory grew apace. More and more fossils were collected, in the Old and New Worlds alike, and reconstructions were made. When the Crystal Palace exposition opened in London in 1856, it included several life-sized statues of dinosaurs. Since they were not labeled, many visitors were puzzled by them. One man guessed that they were intended as an object lesson in temperance, to show what drunkards might expect to see.

In the same year, remains of Neanderthal man first came to light, in Germany. Initially, most biologists denied that this could be an extinct form of human, and various fanciful stories were devised to account for it. Yet evidence continued to accumulate, while the growth of geological knowledge made it less and less easy to believe that such creatures as the dinosaurs had perished in the Biblical flood—that they were, in the phrase of that day, antediluvian.

In 1859 Charles Darwin published *The Origin of Species*. This stunning demonstration of evolution as an understandable, natural set of processes—a hypothesis which had occurred independently, in less detail, to Alfred Russel Wallace—was followed four years later by another intellectual bombshell, Lyell's book *The Antiquity of Man Proved by Geology*. At the same time, field workers such as the Frenchmen Boucher de Perthes and Edouard Lartet were turning up ever more traces of archaic humanity. When Darwin issued *The Descent of Man* in 1871, he did not "prove we are descended from apes." What he did was describe *how* humans and simians could have stemmed from a common ancestor; the idea that this *had* happened was, by then, current.

Of course, it had met with much opposition, both popular and scholarly. Southerners during the American Civil War were fond of saying that maybe Yankees came from monkeys all right, but Mar'se Robert E. Lee couldn't be related to anything with a tail. Most clergymen combated every suggestion that the Book of Genesis was not a straightforward piece of reporting.

In fairness we must add that not all did: indeed, some made important contributions to knowledge in this field, especially in France. For that matter, Thomas Henry Huxley's debating opponent, Bishop Samuel Wilberforce, was by no means a bigoted ignoramus, but a cultivated and philanthropic gentleman.

Nonetheless, the data were accumulating remorselessly. In a paper read in 1865 the Austrian monk Gregor Mendel established the basis of genetics. His work went almost unnoticed for a generation, but came back to light after the Dutchman Hugo de Vries had identified the phenomenon of mutation, about 1895. Here was the decisive last factor that Darwin had not known of, the material on which his principles of natural selection and sexual selection operated. Meanwhile, in 1891 another Dutchman, Eugene Dubois, had found in Java the relics of a being that was unequivocally related to man and yet far too primitive, too apelike, to be *Homo sapiens*.

Meanwhile, too, knowledge was rapidly growing of the world as it had been long before anything like us existed. A clear-cut example is the evolutionary lineage of the horse, established through fossil finds by the American O.C. Marsh.

Out of all this, an understanding developed of much more than fossils. Evolution could be seen in action: that is, the principle of evolution made sense out of observations in science and even everyday life. An obvious case is that of industrial melanism. The peppered moth of England darkened, for better disguise against predators, as trees grew coal-sooty during the Industrial Revolution. In our own lifetimes, with decreasing air pollution, the same species is growing lighter again.

Creationists object that this is not a valid example, but represents mere variability. Nobody, they say, has ever seen a whole new species come into existence. That is true enough, as far as it goes—with some possible exceptions among microscopic organisms. However, evolution takes thousands and millions of years to bring about most of the unmistakable changes that evolutionists describe. The evidence is necessarily indirect. But so, just as necessarily, is the evidence for the reality of events chronicled in the Bible.

Many anomalies have cropped up, but most have turned out to be explainable. Thus, Piltdown man was always an embarrassment, because he did not fit onto any reasonable human evolutionary tree. At last chemical analysis showed that Piltdown man was a hoax. Without the great guiding principle of evolution in general, who would have paid attention to him at all?

Likewise, we have seen the evolutionary principle in sometimes tragically practical application today, as pathogenic microbes gain immunity to antibiotics through the selfsame process of natural selection that Darwin found. On a still deeper level, we find that we can best understand the details of protein chemistry as between different species (for instance, cytochrome-c) in terms of their differentiation through geological time; but it was the concept of evolution that caused researchers to look for such divergences in the first place.

So we have very briefly reviewed the development of evolutionary thought—the evolution of evolution, so to speak—and seen how fundamental it has become to biology. Now we must return to the comparison with physics, and to the philosophy of science in general.

As we have seen, theories are subject to disproof. Else they would have no meaning. (Thus, if I told you that space is pervaded by a fluid so subtle that no instrument or experiment can possibly detect it, you could not prove me wrong, but you would not be obliged to take me seriously, either. As a matter of fact, this is precisely what happened to the "luminiferous ether" about which 19th century physicists had speculated. It turned out to make no difference whether the ether existed or not; therefore nobody had any further reason to imagine that it did exist.)

Thus many theories have fallen by the wayside. But some reveal themselves, in the course of time, to be more fundamental than that. They become basic principles, by which theories themselves are tested. They become touchstones by which observations are evaluated. They become a context within which everything else, in a given field of science, is understandable.

Examples within physics are the two laws of thermodynamics, already mentioned. Without them, we simply could not make sense of our observations of any process involving energy exchange. With them, not only do we comprehend what we see, we are led to new discoveries.

For instance, back in the 1930s, physicists noticed certain curious features of recoil during radioactive decay. The energies and momenta did not balance out as they were supposed to. Either the principles of energy (and momentum) conservation were wrong, or else some ultra-tiny particle was involved, carrying off the excess. Rather than give up their basic principles, which were far too helpful to discard, scientists hypothesized that such a particle did exist: the neutrino. This idea proved fruitful in gaining more knowledge of the nucleus—although not until a generation later was the neutrino actually detected, and then only indirectly.

Granted, basic principles originate in empirical observations. Indeed, the laws of thermodynamics came out of grubby engineering work, and rather late in the history of science at that. Nor are the basic principles Holy Writ. They are subject to modification as our knowledge grows. Thus the separate principles of conservation of mass and energy were unified—modified—into the single principle of the conservation of mass-energy, by Einstein.

However, such principles have become so fundamental that the complete overthrow of any of them would mean the complete overthrow of the sciences with which they are concerned. We would be practically back to Square One. It is therefore both understandable and sensible that scientists will not—cannot—set them aside without an absolutely overwhelming, and hence unlikely, body of evidence.

I submit that evolution is no longer a mere theory. It has become just such a basic principle. It is as much a fundamental of the universe, as we conceive the universe to be, as are the laws of thermodynamics or relativity. There is no scientific argument against it, only an antiscientific one.

The question remains: How shall we persuade a lot of perfectly nice people that they are undermining a cornerstone of their entire civilization?

Of the Sea

-1-

White-maned horses
(hear their neighing!),
gray and gaunt-flanked,
gallop westward.
Wild with winter
winds, they snort
and buck when bearing
burdens for me.

-2-

Clearly the day is, coldly
calling with a wind-voice
to the sea, where tumbles
titan play of billows.
Stood you by my side now,
sweetheart, on the deck planks,
life were full of laughter.
(Long you for me, Freda?)

-3-

Black and cold the breakers
bellow, the thunder inboard.
Ropes and helm turn rebel.
Roaring winds are sleet-cloaked.
Seaman curse and stumble,
sorry they upped anchor.
Bitter is the brew here:
beer of waves is salty.

-4-

Cold and lustful
are the kisses
which Ran's daughter,
white-armed, give us:
laughing, shouting,
shaking tresses
hoar and salt-sweet
high breasts heaving.

Epilogue

-1-

His name was a set of radio pulses. Converted into equivalent sound waves, it would have been an ugly squawk; so because he, like any consciousness, was the center of his own coordinate system, let him be called Zero.

He was out hunting that day. Energy reserves were low in the cave. That other who may be called One—being the most important dweller in Zero's universe—had not complained. But there was no need to. He also felt a dwindling potential. Accumulators grew abundantly in their neighborhood, but an undue amount of such cells must be processed to recharge One while she was creating. Motiles had more concentrated energy. And, of course, they were more highly organized. Entire parts could be taken from the body of a motile, needing little or no reshaping for One to use. Zero himself, though the demands on his functioning were much less, wanted a more easily assimilated charge than the accumulators provided.

In short, they both needed a change of diet.

Game did not come near the cave any more. The past hundred years had taught that it was unsafe. Eventually, Zero knew, he would have to move. But the thought of helping One through mile upon mile, steep, overgrown, and dangerous, made him delay. Surely he could still find large motiles within a few days' radius of his present home. With One's help he fastened a carrier rack on his shoulders, took weapons in hand, and set forth.

That was near sunset. The sky was still light when he came on spoor: broken earthcrystals not yet healed, slabs cut from several boles, a trace of lubricant. Tuning his receptors to the highest sensitivity, he checked all the bands commonly made noisy by motiles. He caught a low-amplitude conversation between two persons a hundred miles distant, borne this far by some freak of atmospherics; closer by he sensed the impulses of small scuttering things, not worth chasing; a flier jetted overhead and filled his perception briefly with static. But no vibration of the big one. It must have passed this way days ago and now be out of receptor shot.

Well, he could follow the trail, and catch up with the clumsy sawyer in time. It was undoubtedly a sawyer—he knew these signs—and therefore worth a protracted hunt. He ran a quick check on himself. Every part seemed in good order. He set into motion, a long stride which must eventually overhaul anything on treads.

Twilight ended. A nearly full moon rose over the hills like a tiny cold lens. Night vapors glowed in masses and streamers against a purple-black sky where stars glittered in the optical spectrum and which hummed and sang in the radio range. The forest sheened with alloy, flashed with icy speckles of silicate. A wind blew through the radiation-absorber plates overhead, setting them to ringing against each other; a burrower whirred, a grubber crunched through lacy crystals, a river brawled chill and loud down a ravine toward the valley below.

As he proceeded, weaving among trunks and girders and jointed rods with the ease of long practice, Zero paid most attention to his radio receptors. There was something strange in the upper communication frequencies tonight, an occasional brief note...set of notes, voice, drone, like nothing he had heard before or heard tell of...But the world was a mystery. No one had been past the ocean to the west or the mountains to the east. Finally Zero stopped listening and concentrated on tracking his prey. That was difficult, with his optical sensors largely nullified by the darkness, and he moved slowly. Once he tapped lubricant from a cylinder growth and once he thinned his acids with a drink of water. Several times he felt polarization in his energy cells and stopped for a while to let it clear away: he rested.

Dawn paled the sky over distant snowpeaks, and gradually turned red. Vapors rolled up the slopes from the valley, tasting of damp and sulfide. Zero could see the trail again, and began to move eagerly.

Then the strangeness returned—louder.

Zero slid to a crouch. His lattice swiveled upward. Yes, the pulses did come from above. They continued to strengthen. Soon he could identify them as akin to the radio noise associated with the functioning of a motile. But they did not sense like any type he knew. And there was something else, a harsh flickering overtone, as if he also caught leakage from the edge of a modulated shortwave beam—

The sound struck him.

At first it was the thinnest of whistles, high and cold above the dawn clouds. But within seconds it grew to a roar that shook the earth, reverberated from the mountains, and belled absorber plates until the whole forest rang. Zero's head became an echo chamber; the racket seemed to slam his brain from side to side. He turned dazzled, horrified sensors heavenward. And he saw the thing descending.

For a moment, crazily, he thought it was a flier. It had the long spindle-shaped body and the air fins. But no flier had ever come down on a tail of multicolored flame. No flier blocked off such a monstrous portion of sky. When the thing must be two miles away!

He felt the destruction as it landed, shattered frames, melted earth-crystals, a little burrower crushed in its den, like a wave of anguish through the forest. He hurled himself flat on the ground and hung on to sanity with all four hands. The silence which followed, when the monster had settled in place, was like a final thunderclap.

Slowly Zero raised his head. His perceptions cleared. An arc of sun peered over the sierra. It was somehow outrageous that the sun should rise as if nothing had happened. The forest remained still, hardly so much as a radio hum to be sensed. The last echoes flew fading between the hills.

A measure of resolution: this was no time to be careful of his own existence. Zero poured full current into his transmitter. *"Alarm, alarm! All persons receiving, prepare to relay. Alarm!"*

Forty miles thence, the person who may as well be called Two answered, increasing output intensity the whole time: "Is that you, Zero? I noticed something peculiar in the direction of your establishment. What is the matter?"

Zero did not reply at once. Others were coming in, a surge of voices in his head, from mountaintops and hills and lowlands, huts and tents and caves, hunters, miners, growers, searakers, quarriers, toolmakers, suddenly become a unity. But he was flashing at his own home: "Stay inside, One. Conserve energy. I am unharmed, I will be cautious, keep hidden and stand by for my return."

"Silence!" called a stridency which all recognized as coming from Hundred. He was the oldest of them, he had probably gone through a total of half a dozen bodies. Irreversible polarization had slowed his thinking a little, taken the edge off, but the wisdom of his age remained and he presided over their councils. "Zero, report what you have observed."

The hunter hesitated. "That is not easy. I am at—" He described the location. ("Ah, yes," murmured Fifty-Six, "near that large galena lick.") "The thing somewhat resembles a flier, but enormous, a hundred feet long or more. It came down about two miles north of here on an incandescent jet and is now quiet. I thought I overheard a beamed signal. If so, the cry was like nothing any motile ever made."

"In these parts," Hundred added shrewdly. "But the thing must have come from far away. Does it look dangerous?"

"Its jet is destructive," Zero said, "but nothing that size, with such relatively narrow fins, could glide about. Which makes me doubt it is a predator."

"Lure accumulators," said Eight.

"Eh? What about them?" asked Hundred.

"Well, if lure accumulators can emit signals powerful enough to take control of any small motile which comes near and make it enter their grinders, perhaps this thing has a similar ability. Then, judging from its size, its lure must have tremendous range and close up could overpower large motiles. Including even persons?"

Something like a shiver moved along the communication band.

"It is probably just a grazer," said Three. "If so—" His overt signal trailed off, but the thought continued in all their partly linked minds: *A motile that big!*

Megawatt-hours in its energy cells. Hundreds or thousands of usable parts. Tons of metal. Hundred, did your great-grandcreator recall any such game, fabulous millennia ago?

No.

If it is dangerous, it must be destroyed or driven off. If not, it must be divided among us. In either case: attacked!

Hundred rapped the decision forth. "All male persons take weapons and proceed to rendezvous at Broken Glade above the Coppertaste River. Zero, stalk as close as seems feasible, observe what you can, but keep silence unless something quite unforeseeable occurs. When we are gathered, you can describe details on which we may base a specific plan. Hasten!"

The voices toned away in Zero's receptor circuits. He was alone again.

The sun cleared the peaks and slanted long rays between the forest frames. Accumulators turned the black faces of their absorber plates toward it and drank thirstily of radiation. The mists dissipated, leaving boles and girders ashine with moisture. A breeze tinkled the silicate growths underfoot. For a moment Zero was astonishingly conscious of beauty. The wish that One could be here beside him, and the thought that soon he might be fused metal under the monster's breath, sharpened the morning's brightness.

Purpose congealed in him. Further down was a turmoil of frank greed. In all the decades since his activation there had been no such feast as this quarry should provide. Swiftly, he prepared himself. First he considered his ordinary weapons. The wire noose would never hold the monster, nor did he think the iron hammer would smash delicate moving parts—it did not seem to have any—or the steel bolts from his crossbow pierce a thin plate to short out a crucial circuit. But the clawed, spearheaded pry bar might be of use. He kept it in one hand while two others unfastened the fourth and laid it with his extra armament in the carrier rack. Thereupon they deftly hooked his cutting torch in its place. No one used this artificial device except for necessary work, or to finish off a big motile whose cells could replace the tremendous energy expended by the flame, or in cases of dire need. But if the monster attacked him, that would surely constitute dire need. His only immediate intention was to spy on it.

Rising, he stalked among shadows and sun reflections, his camouflage-painted body nearly invisible. Such motiles as sensed him fled or grew very still. Not even the great slasher was as feared a predator as a hunting person. So it had been since that ancient day when some forgotten savage genius made the first crude spark gap and electricity was tamed.

Zero was about halfway to his goal, moving slower and more carefully with each step, when he perceived the newcomers.

He stopped dead. Wind clanked the branches above him, drowning out any other sound. But his electronic sensors told him of...two...three moving shapes, headed from the monster. And their emission was as alien as its own.

In a different way. Zero stood for a long time straining to sense and to understand what he sensed. The energy output of the three was small, hardly detectable even this close; a burrower or skitterer used more power to move itself. The output felt peculiar, too, not really like a motile's: too simple, as if a mere one or two circuits oscillated. Flat, cold, activityless. But the signal output, on the other hand—it *must* be signal, that radio chatter—why, that was a shout. The things made such an uproar that receptors tuned at minimum could pick them up five miles away. As if they did not know about game, predators, enemies.

Or as if they did not care.

A while more Zero paused. The eeriness of this advent sent a tingle through him. It might be said he was gathering courage. In the end he gripped his pry bar more tightly and struck off after the three.

They were soon plain to his optical and radar senses among the tall growths. He went stock-still behind a frame and watched. Amazement shocked his very mind into silence. He had assumed, from their energy level, that the things were small. But they stood more than half as big as he did! And yet each of them had only one motor, operating at a level barely sufficient to move a person's arm. That could not be their power source. But what was?

Thought returned to him. He studied their out-landishness in some detail. They were shaped not altogether unlike himself, though two-armed, hunch-backed, and featureless. Totally unlike the monster, but unquestionably associated with it. No doubt it had sent them forth as spy eyes, like those employed by a boxroller. Certain persons had been trying for the last century or so to develop, from domesticated motiles, similar assistants for hunting persons. Yes, a thing as big and awkward as the monster might well need auxiliaries.

Was the monster then indeed a predator? Or even—the idea went like a lightning flash through Zero's entire circuitry—a thinker? Like a person? He struggled to make sense of the modulated signals between the three bipeds. No, he could not. But—

Wait!

Zero's lattice swung frantically back and forth. He could not shake off the truth. That last signal had come from the monster, hidden by a mile of forest. From the monster to the bipeds. And were they answering?

The bipeds were headed south. At the rate they were going, they might easily come upon traces of habitation, and follow those traces to the cave where One was, long before Hundred's males had gathered at Broken Glade. The monster would know about One.

Decision came. Zero opened his transmitter to full output, but broadcast rather than beamed in any degree. He would give no clue where those were whom he called. *"Attention, attention!* Tune in on me: direct sensory linkage. I am about to attempt capture of these motiles."

Hundred looked through his optics, listened with his receptors, and exclaimed, "No, wait, you must not betray our existence before we are ready to act."

"The monster will soon learn of our existence in any event," Zero answered. "The forest is full of old campsites, broken tools, traps, chipped stones, slag heaps. At present I should have the advantage of surprise. If I fail and am destroyed, that ought still to provide you with considerable data. Stand alert!"

He plunged from behind the girders.

The three had gone past. They sensed him and spun about. He heard a jagged modulation of their signal output. A reply barked back, lower in frequency. The voice of the monster? There was no time to wonder about that. Slow and clumsy though they were, the bipeds had gotten into motion. The central one snatched a tube slung across its back. Pounding toward them, through shattering crystals and clangorous branches, Zero thought, *I have not yet made any overtly hostile move, but*—The tube flashed and roared.

An impact sent Zero staggering aside. He went to one knee. Ripped circuits overwhelmed him with destruction signals. As the pain throbbed toward extinction, his head cleared enough to see that half his upper left arm was blown off.

The tube was held steady on him. He rose. The knowledge of his danger flared in him. A second biped had its arms around the third, which was tugging a smaller object from a sheath.

Zero discharged full power through his effectors. Blurred to view by speed, he flung himself to one side while his remaining left hand threw the pry bar. It went meteorlike across a shaft of sunlight and struck the tube. The tube was pulled from the biped's grasp, slammed to the ground and buckled.

Instantly Zero was upon the three of them. He had already identified their communication system, a transmitter and antenna actually outside the skin! His one right hand smashed across a biped's back, tearing the radio set loose. His torch spat with precision. Fused, the communicator of a second biped went dead.

The third one tried to escape. Zero caught it in four strides, plucked off its antenna, and carried it wildly kicking under one arm while he chased the other two. When he had caught the second, the first stood its ground and battered forlornly at him with its hands. He lashed them all together with his wire rope. As a precaution, he emptied the carrier rack of the one which had shot him. Those thin objects might be dangerous even with the tube that had launched them broken. He stuffed the bipeds into his own carrier.

For a moment, then, he lingered. The forest held little sonic noise except the wind in the accumulators. But the radio spectrum clamored. The monster howled; Zero's own broadcast rolled between sky and mountainside, from person to person and so relayed across the land.

"No more talk now," he finished his report. "I do not want the monster to track me. I have prevented these auxiliaries from communicating with it. Now I shall take them to my cave for study. I hope to present some useful data at the rendezvous."

"This may frighten the monster off," Seventy-Two said.

"So much the better," Hundred answered.

"In that case," Zero said, "I will at least have brought back something from my hunt."

He snapped off his transmission and faded into the forest shadows.

-2-

The boat had departed from the spaceship on a mere whisper of jets. Machinery inboard hummed, clicked, murmured, sucked in exhausted air and blew out renewed; busied itself with matters of warmth and light, computation and propulsion. But it made no more than a foundation for silence.

Hugh Darkington stared out the forward port. As the boat curved away from the mother ship's orbit, the great hull gleamed across his sky—fell astern and rapidly dwindled until lost to view. The stars which it had hidden sprang forth, icy-sharp points of glitter against an overwhelming blackness.

They didn't seem different to him. They were, of course. From Earth's surface the constellations would be wholly alien. But in space so many stars were visible that they made one chaos, at least to Darkington's eyes. Captain Thurshaw had pointed out to him, from the ship's bridge, that the Milky Way had a new shape, this bend was missing and that bay had not been there three billion years ago. To Darkington it remained words. He was a biologist and had never paid much attention to astronomy. In the first numbness of loss and isolation, he could think of nothing which mattered less than the exact form of the Milky Way.

Still the boat spiraled inward. Now the moon drifted across his view. In those eons since the *Traveler* left home, Luna had retreated from Earth: not as far as might have been predicted, because—they said—Bering Straits had vanished with every other remembered place; but nonetheless, now it was only a tarnished farthing. Through the ship's telescopes it had looked like itself. Some new mountains, craters, and maria, some thermal erosion of old features, but Thurshaw could identify much of what he once knew. It was grotesque that the moon should endure when everything else had changed.

Even the sun. Observed through a dimmer screen, the solar disc was bloated and glaring. Not so much in absolute terms, perhaps. Earth had moved a little closer, as the friction of interplanetary dust and gas took a millennial toll. The sun itself had grown a little bigger and hotter, as nuclear reactions intensified. In three billion years such things became noticeable even on the cosmic scale. To a living organism they totaled doomsday.

Darkington cursed under his breath and clenched a fist till the skin stretched taut. He was a thin man, long-faced, sharp-featured, his brown hair prematurely sprinkled with gray. His memories included beautiful spires above an Oxford quad, wonder seen through a microscope, a sailboat beating into the wind of Nantucket which blew spray and a sound of gulls and church bells at him, comradeship bent over a chessboard or hoisting beer steins, forests hazy and ablaze with Indian summer: and all these things were dead. The shock had worn off, the hundred men and women aboard the *Traveler* could function again, but home had been amputated from their lives and the stump hurt.

Frederika Ruys laid her own hand on his and squeezed a little. Muscle by muscle he untensed himself, until he could twitch a smile in response to hers.

"After all," she said, "we knew we'd be gone a long time. That we might well never come back."

"But we'd have been on a living planet," he mumbled.

"So we can still find us one," declared Sam Kuroki from his seat at the pilot console. "There're no less than six G-type stars within fifty light-years."

"It won't be the same," Darkington protested.

"No," said Frederika. "In a way, though, won't it be more? We, the last humans in the universe, starting the race over again?"

There was no coyness in her manner. She wasn't much to look at, plump, plain, with straight yellow hair and too wide a mouth. But such details had ceased to matter since the ship ended time acceleration. Frederika Ruys was a brave soul and a skilled engineer. Darkington felt incredibly lucky that she had picked him.

"Maybe we aren't the last, anyhow," Kuroki said. His flat features broke in one of his frequent grins; he faced immensity with a sparrow's cockiness. "Ought to've been other colonies than ours planted, oughtn't there? Of course, by now their descendants 'ud be bald-headed dwarfs who sit around thinking in calculus."

"I doubt that," Darkington sighed. "If humans had survived anywhere else in the galaxy, don't you think they would at least have come back and...and reseeded this with life? The mother planet?" He drew a shaken breath. They had threshed this out a hundred times or more while the *Traveler* orbited about unrecognizable Earth, but they could not keep from saying the obvious again and again, as a man must keep touching a wound on his body. "No, I think the war really did begin soon after we left. The world situation was all set to explode."

That was why the *Traveler* had been built, and even more why it had departed in such haste, his mind went on. Fifty couples scrambling off to settle on Tau Ceti II before the missiles were unleashed. Oh, yes, officially they were a scientific team, and one of the big foundations had paid for the enterprise. But in fact, as everyone knew, the hope was to insure that a fragment of civilization would be saved, and someday return to help rebuild. (Even Panasia admitted that a total war would throw history back a hundred years; Western governments were less optimistic.) Tension had mounted so horribly fast in the final months that no time was taken for a really careful check of the field drive. So new and little understood an engine ought to have had scores of test flights before starting out under full power. But...well...next year might be too late. And exploratory ships *had* visited the nearer stars, moving just under the speed of light, their crews experiencing only a few weeks of transit time. Why not the *Traveler*?

"The absolute war?" Frederika said, as she had done so often already. "Fought until the whole world was sterile? No. I won't believe it."

"Not in that simple and clean-cut a way," Darkington conceded. "Probably the war did end with a nominal victor: but he was more depopulated and devastated than anyone had dared expect. Too impoverished to reconstruct, or even to maintain what little physical plant survived. A downward spiral into the Dark Ages."

"H-m-m, I dunno," Kuroki argued. "There were a lot of machines around. Automation, especially. Like those self-reproducing, sun-powered, mineral-collecting sea rafts. And a lot of other self-maintaining gadgets. I don't see why industry couldn't be revived on such a base."

"Radioactivity would have been everywhere," Darkington pointed out. "Its long-range effect on ecology...Oh, yes, the process may have taken centuries, as first one species changed or died, and then another dependent on it, and then more. But how could the human survivors recreate technology when biology was disintegrating around them?" He shook himself and stiffened his back, ashamed of his self-pity of a minute ago, looking horror flatly in the face. "That's my guess. I could be wrong, but it seems to fit the facts. We'll never know for certain, I suppose."

Earth rolled into sight. The planetary disc was still edged with blueness darkening toward black. Clouds still trailed fleecy above shining oceans; they gleamed upon the darkness near the terminator as they caught the first light before sunrise. Earth was forever fair.

But the continental shapes were new, speckled with hard points of reflection upon black and ocher where once they had been softly green and brown. There were no polar caps; sea level temperatures ranged from eighty to two hundred degrees Fahrenheit. No free oxygen remained: the atmosphere was nitrogen, its oxides, ammonia, hydrogen sulfide, sulfur dioxide, carbon dioxide, and steam. Spectroscopes had found no trace of chlorophyll or any other complex organic compound. The ground cover, dimly glimpsed through clouds, was metallic.

This was no longer Earth. There was no good reason why the *Traveler* should send a boat and three highly unexpendable humans down to look at its lifelessness. But no one had suggested leaving the Solar System without such a final visit. Darkington remembered being taken to see his grandmother when she was dead. He was twelve years old and had loved her. It was not her in the box, that strange unmeaningful mask, but where then was she?

"Well, whatever happened seems to be three billion years in the past," Kuroki said, a little too loudly. "Forget it. We got troubles of our own."

Frederika's eyes had not left the planet. "We can't ever forget, Sam," she said. "We'll always wonder and hope—they, the children at least—hope that it didn't happen to them too cruelly." Darkington started in surprise as she went on murmuring, very low, oblivious of the men:

to tell you of the ending of the day.
And you will see her tallness with surprise,
and looking into gentle, shadowed eyes
protest: it's not that late; you have to stay
awake a minute more, just one, to play
with yonder ball. But nonetheless you rise
so they won't hear her say, "A baby cries,
but you are big. Put all your toys away."'

She lets you have a shabby bear in bed,
though frankly doubting that you two can go
through dream-shared living rooms or wingless flight.
She tucks the blankets close beneath your head
and smooths your hair and kisses you, and so
goes out, turns off the light, "Good night. Sleep tight."

Kuroki glanced around at her. The plaid shirt wrinkled across his wide shoulders. "Poems yet," he said. "Who wrote that?"

"Hugh," said Frederika. "Didn't you know he published poetry? Quite a bit. I admired his work long before I met him."

Darkington flushed. Her interest was flattering, but he regarded "Then Death Will Come" as a juvenile effort.

However, his embarrassment pulled him out of sadness. (On the surface. Down beneath, it would always be there, in every one of them. He hoped they would not pass too much of it on to their children. Let us not weep eternally for Zion.) Leaning forward, he looked at the planet with an interest that mounted as the approach curve took them around the globe. He hoped for a few answers to a hell of a lot of questions.

For one thing, why, in three billion years, had life not re-evolved? Radioactivity must have disappeared in a few centuries at most. The conditions of primordial Earth would have returned. Or would they? What had been lacking this time around?

He woke from his brown study with a jerk as Kuroki said, "Well, I reckon we can steepen our trajectory a bit." A surprising interval had passed. The pilot touched controls and the mild acceleration increased. The terrestrial disc, already enormous, swelled with terrifying velocity, as if tumbling down upon them.

Then, subtly, it was no longer to one side or above, but was beneath; and it was no longer a thing among the stars but the convex floor of bowl-shaped creation. The jets blasted more strongly. Kuroki's jaw clenched till knots of muscle stood forth. His hands danced like a pianist's.

He was less the master of the boat, Darkington knew, than its helper. So many tons, coming down through atmospheric turbulence at such a velocity, groping with radar for a safe landing spot, could not be handled by organic brain and nerves. The boat's central director—essentially a computer whose input came from the instruments and whose efferent impulses went directly to the controls—performed the basic operations. Its task was fantastically complex: very nearly as difficult as the job of guiding the muscles when a man walks. Kuroki's fingers told the boat, "Go that way," but the director could overrule him.

"I think we'll settle among those hills." The pilot had to shout now, as the jets blasted stronger. "Want to come down just east of the sunrise line, so we'll have a full day ahead of us, and yonder's the most promising spot in this region. The lowlands look too boggy."

Darkington nodded and glanced at Frederika. She smiled and made a thumbs-up sign. He leaned over, straining against his safety harness, and brushed his lips across hers. She colored with a pleasure that he found oddly moving.

Someday, on another planet—that possibly hadn't been born when they left Earth—

He had voiced his fears to her, that the engine would go awry again when they started into deep space, and once more propel them through time, uncontrollably until fuel was exhausted. A full charge in the tanks was equivalent to three billion years, plus or minus several million; or so the physicists aboard had estimated. In six billion A.D. might not the sun be so swollen as to engulf them when they emerged?

She had rapped him across the knuckles with her slide rule and said no, you damned biologist, but you'll have to take my word for it because you haven't got the math. I've studied it as far as differential equations, he said. She grinned and answered that then he'd never had a math course. It seemed, she said, that time acceleration was readily explained by the same theory which underlay the field drive. In fact, the effect had been demonstrated in laboratory experiments. Oh, yes, I know about that, he said; reactive thrust is rotated through a fourth dimension and gets applied along the temporal rather than a spatial axis. You do not know a thing about it, she said, as your own words have just proved. But never mind. What happened to us was that a faulty manifold generated the t-acceleration effect in our engine. Now we've torn everything down and rebuilt from scratch. We know it'll work right. The tanks are recharged. The ship's ecosystem is in good order. Any time we want, we can take off for a younger sun, and travel fifty light-years without growing more than a few months older. After which, seeing no one else was around, she sought his arms; and that was more comforting than her words.

A last good-by to Grandmother Earth, he thought. *Then we can start the life over again that we got from her.*

The thrust upon him mounted. Toward the end he lay in his chair, now become a couch, and concentrated on breathing.

They reached ground.

Silence rang in their ears for a long while. Kuroki was the first to move. He unstrapped his short body and snapped his chair back upright. One hand unhooked the radio microphone, another punched buttons. "Boat calling *Traveler*," he intoned. "We're okay so far. Come in. *Traveler*. Hello, hello."

Darkington freed himself, stiffly, his flesh athrob, and helped Frederika rise. She leaned on him a minute. "Earth," she said. Gulping: "Will you look out the port first, dearest? I find I'm not brave enough."

He realized with a shock that none of them had yet glanced at the landscape. Convulsively, he made the gesture.

He stood motionless for so long that finally she raised her head and stared for herself.

-3-

They did not realize the full strangeness before they donned spacesuits and went outside. Then, saying very little, they wandered about looking and feeling. Their brains were slow to develop the gestalts which would allow them really to see what surrounded them. A confused mass of detail could not be held in the memory, the underlying form could not be abstracted from raw sense impressions. A tree is a tree, anywhere and anywhen, no matter how intricate its branching or how oddly shaped its leaves and blossoms. But what is a—

—thick shaft of gray metal, planted in the sand, central to a labyrinthine skeleton of straight and curved girders, between which run still more enigmatic structures embodying helices and toruses and Möbius strips and less familiar geometrical elements; the entire thing some fifty feet tall; flaunting at the top several hundred thin metal plates whose black sides are turned toward the sun?

When you have reached the point of being able to describe it even this crudely, then you have apprehended it.

Eventually Darkington saw that the basic structure was repeated, with infinite variation of size and shape, as far as he could see. Some specimens tall and slender, some low and broad, they dominated the hillside. The deeper reaches were made gloomy by their overhang, but sun speckles flew piercingly bright within those shadows as the wind shook the mirror faces of the plates. That same wind made a noise of clanking and clashing and far-off deep booming, mile after metal mile.

There was no soil, only sand, rusty red and yellow. But outside the circle which had been devastated by the boat's jets, Darkington found the earth carpeted with prismatic growths, a few inches high, seemingly rooted in the ground. He broke one off for closer examination and saw tiny crystals, endlessly repeated, in some transparent siliceous material: like snowflakes and spiderwebs of glass. It sparkled so brightly, making so many rainbows, that he couldn't well study the interior. He could barely make out at the center a dark clump of...wires, coils, transistors? No, he told himself, *don't be silly*. He gave it to Frederika, who exclaimed at its beauty.

He himself walked across an open stretch, hoping for a view even vaguely familiar. Where the hillside dropped too sharply to support anything but the crystals—they made it one dazzle of diamonds—he saw eroded contours, the remote white sword of a waterfall, strewn boulders and a few crags like worn-out obelisks. The land rolled away into blue distances; a snowcapped mountain range guarded the eastern horizon. The sky overhead was darker than in his day, faintly greenish blue, full of clouds. He couldn't look near the fierce big sun."

Kuroki joined him. "What d'you think, Hugh?" the pilot asked.

"I hardly dare say. You?"

"Hell, I can't think with that bloody boiler factory clattering at me." Kuroki grimaced behind his faceplate. "Turn off your sonic mike and let's talk by radio."

Darkington agreed. Without amplification, the noise reached him through his insulated helmet as a far-off tolling. "We can take it for granted," he said, "that none of this is accidental. No minerals could simply crystallize out like this."

"Don't look manufactured to me, though."

"Well, said Darkington, "you wouldn't expect them to turn out their products in anything like a human machine shop."

"Them?"

"Whoever...whatever made this. For whatever purpose."

Kuroki whistled. "I was afraid you'd say something like that. But we didn't see a trace of—cities, roads, anything—from orbit. I know the cloudiness made seeing pretty bad, but we couldn't have missed the signs of a civilization able to produce stuff on this scale."

"Why not? If the civilization isn't remotely like anything we've ever imagined?"

Frederika approached, leaving a cartful of instruments behind. "The low and medium frequency radio spectrum is crawling," she reported. "You never heard so many assorted hoots, buzzes, whirrs, squeals, and whines in your life."

"We picked up an occasional bit of radio racket while in orbit," Kuroki nodded. "Didn't think much about it, then."

"Just noise," Frederika said hastily. "Not varied enough to be any kind of...of communication. But I wonder what's doing it?"

"Oscillators," Darkington said. "Incidental radiation from a variety of—oh, hell, I'll speak plainly—machines."

"But—" Her hand stole toward his. Glove grasped glove. She wet her lips. "No, Hugh, this is absurd. How could any one be capable of making...what we see...and not have detected us in orbit and—and done something about us?"

Darkington shrugged. The gesture was lost in his armor. "Maybe they're biding their time. Maybe they aren't here at the moment. The whole planet could be an automated factory, you know. Like those ocean mineral harvesters we had in our time"—it hurt to say that—"which Sam mentioned on the way down. Somebody may come around periodically and collect the production."

"Where do they come from?" asked Kuroki in a rough tone.

"I don't know, I tell you. Let's stop making wild guesses and start gathering data."

Silence grew between them. The skeleton towers belled. Finally Kuroki nodded. "Yeah. What say we take a little stroll? We may come on something."

Nobody mentioned fear. They dared not.

Re-entering the boat, they made the needful arrangements. The *Traveler* would be above the horizon for several hours yet. Captain Thurshaw gave his reluctant consent to an exploration on foot. The idea conflicted with his training, but what did survey doctrine mean under these conditions? The boat's director could keep a radio beam locked on the ship and thus relay communication between Earth and orbit. While Kuroki talked, Darkington and Frederika prepared supplies. Not much was needed. The capacitor pack in each suit held charge enough to power thermostat and air renewer for a hundred hours, and they only planned to be gone for three or four. They loaded two packboards with food, water, and the "buckets" used for such natural functions as eating, but that was only in case their return should be delayed. The assorted scientific instruments they took were more to the point. Darkington bolstered a pistol. When he had finished talking, Kuroki put the long tube of a rocket gun and a rackful of shells on his own back. They closed their helmets anew and stepped out.

"Which way?" Frederika asked.

"Due south," Darkington said after studying the terrain. "We'll be following this long ridge, you see. Harder to get lost." There was little danger of that, with the boat emitting a continuous directional signal. Nonetheless they all had compasses on their wrists and took note of landmarks as they went.

The boat was soon lost to view. They walked among surrealistic rods and frames and spirals, under ringing sheet metal. The crystals crunched beneath their tread and broke sunlight into hot shards of color. But not many rays pushed through the tangle overhead; shadows were dense and restless. Darkington began to recognize unrelated types of structure. They included long, black, seemingly telescopic rods, fringed with thin plates; glassy spheres attached to intricate grids; cables that looped from girder to girder. Frequently a collapsed object was seen crumbling on the ground.

Frederika looked at several disintegrated specimens, examined others in good shape, and said: "I'd guess the most important material, the commonest, is an aluminum alloy. Though—see here—these fine threads embedded in the core must be copper. And this here is probably manganese steel with a protective coating of...um...something more inert."

Darkington peered at the end of a broken strut through a magnifying glass. "Porous," he said. "Good Lord, are these actually capillaries to transport water?"

"I thought a capillary was a hairy bug with lots of legs that turned into a butterfly," said Kuroki. He ducked an imaginary fist. "Okay, okay, somebody's got to keep up morale."

The boat's radio relayed a groan from the monitor aboard the ship. Frederika said patiently, "No, Sarri, the legs don't turn into a butterfly—," but then she remembered there would never again be bravely colored small wings on Earth and banged a hand against her faceplate as if she had been about to knuckle her eyes.

Darkington was still absorbed in the specimen he held. "I never heard of a machine this finely constructed," he declared. "I thought nothing but a biological system could—"

"Stop! Freeze!"

Kuroki's voice rapped in their earphones. Darkington laid a hand on his pistol butt. Otherwise only his head moved, turning inside the helmet. After a moment he saw the thing too.

It stirred among shadows, behind a squat cylinder topped with the usual black-and-mirror plates. Perhaps three feet long, six or eight inches high...It came out into plain view. Darkington glimpsed a slim body and six short legs of articulated dull metal. A latticework swiveled at the front end like a miniature radio-radar beam-caster. Something glinted beadily beneath, twin lenses? Two thin tentacles held a metal sliver off one of the great stationary structures. They fed it into an orifice, and sparks shot back upward—

"Holy Moses," Kuroki whispered.

The thing stopped in its tracks. The front-end lattice swung toward the humans. Then the thing was off, unbelievably fast. In half a second there was nothing to see.

Nobody moved for almost a minute. Finally Frederika clutched Darkington's arm with a little cry. The rigidness left him and he babbled of experimental robot turtles in the early days of cybernetic research. Very simple gadgets. A motor drove a wheeled platform, steered by a photoelectric unit that approached light sources by which the batteries might be recharged and, when this was done, became negatively phototropic and sought darkness. An elementary feedback circuit. But the turtles had shown astonishing tenacity, had gone over obstacles or even around...

"That beast there was a good deal more complicated," she interrupted.

"Certainly, certainly," Darkington said. "But—"

"I'll bet it heard Sam talk on the radio, spotted us with radar—or maybe eyes, if those socketed glass things were eyes—and took off."

"Very possibly, if you must use anthropomorphic language. However—"

"It was eating that strut." Frederika walked over to the piece of metal which the runner had dropped. She picked it up and came stiffly back with it. "See, the end has been ground away by a set of coarse emery wheels or something. You couldn't very well eat alloy with teeth like ours. You have to grind it."

"Hey," Kuroki objected. "Let's not go completely off the deep end."

"What the hell's happened down there?" called the man aboard the *Traveler*.

They resumed walking, in a dreamlike fashion, as they recounted what they had seen. Frederika concluded: "This...this arrangement might conceivably be some kind of automated factory—chemosynthetic or something—if taken by itself. But not with beasts like that one running loose."

"Now wait," Darkington said. "They could be maintenance robots, you know. Clear away rubbish and wreckage."

"A science advanced enough to build what we see wouldn't use such a clumsy system of maintenance," she answered. "Get off your professional caution, Hugh, and admit what's obvious."

Before he could reply, his earphones woke with a harsh jabber. He stopped and tried to tune in—it kept fading out, he heard it only in bursts—but the bandwidth was too great. What he did hear sounded like an electronic orchestra gone berserk. Sweat prickled his skin.

When the sound had stopped: "Okay," breathed Kuroki, "you tell me."

"Could have been a language, I suppose," said Frederika, dry-throated. "It wasn't just a few simple oscillations like that stuff on the other frequencies."

Captain Thurshaw himself spoke from the orbiting ship. "You better get back to the boat and sit prepared for quick blastoff."

Darkington found his nerve. "No, sir. If you please. I mean, uh, if there are intelligences...if we really do want to contact them...now's the time. Let's at least make an effort."

"Well—"

"We'll take you back first, of course, Freddie."

"Nuts," said the girl. "I stay right here."

Somehow they found themselves pushing on. Once, crossing an open spot where only the crystals stood, they spied something in the air. Through binoculars, it turned out to be a metallic object shaped vaguely like an elongated manta. Apparently it was mostly hollow, upborne by air currents around the fins and propelled at low speed by a gas jet. "Oh, sure," Frederika muttered. "Birds."

They re-entered the area of tall structures. The sonic amplifiers in their helmets were again tuned high, and the clash of plates in the wind was deafening. Like a suit of armor, Darkington thought idiotically. Could be a poem in that. Empty armor on a wild horse, rattling and tossing as it was galloped down an inexplicably deserted city street—symbol of…

The radio impulses that might be communication barked again in their earphones. "I don't like this," Thurshaw said from the sky. "You're dealing with too many unknowns at once. Return to the boat and we'll discuss further plans."

They continued walking in the same direction, mechanically. *We don't seem out of place here ourselves, in this stiff cold forest,* Darkington thought. *My god, let's turn around. Let's assert our dignity as organic beings. We aren't mounted on rails!*

"That's an order," Thurshaw stated.

"Very well, sir," Kuroki said. "And, uh, thanks."

The sound of running halted them. They whirled. Frederika screamed.

"What's the matter ?" Thurshaw shouted. "What's the matter?" The unknown language ripped across his angry helplessness.

Kuroki yanked his rocket gun loose and put the weapon to his shoulder. "Wait!" Darkington yelled. But he grabbed at his own pistol. The on-comer rushed in a shower of crystal splinters, whipping rods and loops aside. Its gigantic weight shuddered in the ground.

Time slowed for Darkington, he had minutes or hours to tug at his gun, hear Frederika call his name, see Juroki take aim and fire. The shape was mountainous before him. Nine feet tall, he estimated in a far-off portion of his rocking brain, three yards of biped four-armed monstrosity, head horned with radio lattice, eyes that threw back sunlight in a blank glitter, grinder orifice and—The rocket exploded. The thing lurched and half fell. One arm was in ruins.

"Ha!" Kuroki slipped a fresh shell into his gun. "Stay where you are, you!"

Frederika, wildly embracing Darkington, found time to gasp, "Sam, maybe it wasn't going to do any harm," and Kuroki snapped, "Maybe it was. Too goddam big to take chances with." Then everything smashed.

Suddenly the gun was knocked spinning by a hurled iron bar they hadn't even noticed. And the giant was among them. A swat across Kuroki's back shattered his radio and dashed him to earth. Flame spat and Frederika's voice was cut short in Darkington's receivers.

He pelted off, his pistol uselessly barking. "Run, Freddie!" he bawled into his sonic microphone. "I'll try and—" The machine picked him up. The pistol fell from his grasp. A moment later, Thurshaw's horrified oaths were gone: Darkington's radio antenna had been plucked out by the roots. Frederika tried to escape, but she was snatched up just as effortlessly. Kuroki, back on his feet, stood where he was and struck with ludicrous fists. It didn't take long to secure him either. Hog-tied, stuffed into a rack on the shoulders of the giant, the three humans were borne off southward.

-4-

At first Zero almost ran. The monster must have known where its auxiliaries were and something of what had happened to them. Now that contact was broken, it might send forth others to look for them, better armed. Or it might even come itself, roaring and burning through the forest. Zero fled.

Only the monster's voice, raggedly calling for its lost members, pursued him. After a few miles he crouched in a rod clump and strained his receptors. Nothing was visible but thickly growing accumulators and bare sky. The monster had ceased to shout. Though it still emitted an unmodulated signal, distance had dwindled this until the surrounding soft radio noise had almost obliterated that hum.

The units Zero had captured were making considerable sound-wave radiation. If not simply the result of malfunction in their damaged mechanism, it must be produced by some auxiliary system which they had switched on through interior controls. Zero's sound receptors were not sensitive enough to tell him whether the emission was modulated. Nor did he care. Certain low forms of motile were known to have well-developed sonic parts, but anything so limited in range was useless to him except as a warning of occurrences immediately at hand. A person needed many square miles to support himself. How could there be a community of persons without the effortless ability to talk across trans-horizon distances?

Irrelevantly, for the first time in his century and a half of existence, Zero realized how few persons he had ever observed with his own direct optics. How few he had touched. Now and then, for this or that purpose, several might get together. A bride's male kin assisted her on her journey to the groom's dwelling. Individuals met to exchange the products of their labor. But still—this rally of all functional males at Broken Glade, to hunt the monster, would be the greatest assemblage in tradition. Yet not even Hundred had grasped its uniqueness.

For persons were always communicating. Not only practical questions were discussed. In fact, now that Zero thought about it, such problems were the least part of discourse. The major part was ritual, or friendly conversation, or art. Zero had seldom met Seven as a physical entity, but the decades in which they criticized each other's poetry had made them intimate. The abstract tone constructions of Ninety-six, the narratives of Eighty, the speculations about space and time of Fifty-nine—such things belonged to all.

Direct sensory linkage, when the entire output of the body was used to modulate the communication band, reduced still further the need for physical contact. Zero had never stood on the seashore himself. But he had shared consciousness with Fourteen, who lived there. He had perceived the slow inward movement of waves, their susurrus, the salt in the air; he had experienced the smearing of grease over his skin to protect it from corrosion, drawing an aquamotile from a net and feasting. For those hours, he and the searaker had been one. Afterward he had shown Fourteen the upland forest…

What am I waiting for? Consciousness of his here-and-now jarred back into Zero. The monster had not pursued. The units on his back had grown quiescent. But he was still a long way from home. He rose and started off again, less rapidly but with more care to obliterate his traces.

As the hours passed, his interior sensors warned him increasingly of a need for replenishment. About midday he stopped and unloaded his three prizes. They were feebly squirming and one of them had worked an arm loose. Rather than lash them tight again, he released their limbs and secured them by passing the rope in successive loops around their middles and a tall stump, then welding everything fast with his torch.

That energy drain left him ravenous. He scouted the forest in a jittery spiral until he found some accumulators of the calathiform sort. A quick slash with his pry bar exposed their spongy interiors, rich with energy storage cells and mineral salts. They were not very satisfying eaten unprocessed, but he was too empty to care. With urgency blunted, he could search more slowly and thoroughly. Thus he found the traces of a burrow, dug into the sand, and came upon a female digger. She was heavy with a half-completed new specimen and he caught her easily. This too would have been better if treated with heat and acid, but even raw materials tasted good in his grinder. Now to get something for One. Though she, better than he, could slow down her functioning when nourishment was scarce, a state of coma while the monster was abroad could be dangerous. After hunting for another hour, Zero had the good luck to start a rotor. It crashed off among the rods and crystals, faster than he could run, but he put a crossbow bolt through its hub. Dismembered and packed into his carrier, it made an immensely cheering burden.

He returned to his prizes. Moving quickly in comparison to the windy clatter of the forest, he came upon them unobserved. They had quit attempting to escape—he saw the wire was shiny where they had tried to saw it on a sharp rock—and were busy with other tasks. One of them had removed a boxlike object from its back and inserted its head (?) and arms through gasketed holes. A second was just removing a similar box from its lower section. The third had plugged a flexible tube from a bottle into its face.

Zero approached. "Let me inspect those," he said, before thinking how ridiculous it was to address them. They shrank away from him. He caught the one with the bottle and unplugged the tube. Some liquid ran out. Zero extended his chemical sensor and tasted cautiously. Water. Very pure. He did not recall ever having encountered water so free of dissolved minerals.

Thoughtfully, he released the unit. It stoppered the tube. So, Zero reflected, they required water like him, and carried a supply with them. That was natural; they—or, rather, the monster they served—could not know where the local springs and streams were. But why did they suck through a tube? Did they lack a proper liquid-ingestion orifice? Evidently. The small hole in the head, into which the tube had fitted, had automatically closed as the nipple was withdrawn.

The other two had removed their boxes. Zero studied these and their contents. There were fragments of mushy material in both, vaguely similar to normal body sludge. Nourishment or waste ? Why such a clumsy system ? It was as if the interior mechanism must be absolutely protected from contact with the environment.

He gave the boxes back and looked more thoroughly at their users. They were not quite so awkward as they seemed at first. The humps on their backs were detachable carriers like his. Some of the objects dangling at their waists or strapped to their arms must also be tools. (Not weapons or means of escape, else they would have used them before now. Specialized artificial attachments, then, analogous to a torch or a surgical ratchet.) The basic bipedal shape was smoother than his own, nearly featureless except for limb joints. The head was somewhat more complicated, though less so than a person's. Upon the cylindrical foundation grew various parts, including the soundwave generators which babbled as he stood there watching. The face was a glassy plate, behind which moved...what? Some kind of jointed, partly flexible mechanism.

There was no longer any possibility of radio communication with—or through—them. Zero made a few experimental gestures, but the units merely stirred about. Two of them embraced. The third waved its arms and made sonic yelps. All at once it squatted and drew geometrical shapes in the sand, very much like the courtship figures drawn by a male dunerunner.

So...they not only had mechanical autonomy, like the spy eyes of a boxroller, but were capable of some independent behavior. They were more than simple remote-control limbs and sensors of the monster. Most probably they were domesticated motiles.

But if so, then the monster race had modified their type even more profoundly than the person race had modified the type of its own tamed motiles down in the lowlands. These bipeds were comically weak in proportion to size; they lacked grinders and liquid-ingestion orifices; they used sonics to a degree that argued their radio abilities were primitive; they required ancillary apparatus; in short, they were not functional by themselves. Only the care and shelter furnished by their masters allowed them to remain long in existence.

But what are the masters? Even the monster may well be only another motile. Certainly it appeared to lack limbs. The masters may be persons like us, come from beyond the sea or the mountains with skills and powers transcending our own.

But then what do they want? Why have they not tried to communicate with us? Have they come to take our land away? The question was jolting. Zero got hastily into motion. With his rack loaded, he had no room for his prizes. Besides, being crammed into it for hours was doubtless harmful to them; they moved a good deal more strongly now, after a rest, than when he first took them out. He simply left them tied together, cut the wire loose from the stump, and kept that end in one hand. Since he continued to exercise due caution about leaving a trail he did not move too fast for them to keep up. From time to time they would stagger and lean on each other for support—apparently their energy cells polarized more quickly than his—but he found they could continue if he let them pause a while, lie down, use their curious artifacts.

The day passed. At this time of year, not long past the vernal equinox, the sun was up for about twenty hours. After dark, Zero's captives began stumbling and groping. He confirmed by direct sense perception that they had no radar. If they ever did, that part had been wrecked with their communicators. After some thought, he fashioned a rough seat from a toppled bole and nudged them to sit upon it. Thus he carried them in two hands. They made no attempt to escape, emitted few sounds, obviously they were exhausted. But to his surprise, they began to stir about and radiate sonics when he finally reached home and set them down. He welded the end of their rope to an iron block he kept for emergencies.

Part of him reflected that their mechanism must be very strange indeed, maybe so strange that they would not prove ingestible. Obviously their cells went to such extremes of polarization that they became comatose, which a person only did in emergencies. To them, such deactivation appeared to be normal, and they roused spontaneously.

He dismissed speculation. One's anxious voice had been rushing over him while he worked. "What has happened? You are hurt! Come closer, let me see, oh, your poor arm! Oh, my dear!"

"Nothing serious," he reassured her. "I shot a rotor. Prepare yourself a meal before troubling about me."

He lowered himself to the cave floor beside her great beautiful bulk. The glow globes, cultivated on the rough stone walls, shed luster on her skin and on the graceful tool tendrils that curled forth to embrace him. His chemical sensor brought him a hint of solvents and lubricants, an essence of femaleness. The cave mouth was black with night, save where one star gleamed bright and somehow sinister above the hills. The forest groaned and tolled. But here he had light and her touch upon his body. He was home.

She unshipped the rack from his shoulders but made no motion toward the food-processing cauldron. Most of her tools and all her attention were on his damaged arm. "We must replace everything below the elbow," she decided, and, as a modulation: *"Zero, you brave clever adored fool, why did you hazard yourself like that? Do you not understand, even yet, without you my world would be rust?"*

"I am sorry...to take so much from the new one," he apologized.

"No matter. Feed me some more nice large rotors like this and I will soon replace the loss, and finish all the rest too." Her mirth fluttered toward shyness. "I want the new one activated soon myself, you know, so we can start another."

The memory of that moment last year, when his body pattern flowed in currents and magnetic fields through hers, when the two patterns heterodyned and deep within her the first crystallization took place, glowed in him. Sensory linkage was a wan thing by comparison.

What they did together now had a kindred intimacy. When she had removed the ruined forearm and he had thrust the stump into her repair orifice, a thousand fine interior tendrils enfolded it, scanning, relaying, and controlling. Once again, more subtly than in reproduction, the electrochemical-mechanical systems of One and Zero unified. The process was not consciously controllable; it was a female function; One was at this moment no different from the most primitive motile joined to her damaged mate in a lightless burrow.

It took time. The new person which her body was creating within itself was, of course, full size and, as it happened, not far from completion. (Had the case been otherwise, Zero would have had to wait until the new one did in fact possess a well-developed arm.) But it was not yet activated; its most delicate and critical synaptic pathways were still only half-finished, gradually crystallizing out of solution. A part could not lightly nor roughly be removed.

But in the end, One's functions performed the task. Slowly, almost reluctantly, Zero withdrew his new hand. His mind and hers remained intertwined a while longer. At last, with a shaky little overtone of humor, she exclaimed, "Well, how do your fingers wiggle? Is everything good? Then let us eat. I am famished!"

Zero helped her prepare the rotor for consumption. They threw the damaged forearm into the cauldron too. While they processed and shared the meal, he recounted his experiences. She had shown no curiosity about the three bipeds. Like most females, she lacked any great interest in the world beyond her home, and had merely assumed they were some new kind of wild motile. As he talked, the happiness died in her. "Oh, no," she said, "you are not going out to fight the lightning breather, are you?"

"Yes, we must." He knew what image terrified her, himself smashed beyond hope of reconstruction, and added in haste: "If we leave it free, no tradition or instinct knows what it may do. But surely, at the very least, so large a thing will cause extensive damage. Even if it is only a grazer, its appetite will destroy untold acres of accumulators; and it may be a predator. On the other hand, if we destroy it, what a hoard of nourishment! Your share and mine will enable us to produce a dozen new persons. The energy will let me range for hundreds of miles, thus gaining still more food and goods for us."

"If the thing can be assimilated," she said doubtfully. "It could be full of hydrofluoric acid or something, like a touch-me-not."

"Yes, yes. For that matter, the flier may be the property of intelligent beings: which does not necessarily mean we will not destroy and consume it. I intend to find out about that aspect right now. If the monster's auxiliaries are ingestible, the monster itself is almost sure to be."

"But if not—Zero, be careful!"

"I will. For your sake also." He stroked her and felt an answering vibration. It would have been pleasant to sit thus all night, but he must soon be on his way to rendezvous. And first he must dissect at least one specimen. He took up his pry bar and approached the three units.

-5-

Darkington awoke from a nightmare-ridden half sleep when he was dumped on the cave floor. He reached for Frederika and she came to him. For a space there was nothing but their murmuring.

Eventually they crouched on the sand and looked about. The giant that captured them had welded the free end of the wire rope to an immovable chunk of raw iron. Darkington was attached at that side, then the girl, and Kuroki on the outer end. They had about four feet of slack from one to the next. Nothing in the kit remaining to them would cut those strands.

"Limestone cave, I guess," Kuroki croaked. Behind the faceplate he was gaunt, bristly, and sunkeneyed. Frederika didn't look much better. They might not have survived the trip here if the robot hadn't carried them the last few hours. Nonetheless an odd, dry clarity possessed Darkington's brain. He could observe and think as well as if he had been safe on shipboard. His body was one enormous ache, but he ignored that and focused on comprehending what had happened.

Here near the entrance, the cave was about twenty feet high and rather more wide. A hundred feet deeper inward, it narrowed and ended. That area was used for storage: a junk shop of mechanical and electronic parts, together with roughly fashioned metal and stone tools that looked almost homelike. The walls were overgrown with thin wires that sprouted scores of small crystalline globes. These gave off a cool white light that made the darkness outside appear the more elemental.

"Yes, a cave in a sheer hillside," said Frederika. "I saw that much. I kept more or less conscious all the way here, trying to keep track of our route. Not that that's likely to do us much good, is it?" She hugged her knees. "I've got to sleep soon—oh, but I have to sleep!"

"We have to get in touch," Kuroki's voice rose. (Thank heaven and some ages-dead engineer that sound mikes and earphones could be switched on by shoving your chin against the right button! With talk cut off, no recourse would have remained but to slip quietly into madness.) "God damn it, I tried to show that tin nightmare we're intelligent. I drew diagrams and—" He checked himself. "Well, probably its builders don't monitor it. We'll have another go when they show up."

"Let's admit the plain facts, Sam," Frederika said tonelessly. "There aren't any builders. There never were any."

"Oh, no." The pilot gave Darkington a beggar's look. "You're the biologist, Hugh. Do you believe that?"

Darkington bit his lip. "I'm afraid she's right."

Frederika's laugh barked at them. "Do you know what that big machine is, there in the middle of the cave? The one the robot is fooling around with? I'll tell you. His wife!" She broke off. Laughter echoed too horribly in their helmets.

Darkington gazed in that direction. The second object had little in common with the biped shape, being low and wide—twice the bulk—and mounted on eight short legs which must lend very little speed or agility. A radio lattice, optical lenses, and arms (two, not four) were similar to the biped's. But numerous additional limbs were long goosenecks terminating in specialized appendages. Sleek blued metal covered most of the body.

And yet, the way those two moved—

"I think you may be right about that also," Darkington said at last.

Kuroki beat the ground with his fist and swore. "Sorry, Freddie," he gulped. "But won't you, for God's sake, explain what you're getting at? This mess wouldn't be so bad if it made some sense."

"We can only guess," Darkington said.

"Well, guess, then!"

"Robot evolution," Frederika said. "After man was gone, the machines that were left began to evolve."

"No," said Kuroki, "that's nuts. Impossible!"

"I think what we've seen would be impossible any other way," Darkington said. "Metallic life couldn't arise spontaneously. Only carbon atoms make the long hookups needed for the chemical storage of biological information. But electronic storage is equally feasible. And...before the *Traveler* departed...self-reproducing machines were already in existence."

"I think the sea rafts must have been the important ones." Frederika spoke like someone in dream. Her eyes were fixed wide and unblinking on the two robots. "Remember? They were essentially motorized floating boxes, containing metallurgic processing plants and powered by solar batteries. They took dissolved minerals out of sea water, magnesium, uranium, whatever a particular raft was designed for. When it had a full cargo, it went to a point on shore where a depot received its load. Once empty, it returned to open waters for more. It had an inertial navigation device, as well as electronic sensors and various homeostatic systems, so it could cope with the normal vicissitudes of its environment.

"And it had electronic templates which bore full information on its own design. They controlled mechanisms aboard, which made any spare part that might be needed. Those same mechanisms also kept producing and assembling complete duplicate rafts. The first such outfit cost hundreds of millions of dollars to manufacture, let alone the preliminary research and development. But once made, it needed no further investment. Production and expansion didn't cost anyone a cent.

"And after man was gone from Earth...all life had vanished...the sea rafts were still there, patiently bringing their cargoes to crumbling docks on barren shores, year after year after meaningless year—"

She shook herself. The motion was violent enough to be seen in armor. "Go on, Hugh," she said, her tone turned harsh. "If you can."

"I don't know any details," he began cautiously. "You should tell me how mutation was possible to a machine. But if the templates were actually magnetic recordings on wire or tape, I expect that hard radiation would affect them, as it affects an organic gene. And for a while there was certainly plenty of hard radiation around. The rafts started making imperfect duplicates. Most were badly designed and, uh, foundered. Some, though, had advantages. For instance, they stopped going to shore and hanging about for decades waiting to be unloaded. Eventually some raft was made which had the first primitive ability to get metal from a richer source than the ocean: namely, from other rafts. Through hundreds of millions of years, an ecology developed. We might as well call it an ecology. The land was reconquered. Wholly new types of machine proliferated. Until today, well, what we've seen."

"But where's the energy come from?" Kuroki demanded.

"The sun, I suppose. By now, the original solar battery must be immensely refined. I'd make a guess at dielectric storage on the molecular level, in specialized units—call them cells—which may even be of microscopic size. Of course, productivity per acre must be a good deal lower than it was in our day. Alloys aren't as labile as amino acids. But that's offset to a large extent by their greater durability. And, as you can see in this cave, by interchangeability."

"Huh?"

"Sure. Look at those spare parts stacked in the rear. Some will no doubt be processed, analogously to our eating and digesting food. But others are probably being kept for use as such. Suppose you could take whole organs from animals you killed and install them in yourself to replace whatever was wearing out. I rather imagine that's common on today's Earth. The 'black box' principle was designed into most machines in our own century. It would be inherited."

"Where's the metal come from in the first place?"

"From lower types of machine. Ultimately from sessile types that break down ores, manufacture the basic alloys, and concentrate more dielectric energy than they use. Analogous to vegetation. I daresay the, uh, metabolism involves powerful reagents. Sulfuric and nitric acids in glass-lined compartments must be the least of them. I doubt if there are any equivalent of microbes, but the ecology seems to manage quite well without. It's a grosser form of existence than ours. But it works. It works."

"Even sex." Frederika giggled a little crazily.

Darkington squeezed her gauntleted hand until she grew calmer. "Well," he said, "quite probably in the more complex machines, reproduction has become the specialty of one form while the other specializes in strength and agility. I daresay there are corresponding psychological differences."

"Psychological?" Kuroki bridled. "Wait a minute! I know there is—was—a lot of loose talk about computers being electronic brains and such rot, but—"

"Call the phenomenon what you like," Darkington shrugged. "But that robot uses tools which are made, not grown. The problem is how to convince it that we think."

"Can't it see?" Frederika exclaimed. "We use tools too. Sam drew mathematical pictures. What more does it want?"

"I don't know enough about this world to even guess," Darkington said tiredly. "But I suppose...well...we might once have seen a trained ape doing all sorts of elaborate things, without ever assuming it was more than an ape. No matter how odd it looked."

"Or maybe the robot just doesn't give a damn," Kuroki said. "There were people who wouldn't have."

"If Hugh's guess about the 'black box' is right," Frederika added slowly, "then the robot race must have evolved as hunters, instead of hunting being invented rather late in their evolution. As if men had descended from tigers instead of simians. How much psychological difference would that make?"

No one replied. She leaned forlornly against Darkington. Kuroki turned his eyes from them, perhaps less out of tact than loneliness. His girl was several thousand miles away, straight up, with no means for him to call her and say goodby.

Thurshaw had warned the insistent volunteers for this expedition that there would be no rescue. He had incurred sufficient guilt in letting three people—three percent of the human race—risk themselves. If anything untoward happened, the *Traveler* would linger a while in hopes the boat could somehow return. But in the end the *Traveler* would head for the stars. Kuroki's girl would have to get another father for the boy she might name Sam.

I wish Freddie were up there with her, Darkington thought. *Or do I? Isn't that simply what I'm supposed to wish? God!*

Cut that out. Start planning!

His brain spun like wheels in winter mud. What to do, what to do, what to do? His pistol was gone, so were Kuroki's rockets, nothing remained but a few tools and instruments. At the back of the cave there were probably stored some weapons with which a man could put up a moment's fight. (Only a moment, against iron and lightning; but that would end the present, ultimate horror, of sitting in your own fear-stink until the monster approached or the air renewal batteries grew exhausted and you strangled.) The noose welded around his waist, ending in a ton of iron, choked off any such dreams. They must communicate, somehow, anyhow, plead, threaten, promise, wheedle. But the monster hadn't cared about the Pythagorean theorem diagrammed in sand. What next, then? How did you say "I am alive" to something that was not alive?

Though what was aliveness? Were proteins inherently and unescapably part of any living creature? If the ancient sea rafts had been nothing except complicated machines, at what point of further complication had their descendants come to life? *Now stop that, you're a biologist, you know perfectly well that any such question is empirically empty, and anyhow it has nothing to do with preserving the continuity of certain protein chemistries which are irrationally much loved.*

"I think it talks by radio." Kuroki's slow voice sounded oddly through the thudding in Darkington's head. "It probably hasn't got any notion that sound waves might carry talk. Maybe it's even deaf. Ears wouldn't be any too useful in that rattletrap jungle. And our own radios are busted." He began to fumble in the girl's pack. "I'm not feeling you up, Freddie. Your spacesuit isn't exactly my type. But I think I could cobble together one working set from the pieces of our three, if I can borrow some small tools and instruments. Once we make systematic noises on its talk band, the robot might get interested in trying to savvy us."

"Sam," she said faintly, "for that idea you can feel me up all you want."

"I'll take a rain check." He could actually chuckle, Darkington heard. "I'm sweaty enough in this damn suit to pass for a rainstorm just by myself."

He began to lay out the job. Darkington, unable to help, ashamed that he had not thought of anything, turned attention back to the robots. They were coupled together, ignoring him.

Frederika dozed off. How slowly the night went. But Earth was old, rotating as wearily as…as himself…He slept.

A gasp awoke him.

The monster stood above them. Tall, tall, higher than the sky, it bestrode their awareness and looked down with blank eyes upon Kuroki's pitiful, barely begun work. One hand was still a torch and another hand had been replaced. It was invulnerable and soulless as a god. For an instant Darkington's half-aroused self groveled before it.

Then the torch spat, slashed the wire rope across, and Kuroki was pulled free.

Frederika cried out. "Sam!"

"Not…so eager…pal," the pilot choked in the robot's arms. "I'm glad you like me, but…ugh…careful!"

With a free hand, the robot twisted experimentally at Kuroki's left leg. The suit joints turned. Kuroki shrieked. Darkington thought he heard the leg bones leave their sockets.

"No! You filthy machine!" He plunged forward. The rope stopped him cold. Frederika covered her faceplate and begged Kuroki to be dead.

He wasn't, yet. He wasn't even unconscious. He kept on screaming as the robot used a prying tool to drag the leg off his armor. Leakseal compound flowed from between the fabric layers and preserved the air in the rest of his suit.

The robot dropped him and sprang back, frantically fanning itself. A whiff of oxygen, Darkington realized amidst the red and black disintegration of his sanity. Oxygen was nearly as reactive as fluorine, and there had been no free oxygen on Earth since—Kuroki's agony jerked toward silence.

The robot reapproached with care, squatted above him, poked at the exposed flesh, tore loose a chunk for examination and flung it aside. The metal off a joint seemed better approved.

Darkington realized vaguely that Frederika lay on the ground close to Kuroki and wept. The biologist himself was even nearer. He could have touched the robot as well as the body. Instead, though, he retreated, mumbling and mewing.

The robot had clearly learned a lesson from the gas, but was just as clearly determined to go on with the investigation. It stood up, moved a cautious distance away, and jetted a thin, intensely blue flame from its torch hand. Kuroki's corpse was divided across the middle.

Darkington's universe roared and exploded. He lunged again. The rope between him and Frederika was pulled across the firebeam. The strands parted like smoke.

The robot pounced at him, ran into the oxygen gushing from Kuroki's armor, and lurched back. Darkington grabbed the section of rope that joined him to the block. The torch was too bright to look at. If he touched its flame, that was the end of him too. But there was no chance to think about such matters. Blindly and animally, he pulled his leash across the cutting jet.

He was free.

"Get out, Freddie!" he coughed, and ran straight toward the robot. No use trying to run from a thing that could overtake him in three strides. The torch had stopped spitting fire, but the giant moved in a wobbly, uncertain fashion, still dazed by the oxygen. By pain? Savagely, in the last spark of awareness, Darkington hoped so. *"Get out, Freddie!"*

The robot staggered in pursuit of him. He dodged around the other machine, the big one that they had called female. To the back of the cave. A weapon to fight with, gaining a moment where Frederika might escape. An extra pry bar lay on the floor. He snatched it and whirled. The huge painted shape was almost upon him.

He dodged. Hands clashed together just above his helmet. He pelted back to the middle of the cave. The female machine was edging into a corner. But slow, awkward—

Darkington scrambled on top of it.

An arm reached from below to pluck him off. He snarled and struck with the pry bar. The noise rang in the cave. The arm sagged, dented. This octopod had nothing like the biped's strength. Its tool tendrils, even more frail, curled away from him.

The male robot loomed close. Darkington smashed his weapon down on the radio lattice at his feet. It crumpled. He brandished the bar and howled senselessly, "Stand back, there! One step more and I'll give her the works! I'll kill her!"

The robot stopped. Monstrous it bulked, an engine that could tear apart a man and his armor, and raised its torch hand.

"Oh no," Darkington rasped. He opened a bleeder valve on his suit, kneeling so the oxygen would flow across the front end of the thing on which he rode. Sensors ought to be more vulnerable than skin. He couldn't hear if the she-robot screamed as Kuroki had done. That would be on the radio band. But when he gestured the male back, it obeyed.

"Get the idea?" he panted, not a communication but as hatred. "You can split my suit open with your flame gun, but my air will pour all over this contraption here. Maybe you could knock me off her by throwing something, but at the first sign of any such move on your part, I'll open my bleeder valve again. She'll at least get a heavy dose of oxy. And meanwhile I'll punch the sharp end of this rod through one of those lenses. Understand? Well, then, stay where you are, machine!"

The robot froze.

Frederika came near. She had slipped the loop of cable joining her to Kuroki off what was left of his torso. The light shimmered on her faceplate so Darkington couldn't see through, and her voice was strained out of recognition. "Hugh, oh, Hugh!"

"Head back to the boat," he ordered. Rationality was returning to him.

"Without you? No."

"Listen, this is not the place for grandstand heroics. Your first duty is to become a mother. But what I hope for, personally, is that you can return in the boat and fetch me. You're no pilot, but they can instruct you by radio from the ship if she's above the horizon. The general director does most of the work in any event. You land here, and I can probably negotiate a retreat for myself."

"But...but...the robot needed something like twenty hours to bring us here. And it knew the way better than I do. I'll have to go by compass and guess, mostly. Of course, I won't stop as often as it did. No more than I have to. But still—say twenty hours for me—you can't hold out that long!"

"I can damn well try," he said. "You got any better ideas?"

"All right, then. Good-by, Hugh. No, I mean so long. I love you."

He grunted some kind of answer, but didn't see her go. He had to keep watching the robot.

-6-

"Zero!" his female called, just once, when the unit sprung upon her back. She clawed at it. The pry bar smashed across her arm. He felt the pain-surge within her sensors, broadcast through her communicator, like a crossbow bolt in his body.

Wildly, he charged. The enemy unit crashed the bar down on One's lattice. She shrilled in anguish. Affected by the damage that crippled her radar, her communicator tone grew suddenly, hideously different. Zero slammed himself to a halt. Her sobbing, his own name blindly repeated, overwhelmed the burning in him where the corrosive gas had flowed. He focused his torch to narrow beam and took careful aim.

The unit knelt, fumbling with its free hand. One screamed again, louder. Her tendrils flailed about. Numbly, Zero let his torch arm droop. The unit rose and poised its weapon above her lenses. A single strong thrust downward through the glass could reach her brain. The unit gestured him back. He obeyed.

"Help," One cried. Zero could not look at the wreckage of her face. There was no escaping her distorted voice. "Help, Zero. It hurts so much."

"Hold fast," he called in his uselessness. "I cannot do anything. Not now. The thing is full of poison. That is what you received." He managed to examine his own interior perceptions. "The pain will abate in a minute...from such a small amount. But if you got a large dose—I do not know. It might prove totally destructive. Or the biped might do ultimate mechanical damage before I could prevent it. Hold fast, One mine. Until I think of something."

"I am afraid," she rattled. "For the new one."

"Hold fast," he implored. "If that unit does you any further harm, I will destroy it slowly. I expect it realizes as much."

The other functional biped came near. It exchanged a few ululations with the first, turned and went quickly from the cave. "It must be going back to the flying monster," said One. The words dragged from her, now and then she whimpered as her perceptions of damage intensified, but she could reason again. "Will it bring the monster here?"

"I cannot give chase," said Zero unnecessarily. "But—" He gathered his energy. A shout blasted from his communicator. *"Alarm, alarm! All persons receiving, prepare to relay. Alarm!"*

Voices flashed in his head, near and far, and it was as if they poured strength into him. He and One were not alone in a night cave, a scuttling horror on her back and the taste of poison only slowly fading. Their whole community was here.

He reported the situation in a few phrases. "You have been rash," Hundred said, shaken. "May there be no further penalties for your actions."

"What else would you have had him do?" defended Seven. "We cannot deal randomly with a thing as powerful as the monster. Zero took upon himself the hazards of gathering information. Which he has succeeded in, too."

"Proving the danger is greater than we imagined," shuddered Sixteen.

"Well, that is a valuable datum."

"The problem now is, what shall we do?" Hundred interrupted. "Slow though you say it is, I expect the auxiliary that escaped can find the monster long before we can rendezvous and get up into the hills."

"Until it does, though, it cannot communicate, its radio being disabled," Zero said. "So the monster will presumably remain where it is, ignorant of events. I suggest that those persons who are anywhere near this neighborhood strike out directly toward that area. They can try to head off the biped."

"You can certainly capture it in a few minutes," Hundred said.

"I cannot leave this place."

"Yes, you can. The thing that has seized your female will not logically do anything more to her, unprovoked, lest she lose her present hostage value."

"How do you know?" Zero retorted. "In fact, I believe if I captured its companion, this unit would immediately attack One. What hope does it have except in the escape of the other, that may bring rescue?"

"Hope is a curious word to use in connection with an elaborated spy eye," Seven said.

"If it is," Zero said. "Their actions suggest to me that these bipeds are more than unthinking domesticated motiles."

"Let be!" Hundred said. "There is scant time to waste. We may not risk the entire community for the sake of a single member. Zero, go fetch back that biped."

Unmodulated radio buzzed in the night. Finally Zero said, "No." One's undamaged hand reached toward him, but she was too far away for them to touch each other. Nor could she caress him with radar.

"We will soon have you whole again," he murmured to her. She did not answer, with the community listening.

Hundred surrendered, having existed long enough to recognize unbendable negation. "Those who are sufficiently near the monster to reach it before dawn, report," he directed. When they had finished—about thirty all told—he said, "Very well, proceed there. Wherever feasible, direct your course to intercept the probable path of the escaped unit. If you capture it, inform us at once. The rest of us will rendezvous as planned."

One by one the voices died out in the night, until only Hundred, who was responsible, and Seven, who was a friend, were in contact with Zero. "How are you now, One?" Seven asked gently.

"I function somewhat," she said in a tired, uneven tone. "It is strange to be radar blind. I keep thinking that heavy objects are about to crash into me. When I turn my optics that way, there isn't anything." She paused. "The new one stirred a little bit just now. A motor impulse pathway must have been completed. Be careful. Zero," she begged. "We have already taken an arm tonight."

"I cannot understand your description of the bipeds' interior," Hundred said practically. "Soft, porous material soaked in sticky red liquid; acrid vapors—How do they *work*? Where is the mechanism?"

"They are perhaps not functional at all," Seven proposed. "They may be purely artificial devices, powered by chemical action."

"Yet they act intelligently," Zero argued. "If the monster...or the masters...do not have them under direct control...and certainly there is no radio involved..."

"There may be other means than radio to monitor an auxiliary," Seven said. "We know so little, we persons."

"In that case," Zero answered, "the monster has known about this cave all the time. It is watching me at this moment, through the optics of that thing on One's back."

"We must assume otherwise," Hundred said.

"I do," Zero said. "I act in the belief that these bipeds are out of contact with the flier. But if nevertheless they perform as they have been doing, then they certainly have independent function, including at least a degree of intelligence." A thought crashed through him, so stunning that he could not declare it at once. Finally: "They may be the monster's masters! It may be the auxiliary, they the persons!"

"No, no, that is impossible," Hundred groaned. Seven's temporary acceptance was quicker; he had always been able to leap from side to side of a discussion. He flashed:

"Let us assume that in some unheard-of fashion, these small entities are indeed the domesticators, or even the builders, of that flying thing. Can we negotiate with them?"

"Not after what has happened," Zero said bleakly. He was thinking less about what he had done to them than what they had done to One.

Seven continued: "I doubt it myself, on philosophical grounds. They are too alien. Their very functioning is deadly: the destruction wrought by their flier, the poison under their skins. Eventually, a degree of mutual comprehension may be achieved. But that will be a slow and painful process. Our first responsibility is to our own form of existence. Therefore we must unmistakably get the upper hand, before we even try to talk with them." In quick excitement, he added, "And I think we can."

Zero and Hundred meshed their intellects with his. The scheme grew like precipitation in a supersaturated pond. Slow and feeble, the strangers were only formidable by virtue of highly developed artifacts—or, possibly, domesticated motiles of radically modified type—the flier, the tube which had blown off Zero's arm, and other hypothetical weapons. But armament unused is no threat. If the flier could be immobilized—

Of course, presumably there were other dwarf bipeds inside it. Their voices had been heard yesterday. But Zero's trip here had proven that they lacked adequate nighttime senses. Well, grant them radar when in an undamaged condition. Radar can be confused, if one knows how.

Hundred's orders sprang forth across miles to the mountaineers now converging on the flier: "Cut the heaviest accumulator strands you can find in the forest. Twist them into cables. Under cover of darkness, radar window, and distraction objects, surround the monster. We believe now that it may not be sentient, only a flier. Weld your cables fast to deeply founded boles. Then, swiftly, loop them around the base of the flier. Tie it down!"

"No," said Twenty-nine, aghast. "We cannot weld the cables to its skin. It would annihilate us with one jet-blast. We would have to make nooses first and—"

"So make the nooses," Zero said. "The monster is not a perfectly tapered spindle. The jets bulge out at the base. Slip the nooses around the body just above the jets. I hardly think it can rise then, without tearing its own tubes out."

"Easy for you to say, Zero, safe in your cave."

"If you knew what I would give to have matters otherwise—"

Abashed, the hunters yielded. Their mission was not really so dangerous. The nooses—two should be ample if the cable was heavy—could be laid in a broad circle around the area which the jets had flattened and devastated. They could be drawn tight from afar, and would probably slip upward by themselves, coming to rest just above the tubes, where the body of the flier was narrowest. If a cable did get stuck on something, someone would have to dash close and free it. A snort of jetfire during those few seconds would destroy them. But quite probably the flier, or its masters, could be kept from noticing him.

"And when we do have the monster leashed, what then?" asked Twenty-nine.

"We will do what seems indicated," Hundred said. "If the aliens do not seem to be reaching a satisfactory understanding with us—if we begin to entertain any doubts—we can erect trebuchets and batter the flier to pieces."

"That might be best," said Zero, with a revengeful look at One's rider.

"Proceed as ordered," said Hundred,

"But what about us?" Zero asked. "One and myself?"

"I shall come to you," Seven said. "If nothing else, we can stand watch and watch. You mentioned that the aliens polarize more easily than we do. We can wait until it drops from exhaustion."

"Good," said Zero. Hope lifted in him as if breaking through a shell. "Did you hear, One? We need only wait."

"Pain," she whispered. Then, resolutely: "I can minimize energy consumption. Comatose, I will not sense anything..." He felt how she fought down terror, and guessed what frightened her: the idea that she might never be roused.

"I will be guarding you all the time," he said. "You and the new one."

"I wish I could touch you. Zero—" Her radiation dimmed, second by second. Once or twice consciousness returned, kicked upward by fear; static gasped in Zero's perception; but she slipped again into blackness.

When she was quite inert, he stood staring at the unit on her. No, the entity. Somewhere behind that glass and horrible tissue, a brain peered back at him. He ventured to move an arm. The thing jerked its weapon aloft. It seemed indeed to have guessed that the optics were her most vulnerable spot. With immense care, Zero let his arm fall again. The entity jittered about, incapable of his own repose. Good. Let it drain its energy the faster.

He settled into his own thoughts. Hours wore away. The alien paced on One's broad back, sat down, sprang up again, slapped first one hand and then another against its body, made long noises that might possibly be intended to fight off coma. Sometimes it plugged the water tube into its face. Frequently Zero saw what looked like a good chance to catch it off guard—with a sudden rush and a flailing blow, or an object snatched off the floor and thrown, or even a snap shot with his torch—but he decided not to take the hazard. Time was his ally.

Besides, now that his initial rage had abated, he began to hope he might capture the entity undamaged. Much more could be learned from a functional specimen than from the thing which lay dismembered near the iron block. Faugh, the gases it was giving off! Zero's chemical sensor retracted in disgust.

The first dawnlight grayed the cave mouth.

"We have the flier!" Twenty-nine's exuberant word made Zero leap where he stood. The alien scrambled into motion. When Zero came no closer, it sagged again. "We drew two cables around its body. No trouble whatsoever. It never stirred. Only made the same radio hum. It still has not moved."

"I thought—" someone else in his party ventured. "Not long ago...was there not a gibberish signal from above?"

"There might well be other fliers above the clouds," agreed Hundred from the valley. "Have a care. Disperse yourselves. Remain under cover. The rest of us will have rendezvoused by early afternoon. At that time we will confer afresh. Meanwhile, report if anything happens. And...good work, hunters."

Twenty-nine offered a brief sensory linkage. Thus Zero saw the place: the cindered blast area, and the upright spindle shining in the first long sunlight, and the cables that ran from its waist to a pair of old and mighty accumulator boles. Yes, the thing was captured for certain. Wind blew over the snowpeaks, set forest to chiming and scattered the little sunrise clouds. He had rarely known his land so beautiful.

The perception faded. He was in his cave again. Seven called: "I am getting close now, Zero. Shall I enter?"

"No, best not. You might alarm the alien into violence. I have watched its movements the whole night. They grow more slow and irregular each hour. It must be near collapse. Suppose you wait just outside. When I believe it to be comatose, I will have you enter. If it does not react to the sight of you, we will know it has lost consciousness."

"If it is conscious," mused Seven. "Despite our previous discussion, I cannot bring myself to believe quite seriously that these are anything but motiles or artifacts. Very ingenious and complex, to be sure...but *aware*, like a person?"

The unit made a long series of sonic noises. They were much weaker than hitherto. Zero allowed satisfaction to wax in him. Nevertheless, he would not have experienced this past night again for any profit.

Several hours later, a general alarm yanked his attention back outward. "The escaped auxiliary has returned! It has entered the flier!"

"What? You did not stop it?" Hundred demanded.

Twenty-nine gave the full report. "Naturally, after the change of plan, we were too busy weaving cables and otherwise preparing ourselves to beat the forest for the dwarf. After the flier was captured, we dispersed ourselves broadly as ordered. We made nothing like a tight circle around the blasted region. Moreover, our attention was directed at the flier, in case it tried to escape, and at the sky in case there should be more fliers. Various wild motiles were about, which we ignored, and the wind has gotten very loud in the accumulators. Under such circumstances, you will realize that probability actually favored the biped unit passing between us and reaching the open area unobserved.

"When it was first noticed, no person was close enough to reach the flier before it did. It slid a plate aside in one of the jacks which support the flier and pulled a switch. A portal opened in the body above and a ladder was extruded. By that time, a number of us had entered the clearing. The unit scrambled up the ladder. We hesitated, fearing a jetblast. None came. But how could we have predicted that? When at last we did approach, the ladder had been retracted and the portal was closed. I pulled the switch myself but nothing happened. I suppose the biped, once inside, deactivated that control by means of a master switch."

"Well, at least we know where it is," Hundred said. "Disperse again, if you have not already done so. The biped may try to escape, and you do not want to get caught in the jet-blast. Are you certain the flier cannot break your cables?"

"Quite certain. Closely observed, the monster—the flier seems to have only a skin of light alloy. Nor would I expect it to be strong against the unnatural kind of stresses imposed by our tethers. If it tries to rise, it will pull itself in two."

"Unless," said Fourteen, as he hastened through valley mists toward Broken Glade, "some biped emerges with a torch and cuts the cables."

"Just let it dare!" said Twenty-nine, anxious to redeem his crew's failure.

"It may bring strong weapons," Zero warned.

"Ten crossbows are cocked and aimed at that portal. If a biped shows itself, we will fill it with whetted steel."

"I think that will suffice," Zero sid. He looked at the drooping shape upon One. "They are not very powerful, these things. Ugly, cunning, but weak."

Almost as if it knew it was being talked about, the unit reeled to its feet and shook the pry bar at him. Even Zero would detect the dullness in its noises. *Another hour,* he thought, *and One will be free.*

Half that time had gone by when Seven remarked from outside, "I wonder why the builders...whoever the ultimate intelligences are behind these manifestations...why have they come?"

"Since they made no attempt to communicate with us," Zero said in renewed grimness, "we must assume their purpose is hostile."

"And?"

"Teach them to beware of us."

He felt already the pride of victory. But then the monster spoke.

Up over the mountains rolled the voice, driven by the power which hurled those hundreds of tons through the sky. Roaring and raging through the radio spectrum, louder than lightning, enormous enough to shake down moon and stars, blasted that shout. Twenty-nine and his hunters yelled as the volume smote their receptors. Their cry was lost, drowned, engulfed by the tide which seethed off the mountainsides. Here and there, where some accumulator happened to resonate, blue arcs of flame danced in the forest. Thirty miles distant, Zero and Seven still perceived the noise as a clamor in their heads. Hundred and his followers in the valley stared uneasily toward the ranges. On the seashore, females called, "What is that? What is that?" and aquamotiles dashed themselves about in the surf.

Seven forgot all caution. He ran into the cave. The enemy thing hardly moved. But neither Zero nor Seven observed that. Both returned to the entrance and gazed outward with terror.

The sky was empty. The forest rang in the breeze. Only that radio roar from beyond the horizon told of anything amiss. "I did not believe—" stammered Seven. "I did not expect—a tone that loud—"

Zero, who had One to think about, mustered decisiveness. "It is not hurting us," he said. "I am glad not to be as close as the hunters are, but even they should be able to endure it for a while. We shall see. Come, let us two go back inside. Once we have secured our prisoner—"

The monster began to talk.

No mere outrageous cry this time, but speech. Not words, except occasionally. A few images. But such occurrences were coincidental. The monster spoke in its own language, which was madness.

Seized along every radio receptor channel there was in him, total sensory and mental linkage, Zero became the monster.

DITditditdit DAH dit-nulnulnulnul-ditditDAH-dah & the vector sum: infinitesimals infinitelyadded from nul-to-INFINITY, dit—ditdit—DAH—ditditditnul (gammacolored chaos, *bang* goes a universe scattering stars&planets&bursts-of-fire BLOCK THAT NEUTRON BLOCK THAT NEUTRON BLOCK THAT NEUTRON BLOCK THAT BLOCK THAT BLOCK THAT NEUTRON) oneone*** nononul—DATTA—ditdit chitter-chitterchitter burning suns & moons, burning stars & brains, burningburning-burning. Burning DahditDahditDahdit give me fifty million logarithms this very microsecond or you will Burn ditditditdit—DAYADHVAM—DAMYATA

and one long wild logarithmic spiral down spacetimeenergy continuum of potentialgradient Xproduct i,j,k but multiply Time by the velocity of light in nothingness and the square root of minus one (two, three, four, five, six CHANGE for duodecimal computation zzzzzzzzz)

integral over sigma of del cross H d sigma equals one over c times integral over sigma partial of E with respect to t dot d sigma but correct for nonsphericalshapentropicoordinatetransformationtop&quantumelectrodynamichargelectricalephaselagradientemperature rising to burning Burning BURNING

dit-dit-chitterchitterchitter from eyrie to blind gnawer and back again O help the trunk is burningburningburning THEREFORE ANNUL in the name of the seven thunders

Everything-that-has-been, break up the roots of existence and strike flat the thick rotundity o' the world RRRIP spacetime across and throw it on the unleaping primordial energy for now all that was & will be, the very fact that it once *did* exist, is canceled and torn to pieces and

Burning
Burning
Burning
Burning

AND the binding energy of a lambda hyperon by a sigma—minus exploding

As the sun fell down the bowl of sky, and the sky cracked open, and the mountains ran like rivers forming faces that gaped and jeered, and the moon rose in the west and spat the grisliness of what he had done at him, Zero ran. Seven did not; could not; lay by the cave entrance, which was the gate of all horrors and corruptions, as if turned to salt. And when God descended, still shouting in His tongue which was madness, His fiery tail melted Seven to a pool.

Fifty million years later the star called Wormwood ascended to heaven; and a great silence fell upon the land.

Eventually Zero returned home. He was not surprised to find that the biped was gone. Of course it had been reclaimed by its Master. But when he saw that One was not touched, he stood mute for a long while indeed.

After he roused her, she—who had been unawake when the world was broken and refashioned—could not understand why he led her outside to pray that they be granted mercy, now and in the hour of their dissolution.

-7-

Darkington did not regain full consciousness until the boat was in space. Then he pulled himself into the seat beside Frederika. "How did you do it?" he breathed.

Her attention remained focused on piloting. Even with the help of the director and radio instructions from the ship, it was no easy task for a novice. Absently, she answered, "I scared the robots away. They'd made the boat fast, you see. With cables too thick to pull apart. I had to go back out and cut them with a torch. But I'd barely gotten inside ahead of the pack. I didn't expect they would let me emerge. So I scared them off. After that, I went out, burned off the cables, and flew to get you."

"Barely in time," he shuddered. "I was about the pass out. I did keel over once I was aboard." A time went by with only the soft rushing noise of brake jets. "Okay," he said, "I give up. I admit you're beautiful, a marvel of resourcefulness, and I can't guess how you shooed away the enemy. So tell me."

The director shut off the engine. They floated free. She turned her face, haggard, sweaty, begrimed, and dear, toward him and said diffidently, "I didn't have any inspiration. Just a guess and nothing to lose. We knew for pretty sure that the robots communicated by radio. I turned the boat's 'caster on full blast, hoping the sheer volume would be too much for them. Then something else occurred to me. If you have a radio transceiver in your head, hooked directly into your nervous system, would that be sort of like telepathy? I mean, it seems more direct somehow than routing everything we say through a larynx. Maybe I could confuse them by emitting unfamiliar signals. Not any old signals, of course. They'd be used to natural radio noise. But—well—the boat's general director includes a pretty complicated computer, carrying out millions of operations per second. Information is conveyed, not noise; but at the same time, it didn't seem to me like information that a bunch of semisavages could handle.

"Anyhow, there was no harm in trying. I hooked the broadcaster in parallel with the effector circuits, so the computer's output not only controlled the boat as usual but also modulated the radio emission. Then I assigned the computer a good tough problem in celestial navigation, put my armor back on, summoned every ounce of nerve I had, and went outside. Nothing happened. I cut the cables without seeing any trace of the robots. I kept the computer 'talking' while I jockeyed the boat over in search of the cave. It must have been working frantically to compensate for my clumsiness; I hate to imagine what its output 'sounded' like. Felt like? Well, when I'd landed, I opened the airlock and, and you came inside, and—" Her fists doubled. "Oh, God, Hugh! How can we tell Sam's girl?"

He didn't answer.

With a final soft impulse, the boat nudged against the ship. As grapnels made fast, the altered spin of the vessels put Earth back in view. Darkington looked at the planet for minutes before he said:

"Good-by. Good luck."

Frederika wiped her eyes with hands that left streaks of dirt in the tears. "Do you think we'll ever come back?" she wondered.

"No," he said. "It isn't ours any more."

TANKA

-1-

Upon a battlefield:

The summer fading,
Chill shall slash the leaves bloody
And the geese trek—where?
Already this ground went red
While the wind called souls away.

-2-

A gentleman to a lady:

In the waning year
My sleeves, which lay over yours,
Are wet as the earth,
Though the rain on them is salt
From a sea of grief for you.

-3-

The lady replies:

Blossoms grew fragrant,
Then faded and blew away,
Leaving bitter fruit.
It fell, and on bare branches
Twig calls to twig through the wind.

Acknowledgements

My name may appear as editor but it takes many people to produce a book like this. The following people helped make this book possible.

Technical help was provided by Dave Grubbs, Alice Lewis, Tony Lewis, Mark Olson and Geri Sullivan.

Proofreading was done by Ann Broomhead, Jim Burton, David Cantor, Gay Ellen Dennett, Tony Lewis, Mark Olson, Priscilla Olson, Joe Ross, Sharon Sbarsky, and Tim Szczesuil.

Dave Grubbs then checked the final copy for errors.

Alice Lewis did her magic in producing the dust jacket.

Special thanks to Mike Resnick for his introduction to the book and Karen Anderson who provided a nifty picture of Poul Anderson.

Rick Katze, editor
May 20 2009